OF
LOVE
AND
LIFE

OF
LOVE
AND
LIFE

Three novels selected and condensed
by Reader's Digest

The Reader's Digest Association Limited, London

The Reader's Digest Association Limited
11 Westferry Circus, Canary Wharf, London E14 4HE

www.readersdigest.co.uk

ISBN 0-276-42994-X

CONTENTS

NIGHTS OF
RAIN AND STARS

MAEVE BINCHY

In a Greek taverna high in the hills above the little village of Aghia Anna, four strangers meet: Fiona, a young Irish nurse; Thomas, a Californian academic; Elsa, a glamorous German television presenter; and David, a shy young English boy. Drawn together by the horror of a tragedy that unfolds in front of their eyes, their dependence upon one another grows— with surprising results.

CHAPTER ONE

ANDREAS THOUGHT HE SAW the fire down in the bay before anyone else did. He peered and shook his head in disbelief. This sort of thing didn't happen. Not here in Aghia Anna, not to the *Olga*, the little red and white boat that took visitors out to the bay. Not to Manos, foolish headstrong Manos whom he had known since he was a boy. This was some kind of dream, some trick of the light. That could not be smoke and flames coming from the *Olga*.

Perhaps he was not feeling well.

Some of the older people in the village said that they imagined things. If the day was hot, if there had been too much *raki* the night before. But he had gone to bed early. There had been no *raki* or dancing or singing in his hillside restaurant.

Andreas put his hand up to shade his eyes and, at the same time, a cloud passed overhead. It wasn't as clear as it had been before. He must indeed have been mistaken. But now he must pull himself together. He had a restaurant to run. He continued fixing the red and green plastic-covered cloths with little clips to the long wooden tables on the terrace outside his taverna. He had laboriously written the menu on the black-board. He often wondered why he did it . . . it was the same food every day. But the visitors liked it; and he would put 'Welcome' in six languages. They liked that too.

The food was not special. Nothing they could not have got in two dozen other little Greek tavernas. There was *souvlaki*, the lamb kebabs. Well, goat kebabs really, but the visitors liked to think they were lamb.

And there was *moussaka*, warm and glutinous in its big pie dish. There were the big bowls of salad, white squares of salty feta cheese and lush red tomatoes. There were the racks of *barbouni*, red mullet, waiting to be grilled, the swordfish steaks. There were the big steel trays of desserts in the fridge, *katai* and *baklava*, made from nuts, honey and pastry. The chilled cabinets of retsina and local wines. People came from all over the world and loved what Andreas, and dozens like him, could provide.

He always recognised the nationality of any visitor to Aghia Anna and could greet them in a few words of their own language. The English didn't like it if you offered them a *Speisencarte* instead of the menu, the Canadians did not want you to assume they were from the United States. Italians did not like to be greeted with a *Bonjour* and his own fellow countrymen wanted to be thought of as important people from Athens rather than tourists. Andreas had learned to look carefully before he spoke.

And as he looked down the path he saw the first customers of the day arriving.

His mind went on to automatic pilot.

A tall man, wearing those shorts that only Americans wore, shorts that did nothing for the bottom or the legs. He was on his own and stopped to look at the fire through binoculars.

A beautiful girl, possibly German, tall and tanned, with hair streaked by the sun or a very expensive hairdresser. She stood in silence, staring in disbelief at the scarlet and orange flames licking over the boat.

A boy in his twenties, small and anxious-looking with glasses that he kept taking off and wiping. He stood open-mouthed in horror, looking at the boat in the bay.

A couple, also in their twenties, exhausted after the walk up the hill; they might be Scottish or Irish—Andreas couldn't quite make out the accents. The boy had a sort of swagger about him, the girl had red hair and a freckled nose.

In their turn, they each saw an old man, slightly stooped, with grey-white hair and bushy eyebrows.

'That's the boat we were on yesterday.' The red-haired girl had her hand over her mouth in shock. 'Oh my God, it could have been us.'

'Well, it isn't, so what's the point in saying that?' her companion said firmly.

For the first time, Andreas realised that it was true. There *was* a fire. Not just a trick of the light. The others had seen it too. He began to tremble and hold on to the back of a chair to support himself.

'I must telephone my brother Yorghis, he is in the police station . . . maybe they don't know about it. Maybe they cannot see it.'

The tall American spoke gently. 'They see it. Look, there are lifeboats already on the way.'

'I can't believe it,' the young girl said. 'Yesterday he was teaching us to dance on that very boat, *Olga*, he called it, after his grandmother.'

'Manos—that's his boat, isn't it?' asked the boy with the glasses. 'I was on his boat, too.'

'Yes, that is Manos,' said Andreas gravely. *That fool Manos with too many people on the vessel as usual, trying to make kebabs with some outdated gas cylinder.* But none of the people of the village would ever say any of this. Manos had a family here. They would all be gathered now, down by the harbour.

'Do you know him?' asked the tall American with the binoculars.

'Yes, indeed, we all know everyone here.' Andreas wiped his eyes with a table napkin.

They stood as if transfixed, watching the distant boats arriving and trying to douse the flames, the bodies struggling in the water. They were too far away to help, but still they couldn't stop looking at the tragedy unfolding below on that innocent, beautiful, blue sea.

Andreas felt a hand on his arm. It was the blonde German girl. 'It's worse for you—this is your place,' she said. 'Why don't you sit down?' Her face was kind. 'There's nothing we can do to help them.'

It was the spur he needed. 'I'm Andreas,' he said. 'You're right, this is my place, and I will offer you all a Metaxa brandy for the shock and we will say a prayer for the people in the bay.'

'Is there nothing, *nothing* that we can do?' asked the English boy with the glasses.

'It took us about three hours to get up this far. By the time we got back I guess we'd only be in the way,' said the tall American. 'I'm Thomas, by the way.'

'I'm Elsa,' said the German girl, 'and I'll get the glasses.'

They stood with tiny glasses of the fiery liquid in their hands and raised a strange toast in the sunshine.

Fiona, the Irish girl, said, 'May their souls and all the souls of the faithful departed rest in peace.'

Her boyfriend seemed to wince at the expression.

'Well, why not, Shane?' she asked him defensively. 'It's a blessing.'

'Go in peace,' said Thomas to the wreckage.

'*Lehaim*,' said David, the English boy with the glasses. 'It means "To life",' he explained.

'*Ruhet in Frieden*,' said Elsa with tears in her eyes.

'*O Theos n'anapafsi tin psyhi tou*,' said Andreas, bowing his head in grief as he looked down on the worst tragedy Aghia Anna had ever known.

They didn't order lunch, Andreas just served them. He brought them a salad with goat's cheese, a plate of lamb and stuffed tomatoes, and afterwards a bowl of fruit. They spoke about themselves and where they had been. They were all in it for the long haul—several months at least.

Thomas, the American, was travelling and writing articles for a magazine. He had a year off, a proper sabbatical from his university in California. Teachers of every kind needed a chance to go out and talk to people of other countries, he said. He looked a little far away as he spoke, Andreas thought, as if he were missing something back home.

It was different with Elsa, the German girl. She seemed to miss nothing she had left behind and had enough money saved to finance a year's travel. She had been on the road for three weeks.

Fiona, the Irish girl, was more uncertain. She looked at her moody boyfriend for confirmation as she spoke of how they wanted to see the world and find somewhere to settle where people wouldn't judge them or try to change them. He just shrugged as though it was all very boring.

David spoke of his wish to see the world while he was still young enough. There was nothing sadder than an old man who found what he was looking for decades too late.

But even as they talked and told each other a little of their lives in Düsseldorf, Dublin, California and Manchester, Andreas noted that they said nothing of the families they had left behind.

He told them of life here in Aghia Anna and how the place was rich today, compared to his childhood when a living was earned in the olive groves or minding goats on the hills. He spoke of brothers long gone to America, and his own son who had left this restaurant after an argument nine years ago.

'And what did you argue about?' asked Fiona.

'Oh, he wanted a nightclub here and I didn't—the usual thing about age and youth, about change and not changing.' Andreas shrugged sadly. 'If I had known how lonely it would be to have my only son in Chicago, far across the world and never writing to me . . . then, I would have had the nightclub.'

'And what about your wife?' Fiona asked. 'Did she not beg you to get him back and open the club?'

'She had died. Nobody left to make peace between us.'

The afternoon shadows grew longer. Andreas served them little coffees and none of them seemed to want to leave. A sunny day had turned into death and disaster. Through the binoculars they saw bodies on stretchers and crowds gathering, people pushing to see if their loved ones were alive. Up here on the hill, even though they knew nothing of each other, brought together like this they talked as if they were old friends.

12

They were still talking as the first stars came into the sky. Now, down in the harbour they could see the lights of flashing cameras and of television teams recording the tragedy to tell to the world. It hadn't taken long for news of the disaster to get to the media.

'I suppose they have to do it,' said David with resignation. 'But it seems so ghoulish, monstrous, preying on people's lives in a tragedy.'

'It is monstrous, believe me, I work in it. Or worked, anyway,' Elsa said, unexpectedly.

'A journalist?' David asked with interest.

'I worked on a television current affairs show. There's somebody like me now, at my desk in the studio, asking questions at long distance of someone down there in the harbour: how many bodies have been recovered, how did it happen, are there any Germans among the dead? I'm glad to be no part of it now.'

'And yet people do have to know about famines and wars—otherwise how can we stop them?' Thomas pointed out.

'We'll never stop them,' Shane said. 'There's big money in this kind of thing.'

Shane was different from the others, Andreas thought. Dismissive, restless, anxious to be somewhere else.

'Not everyone is interested in money,' David said mildly.

Fiona looked up sharply as if she had been down this road before, defending Shane for his views. 'What Shane means is that that's the system—it's not the God in his life nor in mine. I certainly wouldn't be a nurse if it was money I was looking for.'

'A nurse?' Elsa said.

'Yes, I was wondering, would I be any use down there, but I don't suppose—'

'For God's sake, Fiona, get real. What could you do?' Shane protested. Tell them in Greek to keep calm? Foreign nurses aren't in high demand at a time of crisis.' There was a sneer on his face.

Fiona flushed darkly.

Thomas was looking through his binoculars again. 'I don't think you'd even be able to get near to the wounded if you were there,' he said reassuringly. He passed her the glasses and with trembling hands she looked down at the distant harbour and the people jostling each other.

'Yes, you're right,' Fiona said in a small voice.

'It must be wonderful being a nurse, I guess it means that you're never afraid,' Thomas said, trying to make Fiona feel better. 'What a great career. My mother is a nurse and she works long hours but doesn't get paid enough.'

'Did she work while you were a kid?'

'Still does. She put my brother and me through college and we got careers out of all that.'

'What career did you get out of college?' David asked. 'I have a degree in business studies but it never got me anything I wanted to do.'

Thomas spoke slowly. 'I teach nineteenth-century literature at a university.' He shrugged as if it weren't a big deal.

'What do you do, Shane?' Elsa asked.

'Why?' He looked back at her directly.

'Don't know. It's just that the rest of us said. I suppose I didn't want you to be left out.' Elsa had a beautiful smile.

He relaxed. 'Sure, well, I do a bit of this and a bit of that.'

Just then, Andreas spoke very slowly. 'I think you should all call and tell them back at home that you are alive. As Elsa says, this will be on the television news tonight. They will all see, they may know you are here in Aghia Anna, they will think that you might be on the boat of Manos.' He looked around him. Five young people from different families, different homes, different countries.

'Well, my mobile phone doesn't work here,' Elsa said cheerfully. 'I did try a couple of days ago and I thought, so much the better, now it's a real escape.'

'It's the wrong time of day in California,' Thomas said.

'I'd get the answering machine, they'll be out again at some business function,' David said.

'It would only be another earful of "Dear, dear, look what happens when you leave your nice, safe job and go gallivanting round the world,"' said Fiona.

Shane said nothing at all. The notion of phoning home had just never occurred to him.

Andreas stood up at the table and addressed them. 'Believe me, when I hear there has been a shooting in Chicago or a flood or any disaster, I wonder to myself, could my Adoni be caught up in it? It would be so good if he were to ring . . .'

'You see, Andreas, you're the kind of father who *does* care. Some fathers don't,' David explained.

'Every parent cares, they just have different ways of showing it.'

'And, of course, some of us have no parents,' Elsa said in a light voice. 'Like me, a father long disappeared, a mother who died young.'

'But there must be someone in Germany who loves you, Elsa,' Andreas said, and then thought perhaps he had gone too far. 'I tell you, my telephone is there in the bar. Now I will open a bottle of wine to celebrate that we were here tonight, with all our hopes and dreams still left to us as we sit in another night of stars.'

He went inside and could hear them talking out on the terrace.

'I think he really *does* want us to use his phone,' Fiona said.

'Well, you just said what you'd be letting yourself in for,' Shane objected.

'Perhaps it's making too much of it all,' Elsa wondered.

They looked down again at the scene below. And there was no argument, this time.

'I'll call first,' said Thomas.

Andreas stood polishing glasses and listening to their calls. They were a strange little group gathered today in his taverna. None of them seemed at ease with the people they called. It was as if they were all running away from something. Each of them sounded like someone escaping from a bad situation.

Thomas's voice was clipped. 'I *know* he's at day camp, Shirley. I just thought . . . no, it doesn't matter . . . believe me, I had no agenda . . . please, I am not trying to make trouble. All right, Shirley, think what you like. No, I haven't made any plans yet.'

David sounded apprehensive. 'Oh, Dad, you're at home. Yes, well, of course you should be. It's just that I wanted to tell you about this accident . . . no, I wasn't hurt . . . No, I wasn't on the boat.' A long silence. 'Right, Dad, give my love to Mum, won't you . . . no, tell her there's nothing definite about when I'm coming back.'

Fiona's conversation was hardly about the boat tragedy at all. 'I can't give you a date yet, Mam, we've been through this a million times. Where he goes, I go, Mam, and you must make your own plans for that—it would be much better that way.'

Elsa's conversation was a mystery. Andreas spoke German, and he understood perfectly. She left two messages on answering machines.

The first was warm: 'Hannah, it's Elsa. I am in this glorious place in Greece called Aghia Anna and there was a terrible accident today. People died in a boat tragedy. But in case you wondered was I involved in it, I wanted to tell you I'm one of the lucky ones . . . Oh, Hannah, I do miss you and your kind shoulder to weep on. You're such a friend—I don't deserve you. I'll get in touch soon, I promise.'

Then she made a second call and this time her voice was ice cold. 'I wasn't killed on that boat. But you know that there are times I would not mind if I had been. I only called you because I imagine the studio is hoping that I was either burned in that pleasure-boat fire or that I am standing on the harbour waiting to give an eye-witness account. But I am miles away from it, and even more miles away from you, and that's all I care about, believe me.'

And Andreas saw the tears on Elsa's face as she replaced the receiver.

None of them wanted to leave his place, Andreas realised. They felt safe here on his terrace, far from the tragedy unfolding below. And far from their own unhappy lives back home. He left their wine on the table and sat in the shadows with his worry beads moving from hand to hand while they talked. As the night came, and more wine was poured, they were no longer secretive about their home lives.

Poor Fiona was the most eager of all.

'I shouldn't have called, Shane, it just gave them another chance to tell me what a mess I am making of my life, and how they can't get their silver wedding plans organised until they know where I am going to be. I told my mother straight out that I hadn't a notion of where we'd be in five months' time, and she starts to cry. And here we are with all those people down at the harbour who really *do* have something to cry about.'

'Told you.' Shane inhaled. He and Fiona were smoking a joint.

Thomas spoke up. 'I had no luck, either. Bill, my little boy, was out at day camp. My ex-wife, Shirley, was less than pleased by the call. Still, at least the boy won't look at the news and worry about me.'

'How would he know that you were even in this area?' Shane obviously thought the phone calls home were a waste of time for everyone.

'Shirley is meant to put my telephone numbers up on the bulletin board in the kitchen.'

'But has your son called?'

'No.'

'Then she doesn't, does she?' Shane had it all figured out.

'I guess not, and I don't imagine she'll call my mother either.' Thomas's face was set in hard lines. 'I wish I had thought of calling Mom instead. But I wanted to hear Bill's voice . . .'

Finally David spoke quietly. 'When I called, I was getting ready to leave a message on the answering machine—but they were at home and it was my father . . . And he said . . . he said that if nothing had happened to me, what was I ringing about?'

'He didn't really mean that, you know,' Thomas said, soothingly.

David shook his head. 'But he *did* mean it, and I could hear my mother calling out from the sitting room, "Ask him about the award, Harold, is he coming home for that?"'

'Award?' the others asked.

'It's a pat on the back for having made so much money, like the Queen's Award for Industry. There's going to be a big reception. Nothing else on earth matters to them except this.'

'Is there anyone else at home who could go to the ceremony in your place?' Elsa asked.

'That's the problem. That's the whole problem,' David replied sadly.

'You're an only child then?' Elsa said.

'It's *your* life, do what you want to,' Shane shrugged. He couldn't see what the problem was.

'It might be a way of saying, "Come home", mightn't it?' Elsa suggested.

'Everything's a way of saying, "Come home", but "Come home and get a good job and help your father in his business", and that is not what I am going to do.' David took off his glasses and wiped them.

Elsa had said nothing about herself. She sat looking far out to sea over the olive groves at the coastline of the little islands where all those people had thought they would be spending a sunny holiday afternoon. She felt everyone looking at her, waiting for her to talk about the phone call *she* had made.

'Oh, what response did I get? Well, I called two friends, got two answering machines, and they'll both think I'm mad, but what the hell?' Elsa gave a little laugh. There was no hint that she had left a vague, cheery message on one machine and tense, almost hate-filled words on the other.

From the shadows Andreas looked at her. The beautiful Elsa, who had left her job in television to find peace in the Greek Islands, had certainly not found it yet, he told himself.

The phone rang and Andreas started. It might be his brother Yorghis, calling from the police station.

But it wasn't Yorghis, it was a man speaking German. He said his name was Dieter and he was looking for Elsa.

'She is not here,' Andreas said.

'She can't have left,' the man said, 'she only called me ten minutes ago. I have traced the number she called from . . . where is she staying, please?'

'I have no idea, Herr Dieter, no idea at all.'

'And who was she with?'

'A group of people—I think they leave this village tomorrow. Sincerest regrets at not being able to help you, Herr Dieter.' He hung up, and turned to find Elsa standing looking at him. She had come in from the terrace when she heard him speaking German on the telephone.

'Why did you do that, Andreas?' Her voice was steady.

'I thought it was what you would want me to do, but if I was wrong—'

'You were not wrong. You were absolutely right. Thank you very much. Usually I am strong but tonight I could not have had that conversation.'

'I know,' he said gently. 'There are times when it's best not to have to say anything at all.'

The phone rang again. This time it was his brother Yorghis.

Twenty-four people dead.

Twenty from abroad and four from Aghia Anna: not only Manos but also his eight-year-old nephew who had proudly gone out for the day to help his uncle. And the two local boys who had worked on the boat.

'It's a dark time for you, Andreas,' Elsa said, her voice full of concern.

'These are not bright days for you either,' he answered.

They sat there, each thinking their own thoughts. It was as if they had always known each other. They would talk when there was something to say. Elsa spoke eventually.

'Andreas?' She looked outside; the others were talking together.

'Yes?'

'Will you do one more thing for me?'

'If I can, yes, of course.'

'Write to Adoni. Ask him to come home to Aghia Anna. Tell him that your village has lost three young men and a boy, that you all need to see the face of someone who left, someone who *can* come back.'

He shook his head. 'No, my friend Elsa, it would not work. Why do you want to change the lives of people you don't know?'

She threw back her head and laughed. 'Oh, Andreas, if you knew me in my real life, that's what I do all the time, I'm a crusading journalist—that's what the television station calls me. I'm always trying to keep families together, get children off drugs, get integrity into sports . . . It's my nature to change the lives of people I don't know.'

'And does it ever work?' he asked.

'Sometimes. It works enough times for me to want to keep at it.'

'But you've left?'

'Not because of the work.'

He looked at the telephone.

She nodded. 'Yes, you're right, it's because of Dieter. It's a long story.'

'No need to tell me your business, Elsa,' he said.

'You are my friend, I want to tell you.'

But they heard the others approaching.

Thomas was the spokesman. 'We must let you sleep, Andreas, tomorrow will be a long day,' he said.

'We think we should go back down the hill, back to where we are staying,' David began.

'My brother Yorghis is sending a truck up this way for you soon. I told him I had friends who would need a lift; it's a long way.'

'And can we pay you now for our meal—our long day and night with you?' Thomas asked.

'As I told Yorghis, you are friends, and friends do not pay for their food,' he said with dignity.

They looked at him: old and slightly bent, poor, working hard in a restaurant where they had been the only customers all day.

Elsa spoke slowly. 'What do you say that we make a collection for the family of Manos and his little nephew and the others who died today? There will undoubtedly be a fund for them. We can gather what we think our food and drink here would have cost, and then get an envelope and write on it, "From the friends of Andreas".'

Fiona had an envelope in her shoulder bag. She took it out and without a word they poured their euros onto a plate. The sound of the police truck was heard coming up the hill.

'You write the message for the people, Elsa,' Fiona suggested.

And Elsa did with a steady hand.

'I wish I could write in the Greek language,' she said to Andreas, and looked at him as if they shared a secret.

'It's fine—your generosity, all of you, is very fine in any language,' he said, sounding choked. 'I was never good at writing any sort of letter.'

'It's just the first words that are the hardest, Andreas,' she persisted.

'I would begin "*Adoni mou*,"' he said haltingly.

'Now you're halfway there,' Elsa said, and held him to her for a quick moment before they climbed into the truck to go back down the hill to the little town.

None of them slept well that night. They all tossed and turned, the starlight too bright somehow and seeping into their bedrooms.

Elsa stood on the tiny balcony of her apartment hotel and looked out at the dark sea. She was staying at the Studio Apartments, run by a young Greek man who had learned the property business in Florida and had returned with the idea of having six little self-contained units here. Simply furnished, with Greek rugs on the wooden floors and colourful Greek pottery on the shelves. No one balcony overlooked the others.

Elsa knew she wouldn't sleep for hours. There was no point in going to bed. She brought a chair out onto the tiny balcony and sat with her elbows on the little wrought-iron balustrade, looking at the patterns the moonlight was making on the water.

David's little room was too hot and stuffy. It had been fine up to now but tonight was different. The people in the house were wailing too loudly for anyone to sleep. Their son had died on Manos's boat today.

When David had walked into the house and discovered the family and friends comforting each other he had been stricken. He had shaken hands awkwardly and fumbled for the words to express what could not be said. They spoke little English, and they looked at him wild-eyed. They hardly noticed when he came downstairs again to walk in the night air. Their grief was too great.

19

David wondered what would have happened if he had died on the boat. It could so easily have been. He had just chosen one day for a tour rather than another. Would there have been wailing like this in his home? Would his father have rocked forward and back in misery? Or would he have said grimly that the boy had chosen his life and he had to live with that choice and die by it.

Suddenly David felt very anxious as he walked around the sorrowing town. He thought he might go to a small taverna where people were still sitting, talking. He might even meet some of the people he had spent all that time with. He could speak to Fiona about Ireland, a place he had always wanted to go to. He could ask her about nursing, and if it really was as rewarding as people said. Did you get a glow of pleasure as patients got better?

Or he could ask Thomas about his writing: what kind of thing he wrote, why he was going to be away from his university for so long, how often he got to see his little boy. David loved to listen to people's stories. It was why he was so useless in his father's investment-broking business. Clients needed him to tell them what to spend and how. David was much more interested in asking about their houses as homes rather than investments, when what they really wanted to talk about was a quick turnover.

As he walked he saw Elsa on her balcony but didn't call out to her. She was so calm and in control, the last thing she needed was a bumbling fool like him in the middle of the night.

Thomas had booked himself for two weeks into a little apartment over a craft shop. It was owned by an eccentric woman called Vonni. In her late forties or so, she always dressed in a different floral skirt and a black shirt. She looked like someone you would have to give money to for her next meal, Thomas thought, but in fact she owned this splendid luxury apartment which she let out to visitors.

Vonni was Irish originally, he gathered, though she didn't want to talk about herself. She was a perfect landlady in that she left him alone. She offered to take his clothes to a local laundry and she left an occasional basket of grapes or a bowl of olives on his doorstep.

'Where do you live while I stay here?' he had asked at the start.

'I sleep in an outhouse,' she had replied.

Thomas was unsure if she was joking or was in fact somewhat simple in the head. And he asked her no more—he was happy in Vonni's place, where there was a phone in case Bill wanted to call him. He had felt that a cellphone would be intrusive on his travels, and anyway people were always complaining that they couldn't get a signal in remote places. And what did it matter how many euros he spent on an apartment with a telephone? He had nothing else to spend his professor's salary on, and even his poetry was beginning to earn him money.

A prestigious magazine had paid for him to go abroad and write travel articles, in his own style from wherever he wanted. It had been the perfect assignment when he'd realised that he needed to get away. He had wanted to write about Aghia Anna, but the world's press would be arriving tomorrow and Aghia Anna would already be notorious.

Once he had thought it would be easy to go on living in the same town as his ex-wife, seeing his son Bill as often as possible, keeping a civilised and non-combative relationship with Shirley. But now things were different.

Shirley's new boyfriend was Andy, a car salesman she had met at the gym. When Shirley announced that she was getting married to Andy it changed everything. She had explained that she had found a real and permanent love.

Thomas had been surprised to find how much he had resented it. Andy wasn't a *bad* guy, it was just that he'd moved too easily into the house that Thomas had bought for himself, Shirley and Bill.

'Because it's all so much *easier*,' Shirley had explained.

Bill had said that Andy was OK, and that's just what he was: OK. But he was a bit of a jock and not into reading, not into holding a book with Bill at night and saying, 'Come on, you choose what to read and we'll read it together.'

And, to be fair, Andy had sensed the awkwardness of it all. He had suggested that Thomas visit Bill between five and seven when he, Andy, was in the gym.

It had been reasonable, sensible, sensitive even, but that had annoyed Thomas even more. As if he were being tidied away to a place that didn't impinge on their lives. Every time he visited he had come to hate the house more, with the jars of vitamins and health supplements all over the kitchen and bathrooms, the magazines about health and fitness on the coffee tables.

When the chance to get away came Thomas was sure he was right in taking it. He could keep in touch with his boy by phone, by letter, by email. He had convinced himself it was better for everyone. And for the first few weeks it had worked well. He didn't wake up angry any more, nor drive himself crazy thinking about his son's new household. The break had been a good thing.

But the events of today had changed everything. All those people dead, a village plunged into mourning. He could hear the sounds of their crying floating up to him over the harbour. There was no way he could sleep, and his thoughts kept buzzing round like angry insects.

Fiona too was awake in their room in a cramped little house outside town. It belonged to a thin anxious woman called Eleni, who had three little boys. There didn't seem to be any sign of a husband. Fiona and Shane had found the place by knocking at various doors and offering a small handful of euros in return for overnight accommodation.

Now Shane lay sprawled in the chair asleep, the only one who had managed to get a night's rest. Fiona couldn't sleep because Shane had said, out of the blue, that they should move on next day.

She had been startled.

They had both thought Aghia Anna the kind of place where they might stay a while. But now Shane had changed his mind.

'No, we can't stay. It's going to be a creepy place after all this,' he had said. 'We'll get a boat to Athens tomorrow.'

'But Athens is a big city . . . it will be so hot,' she had protested.

But Shane said that he had someone to meet there.

Nothing at all had been mentioned about this fellow when they had set off a month ago. But Fiona knew from experience that it was not wise to upset Shane. It was just that she had wanted to go to the funeral for Manos, the handsome, sexy Greek who had pinched her bottom and said she was *orea*, which meant wonderful, *beautiful*. He was a silly guy, but good-tempered and cheerful, he thought all ladies were *orea*, he drank wine from the bottle and he danced Zorba-like dances for them. But there had been no harm in him, he didn't deserve to die with his little nephew and his work-mates and all those tourists who had been having such a great time.

And Fiona would have liked to see the people from today again. The old man, Andreas, had been so gentle, so generous. Thomas, the college professor, was a wise, good person, and she might even have encouraged David to be more outgoing.

And as for Elsa . . . Fiona had never admired anyone so much, for knowing exactly what to say and when to say it. No wedding ring, and yet she must be about twenty-eight. Fiona wondered who she had telephoned in Germany.

Shane was still asleep in the chair.

Fiona wished that he had not brought out the pot in front of Andreas and the others today, and that he had been a bit nicer to them all. He could be so prickly and difficult. But then he had lived a confused life with no love in it. Not until he had met Fiona, that was. And she alone knew how to reach the real Shane.

The room was very hot and pokey. She wished they could have stayed somewhere a little better. Then Shane might not want them to move on so quickly tomorrow.

During the night, as the stars shone down on the bay, Andreas wrote a letter. He wrote several versions and decided that the last one was the best. By morning he was ready to post the first and only letter he had written in nine years to his son in Chicago.

When the sun came up he got on his putt-putt bike and made the journey to the town.

When the sun came up on Aghia Anna, the phone rang in the apartment over the craft shop.

It was Thomas's son Bill calling him.

'Dad, you OK?'

'I'm great, son, just fine. Your momma gave you my number?'

'It's on the board, Dad. It's just Mom says it's always the middle of the night out there. Andy said I should try anyhow.'

'Say thanks to Andy.'

'I will. He got out a map of the world to show me roughly where you are, when we saw the fire on television. It's a long way away, Dad.'

Thomas yearned to be beside his boy. It was a real ache. But he had to remain cheerful. 'Nowhere's a long way away these days, Bill, the phone is always there. Listen to you! You could be in the next room.'

'Yeah, I know,' the boy agreed. 'I called Gran to tell her you were OK and she said you are to take care.'

'I will, Bill, believe me, I'll take care.'

'I've got to go now. Bye, Dad.'

He was gone but the sun had come up on Aghia Anna and the day was beautiful. His son had called.

Outside the town, when the sun came up, Fiona went to the bathroom and suddenly realised that her period was six days late.

Down by the harbour, when the sun came up, Elsa passed by the church, which had become a temporary morgue. As she rounded a corner, she saw with horror that among the crowds arriving from Athens was a German television crew from her own network setting up shots of the still-smouldering wreck that had been towed into the harbour.

She knew the cameraman and the sound man. And they would know her if they saw her. And then Dieter would know where she was and would be here in a matter of hours.

She backed carefully into a little café and looked around wildly. Some old men were playing a form of backgammon—no help there. Then at a table she saw David, the kind English boy.

'David,' she hissed.

He was overjoyed to see her.

'David, can you go and get a taxi and bring it here for me? I can't go outside. There are people out there I just don't want to see. Can you do that for me, *please* . . .'

He seemed alarmed that she was so different from yesterday.

'Where will I tell the taxi you're going?' he asked.

'Where were *you* thinking of going today?' she asked, desperately.

'There's a place about fifty kilometres away, a little temple and an artists' colony. I was going to get a bus there.'

'We'll take the taxi there,' she said firmly.

'No, Elsa, we'll go out and get on a bus, a taxi would cost a fortune, believe me,' David argued.

'And I *have* a fortune, believe me,' she said, showing him a wad of notes. 'Please, David, just act now, this minute. I haven't committed a crime or anything, but I am in trouble. If you don't help me now then honestly I don't know what I'll do.' She spoke from the heart, not acting.

'There's a line of taxis in the square. I'll be back,' said David.

Fiona had quite a long time to wait until Shane woke up. He lay there in the chair with his mouth open, his hair damp and stuck to his forehead. He looked so vulnerable when he was asleep. She longed to stroke his face but she didn't want to wake him.

Downstairs she could hear Eleni calling to her three little sons. Neighbours kept calling in, obviously telling the story over and over to each other, shocked by the tragedy.

She wouldn't disturb these people by going down, not until Shane woke, until he was ready to go.

When he did wake he was not in good humour.

'Why did you let me sleep in the chair?' he asked, rubbing his neck. 'I'm as stiff as a bloody board.'

'Let's go and have a swim—that will make you feel better,' she tried to encourage him.

'Easy for you—you've been in the bed all night,' he grumbled.

This was not the time to tell him that she had been awake most of the night, and it was certainly not the time to tell him that she could be pregnant. That must wait.

'Will we pack before breakfast?' she asked.

'Pack?' he said, puzzled.

Perhaps he had forgotten the whole idea.

'Don't mind me, I don't know where I am half the time,' Fiona said with a laugh.

'You can say that again . . . Here, I'm going to bed for a bit and you could go and get us a couple of coffees.'

She walked along the beach back towards the town, her bare feet kicking the warm sand at the edge of the sea. She could not believe this was happening. Fiona Ryan, the most sensible of her whole family, the most reliable nurse on the whole ward, had thrown up her job to go off with Shane, the man they had all warned her against.

And she might now very possibly be pregnant.

It wasn't just her mother who had rejected Shane as the other half of her life, it was all her friends, including Barbara, her best pal since they had been six years of age. And her sisters. But what did they know?

And, anyway, love was never meant to be uncomplicated. Think of any of the great love stories and you realised that. Love had nothing to do with meeting a nice *suitable* person, who had a good job, who wanted a long engagement and to save a deposit on a house.

That wasn't love, that was compromise.

She thought about the possible pregnancy and her heart lurched. There had been a couple of times, fairly recently, when they had not been careful. She felt her flat stomach. Was it possible that a child was growing there, someone who would be half Shane and half her? It was too exciting to imagine.

In front of her on the beach she saw the strange baggy shorts and over-long T-shirt of Thomas, the nice American. He recognised her and called out, 'You look happy!'

'I am.' She didn't tell him the way her mind was filling up with wild and wonderful plans for living here in Aghia Anna and bringing up a child with these people, Shane working on the fishing boats or in the restaurants, she helping the local doctor, maybe even as midwife. These were all dreams that would be discussed later when Shane had his coffee. She would tell him then.

'My son called me from the States. We had a great conversation.' Thomas couldn't help sharing his news.

'I'm so very glad. You know I *thought* he might call you back last night—I felt it when you were telling us about him.'

'Let me buy you a coffee to celebrate,' Thomas said, and they walked together along to a small taverna near the beach. They sat down at a table and ordered coffee, and found that they could talk as easily as they had yesterday.

'We were meant to be going to Athens today, but I think Shane's too tired,' Fiona said, when they'd sat there for some time. 'In some ways I'm actually rather glad he's too tired. I like this place. I want to stay on.'

'So do I. I'm going to walk up in those hills, and I want to stay for the funeral.'

She looked at him with interest. 'So do I, and it's not just ghoulish wanting to see it all first hand, I wanted to be part of it.'

'Wanted? Does that mean you'll not stay?'

'Well, we don't know what day it will be and, as I said, Shane wants to go to Athens.'

'But surely if *you* want to . . .' His voice trailed away.

Fiona saw the look on his face. The same look that eventually came over everyone's face when they met Shane. She stood up.

'Thanks for the coffee. I'll go now. If you see the others, David and Elsa . . .'

'I'll say that you and Shane had to go to Athens and you said good-bye,' he said gently. 'I saw them heading out of town in a taxi together this morning. But it's a tiny place. I'll see them again.'

He watched her go and buy some warm bread and a little pot of local honey to take back to that selfish young man and he sighed. A professor, a poet, a writer—and he didn't understand the smallest thing about life and love.

Elsa bent down in the taxi and hid her head under a scarf until they had left the town. Only then did she straighten up. Her face looked strained and anxious.

'Why don't I tell you what I know about this place we are going to?' David offered.

'Thank you. That would be perfect.' She lay back and closed her eyes while his words rolled over her. It was the site of a minor temple that had had some excavation, but the money had dried up so it had been left in a semi-exposed state. There were those who said it was well worth a tour.

And an artist's colony had started there years ago, which was still going strong. Even today, silversmiths and potters came from all over the world. The artists brought their wares to town to sell.

David looked at her from time to time as he spoke. Her face was relaxing. Obviously, she didn't want to tell him what she was frightened of, so he wouldn't ask. Better to go on burbling on about this place they were visiting.

Shane felt a lot better after the coffee, bread and honey. He said that they would have one last day in this crazy place and leave for Athens the following day. It was no big deal. He wondered where they would find a place with some action.

'I don't think there'll be much action today or tonight—the whole town is full of press and officials. The funeral is tomorrow,' Fiona said. She longed to ask if they could leave after the funeral. But she could let that question wait a while. 'There's a lovely little place I saw out on a point—they catch fish and grill them straight from the sea, will we go there?'

He shrugged. Why not? The wine was probably cheaper there than in the fancy places by the harbour anyway.

'We should go now before it gets too hot,' she said, and they walked down the shabby stairs and through the crowded kitchen. She longed to stop and sit there with the family, but she knew that Shane was anxious for his first cold beer of the day. It would soon be noon and it was very hot. They should go to the taverna by the sea straight away.

The day was indeed becoming very hot.

Thomas decided against going up into the hills. He should have left much earlier in the morning for that kind of trip. He looked into the craft shop. Vonni had not opened for business and was asleep in her chair. Suppose she really slept in the henhouse? She could easily sleep in the empty bedroom in the apartment—but he knew better than to ask her.

The shops were closed but he decided to walk along the coast to a simple place on a point that he'd seen a few days back. There had been a wonderful smell of grilling fish when he had passed it then, and it would be just the spot to sit and look out to sea and think. There had been some raggedy umbrellas there that would protect him from the sun, and a cool breeze coming in from the sea. Just the place to go.

Elsa and David's taxi arrived in the old square in the centre of Kalatriada. They stepped out and Elsa paid the driver. Then they stood and looked around. The place had certainly not been discovered by developers. Half the buildings around the square seemed to be tiny restaurants or cafés, and there was a selection of pottery shops. The sea was far below, down a narrow track.

'I'm sure you want to go and find your temple,' Elsa said to David. 'This is a good safe place you brought me, I can hide here.'

'I'm in no great rush to see the temple,' David said. 'I can sit with you for a while.'

'Well, after all those turns and corners, I must say I would love a coffee,' Elsa smiled. 'But truly this is a fine place to come to. You really are my hero.'

'Oh, hero, you say!' David laughed at the idea. 'Not my usual role.'

'Now don't try to tell me that you're normally cast as a villain.' Elsa was cheerful again.

'No, nothing as dashing. The buffoon more often,' he admitted.

'I don't believe it for a moment,' Elsa said.

'That's because you haven't seen me in my real life. I've let my father down in everything, Elsa. Honestly, if he had been given any other kind of son it would have worked. A ready-made business, a position of honour in the community. A lovely home—but it all choked me and made me feel trapped. No wonder he despises me.'

'Shall we sit here, do you think?' Elsa indicated the nearest café and sat down.

The waiter came and spread a piece of waxed paper on another table.

David ordered two *metrios*, the medium-sweet coffees. They soon arrived and the two sipped them companionably.

'I didn't *know* my father, David, but I had many, many arguments with my mother.'

'You see, that's probably more healthy. In my case there aren't any real arguments at all, it's all sighs and shrugs,' David said.

'If you had the time all over again what would you do?' Elsa asked.

'The same, mess it up I imagine.'

'That's so defeatist. You're young. Your parents are alive, for you there is time.' She put down her cup. 'Now, come on. Finish your coffee and we'll go and investigate Kalatriada. And then at lunch I'll tell you my problems and you can give *me* advice.'

Andreas sat with his brother in the police station. Yorghis's desk was piled high with reports about the accident. His phone had been ringing constantly. Now there was a lull.

'I wrote to Adoni today,' Andreas said slowly.

'Good, good,' Yorghis said after a little time.

'I didn't say sorry or anything.'

'No, of course not,' Yorghis agreed.

'Because I'm *not* sorry. You know that.'

'I know, I know.' Yorghis did not need to enquire why his brother had written to the long-estranged son in Chicago. He knew why.

It was because the death of Manos and all the people on the boat had shown them how very short life was. That was all.

Thomas passed the television crews and photographers in the square beside the harbour. It was a job like any other, he supposed, but they did seem somehow like a swarm of insects. They didn't gather where people were having a good time and getting on with life, only where there had been a disaster.

He thought about Elsa, that golden handsome German girl. She had been fairly dismissive of her own role in it all. He wondered where she had been going today in the taxi. Perhaps she knew these German television crews who were gathered around the harbour. Greece was a popular destination for Germans, and it was said that two German visitors had lost their lives on Manos's boat. But even though he looked, she was nowhere to be seen. Perhaps she had not come back from her taxi ride. He walked on to the restaurant on the point.

David and Elsa walked around the ruins of the temple. They were the only visitors. An elderly guide asked them for half a euro and gave them an ill-written and near incomprehensible account of what the temple had once been.

'There could be a fortune made from writing a proper leaflet in German,' Elsa said.

'Or even in English,' David laughed as they wandered back to the square.

'Let's see about this great lunch I'm going to take you to,' she said.

'I'm easy, Elsa . . . look, the waiter where we were before is waving at us, I'm happy to go back there if you are.'

'Of course I am—but then I wanted something more grand because I have to ask another favour of you.'

'You don't have to pay me with an expensive lunch, and I don't suppose Kalatriada has a posh restaurant.'

Their waiter was delighted to see them. 'I knew you come back, lady,' he said, beaming all over his face. He brought a dish of olives and little bits of cheese, he indicated the kitchens where, proudly, he opened up each dish so that they could choose what they would like to eat.

They sat companionably and talked as if they were old friends, wondering what it would have been like to have grown up in a small village like this instead of in big cities. It was only when they were sipping the dark sweet coffee that Elsa said, 'I'll tell you what this is all about now.'

'You don't have to.'

'No, I have to tell you, because I want us to stay here until tomorrow when the funeral in Aghia Anna is over.'

David's mouth opened. '*Stay here?*'

'I can't go back to the town, David, my television crew is there, people will recognise me, they'll tell Dieter, our boss back home, and he'll come and find me. I couldn't bear that.'

'Why?'

'Because I love him so much.'

'So that's bad—if the man you love comes to find you?'

'If it were only as simple as that,' she said, and she took his two hands and held them to her face. He felt the tears splash down over his fingers and onto the table.

'I understand that of course we have to stay here in Kalatriada tonight,' said David, who felt that he was indeed becoming more like a hero as every hour passed.

Fiona and Shane were early and the only people in the restaurant. The waiter left them alone with their fish and some wine by the dark blue sea and white sand. Shane had already drunk two beers and a glass of retsina very quickly. Fiona watched him, waiting for the right time to tell him her news. Finally, she put her hand on his arm and told him that she was six days overdue. She said that since she had been twelve years old she had never been one day late and she felt sure that it really did mean she was pregnant. She looked hopefully into his face.

She saw disbelief written all over it.

He drank another glass of wine before he spoke. 'I can't take this in,' he said. 'We took precautions.'

'Well, we didn't . . . all of the time. If you remember—'

'How could you be so stupid?' he asked

'Well, it wasn't only me.' She was hurt.

'God, Fiona, you really have a way of spoiling everything and wrecking everyone's life,' he said.

'But we *did* want children, we said, you said . . .' Fiona began to cry.

'One day, I said, not now. You're such a fool . . . not now that we're only a month out on the trip.'

'I thought we might stay here, you know, in this place, and we could bring up the baby here.'

'It's not a baby, it's a six-day-overdue period.'

'But it could be a baby, *our* baby.' She struggled to speak through her tears. 'You could get a job in a restaurant maybe, and I could work too . . .'

He stood up and leaned across the table to shout at her. She could hardly hear the things he was saying, so hurtful and cruel were they all. She was a whore, like all women. Scheming and plotting to get him tied down with a brood of children and make him work as a *waiter*. A waiter in a godforsaken place like this.

She must get rid of the baby and never think of coming up with this kind of fairy story again. Never. She was a stupid, brainless fool.

She must have argued with him, none of it was clear, but then she felt the stinging blow on her face with such a shock that she had begun to reel back as he was coming at her again with his fist clenched.

The ground was coming up at her, she felt sick, she was shaking all over. Then she heard the running and shouting behind her and two waiters held Shane back and Thomas, who had arrived from nowhere, was pulling her away, guiding her to a chair.

She closed her eyes as he dabbed her face with cold water.

'You're all right, Fiona,' he said as he stroked her hair. 'Believe me, you're all right now.'

CHAPTER TWO

THE RESTAURANT GAVE THOMAS the number of the police station. Fiona heard Shane laugh when he heard that the call was going to be made.

'Waste of time, Thomas, she's not going to press charges.' He reached for another glass of wine.

The two waiters looked at Thomas as if for advice. Should they let Shane drink or should they restrain him?

But Thomas just nodded slightly. The more drunk Shane became, the worse the impression he would make when the police turned up.

He went into a back room to make the call to the police. He introduced himself to Yorghis, the brother of Andreas, on the phone, who immediately knew who he was.

'You were one of the generous people who gave such a donation to the family of Manos.'

'It was really your brother who did that, he didn't charge us for the meal.'

'Andreas said you were friends.'

'And we are proud to be his friends, but, sir, we have a problem . . .' Thomas explained it all to Yorghis who understood the situation instantly. There was remarkably little red tape. Then Thomas quietly asked the waiters to take Shane into a back room and lock him in. Shane didn't even put up a struggle.

'Leave him some wine, I'll pay,' he said to the waiters, and went to sit down beside Fiona, whose tear-stained face showed someone still in shock.

'It will be fine,' he said, stroking her hand.

'It will never be fine,' she said with a terrible finality. 'We survive, you know, that's why we're all here roaming the earth instead of being extinct.'

And then he didn't say any more while they waited for the police van to arrive. Her face looked sad and empty, but Thomas knew that he was some kind of strength and company for her just by being there.

When Yorghis arrived he told Shane that an assault had been seen by three independent witnesses, that he would be locked up in the police station for twenty-four hours.

'But she didn't mind.' Shane's voice was slurred now and nervous. 'Ask her. I love her, we're together, we might even be going to have a baby—right, Fiona? Tell them.'

She still had her eyes closed.

'That's not important,' Yorghis explained. 'The complaint has not been made by this lady, what she says is irrelevant.' Then he handcuffed Shane and helped him into the police van.

The van had driven off in the sun just as people started to arrive for their lunch. The waiters were relieved. Order had been restored and trade had not been interrupted.

Fiona had said nothing during the whole time but now she started to cry. 'I wish I had a friend, Thomas,' she said.

'I'm your friend.'

'Yes, I know, but I meant a woman friend like Barbara back home, she'd tell me what to do.'

'Do you want to call her? I have a telephone in my apartment,' he suggested.

'It's not the same now. Too many times she offered to help and I didn't listen.'

'I know, you'd have to start too far back.' He was sympathetic.

'I *could* talk to Elsa, but we don't know where she is,' Fiona said sadly, wiping her eyes with a napkin.

'We could find out where she is. I saw her getting into a taxi this morning with David. I don't know where they were going. But why don't we have something to eat to build you up a little? When you are strong enough to walk we'll go and ask the taxi drivers. They won't have forgotten someone like Elsa. She's very warm and sympathetic . . . she's just the person to talk to.'

He was right. They all remembered the German blonde and the small man with glasses. The driver who had taken them to Kalatriada said it had been a wonderful fare.

'Let's go there,' Thomas said, and offered the startled taxi driver his second great fare of the day.

It was certainly a twisty road up through the hills. Once they got to the small town of Kalatriada it was easy to find Elsa and David. Elsa's blonde hair was hard to miss as she bent over some pottery in a little shop.

Elsa panicked. 'Is anyone looking for me?' she asked urgently.

Thomas went straight to the point. 'In a way, Elsa. We were hoping that you and Fiona could have a talk. She's been a bit upset, you see.'

'I can see that,' David said, looking at the livid red mark on Fiona's cheek.

'Next one would have broken her nose,' Thomas said grimly.

'Well, certainly we'll have a talk.' Elsa had her hand on Fiona's arm. 'Sorry for immediately thinking it was about me but I have a few problems, which is why David and I are staying here tonight.'

'Staying here?' Fiona and Thomas spoke together, amazed.

'Sure, it's a nice place, isn't it, and there's a lovely little hotel over there on the other side of the square. We have two rooms. Fiona can share with me and you men can share a room. Is that suitable, do you think?' Elsa's confident smile was back, and they all agreed that it was very suitable indeed.

Ireni, the woman who ran the little hotel, seemed to show no surprise at the ill-assorted group of people with no luggage who had turned up so unexpectedly. She looked tired and bent as she got them towels and a little cake of soap. Her smiles warm but weary, she appeared to do all the cleaning and cooking while three men sat playing a board game in the corner; not one of them helped her.

'A lot of work to be done by the women's movement here in this house, I think,' Elsa whispered to Fiona as they went upstairs to claim their room, leaving Thomas and David downstairs.

'You could probably start with me, Elsa,' Fiona said humbly. 'You don't need to look much further than at me to see a victim.'

Elsa's face was full of sympathy. 'Sleep for a little,' she urged. 'Everything is better after a couple of hours' sleep.'

'I want to tell you about him, and why he does what he does,' Fiona began.

'No, you don't,' Elsa said. 'You want to hear me say you're perfectly right to go back to him and that he didn't mean it.'

Fiona's eyes opened wide.

'Maybe I *will* say that but not now, Fiona. Rest now. We'll talk later. There's all the time in the world. I'll sit here and look at the mountains.'

To her amazement Fiona felt her eyelids become heavy and soon she was breathing deeply.

Elsa sat in the little cane chair and watched the shadows come down over the valley. There was rain tonight, covering the blanket of stars.

They could not eat out of doors, too much rain, Ireni said, but they could sit inside and see the square in Kalatriada. And with the background of old men clicking dice and counters from the backgammon game in the corner, they sat down at a table with a blue and yellow checked cloth and began to eat the kebabs and salad that Irini proudly produced for them. '*Orea*,' David said. '*Poli poli kala!*'

Irini's tired face smiled a big toothless smile. She might only be forty, Elsa thought, less even. It was no life here for her, but she was surrounded by the people she knew and liked, and now four guests were praising the simple food and saying it was beautiful. One of those men at the backgammon tables might be her husband, another her father. There were children's clothes flapping on the line. She probably had a family, little children who knew everyone in the village.

Elsa sighed. Once she would have urged Fiona to look hard at Shane and realise that he would never love her and was probably incapable of loving anyone. She would have said that Fiona should consider all aspects of carrying Shane's child to term. But nowadays Elsa was not at all certain about what was the right thing for anyone to do.

She realised that she had been daydreaming and dragged herself back to the conversation at the table. She had come away to clear her mind, not to sit confused and brooding. She must pay attention and not allow herself to drift off like this again.

Thomas was talking about his landlady. 'Vonni's a real character. She's been here for years, apparently. She never talks about herself, but she speaks Greek like a native. She knows this place Kalatriada well. She comes every few weeks to buy pottery to sell in her craft shop.'

'She's from Ireland, Andreas told me yesterday,' Fiona said. 'I was thinking about her . . . you know, if she could stay here, maybe I could.' Her small pale face looked very sad.

'Did she come here with anyone, do you think?' Elsa wanted to inject some reality back into the discussion before Fiona started living in some fantasy world where she and Shane might raise a family here in the purple Greek mountains.

Thomas didn't know. He told them that although Vonni was so open and friendly you didn't ask her questions. 'But, I think she's fairly pushed for a living. She teaches English, and she sleeps in a sort of shed out back so that she can rent her apartment.'

'How old is she?' Elsa asked.

'Fifty to sixty,' David said.

'Forty to fifty,' Thomas said at the same time. They all laughed.

'Well, so much for dressing up to please men,' Elsa said with a wry smile.

'No, Vonni doesn't dress up, she wears a T-shirt and a coloured skirt and open sandals. I don't expect she's ever worn make-up.' Thomas was thoughtful. 'It's oddly restful, somehow.'

'Do you fancy her then, this restful woman of uncertain age?' Elsa teased him.

'No, not remotely, but she does interest me. I called her before dinner tonight in case she saw no lights in her place and wondered whether I'd disappeared on her.'

'That was thoughtful of you,' Fiona said. It wasn't the kind of thing Shane would have done.

'I told her that I thought we would all probably go back tomorrow for the funeral. I checked that we wouldn't be in the way. She said we should take the bus from the square; one leaves every two hours. Is that OK with everyone?'

'It's fine with me,' David said.

'Yes, and I can go to the police station and talk to Shane,' Fiona said eagerly. 'He will be so sorry and upset by now.'

Elsa was the only one who hadn't spoken.

'Elsa?' Thomas spoke gently.

'I might just stay on here for a couple of days. I could join you all later.' It seemed to need an explanation. She hesitated and then decided to speak. 'It's a little bit awkward, you see. I'm trying to avoid someone and I would prefer to hide out until he has gone away. It would be stupid to meet up with him again in a tiny place like Aghia Anna.'

'And you are certain he's there?' Thomas asked gently.

'Well, this is just his sort of story. No one does human interest better than he does.'

'We could all keep him away from you.' David was busy living up to his heroic role.

'We could tell Yorghis, you know, Andreas's brother, if this man tried to stalk you or harass you.' Thomas was reassuring.

Elsa looked from one to the other. 'No, it's not that. I'm not afraid of him, I'm afraid of myself. Afraid that I might go back to him and then all this—all the business of coming here—would have been such a waste of time.' Her lip was trembling. Elsa the cool, confident Elsa.

They were perplexed.

'I'd stay with you, Elsa,' Fiona began. 'Only I have to go to the police station and check about Shane.'

'You don't *have* to, Fiona, you just want to,' Elsa said.

'Well, I love him, *you* must understand that.' Fiona was stung by this remark. 'Seriously, Elsa. You have to be in love with this fellow otherwise you wouldn't be so afraid of meeting him.'

Thomas intervened. It was getting too serious between the women.

'We've all had a long day . . . suppose we meet here for breakfast at eight. We could get the nine o'clock bus . . . those of us who want to go.

35

Is that OK?' He had a gentle voice, but from years of teaching students he had an air of authority.

They realised he was right, and started to move off.

'Just a moment,' Elsa said. 'I'm very sorry, Fiona, I was rude to you. You have every right to go and see the man you love. And I apologise for putting my own selfish affairs before other people's tragedy. Of course I'll come to the funeral with you and I would be delighted to have the protection of kind friends like you.' She looked from one to the other, her eyes over-bright, as if the smile was hiding a lot of tears.

In the holding cell at the back of the police station, Shane sat with his head in his hands. He needed a cold beer very badly but he was highly unlikely to get one from that ignorant Greek policeman, the brother of the tiresome Andreas up in the taverna.

Where *was* Fiona? He would have thought that she would be here by now. He could send her down to the fish bar at the harbour to get him three cold cans. He banged the plate which had held hard bread against the door.

Yorghis pulled back the shutter and peered in. 'Yes?'

'My girlfriend, I'm sure she's been to see me. Have you kept her away from me? You can't get away with this, you know.'

Yorghis shrugged. 'Nobody came.'

'I don't believe you.'

'Nobody came.' Yorghis began to move away.

'Look—I'm sorry, I didn't mean I didn't believe you exactly, it's just that, you see, we are very close and—'

'It didn't look as if you were very close yesterday,' Yorghis said.

'No, you don't understand, we have a very passionate relationship, naturally it explodes from time to time.'

'*Endaxi*,' Yorghis said.

'What does that mean?'

'It means right, or OK, or whatever you say.' Yorghis moved off. 'I heard she left Aghia Anna yesterday,' Yorghis called over his shoulder.

'I don't believe you!' Shane shouted.

'Believe what you like, I was told she took a taxi and left the place.'

Shane sat there in disbelief. It couldn't be true. Fiona would never leave without him.

'*Kalimera sas*, Yorghis, you look worried.' Vonni stopped to lean on the wall of the police station.

'Well, we have all these crowds of cameramen trampling on everyone for the funeral, the station is full of accident investigators, I have eleven different reports still to compile and I have this young pup in a cell. I don't know what to do with him.'

'The boy who hit the Irish girl?' Vonni asked. Nothing happened that she didn't know about.

'Yes. I wish he were hundreds of miles from here.'

'Well, export him so.'

'What?'

'That's what we used to do in Ireland years ago: if some tearaway was causing trouble the judge or the guards would say that if he was on the mailboat to England that night no further action would be taken.'

Yorghis smiled in disbelief.

'No, it's true, terrible thing to do to England, but we thought, well, England is bigger, it can cope.'

'I see.'

'Suppose you put him on the eleven o'clock boat to Athens. Seriously, Yorghis, he'd be out of here before the funeral starts. It would be an ease to everyone.'

'And indeed Athens is big enough to cope with him.' Yorghis stroked his face thoughtfully.

Vonni's lined, tanned face broke into its wide smile. 'True, Yorghis, Athens is well big enough,' she agreed.

'You can't order me off the island,' Shane said.

'Take it or leave it. We have no time to deal with you now. Locked up here until next week then a prosecution—maybe jail. That's on the one hand. On the other, you get a free trip to Athens. You choose. You have ten minutes.'

'What about my things?' Shane asked.

'One of my boys will drive you past Eleni's house. You can pack your rucksack and be on the boat at ten thirty.'

'I'm not ready to go yet.'

'Suit yourself,' said Yorghis, turning to leave the cell.

'No—wait a minute, come back. I think I'll go.'

Yorghis ushered him out to the police van. Shane got in sulkily.

'Bloody strange way of running a country,' he said.

Back in Eleni's house he noticed that Fiona's things were still there in the room.

'I thought you said she had gone away.'

Eleni explained in Greek that the girl would be back that day. The young policeman knew better than to translate. His boss wanted this violent boy aboard the 11 a.m. ferry and out of his jurisdiction. No point in delaying things because that foolish girl was coming back.

The bus from Kalatriada wound its way through the little hill villages as it headed slowly towards Aghia Anna.

Old women in black got on and off, saluting everyone: some of them carried vegetables, which they might be going to sell at a market; one woman had two hens. A young man played the bouzouki, but the four passengers returning for the funeral were all lost in their own thoughts and concerns about the day that lay ahead of them.

Elsa wondered what were the odds against Dieter turning up in this tiny village where she had run to flee from him.

Fiona hoped that Shane would feel much calmer now. Perhaps she could persuade that nice old man Andreas to put in a word for him; maybe they would let him out for the funeral.

Thomas worked out how he could ask Vonni to sleep in the spare bedroom of her own apartment rather than in that terrible shed.

David looked out at the families of children who waved at the passing bus. He wished he could have had brothers and sisters who would have shared the load. If he had a brother who had trained as an accountant, a sister who had read law and another brother who had gone into Dad's business when he was sixteen and learned it from the ground up—then he, David, would have been properly free to go and learn about pottery somewhere like Kalatriada.

He sighed as he looked out at the hills covered in olive groves. Instead of that, here he was, tortured with guilt. Last night Fiona had touched on Catholic guilt. She didn't even begin to know what Jewish guilt was like!

Vonni gave English lessons to the children in the big room behind her craft shop. She suggested that she would teach them a verse of an English hymn which they could sing at the funeral. It might be a small consolation to the English-speaking relatives who had been arriving on every boat for the past thirty-six hours, coming to the scene of the tragedy. She might even find something in German too.

Everyone thought it was a good idea.

And it would distract the children, take them away from weeping households for a while. The families were grateful to Vonni as they had been for years and years since first she had come to Aghia Anna as a young girl. She had grown older with them all, spoke their language, taught their children, shared the good times and bad. A lot of them could not even remember why she had come here in the first place.

As Thomas went up the whitewashed steps to the apartment above the shop and let himself in, he heard the voices of little children singing: 'The Lord's my shepherd, I'll not want . . .'

38

It had been a long time since he had been in church. Possibly at his father's funeral. That was the last time he had heard it sung. He paused, stricken, in the sunshine.

Andreas and his brother Yorghis, together with a young policeman, stood beside the ferry.

'Is there anything you would like to do before you leave?' Andreas asked.

'Like what? Like congratulate you on your legendary Greek hospitality for example?' Shane sneered.

'Like write a letter to your girlfriend.' Andreas was curt. 'She might like to know that you are safe and well, and free . . . and that you'll contact her when you are settled.'

'I don't have any paper or a pen,' Shane said.

'I do.' Andreas offered both. 'A few short words perhaps?'

'Oh, for God's sake.' Shane turned away.

They blew the whistle to show the boat was about to leave. The young policeman escorted Shane on deck and came back to Andreas and Yorghis.

'It's better he doesn't write to her,' he said to the older men.

'In the long term certainly,' Andreas agreed. 'But in the short term it will break her poor little heart.'

David and Fiona walked with Elsa back to her apartment.

'Look, nobody around,' David said. It was true. The streets that had thronged with press and bureaucrats were quiet now.

'I wish I could stay longer, I just have to check Shane is all right,' Fiona apologised, as she went up the hill towards the police station. From down in the harbour they all heard the hooting of the 11 a.m. ferry as it left for Athens. At midday another boat would arrive carrying even more people coming to the funeral.

'Would you like me to stay with you here, Elsa?' David asked.

'Just for five minutes so that I don't run away again,' she laughed.

'You won't do that.' He patted her hand.

'I hope not, David. Tell me, did you ever in your life love anyone obsessively, foolishly?'

'No. I never loved anyone at all,' he said.

'I'm sure that's not so.'

'I'm afraid it is, and it's not something to be proud of at twenty-eight.' He was apologetic.

'You're exactly the same age as I am!' she exclaimed in surprise.

'You put your years to better use than I did,' he said.

'No, you wouldn't say that if you knew. I'd prefer never to have loved.' She reached out and stroked his cheek. 'You're a dear gentle person, and I'm so happy to have you here. Shall we make ourselves a little lunch together? We could eat on the balcony and see without being seen. Would you hate that?'

'Of course not, I'd love it,' said David.

'Hello, I wonder if I could speak to the police chief, please.'

Yorghis stood up wearily.

Fiona stood there in a little blue cotton dress with a white wool shoulder bag. Her hair falling over her face didn't hide the bruise. She looked frail and unable to cope with the hand that life had dealt her.

'Come in, *Kyria*, sit down,' he said, offering her a chair.

'You see, my friend stayed here with you last night,' she began, as if Yorghis ran some up-market bed and breakfast instead of a jail.

Yorghis spread out his hands in front of him. She looked so anxious to see this boy, so forgiving of what he had done. How did young pigs like that get good women to love them?

'He has gone to Athens,' Yorghis said baldly.

'No, he can't have, not without me, it's not possible.'

'On the eleven o'clock ferry.'

'Did he not leave me a note? Tell me where I should meet him? I must go on the next boat, I must go to him,' she said. She was weeping now. 'I have to be with him . . .'

'There will be no more boats leaving today, because of the funeral. Please, please be calm. It's better that he left.'

'No, no, how could it be better?'

'Because otherwise he would be in jail, locked up. At least he is free.'

'Oh, why did I go away? I'll never forgive myself . . .'

Yorghis patted her shoulder awkwardly as she sobbed. Over her shoulder, down at the foot of the hill, he saw Vonni passing by with her little troupe of children and it gave him an idea.

'Andreas tells me you are a nurse?' he said. 'Do you see Vonni down there, she's looking after the children during the funeral, I know she'd love you to give her a hand.'

'I'm not sure I could help anyone just now . . .' Fiona began.

'That's often when we help best,' Yorghis said.

Thomas went to Elsa's apartment, as he had promised, and was surprised to hear voices inside. Perhaps she had met her friend after all. He knocked on the door and was confused when David opened it.

'It's only Thomas,' David called out. It wasn't much of a welcome.

'Well, I *did* tell Elsa that I'd walk with her to the church,' Thomas said huffily.

'Lord, I'm sorry, Thomas, it's just that we thought . . . we were afraid that . . .'

Elsa came out to join them. She was wearing a smart cream linen dress with a navy jacket.

'Thomas, I asked David to answer the door for me because I still think that Dieter will come calling. Forgive me.'

'What's to forgive?' Thomas was putting on his tie at the little mirror in the hall.

'I should have gone home for a tie too.' David was worried.

'No, you look fine, David,' Thomas said, and they set out together following the crowds to the little church. People stood on both sides of the street winding up from the harbour.

Then a hush came over the crowd and they stood in silence at the approach of the funeral party. Lines of men and women walked behind the coffins in a little procession.

At the back walked the English and German families who had come so unexpectedly to this Greek village to mourn their loved ones.

There was room in the little church for only a tenth of the people gathered to mourn. Crackling speakers relayed the service to the people outside and, unexpectedly, in the middle of the Greek prayers and music, came the sound of children singing 'The Lord is My Shepherd', then a verse from a German hymn.

When the congregation came out of the church and prepared to walk the short journey up to the graveyard, Elsa spotted Fiona. She was with Vonni and the children, all of whom had armfuls of wild flowers.

'Another day, another surprise,' Thomas said. 'Who would have thought she would have got her act together.'

'It's probably to take her mind off Shane,' Elsa decided.

Yorghis made an announcement. The families would like to go alone to the burial service in the graveyard. They thanked people for coming to the church, but now they wanted to be alone. They had asked the café owners and restaurants to open again and for life to carry on. They were sure everyone would understand.

'I don't really want to be alone just now,' Elsa appealed.

'I could treat you to a glass of retsina and a little plate of *kalamari* and olives down at the harbour. Look, they're all putting out chairs,' Thomas said.

'I think Elsa would feel happier out of the public eye,' David said.

'Sure, I forgot. Listen, I have some nice cold retsina in my place, you know, over the craft shop. Is that an OK plan?'

'Very OK,' Elsa smiled. 'I'll just go home and get a scarf for the evening breeze and then I'll get some olives in Yanni's on the way back and see you at your place.' She seemed happy with what had been arranged.

Thomas was soon tidying up his sitting room and getting out glasses. The two men chatted easily for a while as they set out paper napkins and little plates.

Eventually David said what they were both thinking. 'Elsa is a very long time getting the olives, isn't she?'

There was a long pause.

'I suppose she met him,' Thomas said.

'And went off with him,' David said.

Elsa saw Dieter as soon as she came out of Yanni's delicatessen. He was at the end of the street, talking to Claus, the chief cameraman, and looking at his watch. She moved back into the doorway of Yanni's shop but not quickly enough.

Dieter had seen her.

She could see him running towards her.

'Elsa! Elsa!' he called, pushing past the people in the narrow street. His face was flushed and his eyes were bright. She had forgotten how handsome he was, like Robert Redford in his early years.

There was no escape: he was beside her.

'Dieter?' she said uncertainly.

'Darling Elsa, what are you *doing* here, what did you mean by running away?' He stood with his hands on her shoulders, admiring her and drinking her in.

She said nothing, just looked into his very blue eyes.

'Claus heard you were here. Someone from one of the other networks saw you yesterday, but I didn't believe them. Oh, my dearest lovely Elsa—how very, very good to have found you.'

She shook her head. 'You haven't found me, you've just met me by chance. Now I must go.'

She saw Claus move back discreetly: he wanted no part of this lovers' quarrel.

'Elsa, don't be ridiculous—you leave your job, you leave me, no explanation for either . . . you think there is nothing to discuss?' He called out to the cameraman, 'Claus, I'm going to stay the night here, you go back with the others and I'll call you tomorrow.'

'Don't stay for me, Dieter, I beg you. And if you try to force me or threaten me, I swear I'll get the police.'

'Threaten you, Elsa?' He was astounded at the idea. 'As if I would!

I *love* you, Elsa. Is it so demanding and mad that I ask you to tell me why you left me?'

'I wrote to you,' she said.

'Twelve lines,' he said, reaching into his jacket. 'I carry it everywhere, I know it by heart, I am always hoping one day I will read it and it will make sense.' He looked so confused she felt herself softening.

'It's all there,' she said.

'Nothing is there, Elsa. I'll go away, leave you alone, I swear, if you tell me. Just tell me why you threw away two years like that. You owe me that much.'

She was silent. Perhaps she did owe him more than a twelve-line letter.

'Where are you staying? Let me come to your place,' he asked quickly, seeing her hesitation.

'Not my place, no. Are you at the Anna Beach?' It was the one vaguely touristy, comfortable place. She would have expected him to be there.

'Yes, exactly,' he agreed.

'Right, I'll go there with you, we can talk in the conservatory.'

He seemed to expel a sigh of relief. 'Thank you,' he said.

'First I have to leave a message.'

He produced his mobile phone.

'No, I don't know the number.' She went into the delicatessen and gave the olives back to Yanni. There was some discussion and it was agreed. Yanni's little brother would take the bag of olives and a note to the apartment over Vonni's craft shop. She scribbled something on a piece of card.

'You didn't even write twelve lines to this guy—I suppose I should be flattered,' Dieter said.

She smiled at him. 'No, it's not a guy, it's two guys actually.'

'You were so helpful today, Fiona. The parents said to thank you very much.'

'It was nothing, I love children.' Her voice was sad.

'You will have your own one day.'

'I don't know, Vonni, I really don't. Did you have children?'

'One,' Vonni said. 'A son, but it wasn't what you'd call straightforward.' Her tone meant that the subject was closed. She was prepared to talk, but not about her son.

'Vonni, I could be pregnant now,' Fiona said in a rush. 'And . . . well, it's not what you'd call straightforward either.'

'And the young man who has gone to Athens—does he know?'

'Sort of, I told him badly, you see.'

'You shouldn't be on your own now,' Vonni said.

'I'll go to Elsa's place,' Fiona said. But there was no reply there.

The people in David's house said he had not come home, so Vonni escorted her to the apartment above the craft shop.

'I'll wait here until I see you have someone to be with,' she said, and stood in the street as Fiona went up the steps to the apartment.

Vonni saw Thomas open the door and welcome Fiona in, then she went back to the harbour.

At the Anna Beach most of the journalists were at the checkout desk. Another job was over, another disaster recorded, and now they were heading off to the next one.

Dieter and Elsa went over to the big rattan chairs and low tables of the conservatory. Below them the dark blue sea lapped innocently against the rocks.

Dieter ordered coffee for two.

'Sorry.' Elsa called the waiter back. 'I would like an *ouzo* and water, please.'

'Please don't be difficult,' Dieter begged her.

'Difficult? Choosing what I want to drink?' she asked, perplexed.

'No, you know, scoring points,' he said.

'Oh, I'm way beyond that now. Anyway, Dieter, you wanted to talk, so here I am. Talk to me.'

'No, I wanted *you* to talk, I wanted you to tell me why you disappeared, ran out on everything . . . to hide in a backwater like this.'

'I'm not hiding,' Elsa said indignantly. 'I resigned from my work formally; I am here under my own name; when you asked me to come and meet you I came. So where's the secrecy bit? And why do you call it a backwater? Look over at that desk—half the world's media is here . . . plenty of action I'd say.'

'I hate it when you're flippant, Elsa, it's an act, and it doesn't suit you.'

The waiter arrived. Elsa poured some water into the aniseed drink and watched it go cloudy. Then she drained it in one gulp.

'That was fast!' He was startled and amused as he began to sip his coffee.

'Well, why don't you finish yours too—then we can go to your room?'

'*What?*' he looked at her in astonishment.

'Your room,' she repeated as if he were a little deaf. 'You said talk, but you don't mean talk, do you? You mean screw.'

He looked at her. 'Elsa, there's no need to be crude about it all. That's not what we had.'

'Sorry, I thought that's just what we had every night you came to my apartment, and lunchtime too, when it could be managed.'

'Elsa, I love you, you love me, why on earth are you reducing it all to such coarse words?'

'So you don't want me to go to bed with you?' She looked at him innocently.

'You know I do.'

'Well, finish your coffee and get your key,' she said.

David didn't want to go back to the house where he was staying. The family were wiped out with grief over their dead son and he felt in the way. Fiona didn't want to walk all the way out to Eleni's house to sleep there alone in the knowledge that Shane had left her.

'Why don't you both stay here?' Thomas suggested suddenly. 'Fiona can have that room at the back, David can have the sofa bed.' He looked at their faces, both of them very grateful and relieved.

The Hotel Anna Beach had little bungalows facing the sea. Dieter opened his bungalow door with his key and stood back to let Elsa go in first. She didn't sit down but stood looking at the pictures on the walls, big blown-up photographs of the coast.

'This is not what I had expected,' he said.

'But we have agreed that it's what you'd like,' she smiled.

'That's not a real smile, Elsa,' he began.

'You taught me to smile for television. Teeth and eyes, you said. Teeth and eyes. I remember it well.'

'Please, my love, you *are* my love. Please don't be brittle.'

'No, indeed. And let's not waste time either.' Elsa had already taken off her navy jacket. Now she drew the cream linen dress over her head and laid it neatly on the back of the chair.

He was still very unsure.

She removed her lace bra and pants and placed them on top of her dress, then finally she stepped out of her smart navy sandals.

'You are so beautiful, and to think I believed I'd never see you again.' He looked at her in open admiration.

'Not you, Dieter. You get everything you want.' She put her arms around his neck and kissed him. And suddenly it was as if they had never been apart.

In the apartment over the craft shop, Fiona had gone to bed in the small white room that Vonni had furnished with a turquoise bedspread and a bright blue chair. The little white chest of drawers had a blue-framed mirror and some shells and pottery on top. It was cool and welcoming.

Fiona was weary and sad. It had been a nightmare of a day, and further nightmares were ahead. She didn't think she would sleep. Too much had happened and the future was too frightening. She gave a little sob. It was such a tragedy that people misunderstood Shane and brought out the worst in him.

She lay on the bed with its blue cover and cried herself to sleep.

In the room next door Thomas and David heard the sounds of weeping through the wall.

'She's crying over that bastard!' David whispered in amazement.

'I know, it's beyond comprehension,' Thomas whispered back.

And they sat there and waited until the sobs had died down. Then they smiled at each other in relief.

'Do you know what we're like?' David said. 'We're like the parents of a toddler who won't go to sleep.'

Thomas sighed. 'Yes, there was always that moment of not wanting to leave the room until you were *sure* he was asleep, and then just when you crept to the door he'd call you back. They were great days really.' He looked sad, thinking about his son.

David thought hard about what to say. He so often got it wrong.

'It's hard to understand women, isn't it?' he said eventually.

Thomas looked at him thoughtfully. 'It sure is, David, the exact same thought was going through my mind. Fiona crying over that drunken brute who would have beaten her senseless, Elsa going off with the man she had run a thousand miles to escape, my wife who used to tell me she loved poetry and literature and art living with a bonehead who has some exercise machine in every room of my house.' He sounded very bitter.

David looked at him, stricken. It had not been a good thing to say after all.

Dieter stroked Elsa's face.

'I must have been mad to think I had lost you,' he said.

She said nothing.

'It will all be fine again,' he said.

Still no reply.

'You could not love me like that and not mean it?' he said, just a little anxiously now.

Elsa lay there saying nothing.

'Speak to me, tell me that you'll come back with me and it will all be fine again . . .'

She still said nothing at all.

'Please, Elsa . . . please?'

She got up slowly from the bed and put on the big white fluffy robe that was hanging on the bathroom door, then sat in the big bamboo chair looking at him.

'You'll come home with me, Elsa?'

'No, of course I won't. This is goodbye. You know this and I know this, so let's not be foolish, Dieter.'

'This is insane, we were meant for each other. You know it, I know it. Everyone knows it.'

'No. Everyone does *not* know. A few people at work know and say nothing, because they take their lead from you. And, because you do not want us to go public, we have lived a secret life for two years. So less of the *everyone knows we are meant for each other* line.'

He looked at her, startled. 'We went into it, eyes open. Both of us,' he said.

'And I'm walking out of it, eyes open,' Elsa said calmly.

'So what are we talking about then?' He was genuinely bewildered. 'What do you want? Tell me. If you're holding a gun to my head and saying we must be married, then all right. If that's what it takes, all right, that's what we'll do.'

'I've heard of better proposals,' she said with a smile.

'Stop playing the fool. If it's the only way I can have you with me, I'll marry you. Be *proud* to marry you,' he added as an afterthought.

'No, thank you, Dieter. I don't want to marry you.'

'So what *do* you want?' he cried, in near despair.

'I want to get over you, to forget you, to make you no longer any part of my life.'

'You took an odd way to show all that.' He looked down at the bed she had so recently left.

Elsa shrugged. 'I told you. I no longer trust you, I don't admire you or respect you any more. Sex has nothing to do with those things. Sex is just sex, a short amount of pleasure, excitement. You told me that yourself, if you remember.'

'I do remember, but it was in totally different circumstances. We were talking about a meaningless drunken encounter at a film festival with some silly girl whose name I can't even remember.'

'Birgit. And she remembers you.'

'Only well enough to tell you and upset you over something that couldn't have mattered less.'

'I know, I realise that.'

'So tell me, Elsa, if you realise this, what in God's name is all this drama about? Why did you leave?'

'I wrote it in my letter.'

'You did *not* write it, you wrote some rubbish about responsibilities and lines having to be drawn.' His handsome face was working with emotion and his thick hair was tousled.

'Birgit told me about Monika,' Elsa said.

'Monika? Monika? But she was ages before I met you. We agreed that the past was past. Didn't we?'

'Yes.'

'So why bring her up? I swear I never saw her since I met you. Not even once.'

'I know.'

'So explain to me. I beg you. If you know I haven't seen or thought of Monika in years . . . what is this about?'

'You haven't seen or thought of your daughter either.'

'Ah,' Dieter said. 'Birgit really went to work, didn't she?'

Elsa said nothing.

'It was never meant to happen. I told Monika I wasn't ready to be a parent, to settle down. She knew that from the very start.' He was beginning to bluster now.

'How old is she, Dieter?' Elsa's voice was level.

He was genuinely confused. 'Monika?'

'Gerda. Your daughter.'

'I don't know . . . about eight or nine, I suppose. But all that has nothing to do with us, Elsa.'

'You fathered a child. That has got something to do with you.'

'No, it has not. That was not my fault. Monika was in charge of contraception. I have nothing to do with her child. We both began again.'

'But Gerda began with no father.'

'Stop calling her by her name, you don't know her.'

'You should have told me.'

'No. If I had that would have been wrong too. You would have said I was always hanging around a child from a previous relationship. Be fair, Elsa, you would not have liked that either.'

'I'd have liked it a hell of a lot more than a father who opted out and left a child hoping and wondering. It's my own story all over again. My father left home and I spent years waiting and hoping that he would write or call or come to see me.'

'It was different in your case: your father *had* lived at home with you. In my case I had nothing to do with Monika's child. There were no expectations.'

Elsa gave him a long look, then stood up.

'What do you want me to do?' he asked eventually.

'Nothing, Dieter.'

'You'd come back to me if I made some kind of link to this totally strange child?'

'No, I will not come back to you ever.'

'But all this . . .' Again he looked at the bed where they had made love. 'Did it mean nothing to you?'

'You know it did. It meant goodbye,' she said, and put on her dress and her sandals. Slipping her underwear in her bag, she walked to the door.

'You *can't* do this!' he cried.

'Goodbye, Dieter,' she said and walked through the manicured little rock gardens of the Anna Beach towards the gate.

From his bungalow Dieter called after her. 'Don't go, Elsa, please don't go. I love you so much. Don't leave me . . .' But she walked on.

CHAPTER THREE

THOMAS HAD GONE OUT for hot fresh bread and figs for their breakfast. He made a large pot of coffee and rattled the cups.

Fiona emerged pale and tired-looking, but with a grateful smile. David came eagerly to the breakfast table.

'He spoils us, Fiona. Weren't we lucky to find a benefactor?'

'Oh, I know.' Fiona too was fervent. 'I feel much, much stronger today, I'm full of plans now, so I am.'

Thomas smiled at her. 'Tell us your plans,' he said.

'I'm going up to the station to see the chief of police. I'll ask him to help me find Shane. We were only in Athens for twenty-four hours on the way here, but he loved Syntagma Square. Perhaps Yorghis might know some policemen there who could give Shane a message. Then I'll go back to Eleni's and change my clothes—I've been wearing this dress for days—then I'm going to find Vonni and ask her does she need any help with the children.' Her eyes were bright and enthusiastic.

David too seemed to be energised. 'I'm going to walk up to that taverna and see Andreas again.'

'Later on, when they're all awake in California, I shall call my son,' said Thomas. 'But first I'm going to find Vonni. I'm going to *insist* that from now on she stays in her own bedroom. I'm getting antsy just having her living in that place in the yard.'

'*Antsy*?' Fiona asked.

'I know, it's a great word, isn't it. Means something irritates you, gives you ants in your pants.'

'Shane will love that,' Fiona said happily.

Elsa was in her apartment. She knew that she would not sleep so she sat on her balcony and watched the dawn come up in Aghia Anna. Then she went in, had a long shower and washed her hair. She put on a fresh yellow cotton dress and sat down on the balcony again to watch the ferry getting ready to leave.

He would leave on the 8 a.m. for Athens. She was utterly certain of this. Dieter knew she wasn't coming with him, so why wait for the 11 a.m.? He wasn't a person to hang about.

And then she saw him, his hair tousled, wearing an open-necked shirt, and gripping that leather bag she had seen so often. His eyes were raking the crowds around as if he were going to see her in their number. He saw nothing, but he knew her well enough to assume that she was watching. He put down his bag and raised both his arms in the air.

'I love you, Elsa!' he called out. 'Wherever you are I will always love you.'

Some of the young men near him clapped him on the back approvingly. Declaring love was good.

Elsa sat like stone as the little ferry sailed across the sea to Piraeus, the harbour of Athens. The tears dropped slowly down her face and splashed into her coffee and onto her lap.

'David, my friend, welcome, welcome.' Andreas was delighted to see him.

David wished that he could have a father like this, a man whose face lit up when he approached, not a man whose features had set in discontent and disappointment over his only son for as long as David could remember. Andreas and David talked easily about the sad funeral and how Aghia Anna would never be the same again.

'Did you know Manos well?' David asked.

'Yes, we all know each other here, there are no secrets. We know everyone's history. Manos used to come to play with Adoni and little Stavros when he was a child. They made a swing on that tree over there. He used to come up here to escape from his family—there were eight of them. Adoni was an only child so we were happy to have friends come up here to play with him.' Andreas nodded several times. 'Now, come, David. Share a lunch with me. We won't see many visitors today.'

David looked at the open cabinets of food the old man had prepared and he felt a lump in his throat. To have got all this ready and then for nobody to arrive.

'I never tried that big pasta dish,' he began.

'David, if you don't mind, I can freeze that one. I only make it this morning. Could I persuade you to have the *moussaka* or the *calamari*?'

'I'd prefer the *moussaka*. I only said the pasta because I didn't want all your hard work to go to waste,' David said.

'What a kind person you are. Sit here in the sunshine and I will get the glasses and plates . . .'

And David sat wondering what that foolish young man was doing in Chicago when he could be here.

Eleni welcomed Fiona back. It was a shock to see all Shane's things gone, his crumpled shirts and jeans, his canvas bag, his tin of tobacco and whatever else it might contain. Fiona had hoped desperately that he might have left a note for her with Eleni, but it hadn't happened. She felt very dizzy suddenly. Perhaps it was the stuffy room or the realisation that Shane really had gone out of her life. She felt as if she might faint, but she steeled herself in front of the kindly Eleni, whose face was sympathetic and pitying.

Then she felt a hot, wet sensation on her thighs.

It must be sweat. It was such a hot day.

But as she looked down at her sandals she knew what it was.

And Eleni knew too, as she saw the blood. The Greek woman helped her to a chair. '*Ela, ela, ela,*' she said and ran for towels.

'Eleni, could you find Vonni for me, please. Vonni . . . you know?'

'*Xero*, yes, Vonni,' Eleni said, and shouted down to the children.

Fiona closed her eyes. Vonni would be here soon and would know what to do.

Vonni was sitting opposite Thomas in her apartment over the craft shop.

'I've told you before, I'm telling you again, you are paying me an enormous number of euros so that this is your place. Because of you I am a rich woman, so I will not *take* your pity and sleep in your house.'

'Have you no concept of friendship, Vonni?' he asked. 'I am asking you, as my friend: sleep in that little room you decorated so beautifully. Sleep there, not where chickens are crapping all over you.'

Vonni pealed with laughter. 'Oh, Thomas, you are *so* Californian, so hygienic, there are no chickens crapping on me. A couple of hens . . .'

Just at that moment, they heard children shouting something urgently up the staircase.

'I must go,' she said, standing up.

He reached out and grabbed her wrist. 'Vonni, you are not going any-where unless you agree to what I offer. Do you hear me?'

'I hear, I agree,' she said to his surprise.

'Good, well then, OK, you can go.'

'Come with me if you like, you can help, get us a taxi from the square.' To his even greater surprise she snatched some towels from his bathroom and ran down the steps to talk in Greek to two little boys.

'What's happening?' he asked as he ran after her.

'What's happening is . . . that Fiona is losing the baby of that little shit who beat her up.'

Thomas ran for a taxi and Vonni bundled Eleni's two little sons into the back seat, congratulating them for having found her. A taxi ride was a rare treat and they were beaming with pleasure.

When they arrived at Eleni's house, they asked the taxi to wait in case they might need him. Thomas stayed downstairs watching the little boys play and make occasional journeys to stroke the car in which they had travelled. Vonni had gone upstairs and he could hear the women's voices as they spoke in English and Greek. From what he could make out, Fiona would be all right.

Then Vonni came down and reassured him.

'She's going to be fine, she's lost some blood but she's a nurse after all and she's a sensible little thing about everything except that fool. She thinks he'll be upset when he hears. God protect us!'

'Is she all right staying here?'

'I don't think so. They don't speak English in any real sense . . . what I was thinking—' Vonni began.

'Was that she might come and stay with us,' Thomas interrupted.

'No, not that at all. I was going to suggest she spent a couple of days with Elsa, the German girl.'

Thomas shook his head. 'I think Elsa's a bit tied up with her own affairs just now, better if she comes to us,' he said.

'You might find she's not tied up any more,' Vonni said. 'I hear her German friend left on the eight a.m. ferry.'

'I imagine she must be very upset then.' Thomas was pessimistic.

'No, I think it was her doing, but we needn't necessarily say that we know all this?' Vonni suggested.

'I expect you know where she lives?' Thomas said, smiling.

'I know the apartment building, but perhaps you could take the taxi that's outside and ask her?'

'Would I be the right person?' He was doubtful.

'Nobody better. I'll wait here until you come back.'

Eleni's little boys had never known such a day.

A trip in a taxi, people coming and going, sheets and towels being pinned on the line in great numbers to wave in the sunshine. The tall American man with the funny trousers had brought them a big water-melon to share when he came back the second time. They went behind the house and ate it all, then planted the seeds in the earth.

The American man, who was waiting near the taxi, watched them with a pleased expression on his face. Then the woman who had been sick came down with Vonni and their mother and the smart woman in a yellow dress who looked like a film star.

The sick woman's bag had been packed for her, so she must be leaving for good. She kept talking about money and their mother kept shaking her head. Eventually the man with the mad trousers, who must be a millionaire, travelling all day in a taxi, insisted their mother take some notes and then they were all gone.

Except Vonni, who sat down to have coffee with their mother.

'I'll only stay a couple of days until I get myself together,' Fiona promised.

'I'll be glad of your company,' Elsa assured her as she took out Fiona's clothes from the canvas bag, shook them and hung them up. 'There's an iron here, we can get all domestic later on.'

Fiona looked at Elsa's cream linen dress and navy jacket drying on hangers out on the balcony.

'Aren't you disciplined, Elsa, that's what you were wearing at the funeral yesterday, and look, you have it all laundered already.'

'I'll never wear either of them again but I wanted to give them away to someone, so I washed them first.' Elsa spoke calmly. 'Try it on later, and if it fits you, Fiona, and suits you, then you are more than welcome to it.'

Fiona lay back against the pillow and closed her eyes. It was all too much to take in.

Elsa pulled the curtains to darken the room. 'I'm going to sit and read. It's too hot outside so I'll be here in the room with you.'

'Will you be able to read in the dark?' Fiona asked.

'Sure. There's a nice beam of light coming in here.' She settled in a chair by the window.

'Did you meet him, Elsa?' Fiona asked.

'Yes. Yes, I did.'

'And are you glad you did?'

'Well, it was just to say goodbye, really. It had to be said, it wasn't easy, but it's finished now.'

'Dead easy to say, but not to do.' Fiona's voice sounded sleepy. Soon she was asleep, breathing regularly. Elsa looked at her as she slept. She must be about twenty-three or twenty-four, but she looked even younger. Hadn't it all been a great mercy?

Thomas had worked out when best to call his son, Bill. It would be when the boy was having breakfast. He dialled the number, wondering what the chances were that he would get straight through to his son.

As it happened, it was Andy who answered the phone.

'Well, hi, Thomas. Good of you to call the other night. One helluva scene that must have been.'

'Yeah, it was very tragic.' Thomas felt his voice becoming clipped and curt. The man was insufferable, calling a catastrophe that had ripped the soul out of a small village 'one helluva scene'. 'Is Bill around?'

'He's helping his mother do the dishes,' Andy said, as if that's all there was to it.

'Sure, and could you perhaps tell him he might dry his hands and come talk to his father phoning from the other side of the world?'

'I'll see if he's through.' Andy was genial about it. In the distance Thomas was aware that Vonni was watching him from the kitchen door. It didn't help his mood.

'Hi, Dad.' Bill always sounded delighted to hear him.

'How are things, son. Good?'

'Yeah, fine.'

'So what are you going to do today? It's only morning there, isn't it?'

'Yes, well, we'll be going to the shopping mall first. I'm getting new sneakers and then Andy is going to take me for a run to try them out.'

'Sounds great,' said Thomas, in a voice that sounded sepulchral across the thousands of miles between them. 'I miss you, son.'

'Yeah, Dad, and I miss you too. A lot. But it *was* you who went away,' the child answered.

'Who told you that? Was it your mother? Andy? Listen to me, Bill. We discussed this endlessly; better for me to go and give you space together as a family—'

'No, Dad. She doesn't say that,' Bill interrupted. 'And Andy doesn't either. I just said I missed you and that I was still here and you were the one that was gone.'

'I'm sorry, Bill. We're all upset here. So many people died. Please forgive me. I'll call again soon.'

Vonni came towards him with a brandy.

'You made a right dog's dinner out of that,' she said.

'You don't understand what it is to have a son,' he said to her, willing the tears away from his eyes.

'Why the hell do you assume I don't have a son?' she asked him, her eyes blazing.

'You do?' He was astonished.

'Yes, so you don't have a monopoly on being a parent.'

'And where is he? Why isn't he with you?'

'Because like you I made a mess of things.'

Yorghis drove up to the taverna. Someone had given him a big leg of lamb. He thought maybe Andreas could cook it for his customers. Andreas explained, sadly, that nobody but David had come to the taverna today and it didn't look likely that anyone would come tonight. But then Andreas had an idea. Why didn't they cook it at the police station, give all those men who had worked so hard at the funeral a real dinner?

They would ask David and his friends to join them, and Vonni. Andreas scraped up all the salads into a big bowl. He was pleased at the thought of cooking for people rather than sitting in his empty taverna.

'It's not very comfortable, of course, in the police station,' Yorghis said doubtfully. 'Not very welcoming.'

'We'll get those long red cushions. We can put them on benches.' Andreas would not let the idea die. 'David, run up to Adoni's room and get them, will you?'

David looked at him in surprise. Adoni had been gone for years in Chicago yet he still had his own room in this house?

'At the top of the stairs on the left,' Yorghis advised him and David hastened up the narrow steps.

The room had pictures of Panathinaikos, the Athens football team, and posters of a Greek dance troupe; it had images of the Panayia, the Virgin Mary. He was a man of varied tastes, the missing Adoni.

His bed was made as if he were coming back that night, with a bright red rug folded at the end. On the window seats were long red cushions. He grabbed them and went down to help them pack Yorghis's van.

'This will cheer us all up, brother Yorghis,' Andreas said with a smile.

They called first on Thomas and left David there. Thomas sounded pleased at the prospect of the feast and said he would go out to get some wine. Vonni said she'd check out the situation with Elsa and Fiona. She explained briefly to David what had happened to Fiona.

'That's terrible,' David said. 'But maybe it might be all for—'

'Don't even go there, David. You might think it, I might think it, but Fiona most definitely does *not* think it. I thought I'd warn you.'

'Very wise,' David agreed. 'I always say the wrong thing anyway. But what of Elsa? I thought that she had gone off with her German friend?'

'I know,' Vonni said. 'But to be honest, I wouldn't go there either!'

The young policemen were delighted with the great smells of cooking meat, basted with garlic and oregano. It had been an exhausting and draining time. It was good to relax with their boss, his brother, Vonni and the four tourists. One of the girls looked like a beauty queen, the other very washed out, as if she had been ill.

The two men were very different: one tall and lanky in ludicrous baggy Bermuda shorts with pockets, the other small and serious with spectacles.

Andreas carved proudly and the moonlight made patterns on the sea as the clouds raced across the sky.

'It seems so long since we were in Kalatriada,' Fiona said.

'When the night was full of rain beating against the roof and the walls. It was only two nights ago,' Elsa said. 'And so much has happened since!' She reached out and held Fiona's hand as a gesture of solidarity.

Down near the harbour they saw a group of young men gather in front of the little house that belonged to Maria and Manos. And soon they saw other people leave the cafés and restaurants to join them.

'What's happening?' Thomas asked, anxious in case anything was wrong.

Vonni spoke gently. 'It's no problem. Some of the young men said they would like to dance tonight in honour of Manos and his friends, outside his house, in memory of how he used to dance *Syrtaki*.'

'There isn't usually dancing after a funeral here,' Yorghis said.

'This isn't a usual funeral,' Vonni said quietly.

And as they watched, twelve men with black trousers and white shirts lined up, arms on each other's shoulders. The bouzouki players played a few chords and then they began. Bending, swooping, leaping in the night, as Manos and his friends had done until just a few short days ago.

Maria and her children sat on chairs outside their little house. When all this was a long-distant memory, perhaps the children would recall the night that Aghia Anna had come out to dance for their father. The crowd grew ever bigger and they could see people wiping tears from their eyes.

Then the crowd began to clap in time to the music and dancing, every single person joining in. From their verandah at the police station, the group watched too. All of them were wordless, watching the scene. It was so different to anything they had ever seen before.

Elsa passed a paper table napkin to Fiona who was crying openly.

'What a wonderful thing to do,' Fiona said when she could speak. 'I'll never forget this night. And those same stars are shining on Athens and on all our homes everywhere.'

56

CHAPTER FOUR

IN FIONA'S HOME they were talking about her as they did almost every evening. Her mother was looking at the pictures of Aghia Anna in the *Evening Herald*.

'Imagine Fiona being in that very place!' she said in surprise.

'Imagine!' her husband grunted.

'But, Sean, it *was* good of her to ring in case we'd be worried about her. At least she thought that we might be concerned.'

'Why would we be concerned? We didn't know where the hell she was except joined at the hip to that lout.' Fiona's father found very few silver linings in the whole situation, very little cause to see the bright side. He picked up the remote control and turned on the television deliberately to end the conversation.

His wife went over to the set and turned it off.

'Maureen! Why did you do that? I wanted to watch that.'

'No, you didn't want to watch anything, you just didn't want to talk about Fiona. But she's your child as much as mine.'

'She's not a child, according to you . . . she's a woman of twenty-four. She is entitled to make her own decisions, that's what you said.'

'Sean, I said that we were only going to alienate her by attacking Shane, that she was old enough to know the choices she was making. I didn't say that any of them were right.'

'Huh,' he said.

'I want you to listen to me. I invited Barbara around tonight to talk to her about everything. They've been friends for fifteen years and she's as upset as we are.'

'She is not. She's just as bad as Fiona. If a drug-crazed drunken loser like Shane turned up for her, she'd be off too. They're all the same.'

'This is *not* the way we must talk, we must try to keep a lifeline open to Fiona, tell her that we are here when she wants us.'

'I'm not sure that I am here if she wants us. She said some very hurtful things to you as well as to me, remember?'

'That's because we said things to her about Shane that she thought were hurtful.' Maureen struggled to be fair. 'We can't help who we fall in love with, Sean.'

'Yes, we can. We don't all go out looking for lunatics like Fiona did.' He was unbending.

The doorbell rang.

'That's Barbara. Be nice, be reasonable please, Sean, she may be our only link with Fiona; our only hope.'

In David's house in the smart suburbs of Manchester they had been looking at the televised events in Aghia Anna.

'It must have been a terrible thing to see,' David's mother said.

'It must indeed have been terrible if he telephoned us,' his father agreed.

'He has been away for six weeks, Harold, we have had ten letters from him. He does keep in touch.'

'Some of them were only picture postcards,' David's father said.

They sat in silence for a while.

'Miriam, should I have been different, please tell me?' He looked at her begging for the truth.

She reached for his hand and stroked it. 'You have been a wonderful husband, a wonderful father,' she said.

'So why is our son out in this one-horse town in Greece if I was so wonderful? Should I have said something like *be* an artist, *be* a poet, *be* whatever you want to be? Should I? Is this what was needed? Tell me!'

'I don't think so, he always knew you wanted him to run the company, he knew that since his bar mitzvah.'

'So why was that such a crime? I built up this business for my father. He came to England with nothing. I worked day and night to try to show him that his suffering had all been worth while. I try to hand over to my only son a thriving business, that's so bad?'

'I know, Harold, I know all this.' She was trying to soothe him.

'If you understand it, why can't he?'

'Let me tell him, Harold, please let me tell him.'

'No, a thousand times no. I will not have his pity. If I can't have his company, I will not settle for his pity.'

Shirley and Bill came back from the shopping mall. Andy had gone up to the university to motivate some of the students training for a marathon.

Bill helped his mother to unpack the shopping and stack it away.

'You're a great kid,' she said unexpectedly.

'Am I?'

'Sure you are. I've never loved anyone on earth more than I love you.'

'Aw, come on, Mom . . .' He was embarrassed.

'No, I mean it. Truly I do. There's something absolutely earth-shaking about the love you have for your child, it's unconditional.'

'What's that?'

'It means that there are no ifs and buts. You are this special kind of person, nothing can get in the way of it.'

'And would Dad feel the same about me as you do?'

'Totally the same. Your dad and I didn't see eye to eye about a few things, Bill, you know that, but we both thought and do think you were the best thing that ever happened to us. We just want the best for you.'

'Does Dad still love you, Mom?'

'No, honey, he still respects me and likes me I think, but love, no. We just share our love for you.'

Bill thought about it for a while. 'So why doesn't he act like that?' he asked.

'I think he does,' Shirley said, surprised.

'I don't think he does,' Bill said. 'I think he wants me to miss him and be sorry he's not here. But *he's* the one who went away. I didn't. I stayed right here.'

Birgit saw Claus coming into the newsroom.

'You're back from Greece!' she said, delighted.

'Hi, Birgit.' Claus, the chief cameraman, had no illusions that Birgit was happy to see him. If he were back, then Dieter would be back too. That was what interested her.

Claus sighed. Dieter didn't even try, and the women just fell over themselves for him. He waited until Birgit asked about Dieter. He assumed it would be thirty seconds. He was wrong: it was even sooner.

'Dieter back too?' she asked casually.

'No, he stayed on for a bit. He met an old friend out there. Amazing coincidence.'

'An old friend? Some guy he knew in the press corps?'

'No, it was some woman who used to work here, actually. He met Elsa.'

Birgit was a hard woman. It was a pleasing moment to see her face.

'But it's all over between them,' Birgit said.

'I wouldn't hold your breath, Birgit,' Claus said, and moved on.

Adoni looked at the newspaper pictures of the village where he had grown up. He saw the face of his friend Manos, whom he had known all his life. There was a picture of Maria too. Adoni had danced at their wedding.

How extraordinary that newspapers all over America would have pictures and stories of his home town. But he wouldn't tell anyone here in Chicago. The people here in the greengrocer's where he worked knew little about him and his background. If he told them then they would have to know why he didn't stay in touch. They would learn about his fight with his father, the years of silence. They would never understand. These people that he worked with just lived for family, their fathers were in and out of their houses all the time.

Of course he could call his father to offer sympathy over what had happened to Aghia Anna. But then his father would take this as some sign of weakness, a giving in, an admission that Adoni had been in the wrong. His father knew where he was. If he wanted to say something then let him say it.

Shane didn't know how to use the Métro in Athens. When they had been here before Fiona had worked it out. He knew that he wanted to go to the Exarchia area, because he had heard on the ferry that it was full of ouzo shops and tavernas. He still had plenty of grass in his bag, he could sell it there. Then he would sit down, work out what he would do. He was free now, free as a bird. Nobody would be coming at him with cracked notions that he should be a waiter in some backwater. Fiona must have been soft in the head to suggest it.

In the end, of course, like everyone else she had let him down. But then Shane had learned to expect that of people. And she wasn't really pregnant. He knew that. If she had been she wouldn't have gone off and left him when he was in the police station. She could well be on her way home to her awful family in Dublin.

He worked out that he needed the Métro stop called Omonia. God, they had really ridiculous names here, and writing that nobody could read as well.

'Come in, Barbara.' Fiona's mother ushered her in.

'You're out late.' Fiona's father didn't sound very welcoming.

'You know how it is, Mr Ryan, eight a.m. to eight p.m. and we're an hour from the hospital.' Barbara threw herself into an armchair as she had done for years in this house, her red hair tousled, her face tired after a long day's work

'Will you have tea, Barbara, or something stronger?'

'Oh, I could murder a gin, Mrs Ryan, specially if we are going to talk about Shane,' Barbara said apologetically.

'Sean?'

'Well, if we're going to have to talk about him then I need an anaesthetic, too,' he said.

'I was wondering if we could write to Fiona and say that we sort of misunderstood the situation.' Fiona's mother served the gin and tonics and sat down looking from one to the other.

Her husband glowered at her. 'I think we understood the situation only too well. Our daughter is infatuated with a bog-ignorant criminal. What else is there to understand?'

'But it hasn't worked, our saying that. Fiona's hundreds of miles away. And I miss her, Sean, every moment of the day.'

'I agree with Mr Ryan, actually. We didn't misunderstand anything. Shane is a real out-and-out bastard because he manipulates her, he makes things seem to be her fault, not his. He plays the victim card.'

'What I find the hardest is that they say they *love* each other.' Maureen Ryan's face was troubled.

'Shane's never loved anyone but himself. He'll only stay with Fiona for as long as it suits him, and then she'll be alone, miles away with no friends and humiliated. She won't want to come back to us. She'll know that we'll all be thinking, I told you so, even if we manage not to say it.'

'You miss her as much as we do.' Fiona's father sounded surprised.

'Of course I do, I miss her at work every day and I miss going out with her in the evening. I think of a dozen things to tell her and then remember she's gone . . . I was wondering if we could try to build some kind of a bridge?'

'What kind of bridge?' Sean Ryan didn't hold out much hope.

'Well, could you write her a letter sort of implying that we all know now she and Shane will be together in the long run? And I could do the same, like asking would she and Shane be home for your silver wedding or Christmas, something like that?'

'But we can't assume that she's going to be with him for ever, Barbara. What kind of message are we giving the other children if they think we accept Shane as part of their sister's life?'

'Listen, Mrs Ryan, he *is* part of her life. They've gone off to live together, for God's sake. But deep down I've a feeling it's not going to last that long, and if we pretend that we think it's normal then we stop being part of the Bad Cruel World that's beating up on Poor Misunderstood Shane.' Barbara looked from one to the other. 'Believe me, I don't like it either. And I don't like sitting here talking about my friend Fiona behind her back. But I think that we've got to do something or else we'll have lost her entirely.'

The letter was pushed through the door and fell to the floor. Miriam Fine went to see who could possibly be delivering something by hand at this time of night.

It was a big thick envelope addressed to them both. She brought it in to her husband and they opened it together.

It was the confirmation that Harold Fine had won the coveted Businessman of the Year award and details of the ceremony. It would be presented in November at the Town Hall before an invited audience. They hoped that he would ask a group of family and friends to join them for drinks first with the Mayor and dinner later.

'Oh, Harold, I'm so pleased for you, to see it there in black and white,' she said, tears in her eyes. 'David will be so proud and pleased. We'll tell him the actual invitation has arrived. I know he will come home for it all,' Miriam said.

'Let's not be too confident, Miriam. From where David stands, a Businessman of the Year would be the worst thing he could encounter.'

Hannah, a secretary in the television centre, had overheard the conversation between Claus and Birgit. She could hardly credit it. Elsa had gone so far away to leave what had been the love of her life and this catastrophe had brought them together.

'Claus, excuse me, can I have a word?'

'Of course!' Everyone liked Hannah, a bright, helpful, confident young woman. She had been Elsa's friend.

'I just wanted to ask is Elsa coming back?' Hannah asked. She too spent no time beating about the bush.

'I wish I could tell you what has happened, but truthfully I don't know,' Claus said. 'Dieter told us to go home ahead of him. So of course we did. But she looked different. She wasn't the same Elsa that we know. She was changed, somehow, as if she had made up her mind.'

'I see.' Hannah was doubtful.

'I know you probably think that men are hopeless about reading the signs, but, believe me, even you would have found it difficult to know what was happening.'

Adoni decided he would telephone his father. It would be evening in Greece, his father would be at the taverna. It would be busy so his father would not be able to talk for long, which was just as well. Adoni would say that he was very sorry about the tragedy and that he sent his sympathies. They would not talk about what had passed between them.

He could hear the telephone ringing.

It rang and rang and there was no reply. He must have dialled the wrong number. He dialled again. But in the empty taverna the phone rang and nobody answered.

Adoni hung up. In many ways it was probably all for the best.

Shane found exactly the place he was looking for. This was his clientele. It was just the kind of place he would have gone if he had been looking to score. It didn't matter that he didn't know the language. There was an international language over this sort of thing. He spoke to a guy who was some kind of thicko, who understood nothing, then to another who shrugged at him. The third man looked more promising.

'How much?' the man asked. He was small, with quick dark eyes.

'How much do you want?' Shane asked.

'Well, how much do you have?' the man wanted to know.

'Enough,' said Shane.

At that moment there was the flash of a Polaroid camera and then another. Right in his face.

'What the hell—?' Shane began. Then he felt a hand on his collar. The face of the man with the quick dark eyes was an inch from Shane's face.

'Listen to me good. We have two pictures of you, one in this bar, one we will show to the police. If they see you trying to deal again it will be very, very bad for you.'

'You *said* you wanted to buy.' Shane choked the words out somehow.

'This is my father's bar, my family runs this place. I would go very far from here very quickly. That is my uncle holding you. He is expecting you to apologise and leave. In twenty seconds from now.'

'I don't know how to apologise in Greek.'

'*Signomi* will do.'

'*Signomi!*' Shane cried over his shoulder to the older man who was holding him. Then the grip was released and Shane staggered out of the door into the warm Athens night.

CHAPTER FIVE

THOMAS WOKE with a slight headache. It didn't take him long to remember why. The red wine they had drunk last night at the police station had not been allowed to age for any respectable time. Yorghis said it could well have been made last month.

Still, a couple of cups of good coffee would cure that. Maybe he would go out and get fresh oranges and hot crusty rolls for breakfast. Possibly Vonni would have a hangover too.

But when he got up, he saw the door to the spare bedroom was open. The bed was neatly made. No sign of any personal possessions around the place. She was truly using it only as a bed for the night. He wondered where she was now.

She was such a self-sufficient little figure, hair braided around her head, suntanned lined face with its broad smile, that made it impossible to know what age she was. Hard to learn from anyone how long she had been in Aghia Anna. And she told little or nothing about herself, so you would be a long time guessing.

Thomas yawned and went into the kitchen. She had beaten him to it. There were four large oranges on the table and, wrapped in a little check cloth to keep them warm, some fresh bread rolls. Thomas sighed with pleasure and sat down to his breakfast.

Fiona was still asleep, so Elsa left her a note.

> *Gone down to the harbour. Didn't want to wake you. Why don't you come and meet me at noon. Bring a swimsuit if you feel like it and we can have something in that nice place with the blue and white tablecloths. I can't remember its name. I'd like that. Love, Elsa*

She walked through the narrow streets looking at the people washing the pavements in front of their shops, and laying out their wares. In the cafés and restaurants they were laboriously writing their menus on big blackboards. There wasn't the same carefree, cheerful way as before the accident. But at least they were getting on with it. Like Elsa herself.

She was able now to nod and smile at people she passed, saying, 'Kalimera,' here and there. But she had never felt so isolated. No family, no love, no job, and since she had left Germany . . . no home.

Somebody in a shabby van hooted at her. Elsa put up her hand to shield her eyes from the sun and see who it was.

It was Vonni with a load of children.

'We're going for a swim on a really fantastic beach you might not know. Would you like to come?'

'Great, I said I'd meet Fiona at noon in the harbour but I'd be back by then, right? Elsa was glad that she had her bathing suit and straw hat in her basket. She was now prepared to go anywhere.

Vonni nodded at her in agreement. 'Oh, we'll be back by then. I can't expose children to the midday sun.' She said something in Greek to the five- and six-year-olds in the back of the van and they all smiled at her and chorused, 'Yassu, Elsa!'

Elsa felt a sudden lump in her throat as if, in a small way, she did belong somewhere. Just for a while.

David had hired a bicycle and was cycling five miles to where the family he was staying with had told him there was a wonderful beach. He puffed up the hills and sailed down the slopes on the other side. The countryside was so beautiful. Why would anyone want to live in a crowded city?

But when he arrived at the beach, to his disappointment he saw a parked van. And then he saw Elsa and that strange older woman, Vonni, already down by the sea with eight or nine children.

David lay on a grassy mound and watched them all. Elsa was so beautiful in her elegant turquoise swimsuit, her short blonde hair reflecting the sun; she had a light suntan and moved gracefully in and out of the sea, playing with the children.

Vonni, small and swarthy, her hair in plaits over her head, wore a functional black swimming costume that would not have been in fashion twenty years back. She too ran in and out of the little waves calling and encouraging the youngsters to join her, and helping the more timid ones by holding a hand under the chin.

David longed to join them but he felt he would be intruding. Just at that moment, Elsa saw him.

'*Ela, ela*, David, come and swim, it is total magic!'

Awkwardly he went to join them. He had his swimming trunks on under his shorts. He took off his glasses and left them on top of his neatly folded clothes.

He greeted the children. '*Yassas, ime Anglos.*'

'As if they ever thought you were anything but English!' Vonni said, teasing him.

'I suppose so,' David said ruefully.

One of the children splashed him with a handful of water. 'Very good, *poli kala*,' he said.

'I hope you have six children, David, you'll be a wonderful father,' Vonni said unexpectedly.

Fiona woke up and read the note. Wasn't life so odd that she should meet by accident such a kind and generous person? Elsa was almost as good a friend to her as Barbara had been. Shane would be so glad when she told him. She washed her hair and used Elsa's hairdryer. She didn't look too bad. Pale, a bit wishy-washy but nothing that would frighten the birds off the trees, as her father used to say.

Fiona thought about her father. He had been such a loving, marvellous man until she had brought Shane home. She wished in many ways that she could be there for her parents' silver wedding party.

But that was her father's mistake.

He had been so definite about Shane. No time must be spent thinking about it now. She must get on with her life until Shane sent for her. She would dress as well as she could and then walk slowly down to the harbour. She would show her best face.

They left David sitting on the beach learning his ten phrases for the day, then Vonni let the children off in the square and dropped Elsa off from her van at the harbour shortly after 11 a.m.

'Thank you for your company,' Vonni said.

'Why do people in Aghia Anna hand over their children to you, Vonni?' Elsa asked.

'I don't know. They've seen me here for many years now and believe I am fairly reliable, I suppose.' Vonni was not at all certain.

'How many years, Vonni?'

'I came here over thirty years ago.'

'What?' Elsa said in shock.

'You asked me. I told you.' Vonni looked impassive.

'Indeed. Forgive me. I am sure you do not want people to intrude.'

'As it happens, I don't mind people asking reasonable questions. I came to Aghia Anna to be with the man I loved.'

'And were you with him?'

'Yes and no. I'll tell you another time.' Vonni revved up the van and drove away.

'Thomas!'

He looked up at her from where he sat on an wooden box looking out of the mouth of the harbour to sea where the wind was lifting the waves.

'Good to see you, Elsa. Would you like a nice easy chair?' He pulled over another box for her. 'Your hair is damp, were you swimming?'

'Yes, there's a truly beautiful beach in a little lagoon about five miles away. Up that coast,' she pointed.

'Don't tell me you've walked ten miles today!' He was disconcerted.

'No, shamefully, Vonni drove me both ways. We met David there. He's the fit one, he has actually hired a bicycle. Am I imagining it, Thomas, or is the sea much more attractive here than anywhere else?'

'It sure beats my part of California anyway, very flat where we are. Nice sunsets, but no surf, no changing colours like this.'

'No wonder people get inspired by the place. I mean, I know it's meant to be a reflection of the sky, but don't tell me that water isn't dark blue.'

'"Roll on, thou deep and dark blue Ocean—roll!"' Thomas quoted.

To his astonishment Elsa continued, '"Ten thousand fleets sweep over thee in vain; Man marks the earth with ruin—his control stops with the shore . . .'"

He looked at her open-mouthed. 'You can quote English poetry. How dare you be so well educated!'

Elsa laughed, pleased at the praise. 'We had an English teacher at school who loved Byron. If you had picked another poet I wouldn't have done so well!'

'But I mean it. I couldn't quote you one line of German poetry. What am I talking about? I can't even speak a word of the German language.'

'Yes, you can, you said *Wunderbar* and *Prosit* last night,' she consoled him.

'I think I said *Prosit* a little too often last night as it happens . . . oh, I've remembered another German word. *Reisefieber*.'

Elsa pealed with laughter. 'What a marvellous word to know . . . how on earth do you know that?'

'It means "journey fever", doesn't it? Being in a panic at airports and railway stations?'

'That's exactly what it means, Thomas. Imagine you knowing that!'

They sat companionably together as if they had known each other all their lives.

Vonni drove the van back to Maria's house, where Maria was sitting at the kitchen table in front of an empty coffee cup. 'It's getting harder, not easier,' she said. 'I thought that was Manos coming back in his van.'

'Of course it's getting harder. It's sinking in and that's what hurts so much.'

Vonni hung up the keys on a hook on the wall and then produced a pot of hot coffee and some flaky *baklava*. Then she sat down at the table. 'The dancing was beautiful last night. He would have loved it,' she said.

'I know.' Maria was weeping again. 'And last night I felt strong and as if his spirit was still here. That feeling has gone today.'

'Well, it might come back when I tell you my plan,' Vonni said, passing her a piece of kitchen paper.

'Plan?'

'Yes, I'm going to teach you to drive.'

Maria actually managed a watery smile. 'Drive? Me drive? Vonni, stop joking. Manos wouldn't even let me hold the keys of the van.'

'But he would want you to drive now, I know he would.'

'No, Vonni, he wouldn't, he'd think I'd kill myself and everyone in Aghia Anna.'

'Well, we'll have to prove him wrong then,' Vonni said. 'Because you'll have to drive for your new job.'

67

'Job?'

'Oh, yes, you're going to help me in the shop, aren't you? And a lot of your work will involve driving to places like Kalatriada and collecting stuff. Save me trekking for miles on buses.'

'But you can drive there in Manos's van, Vonni.'

'No, I can't. Manos would hate that, he saved long and hard for that van, he wouldn't want you just handing it away. No, he'd be so proud of you if you used it for your work.'

And, magically, Maria smiled again. A real smile this time. It was as if she saw his spirit back in the house again.

'Right, Manos, this is going to amaze you,' she said.

David came across them during the driving lesson up on a big patch of waste ground at the top of the town.

'*Siga, siga,*' Vonni was screaming as the van jerked and shuddered.

'What does *siga* mean? I've often heard it,' David asked, interested.

'Well, you never heard it said with such fervour as this time.' Vonni had got out of the van, mopped her brow and taken some deep breaths. Maria sat gripping the steering wheel.

'It means "slow down", but the lady doesn't get the concept.'

'That's Manos's, isn't it?' David peered at the woman still clutching the wheel. 'Does she need to drive?'

'I thought so this morning, now I'm not so sure. But of course I had to open my big mouth and suggest it.' Vonni sighed.

'I taught my mother to drive when no one else could,' David said slowly. 'Perhaps I could give it a go?'

'How did you do it?' Vonni said, with hope beginning to show in her eyes.

'I was very patient. I never raised my voice once and I spent hours on the clutch,' he said.

'Would you, David? Oh, please would you?'

'Sure. If it would help. You'll have to tell me the words for brake and accelerator and gears, though.'

He wrote them down in his notebook and went over to the van. Maria looked at him doubtfully as he sat in beside her.

'*Kalimera,*' he said formally and shook hands.

'How do you say, "Let's go"?' he asked Vonni.

'*Pame*, but don't say it yet or she'll drive you into that wall.'

'*Pame*, Maria,' David said gently and with a lurch they moved forward.

Vonni looked on, amazed. She watched as he taught Maria to stop the van. He really did have a gift.

'Drive her home when you've finished, will you?' Vonni said. 'I'll cycle down on your bike and leave it for you at Maria's house.'

Before he could answer she had swung her leg over the man's bicycle and was heading off down to the town.

Fiona sat at a table outside the little café and was surprised to see Vonni streaking by on a bike. Vonni saw her and did a wheelie turn to come back.

'All on your own?' she asked.

'I'm meeting Elsa here at midday.'

'Oh, yes, Elsa did tell me. She helped me take the children for a swim.'

'Did she?' Fiona sounded envious.

'Yes, and David came by on his bicycle. He lent it to me and I'm just leaving it at Maria's house for him. David's taking his life in his hands and teaching Maria to drive.'

'Lord, everyone's really settling in.' Fiona was wistful.

Vonni leaned David's bike against one of the empty tables.

'I'll sit with you until Elsa arrives,' she said.

Fiona was pleased. 'Will you have an ouzo?' she asked.

'No, just a *metrios*, please,' Vonni said.

They sat there peacefully, watching the life of the harbour going on around them. That was an interesting thing about Vonni, Fiona observed. She had a great sense of stillness. It was very restful.

'Vonni?'

'Yes?'

'I was wondering . . . could I get some kind of a job here in Aghia Anna? I could learn Greek. I could help Dr Leros. What do you think?'

'Why do you want to stay here?' Vonni's voice was gentle.

'It's beautiful here and I want to be sort of settled when Shane comes back for me.'

Vonni said nothing at all.

'You think he might not come back, don't you?' Fiona cried. 'But you don't know him like I do.'

'True.'

'Believe me, Vonni, he has never in his whole life had anyone who understood him until he met me. We love each other, we went away to be together for ever. Why wouldn't he come back?'

Vonni swallowed and looked away.

'No, please, tell me. I'm sorry I shouted at you, Vonni, I just get so upset when people come out against Shane. I keep thinking that this is going to go on for ever until we're an old, old couple. Perhaps you know something I don't.'

She looked so anxious. She had her hand on Vonni's weather-beaten arm, her eyes were wide, wanting to know more.

Vonni took a deep breath. She had been responsible for Shane going to Athens. She had advised the police chief Yorghis to ship him away from Aghia Anna. She did therefore owe Fiona some explanation.

'No, I don't think I know anything that you don't,' she said slowly. 'But I was going to suggest that Shane might not expect you to stay on here, you know, without him. If he does contact you . . .'

'He will, of course he will. One day he'll get off one of those ferries and I want to be here and settled when he does.'

'It's not realistic, Fiona, this is a holiday place. Not a place to settle down in.'

'You did,' Fiona said simply.

'It was different then, and I came here to live with a man from Aghia Anna.'

'You did?'

'I did indeed, years and years ago. There were hardly any tourists here then. I was considered very unusual, a slut of course. In those days people here, as well as at home, got engaged and then married.'

Vonni looked out to sea remembering it all.

'So then you know it's possible to leave Ireland and come to a beautiful place like this and be happy?' Fiona was trying desperately to find similarities between them.

'In a way,' Vonni said.

'And what happened to the . . . er . . . man . . . from Aghia Anna?' Fiona felt daring to ask such a direct question.

Vonni looked her straight in the eye. 'Stavros? I don't know really,' she said and closed the conversation.

Vonni said she had a hundred things to do and she wanted to thank God above that one of them was not giving Maria a driving lesson.

'Are you all right here on your own?' asked Fiona.

'I'm fine, and thank you so much for being so kind,' Fiona said politely.

She was glad that the older woman was leaving. She should not have asked Vonni what had happened to her man. She saw Elsa coming towards her and waved.

'I'll leave you in good hands then,' Vonni said.

Elsa sat down and told Fiona about the morning on the beach. They ordered a salad and talked easily about life on this island. Just as they were finishing they saw an old van come sputtering past them. It was being driven somewhat erratically by Maria, and David was in the passenger seat.

'Vonni?'

'Come in, Yorghis, sit down.'

'You have nice things here.' The policeman looked around the craft shop.

'Some of it is nice, yes. Thank you again for your hospitality last night, Yorghis.'

'It's not a time to be alone . . . We got a call from Athens, Vonni. That boy we exported, the Irishman . . .'

'Oh, yes?' So he *had* called after all. Fiona had been right. Vonni didn't know whether to be pleased or disappointed. 'What did he say?'

'*He* said nothing. We got a call from a police station in Athens. He had been taken in for dealing in a bar. They found my card on him and wondered what I knew.'

'And what *did* you know, Yorghis?' she asked.

'Nothing as yet. I wasn't there to take his call. I wanted to discuss it with you. She's such a nice little girl.'

'I know. So nice she'd probably get on the next ferry and go to Stand by Her Man.'

'That's what I thought,' Yorghis said. 'I think I'll just tell them that we had a bit of girlfriend battering and drunkenness here. I don't think I'll say anything specific about Fiona, do you?'

'I think you're right. And we might not say anything *to* Fiona either. Do you agree?'

'Is that playing God, do you think?' Yorghis wondered.

'Even if it is, let's do it. Maybe the Almighty needs a hand now and then,' said Vonni.

The sun was setting and there was a gold-red light over the harbour. Thomas saw that Vonni was still working in her craft shop. He thought about going in to invite her to come up for an evening drink with him. But he remembered how much she liked to be left alone. She had only agreed to sleep in the spare bedroom after a lot of reassurance that they would not intrude on each other's lives.

He wanted to call Bill. It had been left so awkwardly hanging in the air last time. He still felt stung by Vonni overhearing him and saying that he had made such a mess of it all.

Thomas climbed the stairs to the apartment and sat down to make a list of things he wanted to tell Bill: that he'd had dinner in a police station; about the men coming out to dance after the funeral; how the Germans learn English poetry even though we don't know any of theirs.

He looked at the headings. What dull, odd things he had picked. A child would not be interested in these things. He sat with his head in his hands, thinking how pathetic he was not to be able to find something to say to the boy that he loved with all his heart.

When Vonni went upstairs much later that night, she found Thomas sitting in the dark. 'Holy St Joseph, you put the heart across me,' she said.

'Hi, Vonni.' He was very down.

'Did you ring your son and annoy him again?' she asked.

'No, I sat here for hours wondering what to say and I couldn't think of anything so I didn't call him,' he confessed.

'Probably wiser in the long run,' Vonni said approvingly.

'What kind of a horse's ass does that make me, not able to find things to say to a nine-year-old?' he asked.

'I'd say it makes you like every father and son in the world, unable to communicate.' She wasn't as unsympathetic as the words might have sounded.

'He's not my son,' Thomas said flatly.

'What do you mean?'

'What I say. Nearly ten years ago when Shirley and I were trying for a baby I went for a medical. Childhood mumps had made me sterile apparently. I walked around all day wondering how to tell Shirley. But when I got home *she* had something to tell me. Wasn't it wonderful— she was pregnant.'

'Did you tell her?'

'No. I needed time to think. I had no idea that she was playing away. Not a clue. And because I didn't speak then I couldn't later. But I love him as much as if he *were* mine. It wasn't Andy, he only turned up years later. Andy thinks Bill's my son.'

'Did you raise it during the divorce?'

'What, and lose any chance of access to Bill?'

'Of course,' she nodded.

'He's a wonderful boy, Vonni.'

'I'm sure he is. I'm very sure he is.'

There was a long silence.

'Go back to him, Thomas. It's breaking your heart to be so far away.'

'I can't. We all agreed it was for the best this way.'

'Agreements can be changed, plans can be rewritten,' Vonni said.

'I'd be worse back there than here. Suppose I had to look at that fool every day, posturing, pretending to be his father.'

'You are his father in every way that counts.' Vonni looked at the floor as she spoke.

'I wish I could believe that,' he said.

'You should believe it, Thomas.' She spoke with quiet certainty as if she knew what she was talking about. His eyes met hers and suddenly it was crystal-clear to Thomas that Vonni really did know what she was talking about.

Vonni and David were sitting drinking coffee at the café with the blue and yellow checked tablecloths. Maria would be out shortly to have her driving lesson.

'She says you are a very good man and you don't shout at her,' Vonni said approvingly to David. 'I told her that you taught your mother to drive. She said your mother was fortunate to have such a son.'

'*She* doesn't think so. She sides with my father over everything: I am so lucky, most men would love to have a business they could walk into.'

'And can you not tell her that you love them both but not the work?'

'I've tried and tried, but it ends in recriminations and arguments every single time.'

'When you go back you'll find that they have softened,' she began.

'I'm not going back,' he said.

'You can't run away, stay here for ever.'

'You did,' David said simply.

'I'm weary of telling people that those were different times.' Vonni sighed.

'I'm taking Maria up some of those mountain roads today.' David changed the subject. 'I thought we'd go up to see Andreas.'

'You like him, don't you?' Vonni observed.

'Who wouldn't like him? He's so kind and gentle. He doesn't pressurise people into doing what they don't want to do.'

'He's set in his ways, of course,' Vonni said.

'But good ways,' David said. 'His son must be a real fool, not to come back from Chicago and help him.'

Vonni stood looking at David quizzically, her head on one side.

'What is it?' he asked eventually.

'You *know* what it is, David. Couldn't someone say exactly the same about you? You have a father and, in your case, a mother too, who miss you and wonder what *you* are doing miles and miles away.'

'It's different,' David said mutinously. 'My father's just never wrong. No one could live with him.'

'Adoni found the very same thing in his father. Andreas wouldn't get lights on the taverna roof, he wouldn't have live bouzouki music in the evening. Adoni could change nothing. Andreas was always right.'

'I don't see him like that,' David said a little coldly.

'No? Well, people are not always courteous to their own sons.' She looked thoughtful.

'You have a son, Vonni?'

'Yes. Stavros, like his father.'

'And are you courteous and polite to him?' David asked.

'I don't see him, to be either courteous or discourteous to. But in the days when I did see him I was going through a period when I was polite to nobody, least of all to him.' She straightened herself up and looked purposeful again. 'Right. I'm taking those children with me so that you can take their mother up the Wall of Death or wherever you want to go with her.'

The bookshop had a small section of poetry, including a book of Goethe's work, German on one side and English on the page opposite. Thomas bought it and went outside and sat on a bench near the shop. He studied the book carefully until he found something appropriate. Then he took out his notebook and was about to write it down, when he felt a shadow fall over the page.

It was Elsa looking over his shoulder to see what he was reading. Then she moved back and spoke the lines to him. '"*Kennst du es wohl? Dahin! Dahin Möcht ich mit dir, o mein Geliebter, ziehn.*"'

'All right, I give in,' he said. 'I haven't read the translation. What does that bit mean?'

'It means . . . "Do you know it perhaps? It is there, there that I would like to go with you, my beloved."'

And as she said it they looked at each other, slightly embarrassed.

'Did Goethe come to Greece?' Thomas asked, steering the conversation into safer waters. 'Until today I've never read a word he wrote,' he confessed.

'And why are you reading it now?'

'To impress you,' he said simply.

'You don't have to, I'm impressed already,' Elsa said.

Andreas got a phone call from Ireland.

'Is that a taverna in Aghia Anna?' the voice asked.

'Yes, it is. Can I help you?'

'Fiona Ryan called her family from your taverna on the day of your terrible tragedy.'

'Yes, yes, I remember. This is Andreas. This is my taverna.'

'I'm Fiona's best friend at home. Barbara. Fiona gave your number in case she got cut off so I rang because . . . well, I was wondering . . . are they still in Aghia Anna?'

'Yes, is there any problem?'

'Fiona's all right, is she?'

Andreas paused. All right? The girl looked wretched. But even though his instinct was to tell this woman Barbara all that had happened, he knew it wasn't his story to tell.

'They all seem to like it here,' he said lamely.

'All? You mean she's been able to make friends with Shane in tow? Usually people avoid them like the plague.'

'Nice people. German, American, English,' he said to reassure her.

'Well, that is a surprise. Listen, Andreas. Is there anywhere I could send her an email or a fax, do you think?'

'Certainly.' He gave her the email address of the police station.

Yorghis was driving around Aghia Anna. He knew he would see Fiona or one of her friends somewhere along the way. He saw her with a straw basket buying vegetables.

'Oh, Yorghis, just the man I need. What's the Greek for watermelon?'

'*Karpouzi*,' he said.

'Good! *Karpouzi, karpouzi*,' she said happily.

'I have a letter for you,' Yorghis said.

'Shane! I just *knew* he would get in touch.' Her face was radiant.

'No, it's from your friend Barbara in Ireland.' He handed over the printed-out email.

She barely looked at it, she was so disappointed. She just put it in her basket. When she had finished her shopping, she sat down at a café and pulled out the email.

You must wonder how Sherlock Holmes Barbara tracked you down, but it was easy: your mother had the number you phoned from, and Andreas told me his brother ran the cop shop. He said you and Shane had nice friends from all over the world. That's great news.

Oh, I do miss you in the hospital, Fiona. Any news on when you and Shane are coming back? It's just that if it were going to be at the end of the summer there are some really great flats coming on the market. You and Shane could easily get one of them, it would only be a ten-minute walk to the hospital.

In fact, I was telling your mam and dad about them, I said that was probably the kind of place the two of you would want to live when you came back. They didn't even flicker an eyelid. Remember when they wouldn't hear his name mentioned? You've certainly laid down the ground rules OK.

They were very pleased you called about that awful tragedy. It must have been terrible.

Anyway, you have my email address now, do tell me how you both like Greece. I always wanted to go there but never got any further than Spain!

Love to you both, Barbara

Fiona sat there stunned.

Barbara sending her love to Shane? Her mother and father accepting the fact that she was going to live with Shane for ever? The world was tilting slightly.

She read the email again and went back to Elsa's apartment to make soup and a fruit salad.

Elsa stopped by Vonni's shop and invited her to join them for supper.

'No, thank you, Elsa, very kind of you, but I have to work. Every week I go to a group of blind people who make rugs. I choose the colours of the wool for them. Then I try to sell the rugs.' She shrugged. 'I had to give something back and I realised that the blind could weave with the best.'

'What do you mean, you had to give something back?' Elsa asked.

'This place was good to me. I was nothing but a nuisance for years, howling and frightening their children. They put up with me until I recovered.'

'I can't believe this . . . you howling and frightening people?'

'Oh, I did, believe me. My husband betrayed me, you see. He saw beautiful Magda, and he forgot everything we had. He was entranced by her. Stavros moved out of our house and into hers. He would not come home to me. I did a lot of stupid things—that's when the people here were so tolerant and good. I had a little boy and they helped me look after him while I worked up in the petrol station. I'll never forget that . . . I was the foreigner and they would have been tempted to side with him rather than me.'

'What kind of stupid things did you do?' Elsa wanted to know.

'Another time possibly.' The shutters came down in Vonni's face.

'It's just that I've done some very stupid things recently. It's comforting to know others did and survived,' Elsa said.

'Is this the man who was staying in the Anna Beach?'

'You know everything!' Elsa exclaimed. 'Yes, it is. And I still love him so much, that's the problem.'

'Why is it a problem?'

'Well, it's complicated. His name is Dieter, he runs the television station where I work . . . used to work. He taught me everything and I became a sort of star there, presenting the big news programme at night. And anyway we fell in love, got together, whatever you'd call it, and have been together for over two years.'

'You live together?' Vonni asked.

'No, it's not as simple as that.'

'Is he married to someone else?'

'No, it's not that. It's just awkward in the Network if people know. People would think I only got my job because I was living with him.'

'Sure.' Vonni was clipped. 'So what are you doing here then?'

'I discovered that he has a child by a woman he knew years back.'

'So?'

'He has a child that he has never acknowledged, he's no part of her life. You don't think that's bad?'

'I think it happens all over the world every day of the week. People survive.'

'It happened to me,' Elsa said. 'My father walked away, didn't give a damn.'

'And look at you! Didn't *you* survive, Elsa? In the end we all have to rely on ourselves. Ourselves and the friends we make, if we are lucky enough to make them. We are not tied to our children, nor they to us. Happy Families is a game people play with cards, it's not reality.'

'I don't know what has made you so bitter and cynical but I'm glad I don't feel like that,' Elsa said.

'You want Dieter to play Saturday Father to some child he probably never intended should exist.'

'But she *does* exist and that's exactly what he should do.'

'That's not why you are leaving him,' Vonni said. 'You're leaving him because you thought that he would eventually admit that he needed you as part of his life. You are such a beautiful young woman, you are accustomed to getting your own way. If you truly loved him you could put this child out of your mind. But no, you can't be sure that he loves you. That's why you are seizing on this episode of his life. You are making it the excuse, aren't you?'

Elsa felt her eyes stinging at the injustice of the attack. 'You're so wrong, he *does* love me. And I have such a huge hole in my heart without him. I've decided that I'm going back to Germany as soon as I can.'

Vonni leaned forward. 'Don't go back there, keep going, leave him be. He's never going to love you the way you want to be loved.'

Elsa stood up, not trusting herself to speak. She wanted to get back to her own apartment.

You're very quiet, Elsa,' Fiona said. 'Don't you like that lovely healthy soup I made you?'

'It's very good. I'm sorry, I just don't feel too cheerful tonight. I had a row with Vonni of all stupid things,' she said. 'I told her about me and Dieter and she wants me to stay away from him.'

Elsa had mentioned nothing to Fiona about her situation up to now.

'But you still love him, don't you?'

'Oh yes, most definitely, and he feels the same,' Elsa said.

'Well, there's no question about it then.' Fiona was matter-of-fact and businesslike about it. 'You have to go back to him.'

They had all agreed to meet at the harbour café after dinner and the four of them talked about their day.

'Do any of you get the feeling that we are just marking time here—that we should be doing something else?' Thomas asked at last.

'I'm happy here. I like it,' David said.

'And I do too,' Fiona agreed. 'Anyway, I have to stay here until Shane gets back.'

'I'll probably go back to Germany next week,' Elsa said. 'I'm just thinking it through. What about you, Thomas?'

'Well, Vonni thinks I should go back to California to see my son. I haven't worked it out either,' he said.

'Vonni's busy dispatching us all home! Once Maria can drive that van, Vonni wants me out too, back to make peace with my parents and work with my father.' David sounded gloomy.

'She doesn't think Shane is coming back and she says there are no jobs here,' said Fiona sadly. 'She says I'd be better to go back to Dublin.'

'She's actually more of a policeman than Yorghis is. She says I should end my relationship with a man who doesn't really love me,' Elsa said, giggling.

'She never put it like that?' David said.

'Almost precisely like that—anyway, I'm different to the rest of you. She wants me to keep on the move and *not* to go home.'

They pooled what they knew about Vonni: she came from the west of Ireland over thirty years ago because she loved a man called Stavros. Somehow she managed to buy him a petrol station, where Vonni worked night and day. She had one son, Stavros, who she didn't see now. Stavros senior had left the island, possibly with Vonni's young son. Vonni had gone through a troubled time but the people of Aghia Anna had looked after her and she felt she owed them in return.

'What kind of a troubled time?' Fiona wondered. 'Maybe she had a breakdown when Stavros left?'

'I think she was an alcoholic,' David said softly.

The others were startled. That quiet, capable, together woman a slave to drink? Impossible.

'Why do you say that?' Elsa asked.

'Well, have you noticed she never drinks any wine or ouzo?'

They looked at him with respect. Only the gentle, sensitive David had noticed what was now so obvious to the rest of them.

CHAPTER SIX

'VONNI, COME UPSTAIRS for a *portokalatha* when you're through, OK?'

'So you've finally noticed I only drink soft drinks,' she laughed at Thomas.

'I didn't, David did. He's the one who notices things. Anyway, what you drink isn't important—I want your advice.'

'I'll be up in ten minutes,' she said. He noticed she was wearing a clean, fresh, yellow blouse with little embroidered roses on it. She must keep her clothes in the craft shop.

'That's pretty,' he indicated the stitching. 'Did you do that?'

'No, it was done by someone else. It's thirty years old.'

'Really? Who did it?'

'It doesn't matter now, Thomas, but she could sew like an angel.'

Thomas swallowed. He had been too intrusive. 'I guess I ask too many questions, Vonni, forgive me. You don't have to talk about it.'

'Well, I do, really. You four are all anxious to know about me . . . I hear that you have been asking everyone in Aghia Anna about me.' She smiled at him innocently.

Thomas looked at the floor. 'I suppose we wanted to know what your husband was like, and what happened to him,' Thomas said uneasily.

'Very hard questions to answer, both of them. His name was Stavros, he was very dark, with brown, almost black eyes, and long black hair. His father was the barber here. He used to say he was ashamed of his wild and woolly son, but the moment I saw him I knew I never wanted any other man.'

'And where did you see him? Here in Aghia Anna?' Thomas asked.

'No, I met Stavros in Ardeevin, a small village in the west of Ireland in the spring of 1966. He came to work in a garage on the main street. We had never seen anything quite so exotic. He was learning English, he said, and the motor trade, and seeing the world . . .' Vonni sighed at the memory. 'We didn't think Ardeevin was the right place to start seeing the world. What about Paris? London? Even Dublin? But he said he liked it, it reminded him of his home town, Aghia Anna.'

'I was still at school, in my last year. My family hoped I would become a primary teacher, but I was so much in love with Stavros I had stopped going to school, abandoned studying. My only purpose each day was to sneak into the back of Ardeevin Motors. I didn't care about anything but being with him.

'But Jimmy Keane, who ran the garage, began to think Stavros wasn't concentrating fully on his work and started making sounds that he was going to sack him. I could neither eat nor sleep with the worry of it all. What would I *do* if Stavros had to move on? Then the most marvellous event occurred in Ireland that summer. There was a bank strike!' Her eyes shone at the memory.

Thomas was enthralled. 'The banks went on strike? Never!'

'Oh, they did,' she said happily. 'And what happened then was nothing short of a miracle,' Vonni said. 'Supermarkets would have a lot of cash and no banks to lodge it in, so they cashed these "cheques" for people they knew. The big town ten miles away had a supermarket where I was known, because the manager was my mother's cousin. So I cashed a cheque for two and a half thousand pounds. And that day Jimmy Keane said he'd have to let Stavros go.' Vonni began to pace the room. 'Stavros told me he would miss me, that I was his true love and that one day we would meet again. He said he would go back to Aghia Anna, open up a petrol station and send for me to come and join him. And I asked what was wrong with going right now? That I had the funds to set him up. I told him that it was my savings.'

'Tell me he was pleased.'

'Oh, he was, but my parents weren't. I told them that day that I was seventeen and a half, in six months I could marry without their permission anyway. What were they going to do? Lock me up?'

'So you wore them down?'

'No. But I told them I was leaving that very night, and we did, on the seven thirty bus.'

'And the money?'

'Ah, yes, the money. We were well in Aghia Anna by the time the bank strike ended. We'd had a wonderful journey, travelling through Switzerland and Italy. I was never so happy in my life.'

'And you arrived here?'

'And it wasn't so great. There was this girl, you see, very pregnant with Stavros's child. She thought he had come back to marry her. She was Christina, the sister of Andreas and Yorghis. When she discovered he had *not* come back for her, she tried to kill herself. But she killed the child she was carrying, not herself. It was a terrible time.'

'What happened to Christina?'

'She went to the hospital on the hill, on the Kalatriada road. I went to see her every week. She didn't speak to me for forty-five weeks, then one day she did. Soon afterwards she met and married a good man. She has children and grandchildren. They live on the other side of the island. I see her often.'

'And what happened to you, Vonni? You married Stavros?'

'In a civil ceremony in Athens. No one thought it was a real wedding— not my family back in Ardeevin, not his family here in Aghia Anna. I learned to speak Greek, I bought the petrol station. I learned how to change wheels, pump up tyres.'

She had begun to sound tired and weary.

'And in 1970 our son Stavros was born. By this time, people were used to me. We had a christening at the church, and even Stavros's father relaxed and sang songs. No word from Ireland, of course. I wrote and told them they had a grandson. No reply at all. I think the money had been the final straw. I was always going to pay it back. And I did.'

David opened the letter. It was the first time his mother had written to him. She had sent him a photocopy of the invitation to the award ceremony and described how the wording was embossed on the thick card.

David knew those awards; businessmen patted each other on the back every year. It was a reward for nothing except making money. His mother wrote on and on—about seating in the Town Hall, what they would all wear, that there would be a table plan.

He would calm himself and write a courteous letter explaining why he would not be there. A letter was wiser than a phone call. No danger of anyone losing their temper.

Fiona went to the Anna Beach Hotel and sent an email to her friend Barbara in Dublin.

> It was good to hear from you, Barb, I'm so glad we chose this place. The accident was terrible, but the people are full of courage. Shane's gone to Athens for a few days on work. I'll write again when I know our plans.
>
> Love, Fiona

'**T**here is a fax for your friend the German woman,' the man at the reception desk said as Fiona was leaving the Anna Beach.

Fiona marvelled at how everyone knew who they all were.

'I'll take it back to the villa,' she said.

She was becoming very familiar with Aghia Anna by now, even knew little short cuts from one side to the other. She laid the piece of paper on the table in front of Elsa.

'I'd have read it but it's in German,' Fiona said.

'Yes.'

'Aren't you going to read it? You don't have to translate it,' Fiona said.

'I know what it says,' Elsa said.

'That's pretty psychic of you,' Fiona said in surprise.

'It's telling me to pull myself together and come back to where I belong, which is in bed with him two nights a week, and no more gestures of independence.'

'Maybe it's not that,' Fiona encouraged her.

'All right—I'll translate . . .' She picked up the paper. 'It's fairly short anyway. "Darling Elsa, Come back to me and we will move together into an apartment openly. We will even be married, if that's what you want. I will write letters and send gifts to that child, if it makes you feel better. We were intended for each other, you know that and I know that. What is the point in playing games? Fax me yes, soonest. Love until the world ends, Dieter."'

In Chicago, Adoni took the letter with the Greek stamp to the men's room and sat down to read his father's spidery handwriting.

'*Adoni mou*,' it began and told simply of the pleasure boat that had burned in full sight of the town with rescuers unable to get to it in time. 'It makes everything else that has happened seem very unimportant,' his father wrote. 'Arguments about the taverna are so small compared to life and death. It would give me great pleasure, my son, if you were to come back to Aghia Anna and see me before *my* death. I assure you that I would not speak to you in that tone of voice that I used when you were here. Your room is always there if you come for a visit, and of course bring anyone you like. I hope there is somebody to bring.'

And Adoni took out a big blue handkerchief to wipe his eyes. And then he cried again because there was nobody to bring.

There was no bail for Shane in Athens, so he was brought back to the cells after the initial hearing.

'I'm allowed to make a phone call!' he shouted. 'You're meant to be in the bloody European Union. One of the reasons we let you in was so as you'd pay some attention to human rights.'

They passed the phone to him without comment.

He dialled the police station in Aghia Anna. He wished he could remember that old guy's name. But what the hell.

'I'm phoning from a police station in Athens,' he began. 'I'm trying to get in touch with Fiona Ryan.'

'We told you before, she is not here,' Yorghis lied smoothly.

'She *must* be there, she's expecting my child, she'll have to get the bail money . . .' He sounded frightened.

'As I say, I'm sorry we can't help you,' Yorghis said and hung up.

Shane begged for a second call. The policemen shrugged.

'Barbara! They took a hell of a time to find you, it's Shane.'

'I was on the wards, Shane, it's called work,' she said.

'Very droll. Listen, has Fiona gone back to Dublin?'

'What? Have you two split up?' She couldn't keep the pleasure out of her voice.

'No, don't be ridiculous, I had to go to Athens . . .'

'For work?' Barbara suggested drily.

'Sort of—and those half-wits in Aghia Anna say she's left there so it's been a breakdown in communications, you might say.'

'Oh dear, Shane, I'm so sorry. How can I help you exactly?' Barbara purred. She had not heard better news since the day her friend Fiona had taken up with Shane.

You paid the supermarket back?' Thomas said.

'It took some time—like nearly thirty years,' Vonni admitted. 'But they got every penny.'

'And do you keep in touch with your family?'

'They used to send a cold little note every Christmas, proving to themselves they are big-hearted, capable of *forgiveness*. I wrote long letters, sent them pictures of little Stavros. And then things changed.'

'Changed? They came round?'

'No, I meant *I* changed. I went mad, you see.'

'No, Vonni. This I can't see.'

She looked tired. 'I haven't talked about myself so much for ages. I'm a bit weary. You can tell the others what I told you, Thomas. I don't want them bothering people here for my story.'

He looked embarrassed. 'They don't need to know. None of us needs to know anything about your business.'

'I'll tell the rest another time . . . you know, like "New readers start here . . ."' She had a wonderfully infectious smile.

Thomas told them the story next day down by the harbour. They had got into the habit of turning up at the place with the blue and yellow checked tablecloths around noon.

David reported on the latest driving lesson, Elsa and Fiona said nothing about their messages from home but told how they had spent the morning helping an old man to paint some wooden chairs, and Thomas told them Vonni's story.

'She did want you to know. It's as if she were going to take it up with one of the three of you.'

They wondered about a country where the banks went on strike. 'I remember my father talking about it. He said that the country ran perfectly well without them. There were a few loose cannons like Vonni who went off with small fortunes, but not many,' Fiona said.

'I wonder who she'll tell the next episode to,' Elsa said.

It turned out to be David. Later that afternoon.

Thomas and Elsa had gone for a walk down the coast; Fiona had gone to ask Yorghis had there been any news from Athens. David sat on the harbour wall with his Greek phrase book. Vonni came to join him and helped him with some pronunciation.

Then David told Vonni about the invitation to his father's award back home. He handed her his mother's letter to read as well. To his surprise she had tears in her eyes.

'You'll go back, of course?' she said.

'No, I can't. Six months later it would be something else. I'd never escape, I'd be sucked back in. You never went back to Ireland, did you?'

'No, but I wanted to, a thousand times. But I was never welcome, so I didn't go. Anyway, I went mad and that sort of changed everything.' She spoke as casually as if she was saying that she'd gone somewhere on the bus instead of out of her mind.

'It wasn't *really* mad, was it?' David asked.

'Oh, I think so. It was because of Magda. She had a terrible husband, very violent, always imagining that Magda was flirting. She was a gentle woman with a beautiful smile. Sometimes she had bruises or a cut but she would say she was clumsy or had fallen. Then one day I went to the café to collect a tablecloth, and she was sitting there, the blood dripping down onto the white material. I ran for old Dr Leros, the father of Dr Leros who is here now. He patched her up and he said that this could not go on, we needed a strong man, someone like Stavros, to do something. Stavros and two of his friends held Magda's husband down on the floor of the café and told him what would happen to him if there was another incident.'

'And did her husband take them seriously?'

'Very seriously, apparently, and Magda stopped being "clumsy", as she called it. That was when people realised that she was very beautiful,' Vonni explained in a small sad voice.

'Did you suspect that Stavros was . . . well . . . interested in her?' David asked gently.

'No, not at all. I was the last to know, the very last person in Aghia Anna, but it finally dawned on me.'

'How?'

'Well, not the best way really. Little Stavros was with me at the petrol station—he was four then, going on five. He asked why Magda was always so tired. She always had to go to bed when she came to our house, and Papa always had to go and sit with her. I felt so dizzy and faint. Magda and Stavros? In our house? In my bed?'

'So what did you do?'

'I closed the petrol pumps and went home early the next day. Little Stavros was playing at a neighbour's house. I opened the door quietly and I heard them laughing. I opened the bedroom door and stood and looked at them. She was beautiful with her long dark curls and her olive skin. I caught a reflection of myself in the mirror. I knew I had lost. Of course he would want her not me.'

David listened, chilled by her intensity.

'I walked away. Out of the door of our bedroom, out of our house, up to the top of the town and into a little bar. I ordered *raki*, the very rough spirit they have, and I drank until I fell on the ground.

'They carried me home, I remember nothing of it. I woke up next day in our bed. There was no sign of Stavros. I remembered her there in the bed and I got up to be very sick. There was no sign of little Stavros either. I went to the bar where I had been the previous day, apologised for my behaviour, and asked them what had been the reception when they took me home.

'Magda had taken my child, *my* child, to his grandfather the barber. Stavros had just pointed them to the bedroom and left. They couldn't help me further. I had brandy this time, good Metaxa brandy to get me over the shock. Four days and nights of drinking, then I realised they had taken my child away from me. I heard like in a dream that Magda's husband had gone away on a fishing boat to another island. And then I remember waking up in the hospital on the Kalatriada road. Christina came to see me. "Pretend to be calm, pretend to be better, then they'll let you out," she said. So that's what I did. I pretended.'

'It worked?' David asked.

'Only for a bit. Stavros would not speak to me, wouldn't tell me what he'd done with my son, and I knew I must not raise my voice again or I would be back in that hospital where they locked every door behind them.'

'And Stavros?'

'Was living with Magda. I bought a bottle here, a bottle there, and drank until I passed out. I don't know how long it went on.

'Then Christina came and helped me pull myself together. And I went to see Stavros. He said I could stay in the house. That our son was living in Athens with his aunt and that I would never see the child again. He explained that soon he would sell the garage, *his* garage, and that he and Magda would settle somewhere new, collect little Stavros, and build a life for him.

'And suddenly I realised that I would be here alone, without my son, without my love, without my garage. Unable to go home, owing two thousand pounds . . . How was I going to find that money now?'

'But in fairness, Stavros knew about the debt, surely he must have said he'd help you?' David was shocked.

'No, he never knew about it. I never told him. He thought it was my savings,' Vonni said.

Then she moved away, and left David sitting on the harbour wall.

'**D**o you know what I don't understand,' Fiona said the same day as the four friends were putting together the jigsaw pieces of Vonni's story.

'Why she didn't get a lawyer?' Thomas suggested.

'She was in no position to do that. Stolen money in her background, he *did* give her the house, and she didn't really know their ways here,' Elsa said.

'No, wait. I don't understand why Andreas said that little Stavros came up to the taverna on the hill to play with his son Adoni and climb trees. He couldn't have done that at four.'

'Maybe Stavros and Magda stayed for a while longer, even a good time longer, and brought Stavros back here,' David suggested. 'That would have been even harder for Vonni to bear.'

'Well, she'll tell one of us, she promised that she would,' Thomas said.

'You're an easy person to talk to, David. I would not be at all surprised if she came back to you,' Elsa said to him with her wonderful smile.

Vonni came back to David sooner than he had expected.

'I have to deliver some potting clay and moulds to the hospital, for their rehab classes. Will you come with me, David? You see, I just hate going there on my own. I keep thinking that they'll lock the door behind me as they did before.'

'But you weren't there very long, were you?' David said. 'Didn't Christina get you out by telling you to pretend?'

'Oh, yes, that was the first time. But I went back. I was there for years on and off really,' Vonni said casually. 'Will we go and pick up Maria's van now and head off?'

'We will, we will.' David smiled.

'Are you imitating my accent, young fellow?'

'Imitate you, Vonni? I wouldn't dare!' he said.

'There's a very nice part of the garden, I'll show you,' she said when the goods had been handed over. And they sat together looking down from one of the many hills that surrounded Aghia Anna, as she picked up her story as if there had been no interruption.

'Once I knew I had lost everything I didn't see any point in pretending. I sold things out of the house, *his* house I always considered it, and bought drink. So I was back in here and out like a yo-yo. Stavros explained to everyone that I was an unfit mother. I saw little Stavros once a week on a Saturday for three hours. There was always someone else there, Stavros's father sometimes or his sister, or Andreas. The visits were not a success. I used to cry, you see, cry over all I had lost. And I would clutch at little Stavros and tell him how much I loved him. He was terrified of me. Andreas used to drive him up the hill to his place, to the swing on the tree, to cheer him up after he had to deal with me, then I would get bladdered with drink to get over it. It went on for years. He was twelve when they took him away.'

'They?'

'Stavros and Magda. Oddly, it was when they were gone that I decided there was still a life to be lived. So I got sober. But it was too late. My son was gone. No point in my trying to find out where. The boy's grandfather, the old barber, was kind to me, but he wouldn't tell me. I wrote to him, young Stavros—letters on his birthday through his grandfather and later through his aunts—every year.'

'And no answer ever?' David asked.

'No answer, ever.'

'Does Andreas not know where your son is? He's such a kind man, he'd understand. His own selfish son won't come back to him from Chicago. Andreas knows what it feels like.'

'David, listen to me. Andreas doesn't know where Stavros is. And there are two sides to everything. I was a pig of a mother when young Stavros was growing up, so how does he know I am mellow and easygoing now?'

'Someone might tell him,' David said.

Vonni brushed it away. 'Listen to me, David, in a similar way, Andreas knew everything about running a taverna when Adoni was growing up, how does Adoni know that his father is lonely and sad, and wants him to come home?'

'As I said, Vonni, someone could tell him. They are *so* foolish, these young men, Adoni in Chicago and Stavros wherever he is. Why they can't see sense and come back to you both is beyond me,' David said.

'There are probably people in England who wonder the same about you,' Vonni suggested. 'In that letter from your mother, she's *begging* you to come home.'

'Where does she say that?'

'In every line. I'm certain your father's ill. He may be dying.'

'Vonni!'

'I mean it, David,' she said.

Elsa had written nothing back to Deiter. She still needed time to think about it. There was no doubt that he had meant what he said. If Dieter said he would marry her then he was prepared to do that. Up to now he had genuinely believed that their lives could run easily together and that there was nothing about the situation that needed to be altered. Now it was up to Elsa to tell him when she would be back home and he would be there, waiting for her.

So what was holding her back?

Elsa walked on her own up one of the windy roads away from Aghia Anna. She had not been this way before, and since she would be leaving soon, she wanted to imprint the whole place on her mind.

No smart restaurants, traditional tavernas or craft shops on this road. Small poor dwellings, sometimes, with a goat or two outside, children playing among the hens and chickens.

Elsa stopped and looked at them. She was smiling at their antics when Vonni came out of a house.

'Heavens, Vonni, you're everywhere!' Elsa exclaimed.

'I could say the same about all of you! I never move but I fall over one of you,' Vonni said with spirit.

'Where does this road lead? I just came up this way to explore.'

'It doesn't really lead anywhere—just more of the same—but I have to deliver something a bit further on. Come and walk with me, I could do with the company.' Suddenly, she looked downhearted.

'Is something wrong?' Elsa asked.

'That house I was in just now, the young woman is pregnant. The father was one of those who drowned on Manos's boat. She doesn't want the child. It's just such a mess. I've been there for an hour saying we'll all help her to look after the baby. But will she listen? No.'

'That's an unusual position for you to be in, Vonni. People not listening to you,' Elsa teased her.

'Why do you say that?'

'Well, we all listen and take notice of everything you say. We spent hours talking to David about your theory that his father might be ill.'

'Not *might* be ill, *is* ill,' Vonni said. 'And what did David decide?'

'He thinks it's all a trap, a way to get him home, and then it will be harder for him to get away again. But you've succeeded—he's going to call his home today.'

'Good,' Vonni nodded her approval. She stopped at a small ill-kept building. 'I'm going into this house—come with me. I have to give Nikolas some magic medicine.'

'You make magic medicines too?' Elsa gasped.

'No, it's an antibiotic cream actually, but Nikolas doesn't trust modern medicine so Dr Leros and I have this little ruse.'

Elsa watched as Vonni moved around the old man's simple house, picking up things here, arranging them there, talking away effortlessly in Greek; and then she produced the magic ointment from her woollen shoulder bag and applied it solemnly to the sore on his leg.

When they left, the old man smiled at them both.

Elsa and Vonni continued to walk companionably down the windy road and Vonni pointed out landmarks as they passed.

'You love it here, don't you?' Elsa said.

'I was lucky to find this place. I'd never live anywhere else.'

'I'll be sorry to leave, I really will,' Elsa said.

'You are leaving? Going back to Germany?' Vonni did not sound best pleased.

'Yes, I have to move on,' Elsa said.

'Move back, more like, move back to what you ran away from.'

Elsa was angry. 'That's not true. Dieter wants to marry me. It will all be out in the open now.' Her eyes flashed.

'And the reason you ran away in the first place . . . that was all about forcing him to propose, was it? I thought you said you felt guilty because he had abandoned his daughter and thought it didn't matter. Has all this disgust with him vanished?'

'We only have one life, Vonni. We have to put out our hands and take what we want.'

'No matter who we take it from? Oh, Elsa, just listen to yourself speaking. I told you before that you were too used to getting your own way. And I mean it.' Vonni sighed. 'But you're not going to take any notice of what I say. You are going to do what you want to. Forget I spoke.'

They walked on in awkward silence until they reached the town.

'Shirley?'

'Yes, Thomas?'

'Is Andy there?'

'You don't really want to talk to Andy?'

'No, I was just hoping that I might be able to talk to my son without Andy-the-athlete breathing down his neck.'

'Are you picking a fight, Thomas?'

'No, of course I'm not. I just want to talk to my kid. OK?'

'Well, hold on, I'll get him for you.' He could almost hear her shrug. 'Hi, Dad.'

'Bill, tell me about your day,' he said and half listened as the boy went on about a track and field event for families at the university. He and Andy had won a three-legged race.

'Father-son race, was it called?' Thomas asked bitterly.

'No, Dad, they don't call them that now—you know so many families have sort of re-formed themselves.'

'Re-formed themselves?' Thomas gasped.

'Well, that's what our teacher calls it, it's got to do with so many people being divorced and everything.'

It wasn't such a bad word, but it didn't begin to hint at the whole story.

'Sure, so what do they call it?'

'A Senior-Junior race.'

'Great. Well, I got you a wonderful book today, there's a bookshop here in this tiny place. It's stories from Greek myths but written for the modern day. I've been reading it myself all afternoon. Do you know any Greek stories?'

'Is the one about the kids who flew off to find the Golden Fleece a Greek story?'

'Sure it is, tell me a bit about it,' Thomas said, pleased.

'It was about this brother and sister and they rode on the back of a sheep . . .'

'Did you read it at school?'

'Yes, Dad, we have a new history teacher and she keeps making us read stories.'

'That's great, Bill.'

'It'll be great when I have a brother or sister next year.'

His heart felt like a lump of lead. Shirley was pregnant again. She and Andy were starting a family and she had said nothing.

'That's *great* news,' he heard himself say through gritted teeth.

'Andy's painting a nursery for the baby. I told him how you made one for me and put in bookshelves even before I was born.'

And Thomas felt the tears in his eyes as he waded in with his two big feet and broke the whole mood.

'Well, I guess Andy will be busy putting up shelves for trainers and trophies and sports gear for the poor little kid. To hell with books this time round.'

He heard Bill gasp.

'That's not fair, Dad.'

'Life's not fair, Bill,' said Thomas, and hung up.

'Tell me about it,' Vonni said when she saw Thomas's face a couple of hours later. 'You messed it up again with that kid, didn't you?'

'Shirley is pregnant,' Thomas said, bleakly. He didn't move from the chair where he had sat since the phone conversation with Bill.

'Your son will need you all the more now if his mother is pregnant. But no, you have to be noble and distant and break that child's heart by giving him space he doesn't want. I get impatient with people like you, Thomas. I know I am a different generation, my son is your age, but I have never indulged in self-pity like you do. Especially since the solution is in your own hands. You love this child, nobody but yourself is putting any distance between you and him.'

'You don't understand, I'm on sabbatical leave.'

'They're not going to get out the FBI if you go back to your home town to see your own son.'

'Would that it were so simple,' he sighed.

Fiona was talking to Mr Leftides, the manager at the Anna Beach Hotel, about a job.

'I could mind the guests' children for you, take them off their parents' hands. I'm a qualified nurse.'

'You don't speak any Greek,' the manager objected.

'No, but most of the visitors here are English-speaking, I mean even the Swedes and Germans all speak English.'

She saw Vonni across the foyer, stacking the shelves of the hotel's tiny craft shop.

'Vonni will speak for me,' Fiona said. 'She'll tell you that I can be relied on. Vonni!' she called out. 'Can you tell Mr Leftides that I'd be a good person to work here?'

'As what?' Vonni sounded curt.

'I'm going to need somewhere to live when Elsa goes back. I was asking Mr Leftides if I could work here in exchange for board and lodging and a little money.' Fiona looked pleadingly at the older woman.

'Why do you need a job? Aren't you going home?' Vonni was terse.

'No, you know I can't leave here until Shane comes back.'

'Shane is not coming back.'

'That's not true. Of course he's coming back. Please tell Mr Leftides that I'm reliable.'

'You're not reliable, Fiona, you are deluding yourself that this boy is coming back to you!'

Mr Leftides, who had been looking from one to the other as if he were at a tennis match, decided he had had enough. He shrugged and walked away.

'*Why* did you do that, Vonni?' There were tears of annoyance in Fiona's eyes.

'You are being ridiculous, Fiona. Everyone was sorry for you and kind when you had the miscarriage and all that upset. But surely by now you must know there's no future for you here, waiting foolishly for a man who will never return. Go back to Dublin and take up your life.'

'You're so cruel and cold—I thought you were a friend,' Fiona said in a shaky voice.

'I'm the best friend you ever had, if you had the intelligence to see it.'

'Vonni? You want a Morning Glory?' Andreas often looked into the craft shop and treated her to a little metal dish with three colours of ice cream across the road in Yanni's delicatessen.

'No, I'd prefer a bottle of vodka with a lot of ice,' she said.

Andreas was startled. Vonni never joked about her drinking, and did not refer to her alcoholic past.

'Is there a problem?' he asked.

'Yes, there is. I've fought with every one of those foreign kids. Every single one of them.'

'I thought you liked them. They're very attached to you.' Andreas was surprised.

'I don't know what it is, Andreas. Everything they say annoys me.'

'That's unlike you. You are always keeping the peace, smoothing things down.'

'Not these days, I'm not, Andreas. I feel like stirring everything up. I suppose it was the boat and all the unnecessary waste of life. It makes everything seem pointless.' She was pacing around her little shop.

'There's a lot of sense in your life,' he said.

'Is there? Today I can't see any. I think I'm a foolish woman, perched here in this place until I die. I used to feel this years back, and then I would hit the *raki* until I was senseless. Don't let me go down that road again, Andreas, my good friend.'

He laid his hand on hers. 'Of course I won't. You've fought so hard to get out of that pit you fell into, nobody is going to let you fall in again. Come with me now and help me make *dolmadhes*. I can't bend the old fingers to stuff the vine leaves and stitch them up. Please close your shop and come up to the taverna with me. As a favour, will you?'

'And of course you'll have plenty of coffee and ice cream to distract me and keep me away from the demon drink?' She gave him a weak smile.

'Certainly. That was my very plan,' he said, and they went out of the door together.

They sat and discussed Vonni at midday by the harbour.

'I can understand her attacking *me*, because, to be honest, a lot of people have a problem with Shane,' Fiona said. 'But the rest of you? I don't get it.'

'Well, it's easy to see where she's coming from with me,' Elsa said. 'I'm a tramp who has somehow blackmailed a poor innocent guy into proposing to her.'

'And did he?' Thomas asked.

'Yes, but it's much more complex than that. Why has Vonni turned on you?' Elsa changed the subject.

Thomas rubbed his chin thoughtfully. 'I truthfully don't know what annoyed her so much about my situation. I just wanted her to agree I was trying to be responsible and do the right thing.'

David tried to stand up for Vonni. 'You can see why she envies you though. If she had been allowed anywhere near her son she'd have been there.'

'You're very forgiving, David, since she lit into you as well,' Fiona said.

'Yes, but she got that all wrong. You see, she doesn't know what kind of people my parents are. I've read my mother's letter over and over and there's nothing in it to suggest that my father isn't well . . .'

'But, David, why did she get angry with you exactly?' Elsa asked.

'Because I was saying what a good man Andreas was and how selfish his son was not to come back and help him. She said I was exactly the same as Adoni, staying away instead of helping my father. But, of course, it's a totally different thing.' He looked round the table and thought he saw a look on all their faces that suggested it might not be so different after all.

Vonni sewed up the vine leaves neatly around their little packages of rice and pine nuts. She was very quiet.

Andreas looked at Vonni from under his big bushy eyebrows. She was right to be concerned. She had the same sense of unease and restlessness that had led her to those frightening drinking bouts all those years ago. He wondered if he should contact his sister Christina. She and Vonni had been good friends and a huge mutual support. But then, he would do nothing without consulting Vonni.

Her face was lined as always, but today she had a worried look.

They worked on the open-air terrace looking down over the town. Twice she got up and went into his kitchen for no reason. He watched her without appearing to do so. Once she reached up to where bottles of brandy and olive oil stood on a line on the shelf. She was breathing fast as if she had run in a race.

'What can I do for you, Vonni? Tell me,' he begged.

'I've done nothing of any use in my life, Andreas. What can anyone do for me? Ever?'

'You've been a good friend to my sister, to me, to all the people in Aghia Anna. That's worth while, isn't it?'

'Not particularly. I'm not looking for pity, I hate that in a person, it's just that I actually can't see any point in the past, the present or the future.' Her voice was flat.

'Well, then, you'd better open the brandy,' Andreas said. 'It's on the shelf in the kitchen. You've been looking at it all morning. Take it down, drink it, then none of us will have to worry about *when* you're going to do it, it will be done.'

'Why are you saying this?'

'Because it's one way to go. You can throw away the work and discipline and denial of years in an hour or so. Because it will bring this oblivion you want.'

'I don't *want* to,' she said piteously.

'No, I know that. But if you see nothing in the past, the present or the future, then I suppose you have to.'

'And do you see any point in anything?' she asked.

'Some days it's harder than others,' Andreas said. 'You have good friends everywhere, Vonni.'

'No, I end up driving them away.'

'Who are you thinking about?'

'That foolish little Fiona, for one. I told her that her boyfriend won't come back. But then, I know where he is. She doesn't know.'

'You did it for the best,' he soothed her.

'I must tell her where he is,' Vonni said suddenly.

'I wonder if that's wise?'

'May I use your telephone, Andreas?'

'Please . . .'

He heard her dial the number and then speak to Fiona. 'I called to say I had no right to shout at you today. To say that I'm sorry. Very sorry.'

Andreas moved away to give her privacy. He knew how very hard it was for Vonni to admit that she was wrong.

In Elsa's villa, Fiona looked at the telephone in her hand, mystified. Whatever she had expected it wasn't this. She was at a loss to know what to say.

'That's OK, Vonni,' she said awkwardly.

'No, it's not OK, as it happens. The reason he didn't get in touch is because he's in jail in Athens.'

'Shane in jail! Oh my God, what for?'

'Something to do with drugs.'

'No wonder I haven't heard from him. Poor Shane—and would they not let him get in touch and tell me?'

'He did try to get in touch eventually, but only so that you'd get him bail, and we said—'

'But of course I'll get him bail. Why did nobody tell me?'

'Because Yorghis and I thought you'd be better without him,' Vonni said lamely.

Fiona was outraged. 'How dare you, Vonni! How dare you meddle in my life? Now he thinks I haven't bothered to get in touch with him.'

'I'll take you to him,' Vonni said. 'I owe it to you. I'll go with you on the eight o'clock ferry to Athens in the morning, take you to the jail, find out what's happening.'

'Why are you doing this?' Fiona was suspicious.

'I suppose I realised that it is your life,' said Vonni. 'I'll see you at the harbour tomorrow morning.' Then she came back and sat down with Andreas.

'Did that work?' he asked.

'I don't know, tomorrow will tell. But I feel stronger somehow.'

'I think we have to keep struggling on, Vonni. Manos and those who died on the boat didn't get a chance to, so I'm going to keep going until the end.'

CHAPTER SEVEN

'MOTHER? I GOT your letter. About the award.'

'Oh, David!' The delight in her voice was hard to take. 'I just knew that you'd call. I knew it. You're such a good boy to phone so quickly.'

'Well, you see, I'm not certain yet what's happening . . .' He did not want to be railroaded into dates of return, times of flights. Already he felt the familiar heavy weight that their pressure always created, it was in his chest and around his shoulders.

His mother was still talking excitedly. 'Your father will be so pleased when he hears you called. It will make his day. He'll be back in about an hour.'

'He's not in the office on a Saturday surely?'

'No, no, just . . . um . . . out . . .'

David was surprised. His father did not go to synagogue every week, only at the High Holidays. Saturdays were always spent at home. He felt suddenly cold. 'Is Father ill?' he asked suddenly.

'What makes you think that?' He could hear the fear in her voice.

'I don't know, Mother. I sort of got the idea that he might have an illness and that neither of you were telling me.'

'You got that feeling . . . far away in Greece?' She spoke in wonder.

'Sort of.' He shuffled. 'But is it true, Mother?'

He felt that time was standing still as he waited for her to answer. It could only have been seconds but it felt like an age.

'Your father has cancer of the colon, David, they can't operate. They've given him six months.'

There was a silence on the line as he caught his breath.

'Does he know, Mother? Has he been told?'

'Yes, that's what they do these days. They tell people. He's very calm. He has a lot of medication.'

David gave a gulping sound, as if he were trying to stifle a sob. 'Why didn't you tell me?'

'You know your father. He is such a proud man. He didn't want you coming back just out of pity.'

'I see,' David said miserably.

'But imagine you sensing from all that distance away, David. It's uncanny, but then you always were so sensitive.'

David had rarely felt so ashamed in his life.

Thomas called his mother.

'Don't call me from so far away, son, wasting all the money on me.'

'It's OK, Mom. I get my full salary, I told you. Plenty to live on like a millionaire out here, and to pay support for Bill.'

'And to send me treats too. You're a good boy, I love those magazines you send me every month. I've been blessed with you and your brother.'

'It's not easy being a parent, is it, Mom?'

'I didn't find it too bad, but then my spouse went and died on me rather than take up with someone else like yours did.'

'It takes two to break up a marriage, Mom. It wasn't all Shirley's fault.'

'No, but when are you finding yourself a partner?'

'One day, I assure you, and you'll be one of the first to know. Mom, I called to ask you about Bill. Do you talk to him at all?'

'You know I do, son, I call him every Sunday. He misses you like hell, Thomas.' She paused. 'He told me you didn't feel good about the baby.'

'I was meant to dance with joy, I suppose,' Thomas said bitterly.

'He said he thought you would love it, like Andy loves him.'

'He thought I'd love the new baby?' Thomas was astounded.

'He's a child, Thomas. He's just nine years of age, his father has left him, left America. He was clutching at straws. He thought that maybe you would come back if there was a baby for you to be stepfather to.'

'What do you think I should do?'

'I don't know. Be near him, not thousands of miles away, I guess.'

'You think that would sort it?'

'Well, at least Bill wouldn't think you had abandoned him.'

Fiona woke very early and saw the dawn come up over Aghia Anna. She was still furious with Vonni and Yorghis for having lied to her. How dare they tell her that Shane had not been in touch? He *had* tried to contact her and these old busybodies had interfered. They said his motive was only to get her to raise the bail money. Well, of course he had to get bail first to get out, to get on with life.

She was not relishing the thought of the ferry trip with Vonni as a companion. She wished too that she hadn't told it all to Elsa last night. Elsa had been less than supportive.

Fiona wished mightily that she could turn the clock back. Why had she asked Elsa to help her raise the money? To lend her a thousand euros, just for a few days until Barbara could send it to her from Dublin.

'Lend you money to get him out to finish off your face?' Elsa had scoffed.

'That was different,' Fiona began. 'He was in shock, I told him the news all wrong, you see.'

Elsa had lifted Fiona's hair. 'The bruises are still there,' she had said softly. 'Nobody on earth, Fiona, is going to lend you money to get that guy out of a place where he should be kept permanently.'

When Vonni and Fiona met at the harbour, Vonni had already bought the tickets. The ferry pulled out of the harbour and Fiona looked back at Aghia Anna. So much had happened since she first came here.

Vonni had gone downstairs to where they were serving coffee and drinks and had returned with coffee and two sticky-looking cakes.

'*Loukoumadhes*,' she explained. 'They're honey fritters with cinnamon. They'll give you energy for the day.'

Fiona looked at her gratefully. The woman was making every attempt at an apology. Fiona knew she must be gracious.

'You have been kindness itself,' she said, patting Vonni's hand.

To her surprise she saw tears in Vonni's eyes. And they sat companionably and ate their honey cakes.

'Are you looking forward to seeing Shane?' Vonni asked.

'I can't wait, I hope he won't be angry that it took me so long.'

'I'll explain, I'll tell him it wasn't your fault.'

'Thank you, Vonni . . . it's just . . . you know . . .' Fiona was twisting her hands awkwardly.

'Tell me,' Vonni encouraged her.

'Well, you've met Shane. He can say things that sound much more aggressive than he intends. I wouldn't want you to think . . .'

'Don't worry, Fiona, I won't think anything,' said Vonni through gritted teeth.

'**E**lsa! I'm delighted to see you,' Thomas called. 'I was going to rent a rowing boat and go out for a couple of hours, would you trust me enough to come with me?'

'I'd love it. Shall we go now?'

'Sure. David's not coming to the café, his father is ill, Vonni was right about that anyway. He's going to arrange a ticket home.'

'Poor David.' Elsa was sympathetic. 'And Fiona's gone to Athens with Vonni. She left this morning.'

'So we're on our own,' Thomas said.

'I'd love a farewell boat journey, I'll help with the rowing if you like.'

'No, lie back and enjoy it. A farewell journey? You *are* going back to Germany then?'

'Oh, yes. I don't know exactly what day, but I am going.'

'Is Dieter very pleased?'

'He doesn't know yet,' she said simply.

Thomas was surprised. 'Why haven't you told him?' he asked.

'I don't know. There are a few things I haven't sorted out in my mind,' Elsa said.

'I see,' said Thomas, in the voice of one who didn't.

'And when will *you* go back, Thomas?'

'It depends on whether I really believe Bill wants me there.' He spoke candidly.

'Of course he does. That's obvious,' Elsa said.

'How is it so obvious to you?'

'Because *my* father left us when I was young. I would have given anything to have had a phone call saying that he was on the way home to live near our street and I could see him every day. That would have been the best thing that could have happened. But it never did.'

Thomas looked at her, astounded. She made it seem so simple, so easy. He put his arm around her shoulder and headed down to where they hired out the brightly coloured boats.

In the crowded harbour of Piraeus, Fiona followed, lugging her heavy bag with her, as Vonni led the way to the *Ilektrikos* and bought the tickets.

'Do you know, I'm a bit afraid of seeing him again,' Fiona said, as they got on the train for Athens.

'But he loves you. He'll be delighted to see you, won't he?' Vonni asked doubtfully.

'Yes, yes, of course. It's just that we don't know how much the bail will be, and really I'm not sure how I'm going to get it when we *do* know. It's not the kind of thing that they're going to help me with from Dublin. I might have to tell them back home that it's for something else.'

Vonni said nothing.

Yorghis had phoned ahead to let the police in Athens know that Vonni and Fiona were on their way. He had given a short thumbnail sketch of who they were and when they would arrive.

Dimitri, the young policeman who had taken the call, only told Shane ten minutes before the visit that Fiona was on her way.

'Has she got the money?' he asked.

'What money?' Dimitri asked.

'The money you bloodsuckers want!' Shane shouted.

'Do you want a clean shirt to wear?' Dimitri was impassive.

'No, I don't want a clean bloody shirt. I want her to see things as they are.'

'They'll be here very shortly.' The policeman was curt.

'They?'

'She has another woman from Aghia Anna with her.'

'Another lame duck. That's just typical of Fiona. She takes her time getting here and then she drags someone else in on the act.'

As he closed and locked the door, Dimitri reflected on the nature of love. They often said that girls liked a whiff of danger. That old policeman in Aghia Anna had said that the young woman who was coming to see Shane was a nurse, a gentle soul, an attractive girl . . .

A short while later, Dimitri returned to the cell and opened the door. 'Your friends are here,' he said tersely.

'Shane!' Fiona cried.

'You took your time.'

'I didn't know where you were until yesterday,' she said, moving towards him.

'Huh,' Shane said, not responding to her arms held out to him.

'I was responsible for all that, I did not pass on the fact that you had been in touch,' Vonni said.

'Who the hell are you?' Shane asked.

'I'm Vonni, from Ireland originally, but I've lived in Aghia Anna for over thirty years. I came with Fiona to help her find you here.'

'OK, thank you. Can you piss off now and leave me with my girlfriend?' he asked with darkened brow.

'Up to you, Fiona,' Vonni said pleasantly.

'Not up to her actually. Up to me,' Shane said.

'Perhaps you could wait for me . . . outside, Vonni?' Fiona begged.

'I'll be there when you need me, Fiona,' Vonni said and left.

Fiona moved towards Shane to kiss him, but he didn't seem to be interested.

'Did you bring the money?' he asked.

'Sorry?'

'The money, to get me out!' he said.

'But, Shane, I don't *have* any money. You know that.' Why was he not reaching out to hold her?

'Don't tell me you've turned up here with nothing to say,' he said.

'I have plenty to say, Shane . . .'

'Say it then.'

Fiona wondered why were they still not embracing, but she knew she must keep talking.

'Well, the good news is that I heard from Barbara. There are lovely apartments very near the hospital and we could easily get one and go back to Dublin. But the sad news is that we lost our baby. It was awful but it happened. Dr Leros said that as soon as we want to try again—'

'*What?*'

'I know you're upset, Shane, I was too, desperately, but Dr Leros said—'

'Fiona, shut up talking rubbish about Dr this and Dr that. Do you have the money or do you not?'

'Of course I don't have the money, Shane. I came to see you, to talk about it, to tell you that I love you and, it will all be all right . . .'

He still hadn't held her or talked about their dead baby.

'Shane, aren't you sad about the baby?'

'Shut up and tell me where on God's earth we're going to find the *money!*' he said.

'We'll ask them, Vonni and I will, how much it is they want and then I'll try to raise it—but that's not the most important thing, Shane.'

'So what's the most important thing?' he asked.

'Well, that I've found you and that I love you for ever. So why don't you kiss me?' she asked.

'Oh God, Fiona, will you shut up about love and think who might get us the money,' he said.

'If we are able to borrow it, then we'll both have to get jobs to pay it back,' she said anxiously.

'*You* get a job if you want to, as soon as I'm out of here I have people to meet, contacts to make. I'll have plenty of money then. I'll hang round Athens for a bit and then I might move up to Istanbul.'

She looked at him levelly. 'And am I to go with you?'

He shrugged. 'If you want. But you're not to nag me about settling down and getting jobs. We left Ireland to get away from all that shit.'

'No, we left Ireland because we loved each other and everybody kept putting difficulties in our way.'

'Whatever,' Shane said.

Fiona knew that tone of voice. It was his switch-off voice. He used it when talking to people who bored him rigid. She had begun to understand that she bored Shane and that he had never loved her. It was staggering and almost impossible to take in, but she knew she was right. It meant that all her hopes and dreams had been for nothing. He would never have tried to get in touch if he hadn't wanted the money for bail.

'You don't love me,' she said in a shaky voice.

'Oh, Lord God above, how often do I have to play the record? I *said* you could come with me if you wanted to.'

There was a wooden chair in the corner. Fiona sat down and buried her head in her hands.

'No, Fiona, this is not the time to go all weepy and emotional on me. Leave it off, will you . . .'

She looked up at him, and her hair was back from her face.

He stared at her. 'What happened to your face?' he asked, as if repelled by the bruising.

'You did it, Shane. In the restaurant out on the point.'

He began to bluster. 'I did *not*,' he said.

Fiona was calm. 'It's not important any more.' She stood up as if to leave.

'Where are you going? You've only just got here. We have to work this out.'

'No, Shane, *you* have to work it out. I've seen you and now I'm leaving.'

'But the money? The bail?' His face was distorted.

She knocked on the door and Dimitri opened it for her. There was a smile on his face.

This drove Shane into a frenzy. He leaped towards Fiona and caught her by the hair.

'You are *not* coming in here playing games like this with me!' he roared.

But Dimitri was more speedy than anyone would have thought. He had his arm across Shane's throat, forcing his chin upwards. Shane was no match for him and was forced to let go of Fiona.

She stood at the door for a moment, watching, then moved out into the corridor and walked to the front office.

Vonni was sitting there with a senior policeman. 'They're talking about two thousand euros,' she began.

'Let them talk about it.' Fiona's head was high and her eyes were bright. 'He's not getting it from me.'

CHAPTER EIGHT

THOMAS ROWED THE LITTLE BOAT back to the harbour. It seemed like coming home.

They looked up towards the hills and pointed to the places they knew. That was the hospital in the Kalatriada road. And that was the road up to Andreas's taverna. And there, finally, was the harbour and the café with the blue and yellow checked tablecloths. It was as if the escapism were over.

'It was good, your voyage?' the old man asked, as they returned the boat.

'Very good voyage,' Elsa said with a smile.

They walked up the harbour road towards the town.

'I wonder if we'll forget this place eventually,' Thomas said.

At exactly the same moment, Elsa said, 'Imagine all this busy world going on without us!'

They laughed at thinking almost the same thought, and as they were passing a café, Thomas indicated that they should sit down.

'Why not?' Elsa was pleased. 'By this day next week there'll be very little chance of dropping into a café.'

'Ah, you speak for yourself,' Thomas said. 'I'll still be here dropping into cafés, rowing boats, reading in the sunshine.'

'No, you'll be on your way back to California,' she said with a great sense of being right about it.

'Elsa! You're as bad as Vonni.' He was puzzled at her certainty.

'I'll send you a postcard. You'll be there to get it,' she laughed.

Andreas came over to their table.

'May I join you? I have some good news to share.'

'Adoni?' Elsa gasped with excitement.

Andreas shook his head. 'No, not as good as that, alas, but still good. The little Fiona has turned her back on Shane, she has walked out on him. She and Vonni are on the last ferry, they will be back by sunset.'

'How do you know?' Thomas asked.

'One of the police telephoned Yorghis with the news. She did not even try to raise his bail—just left.' Andreas spread out his hands at the mystery of it all. 'But it is all very much for the best,' he said. 'And David is coming up to dinner in my taverna tonight to say goodbye. He is leaving Aghia Anna tomorrow afternoon. I wanted to ask you to join us.'

Thomas asked, 'And will Vonni and Fiona join the dinner too?'

'I hope so, yes.' Andreas's smile was warm.

Thomas spoke quickly. 'You are so kind, Andreas, but alas Elsa and I have to meet someone tonight for dinner. What a pity.'

Elsa picked it up quickly. 'Yes, that's such bad timing,' she said. 'Can you tell David we'll see him at the harbour at midday?'

Andreas understood.

He understood more than they realised. Of course, it was very last-minute, he reassured them. But he could read signs as well as anyone. These two wanted to be alone. He left them courteously.

'Amazing to be so centred, so rooted in a place like he is,' Thomas said admiringly, watching the old man leave.

'Why did you say that, about us having dinner?' Elsa asked.

Thomas was silent for a moment. 'I don't really know, Elsa, but I knew you didn't want another run-in with Vonni, and as it happens I share your view. I also didn't want to hear one word tonight about Shane. And . . . and . . .'

'And what?'

'And I'll miss you when you go. I wanted some more time together before you left. Just the two of us.'

David was helping Andreas in the kitchen. 'I'll miss all this so much,' he said.

'Perhaps you could cook for your father? I tell you how to make a good *moussaka*. Do you have *melitzanes* in England?'

'Aubergines? Yes, we do.'

'Then I'll show you. It will please him to see you cook for him.'

'Do you think so?' David was doubtful.

'I don't *think* so, I *know* so,' said Andreas.

Yorghis telephoned from the harbour. He had waylaid Fiona and Vonni and they would be at the taverna in fifteen minutes.

'Yorghis says that Fiona is in great form,' Andreas said.

'She must have got that fool out of jail then,' David said glumly.

'No, on the contrary, I was about to tell you. She turned her back on him. Left him there.'

'For the moment. She'll go back for him.'

'I think not, but I suggest that we let her tell us herself. Do you agree?'

'Oh, yes, that's always my policy,' David said. 'And is she speaking to Vonni still?'

'The best of friends, apparently, according to Yorghis.'

David laughed. 'Aren't you a wonderful pair of old gossips!'

'If you can't gossip with your own brother, I ask you, then who is there to gossip with?'

'Would you like to go to the Anna Beach?' Thomas suggested to Elsa.

'No, it's too . . . I don't know . . . too full of chrome and opulence. Besides, it doesn't have good memories for me. What about that little place out on the point where the waves break?'

Thomas didn't want to go there. 'It reminds me too much of the day that savage hit Fiona.'

'But now she has left him,' Elsa soothed. 'So where should we go? It can't be too public, we did say we were meeting someone . . .'

'Why don't we get some kebabs and wine and go back to my place?' Thomas suggested.

'Sure, that's great. I'll leave a note for Fiona saying I'll be back later and then let's go and buy supper.'

There was a definite change in Fiona, they could all sense it. She held her shoulders back, she smiled more readily.

There were three tables of customers at the taverna, all of them English-speaking. Fiona translated the menu and advised them all to start with *dolmadhes*, which, she explained, were little fat packets of stuffed vine leaves. She suggested the house wine, which was inexpensive and good. Soon she had them so well organised that little Rina, the girl who helped in the kitchen, could serve them.

That meant that Andreas could sit down with his party and look at the lights going on down in the heart of Aghia Anna.

'A pity Thomas and Elsa couldn't join us,' David said.

'Oh, well,' Andreas shrugged. 'And you, Fiona, you are very good with people, you look after them well, would you like to work here?' he said unexpectedly.

Fiona laid her hand on his. 'If you had asked me this last night or even early this morning I would have cried with gratitude. But now,

now I say thank you from my heart, but I will not be able to come and work here.'

'It is too far up from the town?' Andreas asked.

'No, Andreas, not too far. It's just that I'm going home. Back to Dublin.'

She looked around the table at their astonished faces.

Thomas and Elsa finished their meal and sat on the balcony looking out over the rooftops.

'You have a nicer view from your place,' Thomas said.

'You can still see the stars from here, that's all that matters,' Elsa said.

'"What is the stars, Joxer?"' Thomas quoted in a heavy Irish accent.

'Will you say that I am showing off if I say I know where that's from?'

'Go on, tell me, shame me, put me down!' he laughed.

'It's by Sean O'Casey,' she said.

'Top of the class, Elsa. Another devoted teacher?'

'No, Dieter and I went to London, on a secret trip, and we saw it there. It was brilliant.'

'Are you looking forward to being back with him again?' Thomas asked.

'There's a problem,' she said.

'Isn't there always?' he sympathised.

'I suppose so. This problem is an unusual one: although he has promised that there will be no more deception and hiding and sneaking away from people, he never owned up to something else. Like the fact that he and another woman had a child.'

'Since you and he were together?' Thomas asked.

'No, years before, but the point is that he never acknowledged that little girl.'

'Is that what you ran away from?'

'I did not run away, I left my job and went to see the world. But I did think less well of him. Anyone who has a child, either deliberately or accidentally, must be there for that child.'

'And he didn't agree?'

'No, and somehow I was revolted by it. I felt I could never trust him again. I felt ashamed of loving him. I told him all this.'

'And so what has changed? What makes you think that it's right to go back to him now?'

'Meeting him here, knowing he loves me and will do anything for me.' She looked at him, hoping he understood.

Thomas nodded. 'Yes, I would have believed him, too. If you love someone you'll pretend anything to keep that person. I did, I know.'

'What did you pretend?' she asked gently.

'I pretended that I believed Bill was my son. I loved Shirley so much then that I couldn't face her with the absolute proof that he couldn't be.'

'He's not your son?' Elsa was astonished.

Thomas told the story simply and without emotion. The tests that had proved him to be sterile, the joyful announcement of Shirley's pregnancy, and the totally unexpected bonus that when Bill arrived Thomas discovered that he adored the boy.

'Do you still love Shirley?'

'No, I don't hate her either. She irritates me, and now she and Andy are having a child together and that irritates me too. The fact that they *can* for one thing, and for another that Bill is so excited about . . . his new brother or sister.'

'Did you ever think Shirley was having an affair?'

'No, not remotely. But let's put it this way: the very existence of Bill meant that Shirley was not exactly the faithful type. I guess I thought it was just one fling.'

'It probably was,' Elsa said.

'Yes, I think so. But for whatever reason we found less and less to say to each other. And then we got divorced.' He looked gloomy.

'And did you find anyone else?'

'No, I guess I didn't really look. I cared so much about Bill, you see. And I was really very surprised when she brought Andy to meet me so that they could tell me their plans. Shirley said she wanted us to be up-front about everything.' He was scornful.

'Well, what was wrong with that?' Elsa asked.

'Oh, there had been months of secrets and pretence there! People in love can be so smug.'

Elsa was silent. She was thinking hard, working something out.

'Sorry for droning on,' Thomas said.

'No, not at all, you've just clarified something for me.'

'I have?'

'Yes. If Dieter is to be any kind of a worthwhile human being, he must accept the fact that he has a daughter, and recognise her.'

'Even if it means losing you?' Thomas asked.

'He wouldn't lose me over it, if he could genuinely believe that this girl needs a father. The problem is that he might just put on some kind of an act. He thinks that what I want is a diamond ring, respectability, commitment.'

'He doesn't know you very well then, if you have been with him for over two years and he doesn't understand your values.'

'You think I should give him up, don't you?'

'What I think doesn't matter.'

'It matters to me.'

'All right, then. I think you should be with someone who does understand you . . . as well as the other thing.'

'What other thing?' she laughed.

'You know what I mean—sex, love, attraction. All of those are very fine but if you held out for the understanding as well, then you'd be very happy.'

'And where would I find all that in one package, Thomas?' Elsa asked.

'Ah, if I knew the answer to that I'd run the world,' he said, raising his wineglass to her. 'But I suppose I could tell you that we can and do get over loving people and I hope you might contemplate getting over Dieter.'

'Why? You know that Dieter is the love of my life.' She was confused.

'You asked me what I thought, I told you.' Thomas spoke simply.

'But I can't think why you would want me to give him up, get over him . . .'

'Because then I could comfort you.'

She looked at him open-mouthed. 'Thomas, this cannot be true!' she gasped. 'You and I are mates, friends. You don't fancy me, it's only the wine and the stars.'

'You never thought of me in that way at all?' he asked, his head on one side.

'I did think that it would be very easy to love a gentle, thoughtful person like you, rather than a restless, urgent man like Dieter. But then I've often wished idly for things that didn't happen. Couldn't happen.'

'All right, then I think you should go back to him tomorrow. Why hang around?' he said.

'You give up pretty easily,' she said flirtatiously.

'Come on, Elsa. Everything I say is wrong. I did you the courtesy of considering what you said. You are not doing that.'

'I'm only playing with you,' she said.

'Don't,' said Thomas.

She was contrite. 'I'm only playing games because I don't know what else to do. I know what you should do. It's so obvious and easy. And what everyone else—Dieter, David, Fiona, Andreas, Vonni—all of you should do. It's just my own decision that isn't clear.'

'What should Vonni do?' Thomas asked with interest.

'She should get Andreas and Yorghis to find her son and tell him what kind of person she is now. Young Stavros would come home if they told him.'

Thomas smiled at her. 'Elsa the Crusader,' he said affectionately.

In the taverna they talked about Fiona's journey home and when she should leave.

'Perhaps you could come on the last ferry with me tomorrow,' David said. 'We would be company for each other, and you might even fly to London with me.'

'That's not a bad idea, it would make it less hard to say goodbye.'

'For a while,' Vonni said. 'You'll come back again. You've both got friends here.'

'Tomorrow I'll go and say goodbye to Eleni and thank her for everything and call on Dr Leros as well,' Fiona said.

'I'll give Maria a last driving lesson and tell her that Vonni will take over now. Is that right, Vonni?'

'Has she *any* coordination these days?' Vonni asked.

'Much improved,' David soothed. 'And she's great if you can manage not to shout at her but to build up her confidence.'

'Aren't we all great when people don't shout at us and build up our confidence,' Vonni grumbled.

'Have you told them in Ireland that you are going back?' Andreas asked Fiona.

'Not yet. I'll call from the Anna Beach tomorrow.'

'Go in and use my phone,' he said, as he had said all that time ago on the day that Manos had perished with his boat.

'Just a quick call, then, to my friend Barbara. Thank you so much, Andreas.' And Fiona ran into the kitchen.

'Isn't it unusual that you young people don't have mobile phones?' Yorghis wondered.

'Yes, it is odd. Not one of the four of us has one that works here,' David said.

'It's not unusual at all,' Vonni said. 'You have all been running away from something. Why would you want a phone so that you could be tracked down?'

'Barbara?'

'God Almighty, it's Fiona!'

'Barbara, I'm coming home!'

'Well, that's great news! When will the pair of you be back?'

'Not the pair of us. Just me.'

There was a silence at the other end.

'Shane is staying there?' Barbara said eventually.

'In a manner of speaking, yes.'

'Well, that's a pity,' Barbara said neutrally.

'Don't be such a hypocrite, Barbara, you're delighted.'

'That's not fair—why should I be delighted that my friend is upset?'

'I'm not upset, Barbara—could you and I share a flat, do you think?'

'Of course we could. I'll start looking right away.'

'Great, and . . . Barbara, could you sort of tell my ma and da?'

'Sure . . . what exactly will I tell them?'

'That I'm coming home,' Fiona said, surprised that there should be any question about it.

'Yes, but you know the way people of that generation always want to ask questions . . .' Barbara began.

'Oh, head them off at the pass,' Fiona said casually.

Thomas walked Elsa back to her villa and kissed her on the cheek.

'*Schlaf gut*,' he said.

'You're learning German just to impress me?' She smiled at him.

'No, I think I'd have to do much more than say, "Sleep well", to impress you, Elsa,' he said ruefully.

'Like what?' she asked.

'I'd have to be restless and urgent. I could try but it might take a long time.'

'You're better the way you are, believe me, Thomas. See you midday tomorrow at the harbour.'

Fiona was in Elsa's villa already packing her suitcase.

'Before you say anything, I want to apologise, I was completely out of order with you, trying to borrow money and everything,' Fiona said.

'It doesn't matter a bit, anyway I was very short and harsh with you, I am the one to be sorry.'

'It doesn't matter now. I'm over Shane. I'm going back to Dublin. I suddenly looked at him and saw what the future would be like with him, and that it wasn't worth it. I suppose you'll say or think anyway that it can't have been real love if it vanished so quickly.'

'No, it was real love all right,' Elsa consoled her. 'But as you say it has ended, and that will make life easier for you.'

'I didn't give him up to have an easy life,' Fiona explained. 'I just suddenly saw him in a different light, like you all saw him in, I suppose. And then it was quite easy to walk away. I'm sorry of course that he wasn't the person I thought he was. But it's not like your situation, Elsa. In your case Dieter writes begging you to come back to him, promising to change for you. That's real love.'

Elsa ignored this. 'What was it that finally made you choose to walk away from Shane?' she asked quietly.

'I think there was a kind of indifference in his tone. He didn't care.'

'I know what you mean.' Elsa nodded slowly. 'I'm going out on the balcony to look at the sea, do you want to join me?'

'No, Elsa, I'm exhausted. I've been to Athens and back in one day, changed the whole direction of my life. I'm going to have to go to sleep.'

Elsa sat for a long time looking out at the moonlight on the sea, then she went back into the sitting room. She took some paper and began to write a letter which she would fax the next day.

My dear Hannah,

You have been such a good unselfish friend. Asking nothing and always ready to listen. It was, as it turned out, a very good decision for me to come here. And it was even better that I met Dieter again as now I can make a decision based on the facts, not on some fantasy world. I'm still not sure what I am going to do. But a few more days on this peaceful island will make it all clear to me. I heard two things tonight, one from an American man who told me that we can get over people. He just said it casually, like you can get over whooping cough. I don't know if he's right. Then an Irish girl said to me that I was lucky because Dieter had promised to change for me. And I have been wondering why we should want to change people. Either love them as they are or move on.

It's late at night and I am writing this by moonlight. I've been thinking in a way I never did before about my life with Dieter. And then I thought of you, Hannah, and your happy marriage to Johann. On the day you married five years ago, you said there was nothing about him you would change. I envy you that, my dear, dear friend.

Love, Elsa

CHAPTER NINE

MIRIAM FINE HAD PREPARED David's room for him, bought a new lilac-coloured duvet cover and laid out dark purple towels.

'They look nice and manly, somehow. I hope he'll like them,' she said.

'Don't fuss over him, Miriam, he hates fuss,' David's father said.

'You tell me not to fuss? What will you do the moment he comes in the door? You'll start talking to him about responsibility. If there is anything guaranteed to fuss him, it's that!'

'No, I won't talk about responsibility. At least he's seen sense and decided to give up these mad ideas.'

'He's coming home because you're ill, Harold. He worked that out for himself, you saw the letter I sent. I never mentioned it. Not once.'

'I don't want his sympathy, I will not have his pity.' The man's eyes filled with tears.

'But you might want his love, Harold.'

Fiona's father turned the key in the lock. It had been a long tiring day in the office. He had been tempted to go and have three pints in his local pub, but realised that Maureen would have his supper ready. It wasn't worth the hassle.

As soon as he opened the door she ran to meet him.

'Sean, you just won't believe this! Fiona's coming home. This week!' Maureen Ryan was overjoyed.

'How do you know?'

'Barbara rang when you were out.'

'Could that lout not draw his dole money out there?' Sean grumbled.

'No, wait till you hear. She dropped him. She's coming home on her own!'

Sean put down his briefcase and his evening paper and sat down. 'She's really coming back?'

'Tomorrow or the day after. She phoned Barbara and asked her to tell us. She's looking for her old job back and she wants to live in a flat with Barbara.'

'Well, that's all right, isn't it?'

'I think it's all for the very best, Sean,' said Fiona's mother with tears in her eyes.

Bill dialled the number of Thomas's apartment in Greece but there was only an answering machine. He left a message.

'Dad, Andy is driving us to Arizona to see the Grand Canyon. We're going to cross the Sierra Nevada and we're going to meet Gran there. She's going with her book club. Andy says I can call you when we get there so that Gran and I can both say hello.'

Then Andy took over the phone.

'Thomas, just in case you don't get this message before we leave and you want to call Bill, this is the number of my cellphone. I'll try to show things properly to your boy; we have the atlas out now looking at the journey. But I guess there'll be a lot I miss out. Maybe he could go again with you some time when you get back.'

'That's if he *ever* comes back,' Bill said before Andy had hung up.

Because Andy had not yet hung up when Bill said this, it was there on the message when Thomas came back from walking Elsa home and listened to his answering machine.

He sat up for a long time wondering about the world. He saw the torchlight moving around in the henhouse and knew that Vonni would not come to sleep in the guest room tonight. He thought of the strange tortured life she had lived among these people in Aghia Anna. He thought of the beautiful, bright Elsa going back to that selfish German who only looked on her as a trophy. He thought of the simple decent Andy, the man who he had always demonised.

Who was only doing his best.

He thought of his Bill, who believed he might never come home. He sat there thinking until the stars faded from the sky and the early light came up over the hills.

They met for a last lunch at the restaurant with the checked tablecloths.

'I'll miss you all. I don't have very many friends back home,' David said.

'Me neither, but I'd be very surprised if you were without friends for long,' Thomas said. 'And don't forget, you'll make a whole new circle through your driving lessons!'

'It's easy here, but a bit different in England,' David said. 'I don't think I'll set up my own school.'

'Do you have a lot of friends back in Germany, Elsa?' Fiona asked.

'No, hardly any, a lot of acquaintances but only one good friend. She's called Hannah.' She spoke regretfully.

Fiona announced that she was going on the train with David to help smooth over the homecoming for him. 'Will you be here for much longer, Thomas?' she asked.

'No, I don't think so. I think I'll go back to California fairly soon,' Thomas said. His eyes had a faraway look. They didn't want to ask him any more. It was clearly a decision not fully made.

'And when are you going back to Germany, Elsa?' David asked gently.

'I'm not going back,' she said simply.

'You're staying here?' Fiona gasped.

'I'm not sure. But I'm not going back to Dieter.'

'When did you decide this?' Thomas leaned forward and looked at her very intensely.

'Last night, on my balcony, looking out at the sea. I wrote to Dieter. I posted the letter this morning on the way to meet you all. He should get it in four or five days. So now I have time to make up my mind where to go.' She smiled a slow warm smile at Thomas.

'You're not going to go down to the café to say goodbye to them, Vonni?' Andreas asked as he called into the craft shop.

'No, I annoyed them all enough while they were here. I'll let them go in peace,' she said, not looking up.

'You are a difficult woman, Vonni, prickly like a thorn bush. Both David and Fiona said last night how grateful they are to you.' Andreas shook his head, mystified.

'Yes, they did; they were very polite. And by the way, the urge to drink seems to have passed over like a summer cloud. No, it's the other two, Thomas and Elsa, who I really upset. But you and I have heard plenty of advice, Andreas, and did we ever take it? The answer is no.'

'And what would you have changed if you could have your life all over again?' he asked. This was unfamiliar territory for Andreas. Normally he left things as they were, without question or analysis.

'I should have fought Stavros for the petrol station. The people here are fair, they would have known I had bought it for him. I could have raised my son. But, no, I thought the solution was somewhere at the bottom of a *raki* bottle. So it didn't happen.' She looked around her despondently.

'You haven't asked me what I would have changed,' he said.

'I suppose you'd have managed to keep Adoni here. Am I right?'

'Yes, of course I should have done that.' His eyes were sad. 'And I also should have asked you to marry me twenty-five years ago.'

She looked at him, astounded. 'Andreas! You don't mean that. We never even remotely loved each other.'

'I didn't love my wife either, not in any real sense, that is. Not like people read about and sing about. We got on all right and we were company for each other. You and I could have been fine companions.'

'We *are* fine companions, Andreas,' she said. 'It would never have worked out. Believe me. You did the right thing there. You see, I loved Stavros exactly the way you read about, sing about and dream about. I could never have settled for any other kind of love.'

She said it in a matter-of-fact way that brought normality back to their conversation.

'So it was for the best,' Andreas said.

'Definitely. And listen to me, Andreas. Adoni will come back to see you. I know it.'

He shook his big head. 'No, it's only a wish, a fairy tale.'

But Vonni's faith was unshaken. 'He needs time, Andreas. Chicago is a long way away. He'll need to get his head round it. But he'll be here.'

'Thank you, Vonni. You are indeed a good companion,' Andreas said, and blew his nose very loudly.

113

They agreed to meet at the ferry half an hour before departure and then all headed off from the café in their different directions.

Fiona and David went to say their goodbyes, but when they arrived at the craft shop Vonni was not at home.

'She'll come to wave us off,' David said.

'She's very sad these days, she's lost her sparkle somehow,' Fiona said.

'Maybe she's envious with you going back to Ireland . . . something she was never able to do,' David speculated.

'Yes, but she says herself it turned out all right, her love affair, for quite a time, and she did have a son to show for it.'

'Wouldn't it be wonderful if he came back? If he met Adoni somewhere out in Chicago and they decided to go back and swing again on the old tree up at the taverna,' David said.

Fiona pealed with laughter. 'Ah, David, and they say the Irish are the sentimental ones believing in fairy tales.'

Vonni wasn't in her henhouse, nor in her craft shop nor at the police station, so Elsa decided she would go out on the road to the old man who didn't believe in modern medicine. She might find her there.

The sun was high in the sky and she wore her white cotton sun-hat against the heat. The road was dusty. Children came from the tumbledown buildings and waved at her. Elsa wished she had brought some candy, *karameles*, they called it.

She remembered the old man's house and gathered together some sentences in halting Greek to say she was looking for his friend Vonni. But they weren't necessary. Vonni was there, sitting by the old man's bed, holding his hand. She didn't look remotely surprised to see Elsa.

'He's dying,' Vonni said in a matter-of-fact tone.

'Should I go and get the doctor?' Elsa was practical.

'No, he wouldn't let a doctor cross the door, but I'll tell him that you are a herbalist and he'll take what you bring him.'

'You can't do that, Vonni.' Elsa was shocked.

'You'd prefer he died in pain?'

'No, but we can't play games with someone's life.'

'He has about six or seven hours more of life, if that. If you want to help go to Dr Leros. Tell him the situation here, ask him for morphine.'

'But won't I need—'

'You won't need anything. Call into my shop and get a pottery bowl as well. Go quickly now.'

As Vonni had predicted, there was indeed no problem getting the drugs. On her way back up the dusty road, an old van came along. Elsa stopped it and the driver took her back to the old man's house.

'That was very speedy,' Vonni said approvingly, and then she ground up some of the morphine tablets, mixing them with honey in her pottery bowl, and spooned the mixture into the old man's mouth.

The old man mumbled something.

'What did he say?'

'He actually said that the herbalist is very beautiful,' Vonni said wryly.

'I wish he hadn't said that.' Elsa sounded sad.

'Come on, these are the last things he's going to look at—your face and mine. Isn't it good he has yours to concentrate on?'

'Vonni, *please*.' She had tears in her eyes.

'If you want to help, keep smiling at him, Elsa. Think of him as if he were your father, put love and warmth in your eyes.'

Elsa felt that this wasn't the time to remind Vonni that she hardly remembered the father who had abandoned her. Instead she looked at this poor old Greek man and thought of him and his life that was ending with an Irishwoman and a German woman at his deathbed, giving him a very large dose of morphine.

Fiona and David waved until the ferry had turned along the coast and they were out of sight of their friends on the quay.

'I feel desperately lonely,' Fiona said.

'Me too. I could have lived there happily for ever,' David said.

'Could we? Or are we just fooling ourselves, do you think?' Fiona wondered.

'It's different for you, Fiona. You love your job, you have friends, your family aren't going to suffocate you. My father is dying. I shall have to look at him every day and tell him I'll be proud to work in his company.'

'Maybe it won't be as bad as you think.' Fiona was hopeful.

'Yes, it will. You're very good to come and help me break the ice.'

'Will they think I'm your girlfriend, a frightening Catholic coming to destroy your tradition?'

'They already do,' he said gloomily.

'Well, it'll cheer them up enormously when I hare off to Ireland next day,' Fiona said cheerfully. 'They'll be so relieved they'll gather you to their bosoms.'

'We were never slow on the bosom gathering—that's part of the problem,' David said.

And for some reason they both found this incredibly funny.

Elsa and Thomas watched until the ferry was out of sight. Then they walked slowly back up to the town.

'Where were you this afternoon?' he asked. 'I was looking for you, I thought we could take off together in the little boat again.'

'Tomorrow would be lovely,' she said. 'That's if you're free.'

'I'm free.'

'Let's make the most of what time we have left,' Elsa said. 'By renting a boat tomorrow, having a picnic; another day taking the bus to Kalatriada. I'd love to see that place again when I'm not so stressed.'

'That's settled then,' he said. And they both smiled conspiratorially.

To change the subject, he asked, 'You didn't tell me what you were doing all afternoon.'

'I was in a small cluttered house with Vonni, watching an old man die. An old man with no family, no relations, only Vonni and me. I never saw anyone die before.'

'Oh, poor Elsa.' He leaned towards her and stroked her hair.

'Not poor Elsa. I am young, I have my life ahead; he was old and lonely and frightened. Poor old Nikolas. Poor old man.'

'You were kind to him. You did what you could.'

Elsa pulled away from him. 'Oh, Thomas, if you could have seen Vonni. She was wonderful. She fed him honey on a spoon and made me hold his hand. She was like a sort of angel.'

They walked together back to her place.

'Tomorrow we'll take out a little boat again and go to sea,' he said and, as she turned to leave, she gave him a big hug.

'**A**ndy, is this an OK time to call?'

'Sure, Thomas, for me it's fine, but I'm afraid Bill and his mother have gone exploring.'

'Exploring?'

'I mean shopping really, they call it exploring. Could you call in thirty minutes, or make it forty-five? You know what shopping can turn into, I don't want you to waste your nickel just talking to me.'

'I'm happy to talk to you, Andy. I want to ask you something.'

'Sure, Thomas, ask what you want.' He could hear the slightly wary note in Andy's voice.

'I was wondering, if I came back, like a bit sooner than anyone thought, do you think that would be a good thing?'

'Came back? Sorry, Thomas, I'm not entirely with you. You mean came back here to town?'

'Yes, that's what I meant.' Thomas felt cold. The guy was going to say that it would be a bad idea. He knew it.

'But you leased your apartment for a year, didn't you?'

'Yeah, but I thought I'd get a place, a bigger place, with a yard for Bill to play in.'

'You're going to try to take Bill back?' Andy's voice was choked.

'Not back to live, of course not, just a place he could visit.' Thomas tried not to sound impatient.

'Oh, I see.'

God, Andy was slow. It took for ever for an idea to sink in and another age for him to answer.

'So what do you think? Do you think it would be something Bill would like . . . to have me down the street from him? You're the guy on the spot, Andy. Tell me. I just want to do what's best.'

Across thousands of miles, Thomas could almost hear the slow smile crossing Andy's handsome, empty features.

'Thomas, that boy would love it, it would be like Santa Claus and all his birthdays coming together!'

There was no doubting the utter sincerity of the man. Thomas could hardly stumble out the words. 'I won't tell him just yet, if that's OK with you. I'd like to set it up and give him a definite date before I begin talking to him about it. Does that make sense to you, Andy?'

'Sure it does, I'll say nothing until we hear from you.'

'Thanks for understanding,' Thomas mumbled.

'Understanding? That a man should want to be near his own flesh and blood? What's to understand?'

Thomas hung up. Everyone believed that Bill was his flesh and blood. Everyone except Shirley. And indeed for all he knew she might believe it too. After all, he had never told her about the doctor's report. It had been too late to tell her. She might well not know.

Vonni settled herself down in the shed that Thomas called her henhouse. She had seen him talking on the telephone. And earlier she had seen him holding Elsa's hand. They had so much ahead of them, those two. She sighed with envy. It would be wonderful to have years and years ahead. Time to make decisions, to go places, to learn new things. To fall in love again. She wondered what they would do. She wondered about Fiona and David taking a late plane tonight to London from Athens. Would their homecomings be stormy, awkward or emotional? She hoped they would let her know.

She tried to imagine her own son, Stavros, who would never come back and who, as a boy, had once sent a message to say that she had stolen his childhood and he never wanted to see her again. In all her confessions and recitals of her story she had never told any of them that. It was too hurtful to say, even to think about. And as she had done every night for over thirty years she said a prayer for her son. Just in case there might be a God out there and the prayer might do some good.

CHAPTER TEN

ELSA HAD THE PICNIC ready when Thomas came by to pick her up next morning. It was in a basket with a cloth tucked in to cover the food.

'I was wondering . . .' Thomas began.

'What were you wondering, dear Thomas?'

'Don't mock me, I'm a frail poor creature!' he begged.

'I wasn't mocking you, I swear.'

'I was wondering if we might row up the coast to Kalatriada . . . and stay there. For the night. That's what I was wondering.'

'I think you should wonder no more, it's a great idea.' She began to go back into the villa.

'Where are you going?' he asked anxiously.

'To get a toothbrush, an extra pair of panties, a clean blouse. OK?' she asked.

'Very OK.' He had been expecting some kind of resistance. She was out in thirty seconds.

'Will the man with the little boats let us take it away for so long?' she asked.

'I've been down there to check . . . well, in case you said yes . . . and he said it would be fine.' Thomas looked slightly embarrassed.

'Go on, Thomas, what did he really say?' She laughed affectionately.

'He kept talking about you as . . . my *sizighos* . . . it's a partner or a spouse or something, I'm afraid.'

'Well, all right, *sizighos*, let's hit the high seas!' Elsa said cheerfully.

They took a little boat and rowed out of the harbour. The sea was calm and they went up the coast identifying places they knew as they passed. Halfway to Kalatriada they found a big wooden platform about a hundred yards from shore. The kind of place that people might swim out to.

Thomas tied their little boat to one of the posts. It was ideal for their picnic and Elsa climbed out of the boat and laid the cloth out between them. She spread the taramasalata and hummus on the pitta bread, arranged the figs and watermelon on a plate. Then she poured a glass of wine from a bottle and held it out to him.

'You know, you really are quite dazzlingly beautiful,' he said.

'Thank you, but it's not important,' she said in a matter-of-fact voice. She wasn't putting him down. She was just stating a fact.

'All right, it's not *that* important, but it's true,' he said and spoke of it no more.

Kalatriada didn't have a real harbour, so they tied up to a jetty and walked up the steep road to the little village.

Irini remembered them from the last visit. She took their hands in hers and greeted them warmly. She seemed to think it in no way unusual that this happy, handsome couple asked for two rooms.

'We have only one room free, but it has two beds—one for each person,' she said.

'I think we could survive that, don't you, Elsa?'

'Certainly,' she agreed.

I don't think it's a romance,' David's mother said.

'He's never brought a girl home before, Miriam,' Harold Fine said.

'I know but I still don't think so. She's only staying one night, Harold.'

'That's what they say now,' David's father said darkly.

And what in the name of God is she stopping off in Manchester for?' Sean Ryan asked Barbara.

'There wasn't much time to explain but apparently it's someone she met whose father is dying and so Fiona is going to spend a night with the family to ease the situation,' Barbara said.

'Another lame duck,' Fiona's father grumbled.

'Just Fiona being kind,' Barbara said.

'Look where being kind got her before,' he muttered.

'But that's all over now, Mr Ryan.' Barbara sometimes felt that life was all about being relentlessly cheerful both on and off the wards. 'Her plane lands at four, she'll be here before six.'

'I wonder, Barbara, if you were free could you ever . . .' Fiona's mother began.

'Like, be here when she arrives . . .' Fiona's father finished for her.

'To ease the situation?' Barbara asked.

'To stop me saying the wrong thing,' Sean Ryan said bluntly.

'Sure, I'll ask them to let me change my shift,' Barbara said.

It was their second night in Kalatriada and, unlike the time that they had been here with David and Fiona, it was a clear starry night.

Irini set a little table for Thomas and Elsa out in the open air where they could see the square and the people walking up and down. She had put two little sprays of bougainvillaea in a white china vase as a decoration on their table.

As they came to the end of their meal, Thomas took Elsa's hand and stroked it.

'I feel very happy here. Calm, as if the storms have died down.'

'I feel the same,' Elsa said. 'Maybe because we think we can deal with them now,' Elsa suggested.

'How do you mean?'

'Well, you are going back to Bill—the only question is when? And I'm not going back to Germany, so the only question is where?'

'We'll waste no time on regrets, will we?' Thomas said.

'No, regrets are useless. Destructive even.'

'Would you like coffee?' he asked.

'Maybe . . . I'm a little nervous actually, Thomas,' she admitted.

'So am I, but I don't think coffee ever calmed anyone. Shall we go, do you think?' She held his hand as they walked up the wooden stairs.

Irini smiled at them and seemed to understand that this was an important night.

In the bedroom, Thomas went towards Elsa, held her to him and kissed her neck gently. She gave a little shiver.

He drew away.

'Was that gross or something?' he asked, irresolute.

'No, it was exciting and lovely. Come here,' she said.

And first she stroked his face and then she kissed him, holding him close. Her hands went up and down his back and gently he opened her blouse.

'Elsa, I don't know . . . I hope . . .' he began.

'I don't know either, and also I hope,' she murmured. 'Please love me, Thomas. Love me in this beautiful island and let's not think about anything beyond tonight . . .'

David sat and talked to his father along the lines that he and Fiona had rehearsed. Nothing about his illness but a lot about the office and the upcoming award.

'I didn't think you'd care about that kind of thing,' Harold Fine said.

'But they are honouring you, Father. Why should I not care and be very proud?'

His father nodded and smiled. 'Well, I'll tell you frankly, son, it wouldn't have been the same if you weren't here to take part in it.'

In the next room, Fiona talked to David's mother.

'Mrs Fine, you are very kind to put me up for the night. I so appreciate it.'

'Well, of course, any friend of David's is most welcome.'

'He told me all about your lovely home but he didn't do it justice, it's gorgeous.'

Miriam Fine was pleased and confused in equal measure.

'And you live in Dublin, David tells me?'

'Yes, I've been away for many weeks now. I'm so looking forward to seeing them all again.' Fiona's smile never faltered.

'And it was a nice place, this island you were all visiting?'

'Oh, it was lovely, Mrs Fine. They were very kind people.'

'And what exactly were you doing there?'

'Having a career break,' Fiona said blithely.

'And you're a nurse in Dublin?' Miriam Fine was beginning to breathe more easily. This was not a girl with designs on her only son.

'I spent six months on an oncology ward before I went away. They can do so much to help people nowadays, Mrs Fine, you'd be amazed.'

And to her amazement Miriam Fine found herself sitting down and talking to this girl with an Irish accent who was extraordinarily helpful on many different levels. She could not have asked for a better visitor.

At the desk of the Anna Beach Hotel they held several faxes for Elsa. They were increasingly urgent, asking her to pick up her email.

The desk clerk spotted Vonni in the foyer craft shop.

'I wonder could you advise me about these messages? The German woman hasn't come in for a while . . .'

Vonni looked at them with interest. 'I can't read German—what do they say?'

'Some man in Germany saying she can't play games like this, can't leave him. That sort of thing.'

'I see.' Vonni was pleased.

'Do you think we should fax him back saying she isn't around?' the clerk asked, anxious that the hotel should not be blamed for inefficiency.

'No, I'd leave it. If he calls, of course, you could say that you heard she has gone away for a few days.'

Dublin

My dear Vonni,

I swore to you that I'd write when I was home for twenty-four hours. So here goes.

The journey was fine, a plane full of tourists, holidaymakers. David and I felt very superior because we knew the real Greece, not just beaches and discos. We took the train up to David's place. His family have this huge house full of lovely antiques and valuable ornaments. His mother is very innocent and fussy. Mr Fine looks very badly, he only has a few months to live. He was quite frightened but he was able to talk to me about palliative care. He didn't really know what they did and didn't want to ask. David and I cried at Manchester Airport—people thought we were lovers saying goodbye.

Barbara was at home when I got there, to take the edge off things. Dad was walking on eggshells trying not to say anything that would offend; Mam was like some kind of TV commercial about gravy and home cooking, you'd think I'd been in some gulag or other rather than on an island full of wonderful smells and tastes. I still yearn for the smell of the roast lamb and pine nuts up in Andreas's.

Do give him my love, I'll write when I start my job and when Barbara and I get our new flat.

I can never thank you enough, Vonni, particularly for that day in Athens. I have a hope, a dream that you find your husband and son again. You deserve to.

Love, Fiona

Manchester

Dear Vonni,

Oh, I miss you and Aghia Anna every hour of every day. How good it would be to wake up to that bright sky and spend a day without care until the stars came out. I suppose there are stars here, it's been overcast so I don't seem to see them.

My father looks awful. Fiona was wonderful with him, by the way. Talking to him as if she had known him all her life and telling him how great the drugs were to take the edges off pain. Even my mother loved her and was quite sorry to realise that we actually were just friends. We cried at the airport when she left.

Am I glad I came back? Well, put simply, I had to come back. I feel weak at the thought that I might not have done so if it hadn't been for you. The days are dreary, and I will soon be starting work in the office. I have to concentrate because my father wants to talk about it each evening. The man who was running the show naturally hates me, and is very resentful. He keeps wanting to know when I start. I so want to tell him how I feel about it all. But of course I can't. The award is next week.

I dreamed the other night that your son came back. Right into the harbour in a boat with an outboard engine. It could happen, couldn't it?

Love, David

'When should we go back to the real world?' Elsa asked after days spent wandering around the hills and coves of Kalatriada.

'Do you mean back to Aghia Anna or points further west?'

'I suppose Aghia Anna as a base camp,' Elsa said. They had been living a strange life here, totally disconnected from the real world. They had gone shopping in the markets and bought cheese for their lunches on the hills. Because they hadn't really packed for such an extended visit, they bought a couple of extra garments at stalls on market day. Thomas looked splendid in a colourful Greek shirt and Elsa had bought him a pair of elegant cream-coloured trousers in a desperate attempt to get him to abandon the three-quarter-length shorts with all the pockets.

'*Orea*,' Irini said when she saw him dressed up.

'Yes, indeed, he is beautiful,' Elsa agreed.

'I miss my other trousers,' Thomas grumbled.

'You're the only one who does—they're terrible!'

'Oh, Elsa, indulge me, let me wear them. Please,' he begged.

'Hey, this will never do. Wear what you like,' Elsa laughed at him.

'Shall we row back to Aghia Anna tomorrow?' he suggested.

'Yes, it's not as if it were goodbye, we can still be together there,' Elsa consoled herself.

'Of course we can, we're in no hurry to go anywhere,' Thomas agreed.

The following evening, Elsa sat in the Anna Beach with her big organiser diary beside her. For the first time in months she was looking up media contacts back in Germany.

The desk clerk brought her a sheaf of faxes. The last one said that Dieter would be coming out in two weeks' time to find her.

Elsa calmly ripped all the faxes in half and threw them into the wastepaper basket. Then she went to the business centre where she could log on to her email.

> I have written a long letter explaining why I am not coming back. Come out to Greece if you like, Dieter, but I will be gone. It will be a wasted journey.
> Elsa

'Andy, am I disturbing you? It's Thomas.'

'No way. We're down in Sedona today, another canyon, it's real pretty here, Thomas.'

Thomas could hear Bill calling out excitedly.

'Is that Dad? Can I talk to him?'

'Sure, Bill, he called to talk to you. Take the phone and go off to have a real good chat with him.'

'Dad? Is it really you?'

'Nobody else, Bill, just me.'

'What have you been doing, Dad?'

'I went to a little village, a tiny little place, real old-fashioned. One day I'll take you there.'

'Was it lonely for you in this little village all by yourself?' Bill asked.

'Um, no, not lonely . . .'

'So you don't miss us or anything?' the boy asked, sounding very disappointed.

'Oh, I do, Bill, I miss you every single day. And do you know what I'm going to do about it? I'm going to come back there in ten days' time and we'll have a great time.'

'Dad, that's *fantastic*! How long are you coming back for?'

'For good,' he said.

And as he heard the boy who would always be his son shouting out, 'Mom, Andy, Dad's coming home. In ten days' time and he's going to stay for ever,' Thomas felt the tears falling down his face.

'Vonni, do you know what I want to talk to you about?' Takis the lawyer asked her, as he led her into his office.

'Is it something about Stavros?' she asked hesitantly.

'No, not at all,' he said, taken aback. 'It's about Nikolas Yannilakis. As you know, Nikolas died last week. Vonni, he left you everything.'

'But he didn't have anything to leave!' Vonni said, wide-eyed.

'He had enough. He came in here six months ago and made a proper will. Left it all to you. His little house, his furniture, his savings . . .'

'Well, imagine him thinking of doing that!' Vonni was stunned. 'I suppose we should give the house to his neighbours, they have a lot of children, they could do with more space. I could sort of clear it out for them.'

'You haven't asked about his savings,' Takis said gravely.

'Sure, poor Nikolas didn't have any savings to speak of,' Vonni said.

'He left you over a hundred thousand euros,' Takis said.

Vonni looked at him in amazement and sank into a chair. 'That can't be, Takis. The man had nothing, he lived in a hovel . . . where on earth did he get that amount of money?'

'Family apparently.'

'But why didn't he use it to give himself some comfort?'

'Oh, Vonni, I don't know. But Nikolas didn't touch the money, so now it's all yours. And rightly so. You looked after him in a way no one else could have done.'

She sat very still in shocked silence.

Takis wasn't used to Vonni being like this.

'Of course, you don't have to make any decisions yet. I'll arrange all the transfers when you've had time to think about things and feel like giving me instructions.'

'I feel like doing it now, Takis, if that's all right.'

'Certainly.' He sat down opposite her and pulled a pad of paper towards him.

'I don't intend to touch any of that money. Just leave it where it is. I will, as I said, give the little house to the family next door, but I would like them to think it came directly from Nikolas. And I want to make a will . . .'

'Very sensible, Vonni,' Takis said in a low voice. He didn't think it was sensible at all, but it wasn't his business.

'And I would like to leave everything, my craft shop, my apartment, and this legacy from Nikolas, to my son Stavros.'

'I beg your pardon?'

'You heard me.'

'But you haven't seen him in years. He never came back to you despite all your pleas.'

'Are you going to make this will for me, Takis, or do I have to go and find another lawyer?'

It was two days before Thomas would leave for Athens.

'I want you to come up to Andreas's tonight for dinner,' Elsa said. 'We have a lot to talk about. I'll see that we have a quiet table,' she promised.

She wore a simple white cotton dress that night and had a flower clipped in her hair.

'You look lovely and so dressed up. I'm so pleased I wore my smart new Kalatriada trousers,' he said when he saw her.

'I got this dress today to impress you and I have a taxi to take us to the restaurant. How about that for style?'

They went up the winding road to Andreas's taverna, watching the usual starry sky unfold out over the sea.

They had indeed been given a little table for two right at the edge of the terrace with an uninterrupted view.

Little Rina served them. Andreas was indoors. Yorghis, Vonni and Dr Leros were in there with him too. They would talk to them later, when it was time for the second coffee.

'I need to talk to you about my looking for a job,' Elsa said.

'Yes.'

'Why didn't you ask?'

'Because I was afraid you would be offered a big position back in Germany. And, to be honest, I was afraid you might meet Dieter again and . . . and . . .'

'I got a job, Thomas.'

'Where?' he asked in a very shaky voice.

'I'm almost afraid to tell you.'

'Then it is Germany,' he said with a defeated face.

'No. based in Los Angeles, but roaming up and down the west coast. A weekly column for a big magazine, interviews, politics, features. Whatever I can come up with really.' She looked at him anxiously.

'Where?' he asked, dumbfounded.

'California,' she said nervously. 'Is it too much of an assumption? Too soon? I mean I just couldn't bear to lose you . . . but if you think . . .'

A slow smile began to broaden across his face.

'Oh, Elsa, darling . . .' he began.

'I don't have to live with you or anything, I don't want to crowd you out . . . you see, I know that we haven't been together long, but now I couldn't exist without you . . .'

Thomas stood up and went to her side of the table, he pulled her to her feet and kissed her. Someone took a photograph of them but they didn't care, they stood locked in each other's arms as if they were never going to be able to draw apart. Then of course the group in the kitchen came out to join them, and many toasts were drunk. To the couple.

'That man who took your picture, he was German,' said Vonni. 'He recognised you, Elsa, from the television. He asked who Thomas was. I explained you were a high-powered American academic, Thomas, and that you were Elsa's fiancé.'

'What?' Thomas and Elsa spoke at the same time.

'Well, I wouldn't have told them anything, Thomas, if you had been wearing those terrible shorts with all the pockets. But once I saw you in a decent pair of trousers, then I thought it doesn't matter for Elsa if some fan sells the picture to a German newspaper!'

They talked on easily as always, looking down on the harbour way below. The last ferry had come in an hour ago but Andreas's taverna hadn't expected any guests coming from that sailing. It was too late and too far to walk. So they were surprised when they saw someone toiling up the winding path.

It was a man of about thirty. He had a pack on his back and carried a suitcase in each hand.

'There's a dedicated diner,' said Elsa admiringly.

'Maybe he's heard of Vonni's stuffed vine leaves,' said Thomas with a smile. He loved Vonni for calling him Elsa's fiancé even though he was bewildered that everyone hated his lovely shorts with the pockets.

'It's late for anyone to come up here,' Dr Leros said, mystified.

'Unless they really intended to,' said Yorghis in an odd sort of voice, peering at the gateway.

Vonni had stood up to look at the man hesitating at the entrance.

'Andreas!' she said in a choked voice. 'Andreas, my friend, it *is*, it really is!'

Elsa and Thomas looked from one to the other without any idea what was happening. Andreas had stood up and was staggering towards the gate with his arms out.

'Adoni . . .' he cried. '*Adoni mou*! You came back. *Adoni ghie mou*. My son, you came back to see me.'

'I came back to stay, Father, if you'll have me?'

The men embraced in a grasp that looked as if it would never end.

Then Yorghis moved forward, and Vonni and Dr Leros. And they were a little group talking excitedly in Greek and embracing.

Thomas and Elsa held hands very tight.

'We'll never forget this night,' Thomas said.

Elsa said, 'Was I too forward, too pushy? Tell me, Thomas?'

Before he could answer, Andreas and his son came over.

'Adoni, this is the wonderful young woman who told me that I should write to you, when I wondered if you would care. She said everybody loves a letter . . .'

Adoni was tall and handsome. He had a shock of black hair which would one day go grey-white like his father's, but not for a long time and then possibly here in Aghia Anna. Elsa, who could summon words at will on television in front of millions of viewers, was without words. Instead she stood up and hugged Adoni tight as if they were old friends.

'Aren't you just beautiful,' Adoni said admiringly to the blonde girl in the white dress.

'Elsa and Thomas are together,' Andreas said hastily, lest there should be any misunderstanding.

Adoni shook Thomas by the hand. 'You are a very lucky man,' he said with great sincerity.

Thomas agreed. 'I am a very lucky man.' And then he stood up to address the group of friends. He looked straight at Elsa.

'I want to tell you all that Elsa will be leaving with me. We will be going to California together.'

'Yet another reason to celebrate tonight,' Andreas cried out, tears in his eyes.

Thomas and Elsa kissed again, and then they sat with his arm around her shoulders as they watched the homecoming unfold.

Andreas, Yorghis and little Rina ran to get food and wine for the prodigal son.

Vonni sat beside Adoni, her eyes sparkling, flanked on either side by her friends Andreas and Yorghis.

'One night Stavros will come into that harbour,' Andreas said.

'And it will be a night like this,' Yorghis encouraged.

'Yes, yes, I'm sure,' Vonni said, eyes bright, face hopeful.

They knew she was putting on a cheerful manner. At the same time they each stretched out a hand to hold hers. Now her smile was genuine.

'Of course he will come back one day,' she said as she gripped their hands. 'We only have to look at tonight to know that miracles happen. And there is no point in going on if you don't believe that.'

Dr Leros came out of the kitchen excitedly.

'There are two bouzouki players out there, they want to play to welcome you home, Adoni,' he begged.

'I'd love that,' he laughed.

And as the music rang out into the night and the people in the restaurant began to clap to the beat, Adoni stood up and went into the centre of the terrace.

And in front of everyone he began to dance. Adoni danced in front of forty people, some of them customers who knew nothing of what was happening, some like Thomas and Elsa who knew part of the story, and some like his father, his uncle, the doctor and Vonni who knew everything.

His arms high in the air, he swooped and bent and danced, overjoyed to be back where he belonged.

And a little light rain came down but nobody cared.

It didn't get in the way of the stars.

MAEVE BINCHY

Having resolved to turn her back on the 'hurly-burly' of a best-selling author's life a few years ago, much to the distress of her fans across the world, Maeve Binchy says she found herself quite unable to resist the impulse to write. 'In my mind I never really retired from writing, I just retired from promoting books, which is quite different. My health has not been great and I just do not have the energy for book tours. Now I just write at home at my own pace and it works very well.' That's pure understatement. *Quentins*, her first novel after temporary retirement, shot straight into the best-seller lists, and now *Nights of Rain and Stars* is destined to do the same.

Maeve Binchy's latest novel explores the lives and emotions of a group of young tourists who arrive in a small coastal village in Greece. 'I used to love going to Greece when I was a young teacher, and then later I went back there with my husband Gordon. I'm fairly familiar with the country so it wasn't a strange location for me. And people are the same all over the world. They love, hope and dream; they do foolish things, then heroic things. They are unselfish and they are thoughtless; they laugh and they weep in every land. So I don't think it matters if I make them German, American, Irish or English like the four young people in my book—they feel the same as we all do.'

By the same token, then, maybe there is something of Maeve herself in the central character of Vonni, a generous-hearted Irish woman who has spent her adult life in the Greek village of Aghia Anna. 'Yes, there is a lot of me in Vonni. But I'm not a tiny elfin person like she is, and I am not a recovering alcoholic. Also, I am not a mother, and nor did I have a tragic relationship with a husband . . . but on the other hand I did cash a cheque in the 1966 bank strike in Ireland, and I did go off to see the world! And I know I am very bossy and think I can run everyone else's lives for them. So we are alike in many ways!'

It was Maeve's love of holidays in far-flung places that triggered her career. 'I wrote long rambling letters home from trips abroad—editing out bits about falling in love with highly unsuitable foreigners—and my parents were so impressed that they got them typed and sent them to a newspaper, and that's how I became a writer.' She also met and married writer Gordon Snell, with whom she is still blissfully happy, and who 'believed I could do anything'. So she tried her hand at fiction and, as she says modestly, 'that took off fine.'

Looking back over a hugely successful career spanning more than twenty years, does she have any regrets? 'I have no regrets about anything, except that I do miss the kind, enthusiastic faces of readers at book signings. I don't know if it's an addiction, but my head is full of stories. I *love* telling them, and though I think I have said all I have to say about the people we met in *Nights of Rain and Stars*, I know enough nowadays never to say never . . .'

Anne Jenkins

Jojo

The Other Side of the Story

Marian Keyes

*When Gemma Hogan's dad packs his bags
and walks out on her mam after thirty-five
years of marriage, Gemma is astounded.
Her dad has never packed a bag in his
life—her mam always does it for him.
Then she discovers that he has a girlfriend
who is only four years older than she is!
As she comforts her distraught mam,
Gemma wonders what else
can go wrong . . .*

Gemma

To: Susan_inseattle@yahoo.com
From: Gemma343@hotmail.com
Subject: Runaway dad

Susan, you wanted news. Well, I've got news. Although you might be sorry
you asked for it. It looks like my dad has left my mam. I'm not sure how
serious it is. More as and when.
Love, Gemma xxx

WHEN I FIRST got the call, I thought he'd died. Two reasons. One: I've
been to a worrying number of funerals over the past while. Two: Mam
had called me on my mobile; the first time she'd ever done that because
she'd always persisted in the belief that you can only call a mobile *from* a
mobile, like they're CB radios or something. So when I put my phone to
my ear and heard her choke, 'He's gone,' who could blame me for thinking that Dad had kicked the bucket.

'He just packed a bag and left.'

'He packed a . . .?' It was then that I realised that Dad mightn't actually be dead.

'Come home,' she said.

'Right . . .' But I was at work. And not just in the office, but in a hotel
ballroom overseeing the finishing touches to a medical conference
(*Seeing the Back of Backache*). It was an enormous deal which had taken
weeks to pull together; I'd been there until twelve thirty the previous
night coordinating the arrival of hundreds of delegates and sorting out
their problems. Today was finally Day Zero and in less than an hour's
time, 200 chiropractors would be flooding in, each expecting:

a) a name-badge and chair
b) coffee and two biscuits (one plain, one fancy) at 11 a.m.
c) lunch, three courses (including vegetarian option) at 12.45 p.m.
d) coffee and two biscuits (both plain) at 3.30 p.m.
e) evening cocktails followed by a gala dinner, with party favours,
   dancing and snogging (optional).

'Tell me what happened,' I asked Mam, torn as I was between conflicting duties. *I can't leave here* . . .

'I'll tell you when you get home. Hurry. I'm in an awful state, God only knows what I'll do.'

That did it. I snapped my phone closed and looked at Andrea, who'd obviously figured out something was up.

'Everything OK?' she murmured.

'It's my dad.'

I could see on her face that she too thought that my father had bucked the kickit (as he himself used to say). (There I am talking like he actually is dead.)

'Oh my God . . . is it . . . is he . . .?'

'Oh, no,' I corrected, 'he's still alive.'

'Go, go, get going!' She pushed me towards the exit, clearly visualising a deathbed farewell.

'I can't. What about all of this?' I indicated the ballroom.

'Me and Moses'll do it. What can go wrong?'

The correct answer is, of course: Just About Anything. I've been Organising Events for seven years and in that time I've seen everything from over-refreshed speakers toppling off the stage to professors fighting over the fancy biscuits.

'Yes, but . . . ' I'd threatened Andrea and Moses that even if they were dead they were to show up this morning. And here I was proposing to abandon the scene—for *what* exactly?

What a day. It had barely started and so many things had already gone wrong. Beginning with my hair. I hadn't had time to get it cut in ages and, in a mad fit, I'd cut the front of it myself. I'd only meant to trim it, but once I started I couldn't stop, and I'd ended up with a ridiculously short fringe.

People sometimes said I looked a little like Liza Minnelli in *Cabaret*, but when I arrived at the hotel this morning, Moses had greeted me with, 'Live long and prosper,' and given me the Vulcan split-fingered salute. No longer Liza Minnelli in *Cabaret* but Spock from *Star Trek*, it seemed. (Quick note: Moses is not a beardy biblical pensioner in a dusty dress but a hip, sharp-suited blade of Nigerian origin.)

'Go!' Andrea gave me another little push door-wards. 'Take care and let us know if we can do anything.'

And so I found myself out in the car park. The bone-cold January fog wound itself around me, serving as a reminder that I'd left my coat behind in the hotel. I didn't bother to go back for it, it didn't seem important.

When I got into my car a man whistled—at the car, not me. It's a Toyota MR2, a sporty little (very little, lucky I'm only five foot two) number. Not my choice—F&F Dignan (my bosses) had insisted. It would look good, they said, a woman in my position. Oh, yes, and their son was selling it cheap. Ish.

The road to my parents' house was almost car-free; all the heavy traffic was going in the opposite direction, into the centre of Dublin. Moving through the fog that swirled like dry ice, the empty road had me feeling like I was dreaming.

I'd no idea what to expect when I got to my parents' house. Obviously, something was wrong, even if it was just Mam going loola. *'He just packed a bag . . .'* That in itself was as unlikely as pigs flying. Mam always packs Dad's bag for him, whether he's off to a sales conference or only on a golf outing. There and then I knew Mam was wrong. Which meant that either she *had* gone loola or Dad really *was* dead. A surge of panic had me pressing my foot even harder on the accelerator.

I parked, very badly, outside the house. (Modest sixties semi-d.) Dad's car was gone. Dead men don't drive cars.

But my rush of relief circled back and become dread once more. Dad never drove to work, he always got the bus; the missing car gave me a very bad feeling.

Mam had opened the front door before I was even out of the car. She was in a peach candlewick dressing gown and wore an orange curler in her fringe.

'He's gone!'

I hurried in and made for the kitchen. I felt the need to sit down. 'Did something happen? Did you have a fight?'

'No, nothing. He ate his breakfast as normal. Porridge. That I made. See.' She pointed to a bowl which displayed the remnants of porridge.

'Then he said he wanted to talk to me. I thought he was going to tell me I could have my conservatory. But he said that things weren't working out and that he was leaving.'

'"That things weren't working out"? But you've been married thirty-five years! Maybe he's having a midlife crisis.'

'The man is nearly sixty, he's too *old* for a midlife crisis.'

She was right. Dad had had his chance for a midlife crisis fifteen years ago, when no one would have minded, but instead he'd just carried on losing his hair and being vague and kindly.

'Then he got a suitcase and put stuff into it.'

'I don't believe you. Like, what did he pack? How did he know how to?'

Mam was starting to look a little uncertain, so to prove it to me—and probably to herself—we went upstairs and she pointed out the gaps in his wardrobe. He'd taken his top coat, his anorak and his good suit. And left behind a staggering quantity of knitted jumpers and trousers that could only ever be described as 'slacks'. Fawn of colour and nasty of shape, cut and fabric. I'd have left them behind too.

'I thought he'd been a bit distracted for the last while,' Mam said. 'I said it to you.'

And between us we'd wondered if maybe he had the beginnings of Alzheimer's. All at once, I understood. He *did* have Alzheimer's. He wasn't in his right mind. He was driving around somewhere, stone mad. We had to alert the police.

'What's his car reg?'

Mam looked surprised. 'I don't know.'

'We'll have to look it up, because I don't know it either.'

'Why do we need it?'

'We can't just tell the peelers to look for a blue Nissan Sunny bearing a fifty-nine-year-old man. It's a company car, isn't it?'

'Er, I think so.'

'I'll ring his work and someone there, his secretary or someone, should be able to help.'

Even as I rang Dad's direct line I knew he wouldn't answer, that wherever he was, it wasn't at work. Someone answered Dad's phone. Dad.

'Da-ad? Is that you?'

'Gemma?' he said warily.

'Dad, you're at work.' Indisputable.

'Yes, I—'

'What's going on?'

'Look, I was going to ring you later, but things went a bit mad here.' He was breathing hard. 'The prototype plans must've been leaked, the oppo are going to issue a press release—new product, nearly identical, industrial espio—'

'Dad!'

Before we go any further, I have to tell you that my father works in the sales department of a big confectionery company. He's worked for them my entire life and one of the perks of the job was that our house was always littered with bars of chocolate and I was more popular with the kids on the road than I might otherwise have been.

'Dad, I'm here with Mam and she's very upset. What's going on, please?'

'I was going to ring to talk to you later.'

'Well, you're talking to me now.'

'Now doesn't suit me.'

'Now had better suit you.' But alarm was building in me. He wasn't crumbling as I'd expected he would the moment I spoke sternly.

'Dad, me and Mam, we're worried about you. We think you might be a little . . .' How could I say this? 'A little mentally ill.'

'Gemma, I know I've been a bit distant for the past while, I'm well aware of it. But it's not from senility.'

This wasn't going the way I'd expected *at all*. He didn't sound bonkers. Or chastened. He sounded like he knew something that I didn't.

'What's going on?' My voice was little.

'I can't talk now, there's a problem here needs dealing with.'

Snippily I said, 'I think the state of your marriage is more important than a tiramisu-flavoured bar of—'

'*Sssshhhh!*' He hissed down the phone. 'Do you want the whole world to know about it? I'm sorry I ever told you now.'

Fright deprived me of speech. He's never cross with me.

'I will call you when I can talk.'

'Well?' Mam asked avidly when I hung up.

'He's going to call back.'

'When?'

'As soon as he can.'

Chewing my knuckles, I was uncertain of what to do next. I'd never been in a situation like this before and there was no precedent. All we could do was wait, for news that I instinctively knew wouldn't be good. And Mam kept saying, 'What do you think? Gemma, what do you think?' Like I was the adult and had the answers.

'I don't know. Let's watch telly.'

While Mam pretended to watch *Sunset Beach*, I wrote the first email to Susan. Susan had been one-third of the triumvirate, with me and Lily the other two, and after the great debacle she'd taken my side.

Only seven short days ago, on January the 1st, she'd moved to Seattle on a two-year contract as PR for some huge bank. She was lonely and looking for news.

I kept the details brief, then pressed SEND on my Communicator Plus, a huge brick of a thing with so many functions it could nearly read your thoughts. Work had given it to me, in the guise of a present. Yeah, right! In reality it just made me more of a slave than I already was.

When *Sunset Beach* ended and Dad still hadn't rung back, I said, 'This isn't right. I'm going to ring him again.'

To: Susan_inseattle@yahoo.com
From: Gemma343@hotmail.com
Subject: Runaway dad, still at large

OK, more news. You're going to need a Valium when you hear, so don't read any further until you've got it. Go on, go.

Back? Ready? Right. My father, Noel Hogan, has a girlfriend. It gets worse. She's thirty-six. *Only four years older than me.*

Where did he meet her? Where do you think? Work, of course. She's his— God, the tedious predictability of it—his PA. Colette's her name and she has two children, a girl of nine and a boy of seven. The story goes that they'd spent a lot of time working on the new tiramisu bar, and become very close.

I had to leg it home from work (leaving 200 frisky chiropractors in the hands of Andrea) and weasel the info out of Dad like it was a game of twenty questions. 'Do you owe money?' 'Are you sick?' Then finally I hit bedrock with, 'Are you having an affair?'

It's only been going on three months. What's he doing walking out on a thirty-five-year-old marriage for a three-month fling? And when was he planning on telling us? Did he really think he could just pack a suitcase one Tuesday morning and leave for good without having to explain himself?

And the yellow-bellied cowardice of the man. He fesses up to me, on the phone, then leaves me to break the news to Mam. He didn't even have the kindness to let me tell Mam immediately; he had to Share The Joy about Colette.

'She makes me feel young,' he declared, like I should be happy for him. Then he said—and before he even said it, I knew he was going to—he said, 'I feel like a teenager.' So I said, 'I'm sure we can find you one. Male or female?' And he didn't get it at all. Ridiculous old fool.

Telling Mam that her husband had left her for his secretary was literally the hardest thing I've ever had to do in my entire life. It would have been easier to tell her he'd died.

But she took it well—too well. She just said, 'I see.' Sounding very reasonable. 'You know, I think I'd like to speak to him.'

Back out to the phone and this time she rang him and got him at his desk, and they had what sounded like a calm conversation—very: 'Yes, Gemma did tell me. Uh-huh, yes . . . Colette . . . you're in love with her . . . I see . . . I see. Yes, of course you deserve to be happy . . . nice apartment . . . well that's nice. A solicitor's letter . . . I see, yes, I'll look out for it, well, bye for now.'

And when she hung up she said, 'He has a girlfriend.' Like it was news.

Back she went into the kitchen, me following. 'A girlfriend. Noel Hogan has a girlfriend. He's going to live with her in her nice apartment.'

Then she picks up a plate, says, 'My husband of thirty-five years has a girl-friend,' and casually frisbeed the plate at the wall, where it smashed into smithereens. Then another, then one more. She was picking up speed, the plates were twirling faster and the gaps between me having to duck to avoid the explosion of splinters were getting shorter.

'I'm going to drive over there and kill him,' she growled, sounding like she was possessed. And only that

a) she can't drive,

b) Dad had taken the car, and

c) she wouldn't be seen dead in my car

I'm certain she'd have done it.

When she realised she couldn't go anywhere, she began pulling at her clothes—'renting' them, perhaps? I kept trying to grab her hands and stop her, but she was much, much too strong for me. By then I was very scared. She was way out of control and I hadn't a clue what to do. Who could I ring? Ironically enough my first thought was of Dad, especially as it was his fault. In the end I rang Cody. Naturally I didn't expect any sympathy, but I hoped for some practical advice. He answered in non-work mode, i.e. as camp as a row of cerise tents with marabou feather trimming. 'A shock? Do tell.'

'My dad's left her. What should I do?'

'Oh dear. Is she . . . Is that the sound of Aynsley shepherdesses breaking?'

I took a quick look. 'Close enough. What should I do?'

'Hide the good china.' When it became clear that I wouldn't play ball, he said—kindly for him—'Call the medics, dear.'

Round here it's harder to get a doctor to make a house call than it is to eat only one cashew nut. (Absolutely impossible, as we both well know.) I rang and got Mrs Foy, Dr Bailey's foul-tempered receptionist, who always acts like a request for an appointment is a gross imposition on his time. But I managed to convince the old sourball that this was an emergency; the sounds of Mam in hysterics in the background may have helped, of course.

So half an hour later Dr Bailey shows up in his golf clothes and—get this—gives Mam a shot. I thought it was only people who lived in bodice-ripper-land who got given shots by doctors when they became a bit overwrought. Whatever they put in them must be good gear because before our eyes Mam stopped gasping and sagged feebly onto her bed.

'Any more of them?' I asked and the doc goes, 'So what happened?'

'My father has left us for his secretary.'

I expected the good doctor to act shocked, but you know what? Something like guilt skipped across his face and I'm not joking, I could have sworn the word 'Viagra' crackled in the air, like a blue lightning flash. Dad's been to see him recently, I'd put money on it.

He couldn't get away fast enough. 'Put her to bed,' he sez. 'Don't leave her on her own. If she wakes up . . .' He shook two pills onto his hand and passed them over. 'Give her the two. Emergency only.' Then he scribbled a prescription for tranquillisers and hotfooted it back to the thirteenth hole.

I helped Mam into bed—she hadn't got dressed, so there was no undressing to be done—pulled the curtains, then lay beside her, on top of the eiderdown. I was in my Nicole Farhi suit and even though I knew I was going to get feathers all over it, I didn't care. That's how freaked out I was. Anyway . . . After ages more of lying on the bed, I decided I'd better clean up the broken china and I swear to God, you'd want to have seen the kitchen; the smashed plates had gone everywhere—into the butter, floating in the milk jug.

And as for the sitting room, where it was ornaments that had bitten the dust . . . Obviously some of them were so horrible it was a good thing, but I felt really sorry for the poor little ballerina—her dancing days were over.

Then I went back and lay on the bed beside Mam, who was doing these cute little whistley snores. There were some crappy magazines on the floor on her side, and I stayed there for the rest of the day, reading them.

Now, Susan, from here on in, I'm a bit worried about my behaviour—the heating clicked off at eleven and the room got cold, but I wouldn't get under the covers. I think I felt that as long as I wasn't actually *in* bed, I was only keeping her company, but the minute I got in it meant that Dad wasn't coming home. Anyway, I dozed off and when I woke up I was so cold I couldn't feel my skin; so I put on Mam's coat—no point getting hypothermia just cos Dad had gone a bit loola. The next time I woke the bloody sun had come up and I was annoyed with myself. While it was still night-time, there was hope that Dad would come home, and if I'd stayed awake and on guard, morning would never have come. Mad, I know, but that's how I felt.

The first words Mam said were, 'He never came home.'

The second were, 'What are you doing in my good coat?'

So that's you up to date. More news as and when.

Love, Gemma xxx

PS I blame you for all of this. If you hadn't got the job in Seattle, where you know no one, you wouldn't have been lonely and in need of news from home and my life wouldn't have self-destructed just to oblige.

My mobile rang. It was Cody. Cody isn't his real name, of course. His real name is Aloysius.

'OK, Gemma,' Cody says to me, 'you're going to have to be brave.'

'Oh God,' I said, because if Cody tells you you're going to have to be brave, it means the news he has for you is really horrible.

Cody is a funny one. He's very honest, almost gratuitously so. If you say to Cody, 'Now tell me, and be honest, does my cellulite show through this dress?' he will give you an answer.

Now, obviously, no one asks that question if they expect the answer to be yes. But Cody would be the one person to tell you that he can see a hint of orange-peel skin. I don't think he does it out of cruelty; instead he plays devil's advocate to protect his nearest and dearest from ridicule.

'It's Lily,' he said. 'Lily Wright,' he repeated, when I said nothing. 'Her book. It's out. It's called *Mimi's Remedies*. The *Irish Times* are reviewing it on Saturday.'

'How do you know?'

'Met someone last night.' Cody knows all sorts of people. He works in the Department of Foreign Affairs and has a kind of Clark Kent thing going on: serious, ambitious and 'straight' in the daytime, until quitting-time rolls around, when he whips out his poppers and minces for Ireland. He straddles many camps and he's privy to all kinds of advance info.

'Is it a nice review?' My lips weren't responding properly to my need to speak.

'I believe so.'

I'd heard ages ago that she'd bagged herself a publishing deal; I'd nearly gawked at the injustice. *I* was the one who was supposed to write a book; I'd talked about doing it often enough. And so what if my writing career thus far had consisted of me reading other people's books and declaring, 'Such shite! I could do better in my sleep.'

'Thanks for telling me.'

'Has Noel come home?'

'Not yet.'

I closed my mobile and looked at Mam. Her eyes were bulging with anxiety. 'Was it your father?'

'No, Mam. Sorry, Mam.'

We were halfway through Wednesday morning and the mood was very low. I'd been all set to go to work but Mam was so lost and childlike that I rang Andrea to see how things were; she surprised me by saying that the gala dinner had been 'great fun', and I needn't come in, which was decent of her because the post-conference mop-up is a big job.

In return for her decency I told her, briefly, what had really happened with Dad. 'Midlife crisis,' she promised me. 'What car does he drive?'

'Nissan Sunny.'

'Right. Any minute now he'll trade it in for a red Mazda MX5, then soon after he'll come to his senses.'

I went back and relayed the news to Mam, but all she said was, 'Insurance is higher on a red car, I read it somewhere. I want him to come home.'

'Mam, would you mind if I popped out for ten minutes?'

'Where are you going?' Her voice thickened with tears. 'Don't leave me.'

'Just down to the shops. I promise I'll come right back. Can I get you anything? A pint of milk?'

'Why would we need milk? Doesn't the milkman bring the milk?'

A milkman. Another world.

I burned to the local shopping centre and was nearly out of the car before I'd finished parking. My heart was pounding. For the time being the drama with Dad had been relegated to second place. Lily's book was the cause of my dry mouth. I ran across the concourse and entered the bookshop on full alert, adrenalined to the max, feeling like an SAS man breaking into an enemy embassy. I flicked my eyes from left to right, expecting to be ambushed by big displays of Lily's book. Nothing, so far. With my Super-Anxious Vision, I spotted the New Titles wall and in under a second I'd scanned every cover—the Six Million Dollar Man couldn't have done it faster—but there were none by Lily.

Next, the alphabetical listing. The Ws were on the lower shelves, near the floor. Down I sprang. Waters, Werther, Wogan . . . oh Christ, there it was. There was her name. Lily Wright. Done kind of curly and wacky. Like this: *Lily Wright*. And the title was the same: *Mimi's Remedies*.

My heart was banging and my hands were so sweaty they left a smear on the cover. I turned pages but my fingers would only fumble. I was looking for the little bit that tells about the author. And then I found it.

Lily Wright lives in London with her partner Anton and their baby girl Ema.

Sweet Jesus. Seeing it in this book made it more true than it had ever been before. It was *in print*.

Everyone—her publishers, her readers, the bookshop staff—they all thought it was true. Anton was Lily's partner and they had a little girl. I felt excluded from the loop because I was the only person in the whole world who still thought Anton was rightfully mine. Everyone else *every-where* thought Lily's claim to him was legitimate. The bitter injustice. She'd stolen him, but instead of treating her like the common criminal she was, everyone was slapping her on the back congratulating her, 'Well done, that's a lovely partner you've got there.' No mention of the fact that she was thinning on top, of course. Not even a hint that she'd look a damn sight better if she got herself a Burt Reynolds-style hair-follicle transplant—and that's not just me being bitchy, she often said it herself. On the back cover there was a small black and white photo. I gazed at it, my mouth in a bitter-sweet twist. Look at her, all delicate and wide-eyed and blondey and tendrilly, like a long-limbed, slender angel. And they say the camera never lies . . .

I almost felt that I shouldn't have to pay for the book—not only had the author stolen the man I'd loved, but she'd written a book about me.

Somehow I'd paid and I was outside the shop where I stood in the cold, skimming the pages for my name. At first glance I couldn't see it.

I kept looking, then understood that she'd have had to change my name, in case I sued or something. I was probably 'Mimi'. I got as far as page seven before I came out of the trance I was in and saw that I could just as well be in Mam's in the warm, as standing here reading it.

As soon as I let myself back into the house, Mam stood framed in the kitchen doorway and choked, 'He has a girlfriend.'

While I'd been out, she'd talked to Dad and she was experiencing the news afresh.

'This has never happened to anyone I know. What did I do wrong?'

She walked into my arms, sagged against me and cried like a child, proper wa-wa-waaaas, with gulping, coughing and hiccups; my heart nearly broke. She was in such a terrible state I gave her the two emergency tablets and put her back to bed again. As soon as she was breathing peacefully I closed my fist around the prescription Dr Bailey had left—the first chance I got, I'd go to the chemist.

Then, in a rip tide of fury, I rang Dad, who sounded surprised—*surprised*, no less—to hear from me.

'You come home tonight and explain yourself,' I said angrily.

'There's nothing to explain,' he tried. 'Colette says—'

'I don't give a fuck WHAT Colette says. You get over here and have some respect.'

'Language,' he said sulkily. 'All right. I'll be round at seven.'

I hung up the phone and the ground rocked beneath my feet. My father was having an affair. *My father had left my mother.* I settled myself on the bed beside Mam and began to read the book that was all about me.

To: Susan_inseattle@yahoo.com
From: Gemma343@hotmail.com
Subject: What kind of woman steals the love of her life from her best friend, then writes a book and doesn't mention it?

More shocking news just in. Lily's book is out. Yes, Lily 'Every man for myself' Wright. Lily 'Bald Patch' Wright. It's the maddest thing I've ever read, sort of like a children's book, except there's no pictures. It's about a witch called Mimi (yes, you heard me, a witch) who comes to a village, which might be in Ireland or might be on the planet Mars, and she starts interfering in everyone's lives. Making up spells with instructions like, 'Include a handful of compassion, a sprinkling of intelligence and a generous helping of love.' Gag-making. And I'm not in it, you're not in it, even Anton doesn't seem to be in it. The only person I recognise is a spiteful girl with ringlets, who has got to be Cody.

It took me only four hours to read, but I suppose millions of people will buy it and she'll be a millionaire and a big celebrity. Life is such a bastard.

As soon as I'd finished, I had to get Mam up because Dad was coming. She refused to get dressed—she's getting way too fond of that dressing gown.

Then in comes Dad—using his own key which I thought was well out of order—and I got a real fright. Less than two days and already he looks different. Sharper, more defined around the edges, wearing new clothes. Well, I'd certainly never seen them before. A brown suede jacket, and, worst of all, trainers. Oh, mother of God. Blinding white, and so chunky.

'So what's going on?' I asked.

And without even sitting down, he announces that he's very sorry, but he's in love with Colette and she's in love with him.

'But what about us?' I said. 'What about Mam?' I thought I had him there because all my life he's been devoted to us. But do you know what he said? He said, 'I'm sorry.'

Then Mam says in this tiny voice, 'Will you stay for dinner?' I *mean*! So I go, all narky, 'He can't, there aren't enough plates.' Then I tell him, all accusing, 'She broke most of them yesterday because she was so upset.'

But not a bother on him. He just said, 'I can't stay anyway.' Then he gives the front door a furtive look and something clicked into place and I yelled, 'You've brought her with you!'

'Gemma,' he shouts, but I was already at the front door and yes, there was a woman sitting outside in the Nissan Sunny.

Colette spotted me and gave a don't-mess-with-me stare. Like a complete looper I ran over, pressed my face against the window on her side, pulled my bottom lip over my top one and bulged my eyes at her, then I called her the C word and, all credit to her, she didn't retreat an inch, she just gazed at me with roundy blue eyes.

Dad shows up behind me and goes, 'Gemma, let her alone, it's not her fault.' Then he murmurs, 'Sorry, love,' and it wasn't me he was talking to. Deflated, I went back inside, and, Susan, do you know what I was thinking? I was thinking, She has highlights, her hair is nicer than mine.

And next thing you know it's just me and Mam again, sitting in silence, our mouths agape. How had it all happened? But do you know what? In among all the other feelings I've still enough room to feel embarrassed. The thought of my father cavorting, *cavorting* with a woman my age. It's bad enough to think of your parents having sex with each other. But with different people . . .

'After all I did for him,' Mam said. 'What did I do wrong?'

You know what she's like—the perfect wife, always cooking wonderful meals, keeping the house perfect. Even her menopause was carried off with aplomb; not once was she stopped leaving a supermarket with an unpaid-for can of sardines. (Why is it always cans of sardines?)

I'll tell you something, this has made me very bitter about men. What's the point? You give them your life, cook yourself blue in the face, starve yourself into osteoporosis and for what? For them to leave you just when you're commencing your final descent into old age.

'He didn't deserve you,' I said.

But she looked annoyed and said, 'That's your *father* you're talking about.'

But what was I meant to say? Plenty more fish in the sea? Like, Mam is sixty-two; she's soft and comfy and looks like someone's granny.

If you get a chance, call me at Mam's. She's terrified of being on her own, so I'm going to stay here for a little while, just until he comes to his senses and returns home.

Love, Gemma xxx

PS No, I don't mind about you not having a Valium and yes, a rum and Coke was a good substitute. You did the right thing.

Mam let me out to collect clean clothes from my flat, a fifteen-minute drive away. 'If you're not back in forty minutes, I'll be afraid,' she promised. At times like this I hate being an only child.

I got caught on several red lights, which ate into my time, but at least the code on the electronic gate was working. My flat is in a complex that aspires to be 'modrin' and among its many facilities are a (laughably poor) gym and an electronic gate, which is meant to provide 'security'. Except that, on a regular basis, the code on the gate doesn't work.

I flicked through my post—six or seven leaflets advertising power yoga, a flier for colonic irrigation—and checked my answering machine: nothing urgent. Then I flung toiletries, underwear and my mobile charger into a bag and tried to track down clean clothes for work. I found one ironed shirt hanging on the wardrobe door, but I needed two. A rummage through the hangers produced another: it was the one with yellow stains under the arms that washing couldn't shift. Well, it would have to do; I just wouldn't take my jacket off. Finally, I packed my pinstripe suit and four-inch heels. (I *never* wear flats. My shoes are so high that sometimes when I step out of them, people look around in confusion and ask, 'Where'd she go?')

When I got out of the car and came into the house, carrying my clean suit and shirts, Mam said, 'What do you need them for?'

'Work.'

'*Work?* When?'

'Tomorrow.'

'Don't go.'

'Mam, I have to go. I'll lose my job if I don't.'

'Take compassionate leave.'

'They only give it when someone dies.'

'I wish he had died.'

'Mam!'

'I do. We'd get a ton of sympathy. The neighbours would bring food.'

'Quiches,' I said. (Because they do.)

'But instead of having the decency to die he's got a girlfriend and left me. And now you're talking about going to work. Take some of your holidays.'

'I've none left.'

'Sick leave, then.'

'Mam, I *can't*.' I was starting to panic.

'What could be so important?'

'Davinia Westport's wedding next Thursday.'

One of the society weddings of the year, to be precise. The most complex, costly, terrifying job I'd ever worked on and the logistics had occupied me for months.

The flowers alone involved 5,000 refrigerated tulips arriving from Holland and a flower specialist and his six assistants flying in from New York. The cake was to be a twelve-foot-high replica of the Statue of Liberty, but was to be made of ice cream so couldn't be prepared until the last minute. A marquee, big enough to hold 500 guests, was to be set up in a field in Kildare on Monday night and transformed into an Arabian Nights' Wonderland by Thursday morning. Because Davinia had elected to get married in a tent in January, I was still trying to track down enough heaters to ensure we didn't freeze. Among other things . . . Many, *many* other things.

'But if you go to work, what about me?'

'Maybe we could get one of the neighbours in to sit with you. Mrs Parsons,' I suggested, 'she's nice. Or Mrs Kelly.'

Not a great idea, I realised. Relations had been strained—polite, of course, but strained—since Mrs Parsons had asked Mrs Kelly to make the cake for Celia Parsons's twenty-first, instead of asking Mam, who the whole cul-de-sac knew made the cakes for everyone's twenty-firsts; she did them in the shape of a key. (This took place a good eight years ago. Grudge-holding is one of the hobbies around here.)

'Mrs Kelly,' I repeated. 'It wasn't her fault Mrs Parsons asked her to make the cake.'

'But she didn't have to make it, she could have said no.'

I sighed. We'd been through this a thousand times. 'Celia Parsons didn't want a key, she wanted a champagne bottle.'

'Everyone said the sponge was as dry as sand. Mrs Kelly should just stick to what she's good at—apple tarts for funerals.'

'Exactly, and really, Mam, it wasn't her fault.'

It was important to broker closer links with Mrs Kelly because I couldn't take any more time off. Francis and Frances—*yes*, the F&F of

F&F Dignan—had been pleased when I'd won the Davinia account, but if I messed it up, well . . .

'So will I ask Mrs Kelly to come in?'

Mam had relapsed into silence. Then, from somewhere far inside her, came a long, thin keen of pain. It was chilling. Give me plate-breaking over it any day of the week.

She stopped, gathered breath and began again. I shook her arm and said, 'Ma-am. Please, Mam!'

'Noel's gone. Noel's gone.' At that, the noise stopped and she was yelping uncontrollably, the way she had that morning, when I'd had to calm her down with Dr Bailey's emergency tablets. But we were out of pills; I should have gone to the chemist when I'd had a chance. Perhaps there was a late-night one somewhere?

'Mam, I'm just going to get someone to stay with you while I go out and get the tablets.'

She paid me no attention and I pelted up the road to Mrs Kelly and when she saw the state of me at the door, it was clear she thought it was time to start making pastry and peeling cooking apples.

I explained my plight and she knew of a chemist. 'They close at ten.' It was now ten to ten. Time to break the law.

I drove like the clappers and got to the chemist at a minute past. I pounded on the glass door and a man calmly walked over and opened it for me.

'Thank you. Oh, thank God.' I fell in.

'It's nice to be wanted,' he said.

I thrust the crumpled prescription at him. 'Please tell me you have them. It's an emergency.'

He smoothed it out and said, 'Don't worry, we have them. Take a seat.'

He disappeared behind the white partition bit to where they keep the drugs and I sank onto the chair, trying to catch my breath.

He reappeared with the pills and started reeling off instructions—'Take the antidepressants once a day, if you miss a day, don't double up the dose next day, just carry on as normal. Only take the tranquillisers as an emergency, they're highly addictive.' Evidently, he thought these pills were for me and I wasn't sure quite how to go about telling him they were for my mother.

'Um, thanks.'

'Take care,' he called after me.

Normally, I never read book reviews so it took me a while to find them in Saturday's paper. As I skimmed critiques of biographies and a book about the Boer War, I began to suspect that Cody might have been

MARIAN KEYES

wrong for once. But then, my heart gave one big bang that hurt my chest. Bloody Cody was right. There *was* a review.

CHARMING DEBUT
Mimi's Remedies by Lily Wright. Dalkin Emery. £6.99

This debut from Lily Wright is less of a novel and more of an extended fable—and none the worse for that. A white witch, the eponymous Mimi, mysteriously arrives in a small village and sets about working her own particular brand of sorcery. Rocky marriages are cemented and sundered lovers are reunited. Shot through with magic, *Mimi's Remedies* manages to be a charming comedy of manners and a wry social commentary. As comforting as hot buttered toast on a cold evening, and just as addictive.

Shaking, I put the paper down. I think they liked it. Oh God, I was jealous. I was so jealous, it was hot and green in my veins.

I threw the paper from me with a sharp rustle. Why is life such a bastard? Why do some people get every fucking thing? Lily Wright has a gorgeous man—mine—a lovely little girl—half mine—and now a glorious career. It wasn't fair.

My mobile rang and I grabbed it. Cody. 'Have you seen it?'

'I have. You?'

'Yes.' Pause. 'Fair play to her.'

Cody walks a very narrow line between Lily and me. He refused to take sides when the great falling-out occurred and he won't bitch with me about her, even though under normal circumstances he could bitch for Ireland. (If only it was an Olympic sport.) One time he even had the cheek to suggest that Lily stealing Anton from me might have caused her as much pain as it did me. I mean!

It was five days since Dad had gone—*five days*—and he still hadn't returned. I'd been certain he would have by now. It was what had kept me going, thinking that the situation was very temporary; that he'd had a rush of blood to the head, coupled with the stress of the tiramisu situation, but that he'd come to his senses in no time.

I didn't go to work on Thursday and Friday. I couldn't—I was too worried about Mam. But I worked from Mam's, chasing up Davinia's arrangements. I even managed to zip off a couple of emails to Seattle where I vented big time and agreed with Susan that yes, Dad's suede jacket could have been worse, it could have had fringes.

I *had* to go to work on Monday morning. I really, *really* had to. Davinia had requested a face-to-facer, plus I needed to go to Kildare to check that the marquee was being erected in the correct field. I know

148

this seems like a total no-brainer, but it had actually happened to Wayne Diffney, from the boy-band Laddz. His wedding marquee was put up in the wrong field and there wasn't time to take it down, so an extortionate sum had to be paid to the farmer who owned the land. It wasn't our agency, thank God, but nevertheless it shook the foundations of Irish Event Organising.

So, on Sunday night, feeling guilty and defensive, I pressed MUTE on the telly and said, 'Now, Mam, I absolutely *must* go to work tomorrow.'

She didn't answer, just sat staring at the silent images, like she hadn't heard me.

It had been a terrible day—Mam hadn't gone to Mass, and it's impossible to convey how serious this is to someone unfamiliar with the Irish Catholic Mammy. The ICM won't miss Sunday Mass even if she's got rabies and is foaming at the mouth—she'll simply bring a box of tissues and brazen it out. If her leg falls off, she'll hop.

At ten o'clock on Sunday morning, I interrupted Mam, who was sitting passively in front of the telly watching a weekly roundup of the stock market. 'Mam, shouldn't you be getting ready for Mass?'

'I'm not going. They'll all be looking at me.'

I employed the line that she'd fed me throughout my life every time I'd been self-conscious. 'Don't be silly,' I said. 'They're far more interested in themselves. Who'd be bothered looking at you?'

'All of them,' she said woefully and, actually, she was right.

Under regular conditions, eleven o'clock Mass counted as a 'promenade'. If someone in the cul-de-sac got a new winter coat, the first time it was unveiled to the public was at eleven o'clock Mass.

But now that Mam was a deserted wife, she'd knock any new winter coats off today's agenda—and there was bound to be one or two, it was January, it was Sales time.

So Mam didn't go to Mass, she spent yet another day in her dressing gown and now she was refusing to hear me.

'Mam, please look at me. I've really *got* to go to work tomorrow.'

I turned the telly off altogether and she turned to me, wounded, 'I was watching that.'

'You weren't.'

'Take tomorrow off.'

'Mam, I have to go to work in the morning, because over the next four days every second counts.'

'Can't Andrea do it?'

'No, it's my responsibility.'

'So what time will you be home at?'

Panic rose in me. Normally I'd live on site for a job like this, so that

149

every moment that wasn't spent working was devoted to catching up on precious sleep. But it looked like I'd be doing the hour-and-twenty-minute drive from Dublin to Kildare and back, every day.

On Monday morning, when the clock went off at 6 a.m., I was crying. Not just because it was 6 a.m. on a Monday morning but because I missed my dad. Tears spilled onto my pillow. With childlike unreasonableness, I wanted Dad to never have left and for everything to be the way it had always been. I dragged myself from bed and dressed for work.

By 10 a.m. the site in Kildare looked like a film set—lorries and people everywhere. I was wearing a microphone headset so I looked like Madonna on the *Blonde Ambition* tour, except my bra wasn't as pointy.

The marquee had arrived and seventeen of the twenty staff contracted for had shown up to erect it. I had signed for four Portaloos, a team of carpenters were hard at work laying a temporary walkway, and over the phone I had convinced a customs' officer to let the refrigerated lorry full of tulips into the country.

When the ovens for the catering tent were delivered—two days early, but at least they'd come—I sat in my car, turned the heater on and rang Dad at work to ask him, once again, to come home.

Gently but firmly he said no, so then I had to voice a concern that had grown over the weekend. 'Dad, how will Mam manage for money?'

'Didn't you get the letter? It'll explain everything.'

Straight away I rang Mam and she answered by gasping, 'Noel?'

My heart hit bottom. 'No, Mam, it's me. Did we get a letter from Dad? Could you go and look?'

She went off and came back. 'There's an official-looking thing addressed to me.'

'But . . . why didn't you open it?'

'Oh, I always leave those official things for your father to deal with.'

'But this is *from* Dad to you. Could you open it?'

'No. I'll wait till you come home. Oh, and Dr Bailey came, he gave me a prescription for sleeping tablets. How will I get them?'

'Pop down to the chemist,' I cajoled.

'No,' her voice shook. 'I couldn't leave the house. Will you go? The chemist stays open until ten, surely you'll be home by then?'

'I'll do what I can.' I hung up and mashed my face into my hands.

Leaving the wedding site at 8.30 p.m. was almost like taking a half-day. I drove as fast as I could without getting stopped by the peelers, got to Mam's, grabbed the prescription and gunned to the chemist. The nice man popped out from behind the drugs bit and gave me a jaunty, 'Hello.'

He took the prescription and murmured sympathetically, 'Not sleeping?' He surveyed my face, and what he saw there had him shaking his head regretfully. 'Yes, the antidepressants can often have that effect in the beginning.'

His sympathy—though entirely misplaced—was comforting. With a small smile of gratitude, I went home to Mam, where we sat down and opened the scary letter from Dad.

It was from his solicitor. Jesus, how serious was this?

Dad was proposing what he called 'an interim financial settlement'. This had an ominous ring, because it promised a more permanent financial settlement to come. The letter said he would give Mam a certain sum a month, out of which she'd have to pay all housekeeping bills including the mortgage.

'OK, we have to take stock. How much is the mortgage? The electricity bill? The gas bill?'

'I . . . I don't know. Your dad writes all the cheques. I'm sorry,' she said, so humbly I felt I couldn't go on.

'I think we've taken enough stock,' I sighed. 'Let's go to bed.'

'There's just one thing,' she said. 'I've a rash.' She extended a leg and parted her dressing gown. Sure enough, her thigh was covered in raised red bumps.

'You'll have to go to the doctor.' My mouth twitched. Hysteria.

She actually laughed too. 'I can't ring Dr Bailey and ask him to make another house call.'

And I can't go to the chemist again. The man must think I'm a total nutter.

Tuesday morning saw ructions in Kildare. The interior designer and his eight-strong team swanned in to effect the transformation of a tent smelling of damp grass to a glittering Arabian Nights' Wonderland. But the marquee wasn't fully hoisted, so both crews were trying to work around each other, and from the moment one of the marquee men marched along a length of gold satin in his muddy boots, battle lines were drawn.

The interior designer, a bouffed Muscle Mary, called the marquee man 'a cack-handed brute'.

However the marquee man thought being called 'a cack-handed brute' was the funniest thing he'd ever heard and kept saying it. 'Listen, lads, I'm a cack-handed brute. A *brute*!'

Then he called Mary 'a big fat ponce', which was nothing but the truth, but not exactly conducive to a harmonious working environment, and I had to use my considerable negotiating skills to prevent the interiors team from flouncing (what other way?) out.

I didn't get home that night until almost 1 a.m. Mam was still awake, but to my surprise she seemed a bit better. The dead, draggy look in her eyes had lessened. Then I found out why.

'I read that book,' she said, almost jauntily.

'What book?'

'That *Mimi's Remedies*. It was the nicest thing.'

'It was?' I didn't want anyone to like it.

'It cheered me right up. And you never said it was by Lily! It was only when I saw her photo at the back that I realised. What a great achievement, to write a book.' Then she said wistfully, 'I was very fond of Lily, she was always so *kind*.'

'Excuse me, he-llo! She stole my boyfriend, remember?'

'Er, yes. So has she written any more books?'

'One,' I said shortly. 'But it hasn't been published.'

'Why not?' Mam sounded indignant.

'Because . . . nobody liked it.' I was being cruel. Some literary agents had *nearly* liked it. If only she'd take out this character or change the setting or write it in the present tense . . .

For years Lily had rewritten the book—what was it called? Something to do with water? Oh, *Crystal Clear*, that was it. But even when she'd made the requested changes, still no one wanted it.

'I'm going to lend this *Mimi's Remedies* to Mrs Kelly,' Mam said. 'She likes a good read.'

Mam liking Lily's book retriggered the anxiety that my horrible week had managed to obscure; the first chance I got the following day, I rang Cody. 'How's Lily's book doing?'

'Not setting the world on fire.'

'Thank God.'

Then, almost hesitantly, he asked, 'Have you read it?'

'Course! The maddest yoke ever. Have you read it?'

'Yes.'

'And?'

He paused. 'I thought . . . actually, it was beautiful.'

I thought he was being sarcastic, I mean this was *Cody*.

Then I realised he wasn't and the fear nearly killed me. If Cody, the biggest cynic on the planet, thought it was beautiful, then it must be.

To: Susan_inseattle@yahoo.com
From: Gemma343@hotmail.com
Subject: The demon drink

Saturday night was Cody's birthday—need I say any more? He had a knees-up in Marmoset, Dublin's newest restaurant, with twenty of his closest friends.

It's only because I'm more afraid of him than I am of Mam that I was there at all. Anyway, the long and short of it is that the relief of Davinia's wedding going off without too many hitches, coupled with the strain of my home life, meant I went mental.

Clearly I was worried from the off because I constructed a foolproof plan. I wouldn't drink wine because with the constant refills, you can't control the quantities. Instead I'd drink vodka and tonics and—here's the foolproof bit— after each one I'd move the slice of lemon to the fresh glass. When the glass was so full of lemon slices that no more drink could fit in, then it was time to go home. Ingenious, no?

No.

I was one of the last to arrive, not just because Mam kept constructing excuses to stop me from leaving, but because Marmoset is one of those establishments that doesn't advertise its existence—no name, no street number, no windows. Anyway, in I go and there's Princess Cody at the head of the table, receiving his presents. I was in trouble, because that afternoon was the first time Mam had let me go shopping since this business with Dad began, and I couldn't decide where to start or what to buy. So, instead of buying Cody a birthday present, I ended up buying—of all things—a coal scuttle. Don't ask me why, but something about it appealed to me; then—and you're to keep this to yourself—I went to the toy department and bought myself a fairy wand. It's a glittery silver star, backed with lilac fluff. I'm puzzled by how much I wanted it and I've decided it's because with Dad doing a runner I've been robbed of my childhood and this was an attempt to recapture it.

Anyway, what I'm trying to say is that there was only time left to buy Cody a bottle of champagne and stick a rosette on it, and when I gave it to him, he did his haughty, displeased face and sez acidly, 'I can tell you put a lot of thought into that.'

'I don't have to stay here to be insulted,' I said. 'There's loads of other places I can go.'

So he—roll out the flags!—apologised and made Trevor get up so I could sit at his right hand.

It was the usual Cody crowd: screechy, good-looking and great fun. I launched myself with gusto into the V&Ts and all in all I was having a great old time. Then I mentioned to Cody how much I was enjoying eating my dinner off a dinner plate because we've been making do with side plates at Mam's since the day she smashed them all, and I haven't found time to buy new ones.

So Cody jing-jinged his knife on his glass and called for a hush and made me tell the story about Dad leaving. As I was on my sixth vodka, it didn't seem terrible any more, but strangely funny. I had the attention of the entire table as they creased and choked in convulsions at my description of Dad's new look, Colette's highlights, the visits to the chemist.

As I regaled the party, I suddenly saw the funny side. It was HILARIOUS. After that things get a bit hazy. I remember that the bill was horrific and everyone blamed me because the V&Ts were a tenner a pop, and I'd had at least eleven of them.

I paused. If I didn't condense what happened next this email would be as long as *War and Peace*. Because the morning after Cody's party I woke up in my own bed in my own flat, fully dressed but my bra was open under my dress and my knickers were pulled down to the top of my thighs.

As I was wriggling around trying to fix myself I—as you do—glanced over the side of the bed and there, thrown on the floor like a police outline of a corpse, was a man. Dark hair, wearing a suit. I had *no* idea who he was. None. He opened one eye, squinted up at me and said, 'Morning.'

'Morning,' I replied.

He opened his second eye and then I *thought* I knew him. I recognised the face, I was pretty sure of it.

'Owen,' he supplied. 'You met me last night in Hamman.'

Hamman was a hot new bar—I had no idea I'd been there.

'Why are you lying on the floor?' I asked.

'Because you pushed me out.'

'Why?'

'I have no idea.'

'You look very young.'

'Twenty-eight.'

'I'm more than that.' Looking around the room, I said, 'What's my coal scuttle doing in here?'

'You brought it in to show me. You told a lot of people about it last night, you seemed very proud of it. Quite right too,' he added. 'It's a beauty.'

He was taking the piss and I wanted him to go away and for me to go back to sleep and find I'd imagined it all.

'You're in the horrors,' he said, which was pretty observant. 'I'll make you a cup of coffee and then I'll be off.'

'OK.'

And the next thing I knew was I'd jerked awake, my mouth was lined with sheepskin, and I was wondering if I'd dreamt it all. But there was the cup of coffee beside me—stone cold.

When I got out of bed my legs nearly gave way on my first attempt to stand. In the front room the cushions had been knocked off the couch, like someone (me and Owen?) had had a wrestling match on it. Sticky red rings patterned my lovely wooden floor, courtesy of an open bottle of red wine, and there was a horrible bloodlike stain on my eighty-per-cent wool silver-grey rug. It was literally years—well, *a* year, anyway—since I'd gone this mad.

Mind you, something must have changed since the last time I brought home a man I couldn't even remember meeting, because the smart-arse youth had left me a note. I thought those sort of blokes normally scarpered at 4 a.m. The note—scribbled with my eyeliner on a colonic irrigation flier (I'd been sent *millions* of them)—said:

Coal scuttle angel, I find you strangely alluring. Let's do it again sometime. I'll call you, just as soon as my bruises have healed. OWEN

I'll call you.

With those words something made its way through my aching eye sockets, into my swollen brain and I knew that the horrible, ominous feeling weighing me down wasn't just the hangover horrors, but Mam! My eyes went to the phone—I was almost afraid to look. The answering machine light was hopping; it looked *furious*.

Oh the dread. The horrible, awful, dreadful, dready dread.

I wasn't supposed to be in *my* flat. I should have gone back to Mam's last night. I'd promised, it was the only way I had been able to persuade her to let me out at all. How could I have forgotten?

I pressed PLAY and when the flat Margaret Thatcher voice intoned, 'You–have–six–new–messages,' I wanted to die. Then the messages from Mam began. The first one was at five in the morning. 'Where are you? Why haven't you come home?' Another call at six fifteen, then at eight thirty and twenty past nine. She sounded more and more frantic and on the ten thirty call she was wheezing, 'I don't feel well. It's my heart. Where are you?'

The next message was not from Mam but from Mrs Kelly. 'Your poor mother's gone to hospital in a terrible state,' she said coldly. 'If you could find time to contact home we'd all appreciate it.'

To: Susan_inseattle@yahoo.com
From: Gemma343@hotmail.com
Subject: It took three days for the horrors to lift

It's only today that I'm back on solids.

Mam—thanks be to Christ—didn't have a heart attack, just a panic attack.

Dad still hasn't come back. All last week when I was working like a machine, I didn't have time to think about it, really. But now that my routine is back to normal, I've realised it's over two weeks since he went.

This thing has layers. I keep thinking I understand that Dad has left and has ruined everything, then I perk up and think he'll have to come home soon. But then the fact that he hasn't come back yet kicks in again.

And yes, about the wand, thank you for reminding me that I was always partial to cheesy kitsch. Although what's cheesy about my 'Kitty goes to New York' shower cap? It's beautiful, not to mention functional.

I'm back in the office all this week. It's such a relief to be working only ten-hour days.

Anawah, on we trudge. Send me a joke.

Lots of love, Gemma xxx

On the way home from work that evening—like most evenings—I popped into the chemist to get something for Mam. This time it was athlete's foot ointment—I had no idea how she caught that, considering that the most athletic thing she ever did was open a packet of biscuits. But before I even got to ask for it, the nice man behind the counter said, 'You were in good form on Saturday night.'

All the blood that had been milling around in my face began a sudden and speedy exodus.

'Where did I meet you?' I asked through bloodfree lips.

He paused, looked surprised, then said, 'In Hamman.'

'In *Hamman*?' Jesus Christ, who *else* had I met in Hamman on Saturday night?

'This comes as a . . . surprise?'

Too right it did. All of it. That I'd met the man from the chemist in Hamman and remembered nothing about it. *And* that he'd been allowed out from behind the counter. What had he been wearing? I couldn't imagine him in anything except his white coat.

'I was scuttered,' I whispered.

'It was Saturday night,' he said, but then he went just a little bit stern and said, 'Didn't your doctor tell you that you shouldn't drink while you're taking antidepressants?'

Now was the time. 'No, he didn't,' I said, 'because you see, the thing is, the prescriptions that I've been picking up from you, they're not for me, they're for my mother. I'm sorry I haven't told you before now, the time just never seemed right.'

'Was any of the stuff for you?'

I thought back over the long list of medication I had got for Mam; not just the antidepressants, the tranks, the sleeping tablets but the antihistamine stuff for her rash, the antacids for her stomach, the painkillers . . .

'The nail varnish was mine.'

'You know what?' he mused. 'I feel like a right fool.'

'Don't,' I said. 'It was my fault, I should have told you straight away, but I enjoyed someone being nice to me even though there was nothing wrong with me.'

'OK.' He still looked uncomfortable.

'Just out of curiosity,' I asked, 'what's Hamman like?'

'Ah, it's all right. The crowd was a bit too young.'

Straight away I wondered how old he was—up till now I'd never thought of him having an age. In fact I'd never really thought of him as human, just a benign presence who dispensed tablets.

'It's the white coat,' he said, reading my mind. 'Very dehumanising. I'm probably not that much older than you, Maureen, and I've just realised that that's probably not your name.'

'No, it's Gemma.'

'I've a name too,' he said. 'It's Johnny.'

To: Susan_inseattle@yahoo.com
From: Gemma343@hotmail.com
Subject: Wonders never cease

Guess what? The youth rang me. The youth I met the night of Cody's birthday. Owen. He wants us to go out. 'For what?' I asked. 'A drink,' he sez. 'It took you nearly two weeks to call,' I said. 'I was playing hard to get,' he replied.

Anyway I told him I couldn't and he said, 'I understand. You want to spend more time with your coal scuttle.'

Obviously it's not that, it's because there's no way I'll get a pass from Mam at the moment. She only lets me out to go to work and collect her prescriptions.

Anyway, let me know how you are. Any fellas yet?

Love, Gemma xxx

Speaking of prescriptions, Mam was out of sleeping tablets—she was eating them like Smarties—so I hopped into the car and as always the nice man in the white coat was standing behind the counter.

'Hi, Gemma,' he said. 'Not Maureen. Gemma. It'll seem natural after a bit of practice. Look at how they changed Jif to Cif—for a while every-one felt a bit of a thick saying it, but now it's second nature.'

'And Oil of Ulay to Oil of Olay,' I agreed. 'Are you ever not here?'

He thought about it for a moment. 'No.'

'But why? Can't you get another pharmacist to help you?'

'I have someone—my brother. But he was in a motorbike accident.'

Pause where I made a sympathetic noise even though I didn't know the brother. 'When was that?'

'October. And it'll be ages still before he's better. He wrecked his leg.'

More sympathetic noises. 'But do you have to do such long hours?'

'Everyone knows we stay open till ten. Remember that first night when you came here? What if we'd been closed?'

I shut my eyes at the thought. He had a point.

'I don't get out much either.' I didn't want him to feel he was the only one. 'Coming here counts as a social event.'

'How so?' He was very curious and who'd blame him? I'd have been bored out of my skull too, sitting in that shop, reading the back of Anadin boxes. So I told him the whole story—like the *whole* story—the phone call, Colette's highlights, Dad's jacket, Mam's 'heart attack'.

Then someone came in looking for eye drops and I left him to it.

To: Susan_inseattle@yahoo.com
From: Gemma343@hotmail.com
Subject: Hit me, baby, one more time

Guess what? The Owen youth rang again. He said he was looking at his leg and felt that something was missing, which he then realised was the huge bruise I'd given him when I pushed him out of bed that time. He wondered if there was any chance of a repeat performance and he must have got me at a vulnerable time because I said yes. I don't know how I'm going to get it past Mam, but I'll think of something. And I plan to enjoy myself . . .
Love, Gemma xxx

It was good that I was going out. The hours at home with Mam were having a detrimental effect on my grasp of reality. I constructed a vivid, imaginary world where Dad begins to come to his senses. I so badly wanted Mam and Dad to get back together. It was horrible being from a broken home, even though I was thirty-two.

I spent my sleepless early mornings imagining scenarios plucked from various romances, where Mam and Dad ended up being thrown back together. My favourite was the one where Dad dropped in to Mam's, ostensibly to collect his post. Her hair was done, her make-up was flattering, and she was wearing a sarong and bathing suit.

'Noel,' she said, with a warmth that confused him. 'How nice to see you. I was just about to have lunch. Would you like to join me?'

'Aah, depends. What are you having?'

'Toasted cheese and ham sandwiches and a bottle of dry chardonnay.'

'Colette won't let me have cheese.'

'And Helmut thinks I'm a vegetarian,' she said drily. (Helmut is Mam's thirty-five-year-old Swiss boyfriend.)

'That stymies that then.'

'Really?' A slow wicked grin spread across Mam's face. 'Let's be naughty. I won't tell if you won't.'

'Right, so.'

'As it's such a beautiful day let's take it out to the patio.'

They sat at the little table and the sun smiled down. Dad gazed at the lovely mature garden that had once been his pride and joy before he got lured away. 'I'd forgotten what a suntrap this is.'

'I haven't.' Mam extended a toned, tanned leg. 'The Kilmacud Riviera, my dear. So tell me everything. How's life with Claudette?'

'Colette.'

'Oh, I *am* sorry. Colette. Going well, is it?'

'Fine.' Said dolefully. 'How's life with Helmut?'

'Peachy. More sex than I know what to do with. It's all they think about, young people.'

'Aye. They'd have you worn out.' Suddenly the words began to pour out of Dad. 'What's wrong with just a snuggle? Why can't I go to bed and for once *just go to sleep*?'

They sat in silence. (Companionable, of course.)

'And Claudette's two little ones? How are they? Lots of energy at that stage, haven't they?'

'Aye.' Said grimly. 'I'd better go. I've to collect Geri from hip-hop.'

'Wait until that young madam hits adolescence! Then she'll really keep you on your toes!'

Suddenly the thought of returning Chez Colette plunged him into darkest despair. Out in the hall, he nearly left without his post, until Mam reminded him. 'You'd forget your own head, if it wasn't attached,' she said affectionately. 'Lovely to see you,' she said, kissing him on the cheek. 'Do give my best to Claudette. And remember,' she said with a roguish smile. 'About the cheese—it'll be our secret.'

Jojo

Monday afternoon, 2.35

MANOJ STUCK HIS HEAD round the door. 'Jojo, Keith Stein is here.'

'Who's Keith Stein?'

'Photographer from *Book News*. To accompany the piece on you.'

'Oh, right. Two minutes,' Jojo said. She swung her feet off the desk. From her hair she slid out the ballpoint that had been holding it in a makeshift up-do. The auburn waves tumbled to her shoulders.

'Why, Miss Harvey, you're beautiful,' Manoj said. 'Except your mascara's gone flaky.'

He passed her her handbag. 'Put your best face forward.'

Jojo needed no encouragement. Everyone in publishing read the questionnaire in *Book News*; it was the first thing they went to.

She snapped open her compact and reapplied her trademark vamp-red lipstick. She wished it wasn't her trademark, but the one time she'd come to work in 'Crushed sorbet', people looked at her oddly. Mark Avery told her she was looking 'a little peaky' and Richie Gant had accused her of having a hangover.

'More mascara,' Manoj suggested.

'You're so gay,' Jojo said, indulgently.

'And you're so politically incorrect. I mean it about the mascara. Two words: Richie Gant. Let's sicken him.'

Jojo found she was applying her mascara with renewed vigour.

After a speedy colour-by-numbers circuit through the rest of her face—blush, concealer, glow—Jojo pulled a brush through her hair a final time and was good to go.

'Very sexy, boss. Very noir.'

'Send him in.'

Laden with equipment, Keith came into the office, stopped and laughed out loud. 'You look like Jessica Rabbit!' he said in admiration. 'Or that redhead from the fifties movies. What's her name?' He stamped his foot a few times. 'Rita Hayworth.'

Keith unloaded his camera equipment, surveyed the tiny book-lined room, considered Jojo, then looked around again. 'Let's do something a bit different,' he suggested. 'Instead of the usual shot of the desk and you sitting behind it like Winston Churchill, let's sex it up a bit. What about lying on it, on your side, giving a big wink?'

'I'm a literary agent. Have a little respect!' And she was too tall; she'd spill over the ends.

'I've an idea,' Manoj said. 'How about we copy that famous shot of Christine Keeler? You know it?'

'Where she's sat backwards on a kitchen chair?' Keith said. 'Classic pose. Nice one.'

'She was naked.'

'You don't have to be.'

'OK.' Jojo guessed it was better than sprawling full-length on her desk.

Manoj went racing off and returned with a kitchen chair, which Jojo straddled, feeling like a dumbass.

'Fantastic.' Keith knelt before her to start snapping. 'Big smile, now.' But before he pressed the shutter, he lowered the camera from his face and got to his feet again. 'Could you take off your jacket?'

Jojo didn't want to, not at work. Her pinstripe suit held her like a safety harness and, without it, she felt way too busty. But her boobs would be hidden by the chairback so she slipped the jacket off and restraddled the chair, pulling its back to her chest.

'One other thing,' Keith said, 'could you roll up the sleeves of your shirt? And open just one more button at the neck. Just one, that's all I'm asking for. And, you know, shake your hair about, loosen up a little.'

'Think sultry,' Manoj urged.

'Think dole queue, you.'

'Let's get going,' Keith interrupted. 'Jojo, eyes to me.' SNAP! 'They were saying back in the office that you used to be a cop in New York before you got into this game. Is that right?'

SNAP!

'What is *with* you guys?' They all loved that she'd been a cop. Even Mark Avery admitted to sexy imaginings of Jojo kicking down doors, snapping on the cuffs and murmuring, 'I'm taking you in.' 'Like, don't you have any women police of your own?'

'It's not the same here, they have flat shoes and minger hair. So you really were one?'

'For a couple of years.'

SNAP!

'Ever get shot at?'

SNAP!

'Always.'

'Tilt the heat slightly. Ever shoot someone?'

SNAP!

'Yeah.'

'Big smile now. Ever kill someone?'

SNAP! SNAP! SNAP!

Later Monday afternoon

Keith left, Jojo fastened herself back into her jacket and was about to start work when Manoj buzzed her.

'Eamonn Farrell on the line.'

'What now?'

'Apparently Larson Koza got a blinding review in today's *Independent* and why didn't he? Shall I jerk him off and get rid of him?'

'You love saying that. I should never have taught it to you. No, put him through.'

With a click, Eamonn's rage streamed down the phone line and into the room. 'Jojo, I've had it with Koza.'

He let it all out as Jojo 'Uh-huh'd' sympathetically and scanned her emails. One from Mark; she'd save it until she was off the phone.

'. . . plagiarism . . . I was the first . . .' Eamonn was saying. '. . . owes everything to me . . . thinks it's all about image . . . d'you know what they called him? "A Young Turk". *I'm* the Young Fucking Turk around here.'

Poor guy, Jojo thought. She'd been here before with other authors. After their first flush of joy at being published, the craven gratitude dissipated to make room for jealousy. Suddenly they noticed they weren't the only new writers in the world—there were others! Who got good reviews and high advances! It was hard to take on board, especially for someone like Eamonn who had enjoyed a lot of early success.

'So what are you going to do about it? Let's not forget you're walking around with twenty-five thousand pounds of money in commission.'

That's where you're wrong, buddy. Jojo didn't get any of it. You had to be a partner before you pocketed a percentage of any deal.

But she kept it zipped. He was angry and insecure and she didn't take it personally. Anyway, a few more insults later, he stopped abruptly and said, 'Aw, Jojo, I'm sorry. I'm a stupid bastard, doing this to you. It's just the competition is so fierce in this business, it really gets to me.'

He'd want to try being an agent, she thought. Then he'd really know about competition. But all she said was, 'I know, I totally understand.'

'You're a gem, Jojo Harvey. The best. Can you forget all that I said?'

'It's forgotten.'

To: Jojo.harvey@LIPMAN HAIGH.co
From: Mark.avery@LIPMAN HAIGH.co
Subject: Miss

Miss (v.) 1. Feel the want of. 2. Not have. 3. Notice esp with regret the absence of ~ e.g. I miss you.
M xx

To: Mark.avery@LIPMAN HAIGH.co
From: Jojo.harvey@LIPMAN HAIGH.co
Subject: Tough

Tough (adj.) 1. Hard, severe, unpleasant ~ e.g. tough luck, you shouldn't have gone away for whole week to book fair. (Joke (n.) 1. Thing said or done to excite laughter.)
JJ xx
PS I notice esp with regret the absence of you too.

Ten minutes later

Manoj buzzed again. 'On the line we have your cousin Becky, who looks like you, only not so fabulous, if the photo on your desk is anything to go by. I think she wants to hook up with you tonight, she was muttering brokenly about Pizza Express. Do you accept or decline this call?'

'Put her through.'

'No, you have to say, "I accept".'

Jojo sighed. 'I accept.'

Monday evening, 7.10

Most people had already gone home when Jojo started to fill in the *Book News* questionnaire.

Name
Jojo Harvey.

Age
32.

Career path?
Three years in the NYPD (no, really). A few months barmaiding when I first came to London, six months as reader in Clarice Inc. before being promoted to assistant, then junior agent. Made full agent four years ago and moved to Lipman Haigh Literary Agency a year and a half later.

What's your favourite smell?
Mark Avery.

Jojo scribbled, wishing she could inhale him right then.

No, wait; she could *not* write that. Quickly she scored so many lines through it the page almost tore.

Next question.

What makes you depressed?
Richie Gant.

A pause, then more heavy pen scoring. Jesus. She'd badly wanted to be asked to do this questionnaire, but it was harder than she had expected.

Which living person do you most admire?
Mark Avery.

Which living person do you most despise?
Mark Avery's wife? No, no, no. It's got to be me—see next question.

What traits do you dislike most in others?
Women who hit on married men.

What would you change about yourself?
Apart from my boyfriend having a wife and two children?

How about her perfectionism? she wondered. Her tenacity? No, she thought: it had to be her calves. They were too hefty and leather knee-boots were a no-no for Jojo.

Do you believe in monogamy?
Yes. Yeah, I know, how can I? I'm a hypocrite. But I never meant for this thing with Mark to happen. I'm not that kind of person.

Which book do you wish you had agented?
Easy, she thought, not that she'd ever fess up, even under torture. It was *Fast Cars*, the current talk of the town. A great novel except that Richie Gant was the agent—not Jojo—and he'd secured a £1.1 million advance at auction. Jojo had had similar coups but nothing as high and she had been disgustingly envious.

Where do you see yourself in five years' time?
As a partner in Lipman Haigh Literary Agency. And hopefully a lot sooner than five years. Like, as soon as someone retires.

At Lipman Haigh there were seven partners. Then there were a further eight agents who weren't partners, and while there was no way of knowing who the board would pick to replace the next retiree, Jojo had hopes that it might be her.

What are your distinguishing qualities?
I can whistle for a taxi and swear in Italian. I do a great Donald Duck impression and I can fix bikes.

What five things could you not live without?
Cigarettes, coffee, vodkatinis, The Simpsons . . . What else? A regular heartbeat? . . . *More cigarettes.*

What's the most important lesson life has taught you?
Bad hair happens to good people.

She paused. This is total crap, she thought, sticking her pen back in her hair where it was more useful. Manoj would have to do it. It was time to meet Becky.

Monday evening, 8.45
In Pizza Express, Becky was drinking red wine and picking at garlic bread. She waved and beckoned Jojo over.

They hugged, then Becky pulled back and bared her teeth at Jojo in a silent snarl. 'Are my teeth black?'

'No.' Jojo was alarmed. 'Why, are mine?'

'No, but I'm on the red wine. Keep an eye on me.'

'OK, but I will be too, so you'd better keep an eye on me also.'

They scanned the menu and Becky said, 'If I get the Veneziana will you tell me if I get spinach caught in my teeth?'

After they ordered, Jojo said, 'So what's up?'

Becky was an administrator in private health care, responsible for the schemes of large companies, and was going through hell.

'You're not going to *believe* this—she gave me four new clients today.' 'She' was Elise, Becky's boss. 'I've more than I can handle already.'

'Becky, you've got to tell her it's too much.'

'You can't do that. It makes you look like you can't cope.'

'If she's giving you more clients, she must think you're good.'

'No way! She's overloading me so that I'll crack and leave. She's a bitch and I hate her.'

Caught up in the stress of Becky's tale, Jojo produced a box of cigarettes from her bag. 'Back on them.'

'What happened with your acupuncture?'

'Every time I twiddled the pin in my ear, I got a craving for mashed potatoes. Like, *really* bad.'

'We all need a vice,' Becky said.

'I know, but they make it so hard for smokers. If I want to smoke at work I have to stand on the street.'

Becky swigged some wine, then checked her teeth in her spoon. Upside down but not black. Good. 'I feel better,' she said. 'You can't beat a good vent. Now, your go, Jojo. Share the joy.'

'We . . . ll, OK, I haven't sold anything in a while. Nothing good has come my way. Like, *nothing* and Skanky Boy Gant has done two big deals in the past two months and it scares the pants off me.'

Becky wagged a finger. 'Now, now, didn't you just do a deal last week?'

'Oh, that was just for Eamonn Farrell. I'm not talking about my existing authors. I need to keep adding to my client list. If things don't pick up soon I won't make this year's bonus.'

'Bonus, my bum. You should get some of the percentage you negotiate. Become a partner!'

'I'm working on it.'

'So how's your new guy working out?'

'Manoj? Young, keen, smart as a whip, but . . . well, he's not Louisa. Why did she have to get pregnant and leave me?'

'She'll be back in four months.'

'I really miss her,' Jojo sighed. 'I've no one to talk to now.' Louisa was the only person at work who knew about her and Mark.

'What does Manoj look like?'

'Oh no, Becky. Oh, no, no, no. Seventy-five pounds, soaking wet. A bit of a fussy britches. Likes me to look great, thinks it's his job to keep me that way.'

'Gay?'

'Right! And, like I say, he's smart. After two weeks, he already knows about me and Richie Gant.'

'Does he know about Mark?'

'No! Are you insane?'

'When's Mark back from the book fair? Where is it this time?'

'Friday. Jerusalem.'

'Why didn't you just go with him?' Becky asked.

'There were too many others from Lipman Haigh going and staying in the same hotel. Someone would have seen us.' Jojo looked at her pizza a little sadly.

Becky offered solidarity by squeezing her hand, but there was nothing new to say. Since it had started, about four months ago, they'd analysed the situation so much that sometimes soft-hearted Becky began to regret ever getting involved.

'Why don't you come round on Sunday? Andy says he hasn't seen you in ages.'

'It's been less than two weeks. Hey, Becky, am I spending too much time being third wheel with you and Andy? It's just because you're family and you know about Mark.'

'No way, we love it. Come over and we'll read the papers, eat ice cream and complain.'

'About what?'

'Whatever you like,' she said magnanimously. 'The weather. Your job. The way Creme Eggs have got smaller. The choice is yours.'

An hour later, as they kissed good night, Becky asked, 'Are my teeth black?'

'No. Are mine?'

'No. We didn't drink enough. Too bad. See you Sunday.'

Friday morning, 8.57

Jojo heard them before she saw them—the assistants and readers gathered round the latest *Book News* and exclaiming like a flock of sparrows.

Pam was the first to spot her. 'Your questionnaire is in!'

'You look great!'

A copy was thrust into her line of vision and Jojo jumped back. The photo! She looked like a fifties B-movie siren—wavy auburn hair swept over one eye, dark pouting lips—and she was winking. Keith had used the winking photo! It had been a joke and he had promised not to run it.

'Your answers are great. So funny!'

'Thank you,' Manoj said. 'Er . . . on behalf of Jojo.'

What's your favourite smell?
Success.

Which living person do you most admire?
Myself.

What would you most change about yourself?
My lack of modesty.

Which living person do you most despise?
Myself—for my lack of modesty.

What traits do you dislike most in others?
Their filthy minds.

What makes you cry?
Chopping onions.

What makes you depressed?
My lack of psychic ability.

Where do you see yourself in five years' time?
See previous answer.

Which book do you wish you had agented?
The Bible.

Do you believe in monogamy?
It's a board game, right?

What are your distinguishing qualities?
I can whistle for a taxi and swear in Italian. I do a great Donald Duck impression and I can fix bikes.

The only one of the original answers that Manoj had permitted to remain—not that she'd shared the more personal ones with him.

What five things could you not live without?
Fresh air, sleep, food, a circulatory system—and books.

What makes you happy?
When the answer is yes.

What's the most important lesson life has taught you?
Nice girls finish last.

It was a good note to end on. Jojo exchanged a wink with Manoj. Pam watched carefully. She'd once tried to copy Jojo's sexy wink, but she had simply succeeded in dislodging her contact lens.

Lunchtime
Manoj had gone out to buy a hot-water bottle and the whole floor was quiet. Jojo was eating an apple and reading Eamonn Farrell's 'difficult second novel'. She didn't hear anyone come in, but sensed she was being watched and jerked her head up from the manuscript.

It was Mark.

'You're back!'

She sat up straight. Happiness, she thought. A positive emotion triggered by seeing Mark Avery.

Which was kind of nuts because, on paper, Mark Avery wasn't so much of a catch. He was maybe five ten, but seemed shorter because he was bulky. Though his hair was darkish, there was no exotic olive skin colouring, just ordinary English skin and eyes. But it didn't matter . . .

He was smiling. 'I saw your questionnaire. You're a class act, Jojo.'

But before she got a chance to reply, there was the sound of chattering—some of the others back from lunch—and Mark was gone. They were so paranoid about being seen together, that she was often left talking to his slip-stream, the words dying in her mouth.

Thirteen and a half minutes later
Pam burst in, closed the door and leaned against it as though a pack of wild dogs was after her. She was hugging a manuscript tightly to her chest. 'We've got a live one here,' she said.

Pam was Jojo's reader. Each agent had one—it was how Jojo had started in agenting herself. The readers worked their way through the pile of manuscripts that arrived every day at Lipman Haigh Agents. Occasionally they came across a winner, but for the most part they had to discard them and write to the authors urging them not to give up their day job.

'The first three chapters of something called *Love and the Veil*,' Pam said. 'It's great.'

'By who?'

'Nathan Frey.'

'Never heard of him. Gimme.'

Two pages in Jojo was hooked. All her dials were up to ten and she was so psyched she almost forgot to breathe.

When she finished the three chapters, she leapt up. 'Manoj, call this guy. Tell him we've got to see the rest. Send a bike.'

One (record-breaking) hour and fifty-five minutes later
Manoj placed the entire manuscript in her hands, with as much care as if it were a baby.

'Great. Oh *great*. Thank you.'

'Hold all calls?'

'You're way ahead of me.'

Jojo swung her feet up on her desk and disappeared into the book. It was a beautifully written love story about an Afghan woman and a secret service Brit. One of those rare books that had suspense, pathos, humanity and lots of sex.

A long time later

Manoj stuck his head round the door. 'We're going to the pub now.'

'You shiftless brat.'

'It's Friday night. Come to the pub. I've been here nearly three weeks and you haven't bought me a drink yet. They say you got trousered with Louisa all the time.'

'As if! She's been pregnant for the last nine months. I've got to finish these pages, I'm too far in now to be able to stop.'

But Manoj was right, she used to go out more with the people from work. Rowdy Friday-night vodkatini piss-ups, which often ended with the available women going clubbing, scoping for men. But Jojo had met her man . . .

She'd barely started reading again when someone else asked, 'Coming for a drink?'

Jim Sweetman, head of media and the youngest partner.

'Nope.'

'You don't come out any more.'

'Did Manoj send you in here?'

Jim frowned. 'Have I offended you? Did I try to snog you one drunken night?'

'No. And you know how you can tell? Because you still have all your teeth.' She laughed. 'I'm finishing this great, great book. Have a nice weekend. Bye.'

On she read, for twenty, maybe twenty-five minutes, and then she heard someone say, 'Whatcha doing?'

Who now? But it was Mark. Flooded with well-being she smiled her widest smile. 'Reading.'

'When did you learn to do that?'

She tipped back her chair, one foot on her desk and swivelled slightly. It was great to be able to look at him for as long as she wanted. Most times at work she could only allow herself sidelong glances and even then she feared that someone would pounce. 'Aha! Busted! You were *staring* at Mark Avery. What's going on with you and the managing partner?'

'I thought you'd be gone home by now,' she said.

'Stuff to catch up on.'

'How was your book fair?'

'You should have come with me. Don't I get a kiss?'

'I don't know.' She used her foot to swing herself in her chair. 'Do you?'

He came behind her desk and she got to her feet. Arms round his neck, she rested her face against his and took a moment to absorb the sheer relief of his presence. The knot of tension in her gut unwound, and floated free.

'Jojo,' Mark whispered, his face in her neck. They kissed while he tried to slide his hand up under her jacket. In her ear his breath was hot and loud. Then he had opened her jacket buttons, his hand was on the pillowy softness of her breast and she was jelly-legged with longing.

His erection was pressed against her and his hand trying to persuade her to the ground. He was strong and determined but Jojo resisted.

'Everyone's gone,' he said, his fingers finding her nipple. 'It's OK.'

'No.' She slid away from him. 'I'll see you tomorrow.'

No matter how badly she wanted him she would not have sex on her office floor. What did he think she was?

Saturday morning, 9.07

The phone rang: Mark.

'Jojo?' he whispered. 'I'm very sorry. I can't make it today.'

She said nothing. Too disappointed to make it easy for him.

'Sam's in a bit of trouble.' Sam was his son. 'We got a call last night. He went drinking with his mates and got so bad he ended up in hospital.'

'Is he OK?'

'He is now. But we've all had a bit of a fright and I ought to stay close.'

What could she say? Sam was a thirteen-year-old boy. This was serious stuff. 'Where are you?'

'In the shed.'

In the shed. Surrounded by weedkiller, slug repellent and spiders' webs. She nearly laughed—the glamour of an affair.

'Well, take care of yourself, and him and er, the others.' *Your wife, your daughter*.

'I'm sorry, Jojo, you know I am. But there's a chance that tomorrow—'

'Tomorrow, I've got plans. I hope Sam will be OK. See you Monday.'

She disconnected and pulled her comforter up to her chin, having a moment. *Now* she was sorry she hadn't had sex with him on the office floor last night. When you're seeing a married man, you take your chances where you can.

I should never have started this thing with him, Jojo thought. I could be in love with someone else right now, someone who wasn't married.

Even before Jojo had come to work at Lipman Haigh, she'd respected Mark Avery. He was well known in the industry as a visionary. Five years previously, when he had come in as managing partner, Lipman Haigh had been a sleepy little agency. Mark's first act had been to head-hunt several young snappy agents and make three of them partners as soon as the three most doddery incumbents could be persuaded to retire. Then he'd added a foreign rights department and a vibrant media arm and within eighteen months Lipman Haigh had become the hot 'new' London agency.

He was tough—he had to be—but he wore it with grace. In negotiations with publishers he could become as unmovable as cellulite, but he did it decently. Nothing personal, his manner said, but I won't be caving in, so you'd better. Not stern, not slimy, just straight.

But what Jojo had admired most about Mark Avery was his incredible troubleshooting abilities. His instincts were sure, nothing unnerved him, and he was a man with all the answers. Don Corleone without the voice, the entourage and the paunch.

But she hadn't, like, *fancied* him. Then came the night outside the Hilton. She was climbing into a cab after a long, rowdy publishing awards ceremony, when Mark pulled her back. She turned in enquiry and he asked, 'Can I come home with you?'

'You want me to drop you off?'

'No, I want to come home with you.'

'No,' she said, in surprise.

'Why not?'

'You're married. You're my boss. You're drunk.'

'In the morning I'll be sober.'

'And you'll still be married. And my boss.'

'Please?'

'*No.*' She laughed and moved away from his touch and into the cab. Before she shut the door, she said, 'I'll forget this ever happened.'

'I won't.'

The following day she expected a sheepish jokey apology—but there was no apology. She didn't even see him until the afternoon and that was only by accident, when they passed in the hall.

As soon as he saw her his eyes altered visibly. She'd heard about pupils dilating—she got enough romantic fiction sent to her—but she'd never before seen it happen in real life. Now, as if by special request, they dilated until they were almost black. He didn't say one word to her and after that everything was different.

She didn't like it, but she could wait it out. I can outwait anyone, Jojo thought, but, with all that tension flying about, could she help it if she found herself wondering about him? Once she focused on him as a man rather than a boss, her imagination took flight and her resolve began to buckle. The meaningful look in the corridor was the start of a slide into a violent attraction to him and it really pissed her off. Eventually she admitted to Becky, 'I keep thinking about what it would be like to sleep with Mark Avery.'

'Crap. Bound to be. Old guy like him?'

'He's forty-six, not eighty-six.'

'It's only because you haven't had sex for nine months. Not since that Craig. Maybe you should sleep with someone else.'

'But I don't want to go out looking for someone just to sleep with. That's not who I am. I want to sleep with Mark. And not anyone else.'

'Jojo, snap out of it. *Please.*'

'And considering I already like, admire and respect him, I'm doomed,' she continued disconsolately.

More prosaically, she had her career to consider. She hoped to be made partner some day soonish and how would that ever happen if her boss had decided to behave as if she didn't exist?

After five weeks she caved in and made an appointment to see him. She went into his office, shut the door behind her and sat before him.

'Jojo?'

'Mark. Ah . . . I don't know how to say this, but things have been, like, *tense* with us. Is it my work? Do you have a problem with it?'

She knew it wasn't that, but she wanted it clear.

'No, no problems with your work.'

'Riiight. so can we drop the weird stuff? Can we go back to the way we were?'

He considered it. 'No.'

'Why not?'

'Because . . . how can I put this?' he said. 'Because I'm in love with you.'

After a period of silence, Jojo looked up from her lap and said, 'You're married. I would never be with a married man.'

'I know. It's one of the reasons I feel how I feel about you.'

Good, Jojo thought.

'I'm not going to tell you that my wife doesn't understand me. I won't tell you that we never have sex because, very occasionally, we still do. And I love my two children. I don't want to do anything to hurt them.'

'Like leave?'

'Yes. So now it's up to you. You deserve a hell of a lot more than I'm offering, but what I can say is that I've never felt about anyone else the way I feel about you.'

'And you don't make a habit of this sort of thing?'

He looked shocked. 'Absolutely not.'

To her surprise, her eyes were suddenly swimming with tears. It was too much, all of it—his wife and children, his tender humility. *We have to do something.*

It was Becky who came up with the idea of them Getting it Out of Their Systems. 'He might be atrocious in bed,' she said hopefully. 'He might turn your stomach.'

Jojo doubted it but, in jokey embarrassment, ran it by Mark. 'And with a bit of luck you'll go right off me.'

The look he gave her signalled how unlikely that was. 'So where shall we . . .? I mean, I could . . .'

'Come to my place. I'll make dinner. No,' she amended. 'I won't. If I cook for you, I'll never get rid of you.'

He approached sex with her like he approached everything else: with determination, confidence, attention to detail, and he removed her clothes as if he was unwrapping a gift.

Afterwards she asked, 'How was it for you?'

'Disastrous.' He stared at the ceiling. 'I haven't gone off you at all. You?'

'Even worse than I expected.'

'Well? Was he fabulous?' Becky asked the following day. 'Or a bit crap? Sometimes those old guys can be terrible.' Becky had once slept with a drunken thirty-seven-year-old and regarded herself as an authority.

'It's not like that,' Jojo said irritably. 'It's much more than sex, Mark's my favourite person.'

'Sorry,' Becky said, shocked.

'No, I'm sorry.' Jojo was also shocked.

'So what happens now? Now that you've got it all out of your systems?'

'Only a fool would start a relationship with a married man.'

'And you, Jojo, are no fool.'

'No.'

'So when do you see him again?'

'Tonight.'

Sunday afternoon

'Work tomorrow,' Becky said sadly, looking up from a sea of newspaper. 'Last night I dreamt I gave the wrong figures to British Airways and over-refunded hundreds of people, and they're not even my client. Although they will be soon,' she added gloomily, 'the way things are going.'

'This is turning into an obsession,' Andy said. 'You've just got to confront Elise.'

'How?'

'Calmly. Just say what you say to me.'

'What if it turns nasty?'

'Nasty? It's just business, stop being so emotional about it. Be like Jojo. If someone was messing her about at work, she'd tell it to them straight.' Andy stopped. 'Mind you, she's sleeping with her boss, which could turn *extremely* nasty.'

'Enough already,' Jojo said.

'How *is* your adulterous liaison?' Andy asked. 'What's going to happen?'

Jojo squirmed. 'Ask Becky. She's director of emotional affairs.'

'Well?'

Becky considered. 'There are several possible outcomes. I'll make a list.' She scribbled for a few minutes on the 'Style' section of the *Sunday Times* then announced, 'OK. Possibilities.'

a) Mark leaves his wife

b) His wife is also having an affair and she leaves Mark

c) Jojo and Mark gradually go off each other and end up being friends

d) The wife dies tragically. Jojo enters Mark's household as governess to his children and after a respectable time has elapsed, he can go public that he's fallen for her

'Which one do you like the most?'

'None. I don't want him and his wife to break up.'

'So you just want to carry on being a sidecar in the motorbike of his life?' Andy asked.

'No, but . . .' She didn't want to break up anyone's marriage. 'And what about his kids? They'll hate me.'

'They'll live with their mother.'

'But they'll come to us and ruin our weekends. Sorry,' she said a mite defensively. 'I'm just being honest.'

'But you're so good with kids,' Becky said.

'I want kids but I want them to be babies first. Not a teenager who's already showing signs of delinquency and a goofy girl who falls off ponies. I'd spend all my down time at the Emergency Room.'

'So what *do* you want?' This came from Andy.

'For him never to have been married and for there to be no children.'

Becky consulted her list. 'Sorry. That option isn't on it.'

'What a bummer,' Jojo sighed.

'Do you love Mark?' Becky asked.

Jojo thought about it for a long time and concluded, 'Probably. But he's married.'

The thing was, though, that lately Mark had begun half hinting at the possibility of leaving Cassie. *Unprompted* half hinting. Jojo would never instigate it. Perhaps eventually all the cloak-and-dagger stuff would become unbearable, instead of being merely irritating, and maybe then she'd press for more. But at the moment the speculation about their happy future—such as it was—was all coming from him.

Monday morning, 9.00 and ten seconds
Manoj announced Nathan Frey.

He was a wreck. He'd spent three years writing the book; he'd taken out a second mortgage on his house, left his wife and family for six months and, disguised as a woman, lived in Afghanistan. He'd already been turned down by a couple of agents and now that he was this close to realising his dream of getting published, he was falling to pieces.

But when Jojo congratulated him on his wonderful book and explained how she thought it could be sold worldwide, his pallor receded and gradually he took on a healthier colour.

'Is the manuscript with anyone else at the moment? Any other agents?' Jojo asked. It wouldn't be the first time that an author had done a mass mailing and ended up with several agents claiming the author as their own.

'No, I've been doing them one at a time. I couldn't believe it when you rang. I want an agent like you wouldn't believe . . .'

'Well, you've got one,' Jojo said, and immediately two bright spots of raspberry coulis burst onto his cheeks.

'Wow,' he said quietly. 'I can't believe this.' His entire face had pinkened into a pretty strawberry mousse glow. 'So what happens now?'

'I get you a deal.'

'Really?' He seemed startled. 'Just like that?'

'It's a great book. Lots of publishers will want to buy it.'

'I hate to ask . . . I know this sounds a bit funny . . . but . . .'

'Yes, you should make plenty of money. I'll get you the best advance I can.'

'I don't want much,' he said hastily. 'Just to be published is reward enough. But we've had nothing coming in and it's hard for my wife . . .'

'Don't worry. I've the feeling lots of people will want this book and will be happy to pay for it. Give me about ten days and as soon as I have news I'll be in touch.'

Nathan backed out repeating, 'Thank you, thank you.'

Manoj watched him go and when the 'thank yous' from the corridor had faded from earshot, he remarked, 'The honeymoon period. But how long before the abuse starts?'

Jojo smiled.

'So, is he ours?' he asked.

'He's ours.' She thrust the manuscript at him. 'Get copying. I need six perfect copies and I need them half an hour ago.'

'You're going for an auction?'

Jojo nodded. *Love and the Veil* was so wonderful, she was confident that several editors would step up to the plate and engage in a bidding war.

While Manoj inhaled photocopier fumes and groused about having a 2.1 in English and doing work that a monkey could be trained to do, Jojo drew up a shortlist of editors in her head.

First, though, she had to check in with Mark about how Sam was doing. Pretending she cared about his domestic crises was difficult, but because they were important to Mark, she tried. The bottom line was, though, that every time there was a drama, Jojo lost Mark to his family. And they really were the most accident-prone bunch. His wife, Cassie, a primary-school teacher, got debilitating migraines whenever she ate cheese, a fact that did nothing to deter her from tucking into a cheese sandwich whenever she felt like it. Sophie, the ten-year-old daughter, was a danger to herself: in the time Jojo had been seeing Mark, she'd fallen off a pony and got a protractor stuck in her arm. Nor was the drinking incident Sam's first offence—he'd also been caught stealing from the newsagent's. Once again, Mark had to rush home.

To: Jojo.harvey@LIPMAN HAIGH.co
From: Mark.avery@LIPMAN HAIGH.co
Subject: Sam

He's OK now. I'm very sorry. How about Tuesday night?
M

To Mark.avery@LIPMAN HAIGH.co
From: Jojo.harvey@LIPMAN HAIGH.co
Subject: Tuesday

Tuesday it is.
JJ xx

Then Jojo phoned six of the best editors in London, told them they'd been handpicked and promised that a gem was being biked over. A date was set for the auction, a week hence—enough time for the editors to authorise with their higher-ups the big money she was hoping for.

And could this day get any better? When Jojo spoke to Tania Teal at Dalkin Emery about *Love and the Veil*, Tania said, 'Good timing. I was going to call you today anyway, about Lily Wright.'

Lily Wright was one of Jojo's authors, an intelligent, intuitive and gentle woman. When Jojo first took Lily on, she came with her partner, Anton, to see her; they both sat nervously in front of Jojo, finishing each other's sentences and generally being adorable. Lily had written *Mimi's Remedies*, a magical little book about a white witch. Jojo had loved it and really felt it had something very special. But because it was so esoteric, she'd been unable to persuade any publisher to go big on it.

Tania had bought it for the small advance of four grand. At the time she'd said, 'Personally *I* adore it, it's better than Prozac. I have to admit that in my heart of hearts I can't see it going mainstream, but what the hell, I'm going to try anyway.'

'What about Lily?' Jojo asked Tania.

'Lovely news, actually.' Jojo could hear her glee. 'There's a rave review of *Mimi's Remedies* in this week's *Flash! And* we're reprinting. The reports from the reps are good. Would you believe we've almost sold out.'

'You have? Fantastic! And that's on almost *no* publicity.'

'Well, in light of the reprint I've persuaded marketing to run a few ads.'

'Great! And what kind of reprint are we talking? Another five k?'

'No, we thought ten.'

Ten? Double the original print run? The sales reps' reports must be spectacular.

'Looks like we were right about this, Jojo!'

Jojo agreed, thanked her and hung up, high on excitement. It was always good news when, against the odds, a book started to take off, even slightly. But in this case, because the author was such a sweetie, she was overjoyed.

Tuesday morning, 10.15
The first call came. 'I've Patricia Evans on the line. Accept or decline?' Manoj said.

'Accept, accept!' First out of the gate!

A click, then, 'Jojo, I've read *Love and the Veil*.'

Jojo's heart banged as the adrenaline kicked in. This was going to be good.

'I love it,' Patricia said. 'We all love it here and I want to make a preemptive offer.'

'It would have to be a very high offer to take the book off the table right now.'

'I think you're going to be happy. We're offering one million pounds.'

Suddenly her hands were hot and adrenaline was racing through her like an invading army. Jojo was thinking fastfastfast. A million pounds was crazy money, especially for a debut novel. But if Pelham were prepared to go so high, wouldn't some of the other houses also? Maybe in an

177

auction she could get the money higher. Higher than the £1.1 million that Richie Gant had got for *Fast Cars*? . . .

'That's a very generous offer,' Jojo said. Calmcalmcalm. 'I'll talk to Nathan and get back to you.'

'The offer is on the table for the next twenty-four hours,' Patricia said and hung up.

It was Nathan's call. 'Nathan, it's Jojo. We've had an offer from Pelham Press. A high one.'

'How much?'

'A million.'

There was a clatter—the phone might have fallen—then she heard retching sounds. Patiently she waited until he returned and asked faintly, 'Can I call you back?'

Half an hour later Nathan rang. 'Sorry about that. I felt a little dizzy. I've been thinking.'

I betcha.

'If they've offered that much, someone else might too.'

'There's no guarantee, but we're on the same page.'

'What do you think? What are Pelham Press like?'

'Very commercial, very aggressive, they have a lot of best sellers.'

'Eww. They sound dreadful.'

'They're very good at what they do.' Which was piling them high and selling them cheap.

'You see, I have no clue, Jojo. What do I know about any of this? You're the agent, the expert. I trust you.'

'Nathan, a book auction is not an exact science. There's a chance it could all fall apart and I get you nothing.'

'I trust you,' he repeated.

So Jojo was on her own, the decision was hers.

Tuesday morning, 11.50

She'd carried on working—quite a productive couple of hours actually; but all the while, she was playing *Love and the Veil*'s two opposing scenarios off against each other. Accept or reject? Accept or reject?

Accept, she decided. Then Manoj buzzed her. 'Monkey boy here. Any bananas you want eaten?'

'What do you want?'

'I have Alice Bagshawe for you.' Another of the chosen editors.

'Accept or—'

'Accept.' Click. 'Hey, Alice.'

'Jojo. *Love and the Veil*,' Alice said breathlessly.

'Didn't I tell you it was great?'

'It is. Completely. So much so that we at Knoxton House want to make a pre-emptive offer.'

Jojo couldn't help smiling.

'We want to offer a cool . . .' Alice drew the words out for dramatic effect, 'two . . .'

Two, Jojo thought. Two *million*. Thank God she hadn't accepted the Pelham pre-empt—a full million less.

'. . . hundred and twenty thousand pounds,' Alice finished.

It took a moment.

'Two *hundred* and twenty thousand?' Jojo asked.

'That's right,' Alice confirmed, mistaking Jojo's shock for happy incredulity.

'Oh. Oh, Alice, I'm really sorry, we have a much larger pre-empt on the table right now.'

'Jojo, we went to the wire on this. We can't go any higher.'

So Knoxton House were out. Well, there were still five in the game.

'To be honest, Jojo, I don't think it's worth any more than our bid. You really ought to accept the other offer now.'

'Yeah, thanks, Alice.'

Jojo swung in her chair, deep in thought. Alice's call had shaken her faith badly.

The four publishers who hadn't come back to her yet, which way would they jump? There was no way of knowing, not until they called.

I've got to hold my nerve, she thought. I've got to keep it steady.

Tuesday night, Jojo's bed (post-coital)

'So what are you going to do?' Mark asked.

'What would you do?'

'Accept the one million pre-empt.'

'I see . . .'

'It's an astonishing sum, especially for a debut.'

'I seeeeee . . .'

'You're not going to take it, are you?'

'Yes. No. I don't know.'

'You want to beat the one point one million that Richie Gant got for *Fast Cars*, don't you?' Mark wound his fingers in her hair. 'It's not a good way to make decisions.'

'I didn't ask for your advice,' she said haughtily.

'Yes, you did,' he laughed.

She lifted her head, disentangling his hand from her hair, then flopped back against her pillow and sighed. It was 1.15 a.m.

'Time to go home, Mark.'

He sat up, his skin wafting a sweet heat to her. He was sleepy but it was clear he'd been giving this some thought. 'Why don't I stay?'

'Just not go home?'

'Yes.'

'You want to get caught?'

'Would it be so bad?'

'Yes. No matter what happens this isn't the way to do it.' She threw a sock at him. 'Get dressed. Go home.'

Wednesday morning, 10.00

The clock ticked closer and closer to Pelham's deadline and Jojo was still no nearer to fixing on a decision.

Take the million and lose the chance of getting more? Or turn down the million and run the risk of getting far less?

There was no way of knowing: it was just a guess. Although it felt better to call it a gamble.

'Jojo, Patricia Evans is on the line. Do you accept or decline?'

'Decline. I'll call her back in ten.'

Jojo whooshed by Manoj's desk. 'I'm going to see Dan Swann.'

'Your mentor,' Manoj said.

Dan was in his office doing something with a cloth to one of his pieces of war memorabilia.

'Hello, Jojo, you've caught me polishing my helmet.'

Jojo was never sure how many of Dan's double entendres were intentional. All, she suspected, but now wasn't the time . . .

'You're looking a little hot under the collar.'

'I bet I am. I need to say this out loud: I've been offered a one million pounds pre-empt from Patricia Evans. Should I accept it and lose the chance of going a lot higher? Or turn it down and run the risk of getting nothing at all? You're an experienced agent, what do you usually do?'

Dan rummaged in the pocket of his cords and emerged with a coin. 'Heads or tails?'

'Oh, come *on*.'

Jojo looked displeased and Dan said vaguely, 'I can't give you any answers. It's a game of chance and I suspect what you should do is look at what those crass young men call the worst-case scenario.'

Jojo considered it. 'Worst-case scenario? I could lose a million pounds. I could destroy an author's career.'

'Quite.'

'Yes,' Jojo said thoughtfully. 'Thanks, Dan. This has really helped.'

'You'll accept it?'

Jojo looked surprised. 'No.'

'Excuse me, my dear, but you've just said you could lose one million pounds and destroy an author's career. You did say that, didn't you?'

'I said it was the worst that could happen. It's not a matter of life or death. Like, no matter what happens no one gets hurt. No, I'm going all the way. Thanks.'

A one-hundred-and-eighty-degree swivel on her high heels and she was gone. Dan spoke to the air. 'That woman would eat her young,' he observed, with warm admiration.

Later

It was a hard call to make. Patricia wasn't pleased. Not one bit.

'You can still bid on Monday,' Jojo said, gently.

'I've made the only bid I'm going to make.'

'I'm sorry, I really am. If you change your mind . . . I'm going nowhere and you have my number.'

Friday morning, 11.10, the agents' weekly show and tell

'Jojo?' Mark asked. 'Anything to report?'

'Sure have. My author Miranda England is number seven in this week's *Sunday Times* best-sellers' list.'

Murmurs of 'Well done' came from round the table. Only Richie Gant said nothing at all. She knew because she looked hard at him, trying to catch his eye to have a good gloat.

Mark moved on. 'Richie?'

Both Jim Sweetman and Richie shuffled and sat up straighter. They exchanged some kind of look and Richie got the nod. *You tell them.*

'The blinding Mr Sweetman,' Richie sounded like a disreputable used-car salesman, 'and his media department have sold the movie rights of *Fast Cars* for one point five million dollars to a major Hollywood studio.'

Then Richie met her look. A full-on smirk right across the table and into her face.

Friday afternoon, 3.15

Manoj buzzed her. 'I have Tony O'Hare from Thor. Accept or—'

'Accept.'

Jojo's adrenaline was in sudden full spate. This could be good. Another pre-emptive offer, perhaps. A funny time to do it, on Friday afternoon, but . . .

'Jojo? It's Tony. It's about *Love and the Veil*.'

'Yes?' Breathless.

'I'm very sorry but I'm going to have to pass on it.'

Shit.

'Personally speaking, I loved it, but we're pulling in our horns a little here. I'm sure you understand.'

'OK.' She had to clear her throat. 'Don't worry, Tony. Thanks for letting me know.'

'Well?' Manoj came in.

'He's not interested.'

'Why not?'

'Says they're short of cash. Can you open the window?'

'Why? Are you going to jump?'

'I'd like some air.'

'It's painted shut. Don't you believe him?'

'It's hard to know because they'll never say outright if they don't like a book. Just in case it's a huge hit and everyone knows they passed. I'm going out to have a cigarette.'

Jojo stood on the street, inhaling and exhaling thoughtfully. There were still three publishers in the running. There was still everything to play for.

Sunday afternoon, 3.05

Jojo looked up from the Sunday paper and asked, with sudden curiosity, 'Doesn't Cassie ever wonder where you are?'

Mark had shown up shortly after ten. They'd gone to bed, gone for breakfast, then back to bed and now they were making their way through a pile of magazines and newsprint. He seemed in no hurry to go home.

Mark put down Jojo's *Harpers*. 'I don't just disappear. I always tell her something.'

'Like what?'

'That I'm working, or playing golf or . . .'

'And she believes you?'

'If she doesn't, she doesn't say.'

Jojo had seen Cassie once, but that was long before she was interested in Mark, so she hadn't paid her much attention. She remembered her as looking like the primary-school teacher she was: Suzy Hausfrau smiley and cosy with a frosted bob. She was in her early forties but Jojo only knew that because Mark had told her.

Cassie and Mark had been married about fifteen years. Jojo knew the story. Mark was friends with her brother—still was—and he'd met Cassie when they'd all shared a flat. Jojo often wondered if he still loved her; she could have asked him, but she was scared he might say he did and scared he might say he didn't.

Monday morning

Big day. Big, big day. The day the first-round bids for *Love and the Veil* came in. If it was a good auction, and Jojo hoped it would be, it could last all week, with bids and counter-bids.

Tania Teal from Dalkin Emery was the first to throw her hat in the ring. Jojo held her breath and into the silence Tania lobbed, 'Four hundred and fifty thousand.'

Jojo exhaled. Not a bad place to start. If all three came in around this level, there was a chance they would bid against each other until they got to over a million.

'Thanks, Tania. Let me come back to you when I've heard from the others.' She hung up. She felt great.

11.05 a.m.

Olive Liddy from Southern Cross was next.

'Hit me,' Jojo said.

'Fifty thousand.'

Jojo froze and when she unfroze the first thing she did was laugh although, of course, it was no laughing matter.

'Am I way out?' Olive asked, in a small voice.

'Not even in the same zip code.'

'I'll see what I can do.'

11.15 a.m.

And then came Franz Wilder, Editor of the Year.

'I'd like to offer three-fifty.'

'Three hundred and fifty thousand? That's a very healthy bid, Franz. Not the highest I've had but close. If you'd like to come back to me later with a higher—'

'No.'

'Excuse me?'

'That's my final bid.'

Her heart sank and sank and kept on sinking, through the soles of her shoes and into the graphic designers on the floor below.

'Thing is, Franz,' she forced an uplift into her voice, 'Nathan is very hot right now and everyone wants a piece of him.'

'This is a great book, I could really knock it into shape . . .' Franz trailed off, his point made.

'Oh, for sure,' she agreed earnestly. 'But—'

'That's my final offer, Jojo.'

'Yes, but—' If she could only get him up to Tania's bid, then she could push it higher.

'No, Jojo, that's it.'

'OK. Thanks, Franz.' What else could she say?

The full horrible truth kicked in and suddenly she was flailing in empty space. There was only one editor in play: Tania Teal. *How can I have a bidding war with only one bidder?*

How could this have happened?

So, was this it? Going once, going twice, going three times—sold to Tania Teal for £450,000? A mere £550,000 less than Patricia Evans had offered. Not even half. *Oh my God.* Jojo tried hard to get things in proportion: £450,000 was a phenomenal sum of money; it would change Nathan Frey's life for ever.

But she could have got him so much more—and the higher the advance, the higher the marketing and publicity budgets as the publishers sought to ensure they recouped their advance.

And this terrible feeling of loss wasn't just to do with the money. It was because she'd fucked up. She'd been so sure of this book, so certain it would break records, she would have staked her career on it. A horrible thought—perhaps she had. Without realising it, maybe this had been the biggest chance she'd ever get, and she'd blown it.

What if this ruined her chances of being made partner? What if Richie Gant beat her to it? He'd only joined Lipman Haigh eight months ago and Jojo had been there for two and a half years—but he was doing so well. And Jojo wasn't . . .

Manoj came in and took one look at her face. 'Oh, no.'

'Oh, yes.'

'Tell me.'

'Not now. I'm going out to buy something.'

'What?'

'Anything.'

Jojo almost bought a bin for her bathroom; it was blue plastic and had little dolphin shapes cut out of it, but when it came to picking it up and queuing at the cash desk, she was just too disheartened.

She traipsed back to the office and ate a ham and cheese croissant, watching hopelessly as the flakes floated down and stuck to her desk.

When Manoj buzzed with a call her heart nearly jumped out of her jacket.

'Olive Liddy on line one.'

'I only have one line.'

'So? It doesn't mean she's not on line one.'

Jojo sighed heavily. 'Put her through.'

'Olive? What can I do for you?'

'*Love and the Veil*? I hope it's not too late. I'd like to make an offer.'

'Have you had a knock on the head, Olive? You already made your bid. I laughed, remember?'

'I want to increase it.'

'To what?'

'Six hundred thousand.'

'What—? Hey, what's going on, Olive?' *How did you manage to get another £550,000 approved in three hours?*

'I misread the worth of the book. I got it wrong.'

Then Jojo got it. Olive had been hoping no one else was interested and that she'd pick it up cheap. Some nerve! But so what? Everything was back on! Thank Christ.

'I'll get back to you on that.'

Monday afternoon, 3.07
'Tania? We've had some bids higher than yours.'

'How much higher?'

'You know I can't really say . . .'

'Jojo!'

'Six.'

'OK. Seven.'

'Thanks, I'll get back to you.'

3.09 p.m.
'Olive? I've had another bid. Higher than yours.'

'How much higher?'

'You know I can't really say . . .'

'How much?'

'Seven.'

'Eight, then.'

3.11 p.m.
'Tania? We've had another bid.'

'I need more time. I'm not authorised to go any higher.'

'When will you get back to me?'

'Soon.'

Tuesday morning, 10.11
'Jojo, it's Olive. Is the book mine?'

'I'm waiting to hear back from another interested party.'

'I need to know soon.'

'Gotcha.'

10.15 a.m.
'Tania, I'm going to have to hurry you.'
  'Sorry, Jojo. We've been trying to get hold of our publisher. I need him to approve more money, but he's sailing around the Caribbean.'
  'How soon can you get back to me?'
  'I'll try for close of business today.'

4.59 p.m.
'Olive, it's Jojo, can you give me until tomorrow morning?'
  'Well, I don't know . . .'
  'Please, Olive. We're old friends.'
  'OK.'

Wednesday afternoon, 2.45
'Jojo?'
  'Tania?'
  'Nine hundred!'

2.47 p.m.
'Olive?'
  'Jojo?'
  'Nine hundred's the figure to beat.'
  'Fuck! I thought it was mine. Well, I'll have to go further up the feeding chain to get more money approved.'
  'When can you get back to me?'
  'Soon.'

Thursday morning, 10.08
'Jojo, it's Tania.'
  'Still waiting to hear from the others.'
  'I need to know, you know. Nine hundred is a huge sum and I know Olive Liddy is the other editor . . .'
  'What makes you say that?'
  'Word gets around. And she'll never get anything higher authorised. They're hopeless over there.' (Tania had been made redundant from Southern Cross after a bitter falling-out. Feelings still ran high.)
  'Please, Tania, can you just give me until after lunch?'
  'Two thirty, but then I'm pulling out.'

10.10 a.m.
'Olive, Jojo here.'
  'Yes, sorry, look, we're having an emergency meeting this afternoon

with the heads of sales, marketing and publicity. I'll call you back as soon as it's over. Three thirty.'

2.29 p.m.
'It's Manoj. I've Tania Teal on the line.'
　'It's not even two thirty!'
　'What'll I tell her?'
　'Something. Anything. Buy me an hour.'
　'Broken leg?'
　'Maybe not so serious.'
　'*Suspected* broken leg?'
　'Go for it.'

3.31 p.m.
'Jojo, it's Olive. OK.' Deep, deep breath. 'A million.'

3.33 p.m.
'Tania, they've bid a million.'
　'A million!'
　'Are you in or are you out?'
　'In, but I have to try to loosen those purse strings a bit more. By the way, how's your leg?'

Now that she'd got the offer back up to a million, the original pre-empt, Jojo was as high as a kite.
　'What happens next?' Manoj asked.
　'That's it for today, but they'll be back tomorrow.'
　'How are you going to celebrate tonight? Yoga?'
　'Yoga, my ass. Rampant sex with my boyfriend.' *Fuckkkkk.* Shouldn't have said that. Soaring spirits had made her careless.
　Manoj moaned. 'Who is he?'
　'Never mind.'

Friday morning
Tania came back with a further £50,000, which was less than Jojo was expecting. Then Olive counter-bid £20,000.
　'Why so glum?' Manoj asked Jojo. But he knew. 'You think it won't get over the one point one million Richie Gant got for *Fast Cars*?'
　'It's not over yet.'
　But Tania's next bid was for £10,000, and Olive's counter-bid was also for £10,000. Both editors were almost at their ceilings and the bidding stood at £1.09 million.

'You need ten grand more,' Manoj said.

'Twenty. I want to beat him, not just match him.'

In small increments Jojo managed to inch the money up until both editors were at £1.12 million.

'Twenty grand more,' Manoj observed. 'You can stop now.'

But Jojo was going to have to stop anyway. There was no more money and because the bids were equal, a beauty contest would be held, where Nathan would be wheeled round to both publishers, who'd put on a bit of a show, then Nathan would decide who he liked best.

Midnight, Friday, Jojo's flat

Her buzzer rang. Mark. He'd arrived, uninvited, at Jojo's.

She was happy to see him, like, a *lot*, but no way was he to get into the habit of just dropping in for a quick bonk whenever he wanted, before heading home to his wife.

'I could've had my other guy here. How lucky is that?'

'There'd better not be anyone else.'

'The married man tells me I'd better not have someone else!'

'You're right.' He wrestled his mobile from his pocket. 'This has gone on long enough, I'm going to tell Cassie I love you and—'

She grabbed the phone. 'Give me that, you moron. Seeing as you're here, I've got plans for you.'

Twenty minutes later

Jojo rolled off him; they were both slick with sweat and fighting for breath.

'That was . . . that was . . .' he heaved.

'Atrocious?'

'Yes. You?'

'The worst ever.'

'All fired up after the auction?'

'Yeah,' she grinned, 'all that testosterone.'

'So, tell me, did you set out to beat Richie Gant?'

'*Course* I did.'

She buried her face in his neck and inhaled his scent. Oh, he was delicious.

5.45 the following morning

They jerked awake simultaneously, looked at the clock and stared at each other, wild-eyed and sticky-up-haired with fear.

'Shit!' Jojo said. 'Mark, quick, get up, go home!'

'Fuck!' Mark hotfooted it out of the door, still dressing himself. 'I'll ring you later.'

'OK. Good luck.'

Seconds later Jojo heard the main front door slam; he must have body-surfed the five flights. Her stomach was a hard ball of apprehension: this was crunch time. Cassie would know, Mark would tell her, they'd break it to the kids, it would be awful, he'd move out of their home, he'd move in here, they'd be a couple and she wasn't sure she was ready yet.

The day was endless as she waited to hear from him. She went to yoga, on the premise that it was so nasty it would take her mind off the waiting. Which it did, admirably, but only for an hour. When she returned home she half expected to find Mark waiting outside with a suitcase. But nothing. And no messages.

He finally called on Saturday evening when Jojo was at Becky and Andy's.

'Is it him?' Becky mouthed, her eyes wide with apprehension.

Jojo nodded brusquely. She got up and went into the hallway. 'So what happened? Are we busted?'

'No.'

She exhaled, doing it properly for the first time that day. But lacing the relief was some disappointment. In her head, he was already living with her and she'd become quite happy about it, actually.

'So tell me.'

It transpired that Cassie had actually slept right through the night and only noticed that Mark wasn't there when he barged in with his over-rehearsed excuse—long-week-late-night-rowdy-Italians-residents'-bar-comfy-sofa-fell-asleep-here's-their-number-if-you-don't-believe-me.

But Cassie did believe him and Jojo and Mark spent much of Sunday on a subdued post-mortem. 'That was too close for comfort,' they agreed. 'We've got to make sure it never happens again.'

Friday morning

'It's in,' Manoj said, spinning a copy of *Book News* onto her desk nearly a week later. 'Page five.'

Book News, 2 March

RECORD-BREAKING SALE

Love and the Veil, a debut novel set in Afghanistan, has been sold to Olive Liddy at Southern Cross for an alleged £1.12 million, the highest sum ever paid in the UK for a first novel. Described by Ms Liddy as 'the book of the decade', its author Nathan Frey is a former schoolteacher who lived as a woman in Afghanistan for six months while researching the book. The sale was agented by Jojo Harvey of Lipman Haigh who has enjoyed a recent run of success.

9.45 a.m.

Jocelyn Forsyth, one of the elderly partners who Jojo hoped would be retiring soon, knocked on her door. 'Heartiest congratulations, my dear.'

'Thank you.'

'Everything sewn up? All the small print, et cetera, et cetera?'

'Nearly.'

Next to arrive was Jim Sweetman who shone his glorious smile around the office.

'Congratulations. It should be fun selling the movie rights.'

10.56 a.m.

'See you got lucky, Cagney.'

Jojo looked up. Richie Gant was standing at her office door and she put down her pen. 'What? You mean my one-point-twelve-million-pound deal for Nathan Frey?'

'How lucky was that?'

'Yeah,' Jojo smiled. 'And you know what? The harder I work, the luckier I get.'

Four weeks later

'Perhaps you should have a look at this.' Pam handed Jojo a bundle of papers. 'I think it's a manuscript. It's like emails and stuff. And the person who wrote it isn't the person who submitted it. The author is called Gemma Hogan, but her friend Susan is the one who sent it in.'

'Sounds way off.'

Pam shrugged. 'I recommend you take a look. I think it might be great.'

Lily

EVEN THOUGH I made my choice, I shall never forgive myself. This sounds wildly melodramatic, I know, but I mean it simply as a statement of fact. It's the most dreadful thing I've ever done, and even now, though we're together and have Ema, frequently I find myself waiting for a catastrophe. Building one's happiness on someone else's misery is no foundation for long-term stability. Anton says I have Catholic guilt. But I wasn't brought up Catholic—apparently I don't have to be.

Journalists. In my short career as an interviewee I'd met two varieties. Those who displayed their 'serious' credentials by dressing like the homeless (a look I inadvertently favoured myself since becoming a mother). Or those who appeared to spend their entire lives attending functions at foreign embassies. The one now stepping over my threshold—Martha Hope Jones from the *Daily Echo*—was a foreign embassy merchant. She wore a red suit with gilt buttons and high shoes the precise red of her suit.

'Welcome to my humble abode,' I said, and almost bit my tongue. I so did not want to draw her attention to how humble my abode actually was: a one-bedroomed ex-council flat, which housed Anton, Ema and me.

'Delightful,' Martha declared, poking her nose into the kitchen and taking in two clothes horses laden with garments.

'You weren't supposed to go in there.' I flushed. 'Pretend you didn't see.'

But Martha had already reached into her (same red as her shoes) bag, taken out a notebook and scribbled something.

I directed her into the living room, which Anton, bless him, had tidied.

Martha plonked herself on the sofa, yelped, 'Jesus!' and sprang to her feet again. We both looked at the piece of Lego which was the cause of Martha's painfully indented buttock.

'Sorry, it's my little girl's . . .'

Martha scribbled something else in the notebook.

'Don't you use a tape recorder?' I asked.

'No, this is much more intimate.' She brandished her pen with a smile. Yes, and she could misquote me till the cows came home.

'Where is your little girl?' She looked round the room.

'At the playground with her dad.'

Martha accepted tea, refused biscuits, then the interview began.

'I've read part of your biog, but I'm sure you know that Martha Hope Jones's profiles are quite different from the pieces regular hacks produce. I prefer to start with a clean slate, get to know who Lily actually is and *really* get under her skin.'

She made a burrowing motion with her hand and I nodded warily. I so did not want her under my skin.

'You've not always been a writer, Lily?'

'No. Until two years ago I worked in public relations.'

'*Did* you?' Her manifest surprise was insulting even though I knew I didn't look like the archetypal PR person.

'So there you are working away in PR.' Martha's pen was doing overtime. 'Where was this?'

'Dublin, initially, then London.'

191

'What were you doing in Ireland?'

'My mum went to live there when I was twenty and I went with her.'

'And now you're back in the UK. What happened?'

'Cutbacks. I was made redundant. My mum had moved back to the UK, so I did too. Did some freelancing . . .' I stopped.

'And then you got mugged,' Martha prompted.

'And then I got mugged.'

'Could you bear to tell me a little about that?' Martha asked, pressing her hand on mine, her tone suddenly 'caring'.

I nodded. Not that there was ever any doubt. If I held out on the only truly dramatic part of this story, there would be no interview in Britain's fourth-highest-selling daily. I told it quickly, leaving out as much as I could and rushed to the finish, the part where the bloke pushed me over and disappeared with my bag.

'Then he left you for dead.' Martha was scratching furiously at her page.

'Um, no. I was conscious, I was well enough to walk home.'

'Yes, but you *could* have been dead,' Martha insisted. 'He wasn't to know.'

'Perhaps.' I shrugged reluctant approval.

'And though gradually your physical wounds faded, the mental scars remained?'

I swallowed. 'I was rather upset.'

'Upset! You must have been utterly traumatised! Yes?'

I nodded obediently . . . and a little wearily.

'Post-traumatic stress disorder set in,' Martha was scribbling faster and faster. 'You couldn't go to work?'

'Well, I was freelancing at the time—'

'You couldn't leave the house—'

'Yes, I cou—'

'You stopped washing? Eating?'

'But I—'

'You simply couldn't see the point in anything.'

A pause. An exhalation. 'Sometimes. But doesn't everyone feel—'

'And in this dark, lonely place there came a tiny glimmer of light. A vision and you sat down and wrote *Mimi's Remedies*.'

Another pause, then I gave in. 'Go on, then.' She so did not need me here.

'Then an agent took you on, she found you a publisher and hey presto—you're an overnight success!'

'Not exactly. I'd been writing for about five years in my spare time, and I'd actually finished a novel but no one would—'

'How many copies of *Mimi's Remedies* have been sold now?'

'The latest figure is a hundred and fifty thousand. At least that's how many are in print.'

'Well, well,' Martha marvelled. 'Almost a quarter of a million.'

'No, it—'

'Give or take.' Martha's shark smile permitted no argument. 'And you wrote it in a month.'

'Two months.'

'Two?' She seemed disappointed.

'But that's extremely fast! My first novel took me five years, and it's still not published.'

'And you've already got quite a devoted following, I hear. Although the critics haven't always been kind, have they, Lily?'

'Who cares what the critics say?' I said, stoutly. Actually, *I* did. Immensely. I could recite large chunks of the savage reviews I had been getting since *Mimi's Remedies* had begun to haemorrhage from bookshops on word-of-mouth sales. The *Independent* had called it—

'Candy floss for the brain,' Martha said.

'Yes,' I said humbly. I could go on. *This debut novel is a preposterous by-product of the current touchy-feely sensibility. A 'fable', it tells of a white witch, the eponymous Mimi, who arrives unexpectedly in a picturesque village and sets up shop providing magic remedies for the townsfolk and their various neuroses.*

'And the *Observer* said it was . . .'

'"Sweet enough to rot the readers' teeth",' I finished for her. 'I only wrote the book to cheer myself up. I couldn't have known that anyone would publish it. If it hadn't been for Anton it would never have been sent to Jojo.'

Martha's pen speeded up again.

'And how did you meet your husband, Anton?'

'We're not married yet.'

'So how did you meet your *fiancé*, Anton?'

'Partner,' I said, just in case she asked me to produce a ring.

Martha looked at me sharply. 'But you will marry?'

I made vaguely positive noises but in truth it made little difference to me whether or not we did. My parents, by contrast, are great believers in the institution of marriage. They love it so much that they keep doing it; Mum has been married twice and Dad three times. I have so many half-siblings and step-siblings that a family get-together would resemble one of the later episodes of *Dallas*.

'Where did you meet Anton?' Martha asked again.

How ought I to answer this? 'Through a mutual friend.'

193

'Would that mutual friend like to be named?' She twinkled.

'Um, no. Thank you.' I don't think so!

'Oh. Are you quite sure?'

'Quite. Thank you.'

Martha was alerted, she knew there was a story, but she let it go. For the moment, at least.

'And what does Anton do?'

Another tricky question. 'He and his partner, Mikey, run a media production company called Eye-Kon. They made *Last Man Standing* for Sky Digital. A reality game show?' I asked hopefully.

But she had never heard of it. Her and sixty million others.

'And at the moment they're in discussions with the BBC and Channel Five about a ninety-minute feature.'

But Martha had no interest in the ups and downs of Anton's career. Well, I had tried my best.

'Righty-ho, I think I've got plenty here.' She closed her notebook, then nipped to the loo. While she was out of the room I fretted over what I had said, what I had not said and whether or not there were clean towels in the bathroom.

I led her to the downstairs front door and shook her hand. 'Thank you for coming.'

'The picture desk will be in touch about a photo. It was a pleasure meeting you.'

'Goodbye.'

As soon as she had left, I returned upstairs, took some ragged breaths, then rang Anton on his mobile. 'It's safe to come home now.'

'On my way, sweetheart.'

Ten minutes later he gangled in the door, all legs and elbows. Little Ema was fast asleep, bundled into his chest. Whispering, we laid her down in her cot and closed the bedroom door on her.

In the kitchen, Anton took off his coat. 'So tell us, how'dit go with your woman?'

'I'm not sure.'

'Any bickies left?'

'Heaps.'

'I don't get it.'

'Nor me.' The first interview I had done had shamed me utterly by reporting to the world that I had offered only tea or coffee, no biscuits. Ever since then, in a belated attempt to make restitution, we bought top-of-the-range biscuits each time a journalist came, but not one of them ate any.

About Anton. The important thing to remember is that I am not a seductress. To be honest, I'm the least *fatale* of *femmes*.

A potted history of how all this came about: I was brought up in London and my parents split when I was fourteen. The year I turned twenty Mum married dull Irish Peter and moved to live with him in Dublin. Although I was perfectly old enough to live on my own I also went to Dublin and eventually made friends, one of my closest being Gemma. I got a job writing press releases for Mulligan Taney, Ireland's biggest PR firm. But after working there for five years, I lost my job and could not get another one. This roughly coincided with Mum and Peter separating. Mum returned to London and I followed her. Though my heart was not in it, I secured some freelancing work writing press releases. Meanwhile, shortly after I had returned to London, Gemma met Anton; though Gemma visited me occasionally, Anton was too skint to accompany her.

So I never actually met him until he had left a brokenhearted Gemma in Dublin and come to London, to set up an independent media production company.

Anton's version of events was that his one-year relationship with Gemma was over; she said they were just taking a break, that he simply did not realise it yet. Weeping softly down the phone she told me, 'I'll give it two months, then he'll see that he still loves me and he'll be back.'

However, she feared that he might be distracted by a London girlie and as I was *in situ*, I was ideally placed to be Gemma's 'man on the ground'. My brief was to befriend Anton.

'I know I'm a neurotic, jealous, mad woman,' she had said in one phone call. 'I want you to stick close, but please don't get too fond of him. You're good-looking, you know.'

'If you like women who're thinning on top.' (My hair is so fine the pink of my scalp sometimes shows through. Other women say if they won the lottery they would buy themselves bigger boobs or a bum-lift. I would have a hair-follicle transplant.)

'You never know, he might like slapheads. I can just see it, you and he'll be hanging out, then you get an eyelash caught in your eye, he helps you get it out, then Whoops! You're standing right next to each other, close enough for a snog and you'll see that it's been a slow burn and you've been in love with each other for ages.'

I promised Gemma that she had no need to worry and in a way I kept my word. There was no slow burn and caught-eyelash stuff. Instead I fell in love with Anton the first time we met.

Two days after Anton arrived in London, we agreed to meet one Thursday at 7 p.m. outside the underground at Chalk Farm. I was living in a rented hovel in nearby Gospel Oak—walking distance.

As I ascended the hill to the tube station the air was sparkly clean and smelt of lush grass; the cool relief of autumn had just arrived. It was then that I realised that I did not know what Anton looked like. All I had to go on was Gemma's description, which was that he was, 'Gorgeous.' I narrowed my eyes at the distant station, hoping there wouldn't be too many good-looking men there.

But as my eyes searched, I noticed that someone outside the station was watching me. Instantly I knew it was him. I knew it was *him*.

I did not physically stumble, but I felt as if I had. In an instant everything had changed. I know it sounds absurd but I promise it's the truth.

I could have stopped. As early as then I knew I ought to turn back and erase the future, but I continued putting one foot in front of the other, until I was next to him.

His first words to me were, 'I saw you from miles away. Straight away I knew it was you.' He picked up a strand of my hair.

'I knew it was you too.'

While throngs of people hurtled in and out of the station like characters in a speeded-up movie, Anton and I remained motionless as statues, his eyes on mine, his hands on my arms, completing the magic circle.

We went to one of the nearby pretty pubs, where he settled me on a bench and enquired, 'Drink?' His soft, melodious accent conjured up sea breezes and heather-drenched air.

'Aqua Libra,' I answered, afraid to order alcohol because the mix was already too incendiary. He leaned on the bar counter, chatting with the barman, and, in dreadful confusion, I catalogued what I could see. He was all lanky angles and so thin the bum on his jeans bagged; his shirt was a brightly coloured statement, not quite a full-on Hawaiian, but dangerously close. *A geek.* That was how Cody had once described him . . . But his black hair looked slippery silky, he had a beautiful smile and, really, whatever was going on here had little to do with his appearance.

He returned with the drinks and leaned into me, twinkly-eyed with pleasure. He was going to say something nice, I knew it, so I asked several questions, each one more inane than the last. How did he like London? Was his flat near the tube station? Solemnly, he answered them all.

But the real questions were being asked of myself. I analysed Anton's face, wondering, What is it about him that has me feeling this way?

I wondered if it was because he seemed to be the most alive person I had ever met. His eyes sparkled and with every smile or laugh or frown the contents of his head were displayed on his expressive face.

But there was one topic that we had not touched on and the longer we chatted the more its absence took on a presence. In the end I lobbed it in, like a conversational hand grenade. 'How's Gemma?'

I couldn't not ask. She was the catalyst for our meeting and I could not pretend otherwise.

Anton looked at the floor, then up again. 'She's doing OK.' His eyes were apologetic. 'I'm not worth it. I keep telling her.'

I nodded, took another mouthful of my drink, then my head went light and urgent nausea rose in me. On jelly legs I made it to the Ladies, clattered the stall door closed behind me, and retched and retched, until there was nothing but bile left to sick up. I emerged, still wobbly, ran cold water over my wrists and asked my reflection, *What the hell's happening?*

Quite simply, falling in love with Anton had made me sick. All I could think of was Gemma. I loved Gemma; Gemma loved Anton.

I walked back over to him and said, 'I must go home now.'

'I know.' He understood.

He saw me to my door and said, 'I'll ring you tomorrow,' then touched the tips of his fingers to mine.

'Bye.' I ran upstairs to the sanctuary of my flat, but once in, I felt no better. Love at first sight was never meant to be like this. Instead of my entire life simply clicking into place, rendering me joyously whole, I had been knocked entirely off beam.

Even without Gemma, the situation was pretty confusing. But with Gemma . . .

I lay on my couch, therapy-style, and deliberately set about wrapping my heart in resistance. I would not meet him again. It was quite the best way and, once the decision was made, I felt better. Bereft but better.

I had just about calmed myself enough to start concentrating on a film on television when the phone rang. I regarded it fearfully, as I would a ticking bomb. Was it him? Probably. The machine clicked in and Gemma spoke. 'Just calling for a progress report. Please, please ring me the minute you get in. I'm going out of my *mind* here.'

I picked up. How could I not? 'It's me.'

'God, you're home early. Did he talk about me? What did he say?'

'That you're too good for him.'

'Hah! I'll be the judge of that. When are you meeting up again?'

'I don't know. Gemma, isn't this all a bit daft, me spying on him . . .'

'No, it's not. You must meet him! I need to know what he's up to. Promise me you will.'

Silence.

'Promise?'

'OK. I promise.' I was glad to.

I despised myself.

197

True to his word, Anton rang me and the first thing he said was, 'When can I see you again?'

I tried to stay away from him. Goodness knows I tried. But meeting him had shifted my centre of gravity and any element of choice had been removed.

We endured almost six weeks, forty anguished days, saying goodbye to each other, opting for loneliness and honour instead of the guilt of togetherness. Sincerely, I meant every farewell but sooner or later the constant craving forced me to pick up the phone and whisper to him to come over.

The first time I slept with Anton it was almost beyond description. I could feel the emotion flooding from me to him and from him to me, becoming part of each other. It felt like a lot more than sex, it was almost like a mystic experience.

On three occasions we decided to brazen it out and go to Dublin to tell Gemma, but twice I chickened out.

It was impossible. I was prepared to live without Anton rather than destroy Gemma.

'It doesn't matter what you do,' Anton said sadly. 'I'll still never love Gemma.'

'I don't care! Go away.'

But after a few hours of Anton's absence my resolve fell apart and the day eventually came when we got on the plane.

I cannot think about what followed. Not even now. But I will never forget the last thing Gemma said to me. 'What goes around comes around and remember how you met him because that's how you'll lose him.'

Back in the present the phone rang. It was a man from the *Daily Echo's* picture desk, following up on Martha Hope Jones's interview. He wanted to send a courier to collect the photographs of my injuries after I had been 'left for dead'.

'I wasn't left for dead.'

'Dead, injured, whatever. We need those pics.'

'But I don't have any.'

'That puts us in rather a pickle.' He hung up on me.

Though the area I lived in was less than salubrious, I had never expected to be mugged. It was cold and dark and I was keen to get home. Not just to see Anton, who had moved into my hovel six months previously, the day we had returned from the unspeakable visit to Gemma, but because I was three months pregnant and desperate for the loo. Like everything else about Anton and me, the pregnancy had not been planned. We were horribly poor, and we had no idea how we would afford a baby. But it did not seem to matter. I had never been so happy. Or so ashamed.

My need for the loo became more urgent so I speeded up, then, to my surprise, my shoulder was wrenched backwards; someone had caught the strap of my bag and had given it a violent tug. Idiotically, as I turned round, I had a smile prepared because I thought it would be someone I knew, who was being a little rougher than appropriate.

But I did not recognise the young man at my shoulder. He was tubby, with a pasty, sweating face. My eyes were locked onto Doughboy's curranty ones and without a word being uttered, I was giving him my bag.

He took it, stuffed it inside his jacket, then—with the air of a grand finale—shoved me to the ground and ran off.

Feeling dazed and foolish, I clambered to my feet. As I did so I met Irina marching towards me. She was my upstairs neighbour and although we sometimes nodded in the hall, we had never really spoken. All I knew about her was that she was tall, good-looking and Russian.

She stopped and looked at me enquiringly, as I swayed about the pavement.

'I've just been mugged.'

'Mugged?'

'He went that way.' But Doughboy had disappeared.

'Vos there money?'

'A few quid. Two or three.'

'So little? Thanks God.'

She was not exactly tea and sympathy, but she delivered me safely to Anton. However, nothing he said or did could comfort me. I knew what was about to happen: I was going to miscarry. This was divine retribution. Punishment for my wickedness in stealing Anton from Gemma.

Anton insisted on calling the doctor, who did his best to assure me that the chances of me miscarrying my baby were tiny.

'But I'm a bad person.'

'It doesn't work like that.'

The doctor was right and I did not miscarry, but a few days after the mugging, I began a slide into a terrible place. Little by little my vision darkened until all I saw was the bloodiness of human beings and our woeful flaws. We ruin everything we touch.

It was the trauma of being mugged that had triggered such hopelessness, Anton said; I needed to see the doctor again. I disagreed: it was my own wickedness that had reduced me to this wretched state. Anton kept repeating, 'You are not wicked. I didn't love Gemma, I love you.'

That was my very point. Why could he not have loved Gemma? Why must it be so complicated?

I had almost no one to talk to. Since Anton and I had taken the hideous step of going to Dublin and telling Gemma about us, all the Irish girls I knew in London—Gemma's and my mutual friends—had severed contact abruptly.

Anton was out at work all day with Mikey: taking TV executives to lunch and hustling for cash, taking literary agents to lunch and hustling for cheap scripts, and taking theatrical agents to lunch and hustling for actors to play the parts in the cheap scripts, which he had not yet acquired and which he had no financing for.

'No one wants to be the first to commit. If someone else has, they think it's got to be good,' Anton said.

Despite Anton and Mikey's spinning it was taking time for even one of their projects to go into production.

'It'll all come together soon,' Anton promised, when he returned home each evening.

Meanwhile I spent hour after hour on my own, and one day, when the loneliness became too much, I turned on my computer, looking for solace in my book. For almost five years I had been working on a novel, tentatively entitled *Crystal Clear*. It went as follows: chemical company is poisoning the air of a small community, PR girl (a prettier, feistier, thick-haired version of me, of course) sticks her neck out, blows the whistle, tips off the townsfolk and does all the courageous stuff.

Over the preceding four years, I had sent it to several literary agents, three of whom had read it and suggested changes. But even after I had rewritten and redrafted it to their requirements, they still said that it was 'not right for them at this time'.

Notwithstanding, I had retained a nugget of hope that *Crystal Clear* was not utter dross and continued to tinker with it from time to time. But this particular day I simply could not write about babies born with fingers missing and family men succumbing to lung cancer. However, I did not switch my computer off immediately. I loitered, still desperately seeking something. I typed 'Lily Wright', then 'Anton Carolan' and 'Baby Carolan', then the legend, 'And they all lived happily ever after.'

Those words infused me with such unexpected well-being that I typed them again. After I had done it for the fifth time I straightened up my chair, sat four-square to the desk and held my splayed fingers above the keyboard like a virtuoso pianist.

I was going to write a story where everyone lived happily ever after, in a fictional world where good things happened and people were kind. This vision of hope was not just for me. Much more importantly it was for my baby. I could not bring this little human being into the world, burdened with my desolation. This new life needed hope.

That night when Anton came home from a hard day not making films, he was so relieved to find me bright-eyed and enthusiastic that he happily sat and listened to what I had written. And every night thereafter, I read to him what I had written that day. It took almost eight weeks from start to finish and on the ultimate date, when Mimi had remedied all the woes in the village and had to leave, Anton wiped away a tear, then whooped with joy. 'It's fantastic! I love it! It's going to be a best seller.'

'You like everything about me, you're not what one might call impartial.'

'I know. But I swear to God, I think it's superb.'

I shrugged. I was already feeling sad because I had finished it.

'Get Irina to read it,' he said. 'She knows about books.'

Irina and I had become friends after the mugging and I had been upstairs to her flat a few times. I'd discovered that her bookshelves were full of Russian literature; books by Gogol, Dostoyevsky and Tolstoy.

I climbed the stairs, knocked on Irina's door and said, 'I've written a book. I was wondering if you would read it and give me your opinion.'

She did none of that leaping about and yelping that most people do. *You've written a BOOK. How amazing!* She simply nodded, stuck out her hand for the pages and said, 'I vill read.'

'Just one thing, please be honest. Don't be nice to spare my feelings.'

She looked at me in astonishment and I turned away, wondering what kind of humiliation I was letting myself in for. And how long I would have to wait for it.

But the following morning, to my surprise, she showed up. She gave me the bundle of pages. 'I read it.'

'Well?' My heart thudded and my mouth was cottony.

'I like,' she pronounced. 'A fairy tale vhere the vorld is good. Is not true,' she sighed ruminatively, 'but I like.'

'Well, if Irina likes,' Anton said gleefully, 'I think we're onto something.'

I needed an agent, Anton had said. Apparently, I could not send *Mimi's Remedies* directly to publishing houses because they did not look at unsolicited work. He got in touch with his contacts ('This game is all about contacts, baby.'). And that is how Anton and I found ourselves in Jojo Harvey's office in Soho, a fortnight before I was due to give birth.

Lipman Haigh Literary Agency was a big, busy place that inspired excitement, and the best part of all was Jojo Harvey. She was full of energy and absolutely stunning. She welcomed us like long-lost friends and immediately, both Anton and I developed a crush on her.

She said how much she loved *Mimi's Remedies*, how all the people in the office had loved it—I glowed—until she stopped and said, 'Here's the deal. I'm going to be honest with you. It's going to be tricky to sell because it feels like a children's book, but it's got adult subject matter. So it's hard to categorise and publishers don't like that.'

She looked at our woebegone expressions and smiled. 'Hey, cheer up. It's definitely got something and I'll be in touch.'

But then came October the 4th and everything changed for ever. Priorities were immediately realigned; everything slipped down the list a place because at Number One, in with a bullet, was Ema.

I had never loved anyone the way I loved her and no one had ever loved me as much as she did; not even my own mother. My voice could stop her crying and her eyes sought my face, even before she could see properly.

Everyone thinks their baby is the most gorgeous who ever lived, but Ema really was a beauty. The person she looked most like was Anton's mother, Zaga. As a nod to that, although we wanted to call her Emma, we decided to spell it the Yugoslavian way. She was olive-skinned, with a head of silky dark hair. There was no trace of fair, blue-eyed me in her.

She was a big smiler, sometimes she giggled in her sleep, and she was the squeeziest creature ever. She smelt adorable, she felt adorable, she looked adorable and she sounded adorable.

That was the plus side.

On the minus . . . I could not recover from the shock of being a mother. To be entirely responsible for this tiny powerful bundle of life scared me to death and I had never worked so hard or relentlessly. What I found most difficult was that there was no time off. Ever. Anton, at least, had a job in the outside world and got to leave the flat each day but for me, being a parent was twenty-four-seven.

Somewhere in among the blur of twenty-four-hour days, sleepless nights, cracked nipples and colicky screaming, news managed to get through: Jojo had sold *Mimi's Remedies* to a big publishing house called Dalkin Emery! It was a two-book deal and they had offered an advance of £4,000 a book. I was out of my mind with the thrill of having got a publisher; at least I was as soon as I could summon up the energy. And £4,000 was an enormous sum of money, but it was not the life-changing amount that we had hoped for. It looked as if we were destined to remain poor, especially as Eye-Kon's game show, *Last Man Standing*, had made almost no profit and most definitely had not generated a stampede of TV executives to shower Anton and Mikey with cash.

A visit to Dalkin Emery to meet my editor Tania Teal followed. She was in her early thirties and brisk but pleasant. She said they would publish *Mimi's Remedies* the following January.

'Not until then?' That was a year away.

'January's a good time for debut books,' she said. 'Not much else is being published so your lovely book has a better chance of getting noticed.'

'I see. Thank you.'

For a long, long time, nothing happened. At some stage I got sent a print of the jacket, then a proof copy to look for mistakes, of which there was a disturbingly huge number. During this time I ought to have been working on my second book. I certainly made a few stabs at starting, but I was always so tired. Anton tried to be encouraging but as he was nearly as exhausted as I was, he too ran out of steam.

The day came when the finished copies were delivered and I was moved to tears. To hold a novel, with *my* name on the cover, was overwhelming. All those words, words that I'd written *all by myself*, gathered and printed by someone other than me, convulsed me with pride and wonder. Obviously nothing like as intense as having Ema, but a definite second. Publication day was the 5th of January and when I woke up that morning (the fourth time since I had gone to bed) I felt like a child on her birthday. Perhaps slightly over-expectant; teetering on that narrow wire where high-octane good spirits could topple over into tantrumy disappointment at a moment's notice.

Anton greeted me with a cup of coffee and, 'Good morning, published author.'

I got dressed and he kept up a commentary of, 'Excuse me, Lily Wright, but what's your profession?'

'Author!'

'Are you *the* Lily Wright?'

'Lily Wright the author? That's me.'

Then we both bounced giddily on the bed.

Ema picked up on the fizzy atmosphere and gave a long incoherent speech, then slapped her plump knees and shrieked with laughter.

'Enter Ema with news from the front,' Anton said. 'Let's saddle her up, Lily, we're going to visit your other baby.'

I unfolded the buggy for the ceremonial walk to our nearest bookshop, which happened to be in Hampstead.

'We're going to visit Mum's book,' Anton told Ema.

We were on top form. It was a cold sunny morning and we walked with a sense of purpose. I was about to see my first novel on sale, what an experience!

I entered the bookshop with my neck so stretched I felt like a goose and on my face was a happy smile. So where was it?

There were no copies on the display at the front and I swallowed away the pang. Tania had gently explained to me that mine was a 'small' book and therefore would not have big, front-of-shop displays. Nevertheless, I had still hoped . . .

But nor was *Mimi's Remedies* to be found on the New Releases shelf. Or on any Recent Publications tables. Increasing speed a notch, I left Anton and the buggy and moved through the shop, searching and seeking. Though there were thousands of other books I knew I would instantly see mine in among them. If it were there.

When I found myself in the Psychology Department, I stopped abruptly and hurried to find Anton. I met him at the information desk.

'Did you find it?' he asked quickly.

I shook my head.

'Me neither. Don't worry, I'll ask.' Anton nodded at the saturnine youth staring at the computer and endeavouring to ignore us. 'Sorry to cut in on you there but I'm looking for a book.'

'You've come to the right place,' the youth said flatly, indicating the oceans of books on the shop floor.

'Aye, but the one I'm looking for is called *Mimi's Remedies.*'

A few keys were pressed halfheartedly, then the boy said, 'We're not getting it in.'

'Why not?'

'Store policy.'

'But it's brilliant,' Anton said. 'She'— he pointed at me—'wrote it.'

I nodded over-brightly, yes, I had indeed written it.

But far from being impressed, the boy repeated, 'We don't stock it. Talk to your publisher.'

It was a matter of some pride to me that I waited until I was outside the shop before I wept.

'Fucker,' Anton said, his face red with humiliation, as we tramped angrily towards home.

'Fucker,' Ema piped up from her buggy.

Anton and I turned to each other, our faces briefly alight. Her first real word!

'That's right,' I sang, crouching down to her. 'You said it, babe.'

It took about twenty minutes to reach home and I was still shaking when I dialled Tania's private line.

'Can I speak to Tania?'

'Who's calling?'

'Lily Wright.'

'And what's it in connection with?'

'Oh.' Surprised. 'My book.'

'Which is called?'

'*Mimi's Remedies.*'

Two seconds later Tania came on the line. 'Sorry about my assistant. She's a temp. How are you, love?'

Haltingly, not wanting to seem like I was being critical, I relayed what had happened in the bookshop.

Tania cooed and soothed. 'I'm sorry, Lily, I really am. I love *Mimi's Remedies*. But, to put it into context, your print run is five thousand copies. Someone like John Grisham has an initial print run of about half a million copies. Trust me, Lily, your lovely book is out there, but perhaps not in every store.'

I relayed what she had said to Anton. 'This isn't good enough. What about publicity? What about interviews and signing sessions?'

'There won't be any,' I said flatly. 'Forget it, Anton, it's not going to happen. Let's just move on.'

By the end of January it was all over; a total non-event. Basically nothing happened and after the tensest month of my life I realised that nothing would. I was a published author, and aside from a tiny, blink-and-you'd-miss-it review in the *Irish Times* it meant nothing. My life was exactly as it had been and now I had to get used to it.

I remained flattened by anticlimax and when my dad rang a few days later, I found it hard to be animated. Not that it mattered, he had enough animation for ten people.

'Lily, love!' he exclaimed. 'Got some good news for you. A friend of Debs, Shirley—you know her, tall skinny bird—read your *Mimi's Remedies* book and thought it was genius.' His voice dropped low with emphasis. '*Didn't even know you were my daughter*, never made the connection. Her book club is going to read it and when she found out I'm your dad, she went a bit mental, know what I'm saying? She wants signed copies.'

'Well, er, great, Dad. Thank you.' Isolated incident though this was, it cheered me a little.

He picked up on my tone. 'Cheer up now, girl,' he said gleefully. 'This is only the beginning.'

I had once read a newspaper article that described the actor Bob Hoskins as 'a testicle on legs' and that struck a chord: Dad was a little like that. He was short, barrel-chested and swaggery, a working-class boy made good. Then bad. Then, eventually, good again.

My mum—a 'beauty'—had married beneath her. Those were her exact (if jokey) words. She had hooked up with Dad because he had said to her, 'Stick with me, doll. We're going places.' Those were *his* exact words, and he was true to his promise. They went from modest

Hounslow West to detached Guildford splendour to a two-bedroomed flat over a kebab shop in Kentish Town.

(All this has left me with an aversion to house-moving. If the roof fell in on top of me, I would prefer to do a repair job with black bags and masking tape than move.)

Then one Monday morning in early February, Tania phoned. 'There's a fantastic review of *Mimi's Remedies* in this week's *Flash!*.'

'What's *Flash!*?' Anton asked. He hadn't left for work yet.

'A kind of celeb magazine.'

'I'll get it!' He was already halfway down the stairs.

SCREAMING MIMI'S
Mimi's Remedies by Lily Wright. Dalkin Emery 298pp £6.99

Jonesin'? Bum too big? Tattoo gone septic? Then Dr Flash! recommends that you sling on your Jimmy Choos, get down to your nearest bookstore and treat yourself to *Mimi's Remedies*. We know you girls are too busy out caning it to have time to read books but this one's worth it, honest, guv'nor. Witty, cheery and sweet as Kylie, it'll have you rolling in the aisles.

This book is as yummy as an entire bucket of Miniature Heroes—without any of the guilt. Go, girl! *Flash!* Promise: You'll laugh out loud or I'll eat my Philip Treacy.

'They've given you four and a half stilettos,' Anton read, in wonder. 'The maximum number you can get is five. This is a *fantastic* review.'

Then Jojo phoned. 'Great news!' she said. 'Dalkin Emery are reprinting *Mimi's Remedies*.'

'What does that mean?'

'The first print run's sold out and they expect to sell more.'

'But that's good, isn't it?' I stammered.

'Yeah, it's real good.'

I rang Anton and relayed the news.

'Is it just me?' he croaked. 'Or is something happening here?'

About a week later Jojo phoned again.

'You're not gonna believe this!'

'I'm not?'

'They're reprinting.'

'I know, you told me.'

'No! They're reprinting *again*. Twenty thousand copies. Your first print run was five, the second, ten. You're selling on word of mouth.'

'But, Jojo, why? What's going on?'

'The book has struck a chord. You should see your site on Amazon, your sincerity and lack of cynicism is totally touching people.'

I got Anton to help me look up *Mimi's Remedies* on Amazon. There were seventeen reviews and they had all given four or five stars, which was lovely considering that the highest score possible was five stars. I scrolled through phrases like, 'The comfort of childhood . . . magical . . . enchanting . . . transported me to another world . . . the recovery of lost innocence . . . the absence of cynicism . . . hopeful and uplifting . . . it made me laugh . . .'

I was quite stunned. So much so I thought I might cry with pride and happiness. Who were these lovely people? Would I get to meet them? Suddenly I felt as if I had lots and lots of friends.

Just over another week later, news of the third reprint followed, for the staggering figure of 50,000 copies. Then Tania Teal phoned me and asked, 'Are you sitting down?'

'No.'

'OK. Get this. You, Lily Wright, author of *Mimi's Remedies* are number four in this week's *Sunday Times* best-seller list.'

'How?'

'Because you sold eighteen thousand, one hundred and twelve copies of *Mimi's Remedies* last week.'

'I did?'

'You did. Congratulations, Lily, you're a star! We're all so proud of you.'

Later that day Dalkin Emery sent flowers. A small mention in the *Daily Mail* described me as a 'phenomenon'. Far from not being stocked by the bookshop in Hampstead, I now had a stand by the front door and a display in their window. They asked me to come and sign copies and Anton urged me to tell them to fuck right off. But, graciously, I decided to forgive them. I wasn't bitter. Joy and happiness abounded.

And then the *Observer* reviewed my book.

The Observer, Sunday, 5 March
SWEET AND SOUR
Mimi's Remedies by Lily Wright. Dalkin Emery 298pp £6.99

Mimi's Remedies *is sweet enough to turn Alison Janssen sour*

Reviewing books for a living, I'm the envy of my friends but next time they start complaining about what an easy life I have, I shall give them *Mimi's Remedies* and insist they read it right to the very end. That ought to subdue them.

If I say that *Mimi's Remedies* is the worst book I've ever read, I'm probably exaggerating, but you get the idea. The attached material from the publishers describes it as a 'fable'—messaging ahead not to expect realism, three-dimensional characters and believable dialogue.

And, by golly, they're right. It appears to be a cack-handed stab at magic realism without being either magical or realistic. Frankly, I spent the first 100 pages waiting for the punch line.

And so will you when you hear what passes for a plot: mysterious, beautiful 'lady' appears out of the blue in a small village that manifests every version of textbook human dysfunction. A sundered father and son, an unfaithful husband, a young frustrated wife—so far, so *Chocolat*. But, instead of confectionery, Mimi makes spells and even shares the recipes with us—many of which include the emetic instruction, 'Add a sprinkle of compassion, a tablespoon of love and stir with kindness.'

If this is the remedy, I'll take the problem.

The author, one Lily Wright, is an ex-PR girl, so she knows all there is to know about cynical manipulation. And it shows, in every single cloying word. The 'plot' is peppered with coy references to miracles, but the only real miracle is how this candy dross ever got published. It is sweet enough to rot the readers' teeth, yet as unpleasant as sucking a lemon.

Mimi's Remedies is lazy, contrived and verges on the unreadable. So the next time you complain about your job, spare a thought for this wretched book reviewer . . .

It was one of the worst things that had ever happened to me. After reading it my ears began to hum as though I were about to faint, then I sprinted to the loo and sicked up my breakfast. (Perhaps by now it's clear that I am the feeble type who becomes ill after most upsets.)

Jojo rang to cheer me up. 'It's the price of success. She's just jealous. I betcha she's got some shitty novel that no one's gonna touch, so she's pissed with you cos you got published.'

'Do they do that?' I had always thought of reviewers as noble, detached creatures, disinterested and above petty human concerns.

'Sure. All the time.'

The following Sunday, the *Independent* reviewed me: it was just as savage as the *Observer* piece. Otalie, the publicist from Dalkin Emery, rang to offer words of comfort: 'Tomorrow's dog-basket lining.'

I took little consolation in this. So now even the dogs would know how abominable my book was.

An interview with the *Daily Leader* followed; it was quite a positive piece except they said that I had not provided biscuits.

The net result was that I was afraid to open a newspaper.

Then came word of the 'At Home' with Martha Hope Jones. It was an enormous coup and Otalie was beside herself. 'You've arrived, Lily!'

Anton was sent to the shops to buy the best biscuits in the land. The piece had still to run so we were on tenterhooks waiting to see whether Martha would mention them or not.

Amid the bad reviews the book surprised me by continuing to sell. 'The critics may not love you,' Otalie said. 'But your readers do.'

I got the occasional good review. For example, *Loaded* described the book as 'The most fun you can have with your clothes on.' And the press remained interested. But the odd thing was that the good reviews made little impact on me. I could quote the unkind ones verbatim, but I distrusted the good ones.

I opened my eyes and foreboding weighed me down.

Lying beside me Anton said, 'Something awful's happening today, isn't it?'

I sighed. 'The Martha Hope Jones piece is out.'

'I'll go.' Anton pulled on clothes and bounded out of the door.

While he was gone, I automatically went about dressing Ema, while I prayed, *Please let it be nice, oh please let it be nice.*

Then Anton was home again, a rolled newspaper under his arm.

'Well?' I asked anxiously.

'I haven't looked.'

We spread the paper on the floor and flicked over the pages with trembling fingers.

And there it was. Spread across two pages, the headline read 'Wright and Wrong'. Which made a change from 'Lily Wrights her way to Success' and 'Wright On!' What other atrocious puns could they come up with?

At least my photo looked nice; for once I looked intelligent instead of dippy. But underneath Martha's mugshot was a horrible picture of a black and blue shoulder. The caption said, 'Lily's bruises were similar.'

Oh dear.

I began to speed-skim.

Lily Wright is riding high in the best-seller charts with her 'novel' *Mimi's Remedies*. But don't make the mistake of thinking this was laboured over with meticulous care. 'It only took me eight weeks to knock it off,' Lily gloated. 'Most books take five years and even then they don't get published.'

It was like being splashed in the face with iced water.

'I didn't gloat,' I whispered. 'And what does she mean by "novel"? It's a novel, not a "novel".'

Lily's book has been described as 'sickly sweet', but not so its creator. Displaying an arrogant disregard for the opinions of others, Lily said, 'I don't care what the critics say.'

My eyes were drawn once more to my photo: I no longer looked intelligent. I looked calculating.

She went on to quote me: 'Welcome to my humble abode.'

Well, one of us had to say it!

She made reference to the laundry drying in the kitchen . . .

Wright cares not a jot for beauty or hygiene in the home.

The square of Lego . . .

When one is invited to sit down, is it foolhardy to expect that one's hostess has removed all sharp objects from the seat?

My single status . . .

Though Wright has a little girl, she has no interest in legitimising her. And what kind of mother sends her child out to play in subzero temperatures?

It was HORRIBLE.

She quoted the worst parts of the *Observer* and *Independent* reviews just in case one or two people might have missed them the first time round. Then told the story of my mugging. The final paragraph read:

The trauma wrought by her attack still lingers. Though Wright is laughing all the way to the bank, she chooses to remain living in a grubby, one-roomed flat, which, frankly, looks little better than a squat. Is this all she thinks she deserves? And if so, perhaps she's correct . . .

'Which bank am I laughing all the way to?' I asked. 'Apart from my advance I haven't seen a penny. And which am I? Arrogant? Or beset with low self-esteem? And it's not a one-roomed flat. It's a one-*bed*roomed flat.'

For once Anton was clean out of optimism. There was nothing good to be said about this. Nothing at all.

'Ought we to sue?' I asked him.

'I don't know,' he said thoughtfully. 'It's your word against hers, and a lot of what she's said is just her opinion and people can't be sued for that.'

'I'll ring Jojo.' But her machine picked up.

Anton and I simply looked at one other—we were utterly without the emotional equipment to deal with this. Even Ema was unusually quiet.

We remained in silence until Anton said, 'Right, I've an idea.'

He spread the two horrible pages in the middle of the living-room floor and extended his hand to me. 'Up you get.'

'What?'

He was searching through his CDs. 'Let's see. Sex Pistols? Ah, no, this is the one.'

He put on some flamenco music.

Perplexed, I watched him strutting, stamping and arching his arms above his head, as he danced his way onto the article. Ema, relieved that the dreadful atmosphere seemed to have lifted, shrieked and galloped around him. The music sped up and so did Anton, stamping and clapping with great panache until the song ended and he tossed his head back with a flourish. 'Olé!'

'Lay!' Ema yelled, also tossing her head and falling over.

The next song began. 'Come on,' Anton said.

I tried one stamp and liked it, so tried another, then really got into it. I concentrated my stamping on Martha's face, until Anton toed my foot aside. 'Give me a go. Right, Ema, your turn.'

Ema galloped on the spot above Martha's picture. 'Good girlie,' Anton encouraged, 'give her a fine pounding there.'

The three of us stamped and banged until the horrible words and Martha's ugly mug were smeared with print. The grand finale was when Anton held up the page like a matador's blanket and I put my foot through it with a 'Da-dah!'

'Feel better?'

'A little.'

Not terribly, but it was worth a try.

'Will you do something for me?' Anton asked.

'Anything,' I said. Foolishly.

'There's a house for sale in Grantham Road. Will you and Ema come to see it with me?'

After a pause I said, 'What's the asking price?'

'Four hundred and seventy-five thousand.'

'Why do you want to view a house that we will never be able to afford?'

'I see it every day on the way to the tube and I'm curious about it. It's like a fairy-tale house.'

'Why are they selling?'

'It belonged to an old man who died. His family don't want it.'

I had a sudden hard place in my stomach. Anton had researched this without telling me.

'It can't hurt to look,' he said.

I so did not agree. But Anton asked so little from me, how could I refuse him?

'This is it,' Anton said, standing before a detached, sturdy redbrick with a pointy Gothic roof. It was like a miniature castle and looked neither too big nor too small. Just right.

'Victorian,' Anton said, pushing open a waist-high gate and extending a hand. Ema and I followed him up a short tinder path to a tiled porch with a pitched roof. The heavy blue front door was opened immediately by a young suited-and-booted bloke. Greg, the estate agent.

I stepped over the threshold into the hall, the door closed behind me and I was infused with calm. The stained-glass fan window above the front door threw coloured patterns onto the wooden floor and all was peaceful and golden.

Our feet echoed on the wooden floors as we followed Greg into a room that stretched the entire depth of the house. At the front was a pretty bay window and at the back, French windows leading to the garden, which looked crammed with old-fashioned hollyhock-style foliage. A fireplace, patterned with William Morris-style ceramic tiles stood tall by the right wall.

'Original,' Greg said, knocking his knuckles on it.

On the other side of the hall was a cosy little square room, also with a bay window and fireplace.

'This could be your writing room,' Anton said. 'Lily's a writer,' he told Greg. 'Lily Wright.'

'Oh?' he said politely, my name clearly meaning nothing to him.

'I could put my desk here,' I said, stroking the wall. A piece of plaster crumbled into my hand.

'Obviously, the house needs a bit of work,' Greg said. 'Ought to be fun pulling it all together.'

'Yes.' And my assent was sincere.

Then the kitchen, which was a gloomy hidey-hole. 'We could knock through,' I murmured, seizing on the phrase.

Greg led us to the stairs and as I bent down to carry Ema I noticed pinprick holes in the floorboards. Woodworm. How . . . how . . . authentic. It would be impossible ever to be unhappy in this house.

The three bedrooms were each more delightful than the previous. Visions of iron bedsteads, embroidered quilts, rocking chairs and voile curtains billowing in the gentle breeze entranced me.

I took a brief look at the poky antediluvian bathroom and murmured once again about knocking through.

Then Greg took us downstairs for the property highlight: the charmingly overgrown garden.

'Blackcurrant bushes. Raspberry vines,' Greg indicated. 'An apple tree. In the summer you'll have fruit.'

I saw myself sitting in this garden, writing in a pretty notebook, a basket of freshly picked raspberries by my side. In the sunlight my hair was blonde and ripply, as if my highlights had just been done.

Clearest of all was my vision of Ema playing with other children—her brothers and sisters perhaps? For some reason they all had ringlets.

At that moment I wanted the house so badly. I had never before desired something so intensely. I would die without this house. But there was no need for such melodrama because it was my house already. I simply needed to find half a million pounds from somewhere.

I barely remember the walk home, but when I found myself once again in my poky little flat I rounded on Anton. 'Why did you show it to me? We could never afford it.'

'Listen to me a minute.' Anton was scribbling calculations on a paper bag. 'You've sold almost two hundred thousand copies, so you should get roughly one hundred thousand pounds in royalties.'

'I keep telling you, my first tranche of royalties won't be paid until the end of September and that's nearly five months away. The house will be gone by then.'

'We can borrow against future income.'

'Can we? Anton, the house is half a million *and* we'd need knocking-through money.'

'Think of the future,' he urged, his eyes shining. 'At some stage Eye-Kon is going to start turning a profit.'

I remained silent because I did not want to seem unsupportive.

'But much more importantly,' Anton said, 'you have a two-book deal.'

'Yes, but I've written only two chapters of my second one.'

'What about *Crystal Clear*?' It was obvious that Anton had been giving this some thought. 'That's finished. Offer that to them.'

It was strange because the next day, Tania called. She wanted to see my new book. 'To bring out a hardback to catch the Christmas market.'

I had to make the dreadful admission. 'Tania, there is no new book.'

'Excuse me?'

'What with the baby and the tiredness and everything, I just couldn't manage it. I've only done two chapters.'

'I seeee.' Silence.

I mentioned *Crystal Clear*. 'I don't know if you will like it, I sent it to lots of agents—'

Tania cut in. 'Are you telling me you've got another book?'

'Yes.'

'Hallelujah. She's got another book,' she yelled. Someone whooped. 'I'll send a bike.'

213

Later that night, Tania called. 'I love it. Love, love, love it!'

'You've read it? That was fast.'

'I couldn't put it down. It's a different book to *Mimi's Remedies*, very different, but still has the Lily Wright magic. Roll on our Christmas best seller.'

Shortly after that, Jojo spoke to me about signing a new contract for my third and fourth books. 'For a much higher advance than the previous one, obviously.'

'See,' Anton said gleefully.

Jojo said we could sign now while my sales were buoyant, or we could wait until late autumn when, if my new hardback stormed the best-seller lists, my bargaining position would be even stronger.

'But what if my hardback doesn't storm the best-seller lists?'

'That's always a possibility, but it's your call.'

'Anton, what do you think?'

'I don't know why, but I think we should wait.'

'Really? Why don't you want the money immediately?'

He laughed. 'You know me so well. But I'm trying to change the habits of a lifetime. Trying to think long-term, you know. And long-term I think you're likely to get more money if you wait.'

I heard myself say, 'OK, then we'll wait.'

'Oh, poor Lily.' Anton pulled my face to his chest and stroked my hair.

'Careful,' I murmured. 'Don't rub it away.'

'Sorry. Anyway, c'mere, this might put a smile on your little face. You know how I told you our house costs four seven five? They've dropped the asking price! By fifty grand!'

'Why?'

'It's been on the market for nearly four months, they must be getting desperate.'

I made a noncommittal *hmmm.*

He leaned into me, conviction in his eyes. 'I think this house is exactly what we need. There's that lovely room that would be perfect for you to write in, we'd have space for a nanny and we'd never have to move again. OK, we don't have the money yet but *it's coming.* If we wait until all the money is sitting in our bank account, the house will be long gone.' He stopped for breath. 'Lily, let me ask you one thing: do you love this house?'

I nodded. As soon as I had walked in I fell head over heels in love and knew it was the one for me.

'I love it too. It's the perfect house—at a *great price.* We might never get this chance again.'

'Anton! We cannot offer to buy a house when we have no money in place.'

'Of course we can.'

'You're not going to believe it!' Anton cried. 'They've accepted our offer of four hundred grand.'

I felt the colour drain from my face. 'You've offered to buy a house and we've no money! What kind of idiot are you?'

He couldn't stop laughing. He fell onto my neck, giddy with glee. 'We'll get the money.'

'From where?'

'The bank.'

'Do you plan to rob one?'

'I agree with you that we're not standard mortgage application material. What we need is a bank with vision.'

He took to making phone calls, the type that necessitated turning away from me whenever I came into the room. When I asked, 'Who was that?' he would tap the side of his nose and wink.

I thought constantly about the house in a dreamy, lovesick way. In my head I had painted, decorated and furnished all the rooms and I rearranged the furniture constantly, as if it were a doll's house. I had a cream-painted, curvy, antique French bed, with a matching clawfooted armoire, carved trunks, rose borders, potbellied bedside cabinets, plump bolsters, satin eiderdowns, scatter rugs strewn across my shiny wooden floors . . .

I was feeding Ema her breakfast, a protracted, messy experience, which usually left the floor, walls and my hair splattered with clods of wet Weetabix, when Anton frisbeed a letter onto the table. 'Have a read of that.' He was grinning like a loon.

'Tell me.' I was afraid to believe, but what else could it be . . .

'The bank said yes, they'll loan us the money. The house is ours.'

This was my cue to launch myself into his arms and be twirled around the kitchen, both of us laughing our heads off. Instead I stared at him, almost in fear.

He was some sort of alchemist, he had to be. He had got me an agent, who had got me a publisher, he had 'found' my second book when I thought I had none, and now he had secured my dream house even though we had no money up-front.

'How do you do it?' I asked, faintly.

He polished an imaginary medal on his chest, then laughed at himself. 'Lily, take a bow. This is down to you about to bring in a ton of

215

money in September and more when you sign your new deal.'

'Oi!' I wrestled the letter back from Ema, who had been using the back of her spoon to carefully cover it with mushy Weetabix. As I read the typewritten page, joy began a cautious trickle. If the bank had said yes, then everything must be fine. Then I read a sentence that caused my plucky little trickle to make an emergency stop. I gasped.

So did Ema; her eyes were wide and alarmed, just like mine.

'Anton, it says the loan is "subject to survey". What does that mean?'

'Anton! Whazat *meen?*'

'They want to be sure the house is worth what they're lending us for it, just in case we default and they need to repossess.'

I winced. Talk of repossession froze my innards; it brought back the day we left the big house in Guildford.

Anton opened the letter. He read it in silence, but something sombre pervaded the room.

'What is it?'

'OK.' He cleared his throat. 'They've found dry rot in the front room. Quite bad, they say.'

I belly-flopped with disappointment and tears sprang to my eyes. Our beautiful, beautiful house. 'Well, that's that then.'

'It is not. Lily, don't fold on me, dry rot can be fixed! They'll still give us a mortgage, but for less. For three hundred and eighty.'

'Where will we find twenty thousand pounds?'

'We don't. We go back to the vendors and drop our offer by twenty grand.'

'But we still need to fix the dry rot! I repeat, where do we find twenty thousand pounds?'

'There's no way a little dry rot will cost twenty grand to fix. A couple of grand, at most.'

'But the bank said—'

'The bank are just covering themselves. What do you think?'

'OK,' I said. 'Do what you have to do.'

To my utter astonishment the vendors accepted the reduced price. Nevertheless, I got a final-furlong bout of the wobblies: when Anton said, 'Will we buy it?' I heard myself wail, 'No, I'm too frightened.'

'OK.'

'OK?' I looked at him, with suspicion. 'All right then. Talk me into it.'

'Er, right!' He listed out all the reasons we were meant to buy this house: we had royalty money coming in; my career was on fire and I was bound to get an enormous advance in November; we didn't just want *a* house, we loved this *particular* house, it was very us. And finally,

'If everything goes pear-shaped, we can sell the house and get back more than we paid.'

'What if its value drops instead of increasing and we end up owing heaps of money?'

'A house like that, in that area? We can't lose. Nothing can go wrong.'

Gemma

IT WAS EIGHTY DAYS since Dad had left. Or not even three months which, when I put it like that, didn't sound so bad. Not much was going on when suddenly four BIG things happened, one after the other.

The first thing—at the end of March the clocks went forward. No big deal, I know, but wait, that's not actually the thing, that was just the trigger. Anyway, the clocks went forward and the implications didn't hit me until Monday afternoon at work when Andrea put on her coat and said, 'Right, I'm off.' It was still bright so I said, 'It's the middle of the afternoon,' and she replied, 'It's twenty to six.'

Suddenly I got it and nearly choked with terror. The evenings were stretching towards summer; when he'd left it had been the dead of winter. Where had all the time gone?

I had to see him.

I jostled my way out of the office, into the car and drove straight over to his work. His car was in the car park, so he hadn't left for the day. I watched anxiously over my steering wheel as the staff trickled out . . . Oh Christ, here he comes. With Colette. *Shite.* I'd been hoping to catch him on his own.

He was in his suit and looked much as he'd always looked; he was as familiar to me as myself, it was too strange not to have seen him in so long. Colette's hair was still highlighted, it didn't seem like she was letting herself go, now that she'd bagged her man. But on the plus side she didn't look pregnant.

I got out of the car and stepped in front of both of them. It was meant to be kind of dramatic but they were walking quite fast and had almost passed me.

'Dad,' I called.

They turned; blank faces.

'Dad?'

'Gemma. Ah, hello.' He was uncomfortable. He turned to Colette, 'Will you wait in the car, love?'

'Love' gave me a filthy look but swung away towards the Nissan.

'Does she have to be *such* a bitch?' I asked.

'She's just insecure.'

'*She's* insecure. What about me? I haven't seen you in nearly three months.'

'Is it that long?' He shifted in a vague, old-man kind of way.

'Yes, Dad.' In a desperate attempt at humour I asked, 'Don't you want custody of me? You could have weekend visitation rights, take me to McDonald's.'

But he just said, 'You're grown up. It's probably for the best that we don't meet up at the moment.'

'But, Dad . . .' Grief rose like a wave and I began to cry. People walking past were looking but I didn't care. I was bawling and choking like a peanut had gone down the wrong way—and he wouldn't even touch me. I launched myself at him; he stood like a plank and patted me awkwardly. 'Ah, Gemma, ah, don't . . .'

With monumental effort, I forced myself to stop the choking, then cleared my throat, briefly getting it together. 'Dad, please come home. Please.'

'Noel, we have to collect the kids.' Colette.

I swung round to her. 'I thought he told you to wait in the car.'

'Noel, the kids.' She ignored me. 'They'll be wondering where we are.'

'You know what?' I looked at her and pointed at Dad. 'I'm *his* kid and I've been wondering the very same thing.'

She studied me, cool as anything. 'Two minutes,' she said to Dad. 'I'm counting.' She stomped back to the car.

'How's your mother?' Dad asked.

'Your *wife*,' I shouted the word round the car park. The few people who weren't already looking were now. 'Your *wife* is *great*. She has a boyfriend. A Swiss fella called Helmut. He has a red Aston Martin with gull-wing doors.'

'Has she, by the hokey? Listen, Gemma, I have to go now. Geri goes mad if we're late.'

Contempt was all that was left to me. I looked at my father. 'You're a coward.'

In the sanctuary of my car the tears started again. All men are cowards. And this wasn't going to be fixed any time soon; it killed me to admit it but Dad and Colette had started to look permanent. So where did that leave me? What about my life?

Mam was doing her best, she really was trying hard to be brave. She'd found a kind of routine, where she used a string of daytime soaps to get her through the day, like a rope bridge over an abyss. She'd started going to Mass again, she'd even gone to a couple of coffee mornings with Mrs Kelly, but she always came back shaking like jelly. It was still necessary for me to stay with her every night.

I thought of Owen, the youth I'd picked up the night of Cody's birthday (although I had no memory of it). He'd asked me out twice and the second time I'd said yes, but I couldn't name a day because I didn't know how to get it past Mam.

I'd promised to ring him but so far I hadn't.

Second thing—and probably least important of the four—I got a new account at work. The call came the next day—at ten past one, just as I was about to go out to lunch—from Lesley Lattimore, an Irish It girl: in other words she went to lots of parties and spent plenty of money, none of it earned by her. Her dad, Larry 'Wads' Lattimore, had made a fortune from dodgy property developing and fleecing Irish taxpayers, but no one seemed to care. Especially not Lesley.

'I want someone to organise my thirtieth birthday party and I heard you did Davinia Westport's wedding.'

'What kind of event were you thinking of?'

'Two hundred plus. A princess theme. Think Gothic Barbie,' she said, so I did and suddenly I *needed* this job. 'When can you come to see me?'

'Today. Now.'

I grabbed some files, which had photos of some of the more imaginative parties I'd done, and went along to Lesley's city-centre, river-view duplex. She had the super-groomed hair, the St Tropez tan, the clothes sheeny with newness, the all-over gloss that rich people have, like they've been dipped in lacquer.

'Why should I hire you?' she demanded, and I began to list the number of high-profile events I'd pulled together. Then I played my ace. 'I have a wand,' I said. 'A silver star, backed by lilac fluff.'

'So have I!' she cried. 'You're hired!'

She ran off and got it, then circled it solemnly over my head and said, 'I grant you the honour of organising Lesley's birthday party.'

Then she handed it to me. 'Say, "I grant you a castle with turrets."'

Reluctantly I took the wand.

'I grant you a castle with turrets,' I said.

'I grant you a medieval hall.'

'I grant you a medieval hall,' I repeated. I could see this becoming very wearing.

'I grant you a team of jousters.'

'I grant you a team of jousters.'

In between each 'grant' I had to circle the wand over her head and bring it down on each of her shoulders. The mortification was extreme, then she lost interest in the wand and I nearly cried with happiness. Especially as I was meant to be writing down her list of requirements.

And what a list! She wanted a silver empire-line 'gown' (her word) with pointy floor-length sleeves, a white ermine cape, a pointy princess hat and silver shoes (pointy, of course).

I wrote everything down, nodding, 'Uh-huh, good idea.' I didn't address any hard questions, like how the hell was anyone meant to dance to a band of lute minstrels. Now wasn't the time for me to start pulling holes in some of the more impractical parts of her vision. We were still in the warm glow of the honeymoon period and there was plenty of time for screaming matches in the coming weeks.

'And when do you want to have it?'

'The 31st of May.' Two months away. To do this properly I'd have preferred two *years*, but the Lesleys of this world would never be so obliging.

All the same, I went away already buzzing with ideas and everything suddenly seemed a lot easier. Bringing in new business always had a good effect. I was breathing free and clear and it was obvious that this coming Friday night would be perfect for my close encounter with Owen. I could pretend to Mam it was a work do, while being able to enjoy a leisurely hangover the following day. I was doing Mam no favours by lying, but I didn't care. After seeing the togetherness of Dad and Colette I had to try to change things.

Third big thing: my date with Owen.

I rang him and said, 'It's coal-scuttle Gemma. How about Friday night?'

'What time? Nine?'

I hesitated and he said, 'Ten?'

'No, I was thinking more of eight. It's just that for reasons I can't go into now, I don't get out very often at the moment so I need to wring as much enjoyment as I possibly can from the night.'

'We can make it seven, if that's how it is.'

'No, I won't be finished work in time. Now, where will we meet and please don't say Kehoes. You're a young man about town, you know the hot new places, let's go to them.'

'All of them?'

'Like I said, I don't get out very often.'

A thoughtful silence. 'We're only in Dublin, not Manhattan, there aren't that many hot new places.'

'I know, sorry.' I tried to explain. 'I want to go to one of those bars where I'm completely disorientated. I just want to feel I'm living a little, you know?'

'Then how about Crash? There are lots of mirrors and steps. People are always tripping and walking into themselves.'

Perfect. I'd been meaning to check it out for work anyway.

'Eight o'clock, Friday night in Crash. Don't be late,' I warned.

As I stumbled down the mirrored entrance steps of Crash and saw Owen, he wasn't as good-looking as I'd remembered when he'd been lying on my bedroom floor that horrible morning—he wasn't *bad*, just not the criminally young boy-band cutie that I'd remembered. But . . .

'I like your shirt,' I said. It was a picture of a Cadillac driving down a desert highway. Very cool. 'And I like your hair.' Shiny and sticky-up.

'Thanks,' he said, paused, then added, 'I put special stuff in, to make a good impression. Too much information?'

'No.'

'Can I get you a drink?'

'I'll have a glass of white wine now.' I arranged myself on the couch. 'But every second drink will be a mineral water and before I came out I had a glass of milk to line my stomach so I won't be making a show of myself tonight like I did that other time. Too much information?'

'Er, no.' He went to the bar and the back of his shirt showed the same desert highway, this time with the Cadillac driving away.

Then the Cadillac was zooming towards me again. 'Your drink.' He lifted his glass. 'Cheers. To Gemma's big night out.'

We clinked, sipped, replaced glasses on the table, then an awkward pause followed. 'So, how's the coal scuttle working out?' Owen asked.

But it was too late, I'd already pounced. 'Owen, that was an awkward pause and for reasons I can't go into right now, I haven't got time to waste on awkward pauses. We've got to fast-track this thing. I know this sounds mad but could we try to fast-forward through the first three months or so, and get to the comfortable staying-in-and-watching-videos stage?'

He was looking at me a little warily but, to my gratification, said, 'I've seen you without your make-up?'

'Yes, that's the idea. And we don't have sex every night any more.' Then I began to blush: an out-of-control-forest-fire-super-blush, as I realised that we hadn't had sex at all. Yet.

'Oh God.' I put my hands over my fiery cheeks. This wasn't me. 'I'm sorry. I'm not insane, just a bit . . . under pressure.'

There was a moment when the evening hovered on a knife-edge, then

Owen looked relieved at my apology and even began to laugh. 'Let the games begin,' he said. 'Tell me all about you, Gemma.'

Though it had been my idea, I felt embarrassed. 'I'm thirty-two, an only child, I'm an events organiser, which is very stressful but I don't always hate it, I live in Clonskeagh . . . what have I forgotten?'

'Car?'

'Toyota MR2. Yes, I thought you'd like that. Now your go.'

'Honda Civic coupé VTi, two years old and in great nick.'

'Good for you. Other info?'

'Leather seats, walnut dash—'

'You're such a boy.' I was pleased. 'I meant details of the rest of your life.'

'I'm twenty-eight, I'm a middle child and Monday to Friday I sell my soul to the Edachi Electronic Corporation.'

'Doing what?'

'Marketing.'

'Do you have lots of disgusting flatmates?'

'No, I live'—giveaway swallow—'on my own.'

'Right. I'm going to the loo.'

'Good luck.'

When I came back, I was impressed. 'Very cunning how the loos were hidden behind the wash-hand basins and mirrors. It took me ages to find them. You chose well. Now, let's move on to relationship history. Two and a half years ago, my best friend stole the love of my life from me, they're still together and have a child, I've never forgiven either of them and I've never met anyone else. You might think I sound bitter, but that's only because I am. And you?'

'Jesus!' He looked a bit shocked at my onslaught. God, I'd done it again—but he answered, 'Er, I was going out with someone. A girl. And we broke up.'

'When? How long were you going out?'

'We'd been together nearly two years. We broke up just before'— another giveaway swallow—'Christmas.'

'Less than four months ago? After two years?'

'I'm fine about it.'

'Don't be silly. Of course you're not.'

And while he insisted he was, I was thinking, But this is excellent! He'll want *nothing* from me.

Over the next three hours I grilled Owen and learned:

1) He did Tai chi
2) He had a 'thing' about prawns—he wasn't allergic, he just didn't like them

3) One of his feet was half a size bigger than the other
4) His ideal holiday destination would be Jamaica

He matched me question for question. 'What are you most afraid of?'

'Growing old and dying alone,' I said and a little tear escaped. 'No, no.' I waved away his concern. 'It's just the wine. What are *you* most afraid of?'

He thought. 'Being locked in the boot of a ten-year-old Nissan Micra with Uri Geller.'

'Excellent answer! Let's go dancing.'

Hours later, back at his quite-neat-for-a-boy apartment, we wrestled enjoyably in a state of undress on his bed. Of course I thought about Anton, the last man I'd slept with; mind you, this couldn't have been more different. Not just in emotional intensity but even physically— Anton was lanky and lean and Owen much more compact. All the same, I wasn't complaining. Before taking things any further I caught Owen's wrist and said urgently, 'Owen, I don't normally hop into bed with someone on the first night.'

''I know.' His hair was wild and he was short of breath. 'It's just that for reasons you can't go into right now, this counts as three months in. Don't worry. Just enjoy it.'

I did just that.

He awoke as I was climbing into my pants.

'Where are you going?'

'I have to go home.'

He leaned and looked at his alarm clock. 'It's half past three, why are you leaving? Jesus, you're not married?'

'No.'

'Have you got kids?'

'No.'

'Is it the coal scuttle?'

'No.' A bubble of laughter escaped.

'Wait till the morning. Don't go.'

'Have to. Will you call me a taxi?'

'You're a taxi.'

'Fine, I'll just hail one in the street.'

'You do that.'

'I'll call you.'

'Don't bother.'

Another bubble of laughter escaped. 'Owen, our first row! Now, we're really up to speed.'

The fourth thing.

L H Literary Agency
4-8 Wardour Street, London W1P 3AG

31 March

Dear Ms Hogan
(Or can I call you Gemma—I feel I know you already!) Thank you so much for your pages, forwarded to me by your friend Susan Looby. My reader and I loved them.

Obviously the pages are a long way from being a book and the format would have to be decided on—memoir style, nonfiction or a novel. However, I would be interested in talking to you. Please get in touch and we can discuss it further.
With best wishes
Jojo Harvey

Can you imagine? It was Saturday evening. It had been a lovely day, dozing, drinking Alka Seltzers and thinking about Owen, until I felt well enough to get up and pop over to my flat to collect my post, water the cat, look longingly at my own bed etc., when I get this. Even before I opened it, my mouth was as dry as the Gobi; every letter with a London postmark has this effect on me because—fool that I am—I hope that it might be Anton telling me it's all been a terrible mistake, Lily is a balding wolf in hippy-chic clothing and that he wants me back.

So I open it up and it's on nice, creamy paper but my eyes rush to the bottom and it's not from Anton, it's from someone called Jojo Harvey and who on earth is she? I swallow several times and read the letter but instead of being enlightened I'm even more confused. It must be a mistake, I decide. But . . . she'd mentioned Susan. By surname.

I decided to ring Susan. It was midmorning in Seattle and I woke her up, but she insisted she didn't mind and we were so excited at hearing each other's voices that it took time to get to the purpose of the call.

'Susan, listen, I'm after getting this letter. I opened it because it was addressed to me, but it has something to do with you.'

'Go on.' She sounded intrigued. 'Who's it from?'

'Someone called Jojo Harvey, from a literary agency in London.'

There followed the longest silence. So long I was the first to speak. 'Susan? Are you still there?'

'Ah . . . yeah.'

'I thought we'd been cut off. Speak to me.'

After another silence she spoke quickly. 'Gemma, I've got something to tell you and you're not going to like it, at least not straight away.'

My stomach had plunged. 'What? Susan, what?'

'You know since I came to Seattle, you've been sending me emails?'

'Yes.'

'Well, I just thought they were really funny and I've always thought you'd be a great writer, and I know you'd never do anything about it—'

'What wouldn't I do?' But I knew. 'You sent my emails to this agent woman?'

My memory skittered back over everything I'd sent Susan—Dad leaving Mam, Lily's book coming out, my carry-on with Owen—and the breath left my body. 'Not . . . *all* the emails?'

'No, not all,' she was racing through the words. 'I left out some.'

'*Some?*' Some was nothing like enough.

'I left out all the really bad bits, like how much you hate Lily, and . . .'

'And . . .?' I was desperate.

'And how much you hated Lily's book.'

'And . . . ?'

'How you feel about Lily.'

'But you already said that. Did you send everything else?'

'Yes.' It was so low it sounded like a crackle of static.

'Oh, Susan.'

'I'm sorry, Gemma, honest to God, I thought it was the right thing . . .'

I began to cry. I should have been furious, but I hadn't the strength.

I drove back to Mam's. 'Come on,' she said, handing me a glass of Baileys. 'We're missing the *Midsomer Murders*.'

'No, I can't.'

I interfaced with my communicator brick, frantic to read back over what I'd sent to Susan and was currently on some stranger's desk in London. I speed-read through the Sent Items. Ohmigod, ohmigod, ohmigod, it was worse than I remembered. All that private pain about Mam and Dad. Worse still was the mean-spirited stuff that it was OK for my friends to know about, but the thought of anyone else knowing about made me itchy with shame.

On Saturday night and all day Sunday, my mobile rang incessantly, as a mortified Susan tried to apologise. I didn't pick up any of her calls.

'I was only trying to help,' she said, several times a message. 'You're a great writer but I knew you'd never do anything about it yourself.'

That's the trouble with Susan. Just because she went to Seattle and followed her bloody dream, she wants everyone else to do it too.

At work on Monday I realised I should have worked over the weekend, instead of treating myself to a hangover—there were several messages on my voicemail from Lesley Lattimore saying:

1) She didn't like any of the three dress designers I'd put her in touch with.
2) What free cosmetics had I bagged so far?
3) Where was her turreted castle?

I hit the phones in a big, panicky way, putting calls in all over the place—to designers, journalists, cosmetic houses, turreted castles. In the razor-thin sliver of time between me hanging up on one call and beginning another, Cody rang. 'Cody "Kofi Annan" Cooper calling to intercede. Susan says you won't talk to her.'

'No, I won't. This is the worst thing anyone has ever done to me.'

'It is not, you big drama queen. Gemma, I'll say one thing to you and I want you to listen carefully: a literary agent is interested in representing you and you *haven't even written a book*. Have you any idea how lucky you are?'

I shrugged.

'Did you just shrug?'

'Sometimes you scare me.'

'Girl, it's mutual.'

'What are you talking about?'

'You. The way you never do anything any more.'

'Oi, who's the drama queen now? You *know* how hard I work. My job is so demanding and even if I say so myself, I'm extremely good at it.'

'That's right, you're great at pulling in money for the evil twins so they can buy their farmhouse in Normandy or whatever it is this week. What do you get out of it?'

'I'm on good money and, Cody, don't call them the evil twins, sometimes they listen in on my calls.'

'Set up on your own.'

Everyone in the business, it's their *dream* to set up on their own. But you need money and potential clients and F&F have hung me up with a contract that means I couldn't take any existing clients with me. Besides I'd be afraid that F&F would take a contract out on me.

'Maybe someday . . .'

'In the meantime ring this agent woman. If you've any sense.'

'And what if I get published and the whole world reads about my father deserting my mother?'

'Change the details.'

'*They'll* still know it's them.'

'Look, I don't have the answers. You figure it out.'

I remained silent and Cody said, 'Just one more thing. This agent is also Lily's agent.'

'God Almighty . . .'

'So ring her.'

'If she wants me badly enough, she'll ring me.'

'She won't. She's very busy and in demand.'

'Whatever.' I wasn't going to ring Jojo Harvey. If this was meant to be it would happen of its own accord.

OK, I rang her. I gave it until the following Monday—a full-on, Lesley-Lattimore-filled week—waiting for what was meant to be to happen, and, when it didn't, I picked up the phone and rang this Jojo Harvey.

It took a few moments for Jojo to remember who I was but once she did she said, 'Come in and see me.'

'I live in Ireland, it's not that easy.'

'Point taken. So any ideas on format? Fact or fiction?'

'Definitely not fact.' I was horrified.

'Fiction then.'

'But I can't,' I said. 'It's all about my mam and dad.'

'Even that stuff about Helmut?'

'Well, no, *that* was made up. But the basic story, the one of my father leaving my mother, that's true.'

'You know, call me unsympathetic, but it's the oldest story in the book—man leaving wife for younger model. You could change the details a bit.'

'How?'

'The father could work in a different industry—although I love all that stuff about the chocolate—the mom could be different.'

'Everyone would still know it was my parents.'

'They say everyone's first novel is autobiographical.'

I wanted her to keep saying things, to convince me, to talk me into it.

'Gemma, I'm not going to talk you into something you don't want to do. Sorry we've both had our time wasted.'

That stung. But I suppose she was important and busy.

After the night I snuck out on him, Owen never called. So I called him.

'Owen, it's Gemma. Let's go out on Friday night.' Like we'd parted on the fondest terms.

'Will you be sneaking off home in the middle of the night?'

'Yes, but I have a reason. Meet me and I'll tell you it.'

Of course he couldn't resist that and eight o'clock on Friday night saw me once again stumbling down the mirrored steps of Crash.

'*Déjà vu*,' I beamed. 'I like your shirt.' A different one but just as cool.

He wasn't smiling but I kept grinning at him until he gave in and cracked his expression-free face. Then, like he was surprised by what he was doing, he stood up, caught me and kissed me. A very nice kiss, which stopped only when someone called, 'Get a room!'

'So what's your excuse for running out on me?'

'It's a good one. Buy me a drink and I'll tell you.'

I gave it to him chapter and verse, especially how Mam couldn't be left on her own all night or she might fake a heart attack. 'Now you see that me doing a runner was nothing personal, right?'

'I didn't want you to go.' He managed to sound both sulky and sexy.

And under the circumstances I thought it would be nice to reply, 'And I didn't want to go.'

It was a flirty, touchy-feely night, lots of hand-stroking and meaningful eye-locks and we both got a little bit scuttered. We stayed in Crash until kicking-out time, then on the street we stood very close and he said, 'What now? Somewhere else?'

'Let's go back to your place,' I said, fingering a button on his shirt-front in saucy temptress fashion.

'Are you going to sneak out again in the middle of the night?'

'Yes.'

'Then you can't come back. If you can't be bothered to stay for the entire night I don't want you to come at all.'

'But I've told you what's going on! I have to go home to my mother.'

'You're thirty-two years old,' he cried. 'I could get this sort of grief from a sixteen-year-old.'

'So *get* yourself a sixteen-year-old.'

'OK.'

He turned and walked away from me, very angry. I stuck my arm up and hailed a taxi.

Shaking with rage, I got in. 'Kilmacud.'

Just before the taxi took off, the door was wrenched open and Owen bundled himself in on top of me. 'I'm coming with you.'

'No, you're not.'

'Yes, I am.'

'My mother will be thrilled to see you. Not.'

'Stop the car!' Though we were barely moving, we screeched to a kerb-side halt but Owen didn't get out. 'Do we have to go to your mother's house? Can't we go to your apartment?'

'I'd still have to sneak home in the middle of the night.'

'OK, I'll settle for that. Her apartment, Clonskeagh,' he told the driver.

The following day I was pale and subdued. I'd had a drunken row in the street. I'd committed a sex act in a taxi—at least I'd tried but the driver had asked me not to. And I'd slept with a man who called his nether regions 'Uncle Dick and the twins'. But you know what, the sex was glorious. Fast and fabulous and sweaty and sexy—and plenty of it.

Between one of the bouts he'd mumbled into my hair, 'Sorry for saying the thing about the sixteen-year-old.'

I'd been angry at the time, but to hold a grudge you had to care . . . and I didn't.

'I forgive you,' I said magnanimously.

'I saw Lorna today.'

Who? Oh, his ex-girlfriend.

'Were you upset?'

'No.'

No, just devastated. And I got what had happened in the street—he hadn't been arguing with me, he was arguing with someone who wasn't there. So what was my excuse?

We slipped quietly into the fifth month of Dad's absence. I managed to keep it from myself for a couple of days because I was so depressed about other things, mostly my stillborn writing career.

Jojo was right—a husband leaving a wife for a younger woman really was the oldest story in the book. Even though my novel wasn't going to happen, it all began to unfold in my head.

In the book I could have a different job—in fact, I didn't have to have a job at all: I could be a housewife (oh, the happiness!) with maybe a couple of children of my own.

I could give myself two sisters, or maybe a brother and a sister; I played around with various scenarios and in the end I settled for an older sister called Monica.

'My' name is Izzy and I have chin-length corkscrew curls in great condition. Much as I'd have loved it, I couldn't imagine being a house-wife so Izzy works in PR, and yes, she organises events.

Izzy was having a love/hate flirtation thing with one of her clients. He was called Emmet, a grand sexy name, and he ran his own business (still undecided as to exact nature thereof) and Izzy was organising a sales conference for him. He was a bit narky—but only because he fancied her—and when she booked all the delegates into the wrong hotel, because she was upset about her ice-cream salesman dad leaving her mother, Emmet didn't sack her as would so happen in real life.

Other modifications: the dad wasn't having an affair with his secre-tary, that was too much of a cliché. Instead it was his golf partner's eldest daughter. And the mammy wasn't quite as incapable as my mother—I suspected that people simply wouldn't believe it.

Some things stayed the same: my car, for instance. And I kept the nice man in the chemist but changed his name to Will.

It was a funny exercise—like being a different version of me, or perhaps knowing what it was like to be someone else. Either way, when I woke into the acid-bright early morning, paralysed with screaming despair, it took my mind off things.

To: Susan_inseattle@yahoo.com
From: Gemma343@hotmail.com
Subject: I've started to write it

Thank you, thank you, thank you for making it happen. You're right, I'd never have done it if it had been left to me. I'm so sorry for not taking your calls, I wasn't trying to be mean. Anyway, I've been thinking about it so much that I felt I'd burst if I didn't write it. I work at it in the early mornings and in the evenings. Mam goes to bed at nine thirty, sleeping the sleep of the heavily tranquillised and I'm able to clatter away on the PC. But even while I'm watching *Buffy* I'm thinking about it and itching for Mam to go so I can get started.

Is this what it means to be a tormented artist? Answers on a postcard, please.

Love, Gemma xxx

Back in the real world, I'd finally found a castle with turrets. I'd also run to ground a dress designer so down on her luck that she was prepared to take on Lesley and her unreasonable requests. And I was in the final moments of securing coverage from a glossy magazine and if the cosmetics people were guaranteed publicity, they were a lot more likely to sponsor us.

Even though I say it myself, I'm GREAT at my job.

To: Susan_inseattle@yahoo.com
From: Gemma343@hotmail.com
Subject: I rang Jojo

and told her that I'm going to write the book and she said, 'Well, congratulations, you've got yourself an agent!' Then she asked if it was all OK with Mam and I just said, 'Mmmm.'

I'll jump off that bridge when I come to it.

Love, Gemma xxx

I didn't tell Susan what happened next.

I cleared my throat because I had something important to say. I hovered on the moment, then, 'Jojo, I know one of your clients.'

'Yeah?' Not interested.

'Lily. Lily Wright.'

'Oh, Lily's doing great! Really, like, super-great.'

'Yes, well, tell her Gemma Hogan says "hello".'

'Will do.'

See, I wasn't sure Susan would approve. She was my friend, but she was regarding all this agent stuff as very positive and I have to fess up to coming at it in a more mean-spirited way. I wanted to unsettle Lily with my message: I'm in the same business as you now and I'm on your tail.

Well, come one, she'd stolen the love of my life, she was a millionaire and she was in loads of newspapers. What would you do?

Friday nights with Owen had become a regular thing *and* we usually managed a quick midweek ride. Owen was great fun and there was no pesky churning-stomach, wobbly-kneed, tongue-tied stuff you get when you're mad about someone. I didn't think about him when I wasn't with him, but I was always glad to hear from him. And he felt the same way about me.

Funnily enough, we nearly always had some sort of a row—either he was mean to me or I was mean to him—I'm not saying it was healthy but it was a regular event.

Owen and I were lying in bed in a post-ride rosy glow, fashioning imaginary, happy futures for each other.

'What do you think will happen?' I asked him.

'Your book will get published,' Owen said. 'You'll be famous and Lily 'Every man for myself' Wright's publishers will be dying to have you, but you won't go to them unless they drop Lily.'

'And Anton will leave Lily and come back to me and revenge will be mine! No offence.' I punched his shoulder to soften the blow. 'Because you'll be married to Lorna and we'll all be friends. We'll hire a *gîte* in the Dordogne and go on our summer holidays together.'

'And I'll always be fond of you.'

'Exactly. And I'll always be fond of you. Maybe you could be god-father to my and Anton's first child. No, actually, scratch that. That's going too far.'

'How will I get Lorna back?'

'How do you think?'

'She'll see you and me together and realise what she's passed up.'

'Precisely! You learn fast, my little one.'

'Thank you, grasshopper.'

I looked at his alarm clock. 'It's ten past eleven. I've a few hours of my curfew left, let's go out for a drink.'

Later, in Renards, with several speedy drinks under our belts, Owen said, 'Am I coming to this Gothic Barbie party?'

'No.'

'What? Ashamed of me?'

'Yes,' I said, although I wasn't. He couldn't come because it was a work do; I wasn't a guest at Lesley's bash, I was a slave.

I shoved my chair back so there was room for him to storm out. 'Off you go.'

Off he went and I sipped my wine and thought nice thoughts, when through the crowds I noticed a man down by the bar, looking directly at me and smiling warmly.

But he wasn't a comb-over lech, he was In The Zone—you know, the right age and nice-looking. The novelty of it nearly made me laugh out loud; I was being *picked up*. In an Irish nightclub!

And he was coming over. She shoots, she scores!

I knew him, though. I just couldn't place him. He was frustratingly familiar, who the hell . . . oh, of *course*, it was Johnny the Scrip, from the chemist. I got a funny warm feeling in my stomach, but that could just have been the wine.

'Who's minding the shop?' I called.

'Who's minding your mammy?'

We wheezed with empathetic mirth.

He nodded at my glass of wine and said, all high-spiritedly, 'Now, Gemma, I'd love to buy you a drink, but should you be drinking while you're on medication?'

'It's notmine, youthick. It's memammy's.' I was a little more jarred than I realised.

'I know,' he winked.

'I know you know,' I winked back.

''Scuse *me*.' Owen jostled his way back in, his little face like thunder, jogging Johnny's elbow and slopping his pint.

'I'll leave you to it.' Johnny passed me a your-young-friend-is-a-bit-pissed look and sloped away back to his friends. 'Nice to see you, Gemma.'

'Who the fuck is he?' Owen scowled.

'Just someone I fancy.' Now, what was that all about? There was no need to say that—even if it was true.

And it might be.

Owen gave me a baleful look. 'Gemma, I'm fond of you, but you're more trouble than you're worth.'

'*Me* trouble?' I did a mirthless, 'Hah! And you're the person who's had more comebacks than Frank Sinatra.

'Drunk,' I listed off on my fingers. 'Immature. Unreasonable.' I paused. 'And that's just me. I'm not normally like this.'

I stopped, my eyes suddenly filled with tears. 'I dunno, Owen. Am I going mad here? I don't like who I become when I'm with you.'

'Neither do I.'

'Fuck off.'

'Fuck off yourself,' he said, taking my face in his hands with odd tenderness. He kissed me full on the mouth—he was such a lovely kisser—then he kissed my tears away.

The week of Lesley Lattimore's party was seven days of hell. When God created the world, I swear he didn't work as hard as I did that week.

On the first day . . . Lesley took a notion that she wanted the outside walls of the castle to be painted pink. So I asked the owner, Mr Evans-Black, and he told me to fuck off. Literally.

I went back and told Lesley it was no go. 'Fine,' she said airily, 'we'll find another castle.'

And it took a very long time and all of my diplomacy to convince her that actually, no, we wouldn't find another castle.

On the second day . . . We had the fitting of Lesley's pointy-sleeved dress, her pointy shoes and pointy hat. But as she twirled in front of the mirror she placed a finger to her mouth and said thoughtfully, 'Something's missing.'

'You look *fabulous*,' I yelped, feeling the jaws of hell opening. 'Nothing's missing.'

'But there is,' she said, swinging back and forth and behaving all little-girlie. 'I know! I want a hairpiece, a huge fall of ringlets from the crown of my head all the way down my back.'

The designer and I shared a moment of despair.

On the third day . . . I was overseeing the installation of huge drops of pink silk from ceiling to floor when I heard someone boom, 'So this is the woman who's spending all my money.'

I turned round. Christ, it was Lesley's Dad, Wads! And Mrs Wads, who was a too-much-money-meets-too-much-Librium train wreck.

'Mr Lattimore. A pleasure to meet you,' I lied.

'Tell me now, is there good money in this party-organising lark?' he asked. I'd lay bets that if he met the Queen, he'd ask if there was good money in being a monarch.

I tittered in terror. 'I'm not really the person to ask.'

'Who should I ask, then? Francis and Frances?' he asked. 'The evil twins? They're the ones who keep all the profit?'

What could I say?

'Yes, Mr Lattimore.'

'Don't bother with that Mister stuff, no need to stand on ceremony with me. The name,' he said with ominous calm, 'is Larry.'

Oh Jayzus, there go my kneecaps.

On the fourth day . . . The wind machine to move the fabric about had arrived, the furniture was on its way, Andrea and Moses had come down to help me and things were starting to seem less dangerously out-of-control, when Lesley had a sudden fit. 'The bedrooms are too ordinary! We have to get them decorated.'

I held her still, looked into her eyes and said through clenched jaws, 'There. Is. No. Time.'

Steadily she eyeballed me back. 'Make. Time. I want those things that go over the bed, like mosquito nets but pretty. In silver.'

I thought of Wads and my kneecaps.

'Phone!' I shrieked at Andrea, dangerously close to losing it. 'Excuse me while I just buy up all the silver lamé in Ireland.'

On the fifth day . . . The glasses arrived and half of them hadn't survived the journey. Freak stations, trying to get more; they weren't just any glasses, they were pink Italian crystal. But it was the silver lamé mosquito nets that were breaking my heart. Only a few lone operators would take the job at such short notice so I sewed them myself.

On the sixth day . . . The day of the party. I'd had no sleep, my fingers were covered in cuts, but I was keeping it together. I was Keeping. It. Together. Ear to the ground, finger on the pulse, that was me. Picking up on any imperfections, including the two bullet-headed-thug types bursting out of too-tight suits. Bouncers. God, but they were rough-looking.

I collared Moses. 'That pair. Couldn't we have got bouncers who didn't look quite so psycho?'

'Them? They're Lesley's brothers.' And Moses dashed away to welcome the lute minstrels and give them their tights and curly-toed slippers.

And for the rest of the day and night, it was just a succession of people running up to me and saying: 'Gemma, someone's collapsed in the hall.'

'Gemma, have you any condoms?'

'Gemma, Wads wants a cup of tea but Evans-Black has barricaded himself into his room and won't give up the kettle.'

'Gemma, they're booing the lute players. It's quite ugly.'

'Gemma, Lesley's brothers are beating the shit out of each other.'

'Gemma, Mrs Wads is having sex with someone who isn't Mr Wads.'

And on the seventh day . . . She lied to her mammy and said she had to go back for the clean-up operation when in fact Andrea and Moses were doing it. Instead she went to Owen's and said, 'I want to have sex with you, but I've no energy. Would you mind if I just lay there and you did all the work?'

'So what's new?'

Which wasn't true; she was quite inventive and energetic in the scratcher with Owen. All the same, he did what she asked, then he made her slices of cheese on toast and she lay on the sofa and watched *Billy Elliot*.

The week after Lesley's party I had to collect a prescription (anti-inflammatories, Mam had pulled a muscle in her hand, God only knows how—pressing the remote?).

'Hi, Gemma.' Johnny smiled and I smiled. There was just something very nice about him. Such a lovely manner. Mind you, he didn't look like he'd looked in Renards when he'd been sparkly and alive and a little bit bold. Cinderella syndrome: suddenly I understood that he was exhausted. For as long as I'd known him he'd been working twelve-hour days, six days a week and even though he was kind to his clientele, I wasn't seeing him at his best. If only he didn't have to work so hard . . .

I submitted my prescription and asked, 'How's your brother?'

'It'll be ages before he's back on his feet. Um, listen, I hope I didn't upset your boyfriend that night in Renards.'

I took a breath. 'He's not my boyfriend.'

'Er . . . right.'

I just didn't have a clue where to begin an explanation of the weirdness that was me and Owen, so jokily I said, 'Yes, I *am* in the habit of kissing men who aren't my boyfriend.'

'Great. I'm in with a chance then.'

'Oh, so you don't want to be my boyfriend?' It was meant to be arch and, you know, *good fun*, but first a red tide roared up his face, then up mine. Mortified and mute, we radiated heat at each other and my armpits were itchy.

'Christ,' I tried to save the day with my scintillating wit, 'we could roast marshmallows on the pair of us.'

He laughed redly. 'We're both a bit long in the tooth to be blushing like this.'

Once Lesley Lattimore's life-sapping bash was over, I could focus on my book, which was motoring along beautifully; I reckoned I was over three-quarters of the way through. The only fly in the ointment—a very big one—was my mother. I suspected she'd never OK my novel being published, even though, as I kept saying to myself, it was the oldest story in the book. *And* the people were no longer anything like us. I mean, Izzy persisted with an attraction for the man in the chemist, for goodness' sake!

I was thinking all kinds of panicky things, like I'd have to publish under a pseudonym and pay some actress to pretend to be me. But then I wouldn't be able to gloat at Lily and show Anton what a success I was.

I went to Susan for advice. 'Just be honest with your mammy,' she said. 'It never hurts to ask.'

Now there she was wrong.

I broached it during an ad-break. 'Mam? I'm thinking of writing a book.'

'What sort of book?'

'A novel.'

'What about? Cromwell?'

'No . . .'

'A Jewish girl in Germany in 1938?'

'Listen . . . ah. Switch off the telly a minute and I'll tell you.'

To: Susan_inseattle@yahoo.com
From: Gemma343@hotmail.com
Subject: Breaking the news

Dear Susan,

I took your advice and told her. She called me a bitch. I couldn't believe it and nor could she. Even Colette hadn't been called a 'bitch'.

But when Mam heard my story line, her mouth fell further and further open and her eyes became more and more bulgy.

'Well . . . you little'—big long dramatic pause—'*bitch!*'

It was as if she'd slapped me—and then I realised she actually had. A belt across the face from the palm of her hand.

'You want the whole world to know how I've been humiliated.'

I tried to explain that it wasn't about her and Dad, at least not any more, and that it was the oldest story in the book. But she grabbed the bundle of pages that I'd printed out for her. She tried to rip it in two, but it was too thick, so she broke it up into smaller pieces and then *really* went for it. Like, *savaged* it.

'Now!' she declared, when every page was reduced to shreds and strips of paper were fluttering around the room like a snowstorm. 'No more book!'

And I hadn't the heart to explain about how it's all backed up on the computer.

I really *am* a tormented artist.

Love, Gemma

It badly damaged things between me and Mam. I felt guilty and ashamed—but very resentful. Which made me feel even more ashamed. And still I wouldn't stop writing. If I really loved her, wouldn't I just knock it on the head?

Meanwhile, Mam, who had been improving, went back into suspicion overdrive and tried to monitor my every move. Something had to give—and it did.

It was an ordinary workday, I was running around like a blue-arsed fly, getting dressed, and she cornered me. 'What time will you be home tonight?'

'Late. Eleven. I'm having dinner at the new hotel on the quays. The one I want to hold the conference in.'

'I don't want you to go.'

'Well, that's tough, because I've no choice. I have to do my job.'

'Why?'

'I've a mortgage to pay.'

'Why don't you sell up that old flat and just live here?'

AAAAAAARRRRRRGGGGGGGGHHHHHHH! My worst fear, by eight million miles. Something snapped.

'I'll tell you why,' I said, too loudly. 'What if Dad marries Colette and we have to move out of here? We'll be glad then to have my flat to live in.'

I regretted it immediately. She began fighting for breath and between gasps, said, 'It *could* happen. It's been six months and not once has he picked up the phone. He has no interest in me.'

And you know what? The following day, with almost spooky timing, a letter arrived from Dad's solicitor, asking for a meeting to discuss a permanent financial settlement.

I read it, then handed it to Mam, who stared at it for a long, long time before speaking. 'Does this mean he's going to sell my house?'

'Maybe.' I was very nervous, but I didn't want to lie. 'Or maybe he'll let you have it, if you give up any further claims.'

'To what?'

'His income, his pension.'

'And what am I to live on? Fresh air?'

'I'll look after you.'

'You shouldn't have to.' She stared out of the window and she didn't look quite so bewildered and beaten. 'I ran his home all his life,' she mused. 'I was his cook, cleaning woman, concubine, the mother of his child. Have I no rights?'

'I don't know. We'll have to get a solicitor.'

Another silence. 'That book of yours? What kind of light did it show your father in?'

'Bad.' Correct answer.

'I'm sorry now I tore it up.'

'How sorry?' Proceed with caution.

'You couldn't write it again, could you?'

To: Susan_inseattle@yahoo.com
From: Gemma343@hotmail.com
Subject: She said yes!

She says she wants Dad named and shamed, that everyone knows about her situation anyway and that she might even go on *Trisha* and name and shame Dad there too. And guess what? I've finished my book! I thought I had a good bit still to go but it all came together very quickly. OK, the ending is a bit fairy-tale and I might laugh at it in someone else's book but, like everything in life, it's different when it's your own.
Love, Gemma xxx

I rang Dad to find out what his permanent financial settlement comprised. It was as I'd feared: he wanted to sell the house so he'd have money to buy a new one to house Colette and her brats. Mam and I hired a family lawyer, Breda Sweeney, and went to see her.

'Dad wants to sell the house. Can he do that?'

'Not without your consent.'

'Which he won't get,' Mam said.

'But when you've been separated for a year, he can go to court and plead his case.'

'Which is?'

'That he's got two families to support and that a lot of equity is tied up in the erstwhile family home. What usually happens is that the judge will make an order for the house to be sold and the proceeds to be shared.'

Fear seized me and Mam asked—whispered, kind of—'Does that mean I'll lose my home?'

'You'll have money to buy a new one. Not necessarily fifty per cent of the proceeds, the judge will decide on that, but you'll have something.'

'But Dad will have to continue to support her?' I asked.

'Not necessarily. By law Maureen is entitled to be given as much as can be given to maintain her lifestyle without impoverishing him.' Breda made a gesture of impotence. 'There's only so much money to go round.'

'I'm running low on tranquillisers,' Mam said, when we got home. 'I don't want to run out of them. Not now, not with this news. Will you go to the chemist?'

'Oh. OK.' I found I felt funny about going. I hadn't seen Johnny for a couple of weeks, not since our bout of flirting.

Why was I reluctant to see him? I asked myself. After all, he was lovely. It was because I knew what I was doing was wrong. Owen—for good or ill—was my boyfriend and it wasn't fair on him to flirt with Johnny. Not unless I was planning to do something about it: like break it off with Owen and boldly go into the chemist looking to have more than my prescription filled. And was I going to do that?

It was one thing to spend a lot of my time with Owen, fantasising out loud about Anton, but Johnny was different. He was real. He was near.

He was interested.

I knew I had an opportunity with him, and although it gave me the stomach-churnies (the good ones), I was afraid. I didn't know why, all I knew was that I wasn't afraid with Owen.

Jojo

***Book News*, 10 June**

MOVIE RIGHTS SOLD

Movie rights for *Love and the Veil*, the debut novel from Nathan Frey, have been sold to Miramax for a seven-figure sum, rumoured to be $1.5 million. Brent Modigliani at Creative Artists Associates brokered the deal with Jim Sweetman of Lipman Haigh. The novel, which was agented by Jojo Harvey from Lipman Haigh, will be published in spring next year by Southern Cross.

Nothing like some good news to get the old spending instincts into gear. It was lunchtime. Nearly.

'Manoj, I'm going out. I may be some time.'

'Looking at nail colours?'

'Nail colours, handbags, who knows? I'm wiiide open.'

But not for long. Out in the sunshiny street, she was hooked by a pale blue leather jacket in Whistles window; such an object of desire, her mouth went dry.

She went inside, found it in her size, held it at arm's length and stroked it like it was an animal. The leather was as thin and supple as skin and it was so beautiful it crimped her insides. It was also expensive, impractical and wouldn't survive more than a season—but who *cared*?

Right on the shop floor, she shrugged it on, found a mirror—and abruptly the buzz drained away. It made her chest look as if it had been inflated with a bicycle pump. It was *obscene*. Mark would love it, of course, but where would she wear it with him? Her living room? Her bedroom? Her kitchen?

She reconsidered. It was way pricey for something that would never be worn outside her flat. She was going to think about it.

Back in the office, she ate her sandwich and checked her emails.

To: Jojo.harvey@LIPMAN HAIGH.co
From: Mark.avery@LIPMAN HAIGH.co
Subject: Monday night?

Can I pencil it in? I'm sorry about this weekend. Bloody parents' golden wedding anniversary. Have a nice—but not too nice—weekend without me.
M xx
PS Yvooluie

It had snuck up on them but in the past few months she and Mark had been spending more and more time with each other.

Since the night when Mark had accidentally slept through to morning, he now stayed over in Jojo's about once a week. Cassie didn't complain about him not coming home and Jojo was baffled by her passivity. 'What do you *tell* her?'

'That I'm talking to the West Coast or I'm entertaining publishers and that I don't want to disturb her by staggering in at three in the morning when she's got work the next day.'

'She buys it?'

'She seems to. She just asks that I let her know by midnight so she can put the mortise lock on the door.'

'Where does she think you sleep?'

'In a hotel.'

'No way would *I* buy that. No way.'

'Not everyone's like you, Jojo.'

'Yeah.' And she understood that sometimes it's too painful for people to see what's under their noses. That hurt. She didn't want to cause Cassie—anyone—pain.

To: Mark.avery@LIPMAN HAIGH.co
From: Jojo.harvey@LIPMAN HAIGH.co
Subject: Nice weekend?

Monday night good. Far away but good. But excuse me? Have a nice weekend? How can I have a nice weekend? I will never forgive you for the way you treated me on my birthday.
JJ xx
PS Eoovilyu too

Four weekends previously, on the 12th of May, Jojo had turned thirty-three. Some time before it, Mark said to her, 'I'm taking you away for your birthday.'

'Yeah?' Hot with pleasure at his thoughtfulness. 'Where?'

He paused. 'London.'

'London? This London?'

Before she had time to tell him to go fuck himself, he passed her a sheet of paper. 'It's a timetable.'

Jojo's Birthday Weekend

Friday 3.30 p.m.:   Skive off work early. Proceed separately to Brook Street and check into Claridge's hotel.

'Claridge's! I've always wanted to stay at Claridge's!' It figured large in her fantasy, Agatha Christie-style Britain—cream teas and snooty butlers and 'gels' up from the country for the day.

'I know,' he said.

Friday 4.00 p.m.:   Try out the facilities of the suite paying particular attention to the bed, then step out onto nearby Bond Street to look for Jojo's birthday gift.

She looked up again. 'Bond Street is *way* expensive.'

'I know.'

She eyed him with admiration. 'What a guy.'

Friday 7.00 p.m.:   Drinks, then dinner in a restaurant where I had to promise to get the chef a book deal, in order to get a reservation this side of Christmas.

***

Saturday morning: Breakfast in the suite, followed by a swim in the hotel pool, then return to Bond Street to continue the search for Jojo's gift.

Afternoon at leisure: Perhaps measuring the bounce of the bed.

Saturday 7.00 p.m.:   Cocktails, then dinner in a different but still insanely difficult-to-get-into restaurant.

***

Sunday morning: Breakfast in the suite, another swim and a final test of the bedsprings.

12 noon: Check out and home.

It had been the perfect weekend. When they'd arrived, flowers and champagne were waiting in the room. They'd had sex about sixty times, even in the swimming pool when they'd been the only people there.

Patiently he went from shop to shop with her, admired handbag after handbag, even though she knew they seemed identical to him.

They had afternoon tea in the Garden Room, they drank the champagne with their room-service lunch on Saturday afternoon and the only hiccup in the two days was when he'd steered her towards the rings in Tiffany's.

'Maybe you should pick one,' he said.

'Don't be a dumbass,' she said, suddenly angry with him. The last thing she wanted during this precious time was to be reminded that he was married.

That night, in the restaurant, as they looked at their menus, he took her hand. She twisted it out of his grasp but again he went for it.

'Mark,' she frowned. 'Anyone could see us.'

'Your point?'

'While we're in London we have to play it safe.'

'Playing it safe is the most dangerous thing a woman like you could do.'

She burst out laughing. '*Moonstruck*? Nicolas Cage says it to Cher? Am I right?'

Mark sighed. 'You were meant to think I made it up. You are the most amazing woman I've ever met. You know everything.'

To: Jojo.harvey@LIPMAN HAIGH.co
From: Mark.avery@LIPMAN HAIGH.co
Subject: Birthday weekend

Didn't you enjoy it?

To: Mark.avery@LIPMAN HAIGH.co
From: Jojo.harvey@LIPMAN HAIGH.co
Subject: Enjoy it?

Yes. Far too much. Nothing will ever be as nice ever again.

Monday morning, opening her post

One was marked personal and Jojo thought she recognised the handwriting. She tore the envelope and tipped out the letter. 'Oh no!'

Dear Jojo,
There's no easy way of telling you this but I have decided not to return to work. I know I promised you that I would. I meant it when I said it, but I wasn't prepared for how much I love Stella and I can't bear the

*thought of leaving her every day with a minder. When it happens to you,
you'll know what I'm talking about.
With lots of love,
Louisa and Stella*

This was not good news. She loved Louisa. She was her sidekick, a
smarty who always delivered. Right away she went to see Mark.

'Louisa isn't coming back.'

'Aaaahhhhh.'

'You knew?'

'I thought she might not. It happens. Should we advertise for someone new, or do you want to keep Manoj?'

'Manoj is fine. OK, he's very good,' she admitted reluctantly. 'It's just
that Louisa was my friend. She knew about you. Now I've no one to
talk to.'

Mark said nothing. He let the silence endure and Jojo was the one to
crack.

'Hey, it's your birthday Friday.' She went for levity. 'Eight o'clock, my
bed, for a very special gift.'

A second too long before he spoke. 'I can't.' He sounded pained.
'Cassie's organised something.'

'Oh. What?'

'A night in a country house hotel. Weymouth Manor or something.
I'm so sorry.'

Jojo got it together. 'Come on, Mark, she *is* your wife.'

'How about Sunday?'

'Sure.'

Then she went back and broke the news to Manoj that he was going
to be made permanent. He was so happy he almost cried. 'You won't
regret this,' he wobbled.

'I already am. Pull yourself together. Any messages?'

'Gemma Hogan rang. She was wondering if you've sold her book yet.'

Jojo rolled her eyes. Gemma Hogan was an Irishwoman who had sent
sheaves of emails to her friend detailing her elderly father leaving her
mother. When the bunch of pages arrived on Jojo's desk they weren't in
book format, but were entertaining and funny enough for her to be
semi-interested. When the finished product arrived, it belonged in the
category of books that Jojo called the So-What?s—not special enough to
be sold via auction. Instead Jojo would have to approach each house
individually and, if they passed, carry on to the next bunch.

The heroine, Izzy, starred in a cookie-cutter love story with a little
twist. It had signalled from page one that she would end up with the
brooding, cleft-chinned Emmet, a hero straight from central casting;

instead she falls for the quietly sexy pharmacist who has been dispensing the mom's happy pills. It was the mom's journey that was much harder to stomach. Sixty-two years of age, so ditsy and dependent that she'd never learned to drive, she was running her own business by page seventy-nine (importing Swiss skincare into Ireland, hand in hand with her Swiss toy boy).

Despite its flaws the book was fun and would probably sell.

When Jojo rang to tell Gemma that she would represent her and her book, Gemma chuckled quietly. 'I'm screaming my head off on the inside, but I'm at work,' she'd said apologetically. 'So you really liked it?'

'I *loved* it.' Well, she had enjoyed it. 'I'll start sending the book out straight away.'

'There's no need to send it to lots of people. I'd like to be with Lily Wright's publisher. Dalkin Emery?'

'Woah.' For a first-timer Gemma was surprisingly knowledgeable about publishers. Then Jojo thought about it—not a bad idea. Dalkin Emery were good with women's fiction.

'We can try Dalkin Emery but I'll send you to a different editor. It's not a good idea for friends to share editors. You might find it hard to believe now, but this could start a huge rivalry and ruin your friendship.'

'We're not really friends. We just . . . know each other.'

Nevertheless, Jojo decided against it—the client is *not* always right—and sent it to Aoife Byrne instead.

But Aoife rang her and said, 'Jojo, this Gemma Hogan book is more Tania Teal's thing. I've passed it on to her.'

The weird thing was that as soon as Jojo hung up, Gemma rang for a progress report, and when she heard that Lily's editor was considering her book she said, 'I knew it. I'm meant to be with that editor.'

And although Jojo didn't believe in any of that 'meant to be' crap, she was a little impressed.

For about five minutes. Tania passed. She said it was a sweet book, actually reminiscent of Miranda England's earlier work, but it just wasn't special enough.

Damn, Jojo thought. These so-what books put varnish on her nails but they were a lot of work for little reward. So even though she had no good news, she rang Gemma. She had a policy of returning calls to all her authors, no matter how unlucrative they were—and giving it to them straight.

'No sale yet, Gemma. We've had a couple more passes. But not to worry, there are plenty of publishers out there.'

'Couldn't we try Lily Wright's editor again?'

'No, we totally can not.'

Friday afternoon

Eamonn Farrell, author and piss-head, was her three-thirty. He showed up at five to four, smelling of tobacco, fast food and Paco Rabanne. As one of Jojo's star authors, second only to Nathan Frey, she had to kiss him. It doesn't happen often but sometimes I hate my job, she thought dolefully.

He sat in front of her in clothes that looked like they'd been tied to the back of a car and dragged around town for a couple of hours, and complained for a solid forty-five minutes about every other male author on the planet. Then he stood up and said, 'Right, I'm off to get pissed.'

'I'll walk you to the lift.'

She hustled him and his smelliness in. 'Take care, Eamonn. Missing you already.'

The doors slid shut, taking Eamonn Farrell away from her. The relief! Her usual author's bedside manner had deserted her today. With a lighter heart she turned to go back to her office—and at the far end of the corridor she saw Mark with a blonde woman. Every nerve-ending prickled when she realised that it was Cassie.

Who wasn't exactly as she'd remembered her. Taller and slimmer, wearing jeans, a white shirt and—WHAT? Oh my GOD! It couldn't be. But she looked again—it was! *She's wearing my jacket.*

Mark saw her, his face lit up with alarm and they exchanged a stare that flashed the length of the hallway. Jojo would have spun on her heel and sprinted to the lift except it might have looked a little obvious; she *had* to walk towards them. Cassie was walking faster than Mark, her voice was loud and she sounded like she was telling him off for something. 'You silly man,' she was saying, then she laughed.

When she reached them, Jojo ducked her head, mumbled, 'Hi,' and slid past. But then she heard Cassie say, 'Hello.'

Both Mark and Jojo attempted to keep moving, but Cassie was going nowhere so Mark had to introduce them, which he did with all the enthusiasm of a man en route to the electric chair. 'This is Jojo Harvey. One of our agents.'

'Jojo Harvey.' Cassie took Jojo's hand in both of hers, looked her in the face and said, 'My God, you gorgeous creature.' Her eyes were blue, proper Scandinavian blue, and, although they were lined, she was very attractive. 'And I'm Cassie, Mark's long-suffering wife.'

Fuuckkk. But Cassie twinkled and Jojo understood that she was joking.

'I've been meaning to write to you, Jojo.'

Fuuckkk. 'You have?'

'You have so many good authors. I loved *Mimi's Remedies*,' Cassie exclaimed. 'It was brilliant, a wee gem.' Exactly what Jojo thought. *Fuuckkk*. 'And I hope you don't mind, but I asked Mark to steal a copy of Miranda England's latest from your office. She's great, isn't she? Pure escapism.' Exactly what Jojo thought. *Fuuckkk*.

'You read a lot.' She sounded robotic but, hey, she was in shock.

'I love books,' Cassie sparkled with glee, 'and the only thing better than a book is a *free* book.' Exactly what Jojo thought. *Fuuckkk*.

'Hand. Y. For. You,' she said, in her Dalek monotone, 'Know. Ing. Some. One. In. Pub. Lish. Ing.'

Cassie smiled affectionately at Mark. 'He has his uses.' Then she giggled. Giggled! Like she'd thought of other uses for Mark. She tugged him by the tie, 'Come along, birthday boy.'

Feeling worse than she had in the longest time, Jojo went to Becky and Andy's, where they poured her wine and let her vent.

'I had the shittiest day. I've just met Cassie Avery and she's a babe.'

Becky snorted.

'No, really. She was warm and fun and her hair was beautiful. She called me a gorgeous creature. And this is the fur-eek-iest thing, she was wearing the blue leather jacket that I nearly bought.'

Becky couldn't mask her shock at that.

'I reckon she knows all about you,' Andy said. 'She's had you followed and was sending you a message with the jacket. Good job you don't have a rabbit.'

'You watch too many low-rent thrillers,' Becky said. 'But, Jojo, I think she must suspect about you. Sounds like she was putting on a show. I mean come on, the jacket. And you say her hair was nice. Like she'd just had it done?'

'Yes.'

'See?'

'It wasn't like that. I honest-to-God think the jacket was just a coincidence. I mean, it was pure chance that I met her at all. I really don't think she knows about me.'

'I thought she was just a silly woman who ate cheese sandwiches even though she knew they gave her migraines,' Andy said.

'And me. What a difference a week makes. Last Friday I felt so guilty, I didn't want Mark to ever leave her, this week I want him to, so bad, but I'm afraid he never will.'

She went hot and cold with fear. Until now, she'd been in control, but that one short encounter with Cassie had cast her adrift.

Ages ago Andy had said something about the danger of getting involved with your boss. He'd been right.

'I feel sick. What if he picked me to have a fling with because he thought I'd never ask him to leave her? And why did he make me think she was a frump?'

'But did he?'

Jojo thought. Maybe not. And hadn't he told her right at the start that his wife understood him? He'd even said that sometimes they still slept together. But she felt so shaken and uncertain . . .

She told them the rest of what happened and Becky concluded, 'At least she didn't put the cigarette in his mouth, so that they drove away looking buddy-buddy, like Thelma and Louise.'

'And you're a bit pissed,' Andy said. 'Things always seem worse when you're pissed.'

'They always seem *better* when you're pissed, you moron.'

'Oh, right. Sorry.'

Saturday morning

Flowers arrived. It had happened once too often. They represented broken dates, bikini lines which had been waxed for no reason, punnets of strawberries she'd had to eat all on her own. Now she hated flowers.

Shortly afterwards her phone rang. She checked caller-display: Mark's mobile. She picked up and, dispensing with pleasantries, asked, 'Where's Cassie?'

'Oh. In the spa.'

'How was your seven-course dinner?'

'Wha—?'

'And your four-poster bed?'

'The—?'

'And the Romanesque pool. Look, stop sending me flowers.'

'But they're to let you know I love you when I can't be with you.' He sounded hurt.

'I know, yeah, I know, but arranging them, picking up dead petals from the floor and fitting dead bunches in a garbage bag without getting stem-slime on my fingers—you know what? I seem to do fuck all else and I've had it.'

'This is about Cassie.'

'I guess.'

There was the longest silence, then he said in a heavy, resigned voice, 'We've got to talk.'

She was shot through with a thrill of something very nasty.

Then he said, 'This couldn't have gone on for ever,' and her head lifted with shock.

She wasn't ready for this to be over yet. 'Talk to me now, Mark.'

'I can't. Cassie will be back soon. I'll see you tomorrow.'
She hung up. Fuck. Twenty-four hours to get through.
Right away, she rang Becky, who arrived an hour later with Andy.
'You must be in agony,' Becky observed.
Jojo shrugged.
'You're being ever so brave.'
'That's me, Becks. Tough. Stronger than the average woman.'
'Yes.' Becky and Andy exchanged a look, acknowledging the bottle of
red wine that Jojo was ploughing through, the cigarette smouldering in
the ashtray, the other cigarette between her fingers.
'One good thing,' Jojo mused. 'At least I didn't spend all my money
on a first edition of *The Grapes of Wrath* for his birthday. I just got him a
first edition of *The Pearl* because *The Grapes of Wrath* was way pricey.'
'Don't give it to him. Resell it on the Internet,' Becky said.
'Give it to him,' Andy said. 'Stay on his right side. Whatever happens,
he's still your boss.'
'I'm sure her career is the least of her worries,' Becky chided.
'This is Jojo,' Andy chided back. 'Not you.'

The following day Mark arrived at Jojo's at one fifteen. He tried to
embrace her and she stepped away from him. He followed her into the
front room where they sat in sombre silence.
'I love my kids,' he said.
'I know.'
'I never wanted to leave them. I told you that right from the start.'
'Always.'
'I've been looking for the right time to leave them. I wanted them to
have one last happy-family holiday, so I thought I'd go after we come
back from Italy in August, but then they're about to start a new school
year, so that's a terrible time.' He hitched and dropped his shoulders.
'Jojo, I've realised there'll be no right time. Ever.'
Her heart seemed to stop.
'So let's do it now,' he said. 'Today.'
'Excuse me?'
'Today. I'll tell Cassie today. I'll leave her today.'
'*Today?* Waitaminute, you're way ahead of me. I thought you were
breaking up with me.'
'Break *up* with you?' He was a picture of confusion. 'Why would you
think that? I love you, Jojo.'
'Because you said we had to talk. And because you never told me
Cassie was so, like, attractive.'
'But you'd seen her before. You knew what she looked like.'

'I don't remember her looking like that.'

She lit a cigarette; the turnabout had been too speedy. She'd thought she was losing him, she'd half come to terms with it, and instead things were accelerating in the other direction. He was coming to live with her. Today.

After thinking she'd lost him, she wanted him with an intensity that frightened her. But first there was a question she needed the answer to. 'Mark, did you sleep with her this weekend?'

He laughed. 'No. Since I've been with you, I couldn't be with anyone else.'

She had to believe him.

He got to his feet. 'I'm going to go home now and tell her. I don't know when I'll be back—'

'Wait, wait, no wait. Today is too soon.'

He looked at her curiously. 'When, then?'

She thought about it. When would be the best time to deprive Sam and Sophie of their dad? Next week? Four weeks' time? When? The procrastination couldn't go on for ever, they needed a definite date. 'OK,' she said finally. 'Have your family holiday in August.'

'Are you sure?'

'I'm sure.'

'OK. The end of August. Now can we go to bed?'

Monday morning

To: Jojo.harvey@LIPMAN HAIGH.co
From: Mark.avery@LIPMAN HAIGH.co
Subject: Meet me for lunch

I've something to tell you. Antonio's in Old Compton Street at 12.30.

To: Mark.avery@LIPMAN HAIGH.co
From: Jojo.harvey@LIPMAN HAIGH.co
Subject: Re: Meet me for lunch

ANTONIO'S??! Last time I was in that dump, I was working as a bargirl and Becky got poisoned. This'd better be good.

Mark was already there when she arrived, a coffee in front of him.

She squashed into the too-small booth.'What's up?'

'Jocelyn Forsyth is retiring.'

Her breath caught. 'Yay! When?'

'November. It'll be announced when he's told his clients, but I thought you'd like to know a.s.a.p.'

'Thank you.' She was suddenly excited and bright-eyed. 'Sometimes it can be very handy sleeping with the managing partner. So Lipman Haigh will be taking on a new partner, right?'

'Right.'

'Who's it going to be?'

He laughed regretfully. 'I don't have that much power, Jojo. That's up to all the partners to decide.'

'So I'd better be real nice to all the partners.'

'Starting with me.' He slid his thigh between hers. 'Shall we order?'

'I dunno. Eating in here is a form of extreme sport.'

He nudged his thigh in a bit further. 'A little more,' she said, shifting down slightly in her seat, letting her legs fall open.

'Bingo,' she said quietly. 'I could get to like it in here.'

'Jojo. Jesus Christ,' he said with low intent. He gripped her hand and stared at her mouth, then at her nipples which were straining through her bra, her shirt and her close-fitting jacket.

He began to move his knee against her and she caught his hand in her mouth then, all of a sudden, she was dropping his hand like it burned; someone she recognised was coming in. It was Richie Gant.

Eye contact was made, like a complicated knife-throwing trick and everyone froze, locked in mortification.

Fuck, Jojo thought, feeling strangely dislocated.

He backed out of the door and Jojo and Mark looked at each other.

To: Jojo.harvey@LIPMAN HAIGH.co
From: Mark.avery@LIPMAN HAIGH.co
Subject: I've been thinking . . .

Maybe we should wait until after the partnership appointment in November before we become official. I don't want 'us' to damage your trajectory.
M xxx

Jojo stared at her screen in dismay. Was Mark bailing on her? November was a long, long way away; so long that it might never happen. Was he getting cold feet?

The possibility scared her so much, she was actually surprised.

She went to his office and walked in. 'What's going on?'

'With what?'

'We agreed on August, now you want to change it to November. If you're trying to bail on me, forget it.'

Mark raised his eyebrows in polite enquiry. 'I made the suggestion with your career—and only that—in mind.'

She nodded, a little intimidated by his clipped tones. 'I bet Richie Gant has told the partners he saw us together.'

'Maybe. But an affair is different from my having left my wife to set up shop with you.'

She thought about it: he was right. It would be better to wait. And November was only a short while after August. It was just that . . .

'I'm usually the one who keeps deferring our big day,' she admitted.

'I had noticed,' he said, drily.

'You've been very patient.'

'I would wait for you for ever.' Then he added, 'Although, obviously, I would prefer not to have to.'

'November it is. When? The day of the decision?'

'Why not wait until it's official and published in *Book News*? No point spoiling the ship and all that.'

'You're doing it again.'

'What?'

'Scaring me.'

'There's nothing to be afraid of.'

Thursday afternoon

'Tania Teal on line one for you. Accept or reject?'

'I'd rather stick a rusty compass in my eye.'

'I didn't ask you that. Accept or reject?'

'OK. Accept.'

Click, then Tania's anxiety was pouring down the phone line. 'Jojo, that Irish thing you sent me,' Tania said. 'Have you managed to sell it?'

She meant Gemma Hogan's book: the one Jojo couldn't even give away.

But she wasn't telling Tania that. 'You might just have got lucky,' she said. 'It's still available but only just. I've got two houses about to bite—'

'How much?' Tania interrupted. 'Ten grand?'

'Er—'

'Twenty? Thirty, then.'

Jojo said nothing. Why should she? Tania was doing the bidding for her.

'Thirty-five?'

Jojo made her pitch. 'A hundred for two.'

Tania whispered, 'Christ.' Then in a proper voice asked, 'Is there a second book?'

'Sure.' She didn't know for certain, but there probably was.

'Sixty for one,' Tania said. 'And that's it, Jojo. I don't want another author, I've too many as it is. I just need a stopgap.'

It wasn't perfect. A two-book deal was always better because it meant the house was committed to the long-term future of the author.

But still a deal was better than no deal. Sixty grand was better than a thousand. And who knows, if the book did well, she could get Gemma a second deal for a lot more.

'OK. *Runaway Dad* is yours.'

She could actually feel Tania wince. 'That name will have to go.'

Then Jojo rang Gemma, who was thrilled she'd been sold to Lily Wright's editor.

'Thank you for trying again for me. I knew you could convince her.'

Authors, Jojo thought. Buncha know-nothings. Then Jojo told Gemma about the money.

'*Sixty* grand. Sixty *grand*. Oh, great! Fabulous! Fantastico!'

Fantastico, indeed. No need to tell Gemma she was the literary equivalent of a Band-Aid, because this might work out very nicely.

Lily

***Book News*, 5 August**

RECENT ACQUISITIONS

Tania Teal from Dalkin Emery has bought *Chasing Rainbows*, the debut novel from Irish writer Gemma Hogan. Agented by Jojo Harvey from Lipman Haigh, the book sold for a reported £60,000. Described as a cross between Miranda England and Bridie O'Connor, it will be published next May as a paperback original.

I was skimming through *Book News*, looking for any excuse not to write, when the words 'Gemma' and 'Hogan' leapt off the page, waited until they had my full attention, then punched me in the stomach. Gripping the page too hard, I read the piece properly. *Gemma. Book. My agent. My editor. Lots of money.* I sank my face into my hands; this was a message, like the horse's head in the bed in *The Godfather*.

I am gifted at intuition, at premonitions even, and I knew the game was up. Although I had feared some form of retribution, so much time had passed that I had begun to hope that Gemma had moved on with her life and perhaps even quietly forgiven me. But I had been mistaken: all this time she had been planning revenge. I was not sure exactly how she was going to ruin my life, I could not have given precise details there and then, but I knew this was the start of an unravelling.

I picked up the phone, blew the dust off it through trembling lips and rang Anton.

'Gemma's written a book.'

'Gemma Hogan?'

'It gets worse. Guess who her agent is? Jojo. And guess who her editor is? Tania.'

'No! That can't be right.'

'It is, I promise. It's in *Book News*.'

Silence. Then: 'Christ, she's sending us a warning shot across the bows. It's like the horse's head in *The Godfather*.'

'That's just what I thought.'

'Ring Jojo, find out what it's about. But it's got to be about us, right?'

'Yes, and the worst bit of all'—I could hardly utter the words, so great was my jealousy—'she got a huge advance.'

'How much?'

'Sixty thousand.'

Anton became quiet for a long, long time, then I heard a whimper.

'What?' I almost shouted.

'I picked the wrong girl!'

'Oh, ha bloody ha,' I said crossly.

I phoned Jojo. I managed the polite 'Howareyou?' thing, then striving for casual but sounding half-strangled, I said, 'Er, I read in *Book News* that you have a new author called Gemma Hogan. I was wondering—'

'Yeah, it's the one you know,' Jojo said. 'She said to say hi to you. Ages ago. I'm sorry I forgot.'

'She . . . she had a message for me?'

'She just asked me to say hello.'

Dread swamped me. Any hope that this was a bizarre coincidence dissolved. Gemma had planned this. It was deliberate and targeted.

'Jojo, can I ask . . . do you mind, is it breaking client confidentiality . . . what's her book about?'

'Her dad leaving her mom.'

'And a best friend stealing someone's boyfriend?'

'No, just the dad leaving the mom. It's fun! I'll get a copy to you, soon as they're proofed.'

'Thanks,' I whispered, and hung up.

Ema has run away with a marauding gang of chartered accountants, I thought. *Anton has a touch of dry rot in his left leg and I lost my mother in a card game.*

I forced myself to concentrate hard on the horridness of this scenario.

Then I did the mental equivalent of elbowing myself and saying, 'Silly! None of those things are true!'

This exercise usually makes me grateful for my lot.

Not today, though.

Anton rang back, 'Have they turned up yet?'

No need to ask who 'they' were: the builders. Our obsession, our fixation, the centre of our lives.

We bought our beautiful redbrick dream house and moved in at the end of June. Spirits had been sky-high. I was so happy I thought I might die. Before we had even moved in, we had a building firm lined up to repair our dry rot as a prelude to 'knocking things through'. We had not even fully unpacked when a small army of Irish labourers descended upon us.

The Mad Paddys wielded their claw hammers and set to work with zeal, behaving as though they were on a demolition job—they ripped the plaster from the walls, then the bricks, then pretty much removed the entire front of the house; the only thing that kept it from toppling over into the front garden was a mesh of scaffolding.

For almost a week they slashed and destroyed and just at the point when they were meant to start reassembling our ruined house, they discovered the dry rot was a lot worse than originally thought.

And the cost of the job? In light of the new discoveries, the original quote doubled overnight. Those in the know told us this was textbook, but I took it personally.

Muttering something about needing new window lintels—whatever on earth they were—and not being able to do anything until they arrived, the boys disappeared. Once more, I took it personally. For two full weeks we saw nothing of them. Gone, but not, however, forgotten.

Anton, Ema, Zulema—I will get to Zulema—and I, were existing in squalor. Builders' tools were strewn about the house and one of them, a foot-long wrench, had become the unlikely object of Ema's affections. She had become so attached to it, she now insisted on sleeping with it. Other children become fixated with velveteen rabbits or small blankets; mine had fallen in love with a builder's wrench and had named it Jessie.

But worse than all the other plagues put together was the omnipresent dust . . . Beneath our fingernails, between our bedsheets, behind our eyelids—it was not unlike living in a sandstorm.

It was wretchedness beyond description, especially for me, because I 'worked' from 'home', but when I begged Anton to do something, he insisted the men would return when the lintels had arrived from wherever lintels come from.

'No, Anton, no sign of them yet.'

'It's your turn to ring them.'

'Excuse me, I think not. I rang them first thing this morning.' We rang them four or five times daily.

'You didn't, Zulema did.'

'Because I bribed her to.'

'What was it, this time?'

I hesitated. 'My toner.'

'The toner I bought you? The Jo Malone stuff?'

'Yes,' I said. 'I'm sorry, don't be cross. I did love it, I do. But I loathe ringing them so much and she's quite good at it. They don't laugh at her.'

OK, Zulema: Zulema was our au pair. She was part of our brave new world—new house, me writing my next book, etc. She was a tall, good-looking, strong-willed Latina who had arrived three weeks ago from Venezuela.

I was terrified of her. So was Anton. Even Ema's perpetual grin dimmed a little in her presence.

Her arrival in our lives had originally been planned to coincide with the end of the building work. We had hoped to welcome her into a beautiful dry-rot-free home, but the house was still a wreck on her arrival date. Zulema took one look at the scaffolding-clad house and its all-pervasive dust and announced, 'You leeve like animals. I weell not stay here.'

With terrifying speed she found a boyfriend—someone called Bloggers (Why? I have no idea.), who had a nice flat in Cricklewood—and moved in with him. 'Do you think she'd let us come too?' Anton had asked.

Zulema was very helpful. Dreadfully helpful. All day long she policed Ema so that I was entirely free to write, but I missed Ema and I loathed the very concept of having an au pair.

'Zulema?' I called.

She pushed open my study door. She looked displeased. 'I feed Ema.'

'Yes, um, thank you.' Ema appeared between Zulema's legs, winked at me—conspiratorially? But she was only twenty-two months . . . much too young to wink conspiratorially . . . then clattered away. 'Zulema, would you mind ringing Macko again? This time, *beg* him to come?'

'What weell you geeve mee?'

'Er, cash? Twenty pounds?'

'I like Super Line Corrector from Prescriptives.'

I looked at her beseechingly. My beloved night cream. And it was new. But what choice did I have?

'OK.' At this rate I would have no skincare left at all.

She returned within seconds.

'He say he ees comeeng.'

'Do you think he meant it?'

She shrugged and stared at me. What did she care? 'I weell take Super-line Corrector.'

'You do that.'

Zulema thumped upstairs to spirit away my night cream from my dressing table, and I resumed staring at my desk. Perhaps they would come this time. Just for a moment, I let myself hope and my spirits inched upwards. Then my copy of *Book News* caught my eye and I was reminded of Gemma's huge book deal—I had forgotten briefly—and my spirits lowered themselves back to base. Cripes, what a day.

My new book was about a man and a woman who had been childhood chums and had met again as adults on Friends Reunited. Almost thirty years earlier, when they had both been five years old, together they had witnessed a murder. At the time they had not understood what they had seen, but their reunion had unlocked long-dormant memories. They were both married to other people, but as they began to explore what they thought might have happened, they became closer to each other. As a result their marriages were suffering. It was not what I wanted to write, it made me unhappy, but it was still what my fingers persisted in typing.

I frowned at my screen to show that I meant business, and off I went. I did my best. I typed words, yes, they were definitely words—but were they any good?

All at once, I became aware of the noise of a lorry chugging outside. At that moment the doorbell rang and voices sounded from the front step. Male voices. Shouty, tarry, cement-coated male voices. Could it be . . .?

I glanced through my little window. They had arrived! Macko and his team had finally arrived to fix my house! It had been worth losing my toner and night cream. I could have kissed Zulema. Had I not been afraid of being turned into a pillar of salt.

I opened the front door and let the Mad Paddys stomp in. Because they all looked the same, I was never sure exactly how many there were, but today there appeared to be four. The pick-up that chugged on the spot outside contained big, thick pieces of wood—the elusive lintels! Shouting and trying to order each other about, the Mad Paddys carried them upstairs, dislodging lumps from the walls and sizable chips from the coving. (Original, irreplaceable, but at the time I was happy enough to overlook it.)

I rang Anton. 'They're here! With the lintels! They're removing the old ones as we speak! Leaving enormous holes in the walls!'

Silence. More silence.

'Anton? Did you hear me?'

'Oh, I heard you all right. I'm just so happy I might puke.'

For the rest of the day I sat in my study trying to write, while a team of builders swarmed over my house shouting and banging. I sighed happily. All was well with the world.

Tania Teal biked over a completed copy of *Crystal Clear*. It was a beauty, with a cover similar to *Mimi's Remedies*. That cover had been a slightly blurry oil painting of a pretty, witchy woman against a background of duck-egg blue. This was a slightly blurry oil painting of a pretty, witchy woman against a lavender background. It actually looked like the same slightly blurry oil painting, but the *Mimi's Remedies* woman had blue eyes and wore button boots, whereas the *Crystal Clear* woman had green eyes and wore kitten heels. Tons of differences.

It would go on sale in two months' time, on the 25th of October, but from tomorrow would be on sale in the airports. 'Good luck, little book,' I said, and kissed it. If I had not died of exhaustion by tonight, I would take it to Irina's.

Irina's circumstances had changed. She had met a Ukrainian 'businessman' called Vassily, who had plucked her from grim old Gospel Oak and installed her in a serviced apartment in St John's Wood. She still worked part-time in her job as a cosmetics assistant, but this was only out of love of Clinique, not because she needed the money. 'I think of having to live vithout the free semples and I think I might die.' (She had struck her breast dramatically, then flipped a compact to examine her lipline.)

I had already visited her in her new home: a large three-bedroomed apartment in a purpose-built block. Green leaves clustered at the second-floor windows and even though this was the home of a Russian kept-woman who was being bankrolled by a Ukrainian gangster, it felt terribly respectable. I especially admired the lack of dust.

September saw both advances and reverses in our fortunes.

Anton and Mikey had spent much of the summer pulling together a big, glitzy deal that would make Eye-Kon. It was all gelling satisfactorily and contracts were ready to be signed, when the script attracted sudden Hollywood interest and the whole deal collapsed like a house of cards. It plunged Anton into a black depression.

Witnessing his despair was truly frightening, because his default state was irrepressible optimism. But too many deals had gone wrong for him to bounce back this time. He talked about what a failure he was, how he had let me and Ema down, and he began making noises about seeking out an alternative career. 'Bartending, perhaps,' he said, prone in bed. 'Or beekeeping.'

On the plus side, something about his brooding despair affected the builders. Without us even having to chivvy them, they quietly installed three out of four of the new lintels and even began to replaster the main bedroom.

For a whole week Anton stayed away from work. 'I've no stomach for it,' he said.

He spent a lot of time with Ema. He had somehow managed to shake Zulema for the week. I suspected—but did not ask—that he had had to pay her to stay away.

Anton stood at the door of my study and watched me typing. Several emotions fought on his face. 'You work so hard,' he said, then called, 'Ema, where are you?'

Ema marched in, wearing a red and blue horizontal-striped all-in-one vest and shorts. Anton watched her tenderly.

'You look like a Hungarian weightlifter,' he said, then, after further scrutiny, '*circa* 1953.'

I knew then he was getting better.

However, he never fully returned to his old self. He made countless references to how hard I worked, to the fact that any money coming in was generated by me and that if it wasn't for me, we would have nothing. It frightened me because I did not enjoy the feeling that everything—from our home to our food—depended on me.

On the last day of September, my first royalty cheque for *Mimi's Remedies* arrived. It was for such a ridiculously large sum—£150,000— that it seemed like a joke cheque. I wept with pride.

Anton took a photo of me holding the cheque, like a Pools' winner— then I kissed it goodbye because almost all of it was committed elsewhere. To the bank, the builders, the credit-card people . . .

'Only you and I could get a cheque for a hundred and fifty grand and two days later be left with almost nothing!' I said to Anton.

'But we've spent it on good stuff,' he said. 'Look at us—responsible adults. We've paid the first instalment on the house to the bank, now they won't repossess.'

'And our next instalment is due—'

'On the 30th of November, when you've signed your new contract with Dalkin Emery.'

'But, what if everyone hates *Crystal Clear*?' I said. 'What if no one buys it? Dalkin Emery won't give me a new contract. And without a new contract, we won't have enough money to pay the next instalment on this house.'

Losing this house! My scalp crawled with terror. I could not imagine anything worse.

Calmly, Anton began to intone, '*Crystal Clear* is a great book. Dalkin Emery are doing a massive campaign for it. It will be a great success. Dalkin Emery have talked about it being a Christmas number one. In a month's time Jojo will go to them and they will offer you a new contract with a huge advance. Everything will be fine. Everything *is* fine.'

Jojo

Monday morning, early November

To: Jojo.harvey@LIPMAN HAIGH.co
From: Mark.avery@LIPMAN HAIGH.co
Subject: News. Possibly bad

Jocelyn's changed his leaving date to January. He started with Lipman Haigh in January thirty-seven years ago and, ever the traditionalist, he wants a nice round sum.

This means the partnership decision won't be until January either.

Monday night, Jojo's flat

'What do we do now?' Mark asked.

'About what?'

'About us.'

Jojo lapsed into thought. 'We said we'd wait until after the partnership decision. Nothing's changed. We just push it back a couple of months.'

'What's the point in waiting? Everyone in work knows anyway, thanks to Richie Bigmouth.'

'But everyone knowing we're having an affair isn't as bad as you leaving your wife and setting up home with me. C'mon,' she cajoled Mark. 'You were the one who wanted to wait until after the partnership decision!' she said.

'But now that everyone knows, it's kind of moot. I'm going home.'

Wednesday morning

Jojo switched on her computer. She was anxious. The new best-seller list appeared at nine o'clock every Wednesday morning, and she was a little spooked about how Lily Wright's new hardback was doing. After the runaway success of *Mimi's Remedies*, everyone had expected it to be a Christmas number one. But, initially at least, Jojo had had slight, niggly doubts; *Crystal Clear* was a very different book to *Mimi's Remedies*. Extreme realism, as opposed to *über*-escapism.

Jojo scrolled down through the top ten: nothing. The top twenty: nothing. There was Eamonn Farrell, at 44, and Marjorie Franks, one of her thriller writers, holding steady at 61. But where was Lily? On she scrolled, down, down, down. I must have missed it, she thought—and then she spotted it, buried deep at number 168. In its first week on sale it had sold a pitiful 347 copies. Shit. *Crystal Clear* had been expected to debut in the top ten but it looked like it was sticking to the shelves.

'*Mimi's Remedies* was a slow starter,' Manoj reminded her.

'*Mimi's Remedies* didn't have a two hundred k campaign behind it.'

Jojo's game plan had been to open negotiations for Lily's new contract the week after *Crystal Clear* came out—like, *today*—when, if everything had gone as it should, Lily's star would be at its zenith and all she would have to agree with Dalkin Emery was whether they'd like to give Lily an obscene amount of money, or simply a disgusting quantity. Now she wasn't so sure.

She rang Tania Teal. Making sure she sounded upbeat and confident, she sang, 'Time to talk turkey. Lily Wright's new deal. We're ready for our close-up.'

'Close-up of what?'

Shit. Jojo kept it steady. 'Of her new contract.'

'Rii-iight. I see. You said she was working on something new? It would probably be best if I took a look at it. Before we settle on a figure.'

This was not the enthusiastic response Jojo had hoped for.

But staying cheery, she said, 'Seven chapters of Lily Wright's FABU-LOUS new book being biked over to you right now. Get your cheque-book ready!'

Wednesday evening

She met Becky after work for a quick pizza.

Once they were settled Jojo said, 'My period's late.'

Becky became very still. 'How late?'

'Three days. I know it's nothing, but I'm always way regular. And I feel weird.'

'How?'

'Sort of . . . dizzy. And I sort of don't want to smoke.'

'Christ. Oh my God.' Becky bit her knuckles. 'Have you done a test?'

'This morning. Negative. But it's early, like, too early?'

'Could it have happened?'

'Mmmm, we use condoms but . . . accidents happen. And we did it right in the middle of the month. Easy to remember exactly when, when you're seeing a married man.'

'Less of the violins,' Becky said. 'How d'you think Mark will take it?' Becky chose her words carefully. 'Is there a chance he might not be happy?'

Jojo considered. 'Sure.' She half laughed. 'But he might be psyched. But what about me? It's not the right time to have a baby.'

'But it's never the right time—for anyone, not just you.' She sighed. 'I'd love to get up the duff, but we really can't afford to have a baby yet.'

'If I become a partner my income is actually going to drop over the next three years.'

'You what?'

'Partners have to invest money. Now that Jocelyn is leaving—if he *ever* does—the new partner will have to replace his moolah.'

'How much?'

'Fifty grand.'

'*Fifty grand?* Where are you going to get that sort of money?'

'I'm not. So how they do it is they deduct it from future earnings and pay me fifty grand less over the next three years.'

Friday evening, Jojo's flat

'Guess what?' Jojo said.

Mark looked at her, did a once-over, and something changed in his eyes, as if he'd retreated. 'You're pregnant.'

She paused, startled. 'Damn, you're good. Well, my period is five days late, but the test is negative.'

'Doesn't mean a thing. Same with Cassie. Test kept showing up negative but she was pregnant all right.'

They stared at each other, taking in that statement, then both dissolved into horrified giggles.

'Fuck!' Jojo breathed. 'You should know this: my dad will go apeshit and want to kill you. He'll call on you late some night with my three brothers and a shotgun.'

'I'd better make an honest woman of you, in that case.'

Then the news seemed to hit him and he lapsed into silence. He wiped his hand across his mouth once, then again. 'Um, this is big stuff, Jojo. Big, unplanned stuff.'

'Duh! I had noticed.'

'I reckon I always assumed this would happen *sometime*. Us. Babies.' He paused and added dismally, 'But not this soon.'

'How bad do you feel?'

'Quite honestly, Jojo, I would have preferred us to have some time together on our own, before children came along.' He furrowed his brow. 'How did this *happen*? I mean, we've been careful, haven't we?'

'Accidents happen.'

He acknowledged that. 'Yes, I suppose they do. I have to tell Cassie right now. It can't be put off any longer.'

Jojo's insides crumpled with shame. 'Me being pregnant is going to make it far worse for her.'

'I know. But it's not fair to her not to tell her.'

'You're right but could you wait until I get a positive result and we know for sure?'

Mark looked irritated, then he became sorrowful and took her hand. 'Jojo, listen to me, the partnership decision is in eight weeks' time. Then I am leaving my wife and coming to live with you. If that's not what you want, you'd better tell me.'

She felt panicky. 'I do want it. But this is hard for me. These are not the values I was brought up with.'

'They're not the values I was brought up with either, but I'm doing it because I love you. And I'm beginning to feel we're not on the same page.'

Some instinct was telling her she was suddenly a hair's-breadth away from losing him.

'Mark, you were the one who said we should wait until after the partnership decision. I don't recall being any too thrilled about that.'

'Not straight away. But once you got over your suspicion that I was stalling, then you were keen. Slightly too keen, in my opinion.'

That was the trouble with Mark. He was way smart.

She had a choice to make here: jump, or get off the bridge. OK, she would jump. 'Wait until I know for sure that the test is positive, then we'll tell her. OK?'

He stared at her and said, slowly, 'You're on notice but OK.'

'"On notice"? Don't speak to me like that. I'm not a fucking publisher who's late paying royalties.'

But he didn't apologise. He left without saying anything.

Wednesday morning

When Jojo's period arrived, ten days late, she was actually a little embarrassed; she wasn't usually a drama queen. But she was vaguely interested in what had caused the delay: anxiety about Mark leaving Cassie?

Waiting too long for the vote on the new partner? Work stress? And, yeah, there was *lots* to be stressed about.

On Lily Wright's second week on sale, there had been an improvement, but nothing like enough. She 'shot' from 168 to 94, selling a paltry 1,743 copies. Considering there wasn't a railway station in the land that wasn't plastered with ads for *Crystal Clear*, this wasn't good.

Poor Lily had dragged her sorry ass around the country, doing one gnarly reading after another. Daily, either she or Anton phoned, their voices small and scared, as they asked, 'Is there any news? Any word on the new deal?'

They were horrified that Dalkin Emery were taking so long but the situation was too delicate for Jojo to force.

Tuesday afternoon, end of November
'Tania Teal on line one.'

'Accept!'

This was the call, Jojo knew. The one that would condemn or save Lily Wright.

'Tania, hey.'

'Sorry, Jojo, it's no go on Lily Wright. We're not going to renew her contract.'

'Tania, you cannot be serious. Have you read her new book, do you know how great it is—'

'Jojo, I'm going to say what everyone is thinking. *Mimi's Remedies* was a one-off, a one-hit wonder. Readers' loyalties are not to Lily Wright the author but to *Mimi's Remedies*, the book. *Crystal Clear* is the biggest disaster we've ever had.'

'OK, the hardback sales are slow but you know what this means?' Jojo forced herself to sound wildly cheerful. 'The paperback will go through the roof! Just like *Mimi's Remedies* did!'

'If Lily Wright wants to write another *Mimi's Remedies*, I'd be happy to publish it,' Tania said. 'Otherwise it's no go. I'm sorry, Jojo, I really am.'

'Lily Wright is one of the hottest authors around,' Jojo said. 'If you don't want to publish her, there are plenty of others who will.'

'I understand, and good luck with it all.'

'Your loss,' Jojo said. She clattered the phone back and sat in gloomy contemplation. Rats. Now she had to tell Lily and she would prefer to shoot herself in the head. With a sigh, she lifted the phone again. Better to get it over with.

'Lily, I've heard from Dalkin Emery about the new contract.' Very quickly, before Lily had time to get any false hope, she said, 'I'm sorry but it's bad news.'

'How bad?'

'They don't want to buy the new book.'

'I can write another.'

'Unless it's another *Mimi's Remedies*, they don't want to renew the contract. I'm so, so sorry,' Jojo said, and meant it.

After a period of silence, Lily said quietly, 'It's OK. Please, Jojo, it's really OK.'

That was Lily all over: too sweet to start yelling and blaming.

'I feel lousy that I didn't get you to sign with them last May.' *When they still wanted you.*

'Don't feel bad. No one forced me to wait,' Lily said. 'It was my choice. Mine and Anton's.'

Jojo hung up, wiped out. Passing on bad news was as much a part of the job as delivering good stuff, but she was feeling more shitty than she had in a long, long time. Poor Lily.

And, on a selfish note, this wasn't such a great time for Jojo to fuck up. She didn't often make mistakes and hated when she did. But with the partnership decision coming up, this miasma of high-profile failure was not welcome. She was still in line to generate more income than any other agent this year but the gloss was gone from her crown a little.

Gemma

YOU KNOW, WRITING a book isn't as easy as it looks. First, my editor (I love saying that: 'my editor') made me rewrite loads of it, making Izzy 'warmer' and Emmet 'more human and less of a Mills & Boon caricature'—the cheek of her. Sorry, I mean, the cheek of 'my editor'. Then when I'd done that—and it took ages, all of August and most of September—some copy editor went through it and came back with eight million queries. *Then* I had to proofread it.

Mind you, with the advance they'd given me I wasn't complaining. I'd nearly collapsed and died when Jojo told me: sixty grand. *Sixty grand.*

My imagination, fevered at the best of times, went wild at the thought of all that loot: I'd give up my job and travel the world for a year. I'd replace my heartbreaking car. I'd go to Milan and buy up all of Prada.

Until I returned to earth and saw that this windfall was a result of my mother's misfortune. She was going to have to move house early in the new year; the advance money could make the difference between a hell-hole and a hovel.

We'd finally agreed on a name. No one had liked my suggestion of 'Sugar Daddy'. Or 'Mars Attack'. 'Shockolat' was a runner for a while, then someone at Dalkin Emery suggested 'Chasing Rainbows' and suddenly everyone was happy. Except me. I thought it sounded a bit *nice*.

The day the cover arrived was a great one. A soft-focus watercolour, in blues and yellows, it was a smudgy image of a girl looking like she'd lost her purse. But it had my name on it. My name!

'Mam, look!'

Even she got excited. She was nothing like as pitiful and bewildered as she'd been in the first post-Dad months. Dad's desire for a permanent financial settlement had changed her—it made her angry; no bad thing.

In the summer, Dad had sent us a letter confirming that the minute the year's separation was up, he'd be applying to the courts to sell the house. From the day he'd left, Mam and I had regarded his absence as temporary, like our lives had just hit the pause button. But after we got this letter, I had to negotiate some changes; we couldn't go on as we were.

It wasn't easy—Mam produced rivers of tears and a selection of ill-nesses, both fake and some real—but then she seemed to come to terms with my need for space, and by the end of the summer I got to sleep in my own flat three or four nights out of every seven. I saw her a lot more than most thirty-something women see their mothers, but it still felt like glori-ous freedom.

She studied the girl on my book cover. 'Is she meant to be you?'

'No, only figuratively.'

'You'll have to show it to Owen,' she said slyly.

She knew about Owen: in fact she'd met him. And, oddly enough, con-sidering her suspicion of anything that interfered with my time with her—like my job—she approved of him. I told her not to bother, because he wouldn't be around for long, and yet we had carried on, bickering enthusiastically, past the summer and into the autumn. And now here we were in November and we were still an item.

'Owen.' I shrugged dismissively.

'Don't play it down for me,' she said. 'You girls talk about finding The One, but The One comes in all shapes and sizes. Often you don't realise that that's who you've met. I know a woman who met her The One when she was on a ship following a man out to Australia. On the journey out she palled up with a lovely chap but she was so fixated on the man in Australia that she didn't realise the chap on the ship was her The One. She tried to get the first fellow to marry her, then came to her senses. Luckily the second chap was still interested. And I know another girl who . . .'

I tuned her out. I felt slightly uncomfortable because there was some-one besides Owen I wanted to show the book jacket to: Johnny the Scrip. It seemed only fair because he knew all about the book; he'd been so encouraging about it, when I used to be a regular visitor.

I didn't see him so much any more, and not just because Mam no longer needed so many tablets. No, around the time the flirting with Johnny was starting to blossom into something more meaningful, I'd had a little think. Owen was my boyfriend. For as long as it continued, I was going to treat him right.

Johnny must have been having similar thought processes because the next time I went to him, he asked, 'How's your non-boyfriend?'

I coloured. 'OK.'

'Still seeing him?'

'Yes.'

'Ah.' The word, as they say, spoke volumes.

He didn't say that he wasn't going to step on someone else's toes, but it was clear that that was what he meant. So, by silent mutual agreement, we both retreated.

'Mam.' I interrupted her story about someone else who'd missed her The One when he'd been right under her nose. 'Do you need anything from the chemist?'

She thought about it. 'No.'

'Oh, OK.' I'd go anyway.

Echinacea, I decided. That was a reasonable thing to buy, especially at this time of year. At the chemist Johnny greeted me with a smile. Mind you, he did that to everyone, even those with all-over-body psoriasis.

'Name your poison,' he said.

'Echinacea.'

'Coming down with a cold?'

'Er, no. Just precautionary. How's your brother doing?'

'Recovering nicely. He's doing a lot of physiotherapy on his leg and he's not enjoying it.'

I made a couple of 'ah, well' style noises, then went 'Oh!' like I'd just remembered something and pulled the cover from my bag. 'I thought you might like to see it.'

'What's this? The cover of your book!' He lit up. He looked genuinely happy for me. 'Congratulations!'

He studied the cover for ages, while I studied him. You know, he really was very nice-looking, his intelligent eyes, his lovely shiny hair. Mind you, it would be a disgrace if his hair *wasn't* shiny with him having access to all those hair products . . .

'It's really good,' he said finally. 'It's only smudgy lines but they've managed to make her look bereft. I'm looking forward to reading it.'

I got a twinge of something peculiar. Of course! In my book there was page after page about the loveliness of 'Will', i.e. Johnny, and I marvelled at the size of my stupidity. Johnny was bound to recognise himself; he was going to know I fancied him. Or had fancied him. He probably knew anyway, but still, how mortifying . . . Flustered, I took my leave.

'Your echinacea,' he called after me.

Liby

FIRST NATIONAL BANK
23A Edgeware Square, London SW1 1RR

5 December

Dear Mr Carolan and Ms Wright,

<u>Re: 37 Grantham Road, London NW3</u>

I refer you to clause 7(b) subclause (i) of the agreement drawn up between The First National Bank and Mr Carolan and Ms Wright on 18 June of this year. The clause states that a payment of £100,000 (one hundred thousand pounds sterling) is payable by Mr Carolan and Ms Wright to the bank no later than the 30th of November. As of the 5th of December such payment has not been received (and a telephone conversation with Mr Carolan has confirmed that the payment will not be received in the foreseeable future). I am left with no choice but to refer you to clause 18(a) which states, 'In the event of non-payment of any of the scheduled monies, the property is immediately forfeit.'

Therefore the property at 37 Grantham Road must be vacated by the 19th of December, two weeks from this date, and all keys for the property must be posted by first-class mail to the above address.

Yours sincerely,

Breen Mitchell

Special Loan Executive

It was like the end of the world.

Anton responded with, 'They can't do that' bluster and swore to me, 'We won't lose our home, baby.' But I knew he was mistaken.

Of course we rang the bank and did all we could in an attempt to convince them to give us until March, when everything could hopefully be salvaged. I pleaded, Anton implored, we even considered (briefly) putting Ema on the line to sing 'Twinkle, twinkle, little star'. They refused.

Some time in this hellish period, Zulema gave notice with immediate effect. It was not a good time for her to leave, but I acknowledged we could no longer afford to keep her.

By then, with all the to-ing and fro-ing with the bank, we had already wasted one of our two weeks of notice. It was twelve days before Christmas and we had a week to find somewhere to live.

So Anton bought the *Standard* and racked up several flats to view. Before I even saw the first one, I hated them all.

I know the letting agents thought Anton and I slightly weird. Anton, habitually so charming and likable, was absent. The person looking out from behind his eyes was not the Anton I knew. With a shock, I noticed he suddenly looked a lot older.

As for me, I found it hard to maintain proper eye contact because my eyes kept scudding from side to side, doing that constantly-moving-fish thing, that happens to extremely stressed people. But the agents could not know that, they must have simply thought I was a dodgy prospect.

After three days of viewing, we were obliged to make a decision and I opted for the last flat we had seen because it was the only one I could remember. It was in Camden, not far from our current home, and was new and characterless, with white boxy rooms. We signed a lease for three months. We had to pay cash because we were in such a hurry to move in. Also, because our bank references would not have passed muster.

And then we were on our knees, on a dusty floor, working through the night, packing an infinite number of boxes. Then it was the final morning, the removal van had arrived and a team of young Kiwi blokes in red shorts were loading it up. I leaned against a wall and wondered, Is this really happening? Any of it? Especially the red shorts?

Then the house was completely empty and there was no further reason to stay.

'C'mon, Lily,' Anton said gently.

'OK.'

But leaving my dream house buckled me. As I waited just a second too long to shut the front door behind me for the last time, I actually felt something change irrevocably within me. I was saying goodbye not just to four walls (three and a half, in any case—the builders had still not finished the small bedroom, not that it mattered any more) but to a life that Anton and I would never now get to live.

If it had been just me, I am not sure I would ever have unpacked in the new place. I would have located my duvet and a pillow and lived quite comfortably in the forest of cardboard boxes. However, because of Ema, it was necessary to get some things immediately functional. The TV, of course, was something she insisted upon. As was the sofa, to facilitate comfortable viewing.

By eight o'clock that night, most of the essentials were in place, and the speed of the transition was too much for me. This was our home now. I stared around at the smooth white walls; it was like being inside a cube. I loathed it. Perplexed, I looked at Anton and asked, 'How did things go so horribly wrong?'

Anton grabbed me by the wrist, trying to get my attention. 'At least we have each other.'

I was still surveying the bleak white walls. 'What?'

He looked at me in despair. 'I said, at least we have each other.'

Gemma

CHRISTMAS DAY, with just me and Mam, was horrendous. I only survived it by drinking nearly a litre and a half of Baileys.

All through the day, like a broken record, she kept saying, 'This is our last Christmas in this house.'

Last Christmas? It could be our last *month*. January was looming, when Dad would be applying for the court order. How quickly would it happen? How soon would the house be put on the market? Breda, our solicitor, said it could take months.

Anyway, you'll never guess what happened next . . .

No, go on. Try. OK, brace yourself.

On the 8th of January, a year to the day since he left, Dad came home. Just like that. I don't think he was even aware it was the anniversary of his leaving, it was just another weird turn in the weirdness that was the whole episode. His return was as low key as his departure: he simply showed up at the front door with three bags full of his stuff and asked Mam—at least he had the decency to ask—if he could come back.

Mam responded by pulling herself up to her full height and saying, 'Your floozy thrown you out then, has she? Well, you'd better make it up with her because there's no welcome for you here.'

Ah no, only joking. I wasn't there at the time, so I don't know exactly *how* quickly Mam hustled him into the house, but I'd put money on it being very, *very* fast.

By the time I came home from work that evening, he was settled in his chair, doing the crossword. Mam was in the kitchen cooking up a storm, and I had a moment when I genuinely wondered if I'd just dreamt the entire past year.

I ignored a nervous-smiling Dad and cornered Mam at the chopping board. 'Why did you let him back straight away? You could at least have made him suffer for a *while*.'

'He's my husband,' she said, going all weird and devout and unreachable. 'I made my wedding vows before God and man.'

Ah, vows. Them yokes; they'd made martyrs and eejits of generations of women. But what can you do? There's no reasoning with that sort of lunacy. And from a selfish point of view, his return was my get-out-of-jail card. Life could get back to normal.

'Why did he come home?'

'Because he loves me and doesn't love Her any more.'

'Any explanation for why he spent the last year living with a thirty-six-year-old?'

'Something to do with facing turning sixty.'

Right. Late-onset midlife crisis—nothing we hadn't figured out for ourselves.

'How do you know he's not going to turn round in a month's time and do it again?'

'He won't. He's got whatever it was, out of his system.'

'But he's going to see Colette every day at work.'

'No, he's not.' The way she said it got me interested—she sounded kind of triumphant. 'He's taking early retirement. Do you think I'd let him go into that place where she is every day? I told him to sack her or to leave himself.'

Suddenly I had a great idea. 'Come on,' I urged, 'let's drive over to their work and laugh at her.'

Briefly a light lit Mam's eyes, then she said, 'You go. I've to get your father's tea on.' Then she said halfheartedly, 'We have to forgive her.'

Pah! Too much was made of forgiveness. There was no way I was ever going to forgive Colette and I had no problem with that. A little bit of hatred never hurt anyone. Look at how I'd hated Lily for *years* and it had never done me any harm.

Speaking of hatred, there was something I had to tell Dad.

'I'm getting a book published.'

He expressed great delight—as much to do with the fact that I was talking to him, probably—and when I showed him the proof copy, he declared, 'Would you look at that: Gemma Hogan, my little girl. *Chasing Rainbows*, now that's a marvellous title. What's it about?'

'You leaving Mam and taking up with a girl only four years older than me.'

He was deeply shocked and looked, open-mouthed, at Mam to see if I was having him on.

'It's no joke,' I said.

'It's not.' Mam looked extremely uncomfortable.

'Jesus, Mary and Joseph,' he sounded panicked, 'I'd better read the fecker.' Six pages in he looked up, ashen-faced, 'We'll have to put a stop to this immediately. Im*med*iately. This can't get out.'

'Too late, Dad. I'm under contract.'

'We'll see a solicitor.'

'And I've spent loads of the advance.'

'I'll give you the money.'

'I don't want your money. I want my book to be published.'

'But look at it.' He smacked the pages with the back of his hand. 'All that personal stuff. And I wouldn't mind but plenty of it isn't even true! If this comes out I'm going to be very embarrassed!'

'Good,' I said, putting my face too close to his. 'It's called living with the consequences of your actions.'

'Gemma!' Mam summoned me into the kitchen. 'He's said he's sorry,' she said. 'And he means it. He was going through a crisis. In a way he couldn't help what he did. You're being very hard on him, in fact you can be very hard on everyone.'

That very night, I removed all my belongings from my parents' and officially moved back into my own flat.

I rang Owen to report the good news. 'We can see each other all the time now, if we want. Come over now, let's try out our new life for size.'

Half a *Coronation Street* later he arrived.

'I need to talk to you,' he said.

'Why?'

'Guess what?' He was smiling, but in a strange way.

'What?'

'Lorna rang me.' Lorna was his twenty-four-year-old ex and the prickly feeling on my scalp told me what was coming next. 'She wants us to get back together.'

'She does?'

'It happened exactly like you said it would: she saw us together on

271

Saturday, when we were in town shopping, and she realised what she was missing. You're brilliant!'

'That's me.' My voice was annoyingly wobbly.

'Christ, you don't mind, do you?'

'Of course I don't mind,' I choked, overwhelmed by ridiculous tears. 'I'm really happy for you. We always knew it was going nowhere.' But it had gone nowhere for nearly nine months.

He was silent, and when I looked up from my crying jag I saw why: he was crying too. 'I'll never forget you,' he said, wiping fat tears away from his face.

'Oh, stop being so melodramatic.'

'OK.' As if by magic, the tears disappeared and, really, he couldn't hide his happiness and how keen he was to get going.

Just before he got into his car, he yelled, in frothy high spirits, 'We'll all go out soon, me and Lorna and you and Anton. We'll plan the route for our holiday in the Dordogne!'

'And don't forget to call your first child after me,' I managed.

'Consider it done. Even if he's a boy.'

Then he gunned the car away, beeping and waving like he was in a wedding cavalcade.

Jojo

January

Jojo returned to London, full of hope for the new year. She'd had a happy holiday in New York with her family but knew that her next year's Christmas would be different. Not in NYC. More likely to be sharing space with accident-prone Sophie and dipso Sam, in Mark's and her new home, wherever that might be.

On her first day back, Manoj came in and dumped a box on her desk. 'Proof copies of Gemma Hogan's *Chasing Rainbows*.' The jacket was a pastel watercolour of a woman.

It was a cute little package, and Jojo gathered up ten copies and took them through to Jim Sweetman, to send to his movie contacts. 'Do your magic.'

The partnership vote was due on Monday, the 23rd of January—three weeks away. The first week passed without incident. Then the second week. The countdown for week three was under way—Monday, Tuesday, Wednesday was gone—then on Thursday morning the email arrived.

To: Jojo.harvey@LIPMAN HAIGH.co
From: Mark.avery@LIPMAN HAIGH.co
Subject: News. Possibly bad

I need to talk to you. My office a.s.a.p?
M xxx

What now?

Mark was sitting behind his desk, looking super-serious. 'I wanted to tell you in advance of tomorrow's meeting, Richie Gant has come up with something.'

'What?' Instantly Jojo was nervous. Skanky Boy was full of surprises, none of them nice.

'He's made friends with some of the marketing people from Lawson Global. They own soft drinks, cosmetics, sportswear . . . and it looks like they're interested in paying for mentions in some of Lipman Haigh's authors' books.'

She opened her mouth, she could barely speak. 'You mean, corporate sponsorship?'

'Not actual sponsorship of a title, not like *Coca-Cola's Horse Whisperer*, just mentions of a particular brand in the text.'

'Corporate sponsorship,' Jojo repeated. 'Exactly what you and I discussed, like, a year ago. We thought it sucked. I still think it sucks.'

'With the right fit, it doesn't have to be offensive.'

She gave him a long, perplexed look. 'This isn't happening. Mark, you're way off here. It's a cruddy idea.'

'Jojo, it's business, possibly very lucrative.'

He let this hang and the implication was clear. Leaving Cassie and setting up a second home with Jojo was going to cost them.

Jojo shuddered. 'You know what, Mark? I'm disappointed in you.'

He became very calm. Scary calm. 'I'm running a business. It's my job to explore the idea of bringing in more money. I have principles but being too high-minded doesn't work in a commercial arena. And, yes, I did think it was a crass idea, but I reserve the right to change my mind. Especially when it's presented as a fait accompli.'

'Gotcha,' Jojo said. 'Loud and clear.'

She powered out and he made no attempt to follow her, then she stood on the street and smoked with so much fury a passing man said, 'What did that poor cigarette ever do to you?'

Friday-morning meeting
Everyone already knew about Richie's new corporate connections, so at least Jojo didn't have to endure everyone going 'Ooohhh' approvingly, like he'd just pulled a cruddy old silk hanky out of a cruddy old silk hat.

But it wasn't over yet. Ever the showman, Richie gave possible scenarios. He turned to Jojo. 'Don't worry. I'll do my best with your authors. See if we can't earn them a little sponsorship money.'

'No need,' Jojo said crisply. 'My authors earn enough from *writing books*.'

'Up to them,' Richie shrugged, 'if they want to turn down free money. Just seems like a funny thing to advise them, that's all. Glad you're not *my* agent!'

'Not as glad as I am, dog-breath.' Although she only said 'dog-breath' in her own head. Ever the professional.

'Let's take Annelise Palmer,' Richie continued. 'A writer of racy bonk-busters, she'd be a good match with one of the expensive champagnes in Lawson Global's portfolio. If Annelise was game, and I know that old bird, I bet she would be'—he chuckled with such audience confidence that Jojo had to sit on her hands in case they hit him without her say-so—'that could net her up to a million quid. We get ten per cent and if we ask nicely they'll throw in a couple of crates of champers.'

'Have they actually proposed this?' Mark challenged. 'Have they actually mentioned this kind of money for individual authors?'

'Mentioned? You mean *promised*. For real,' Richie nodded seriously. 'Believe me, this is going to happen.'

The entire room went into shock. Even the ever-restless molecules of air seemed to pause their perpetual circling. A million smackers just for mentioning champagne!

Jojo watched everyone's expression change—they were looking at Richie like he was an alchemist. And they were already spending the loot. A new Merc. A holiday home in Umbria. A retirement spent on the QE2. Enough cash to leave your wife and set up a comfortable, worry-free home with your girlfriend. Jojo had to do something.

'So I could ring them right now,' she said, 'and tell them that Annelise is on for it, and to bike us over the million big ones in used fivers.' She pulled her handbag onto the table, produced her mobile phone.

Once again the room froze into stillness. All that moved were optic muscles as everyone played eye-tennis between Richie and Jojo. The seconds ticked for too long, Jojo's hand beneath the phone became slick with sweat, then Richie caved. 'Obviously this is only an example. Like, *obviously*.'

'Oh,' Jojo feigned breathy surprise, 'it's only an *example*.'

As people watched their dreams waver and dissolve, suddenly they were staring at Richie like he was a trickster.

But the sting in the tail was the announcement that the following day three of the Lawson Global guys were going with Richie, Jim Sweetman and Mark to a luxury country hotel to play golf and bond. Jojo tried to hide her disbelief. Mark had not told her about this and also, when did that shit-head Gant learn to play golf?

'How come I'm not invited?'

'Why should you be?'

'I brought in more money than any other agent last year and I'm on course to do it again this year.'

'Can you play golf?' Richie asked.

'Sure I can.' Like, how hard could it be? Especially if she pretended every golf ball was his head.

'Shame,' Richie wall-eyed her. 'It's already booked and there are no more places.'

After the meeting ended she went to Mark's office, closed the door behind her and said, 'You never told me you were going away to play golf with these guys.'

'You're right, I didn't.'

'Why not?'

'You're not the boss of me.'

It was like a staple gun to the heart. 'Mark! What's happening? Why are you being so horrible?'

'Why are *you* being so horrible?' He was far too calm and at times like this she remembered, *really* remembered why she'd fallen for him in the first place: his strength of character, his ability to see the big picture . . .

'I'm not being horrible, Mark.'

He shrugged. 'And I'm just doing my job.'

'Even when it conflicts with me?'

'I don't see it that way. You may not believe me, but everything I do, I'm doing for us.'

Thanks to Slimeball Gant things with Mark were starting to get messy; she would not allow it. She made a big, almost superhuman effort to get over herself.

'I believe you.'

Saturday morning, Jojo's flat
Before Mark left for his golf weekend, Jojo said, 'You're not to tell those Lawson guys what I'm like in bed.'

'Why would I do that?'

'I know what guys are like, telling sexist jokes and discussing women.'

'How?'

'Because I'm one of them.'

He put his hand on her waist, then slid it upwards. 'I don't think so.'

He took his hand away and she replaced it.

'Jojo, we don't have time for this.'

'Yes, we do.'

'I'll be late.'

'Good.'

Sunday afternoon, Jojo's flat

Mark came straight from the hotel to her.

'Hey, baby.' She gathered him in her arms like he'd just come home from war. 'It's OK, you're OK now.'

She followed him into her living room and asked, 'How bad was it?'

He smiled. 'Bad. I had to smoke a cigar and you know how you have to cut a bit off the end?' Jojo didn't.

'Well, one of the Lawson blokes kept making circumcision jokes about it.'

'Eeewww. Worst moment of the entire weekend?'

Mark thought about it. 'When one of the Lawson blokes described another man as, "He's the one guy who if he fell into a pool of tits would come out sucking his thumb."'

'Eeewww,' Jojo repeated. 'How was Gant?'

Mark just shrugged.

'Help me out here?' Jojo burst out. 'Just tell me how anyone could like him. Like, what am I missing?'

Mark thought about it. 'He's good with people, he intuits what they like and then homes in on it.'

'He doesn't do it with me.'

'He doesn't need you to like him.'

'He will when I'm a partner and he isn't.'

Her words hung in the air and when Jojo spoke, the anxiety that had dogged her all weekend, and made her buy an impractical, ridiculously expensive clutch bag, broke through. 'Can we talk about tomorrow? Do you think I'll get it?'

'You deserve it.'

'But do you think I'll get it?'

'It's between you and Richie Gant.'

'Yeah, and *let's* look at the facts. I'm a great agent, I make more money than anyone else including Gant. Can I do more than that? I don't think so.'

She believed in thinking positive. But she woke up in the middle of the night, thinking not so positive. Mark had gone home and she was glad; she didn't want him to see her like this. She was imagining what it would be like if she wasn't made partner tomorrow. Apart from the shock and humiliation, Richie Gant would be her new boss, well, one of them. And he would not be a gracious winner. She'd have to leave Lipman Haigh and start all over again for someone else. Prove herself, build alliances, generate income. It would set her back at least two years. The panic was starting to spiral within her, moving up and up to block her throat.

She got it together. Richie Gant was good—and sneaky. But his corporate sponsorship project was all talk. No one was in any immediate danger of making any money from it. She was a better agent. Fact. She generated more income. Her authors were excellent long-term prospects. How could she not get it?

Liby

ANTON WAS HOME from work. He shot into the room and said, 'Look at what I got sent today.' I had not seen him so animated in a long time.

He brandished a book and when I saw that it was Gemma's book, *Chasing Rainbows*, I lunged and grabbed it, desperate to read it. Nausea set up a familiar churning.

'How did you get this?'

'Proof copy. Jim Sweetman, the media fella over at Lipman Haigh, sent it to me. And,' Anton said, all aglow, 'it's not about us.'

'What's it like?' I asked. 'Is it good?'

'Nah.' But excitement was hopping from him, zigzagging like colour through the air.

Surprised, I accused, 'You like it.'

'I don't.'

I held my breath because I knew there was a 'but' coming.

'But,' he said, 'I'd like to option it.'

I was stunned into silence. All I could think was that he had not optioned my book. Either of them.

It was five weeks since we had moved out of our house, but it felt a lot longer. Losing our home had been catastrophic, but I was under no illusions that there was still a lot further to fall. Anton and I were unravelling. I was watching it happen from a distance, like it was happening to another couple.

We no longer had anything to say to each other; our disappointment was too huge a presence. I bitterly resented Anton's recklessness with money. I was obsessed with the house we had lost and felt it was all his fault. And, although Anton did not articulate it, I knew *he* blamed *me* for not writing another hit book. Briefly, we had been on the crest of the wave and it was difficult to adjust to all that excitement and hope being whipped away.

We barely spoke and when we did, it was simply to snap child-care instructions at each other.

It felt like a long, long time since I had drawn a proper breath. Every inhalation was a shallow panicked little effort, which brought no relief, and I never slept more than four hours a night. Anton kept promising me that life would improve. And he seemed to think it just had.

'Chloe Drew would be perfect for the lead!' he enthused.

'But Eye-Kon have no money to option the book.'

'The BBC are interested in a co-production. They'll put up the money if Chloe is on board.'

'Gemma will never let you option it. After what we did to her, you haven't a hope.'

But he had a hope. I could see it in his eyes. Already he was persuading her and using whatever means necessary. I knew that Anton, for all his shabby, laid-back charm, was ambitious, but the extent of it impacted like a blow to the chest.

'Lily, this will be the saving of us!' He was a ball of fervour. 'It's got fantastic commercial potential. Everyone could make a pile of money from it. Life would get back on track for us.'

Anton needed this for his pride. And he needed to feel something good could happen to us. But to secure the rights to her book, how far would he go with Gemma? Because of the fierceness of his desperation, I was hit with a powerful conviction that it could be quite some way. Her last words to me flashed into my head: *remember how you met him because that's how you'll lose him.*

'Don't get involved in this,' I urged, low and desperate. 'Please, Anton, nothing good will come of it.'

'But, Lily,' he insisted. 'What an opportunity! It's exactly what we need.'

'It's Gemma!'

'It's business.'

It was then that I discovered I no longer had faith in me and Anton. I had once thought that, as a unit, we were indestructible. Now we seemed small and fragile and perched on the rim of a catastrophe. I didn't know the precise nature of it, or exactly how it was going to come about, but with hideous certitude, I saw my future set in stone: Anton and I were going to split up.

Jojo

Monday morning, 9.00
Probably the most important morning of Jojo's entire career. On her way to her office, she passed the boardroom—behind the closed door, all the partners were in there. *Vote for me.* She tried to send voodoo thought waves. Then she laughed at herself: she didn't need voodoo thought waves. She was a good enough agent.

All the same she was very jumpy. She accused Manoj of banging her coffee cup too loudly on her desk and when her phone rang her heart almost pushed out through her rib cage.

'We'll know by lunchtime,' Manoj soothed.

'Right.'

But just after ten, someone appeared in her doorway. Mark! But it was far too soon. Could be they were on a break . . .

'Hi . . .'

In silence, Mark closed the door behind him, leaned against it, then looked her in the eye. Immediately she knew. But couldn't believe it. She heard herself say, 'They gave it to Richie Gant?'

A nod.

She still couldn't believe it and for a moment felt she might burst from her body. This wasn't happening.

Mark moved towards her and tried to hug her but she moved out of his arms.

She stood by the window and stared at nothing. It was over. The vote had happened and she hadn't got it. She was trying to think logically but her processes were hit hard. 'Is it because of you and me, do you think?'

'I don't know.'

Mark looked grey and exhausted and Jojo had a momentary insight into how horrible this was for him.

'I so don't get it. I've great authors who're going to have long careers. Short-term *and* long-term I'm a better bet. What d'you think happened? Seeing as I bring in more money than Gant.'

'Only just.'

'Excuse me?'

'That came out wrong. What, I mean, is they looked at this year's income and you and Richie are neck and neck.'

'No, we are so not. I'm ahead, by lots. How can we be neck and neck?'

Mark looked like he wanted to die and she was sorry for taking it out on him. He couldn't control the other partners, they made their own decisions. But she needed to know. 'Tell me.'

'I feel so bad for you.' His eyes glistened with unshed tears. 'You deserve it and it means so much to you. But the way they look at it is, if Richie pulls off even one corporate deal, that puts him way ahead of the game.'

'But he's delivered zilch. He's talking the talk and they fell for it. It's a crass, crap idea and I bet no one will go for it. Writers still have some self-respect.'

Mark shrugged and they stood in silence, miserable and separate.

Then Jojo got it and surprise, more than anything, made her blurt, 'It's because I'm a woman!' She'd heard about this—the glass ceiling—but never thought it would happen to her.

'This has got nothing to do with you being a woman.'

'The bottom line,' Jojo said slowly, 'is they made him partner because he might pull off a deal with one of his golf-course cronies.'

'No, they made him partner because they think long-term he'll bring in more money.'

'And how's he going to do that? By playing golf with other men. Stop peeing in my ear and telling me it's raining. This is a case of glass ceiling.'

'It isn't.'

'It is.'

'It isn't.'

'Whatever.' Jojo wanted Mark out of her office. She needed to think. 'We'll talk about it later.'

'What are you going to do?'

'What do you think? Whack Gant?' She pointed towards her desk. 'I've got a job to do.'

He looked relieved. 'I'll see you later.' He tried to hug her again and she slipped away from him. 'Jojo, don't punish me.'

'I'm not.' But she didn't want anyone touching her. She didn't want anything. She was on autopilot until she had figured out what to do.

Ten minutes later

Richie Gant stood in her doorway, waited until he had her attention, then grinned nastily at her. 'So, even your boyfriend didn't vote for you.'

'Get out of my office,' Jojo said.

'He didn't vote for you. He voted for me.'

She felt herself flash white with shock but kept it steady. 'Get out.'

He backed away, still grinning, and when he'd disappeared from sight, she began to shake. One thing she'd learned: the *SkankMeister* didn't lie. If he said Mark didn't vote for her, then Mark didn't vote for her. There was only one thing to do.

Mark's office

He looked up, as she came in.

'Mark, tell me the truth because I'll find out anyway. Did you vote for me?'

A too-long silence. Then, 'No.'

She pulled up a chair in front of his desk. 'Why not? And this'd better be good.'

'Actually, it is.' He sounded so sure of himself that Jojo was surprised—and super-relieved. This was going to be OK, this was going to be all right. This was *Mark*.

'Do the sums, Jojo,' Mark said. 'Me leaving Cassie and you and me setting up a home together is going to cost shedloads. Richie said that if he wasn't made partner he'd leave, taking his money-spinning idea with him. Plus, if you were made partner, your—*our*—income would go *down* for three years. And after you had the pregnancy scare, it made me realise that you might be planning to give up work anyway. It sounds a bit made-for-TV, but I did it for us. And there's more. Everyone knows we're together and they're watching for signs of favouritism. If I wanted to retain the respect of my partners, I *couldn't* vote for you.'

Mute with frustration she stared at him. 'Why didn't you talk to me about it?'

'Because I know you, Jojo. I knew you'd choose the job over me. Us.'

She couldn't keep her anger from busting out. 'You wrecked my chance of being a partner so we'd have the money to be together.'

He eyed her shrewdly. 'Put it another way. You'd risk wrecking the chances of us being together just so you could be a partner.'

It took her a long time to answer. 'I didn't realise it was a choice.'

She left, sunk deep in a crisis of the soul. Was Mark right? Was she too ambitious? But that description was never applied to men—in the same way it was impossible for a woman to be too thin, it was impossible for a man to be too ambitious.

Rising up in her again was something she wanted not to see—Mark had had no right to take that decision for her.

But she loved Mark. Like, she *loved* Mark. Something her dad used to say came to mind: Which would you rather be—right or happy?

Back in Jojo's office

Something clicked and suddenly she was left with no choice. Worth trying anyway . . .

She said to Manoj, 'I need you working late every night for the rest of this week.'

'On what?'

'It's a secret.' She leaned in close to him. 'And if you tell anyone, I will kill you.'

'Fair enough.' He swallowed and she felt a little bad; she shouldn't go round scaring him but it was so *easy*.

'I want phone numbers for all my authors.'

'Why?'

'What did I just tell you?'

Gemma

AFTER OWEN DUMPED ME, to my great surprise, I was devastated. Even though I knew it was silly, I cried all the way driving to work the next day, I cried *at* work and I cried at home that evening. Then I got up the following day and repeated the pattern exactly. It was like being fifteen all over again.

It was very different when Anton had dumped me—that made me bitter and warped, it had changed me. But I didn't call Owen a bastard and I didn't fantasise about getting him back. I had no intention of even trying. Instead of generating bile his departure had opened up a big boxful of sad.

Even work was breaking my heart. I was working on a very unusual event—Max O'Neill, a young man, only twenty-eight, was terminally ill and had hired me to plan his memorial service. Initially I'd been touched and flattered that he'd picked me. (Although F&F hadn't been. Frances had grumbled, 'It's not like we're going to get much repeat business from him.') Every time I saw him and we made videos in which he told his friends not to grieve for him, or when we planned the drinks for the 'party', I came away a wreck.

And in the middle of all this lachrymosity I descended on Johnny. After a particularly wrenching session with Max, I'd been driving past the chemist and, on a wild whim, called in, looking for comfort, emotional ice cream. After we'd exchanged New Year felicitations, he asked, 'What can I get you?'

I hadn't given this any thought. 'Oh, ah . . . a glucose lollipop. And— what's this? Surgical gauze? OK, I'll take a packet.'

'Are you sure about that, Gemma?'

'No, no, I'm not. Just the lollipop.'

Even after I'd tried to pay (He wouldn't let me, 'For God's sake, it's only a lollipop.') I still wouldn't leave.

'How are things?' he asked.

'Great,' I said miserably. 'Dad's back. How's your brother?'

'Very good, he'll be back at work soon and my life will be my own again. Your book should be out soon, shouldn't it?'

'May. And it goes on sale in airport duty-frees sooner than that. Some time in March.'

'You must be very excited.'

'Mmmm.'

'I'm looking forward to reading it.'

'I'll try to get you a free copy.' My worry about him reading about himself had diminished, washed away by sadness.

Eventually he asked—and it wasn't like I hadn't been fishing for him to—'And, er, how's your non-boyfriend?'

'Oh, that's all over. He went back to his old girlfriend. It was very amicable.'

My eyes filled with tears, not the shame of full-blown crying, but enough for Johnny to hand me a tissue. Well, he had a shopful of them.

Later, in the comfort of my own home, I realised that the kindness of the tissue gesture was what prompted the ensuing insanity. I dabbed my eyes and heard myself say, 'You know, maybe we should go out for a drink some time, you and me.'

I cocked my head to listen. *Did I really say that?*

Then I saw his face. You'd want to have seen it. He looked really insulted.

'Oh God, I'm sorry,' I said, hurrying away. 'I'm very sorry.'

I got into the car, clutching my free lollipop. Dad was back and I was worse mad now than I ever was.

Little did I know that life was about to change in a major way.

It began with a phone call from Jojo.

'Like, totally great news,' she said. 'I've had a call from a production company called Eye-Kon. They're interested in optioning *Chasing Rainbows* for a made-for-TV feature. Anton says—'

'*Anton?*'

'Yeah, Anton Carolan. Hey, he's Irish, you probably know him.'

'I know him.'

Pause. 'I was only kidding. But you know Lily, so of course you know him.'

'I knew him before Lily did.' But I didn't really try to score points. I was way too stunned: Anton wanted something I had. *I had something that Anton wanted.* Even in my most elaborate fantasies, I'd never imagined this situation. I thought back to three and a half years previously when I'd been almost suicidal without Anton. When I wanted him so badly and I was totally and utterly powerless. How insane life is. Breathlessly, I urged, 'Jojo, tell me more.'

'I've told you all I know. They've no money but the BBC has. So you're interested, in theory?'

'Of *course* I'm interested!'

'I'll tell them. These things take time, don't hold your breath, I'll keep you in the loop.'

'But—'

She was gone and I sat staring at the phone, too astonished to carry on with my day. Anton! Out of the blue! Wanting my book!

For the first time in a long time I wondered about him and Lily. Lily can't be much fun at the moment, I thought, what with her new book having tanked. Maybe Anton had had it with her, maybe he was ready to jump ship.

What should I do? I wondered. Should I let this option thing go through the official channels or should I contact him directly? After all, we were old friends . . .

For the next two days I thought of nothing else; in fact I was so caught up in it I almost forgot to cry.

Then Jojo rang again. 'Gemma. Can you talk? I've got a proposal for you.'

'Another one? Go ahead.'

'I have decided,' she sounded excited, 'to set up on my own and I'd like to take you with me.'

The lucky cow. I'd love to do that, set up my own agency. But I enjoyed my facial features in their current configuration.

'So whatcha say? Are you in or out?'

It was a total no-brainer. This was the woman who'd got me sixty grand. Why wouldn't I stay with her? 'Count me in. What other authors are coming with you?'

'Miranda England, Nathan Frey, Eamonn Farrell . . .'

'Lily Wright?'

'I haven't spoken to her yet, but yeah, I hope so.'

Friday morning

Jojo went to Mark's office and handed him a letter. He looked at it. 'What's this?'

'My notice. I'm leaving.'

Mark looked weary beyond weary. 'Jojo, for God's sake . . . Don't do this,' he beseeched. Horrified, she realised he might cry. 'You need a job.'

'I have a job.'

'Working for who?'

'Myself. I'm setting up on my own.'

Mark made a jaded sound, halfway between a laugh and a sigh.

'I have to, Mark. I can't stay here. And no way am I going to work for another agency and watch the same shit happen again.'

He laughed in a beaten way, then asked, 'Jojo, what about us? You and me? Are you setting up on your own in a personal capacity as well as a professional one?'

Funny, she hadn't really decided what to do, not until that moment. She looked at him, at his beloved face, so familiar and handsome to her; she thought about their affection and fondness for each other, their friendship, their hope for their future.

'Yes,' she said. 'It's over, Mark.'

He nodded, like it was what he'd expected to hear.

Then for the first—and last—time she did something she never did on work time: she hugged him. She pressed herself against the length of him, in the hope that she could remember how he felt, how he smelt, the hard heat of his body. She held him fiercely, trying to stamp him for ever on her memory. Then she walked away.

Clearing out her desk Jojo wondered where were the cardboard boxes that always materialised when people in movies left their jobs at short notice. Not that she had much, she wasn't a pot-plant kind of person, they were so *needy* . . .

Her phone rang and absently she picked it up. Miranda England.

'Jojo, I've been thinking . . .'

Jojo went cold.

'In your new company you don't have a foreign rights department, do you?'

'Not yet. But I will.'

'And you don't have a media department yet?'

'But I will.'

'Jojo, I need the income from my overseas sales. Germany pays me almost as much as the UK. And the movie options bring in plenty too.'

'Miranda, who got to you? Richie Gant?'

'Nobody did!'

'What did he offer? Nine per cent? Eight? Seven?'

Miranda paused and admitted unhappily, 'Eight. And he's right about the media and foreign rights department.'

'Miranda, I'll offer you seven per cent and I'll have media and foreign rights departments up and running in three months.'

'I'll think about it.'

Gemma

I CAUGHT THE 6.35 A.M. from Dublin and went straight from Heathrow to Eye-Kon's offices. I wore my new black suit. By Donna Karan. No, Prada. Either way it made me look tiny-waisted and chic.

Meeting Anton for the first time in three and a half years was weird. He looked exactly the same: same dancing eyes, same through-a-hedge-backwards chic. And same charisma, of course—lots of it. Some things never change.

'How's it going, you mad woman?' He grinned. 'Come in, sit down. Drink? Take a seat. You're looking fantastic.'

The last time I'd seen him, I'd been sick with love for him. Back then Anton had had all the power. But now, due to some mad quirk of fate, due to life being, for once, *fair*, I held his future in my hands.

He smiled at me, a wide, winning smile. 'Sell us your book, Gemma. Go on, it's great. We'll make an excellent movie out of it. I promise we won't let you down.'

'Is that so?' I asked coolly. 'Anton, I've done a little research. Eye-Kon is screwed. You really need this book.'

That knocked some of the skittishness out of him. 'Maybe.'

'No maybe about it. And the good news is, Anton, you can have it. Without it costing you a penny.'

'I can?'

'Under certain conditions.'

'And they are?'

I waited a moment, building dramatic tension. 'How's Lily?' I asked. 'How are you two getting on?'

To my surprise—I hadn't expected him to admit it so quickly, things must be AWFUL—he hung his head.

'Not great.'

'Not great? Good. That'll make leaving her easier for you.'

I expected a flurry of what-are-you-talking-abouts and don't-be-mads. But he just nodded and said quietly, 'OK.'

'OK?' I queried. '*OK*? That simple? You can't love her very much if you're prepared to put your career before her.'

'I don't. I don't love her at all. I never did. It was all a mistake. I was lonely when I first came to London and I mistook friendship for love. Then she got pregnant and how could I leave? But then I read your book and it's so *you*. It reminded me of what a great girl you are and the laughs we used to have. Seeing you here today, in your lovely Prada suit, I've no doubt in my mind that it was you I loved all along.' He stood by the window and stared out at the porridge-coloured London sky. 'I've known for a long time that being with Lily was a mistake. Ever since she got the Burt Reynolds-style hair-weave to cover her bald patch.' He sighed heavily. 'I should have left then, but it would have been criminal to walk out . . .'

I paused. No, it was no good. The fantasy wasn't working any more. There was no way I'd be able to go to London and proposition Anton, in an attempt to destroy Lily. I was almost disappointed with myself. It was one thing to want to drive over to Colette's work and make fun of her in the company car park after Dad had left her. But this kind of revenge-style fantasy—would any real person be able to do it?

And what kind of pitiful creature would be happy to bag a bloke by kick-starting his career? It would be like buying someone.

Jojo

Jim Sweetman's office

'Jim,' Jojo asked. 'I'd like to offer you a job.'

'Wha-at?'

'Yeah, as my media person.'

'Jojo, I—look! No—'

'Think about it,' she said. 'Equal shares. We'll make a ton.'

She got up to leave and he yelled after her, 'Jojo, I want to talk to you about something else.'

'What?'

'I don't know if you're still interested, but Gemma Hogan's book? *Chasing Rainbows*? Eye-Kon were pulling a deal together with the BBC and Chloe Drew?'

'Sure I'm interested. Gemma's still my author.'

'Heard at lunch that Chloe's had a major coke and alcohol meltdown and gone into rehab. I've made a few calls to confirm.'

'Say it ain't so.'

'Sorry, Jojo. The deal is off. Chloe was the clincher. Without her the BBC won't make with the readies. But no one wants to work with a drunk, even an ex-drunk. The insurers won't touch her.'

Liby

THE FUNNY THING was that less than an hour after Jojo called, explaining that she was setting up on her own and asking me to stay as her client, Anton found out that Chloe Drew had had some sort of breakdown. She had been pivotal to *Chasing Rainbows*; without her the BBC were not interested and the deal was not going to happen.

I should have been happy. Anton and I were safe now, were we not?

Unfortunately, no: Anton's brush with Gemma, or at least her book, had revealed the full extent of the rot in Anton's and my relationship.

And the fact that, once again, another of Anton's business ventures had collapsed, convinced me that life with him would always be a financial roller coaster. I could not live that way. I owed it to Ema to seek stability.

In the weeks since the move, we had been so silent with each other that I genuinely believed we were finished in all but name. I was sure that he would let me go quietly, acknowledging sadly that it was a shame it had not worked out, but that under the circumstances it was a miracle we had stayed together as long as we had, etc.

But he went wild.

When Ema had gone to bed that night, I picked up the remote and, without preamble, turned off the TV.

He looked at me in surprise. 'What?'

'Irina has said Ema and I can stay with her for a while. I think we should go sooner rather than later. Tomorrow?'

'What are you talking about?' He gripped my wrist so hard that it hurt. 'Lily?' he questioned. 'Lily? What?'

'I'm going,' I said, faintly. 'I thought you knew.'

'No.' He looked utterly horrified. 'Lily, please,' he choked. 'I beg . . . *implore* you to think about it. I thought things would get better. I thought they were getting better.'

'But we never speak to each other any longer.'

'Because we've lost our home, a terrible thing has happened. But I thought we were regrouping!'

'We're not regrouping. We will never regroup. We should not have been together ever, it was wrong from the beginning and it was always going to end horribly. We always *knew* this.'

'I didn't.'

'You persist with looking on the bright side but the reality is that we are disastrous together,' I reminded him. 'Look at the mess we've made of our lives. We had a lot going for us and we've screwed it all up.' I said 'we' but what I really meant was, '*I* had a lot going for me and *you* screwed it up.' I did not need to say it; he was no fool, he would have already grasped that.

'We were unlucky,' he insisted. He leaned heavily against the door. 'It's because of your history, your dad losing the family home. It had a terrible effect on you.'

I said nothing. It was probably the truth.

'You're angry with me,' he said.

'Absolutely not,' I said. 'I hope eventually we will be friends. But, Anton, we're bad for each other.'

He looked at me, his face stricken, and I dropped my eyes. 'What about Ema?' he asked. 'Us breaking up can't be good for her.'

'I'm doing this *for* Ema.' Suddenly I was furious. 'Ema is my number-one priority. I want security for her.'

'You're angry with me,' Anton repeated. 'Very angry.'

'I'm not! But keep on insisting that I am and I probably will be.'

'I don't blame you for being angry. I could shoot myself for getting it all so wrong.'

I decided to ignore this. It did not matter what he said, he would not change my mind. Anton and I were finished completely and I actually felt it was necessary for us to part, that we would both be dogged by bad luck, until we had righted the wrong we had committed when I first stole him from Gemma.

When I told him that, he exploded. 'You're just being superstitious. It doesn't work like that.'

'We were never meant to be together, I always knew it would end in disaster.'

'Lily, but, Lily . . .'

'It doesn't matter what you say or do,' I said. 'I'm going. I have to.'

He tried to talk me out of it, right up to the last minute. Even as I was getting into the taxi, he said, 'Lily, this is only temporary.'

'This is not temporary.' I held his eyes. I had to let him know this. 'Please get used to it, Anton, because this is for ever.'

Then the car drove away, taking me to my new life, and I know this sounds cruel but, for the first time since I had met him, I felt clean.

Jojo

ON FRIDAY EVENING, Manoj helped Jojo carry her cardboard boxes down to the taxi.

'I can't believe you're leaving,' he quavered.

'Don't be such a girl,' she said. 'I'll send for you. Soon as I'm up and running.'

Her mobile rang. She checked caller display—Mark—and let it roll over to message service. Once in her flat, she dumped the boxes and noticed that her machine was flashing with messages. Already?

The first was from Jim Sweetman. 'Jojo, I'm flattered by your offer, but I'm staying with Lipman Haigh.' Damn, she thought. Then—So what? She'd get another media person, and find someone to do foreign rights.

The second message was from Mark. 'There's no need for any of this, Jojo. I've already torn up your resignation letter. Just come in on Monday, same as ever, and we'll get everything back on track. And as for you and me, you're the most important person in my life, the most important person I've ever met, we *have* to work this out, Jojo, we *have* to, because the alternative is unthinkable—'

In all there were six messages from him.

She went to stay with Becky and Andy for the weekend.

'Because you want to be with people who love you,' Andy said sympathetically, as he opened the door.

'No, because I just bet Mark will call round to my apartment in the middle of the night and lean on the buzzer until I let him in.'

'Have a glass of wine, put your feet up and forget about it all for a while,' Becky soothed.

'I can't.' Right on cue her mobile rang. She looked at caller display. Not Mark, not this time. She hit TALK.

'Hey you, Nathan Frey! Yeah, I did call earlier. I was, like, wondering if you'd had a call from Richie Gant, offering, like, *the earth*.'

Jojo took the call into the hall, where she paced back and forth, talking up a storm. Then she came back and collapsed onto the couch. 'That was Nathan Frey. Looks like Gant's got to all my authors. All the big ones, anyhow. Gonna spend my weekend doing damage limitation, trying to get them back on side.'

All weekend and through into the following week, her phone was on fire, but with the wrong sort of calls. Her resignation had—understandably—generated great furore in publishing circles. Theories abounded. She'd discovered that Richie Gant was the illegitimate son she'd had and given up for adoption (from an editor who specialised in sagas). She'd been having an affair with Mark Avery, who hadn't voted for her, then dumped her (from the vast majority of London publishing).

But far worse than the people exercising their naked curiosity were the calls from her authors. On Tuesday afternoon, there was a call from Miranda England. She was making it official—she was going to Richie Gant. It hit Jojo like a blow from a baseball bat.

On Wednesday, Marjorie Franks signed to Richie. On Thursday, Kathleen Perry, Iggy Gibson, Norah Rossetti and Paula Wheeler jumped ship and on Friday a trio of thriller writers went, all of them steady sellers.

Every time an author walked, the chances of her making it as a solo agent shrank further.

And all the time, she was bombarded with messages from Mark; day and night he emailed, texted, wrote letters, sent flowers and a box of goodies from Jo Malone. He rang on her home phone and mobile and he loitered outside her apartment.

The amazing thing was that, despite him almost stalking her, she never spoke to him or even saw him. And yeah, that made it easier to stick to her guns. She suspected that if they saw each other, she would crumble. Things, right now, were so scary and bad that walking back into the cocoon of her old life, where she was loved and secure, would be just too hard to resist.

Monday morning
Her second Monday as a self-employed agent. She felt confident and hopeful, like she was turning a corner.

The phone rang. It was Nathan Frey's wife, to say that Nathan's new agent was Richie Gant.

Fuccckkk.

She had only one big author left: Eamonn Farrell.

On Tuesday, only two smaller authors walked.

But Wednesday was Meltdown Day.

When she switched on her computer, waiting was an email from Eamonn Farrell, saying he had found new representation. She leaned her forehead against the screen. That was it, her last big author gone.

Then the phone rang: Mark. He left a frantic, pleading message for her every morning around this time. But today he sounded different.

'Jojo,' he said, 'I'm going to stop bothering you now. I'm sorry we didn't manage to work it out, I've never been sorrier about anything. We were one inch away from perfection, we were almost there, but I know when I'm beaten. Good luck with everything. I mean that.'

Then he clicked off and she almost felt the molecules of her phone relaxing after its recent spate of very demanding work.

This wasn't some dumbass trick of Mark's to get her to change her mind. She knew his MO; he had given this his all, it hadn't delivered the desired results, so he was quitting. Game over.

This was what she wanted. She had never intended to go back to him.

But, like an out-of-body experience, she saw herself, sitting in her apartment on a bleak morning in February, with her best friend gone and her career in ruins.

At that Jojo cried so hard and for so long she barely recognised herself in the mirror. When she stuck her face in a basin of cold water to calm the red swelling she found herself considering just staying there and letting herself drown.

For about half a second.

Then she got it together. Authors? Who needs 'em? Hey, plenty more where they come from. And another Mark? Plenty of them too, if she could be arsed.

Lily

I LIKED MY NEW LIFE. It was peaceful, devoid of drama and very little happened. I had no grand plans, no vision for the future, all I wanted was to get through the day. I enjoyed my life's smallness. Until recently everything had been done on a grand scale—novels and book deals and houses—and I was happy that it had all been reduced to bite-sized pieces.

One day clicked over into the next and all of them were interchangeable and without character. Not once did I contemplate the future, except in terms of Ema. She had always been a hardy little creature, and perhaps her physical robustness was also an indication of emotional resilience. I had to admit she certainly did not seem shaken by her ruptured life.

Even though she was living separately from him, she saw Anton frequently. Most days he took her to the park after work, and she stayed overnight with him on Saturdays. After the first few visits, when his eyes were bleak with heartbreak, I could not bear to see him and asked Irina if she could oversee him picking up Ema and again when he returned her home. To my extreme gratitude, Irina agreed. This arrangement worked well, until one evening, perhaps three weeks after I had left him, when Irina was in the bathroom at precisely the wrong time and I had to open the door to readmit Ema.

'Lily.' Anton looked shocked to see me. As I was shocked to see him. He had always been thin but during the weeks since I had seen him, he had become haggard. Not that I was in imminent danger of gracing a fashion shoot myself. (If it had not been for Irina's lavish generosity with her pore-minimiser, I would have needed a head transplant.)

Ema scooted past me into the apartment and seconds later I heard the opening notes of *The Jungle Book*.

'I wasn't expecting to see you . . .' Anton said. 'Look . . .' He fumbled in his leather jacket and produced a letter. It was so crumpled and battered it looked as if it had been in his pocket for weeks. 'This is from me. I wanted to give it to you by hand, to make sure you got it. You won't want to read it now, but you might want to some time.'

'Fine,' I said stiffly, unsure what to do. I wanted to read it but instinct was warning me not to. Horribly shaken by seeing him, I said goodbye, closed the door on him, then went into my bedroom, put the letter in a drawer and waited to forget about it.

It took me the rest of the evening and a quarter of a bottle of dog-rough vodka to regain my equilibrium. But then I was fine. I understood that inevitably this would be painful. Anton and I had been in love, we had had a child together and we had been each other's best friend from the moment we had met. The ending of something so precious could only be bloody. But at some stage in the future the pain would stop and Anton and I would be friends. I just had to be patient.

I knew that one day my life would be utterly different; full of feelings and friends and laughter and colour and with an almost entirely new cast to the one currently peopling it. I was wholly certain that some day there would be another man and more children and a different job and a proper home. I had no idea how I got from the small bare life I was now living to the full, colourful one I envisioned. All I knew was that it would happen. But right now it was a long way away.

So complete was my passivity that I could not even feel guilty about Irina's staggering generosity with her home and caretaking Ema. Sometimes I had to borrow money from her—I was working as a copy-writer but it paid spasmodically—and I even had no shame about that. Invariably, she handed it over without comment, except for once when I came in from yet another feeling-free walk in the park and said, 'Irina, the cashpoint wouldn't give me any money. Can you loan me some until I next get paid?'

She replied, 'Why do you hev no money? You got big cheque last week.'

'I had to pay you back, then I bought Ema a tricycle, all the other little girls have tricycles, then I had to get her hair cut into a Dora the Explorer bob, all the other little girls have Dora the Explorer bobs . . .'

'And now you do not hev enough to feed her,' Irina said. Slyly, she added, 'You hate Anton for being bed vit money but you are werry bed too.'

'I never said I wasn't. It just goes to show what a mismatch Anton and I were.'

She sighed and indicated a biscuit tin. 'Help yourself.' Then she handed me a postcard. 'Mail for you.'

I looked at it in surprise: a picture of three grizzly bears, standing in a stream, against a backdrop of pine trees and the great outdoors. It looked as if it had been sent from Canada. The biggest bear had a huge salmon between its jaws, the medium-sized bear was scooping a fish from the water and the smallest bear held a flipping fish in its paws. I turned it over and the caption read, 'Grizzly bears at a weir'. But someone—a person with Anton's handwriting—had crossed out the official caption and handwritten, '*Anton, Lily and Ema enjoy a fish supper.*' To my enormous surprise I heard myself laugh.

He had also scribbled, '*Thinking of you both. All my love, A.*'

It was utterly imbued with the spirit of Anton; funny and clever and mad, and, I thought joyfully, This is the start of the happy memories. I am finally getting to the point where I can look back at my time with him without feeling wretched.

I felt happy all day long.

A few short days later the post yielded up a postcard of Burt Reynolds, looking very matinée idol and luxuriant of moustache. Anton had written: *I saw this and thought of you.* Again I laughed and felt hopeful about the future.

I was starting to look forward to the postcards and soon another one arrived, this time of a vase bearing Chinese-style line drawings of people and cups and stuff. The caption read, 'Ming vase depicting tea ceremony', but Anton had crossed it out and written, '*Anton, Lily and Ema, circa 1544, enjoying a cup of tea after a hard day's shopping.*' When I looked again, it even seemed like there were shopping bags beside the figures.

I turned to Irina and said, 'I've been thinking. When Anton comes for Ema today, I think I can deal with it.'

'Very well.'

That evening when I opened the door to him, Anton did not even seem surprised. He simply exclaimed, 'Lily!' As if he was thrilled to see me.

He looked a lot better than he had at our previous encounter, not remotely as drawn and gaunt. His aura of shine and vitality had returned; clearly he was on the mend, we both were.

'Where's Irina today? What's up with her?' he asked.

'Nothing. Just . . . you know . . . I'm ready, it's time . . . Anton, thank you for the postcards, they're so funny, they made me laugh.'

'Great. And I'm glad I've met you because I wanted to give you this.'

He handed me an envelope which triggered a guilty memory of the unread letter in my underwear drawer.

'What's this?'

'Dosh,' he said. 'Lots of it. Now that I'm back making infomercials, the money is rolling in.'

'Is it really?' This was the final sign I needed that we were better off apart.

'Buy yourself and Ema something nice. I read in the paper that Origins has a new perfume out—and don't forget to get yourself something too!'

The twinkle was back in his eyes and I felt a huge rush of affection towards him that almost translated into me lunging at him in a hug. I restrained myself this time but wouldn't have to for much longer. Soon we could embrace as friends.

A visit to Mum in Warwickshire was long overdue. I needed a break from work, so now seemed a good time to go. I rang Mum and gave her the good news about our visit.

'How long do you plan to stay?' she asked. Anxiously?

'Ages,' I said. 'Months. Before you start to hyperventilate, about a week. OK?'

'OK.'

I went to pack and, a couple of strata down in my underwear drawer, I ran into the battered letter from Anton. I itched to open it. Instead I left it where it was. Then I loaded up the car (Irina had let me borrow her new Audi), mostly with cuddly toys.

It was a clean spring morning and it felt good speeding along, as if I was leaving danger behind me in London. Less than two hours after we had left we were turning off the motorway. 'We're almost there!' Then, 'Whoops!' as my carefree twists and turns brought us up right behind a lorry laden with columns of concrete bollards, rumbling along at about fifteen miles an hour. The road was too narrow and bendy to overtake, but, 'We're in the country now, Ema. No need to rush.' Ema agreed and we launched into the four millionth verse of 'The Wheels on the Bus'.

Bellowing, 'Swish, swish, swish!' we crawled along behind the lorry when suddenly—and it was rather like watching a film—it bumped over a hump in the road and the bollards had broken free of their chains and were flying loose, like so many concrete skittles. Raining down on us, bouncing off the road, flying right at me; there was not even time to be surprised. Some hit the roof of the car and it buckled down on us. I could not see in front of me, my foot was on the brake but we were still moving. At some stage we had stopped singing and I knew, with crystal clarity, that we were about to die. I was about to perish with my child on an A-road in Warwickshire. *I'm not ready . . .*

The skid went on for ever. It was like being in a dream, where you want to run but your legs refuse to work; the brake was pressed to the floor but would not respond.

Finally, eventually, we reached a halt. I sat for a moment, barely believing the stillness, then turned to Ema. She extended her hand. There was something in it. 'Glass,' she said.

I got out of the car and my legs were so light I seemed to be floating. I retrieved Ema from her baby seat and she too seemed to be weightless. Her Dora the Explorer hair was studded with hundreds of little nuggets of glass—the back window had caved in on her head, but the strange thing was that she did not appear to be injured. Neither was I. Nothing was painful and neither of us bore any sign of blood.

The driver of the lorry was a gibbering wreck. 'Oh my God,' he kept saying. 'Oh my God. I thought I'd killed you, I thought I'd killed you.'

He whipped out a mobile and made a call—sending for help, I thought passively—and I stood, holding Ema and looking at the battered car and bollards everywhere, strewn back along the road. I felt an urgent need to sit down, so I lowered myself on my not-there legs onto the grass verge and pulled Ema to me.

We were taken to hospital, pronounced to be in health as perfect as it was remarkable, then Mum came to ferry us to her home: an idyllic little cottage on the edge of a farming community. Mum's garden bordered a field containing three solid sheep and a baby lamb skipping about like a happy half-wit.

Ema, a city girl, was dazzled by her first real-life sheep.

'Bad dog,' she shouted at them. 'BAD dog!'

'Come inside,' Mum said to me, 'you've had a dreadful shock, you need to lie down.'

I was reluctant to leave Ema or even to take my eyes off her, after I had so nearly lost her.

But Mum said, 'She'll be quite safe here,' and somehow I believed her. Moments later she had installed me in a wooden-beamed, rose-patterned room, and I was sinking into a soft bed with smooth, cotton sheets. Everything smelt clean and nice and safe.

'I have to sort out Irina's car,' I said. 'And I have to contact Anton. And I have to ensure that nothing terrible happens to Ema ever again. But first I have to go to sleep.'

And then it was morning and I opened my eyes to find Mum and Ema in the room, Ema grinning her melon grin.

The first thing I said was, 'We didn't die yesterday.'

Mum gave me a 'Not in front of Ema' look and asked, 'How did you sleep?'

'Wonderfully. I went to the bathroom in the middle of the night but I didn't walk into the doorjamb and damage my optic nerve, ensuring double vision for the rest of my life.'

'Your father is on his way from London. He has to see for himself that you've been saved from the jaws of death. But we're not going to get back together,' she added quickly. She always had to say that to me whenever she and Dad met. 'And I rang Anton.'

'Don't let him visit.'

'Why not?'

'Because I don't want to do anything rash.'

She looked sad. 'It's a terrible shame about you and Anton.'

'Yes,' I acknowledged. 'But at least I never caught him wearing a red basque and black stockings.'

'What on earth,' she frowned, 'are you talking about?'

I frowned back. 'Nothing. I'm simply saying how good it is that that never happened. It would make things considerably more difficult between us because each time I saw him I might want to laugh.'

'And what was that about not walking into the doorjamb?'

'Just that I am happy that it didn't happen.'

A shadow crossed her face and she pulled Ema to her protectively and said, 'Let's make pancakes, shall we?'

They disappeared into the kitchen and I dressed slowly and sat in the sunny window seat until the wheels of a twenty-year-old Jag crunched on the gravel outside announcing Dad's arrival from London.

Mum watched Dad getting out of the car and rolled her eyes. 'Just as I expected, he's in tears. He has such an obnoxious streak of sentimentality. It's terribly unattractive.'

She opened the front door and Dad gathered me in his arms, so tightly that I began to choke.

'My little girl,' he said, his voice thick with tears. 'I haven't been right since I heard. You were so lucky.'

'I know.' I managed to break free and take a breath. 'When you think about it, all my life I've been lucky.'

He looked slightly puzzled, but because of my brush with death he was obliged to humour me.

'Think about it,' I said. 'Of all the times I drank from a can of Coke on a summer's day, and not once was I stung by a wasp which had crawled in. Never did I go into anaphylactic shock so that my tongue swelled up like a rugby ball. Isn't it wonderful?'

Mum looked at Dad. 'She keeps saying things like that.'

We lapsed into awkward silence, all the better to hear the happy shouts of Ema tormenting the sheep. ('Bad dog. NASTY dog.') Mum looked in the direction of the racket, then snapped her head back and pounced. 'What are you thinking now?'

'Nothing! Just how happy I am that all my toenails grow in the right direction. Having ingrown toenails must be dreadful.'

Mum and Dad gave each other a look.

'You ought to see a doctor,' Mum said.

I ought not. I was simply in the grip of one of those bouts of gratitude which sometimes assail me post-disaster. I tried to explain. 'Yesterday, there were so many ways Ema and I could have died. We could have been hit by a bollard, I could have driven the car into a ditch because I couldn't see where we were going or we could have ploughed into the back of the lorry. Being saved in so many different ways has made me think about all the terrible things that could happen but actually don't. Even though not everything is going well for me at the moment, I feel lucky.'

Dad was full of talk of taking me to Harley Street, nothing but the best, but Mum slapped him down. 'Please don't talk such nonsense.'

'Thanks, Mum.' At least one of them understood.

Then Mum added, 'The local chap will do fine.'

I tried to hide it but could not. It was like when I had been mugged, except the entire opposite, if you know what I mean. Back then all I saw were the terrible things that could happen to human beings. This time all I saw were the bad things that *did not* happen.

The following day Dad returned reluctantly to London—Debs needed him urgently, to open a jar of jam or something—and it was just Ema, Mum and me. The weather was glorious and so was my mood. I thought I might burst with the joy of not having tinnitus. Or leprosy.

With shining eyes I said to Mum, 'Isn't it wonderful to not have gout?'

She snapped, 'Right, that's it!' lifted the phone and requested a home visit.

Dr Lott, a young, curly-haired man, appeared in my rose-covered bedroom, less than an hour later. 'What appears to be the problem?'

Mum answered for me. 'Her relationship has failed, so has her career, yet she feels very happy. Don't you?'

I assented. Yes, that was all true.

Dr Lott frowned. 'That is worrying, but not actually a sign of illness.'

'I was almost killed,' I said. I explained about the accident.

'Ah,' he said. 'This makes perfect sense. Your body is so surprised at still being alive that you're experiencing a massive rush of adrenaline.

This explains your elation. Don't worry, it should soon pass.'

'I should be feeling depressed again shortly?'

'Yes, yes,' he reassured. 'Possibly even worse than usual. You may experience what's called an adrenaline crash.'

'Well, that's a relief,' Mum said. 'Thank you, Doctor, I'll see you out.'

She walked him to his Saab and their voices floated in through the window.

'Are you sure you can't prescribe something for her?' I heard Mum ask.

'Like what? Don't worry,' Dr Lott promised Mum. 'Lily's elation will pass soon.'

'And while we're waiting?'

'She's a writer, isn't she? Why don't you try persuading her to write about all of this. At least if she's writing about it, she won't be talking.'

He had barely finished his sentence when I had reached for a pen and notebook and watched my hand write, 'Grace woke up and discovered that once again a plane had not landed on her during the night.' It was a good opening sentence, I thought.

And so was the paragraph which followed, where Grace had a shower and did not scald herself, had a bowl of muesli and did not choke to death on a nut, thrust her hand into a drawer and did not sever a vein on a knife, left the house and did not skid on a stray apple core into the path of a speeding car. On the way to work, her bus does not crash, and nothing heavy falls out of the sky to land on her workstation—all before nine o'clock in the morning! I already knew my title. *A Charmed Life*.

Jojo

JOJO WOKE UP—thought the two thoughts she had every morning—and knew that today was the day that something had to change.

In the first two weeks after she had left Lipman Haigh, life was busy. The phone rang all the time—authors telling her they were jumping ship to go to Richie Gant, Mark begging her to come back, publishing people desperate to know what the story was—then, like the flick of a switch, everything suddenly went very quiet.

Jojo discovered that sitting in her living room, trying to run a literary agency with almost no authors, sucked. The final shakedown showed she had lost twenty-one of her twenty-nine authors to Richie Gant and only the small—unlucrative—ones had stayed.

No money was coming in—like, *nothing*—and it freaked her out.

For thirteen straight weeks, every single morning, it was the second thing she thought of when she woke up. All through February, all through March, all through April. Now it was the start of May and nothing had changed.

But today was the day that something had to give.

There was no money left; she had sold her small holding of stocks, cashed in a pension scheme and had run her overdraft and cards to the hilt. She had used everything up, she had a mortgage to pay and whatever else happened, she was not going to lose her apartment.

She had two options, neither of them attractive—she could remortgage her apartment or return to work for a big agency. It was going to be hard (like, impossible) to remortgage her apartment without a steady job. So really, she had one option left, but saying she had two made it seem better.

Feeling a little weird, a little sad, she picked up the phone and rang her number-one agency, Curtis Brown. The person she needed to speak to wasn't available so she left a message.

When the phone rang she thought it would be someone from Curtis Brown returning her call, but it wasn't.

'Jojo, it's Lily. Lily Wright. I have a manuscript for you. I think, I mean, how can anyone ever be sure, but I think you're going to love it. Like it, in any case.'

'You think? Well, let's take a look!' Jojo had no hope for this. Lily, a totally great person, was a literary untouchable. After the train wreck of *Crystal Clear*, she would never be published again.

'I live quite nearby,' Lily said. 'In St John's Wood. I could drop it over to you now. Ema and I would enjoy the walk.'

'Sure! Why not!' OK, so she was humouring her, but it was better than telling her not to bother, right?

Lily and Ema came, Lily had a cup of tea, Ema broke the handle off a mug and hung it from the inside of her ear like an earring, then they left again.

Some time in the afternoon the woman from Curtis Brown rang back and gave Jojo an appointment for later in the week. And, slooooowly, the day passed. She spoke to Becky several times, went to yoga, came home, made dinner, watched TV and, at about eleven thirty, decided it was time for bed. Looking for something to read to ease her into sleep, her glance bounced off Lily Wright's bundle of pages. Might as well take a look.

Twenty minutes later

Jojo was sitting straight-backed in bed, her hands gripping the pages so tightly that they buckled. She was only a short way into the book, but she *knew*. This was IT! The manuscript she had been waiting for, the book that would reignite her career. It was *Mimi's Remedies* mark two, only better. She would sell it for a *fortune*.

Gemma

IT WAS NEARLY a week since I'd last seen my parents—just like the good old days. When I did finally get it together to call over, Mam said, 'This came for you.'

She handed me an envelope that had several addresses crossed out then written over. It had originally been sent to Dalkin Emery and they'd forwarded it on to Lipman Haigh, who'd sent it to my parents. It had a Mick stamp on it.

I opened the letter.

Dear Gemma,
   I just wanted to let you know how much I enjoyed Chasing Rainbows. *(I got it in the airport on my way to Fuerteventura.)*
   Congratulations on a great read. I was happy that Will and Izzy finally got it together after all their trials and tribulations. I didn't think it was going to happen, especially when that other man was knocking around. I was concerned that Izzy was on the rebound but now I'm convinced—they make a lovely couple.
Love, Johnny
PS Come and see me. I have some new surgical gauze in that you might find interesting.

Johnny. Johnny the Scrip. From the chemist. I didn't know any other Johnny. And he'd signed it 'Love'.

It was like someone had drilled down and filled up every part of me with relief. He'd read the book. He didn't hate me. He'd forgiven me for treating him like a stopgap.

He wanted to see me . . .

How did I feel about that? I felt that I'd call in on the way back to my flat, that's how I felt! I understood something: I was finally ready. For the past year—more—I'd been way too mad to pursue anything with Johnny and I think I'd wanted to wait until I was myself again before trying to embark on anything with him. I reckon it was why I'd stayed with Owen—being with him kept me from pushing for anything with Johnny.

Then I noticed the date on Johnny's letter and I was shocked. It was the 19th of March—six weeks earlier. It had spent all that time passing from publisher to agent to parents. Suddenly it seemed imperative to leave.

'What is it? A fan letter?' Dad asked.

'Look, I'm off.'

'But you've only just got here.'

'I'll come back.'

I drove as fast as I'd driven that first night long ago when I was on a mission to secure drugs to stop my mammy going totally doolally. I parked outside, pushed open the door, and there he was, in his white coat, bending solicitously over some old lady's hand. My heart swelled.

Then he looked up and I got the fear: it wasn't him. It was very like him but *it wasn't him*. For a mad moment I feared body snatchers, then I realised this must be Hopalong the famed brother.

'Can I help you?' Hopalong asked.

'I'm looking for Johnny.'

'He's not here.'

Something about the way he said it gave me a bad feeling. 'He hasn't, by any chance, emigrated to Australia?' It would be just my luck. And he'd possibly meet his The One on the boat . . .

'Um, no. Well, he didn't mention it yesterday evening, if he has.'

'OK.'

'Can I give him a message?'

'No, thanks. I'll call back.'

The following day I called again but, to my great dismay, Hopalong was still manning the decks.

'You're sure he hasn't gone to Australia?'

'No, but if you want to see him, why don't you come in the daytime?'

'Because I have to work in the daytime. He used to work evenings.'

'Not any more. He only does one evening a week now.'

I waited patiently. Hopalong continued rearranging the packets of Hacks.

'And what evening is that?'

'Hmmm?'

'*And what evening is that?*'

'Oh! Sorry. Thursday.'

'Thursday? Tomorrow is Thursday. You're sure about that?'

'Yes. Well, *nearly* sure.'

I was clambering into my car when he called after me, 'Don't forget, we close at eight now.'

'Eight o'clock? Not ten? Why?'

'Because we just do.'

Lily

JOJO SET THE AUCTION date for *A Charmed Life* a week hence but, as she predicted, there was a flurry of pre-emptives. Pelham Press offered a million for three books. 'No,' I said. 'There won't be a second or third book. This is a one-off special.'

Knoxton House offered eight hundred for two. I repeated that this book was a stand-alone event. The weekend intervened, then on Monday morning, Southern Cross offered five hundred for one.

'Take it,' I told Jojo.

'No,' she said. 'I can get you more.'

Three days later, on Thursday afternoon, she sold it to B&B Halder for £650,000. Giddy and giggly, she said, 'We have to celebrate. Come on, meet me for a drink. Don't worry, I won't keep you late, I've got a do this evening.'

We agreed on six o'clock in a wine bar in Maida Vale. When I arrived, Jojo was already there, with a bottle of champagne.

After a couple of glasses she asked me—as I had known she would— 'Why were you so insistent that you would only sign for one book? I could have got you *millions*.'

I shook my head. 'I'm not going to write another book. I plan to go back full-time to copywriting. It's steady money, I quite enjoy it and no one humiliates my efforts in the Sunday newspapers.'

'You know what they say?'

'A hazelnut in every bite?'

'How to make God laugh? Tell him your plans.'

'OK,' I conceded. 'None of us know what's going to happen. But if I have anything to do with it, I won't write another.'

Some time later, Jojo looked at her watch. 'Seven thirty. Gotta go. Meeting up with my cousin Becky. She's coming with me to the Dalkin Emery author party tonight.'

'The Dalkin Emery author party?' I put my head to one side. 'Wasn't I one of them once? Well, I wasn't invited to the party.'

'Guess what?' She leaned in to me, laughing. 'Neither was I, until about five minutes ago. They biked me over an invite yesterday. Thanks to you and your fabulous new book, I'm back in the game.'

'How fickle of them. How rude. And you're going to go? I'd tell them to get lost!'

'I've got to go,' she said, lapsing into an unexpected dark mood.

I said nothing, but I, like everyone else, had heard the rumours. Something to do with an affair with her boss and her having to leave because he had broken up with her or some such. Then her cousin phoned and she left to meet her.

I walked home, put Ema to bed, then braced myself. It was time to read Anton's letter.

I had no choice. I knew it would not go away.

I lay down on the sofa and slid out three crumpled handwritten pages:

My dearest Lily,

When are you reading this? Six months after we've broken up? A year? No matter how long it is, thank you for doing so. There is only one thing I want to say in this letter and that is to let you know how very sorry I am for all the unhappiness I've caused you.

When we first met, the choice you had to make—between Gemma and me—was a horrible one. I tried to understand, I thought I understood, but at the time I was just one big, insanely happy eejit, so bowled over at our 'rightness', that I didn't really get it. In retrospect, I don't think I ever fully understood the depth of your guilt and the fear that you would be punished. In my defence, I tried, but the happiness at our being together kept rushing in and sweeping it away.

I don't know if you can ever be convinced that our being together was right. But would you please try? Don't ruin the rest of your life by dragging around a big sack of shame with you. Would it help if you looked at Ema? She's such a sparky little soul, she makes the world a better place, and we made her, you and me. Some good has come out of us.

I would also like to apologise about losing you and Ema your home. Words are ridiculously inadequate at conveying the extent of my shame.

I was afraid that if we didn't buy a home for the three of us that we'd fritter away all your hard-earned royalties and end up with a load of crap (cars, stereos, Barbie merchandise) but no security (you know what we're like). It was a stab at behaving like a responsible adult. Buying beyond our means seemed like the smart thing to do. Like the fool I was, I thought I had vision. But none of that matters now. I didn't listen to your fears, it all fell apart and I hate listening to my pathetic attempts to justify myself.

I regret the mistakes I made, I bitterly regret the unhappiness I caused you but I will never regret our time together. When I'm eighty and looking back on my life, I'll know that there was at least one good pure thing in it. From that first time we met outside that tube station, I felt like the luckiest bastard on the planet and that feeling never went away. Every single day that we were together I couldn't believe my luck—most people don't have in a lifetime what we had in three and a half years and I will always be grateful for that. You will go on and meet someone else and I'll just be a chapter in your tale, but for me, you were, you are and you always will be, the whole story.
Yours always,
Anton

I put down the letter and stared at the ceiling. Stared and stared.

I had known this was coming. I had known for weeks, since before I had gone to Mum's. It had been *why* I had gone.

Even then I had known that I would have to make this choice. My love for Anton had crept stealthily back; banished for a while by my heartbreak over the house, it had returned in force, clamouring for me to address it.

And how should I do it?

I had an idea.

At least now I understood what had been going on inside me: I had been very angry with Anton—losing houses was a touchy subject for me. But, and I did not know why—time? Distance?—I no longer blamed him. I had thought I could never forgive, but I had.

Even before I had read this letter, I understood what he had been trying to do with the house: he had taken a risk, but as risks go, it had been quite an unrisky one. He had been unlucky.

And what about me? I had been there too, I could have stepped in. Instead I had been complicit and passive, clinging to the position where I could blame if I needed to.

Anton was undeniably careless with money. But I was not any better. Let she who is without debt write the first cheque.

I sighed long and wearily, still looking up at the ceiling, hoping to see answers there.

Happiness is a rare thing and you have to take your chances where you find them. I wanted to do the right thing—but how do we ever know? There are no guarantees.

I decided to make a list, as if the biggest decision of one's life could be made by writing out bullet-points on the white margin of the TV guide. Well, it was as good as any other way . . .

- Ema would be better off if her parents were together.

- I felt able to get past my guilt with Gemma.

- I had forgiven Anton for the house and we would be more sensible with our finances in the future.

- He was my most favourite person in the whole world. By a million miles. (Apart from Ema.)

Hmmm . . .

Well, I thought, it couldn't hurt to *talk* to Anton. So, invoking the forces of the universe, I made a decision. I would ring him—right now and just this once—and if I did not get him, I would take it as a sign that we were not meant to be. Carefully I picked up the phone, hoping to convey to it how important its next mission was. I wondered where Anton was right now, what the plan for us was. Then I pressed the numbers, put the phone to my ear, heard it begin to ring and prayed.

Gemma

ALL DAY THURSDAY I was a bit flaky at work—excitement, see? About finally seeing Johnny that evening, see? But everything conspired against it because I had to work until six thirty, then I had to collect Dad from the day hospital. He'd had a minor operation (something to do with his prostate, I *so* did not want to know), and because he'd had an anaesthetic, he wasn't allowed to drive himself home. But he took forever to leave, saying goodbye to the nurses as if he'd been there for six months and not six hours, and by the time we left the hospital it was seven forty-five. Johnny's chemist closed at eight, so I took an executive decision.

'Dad, before I drop you home, I've got to go to the pharmacy.'

'What do you need?'

'Plasters.'

'But you haven't cut yourself.'

'Tissues, then.'

'Have you a cold?'

'All right, Hedex,' I said irritably.

'Have you a headache?'

'I do now.'

I parked outside and he clipped off his seat belt. Anxiously, I said, 'Dad, stay in the car. You're not a well man.'

Not a chance. He'd got wind something was up. 'I need to buy something myself.'

'What?'

'Er . . .' he scanned the window for ads '. . . Oil of Evening Primrose.' Clutching his groin, he followed me in.

There was a man behind the counter, he was wearing the regulation-issue white coat, he had the right-size body, but I couldn't see his face.

If he turns round and I'm looking at Hopalong, then I'm giving up, I thought. Me and Johnny the Scrip are just not going to happen.

Then, with excruciating slowness, the man turned and—*oh, thank you, God*—it was Johnny!

'Gemma!' His face lit up, then he looked enquiringly over my shoulder.

'Oh, that's my dad,' I said. 'Just ignore him.'

'Right.'

I stepped closer. 'I got your letter,' I said shyly. 'Thank you. Did you really like the book?'

'Yes. Particularly the love story between Izzy and Will.'

'You did?' I'd gone the colour of a fire engine.

'It was nice the way they got it together in the end. He seemed like a nice bloke.' He flicked a slightly perplexed look behind me, at Dad.

'Oh, Will *is* a nice bloke,' I tried to focus on the job in hand, which was securing the heart of Johnny. 'He's great.'

'So's Izzy.'

Behind me, I heard Dad exclaim, 'Christ Almighty, you're Will! Out of the book!' He hobbled forward. 'I'm Declan Nolan, the father that does the runner—'

I stopped him; this was getting way too pally. 'And I'm Izzy.'

'Good girl.'

'As in Will and Izzy.'

He finally got it. 'I'll, ah, leave you to it.' He stepped towards the door and I turned back to Johnny.

'Gemma?' he said.

'Yes?' I was holding my breath.

'I was thinking.'
'Yes?'
'Something you said ages ago.'
'Yes?'
'About going out for a drink.'
'Yes?'
'Well, isn't it about time . . .?'
Yesssssssss!!!!!

Some time later, back in the car, Dad said, 'I can't believe that. You drove over to a man and laid your cards on the table. What's the world coming to?'

'Come on, Dad, what's the big deal? It's not like I asked him to leave his wife of thirty-five years, is it?' *Did I really say that?* We looked at each other, watching warily.

Eventually, Dad spoke. 'I think we might have to go for family counselling or something. What do you think?'

'Dad, don't be ridiculous, we're Irish.'

'But this sort of bad feeling can't go on.'

I thought about it. 'It'll pass. Just give me time.'

'Time heals everything, doesn't it?'

I thought about it. 'No.' Then I conceded, 'But most things.'

Jojo

AT THE DALKIN EMERY author party, halfway through flicking her hair over her shoulder and into Kathleen Perry's drink, Jojo saw him—at the far wall and wearing a dark suit; he was watching her. Their eyes connected and it hit her like a punch in the stomach.

Her heart was pumping hard, the hand round her glass was instantly sweaty and everything felt super-real. He mouthed something at her: 'Wait.' Then, 'Please.' Then he turned his shoulder and began pushing through the people, moving in her direction.

He disappeared from view and then reappeared, right in front of her.

'Jojo?' It sounded like an enquiry, as if he was checking she was real.

'Mark.' Even saying his name felt like a relief.

'You look'— he sought a good enough word—'great.'

'That's me,' she quipped. He lit up with delight and for a moment it was like old times. Until Jojo asked, 'How're Cassie and the kids?'

Warily he answered, 'OK.'

'You and Cassie are still together?'

He hesitated. 'She found out about, you know, us.'

'Shit. How?'

'After you left it was obvious that something was wrong.' He half laughed. 'I went to pieces.'

She hadn't exactly been, like, on cloud nine herself. 'Had she known?'

'She'd guessed there was somebody. She didn't know it was you.'

'I'm sorry. I'm sorry to hurt her.'

'She says it was a relief to finally find out. She says pretending not to notice that I was never there was doing her in. For the past few months we've been trying to patch things up.' He stopped. 'But I still think about you all the time.'

She'd been moving closer, reeled in by him. Straightening her shoulders, she shifted away—too scared of catching even a hint of how he smelt, that would be the undoing of her.

'Could we meet some time?' he asked. 'Just for a drink?'

'You know we couldn't.'

People were looking at them, their intimacy all too obvious.

'Mark, I have to go now.'

'Do you? But—'

She pushed her way through the crowds, knowing everyone, smiling, smiling, smiling her way to the door.

Once outside, she walked at speed, Becky skipping in her wake, trying to keep up. When they were at a safe distance, she abruptly stopped in a doorway and jackknifed over, clutching her stomach.

'Are you going to throw up?' Becky whispered, circling her hand on Jojo's back.

'No,' she answered, thickly. 'But it hurts.'

'You could get back with him, you know.'

Jojo straightened up. 'That will never happen. It is over.'

'How can it be? You miss him terribly.'

'So what? I'll get over him, hey, I'm nearly there already. And if I want, I'll meet someone else some time. I mean, look at me—I run my own business, I've got all my own teeth and hair, I can fix bikes—'

'You look like Jessica Rabbit.'

'I'm a cryptic crossword ninja.'

'You do a brilliant Donald Duck impersonation.'

'Exactly. I'm *fabulous*.'

Lily

ANTON'S PHONE RANG once. It rang twice. My heart was pounding, my hands were slippery, I was mouthing, 'Please God.' It rang three times. Four times. Five times. Six times.

Shit . . .

On the seventh ring, there was a click, a burst of pub-like chatter and laughter, then someone—Anton—said, 'Lily?'

Joy rendered me light-headed. (Though I must admit I had called him on his mobile. I had not taken any chances.) And before I had uttered a word he had known it was me! Another sign! (Or else he had caller display.)

'Anton? Can I see you?'

'When? Now?'

'Yes. Where are you?'

'Wardour Street.'

'Meet me at St John's Wood tube station.'

'I'll leave now. I'll be with you in fifteen, twenty minutes at the latest.'

Infused with wild energy, I ran to the mirror and pulled a brush through my hair. I rummaged through my make-up bag but I didn't need any, I already looked transformed. Nevertheless, I quickly rubbed on blusher and lipgloss, because it couldn't hurt. Then I went to ask Irina to watch Ema. 'I'm popping out for a while.'

She asked, 'Why?'

'I'm going to do something rash.'

'Vit Anton? Good. But you kennot go looking like that. You need pore-minimiser.' She reached for her crate of cosmetics but I fled.

I had to leave the apartment. Although Anton would not yet have arrived at the station, I had far too much nervous energy to be contained within walls.

Dusk was falling, the light was navy-blue and at the speed I was walk-ing, it took me less than five minutes to walk to the station.

The vision of my future I had had when I was in the numb stage of grieving for Anton returned with force; I had been convinced that a new life was waiting for me, full of feelings and laughter and colour and with an entirely new cast of people to its current one. I had not stopped believing in that vision, but some of the cast were the same. Anton was still the leading man, he had made the part his own.

I rounded the corner to do the last stretch and, through the gloom, fixed my eyes on the station entrance, the magical portal that would deliver him to me.

Then I noticed that a rangy figure outside the station was watching me. Although it was too dark to see properly and too soon for Anton to have arrived already from central London, I knew instantly that it was him. I knew it was *him*.

I did not physically stumble but I felt as if I had. It was like seeing him for the first time.

My footsteps slowed; I knew what was going to happen. Once I was beside him, that would be it. There would be no talking; we would be fixed, fused, for ever.

I could have stopped. I could have turned back and erased the future, but I continued putting one foot in front of the other, as if an invisible thread led me directly to him.

His first words to me were, 'I saw you from miles away.' He picked up a strand of my hair.

I moved closer to his height, his beauty, his Anton-ness and into the light of his presence. 'I saw you too.'

While people hurried in and out of the station like characters in a speeded-up movie, Anton and I remained motionless as statues, his eyes on mine, his hands on my arms, completing the magic circle. And I said what I had always known, 'As soon as I saw you I knew it was you.'

EPILOGUE

ALMOST NINE MONTHS to the day that Owen broke it off with me, he and Lorna had a little girl and called her—wait for it!—Agnes Lana May. Nothing that could remotely be construed as 'Gemma'. They didn't ask me to be her godmother. Currently, there are no plans to go to the Dordogne together.

My book came out in the middle of May and it bombed. They blamed the cover, the title and the atrocious reviews. The general tone was '. . . escapist pap.'

It was horrifically humiliating. The only nice reviews were in crappy magazines that print a lot of 'I stole my daughter's husband' type stories. One of them called it Revenge Literature and clearly this was something they approved of.

But even that wasn't enough to sell my books and I must admit I didn't help: just before the book came out, Dad asked me not to do publicity where I told the real story behind the book, and something must have softened in me because I took pity on him and agreed.

There won't be a second book; I have no imagination and nothing bad has happened to me—apart from my first book getting horrible reviews and not being able to write a second book, but that's all a little post-modern. The fact is that my life is too nice and there are worse complaints.

I still have most of the advance money (they didn't make me give it back even though the book sold almost nothing) and maybe one day in the misty future I'll set up on my own. Not as easy as it sounds, we're not all Jojo Harvey, who now has fabulous coloured-glass offices in Soho and four people working for her, including her old assistant Manoj.

Lily's career goes from strength to strength. She wrote a new book called *A Charmed Life*, which was like another *Mimi's Remedies* and sold in its millions. Then *Crystal Clear*, the book that nearly broke Dalkin Emery, surprised everyone by getting short-listed for the Orange Prize and *that* also sold in its millions. Apparently she's writing something new, they're all very excited.

I actually met Anton and Lily at a publishing do, shortly after *Chasing Rainbows* came out and my publishers were still talking to me. I was moving through the throng, trying to find the Ladies and suddenly me and Lily ended up standing before each other.

'Gemma?' Lily croaked. She looked absolutely terrified.

And after all the fantasies I'd entertained over the years—splashing a glass of red wine in her face, zapping her with death stares, shouting out to the roomful of her peers about what an evil bitch she was—I watched myself take her hand, hold it and say with a certain amount of sincerity, 'I enjoyed *Mimi's Remedies*, and so did my mother.'

'Thank you, thank you so much, Gemma. And I loved *Chasing Rainbows*.' She did her sweet-girl smile, then Anton appeared and that was fine too. We made a few moments of innocuous chitchat, and as they left Anton tried to hold Lily's hand, but she wouldn't and I heard her say, 'Have some consideration.' Meaning, I think, for me.

And, yes, I felt sad then. That sort of gesture was Lily all over; she was very mindful of other people's feelings. It was a pity we couldn't be friends because (apart from that one boyfriend-stealing incident) she was a lovely person. I'd been so fond of her.

But onwards and upwards.

When Mam met Johnny the Scrip for the first time, she took in his broad shoulders, his air of kindness and the twinkle in his eye that is a permanent feature now that he's no longer working round the clock, and she leaned over to me and murmured, 'Looks like the professionals have arrived.'

She likes him. Shite.

But even that wasn't enough to put me off him.

As for Mam and Dad . . . well, he does the crossword and plays golf, they watch murder-mysteries and go for drives. Apart from the fact that I've had a book published and we have access to all the surgical gauze we can eat, you'd swear he'd never been away . . .

MARIAN KEYES

The road to success has not been an easy one for Marian Keyes. The eldest of five children, Marian grew up in Dublin. Having gained a law degree, she moved to London to work, but during this time her lifelong low self-esteem gradually turned into a drinking problem. 'By the time I was thirty,' Marian states, 'it had all come to a terrible head and, after a suicide attempt, I was lucky enough to get into rehab. (Mind you I didn't feel lucky at the time! I thought my life was over.) I began writing short stories four months before I finally stopped drinking and, after I came out of rehab, I decided to send them off to a publisher. So that they'd take me seriously, I enclosed a letter saying I'd written part of a novel. Which I hadn't.'

When the publisher wrote back asking to see what she had written, Marian dashed off four chapters of what would eventually become her first novel, *Watermelon*, and was offered a three-book contract. 'Having felt pain, I can now describe pain to other people,' Marian Keyes explains. 'Every miserable moment I've had has made me what I am today. I think I write the stories I write, which are ultimately cheery and optimistic, so that I can feel hopeful myself.'

In 1995, Marian married Tony, a friend of one of her flatmates in London, and in 1997, with Marian now writing full-time, they moved back to Ireland. 'We live in the suburbs, in a place called Dun Laoghaire, near to my mother and father—it's a ten-minute walk—and we go there on Thursdays. I've a brother and sister living in Dublin too, so it's a chance for us all to catch up. Dinner is either spaghetti bolognaise or chicken casserole on a strict rotation system. It's a certainty. Mum also keeps the freezer full of mini Magnums, just for me!'

Marian Keyes's writing regime is rather unorthodox but works well for her. After breakfast in bed—porridge and coffee brought to her courtesy of Tony (who gave up a successful career in IT to work as her personal assistant or 'dogsbody' as they jokingly refer to him), Marian sits in her pyjamas and types for six hours straight. 'I write in bed with my laptop. Our room overlooks the garden, which is not that big but it's a disaster. We're away so often and it's really difficult to maintain. But because I'm so shortsighted, I can only see the greenery, so it looks OK to me!'

Happiness, for Marian Keyes, has less to do with her writing success and more to do with family and friends. Family is important to her, and she's particularly sad that she and Tony have been unable to have children. 'It has been a source of grief for both of us. We haven't adopted because I didn't want *any* child, I wanted his child. My brother and his wife are very generous, though, letting us mind their babies.

'I was always dissatisfied with myself and my life,' the author continues, 'and now I like what I do. I just want to write good books, and I want to write the best book I possibly can write each time.'

Jane Eastgate

The Wedding Day

Catherine Alliott

*Annie O'Harran can hardly believe her luck when
Dr David Palmer asks her to be his wife. But then,
neither can anyone else. Her ex-husband Adam is
convinced Annie is still in love with him; her sister
Clare is jealous that Annie has found happiness just
when her own marriage is on the rocks; and her
daughter Flora thinks Annie will need to smarten up
her act to keep David interested.*

*But the wedding plans are going ahead—David is
making sure of that. Meanwhile, Annie is heading off
to Cornwall for some much needed peace
and quiet. Or so she thinks!*

Chapter One

'SO YOU DON'T THINK she'll mind?' I asked again, coming back to the breakfast table with two slopping mugs of coffee. I handed him one.

'Annabel, for the last time, I *know* she won't mind.' David reached for a piece of kitchen towel and carefully wiped the bottom of his mug before setting it down. 'That house stands empty for months on end, for heaven's sake. She'll be delighted to have the place occupied.'

'And you won't mind us going?' I perched on a chair opposite him in my threadbare blue dressing gown, cradled my mug in my hands and peered anxiously at him over his propped-up newspaper. 'You'll be here all on your own, David, for the whole summer.'

With a sigh, he folded *The Times* carefully into quarters, laid it aside and smiled. 'I think I'll survive.'

'It *would* be rather marvellous,' I went on abstractedly. 'And just what I need right now. Nearly two months of peace and quiet to finish this wretched book, and by the sea, too. And without . . . well . . .'

'Shopping to do and beds to make and the telephone ringing constantly and your bloody sister popping round every five minutes, yes, yes, I agree. We've been through this a million times, Annie, *take* the house in Cornwall and *finish* the wretched book and get it over and done with.' He grinned and propped up his newspaper again.

'And we'll get married the moment I get back,' I said. 'In the church at the bottom of Cadogan Street because Mum was cheated out of the church bit the first time round and would love it so, and—'

'Look,' he interrupted, shaking his paper irritably. 'We've been through this, Annie. We've been through the unsatisfactory nature of your charmless wedding to your faithless first husband, and the not unreasonable demands of my future mother-in-law for church nuptials the second time around, and I've *said* yes,' he implored plaintively.

'And Flora would love it too,' I mused, picking up my plate and drifting absently to the sink, stacking it high on top of an already tottering pagoda of dirty dishes. 'The wedding, I mean. Being a bridesmaid.'

He caught my wrist suddenly as I floated back and kissed the palm of my hand hard. In a swift movement he'd drawn me down on to his lap. 'Yes, she would,' he murmured, kissing me purposefully on the mouth. 'Now, stop it. We've agreed. You go to Cornwall, you take my dippy aunt's house, and you finish your book. Then you return, six weeks later, a woman of letters—and in a matter of days you'll have a ring on your finger and all the bourgeois respectability that goes with being Mrs Palmer, the doctor's wife. Frankly, I don't mind what you do so long as you stop burning the toast and making me drink coffee in Flora's chipped Groovy Chick mug.' He peered balefully into its pink depths.

'I'll have it back then, shall I? Since you're fussy?' Flora, having pounded downstairs, came through the door in her school uniform. 'And, Mum, stop hopping around,' she added as I hastily got off David's lap, blushing. 'You're sharing a bed together, for God's sake, I don't see that a cuddle at the breakfast table makes any difference.' She grinned conspiratorially at David, clearly relishing her role as the mature observer of impulsive love-birds. He winked good-naturedly back.

'Flora's right. Stop behaving as if we're just playing Scrabble up there and give her a little credit. And, incidentally, where exactly does my new step-daughter fit into this great summer scheme of yours?'

'What scheme?' demanded Flora. She threw back her head and gathered a sheet of silky dark hair into her hands, ready for the scrunchy poised between her teeth.

'Well, Flora, nothing's set in stone,' I began nervously, 'but you know this book I've been trying to—'

'Oh God, is it ten past?' Her eyes flew to the clock. 'My bus!' She seized a piece of burnt toast from the toaster and simultaneously stuffed books in a bag with the other. 'Yes, I know your book.'

'Well, Gertrude has a place by the sea, apparently.' I twisted my fingers anxiously, following her as she dashed round the kitchen gathering together gym kit, pencil case, trainers. 'You know, David's aunt—'

'Yes, of course I know Gertrude. Has she? I didn't know that.'

'And . . . well, I thought I might go there. Borrow it, just for the summer. Just for six weeks or so—'

'Six weeks!' She paused. Stopped her packing and gazed. 'What, you mean . . . and I'll stay here? With David?'

'Oh no! No, I didn't mean that. No, it'll be during the school holidays, so you'll come with me. I'll be working, obviously, but I could get a nanny or something . . .'

'A *nanny*. God, Mum, I'm twelve. I don't need a nanny.'

'Well, you know, a girl, a teenager or something. Just to keep an eye on you.'

She shook her head and resumed her packing. 'I can amuse myself. And, anyway, I think I'd rather be in London. All my friends are staying in London for the summer, and I could stay here with David, couldn't I?'

'Doesn't matter a jot to me,' said David equably, getting up from the table and reaching for his suit jacket on the back of a chair.

I looked at him gratefully, loving him for playing to her bravado. For not saying: 'What friends, Flora?' or: 'Flora, do me a favour, you can't even manage a *sleep*over without your mum, let alone six weeks.'

'You girls sort it out between yourselves,' he went on, glancing at his watch. 'I'll see you both later.' He kissed me again and tweaked Flora's pony-tail on the way out.

When he'd disappeared down the front hall and the door had shut behind him, I turned anxiously to her.

'But you will come with me, won't you, Flora? I hadn't planned on doing this without you, you know.'

'Hadn't talked to me about it though, had you?'

'Well, no.' I hesitated. 'Obviously I had to talk to David first.' I paused, letting this new level of hierarchy sink in, then lost my nerve. 'I mean,' I said quickly, 'he's the one being left behind, and anyway, I haven't even asked Gertrude if I can borrow the house yet.'

'Where is this place, anyway?'

'Down on the north coast of Cornwall, near Rock. It's really pretty. And perched high up on the top of a cliff and—oh, Flora, you can surf and water-ski, sail dinghies. You'll have a terrific time! You'll make friends—'

'OK, OK, stop selling it. You'll be throwing in sing-songs round the campfire next. And what about David? Why isn't he coming?'

'He will, of course he will, for weekends. But he can't take all that time off, particularly if we want to have a honeymoon later on in the year.' I hesitated. 'Flora, you do realise we will *have* a honeymoon . . .'

'Oh God, I'm not coming on that!'

'No no,' I said quickly. 'Just checking you knew.'

'Mum, do me a favour.' She made a gormless face. 'Anyway, Granny will come and look after me, won't she?' She contrived to look nonchalant but her dark eyes were anxious and my heart lurched for her.

'Of course she will. Now go, darling. The bus will be at the corner any minute.'

We both glanced up as the familiar rattle heralded its approach.

'Go!' I yelled.

She went, snatching up her bags, flying down the passage and through the front door as I followed behind.

I stood at the door, watching as she boarded the bus. I saw her glance nervously over her shoulder as a couple of the older girls bounded noisily up behind her. This morning they smiled as she turned, so she smiled back, then glanced quickly at me, to see if I'd noticed she'd been included. I held my smile, a lump in my throat.

The bus purred off and I stayed in the doorway, leaning on the frame and glancing up and down the quiet, tree-lined London street. The Victorian villas were more or less identical, give or take the window-box planting or the variety of geraniums artfully arranged round the front doors. Periodically, doors would open and spew out their occupants: schoolchildren followed by harassed mothers, yelling enquiries to their offspring about violins and book-bags; fathers, in their dark suits, firmly shutting garden gates behind them and forgetting, in that instant, the spilt Rice Krispies packets within, focusing only on the day ahead as they headed purposefully for the City. Men who looked a whole lot like David, I reflected as I stood there, pleased, for once, to have a man who fitted in. Who conformed. Unlike Adam.

David was a GP, with salubrious premises in Sloane Street, which he was doubtless striding towards even now, where his late uncle, Hugh, Gertrude's husband, had practised before him. And it was here, near to his Sloane Street surgery, that he'd saved me, too. In so many ways.

The first thing I'd noticed about David had been his eyes, huge with horror as he ran towards me.

'Look out!' he cried as a sheet of plate glass, the one in the window of Boots the Chemist's, had been about to receive a mighty blow from a parcel of bricks swinging precariously from a rope as they were incompetently raised by workmen to scaffolding on the roof above. As the bricks lurched perilously close to the window, David simultaneously launched himself at me and Flora—just as the glass smashed to smithereens. As we were flung across the pavement with David prone on top of us, he looked up and let loose a stream of abuse at the workmen, the first and last time I ever heard him swear.

Thankfully the glass hadn't injured us, but David wasn't satisfied. As he picked himself up from the pavement and helped us to our feet, he took one look at the two tremulous females before him—who for various reasons hadn't been in the best of health even before the glass had shattered—and insisted we accompany him back to his surgery so he could check us over. I protested, but he was adamant.

So, with Flora trailing behind us, David helped me round the corner to his rooms on Sloane Street. On the second floor, the smooth blonde receptionist was instantly all tea and sympathy at the sight of us, which Flora and I—completely overwhelmed now by the opulence of our surroundings—meekly lapped up. As we trooped into David's consulting room, the deep shine of the furniture, the pall of antiquity on the oils hanging from the panelling and the chesterfield sofa I was invited to sit upon, all further contrived to render us mute and helpless.

David shone a torch in my eyes, and then carefully looked at my face.

'I'm checking for minuscule shards of glass . . .' he murmured, really very close up now. 'But actually . . . you look . . . perfect.'

I flushed to my roots at this and, for a split second, he caught my eye. And that's where it all began, I think. In the eyes.

He cleared his throat and moved swiftly across to examine Flora, who was perched on an identical sofa on the opposite side of the room. This not only gave me an opportunity to breathe, but also to look at him.

God, he was handsome. Crouched as he was at my daughter's feet in his immaculate charcoal-grey suit. His hair was fair and soft and swept back in a rather up-market way, and his intelligent face was concentrated into a look of deep concern. Flora sat before him, quiet as a mouse.

'You both look fine,' he declared suddenly, springing athletically to his feet. 'Though a little shaky. But if I were a betting man, I'd put your pallor down to exhaustion rather than the shock of that plate-glass window shattering. When did the pair of you last eat?'

I cleared my throat and tentatively admitted that we'd missed breakfast. Oh yes, and lunch to, on account of Flora being unable to face a thing due to appalling tummy cramps and me being too tired to contemplate food having been up all night trying to write. He frowned.

'I see. And you thought, having been up all night, that a little shopping spree in Knightsbridge might revive you?'

I smiled at his irony and gave him some of mine.

'Flora had set her heart on a pair of combat-style trousers that can't be found locally. Without them, her life would not be complete. It had to be Knightsbridge.'

He looked perplexed and said that he thought a decent breakfast was a bit more important than a pair of trousers, and that since he'd been on his way to lunch when he'd literally bumped into us, why didn't we accompany him to Starbucks for coffee and sandwiches?

The hot chocolate and egg mayonnaise rolls in the window of the sunny café went down a treat and Flora and I guzzled greedily as dust motes gathered in shafts of light around us. Afterwards, equilibrium restored, my daughter announced that she was going down to Gap to secure the trousers. Promising to be no longer than twenty minutes, she disappeared, leaving the stage free for David to use those twenty minutes to extract from me a promise to be allowed to restore my blood-sugar levels further at a restaurant of his choice the following evening.

That next night, after dinner, he'd taken me to bed. To my bed, in Fulham, becoming the only man to occupy the slot on the left-hand side of the Heal's summer sale bargain since my ex-husband Adam had vacated it. And I knew it was no mistake. Happily, he'd known it too, and a year later—almost to the day—here we were, on the brink of a wedding and a future together.

David moved into my tiny, bijou Fulham house, full of scatter cushions and twee clutter and rickety pine furniture, and left behind his spacious, minimalist, flat in Islington. The plan was to marry in the autumn, to sell both the properties and to buy in leafy Hurlingham, where, David predicted, the garden would soon play host to a pram, a paddling pool and, later, a tricycle or two.

All of which, frankly, made me want to pinch myself. In fact, as I confided to my sister Clare a few weeks after the Sloane Street incident and the Italian dinner, it almost made me want to believe there was Someone Up There rooting for me after all.

It was to Clare's that I hurried round to now to share my news.

Clare lived three streets away from me, in a much taller, more elegant, cream town house and where she'd been a lot longer. When I'd finally left Adam I'd flown geographically to her side, buying a place literally round the corner, unashamedly clinging to the small but strong residue of family I had in her: my big sister, who, from the moment she'd set eyes on Adam all those years ago, had folded her arms and declared, 'He's gorgeous, I grant you, but a *boy*, Annie, who looks and behaves like a red setter puppy. He'll need regular meals and exercise, but the moment your back's turned, he'll go for a walk with anyone who jangles a lead.'

Well, naturally, I'd been proud to prove her wrong. I'd been proud to go out with him for three, glorious years, and have him propose to me on a Hawaiian beach, and get married there, barefoot and with flowers in my hair, three days later. I'd returned home the proud owner of a dashing up-and-coming-actor husband and a dear little ring set with tiny seed pearls. I also had a baby on the way, and all this before my sister—four years older than me, mind—had even got off the starting blocks.

Yet, as ever, her foresight had proved to be horribly accurate. He'd wavered when I was big with child, seeking solace in candlelit restaurants with various supportive supporting actresses. He absented himself regularly on theatre tours during Flora's toddlerhood, and finally flitted off to Lyons on her first day at school with a nubile cycling enthusiast keen to introduce him to the joys of the Tour de France. He returned a week later, breezing brazenly through the back door and flicking on the kettle as if he'd just been to the paper shop.

So what had attracted me to this man in the first place, you might wonder? Well, apart from fabulous dark good looks, Romany gypsy curls, and charm that would have the birds dive-bombing from the trees, there was also his strong gravitational pull. Charisma, I believe it's called, and to a nineteen-year-old farmer's daughter from Devon, his brand of London-based, theatre-world charisma was pretty irresistible.

I gave up my place at the local technical college and trailed round the country with him, sitting in cold repertory theatres smoking Gitanes in black roll-neck jumpers and helping him learn his lines. There I'd be during every performance, always in the front row, always word perfect, and then, during the day, when I wasn't needed for prompting at rehearsals, waiting for him in some seedy bed-sit, writing short stories to pass the time. One or two were taken by *Woman's Realm*, which helped to pay the rent, and very occasionally I reached the dizzy heights of *Woman's Own*. I suppose, in retrospect, that that was the one productive thing to come out of our union together, besides Flora.

Our coming unstuck was a gradual process. There was the first phase in our marriage when I knew about the infidelity and was heartbroken, but loved him so much I couldn't do anything about it. Then there was the second phase, when I confronted him, he broke down and said it would never happen again and I believed him. Finally though—and I'm talking an embarrassing number of years here—I mustered the strength to take Flora away and live elsewhere. I put down a deposit on the house in Fulham with some money Dad had left me, and told Adam it was for ever.

He didn't believe me and visited us daily. In fact, he practically camped out in our front garden. Ostensibly he was there to see Flora, for which I was grateful, but principally it was to try to woo me back. He was honestly unable to understand why a few dalliances with other women had caused me to up sticks and file for divorce.

'But, Annie, you're my wife! You're literally the only person in the world apart from Flora that I really love, you must know that,' he'd cried, the decree nisi poised and awaiting his signature on my kitchen table. 'It's only *ever* been you, Annie. Don't do this to me!'

Me doing it to him, note. But by now I'd met David. Just. And I was slightly stronger, was eating properly, and sleeping a little bit more. My defences were not quite so low. I gave a tight smile.

'Sorry, Adam, it's me, I know. My fault. Call me old-fashioned, but I've got this thing about monogamy.'

He sighed and scratched his head. Shook it incredulously.

'Annie, men are different,' he explained patiently. 'Surely you know that by now? Staying constant to one woman for the rest of our lives, however much we love her, is terribly, terribly difficult. But I do love you, Annie, I swear it, and it's only ever been you.' He paused. 'All right if I borrow the lawnmower?'

I blinked. 'The lawnmower?'

'Francine's lawn needs mowing. She's playing Titania to my Oberon and I'm staying with her now that I've given up the flat. I couldn't face being there without you and Flora'—he shot me a bruised look—'so I've gone over to her place. I said I'd help out a bit. In lieu of rent.'

'Staying?' I folded my arms, eyebrows raised.

'Yes, just staying, Annie,' he said, affronted.

'Spare room?'

'Well, no . . .' He hesitated. 'She hasn't got one.'

I smiled. 'The lawn mower's in the shed, Adam. Help yourself.'

And so he went. In a huff. Really offended. Firmly convinced that I was the guilty party here. How *could* I leave him? How could I walk out on him and render him homeless?

And I knew, too, that a smidgen of what he'd said was true. That plenty of husbands did conduct themselves so, and plenty of women accepted these marriages. And I didn't deride those wives either, because I knew how much easier it was to accept it, as I'd accepted it too, for a time. All right, for years. Eleven. But when Flora was old enough to know what was going on too, I knew I had to escape with a few shreds of dignity intact. For her sake.

But it was hard. Bloody hard. Because I loved him. And just as I was wondering if dignity was such a big deal, or if being with the man I loved even if he did have the morals of an alley cat was more important, David stepped in. And saved us. Just in time. He arrived, as Clare often drily said, like the Seventh Cavalry, just as I was wavering.

I rang Clare's doorbell and heard sharp high heels echoing down the passageway. A moment later the door opened and Clare stood before me, dark hair swept up in a chignon, fully made up and immaculate in a charcoal-grey Joseph suit.

'Oh, it's you.'

She turned and stalked quickly back to the kitchen. I wasn't affronted. A typical early-morning greeting from a woman who's already got a husband off to work, two children to school, and is spooning Milupa into another while trying to get to the City herself.

'Bad moment?' I called, shutting the door behind me. 'I thought you didn't go in 'til later on Fridays?'

'Not this Friday,' she called back. 'There's a partners' meeting and I have to be there. I'm leaving in ten minutes.'

I followed her down to the kitchen where Henry, her toddler, was banging a spoon impatiently in his high chair, annoyed that the flow of nutrition had been interrupted. I boggled as Clare efficiently threw a white sheet over her head and stuck her arms through a couple of holes.

'What's that for?'

'I made it. Michael calls it my shroud. I use it to feed the children in.'

I giggled. 'Surprised you haven't got gloves and a surgical mask!'

'Oh, don't tempt me.'

She dragged out a chair for me and perched on the edge of hers, resuming spooning duty as Henry opened, shut, swallowed, opened, shut, swallowed, faster than she could get it in.

'Eats well,' I hazarded, sitting down at the immaculate breakfast table, cleared for action already save for a jar of tulips and Henry's bowl. How unlike mine, I thought, with its jumble of cereal packets, dog-eared paperbacks and piles of bills and junk mail still mouldering peacefully.

'He has to,' she replied darkly. 'He knows it might be the only square meal he'll get today. If Donna can bear to tear herself away from her mobile phone to throw him a rusk he'll be lucky.'

'Now you know that's not true,' I soothed. 'Donna does a brilliant job. Michael was telling me only the other day what an asset she's been.'

'Oh yes, a marvellous asset, particularly from his point of view. If you had someone hanging on to your every word and asking if they could possibly iron your underpants, you'd consider them an asset too.'

'You're making it up as you go along,' I said coolly. 'Donna doesn't give two hoots for Michael, and vice versa. You're just oversensitive.'

'Oversensitive, am I? Ah. And why might that be, I wonder?'

'Clare . . .' I sighed.

'Because my husband was caught fumbling up his fund manager's dress at the Christmas party while the rest of his department tittered and watched? But surely that wouldn't render me oversensitive, Annie?'

'He wasn't caught,' I said, 'he admitted it, and the only reason *he* told you was because the guilt was killing him. Anyway, he was drunk and it was a one-off snog and it was *months* ago. When are you going to let him off the hook, Clare?' I got up impatiently and filled the kettle.

She put the spoon down. 'Oh, you think I should, do you? Like you did all those years with Adam?'

Henry yelled indignantly. She picked up the spoon again.

'No,' I said evenly, 'I don't. And if this is about not turning into me, Clare, then I have to tell you there's little chance of that. You're not nearly as stupid.'

I turned and faced her defiantly. She gazed at me, two pink spots appearing in her cheeks. Suddenly her shoulders sagged and she sighed.

'OK,' she caved in. 'Sorry. I didn't mean that. Didn't mean you were stupid. It's just . . . well, it eats away at me, Annie. Every time he touches me, I see his arms round her. Picture him kissing her, and—'

'So walk out,' I interrupted, sharply.

She stared. 'Oh, don't be silly. I can't do that.'

'Why not?'

'Well, because there're the kids and the house and everything, and—'

'Exactly, so forget it.' I banged a coffee cup down in front of her, spilling half of it. 'Hell, Clare, don't wreck the rest of your married life together just because of it!'

'You see,' she said gloomily, instantly reaching for some kitchen paper to wipe the coffee I'd spilled, 'that's the trouble. That's the difference between you and me. I can't forgive. Can't forget. I'm paranoid now, and I can't help feeling it'll happen again. And be more serious next time. And that I'll be left with four children under twelve because I took my eye off the ball and was never there for my husband. Never having my nails done, or getting trim at the gym, or having my hair cut at Michaeljohn.'

'Oh, you mean like the rest of us stay-at-home mothers,' I said acidly.

'No, I didn't mean that either.' She swept a hand over her perfect chignon. 'It's just . . . well, I do wonder whether it was my fault. Michael and that girl. Because I take on too much, work so hard to be the best investment banker and don't notice everything coming apart at the seams.'

'You're just tired,' I said firmly, lifting Henry out of his chair and setting him down. 'You've got too much on your plate.' I wiped Henry's mouth with the bottom of his T-shirt and saw Clare blanch.

'Yes, well, you didn't come to my door at this hour in the morning to hear about my marital disharmony. What gives? More doctors-in-love-true-romances? Tell me again about how he lit candles in the bathroom, the lovely, lovely man, and tell him Michael's only ever lit a candle in a power cut. Go on, make me drool.'

'No,' I said, 'not candles, but . . . oh, Clare, I'm so thrilled.' I couldn't suppress a beam. 'You know his aunt, the one who brought him up?'

'Gertrude in Onslow Gardens? I've formed a mental picture of the woman, got her swathed in fur stoles with those yucky fox heads on the end with tiny veiled hats, but no, I've never met her. Why?'

'Well, she's got this fabulous house in Cornwall, near Rock. It's that one right on the coast, up an inlet, all sort of Frenchman's Creekish . . . near where Dad used to take us when we were little. Remember we used to take the boat past?'

Clare shook her head abstractedly, reaching for her briefcase. 'No.'

'Well, the thing is, it lies empty for most of the year, and David says he's pretty sure Gertrude'll let me take it for the summer!'

Clare looked up from stuffing documents into the briefcase. 'Near Rock? But that's brilliant. You know we'll be down again this year?'

'You will?' I blinked. 'Hang on, I thought you said you'd had it with Cornwall? Said if you saw another sandcastle you'd detonate it.'

'Did I?' She looked vague. 'Must have been premenstrual. Oh no, we're *definitely* going. We're taking that cottage again.'

'Are the Mitchells going with you again?' I asked innocently.

'You know damn well they're not,' she snapped. 'Serena Mitchell proved to be a complete pain last year. All that sucking up to me and doing all the shopping in Wadebridge while I sat on the beach, and: "Oh, I in*sist* on cooking lobster for everyone tonight, Clare, *do* let me", all because she wanted Michael to give her wally husband a job. As soon as Schroders offered him something she dropped us like a cup of cold sick. We haven't heard from them since.'

'So who are you going with then?' I asked. 'You're surely not taking that house on your own, are you?'

'Oh, no, we're not going on our own. We've asked the Howards.'

'The Howards!' I stared at her incredulously. Two familiar spots of colour were rising in her cheeks. Rosie Howard was my best friend, and had been ever since our hips had welded together in the dormitory of St Mary's Convent, Dorset, at the age of twelve.

'Golly,' I said, stunned. 'What did they say?'

'They said they'd love to. They're not doing anything this summer. Said they hadn't got any plans.'

'Because they haven't got a bean,' I said shortly. 'Oh, yes,' I went on tartly, 'I'm sure they'd love to come and share some all-expenses-paid accommodation. When did you ask her?' And why on earth hadn't I heard, I wondered?

'Only yesterday,' she said hurriedly. 'So she probably hasn't got round to ringing you yet.'

Suddenly my anger dissipated. I felt embarrassed for Clare. God, it couldn't have been easy to go through her address book and end up asking my best mate. And why should I be annoyed with Rosie? With an unemployed husband and no prospect of a holiday this year, who on earth wouldn't leap at the chance of giving their kids a run on the beach at my sister's seaside house?

'Great.' I smiled, nodding. 'That's brilliant.'

'Oh, Annie, I'm so pleased.' She looked hugely relieved. 'I was a bit worried you might think . . . you know. Muscling in and all that.'

'Not a bit of it. I'm delighted.'

'And we can all muck in,' she said eagerly. 'You know, meet on the beach every day, share picnics.'

'Yes, except this isn't a holiday for me, Clare. David and I are having our break later on, in Mauritius. This is for me to work, remember?'

'Oh, yes, I know. But not every day, surely?'

'Well, we'll see.'

'The Todds are going too, you know.'

'Doesn't surprise me,' I said grimly. 'That man thinks he owns the place. He walks into Rick Stein's and pauses at the door as if everyone should drop to their knees and genuflect.'

'Well, he's very successful. And very attractive too, I think.'

'If you like the over-fifties in tight jeans and pink shirts with a paunch and arrogance to match. No, thanks.'

'He kissed me last year, you know. After the Elliotts' drinks party.'

'No! What—a snog?'

'Not a snog exactly, but when he said goodbye he deliberately planted one full on the mouth. Wiggled his tongue a bit.'

'Oh, yuck!'

'Oh, no, quite nice actually. I'm definitely on for more this year.'

'Clare!' I was genuinely shocked.

'And maybe I'll let Michael find out, too.'

'Ah, right. So that's what this is all about.'

'I can't help it, Annie, but I can't find it within me to forgive him. Thought this might help.'

I gave a wry smile. 'I doubt it. But I don't suppose you'll take any notice of me.'

'Doubt it,' she said cheerfully. 'Never have before, have I?' She snatched up some earrings from an ashtray and popped them in, then turned back to me, frowning. 'Anyway, I thought you'd done most of your book. Didn't you say you'd finished it?'

'No!' I flushed, alarmed. 'God, did I tell you that?'

'Yes, you said someone had rung from the publishers and you'd said—'

'Oh, yes, I *said* I'd finished, but I've only actually done three chapters!'

'So why did you tell them you'd finished?'

'Because when this chap Sebastian rang,' I blustered, 'and said he liked the first bit and could he see the rest, I couldn't exactly say I hadn't written it, could I? So I said it needed a bit of polishing. But the thing is, I've got to write the whole bloody thing! So all I'm saying is I need a bit of space to do some work!'

'Right.' She looked really miffed. 'We'll keep ourselves to ourselves, then. Keep *right* out of your hair.'

'Oh, no, I didn't mean that either,' I groaned. 'It's just . . .' I hesitated. 'I can't do open house. I have to get my head down, because . . . well, this is my big chance, Clare! It's my dream to be published one day, and this is the first time I've ever offered up a manuscript which anyone's ever been remotely interested in. And you know how many times I've tried.'

She nodded. 'I know.' She was silent for a moment, then she sighed. 'OK, so what about Flora? Is she to keep out of your way, too?'

I hesitated. 'I thought I might get a nanny for Flora.'

'Oh, don't be ridiculous. She's twelve! We'll have her.'

'Oh, no, I couldn't, Clare,' I said, horrified. 'This is your only break of the year. No, no, I'll sort something out.'

'Don't be silly,' she said staunchly. 'One more doesn't make any differ-ence. I'll cope. And we're very open house,' she added piously, posi-tively reeking of burning martyr now. 'Very easy-going.'

'Well.' I bit my thumbnail nervously. 'We'll see.'

'And what about David?'

'He'll be down at weekends, if he can get away. But it's a hectic time of year for him.'

'Of course it is. And you've got the wedding to organise too, you know,' she warned, busily buttoning up her jacket. 'You can't just leave it all to David, he's a busy man. And it takes longer than you think, there's masses to do. I don't think you've even considered flowers and headdresses yet, have you?'

'No. No, I'll get on to it,' I agreed, biting my nail practically down to the quick. She always made me feel about the same age as Flora.

'And don't forget Mum wants a church.'

'I haven't forgotten,' I snapped.

My phone rang in my jacket pocket and I answered. It was David.

'I've just rung Gertrude, Annie, and she said she'd be thrilled.'

'Oh!' I perked up a bit. 'She doesn't mind?'

'Not in the slightest. I told you, she's delighted to have it occupied, but I said you might pop round and see her this morning, if that's all right. Is that OK? You know, to chat it through?'

'Of course,' I beamed. 'What time?'

'About ten, I said. Any good?'

I glanced at my watch. 'Perfect.'

I rang off and turned round to Clare, who'd disappeared down the hall with Henry.

'Donna!' she yelled up the stairs. 'I'm away!'

'Coming!' came back the cry and, sure enough, moments later, a pair of wide denim flares tripped lightly down the stairs, followed by a pretty freckled face and long blonde hair. Henry's face lit up as he toddled away from Clare to meet her.

331

'Do-nnaa!'

'Hey, my prince!' She scooped him up in her long brown arms and kissed his nose. Henry chortled, and Clare had the grace to smile.

'At least he likes her,' I said quietly in the garden after the door had shut behind us.

She looked at me, surprised. 'Oh, he loves her. And actually I'm not jealous at all. I love my kids too much to be small-minded about that. No, no, I'm delighted.'

'And you don't ever think . . . I'd rather be her? When you leave him?' I asked tentatively as I followed her down the path.

'Oh, sure I do, of course. Every morning.' She swung round incredulously. 'God, Annie, I wouldn't be human if I didn't think that! But it's not that simple, is it?'

I couldn't help smiling as Clare stalked off down the steps to the District Line, her back ramrod straight in her nipped-in grey jacket, handbag swinging jauntily. I watched her go; so outwardly prickly, so defiant sometimes, yet inside, so desperately wanting to be loved.

And Dad had been hard on her, I thought, as I turned to cross the road to the bus stop. Dad had expected so much from the girl who should have been a boy. She'd been pushed and chivvied out of that farmhouse whether she'd liked it or not. All to live up to his expectations and not be a farmer's wife like Mum and his mother before her.

Yet I, four years behind, had been allowed to wallow in the slipstream; be Mummy's concern, not Daddy's. I'd led a happy, charmed childhood, while Clare, growing up in the same house, hadn't.

I'd read voraciously, helping myself to what I felt like in the local library—romantic novels, sagas, not the classics Clare was force-fed—and then later, as a teenager, I developed a passion for the poetry of Emily Dickinson. I'd sit for hours and read it on the back step. No one took much notice though. Expectations were lower, you see.

So had Dad enhanced Clare's life? I wondered now as I stepped on to the bus. Would he be proud of her? Or, with the hindsight I was sure heaven afforded, would he be looking down and wondering if he hadn't 'bin a bit hard on the lass'? Wished she were at home now, with Henry, cuddling him on her lap as they watched *Teletubbies* together, or would he still be up there thinking: That's my girl. Off to show those boys a thing or two in the money markets. Off to kick some ass.

I sighed as I got off the bus at my stop and walked along the high street. Who knows. Certainly Mum had quietly questioned Clare's life since Dad had gone, wondered if she wasn't pushing herself and her family too hard, but everything Mum suggested was hesitant. Timid.

Clare, like her late husband, knew best. On the other hand, Dad's death had made Mum dare to champion me.

It was she who urged me to write a novel. I didn't tell her that what I really wanted to do was write a biography about a certain poet I admired, although, to be fair, had she known, I'm sure she would have encouraged me.

I turned the corner into Gertrude's road. Tall, elegant cream houses reared up at me out of a sailor-blue sky. Yes, encouragement, I mused. That's what I could have done with when Dad was alive. Yet maybe he'd known I couldn't cut the mustard. After all, three attempts later and I still wasn't published, even though this time, amazingly, a publishing house had responded, not with the usual polite rejection slip, but with a personal letter from a senior editor. I knew it by heart.

Dear Mrs O'Harran,

Thank you for sending me the first three chapters of your manuscript. I think you show great promise and have considerable talent. I do hope the novel continues in the same vein. I have to tell you, however, that the reading public nowadays demands a great deal more sexual explicitness from romantic fiction. So far, your characters seem reluctant to move in this direction. Perhaps Lucinda could get her kit off in chapter four?

Yours sincerely,

Sebastian Cooper (senior editor)

Now, admittedly that last line had startled me. Shocked me, in fact. But then again, I reasoned, I wasn't used to the lingo of trendy publishing houses. I was merely a housewife from Fulham penning my love stories and, actually, straightforward advice was just what I needed right now. And if sex sold, then surely I could steel myself to write it?

I raised my chin defiantly and mounted the steps to Gertrude's gleaming black front door, remembering how awestruck I'd been by these exclusive South Kensington surroundings a year or so ago. David had brought me to meet his only living relative, with the vague proviso that she was a bit dippy and rather bohemian. Expecting a sweet old thing in a chaotic flat full of cats, I'd bounced up these same steps to find a very grand old lady in grey flannel trousers and a Katharine Hepburn black polo neck, opening the door to the largest London house I'd ever seen. Despite a rapidly fading memory, she still, at eighty-odd, had the power to scare the pants off anyone and I had to keep telling myself that she must be kind at heart to have taken on her eight-year-old nephew when her sister and husband had been tragically killed in a boating accident.

I smiled as the door opened and Gertrude peered down at me: tall and commanding in an ankle-length purple waistcoat, corduroy trousers and ropes of beads round her neck. Her steel-grey hair was cut in a sharp, uncompromising bob. Her pale blue eyes were cloudy though, over her hawklike nose.

'Annabel! My dear, how delightfully unexpected.' She presented me with her floury cheek, indicating it should be kissed.

'Unexpected, Gertrude? Didn't David say I was coming?'

She stared down at me. 'D'you know, you're quite right. I believe he did. Rang not half an hour ago.' She clapped a hand to her forehead. 'Stupid of me! Come in, come in!'

Her voice echoed flutily down the hall as she strode off into the depths of the house, then paused at the entrance to the lofty drawing room, bowing her head low to indicate I should shuffle through first.

The room was high, with an elaborately moulded ceiling, and painted a delicate shade of duck-egg blue. At the tall sash windows, drapes of deep plum damask hung in heavy folds, and all round the room were dotted Gertrude's potted palms and elegant but delicate antiques.

'Coffee?' She gave a dangerous twinkle. 'Good and strong and black?'

It was a private joke between us, except the joke was firmly on me. The only way I can take my coffee is white and very milky, but on that first disastrous visit, I'd been offered it good-and-strong-and-black. Desperate to ingratiate myself, I'd accepted with alacrity.

I remember sitting there, watching as she poured the filthy treacle from a percolator. I'd stared at it for twenty minutes, raising it to my lips occasionally but unable to get a drop down. Later, when she and David briefly left the room to attend to a broken window lock in the kitchen, I threw it, in desperation, into the nearest pot plant. Latterly, of course, I'd come clean and she'd deigned to add a drop of milk, but it was still very strong and quite filthy, and I was still too timid to refuse.

'I'd love one, Gertrude,' I said, cranking up a vivacious smile. 'Although'—I licked my lips bravely—'I've been reading more and more about how bad coffee is for you. I'm thinking of switching to tea.'

'Stuff and nonsense.' She glared, fumbling with cups and saucers on a tray. 'I've been drinking five cups a day for the last sixty years and I've never felt fitter.'

Could account for the violent hand tremor though, I thought as the cup and saucer rattled its way precariously towards me.

'Absolutely,' I agreed. 'They'll print anything in the papers these days.'

Gertrude sat down opposite me and fixed me with a stare of stern disapproval. 'Now. I gather you're after the house.'

I flushed. Oh God, that sounded awful! Like some terrible, grasping arriviste, intent on my future husband's chattels.

'Well, n-no,' I flustered. 'It's just that David said it was empty and . . . But if it's not convenient . . .'

'It's more than convenient, my dear, I'm delighted to have it used. You've seen it, I take it?'

'Er, I know where it is, vaguely, but—'

'But I've shown you the painting in the dining room?' she persisted.

'No, never.'

'Didn't I show you last week? Showed someone.' She pursed her lips and narrowed her eyes accusingly.

'No, Gertrude,' I said firmly. 'Not me. Must have been someone else. Cecily, perhaps?'

Cecily was a niece on Hugh's side who popped in occasionally to visit and quake, like me. We swapped horror stories.

She kept her eyes trained suspiciously on me for a few long moments, convinced that I was trying to trick her. I tried not to flinch. Abruptly her face cleared. 'You're quite right,' she said quietly. 'It was Cecily. Came in to fill in some forms for me. I remember now. We did it in the dining room, that was it. So.' She put aside her cup and rose to her feet. 'Come.'

Hurriedly I put down my cup and followed as she strode towards the double doors that connected the two rooms. She opened them with a flourish and swept through into the dining room. Her waistcoat fanned out behind her like a cloak as she skirted the vast Regency table and came to a halt by the Adam fireplace. She gazed up at a picture above it.

'There.' She raised her chin imperiously. 'What do you think?'

I followed her eyes. 'Oh,' I breathed. 'It's gorgeous!'

I'd only been in this room once before, and never noticed the painting. It was a large watercolour of a low, long, Elizabethan house, timbered and covered in wisteria, and with a sweeping lawn in front. Flanked by rhododendron bushes, it stood proudly on a cliff top overlooking the sea.

'Will it suit?' she demanded sharply.

'Suit? Golly, Gertrude, it's fantastic. I mean—to be literally right on the sea like that . . .'

'Yes,' she agreed, head on one side, considering it. 'It is a lovely spot. Just at the end of the creek. And the beach is pretty much private. We own the land at the top. So Joe Public can only get to it by boat, or else scramble across the rocks and get marooned. Silly asses. We've had the odd drowning incident, you know. Always a bit tricky.'

For whom, I wondered nervously. Her, or Joe Public?

'And we had a whale of a time there as children, of course,' she mused. 'Pammy and I. Picnics and bathing and whatnot. Such larks.'

Her blue eyes clouded for a moment and I thought how awful it must have been to lose her sister like that, suddenly, at only thirty-two.

'Anyway.' She came to. 'Take it, my dear. I couldn't be more pleased. Have it with pleasure. Here, I'll give you a key.'

She crossed to a writing table in the corner and pulled out a drawer.

'Somewhere . . . in here . . . ah.' She took out a ring with half a dozen identical keys on it. 'Always keep a few because I lose them. Hopeless . . . here, my dear.' She pulled one off finally and handed it to me. 'Now. David can tell you how to get there—'

'Actually,' I broke in eagerly. 'I know the spot quite well. I grew up in Devon, and Rock's only an hour or so away—'

'Of course, you're a West Country girl. Well, then, you'll be quite au fait with the beating of the waves and the seagulls screeching endlessly overhead. And you never know, you might get some inspiration for that book of yours. Might do some writing?'

'Well, that is rather the idea,' I said, confused. 'Didn't David say?' I added anxiously. 'That's the whole point. I wanted somewhere quiet to, you know, write in peace.'

She frowned down at me. Blinked. 'D'you know,' she said slowly, 'I believe he did mention that. Tell me.' She seized my arm urgently and brought her face down to mine. 'Is it saucy?'

'Heavens no!' I said, terrified.

'Oh.' She looked disappointed.

'B-but I haven't written it all yet. Gertrude,' I said. 'And I *have* been asked to spice it up a bit—'

'Oh, I should!' she urged.

'Yes,' I gulped. 'Um, are you sure I can't give you any rent for the house?'

'Heavens no, I wouldn't hear of it,' she said firmly, taking my arm and propelling me back through the drawing room and down the hall to the front door. 'You're family now, Annabel. No, no, just go and enjoy, and send me a PC letting me know all is well.' She stopped suddenly in the passage, short of the door. 'Oh Lord. I am a poor hostess, I haven't offered you a thing! Won't you have a coffee with me before you go?'

'You've . . . just given me one, Gertrude.'

She frowned, and I knew she thought I was tricking her again. I made a helpless gesture to the drawing room. She popped her head suspiciously round the door and spied the tray.

'Good heavens, so I did!' She clapped her hand to her head. 'I am an absent-minded old ninny.' She opened the door with a flourish. 'Send my love to David, and Flora too.'

'I will,' I promised. Dear old thing. She really was losing it a bit. I made a mental note to tell David. 'And thanks so much for the house.'

THE WEDDING DAY

When I got back home I found Rosie on my doorstep. Her short red hair looked wild and mussed as if she'd forgotten to brush it. She had Phoebe, her four-year-old, on her hip and looked about to leave when she saw me come round the corner.

'Oh! I was about to go!' she yelled.

'Sorry, I was round at Gertrude's. Did you say you were coming?'

'No, just popped in on the off-chance. Have you spoken to Clare?' She looked anxious as I walked up the path towards her.

I smiled as I rooted in my pocket for my key. 'I have.'

'Oh, Annie, I'm sorry. I meant to ring you last night and tell you. D'you mind?'

'What, that you're going on holiday with my sister? Of course not.' I let her in.

'You're just saying that,' she said nervously as she hastened after me down the long passage to the kitchen. 'I can tell by your tone you're not amused, but when she rang . . . God, I was at such a low ebb, Annie and I thought: Bugger it. A couple of weeks by the sea is just what we need right now, Dan and I, but more particularly the kids. I mean, we haven't had a holiday for nearly two years now and . . . Oh, I know she's your sister and not really my friend . . .' She tailed off miserably and sank down in a heap at my chaotic kitchen table with Phoebe on her lap.

'Listen, Clare's under no illusions,' I said as I whisked round behind her clearing the table, slinging cereal packets in cupboards. 'She knows you're my friend, but she likes you and desperately wants . . . well, sounds sad, but more mates. Particularly to go on holiday with.'

'And I like her too,' Rosie said quickly. 'And would like to spend more time with her, get to know her better. It's just she can be a bit . . .'

'Scratchy? High-handed? Bossy?' I squirted some Fairy Liquid in the sink and turned the taps on hard. 'God, you don't have to tell me, Rosie, I grew up with her. But don't worry, my friend, you won't be alone. I'll be there for you. Round the corner, up the creek, as it were.'

'What creek?'

I plunged my hands into the soap suds and gazed dreamily out of the window. 'The one that snakes sleepily off the estuary under an umbrella of leaves into a thicket of green, far, far from the madding crowd.' I smiled as I took a gleaming plate out of the water. 'Gertrude's lent me her house,' I informed her. 'The one I told you about.'

'Annie, that's fantastic! So you'll be down there too. Brilliant. I'm so relieved.' She put her hand into her old suede bag to pull out a tin of Old Virginia and a packet of Rizlas—her latest economy drive.

'But golly,' she murmured, 'if *you're* there it'll make all the difference. No, Phoebe, please let Mummy do it.' She retrieved a paper from her daughter's hand, which Phoebe surrendered with unusual complicity.

'Why didn't you leave her with Dan?'

She shifted Phoebe on her lap. 'Dan's got an interview.'

'Oh?' I turned from the sink.

'Don't get excited. He's had interviews before.'

'Yes, but you never know.'

'How true. You never know. This could be the one to raise us from the depths of despair and take us sailing into the ranks of the gainfully employed. To take us back into mainstream society, with our bank balance flashing miraculously from red to black. I could even tell our vulturine estate agent to piss off.'

I turned to look at her from the sink. She was lighting an appalling rolled cigarette that drooped down at one end. It was shaking a bit.

'You're selling?'

'We're having it valued,' she muttered. 'That's all. But with a view to selling, yes, and maybe renting and then buying again when the market finally crashes. Dan says it makes sense.'

'Of course,' I said quietly.

Rosie had the prettiest pink Fulham house which they'd bought for a song in the days when one could. Painstakingly, over the years, she and Dan, without builders, had laid a reclaimed slate floor in the kitchen, punched out a bay window in the sitting room, opened up every fireplace, quarry-tiled the bathrooms, and agonised in salvage yards over Victorian light-switches and doorknobs. It had been a labour of love.

I turned back to avoid her eye and rinsed a cup under the tap. 'Well, you never know. He might get the job this morning.'

'He might. And then we could relocate to Birmingham. Super.'

'Birmingham!'

'Oh, don't worry, he won't get it,' she said drily. 'He's too old. Anyway, I've told him if he does get it he'll have to weekly commute. Either that or I'll divorce him. He's quite keen on option two, actually.' She grinned and looked around for an ashtray. Not finding one, she flicked her ash into a pot of half-dead azaleas.

'Thanks.' I shoved a saucer under her nose.

'Makes great compost,' she advised. 'No, what we were actually thinking was that maybe Michael could give Dan a job at Schroders?'

The telephone rang.

'Oh!' I whipped round in horror. 'God, that's what the Mitchells did last year and Clare twigged and went totally insane! Please tell me you won't do that,' I implored her, one hand hovering on the receiver.

'All right, all right, keep your wig on,' she muttered as I lifted the phone. I was still gazing anxiously at her as I said hello.

'Ah. Bad moment?' It was David.

'Um, no, not at all. Just got Rosie here.'

'Oh, right. So if I were to pop back for lunch and a bit of Midweek Sports Special, would that be inconvenient?'

I giggled. 'Not at all, I'll get rid of her. She's only popped round to apologise for using my sister. I'll see you later.' I put the phone down.

Rosie eyed me suspiciously. 'Who was that? You've gone all pink.'

'David. He's coming back for lunch, and then we're going to make babies, so you'll have to shift your ass.'

She boggled. 'He comes home for lunchtime sex?'

'Only because it's that time of the month, and David being David knows precisely where I am in my menstrual cycle, which is more than I do, I might add. He took my temperature this morning and decided I'd be peaking at precisely twelve thirty-two.'

'Blimey, he is keen,' she said, hastily gathering up her Rizlas and stuffing them in her bag. She stood up and hoisted her daughter on to her hip. 'Right, come on, young Phoebe, you're too young to witness Dr Finlay bursting through that door, tongue hanging out, hips thrusting, ready to start his dynasty. It's back to the cat food for us.'

At that moment the milk bottles rattled on the step outside and a key went in the door. Rosie and I stared at one another, astonished.

'Bloody hell, that was quick!' Rosie boggled. She laid a hand on my arm. 'No, don't tell me,' she whispered. 'He was in a phone box, he twirled round a few times, and now he's standing outside with his pants over his tights. I always thought he looked like Clark Kent.'

'Either that or he was en route with his mobile when— Oh!'

The door opened and we both turned to see that it wasn't David at all. Sauntering into my house was my ex-husband, Adam.

Whistling, he came towards us. Tall, dark and disreputably handsome, he was wearing a grey T-shirt, cargo pants and trainers. On his head, in the manner of a gauche fourteen-year-old, a baseball cap was turned back to front. Adam is nearly thirty-eight.

When he saw us, he looked surprised. 'Shit. Didn't see you in here.'

'Adam.' I leaned back against the sink and gripped the rim hard.

'Hi, sweetie.' He planted a kiss on my cheek, then cast a nod in Rosie's general direction. 'Rosie.'

Rosie couldn't speak.

'Sorry to bust in but I had a break in rehearsals and I wanted to check the diary.' He sauntered round the room and stopped at the cork notice board. 'Thought you'd be out shopping actually, but still chained to the sink, I see?' He grinned and I loosened my grip on it. 'That's what I like about you, Annie, it's either the kitchen or the bedroom and you know what to do in both. Know the quickest way to a man's heart, as Jerry Hall once famously said.'

'Although, as Ruby Wax once famously said, the quickest way to a man's heart is actually through his chest,' I quipped back.

He gave a bark of laughter. 'That's what I like to see, still coming out fighting. What's this then?' He moved across to the stove and peered in the pan. 'Enough for three?'

'Rosie's not staying,' I said quickly. 'It's just—for me. And David.'

'David's popping home for lunch?' His eyes widened. 'Really. And then, no doubt, availing himself of your other area of expertise in the bedroom? Oops, spot on,' he muttered as, maddeningly, I flushed. 'Well, I'd better make myself scarce in that case, once I've checked a few dates with you. All right if I help myself to one of lover boy's Stellas?'

'Help yourself,' I muttered, as he did just that.

Rosie finally found her tongue. 'He just walks in here,' she exploded, her face pink with outrage, 'without a by your leave, *with* a key, helps himself to your fridge—why the hell don't you change the locks, Annie!'

'Ah, but that wouldn't be fair,' said Adam. He crossed to the larder door where my calendar hung and began coolly to flick through it. 'Annie gave me this here key back in the days when I visited regular, like. Every day, to be precise, and nights too sometimes, eh, Annie?' He grinned over his shoulder at me. I flushed and stared at my feet.

'Oh, yes, up until a year or so ago I still had a foot firmly in this door, and a place in her heart, too. Until the flying doctor came winging by and usurped me. Bastard.' He grinned. 'And anyway, apart from anything else, my child lives here,' he reminded her, letting the pages of the calendar fall back. 'So it wouldn't be entirely friendly to lock me out, would it?' He glanced back at the calendar. 'This when her school holidays start then, Annie?' He prodded a date I'd circled in red.

'Yes. That's it,' I muttered.

'Great. I'll have her that weekend then, shall I? That's what I came to say, that I may need to juggle my dates a bit.' He pulled a diary from his pocket. 'I think I've got her every other weekend till then, but we're going to Cornwall soon so I need to change all that.'

'Cornwall?' My heart stopped. 'Whereabouts?'

'Oh, usual place,' he said airily. 'Near Polzeath. Where we went last year, remember? Cozzy's parents have a bungalow down there.'

So Cozzy had lasted a year. Unlike Francine. And I did remember him motoring off from this very house after an illicit night with me, in the days when, to my shame, I still let him into my bed, even though he didn't live here. Yes, off he'd gone to frolic in the surf with Cozzy. 'Right.' I swallowed. 'It's just that we're going to Cornwall too. For six weeks.'

His beer froze at his lips. 'Six *weeks*? Without consulting me? A whole summer, without me seeing my daughter?'

'Well, I would have consulted you, naturally, Adam,' I said hastily. 'But it's only just been decided. And since you're going to be down there too, it's actually quite convenient. I could drive her over to you.'

'Yeah,' he agreed as he weighed it up, considering. 'Or I could come and get her. Where are you staying?'

'David's aunt's got a place on the Camel estuary.'

'Cool. Big pad?' Adam thought it took years off him to talk like a hippie.

'Um, I'm . . . not sure.'

'Oh, huge,' said Rosie, reading his mind. 'With a pool, and a billiard table, and a tennis court. You'll have to come over, Adam, use the facilities. Raid the fridge.'

'Might take you up on that.' He winked at her, unruffled. 'Unless you're there already, Rosie, which I have a shrewd suspicion you might be, in which case there may be a conflict of interest. Dan and I could hang out quite happily together by the pool but I suspect you'd get on my tits after a while. How is dear old Redundant Man, anyway?'

'He flourishes, thank you, Adam,' she snapped. 'At least he actually tries to get work and doesn't just pose about in back-to-front baseball caps pretending he's a teenager.'

'All right, you two,' I said wearily. 'Can we get back to why you're here, Adam? Obviously you want to see Flora over the summer and since we're both in Cornwall it makes things logistically easier, if not . . .'

'Emotionally easier?' he pounced, delighted. 'Surely you weren't thinking what a blessed relief it would have been *not* to see Adam for six weeks? To get out of the mind-set of lusting after a wayward, impoverished actor and into the mind-set of marrying handsome, successful, *sensible* Dr Kildare? Surely you weren't thinking *that*, Annie?'

'Get out, Adam,' Rosie seethed. 'If she won't tell you, I will. You're half the man David is and you know it. You're just scared witless she's going to end up with someone loyal and honest and devoted.'

'All of which are excellent canine attributes, I grant you, but are they entirely the spice of life? Does loyalty make the party go with a zing, say, or does—Ah! The man himself. Or hound dog, should I say. Let him speak for himself. David, welcome!'

David appeared in a shaft of light down the hall as the front door opened. He closed it behind him and advanced warily down the passageway in his pinstripe suit, carrying his briefcase.

'Welcome to this small kitchen party,' went on Adam, spreading his arms wide. 'Rosemary I believe you know, and of course my ex-wife, Annabel, and I am merely a wallflower. How cosy is that. Stella?'

'No, thanks, Adam, and while I don't begrudge you a beer, I'll thank you not to help yourself to another, because on the one hand I've got things to do here and on the other, there's a disgruntled-looking blonde outside in an ancient MG that I seem to recall belongs to you.'

'Shit! Cozzy!' Adam clapped a hand to his forehead. 'Forgot she was out there. I was going to tip her the wink at some point and bring her in and introduce her to you, Annie, but I suspect now is not the moment?' He took in my flushed face and the two icy ones flanking me. 'Ah. No. Thought not. Oh, well, at some stage it might be a good idea to get to know each other. Flora thinks she's terrific, and now you've got yourself a man, there'll be less angst all round, eh? Less hell hath no fury. Yes. Well.' Even Adam seemed to sense the atmosphere was against him. 'I'll be on my way. Rosie, David.' He nodded at them. 'Thanks for the beer, mate, and, Annie, we'll swap holiday addresses and phone numbers soon, eh? Might even all get together for a barbie on the beach!'

Grinning at David's horrified face, he slid out of the kitchen and slunk down to the front door, whistling merrily again.

Rosie, gathering up her by now sleeping child, and her old suede bag was, after a swift goodbye, gone pretty much in his wake.

When the door had shut behind them, David turned to me, appalled. 'He's coming to Cornwall?'

'Er, yes.' I bit my lip. 'Always does, I'm afraid. Well, since last year. Cozzy's got a place down there, you see.' I avoided his eye.

'I didn't know that,' he said despairingly, scratching his head. 'You didn't mention it, Annie.'

'I forgot,' I said simply. 'And anyway'—I went across and put my arms round him. 'He won't spoil our fun.' I kissed him softly on the mouth.

Chapter Two

'COME ON, FLORA!'

I crammed the suitcase into the boot and slammed it shut, glancing back through the open front door to where she stood in the hall talking to David, his fair head bent over her dark one. I paused for a moment, watching, as David got some batteries from his briefcase and gave them to her. Fumbling a bit, she slotted them into her personal stereo.

I smiled. It was typical of the man that he should check her batteries before a long journey, but then get her to fit the new ones herself. He was supportive, but not too over the top. He was alive to the delicacy of the situation, just as Flora was alive to it too, but in a different way.

A year ago, when Adam had first heard about David, he'd rung us, distraught. Flora had answered.

'It's Dad,' she whispered. 'He's heard you've met someone. He wants to come back. For good.'

My heart, and I know it shouldn't have, leaped. But her dark eyes had filled with tears. She shook her head. 'No, Mum,' she whispered.

I'd stared at her for a long moment. Then I swallowed hard and took the mouthpiece from her. 'Sorry, Adam, we don't want you back.'

And that was that. But the awful thing was, if it hadn't been for my eleven-year-old daughter I'm not sure I would have got off the roundabout. Not sure I wouldn't still be spinning round now, sharing a niche with his harem of women. But Flora, who loved her daddy more than anyone, knew better, knew that he wasn't good for me.

'Ready, love?' I walked up the path, smiling at them. At my two.

'Ready. But, David, *please* don't forget my fish. They hate slimy water and it only takes a second, I promise.'

'It takes precisely twelve minutes because I did it for you last weekend, and no, I won't forget them. Or your plants,' he added to me. 'Although someone should really tell your mother, Flora, that those spider things with trailing babies went out with hostess trolleys and Arctic Rolls. I've half a mind to replace them while you're away.'

'Don't you dare,' I warned. 'Now, Flora, map?'

'Got it.' She tapped her bag. 'Come on, Mum, let's go. Bye, David.' She reached up and gave him a kiss.

'Bye, hon. Take care and look after your mum.' He took me in his arms. 'I'll be down in a couple of weeks to check up on the pair of you.'

'A couple of weeks? Can't you come this weekend?'

'I'll do my best,' he said, walking us to the car, 'but I'm up to here with paperwork at the moment and it is a long way for the weekend.'

My heart lurched. 'I know, but you said you didn't mind.'

'I don't.' He opened the car door for me. 'Now, for God's sake drive carefully, and stop for lunch, and *don't* drive if you're tired.'

'I will,' I promised, glowing slightly under his protection. When had Adam ever exhorted me to drive carefully?

He waved us off and, as my ancient Fiat pulled out into the sunny Fulham street, I gave a hoot and a backward wave to him.

'Lovely man,' I said, admittedly a trifle smugly, as I eyed him in the rearview mirror. 'Can't quite believe he's marrying me.'

'Neither can anyone else,' murmured Flora.

'What d'you mean?' I said sharply. ' "Neither can anyone else"?'

'Only joking,' she grinned. 'No, I just meant he is quite cool. I mean, for us,' she added, generously offering herself into the equation. 'Let's face it, we are a bit scruffy, Mum.'

I negotiated the sunny streets out towards the A4 and regarded my daughter beside me in her cropped jeans, immaculate white T-shirt and freshly washed hair caught back in a ponytail. She looked, as ever, with her beautiful heart-shaped face, like a Ralph Lauren advert.

'Well, you're not,' I said shortly. 'So you must mean me.'

'Well, you must admit,' she said, regarding my filthy old espadrilles and faded man's shirt, which was hanging over the top of my trousers because the zip had gone at the side, 'you're not exactly Coco Chanel.'

'David doesn't mind about that,' I retorted.

'Just as well, with your wardrobe. But honestly, Mum, you might try. I saw your pants in the bathroom the other day, and they're outrageous. All that crumbling grey elastic. You should throw them away.'

'Right,' I said shortly. 'Anything else destined for the rubbish bin?'

'Well, those trousers you're wearing now, and those horrid stained espadrilles and your *dressing* gown, with that huge great coffee stain on the back that you wander around in from nine o'clock onwards every evening. Honestly, Mum, it puts men off.'

'Men? You mean David?'

'I don't know, do I? All I'm saying is . . . don't let yourself go.'

She stared out of the window fixedly, her face and neck pink. I got the impression she'd been meaning to tell me this for some time.

'So what else?' I insisted furiously.

'Oh, I don't know,' she muttered. And then rather bravely: 'Well, OK, the house. You never bother to tidy up, just wait for Yvonne to come in once a week, and all the washing up in the sink builds up—'

'But I do it, eventually. It does get done.'

'I know, but in between, it's such a mess. And David's so immaculate, and . . . well, I mean look around you. Look at this car, Mum.'

I looked. Sweet wrappers rolled luxuriantly on the floor; an empty McDonald's carton basked in the sunshine on the back seat; a shrivelled apple core festered on the dashboard. All my detritus. Nothing I could blame Flora for. Caught and shamed, I retorted angrily.

'Oh, don't be so prissy, Flora!' I roared. 'D'you want a gleaming four-wheel-drive that's never seen a spot of mud? Is that what you want?'

'No, but you deliberately go the other way,' she persisted.

'Right!' I said, fury mounting. 'Well, I'm so glad that you spoke up, darling.' I swung into a BP garage and joined the queue for petrol, fuming. 'Clearly I've got some thinking to do if I want to keep a man.'

'Mum . . .' she muttered miserably, picking at the seam of her jeans.

'Oh, no, I'm obviously totally out of touch with my feminine side. Instead of trying to write a novel in the attic, I should be languishing between designer sheets painting my nails! I should be wiggling my pert little backside as I vacuum the car with a Dustbuster! Well, let's start now, shall we?' Furiously, I leaned across her, grabbed a grotty plastic bag from the floor by her feet, and began madly stuffing it with rubbish.

'Mother, chill.'

'In fact, let's get this whole flaming shooting match sorted out now, shall we? Look, there's a car wash!'

I shunted triumphantly into reverse gear, lurched backwards, and then jerked to a halt in front of it.

'Mum, no.'

'No? *No?*' I turned to her with mock incredulity. 'Why not? Golly, perish the thought we should drive to Cornwall in a dirty car!'

I jumped out and dashed to the kiosk. Happily there was no queue so I quickly secured my ticket and raced back.

'Right, in it goes!' I panted, shoving the ticket in.

The little light on the control box flashed to green and I sped grimly up onto the ramp.

'You're supposed to put the aerial down,' muttered Flora. 'Most cars have a button to retract it, but since ours is practically prewar, it'll get snapped off.'

'So be it!' I barked. God, even my *car* was too old.

She shook her head in wonder, folding her arms. 'Right. Fine. Leave it. A five-hour drive to Cornwall with no radio. Perfect. I've got my CD player, of course, so I'm all right. Your lookout, Mum.'

I glanced at her. A triumphant little smile played on her lips. She knew she'd won. Well, bugger that. I jumped out of the car.

'It's too late, Mum, you've put the ticket in!'

Bugger that, too. Quickly I nipped round the bonnet, reached up and deftly pushed the aerial down. The concrete was wet and slippery under-foot though, and as I started back I lost my footing and fell to my knees with an agonising crack. A white light of pain shot through me and I swore furiously, just as jets of water shot at me from every direction in great horizontal sheets. While I shielded my face from the onslaught and tried to breathe, huge rolls of blue polyester fabric lunged towards me, fringed and whirring, knocking me flat to the ground. More and more water was fired at me as I clawed my way back onto the bonnet and clung there, spread-eagled like a sacrifice. I wondered if I was going to be killed. Was that possible? In a BP service station in West London?

As I struggled for air, the machinery miraculously halted for a moment. Gasping, I lurched upright, turned and staggered, arms outstretched blindly, towards the drier concrete of the forecourt. I made it by a whisker, just as the mechanical rolls whirred up again.

On the forecourt, all business had come to a standstill. On this swelteringly hot, busy day in West London, people stood transfixed as a woman, pouring with water, staggered out of the car wash. As I glanced back, I saw Flora shrinking down in her seat.

A young Indian attendant in a turban came running out of the kiosk. 'What happen!' he shouted. 'You no supposed to get out!'

'I thought I had time!' I gasped.

'Time? You have no time! Once you put ticket in, you had it! Bingo!'

'Clearly.'

I turned back to the car just in time to see it being deposited by the ramp, gleaming, onto the forecourt. I lurched towards it, swinging my wet legs wide like John Wayne, the water squelching out of my shoes. I went to the boot and opened it. Found my case. Flora shot out of the passenger seat and ran round to me.

'Are you all right?' she shrieked.

'I'm fine,' I muttered grimly.

She gaped at me, speechless, as I rooted for a towel and some dry clothes. Then, with my togs rolled up under my arm, I made sodden progress, with as much dignity as I could muster, towards the kiosk.

I cried aloud at my first view of Taplow House. Although to be fair, of course, it wasn't my first view. I'd spied it, as I'd told Gertrude, years ago, when I was about twelve, on a family holiday.

The first time was in a little boat that Dad had hired to take us up the estuary. As we floated past the mouth of the creek, I caught a glimpse of an old stone house covered in creeper, up a secret, green alley.

'Look!' I'd pointed.

'Mmm. Lovely spot,' Dad had murmured, his eyes gleaming with envy, hand on the tiller, puffing his pipe as he guided us past.

Later, I remembered my astonishment when David described the house his aunt owned.

'She *owns* it! The one up the little creek, the one all on its own—are you sure? Sure it's the same one?'

'Quite sure.'

'But, David, that was the house I dreamed about! As a child! I made up stories about it, fantasised about the family who owned it. I imagined all these brothers and sisters, you see, and a beautiful mother who was an artist's muse, and a domineering father who was terribly jealous of the French artist who painted his wife. And I made friends with one of the sisters—Tabitha, she was called—and there was this tall, frightfully attractive brother who wrote poetry and—'

I'd stopped at his astonished face. Yes. Steady on, Annie.

Now, though, as I got out to swing open the five-bar gate at the end of the drive, my heart was pounding just as fast as it had twenty years ago. We purred down the gravel drive, Flora and I, round a bend and, as the rhododendron bushes parted, it appeared out of a sweep of gravel. A long, low, stone house, its crumbling grey façade almost entirely covered by wisteria, its bay windows so low they almost touched the ground, while the upstairs windows, under deep eaves, glinted in the sun like sharp eyes under brows. I stopped the car and my eyes feasted. I gazed at the overgrown garden: a tangle of weeds that gave way to a lush lawn, almost field-like it was so strewn with daisies and buttercups and cowslips, which swooped down in turn to thick undergrowth and trees, and then gave a glimpse of the sea beyond.

'Pretty,' commented Flora, scratching her leg.

'Pretty!' I squealed, reaching for the door handle. 'Flora, it's heaven!'

'Bit neglected, though. That lawn could do with a mow.' She peered around. 'Did you know it was going to be like this?'

'I had an idea, but I was willing myself not to be disappointed. I'd only ever seen a glimpse.' I shielded my eyes with both hands against the sun, taking in the peeling green shutters at the windows. Greedily I drank in every detail.

'So how do we get to the sea?'

'Through those woods, I imagine.' I pointed. 'Come on, let's see.'

We walked quickly across the mossy gravel and the overgrown lawn, both tacitly agreeing to deal with the cases and interior later.

'Oh, I can see where, because look, there are steps!' She ran ahead of me, and I revelled in her excitement. On the cusp of her teens, but happily still such a child. Still longing to kick off her shoes and run down the steps, to show me first.

Sure enough, the thick undergrowth at the bottom of the garden yielded to granite steps, and then a track leading downwards, twisting and turning sharply through the woods. As I hurried to follow her, plunging into sudden shade, she cried out.

'Except it's not the sea, it's a river! Our own river, and a beach!'

I hastened to join her, loving the excitement in her voice. As I reached the shore, I caught my breath. It was indeed a very private little beach on a slip of a creek that snaked in from the main estuary.

I gripped Flora's shoulders from behind. 'Like it?'

'Totally love it,' she murmured back. Then: 'So quiet!'

'I know.'

'And so private.'

'Isn't it,' I agreed, glancing about. No one, literally no one in sight, not a house, not even a boat. 'This solitude is what I came for. I can see myself sitting on that rock with my notebook, sunhat on, words flowing copiously, inspired by the glorious seascape—oh, I can't wait.'

'While I, meanwhile?' She raised her eyebrows.

'You, meanwhile, will . . . skim stones, paddle, make castles—'

'Castles! I'm not six.'

'Well, I don't know . . .'

'Cycle round the lanes? Pop into Polzeath and hang out at the beach café like you and Clare used to?'

I hesitated. 'Flora, there were two of us, remember.'

'So?'

'And times were slightly different then. Safer.'

'Rubbish,' she scoffed. 'You told me you slipped away from Grandpa and had a whale of a time with local boys on the beach.'

'Well, we'll see,' I said curtly, wishing I hadn't been quite so sisterly with her in what had clearly been a rash, confidential moment. 'Come on, let's see the house.'

Linking her arm with mine, I walked her back up through the woods, crossed the garden and went round to the front door, ducking under the little wooden porch as I dug in my pocket for the key. It was stiff in the lock, and for an awful moment I thought it wasn't going to turn, but it did, and we went into the dark, flagged hall, gazing round, blinking in the gloom. If the interior was distinctly cool, it was, in a way, rather comforting after the intense glare of the sun and sea without. Dark beams loomed low over bulging, cream walls, and bits of ancient Persian carpet made a poor fist at covering the plain oak boards. In the sitting room there was a scuffed old leather sofa, two upholstered chairs with exploding arms, and an oak bookcase that ran the length of one side of the room, groaning with books. We wandered on.

The kitchen, with its chipped blue lino floor, yellow Formica work surfaces, glass cupboards on the walls and ancient Rayburn, was straight out of the 1950s. There was also, we discovered, a rather austere dining room and, off the hall, a small, surprisingly light study— which I made a mental note to make use of in bad weather—with a vast leather-topped desk and a captain's chair.

Upstairs, Flora had discovered three bedrooms and a bathroom on the first floor, and then right in the attic, where I followed her up to now, two tiny ones with faded rose wallpaper, and another bathroom.

'Perfect,' I said, throwing up the sash window in the larger of the two bedrooms and sticking my head out. I looked straight across the creek to the other side, where cows grazed in a patchwork of lush fields, and where, in splendid isolation, a little grey church nestled in the fold of a hill. I shut my eyes and breathed deeply.

'I'll be up here then,' said Flora decisively, flopping down on the bed behind me.

'And I'll be on the floor below,' I said, turning. 'In the main bedroom, overlooking the garden.'

She sat up quickly. 'Not the one right at the end of the corridor?'

'No,' I said patiently, 'just below you. Literally just down the stairs.'

'Oh. Good.'

I sensed the relief in her voice and tactfully avoided her eye. She wanted to appear independent, but still wanted me close by. She'd never quite grown out of that. I glanced at the eczema on her legs, which hopefully would abate in the sun. She saw me looking and scratched it.

'What?'

'Nothing. Come on, let's go downstairs.'

We spent the rest of the afternoon unpacking and making beds, and then I scrambled some eggs for supper. No garden furniture apparently, so we ate side by side on the warm stone steps that led down from the kitchen to the garden. As we sat, gazing into the last rays of the sun as the mayflies gathered, Flora scraped her plate thoughtfully.

'Anyway, the others will be down soon, so I can cycle round to see them, can't I?'

'You can,' I affirmed graciously. 'I don't mind that at all. Just no wandering about on your own.'

'And if I'm at Clare's, you'll have David. I mean, at the weekends.'

I smiled at her attempt to give me some space. 'I will, my darling.'

A silence ensued.

'Will you miss him?' she ventured, at length.

'During the week? Yes, I'm sure, but you know I'll be terribly busy.'

Privately I couldn't help thinking: Golly, what heaven. No man to cook for, no house to clean. We'd live outside mostly, I decided, and anyway, it was so dark inside no one would notice if I didn't dust. Didn't hoover. But then—suddenly I brought myself up sharp—that wasn't the attitude, was it? The new attitude . . . A plan was beginning to form.

'Flora,' I said eventually, 'would you mind very much if I nipped into Rock? Would you be all right here on your own?'

'What, now?'

'Yes, just for an hour or so. The shops will still be open. I thought I'd look around. Will you be OK?' I challenged her briefly with my eyes.

'Of course,' she said, rising to it. 'I'll raid the bookcase. I notice there's no telly, but there are masses of books. Why? What d'you need?'

'Oh, this and that.' I smiled and took the plates inside.

I left her humming to herself in the sunshine and nipped upstairs. Pulling open all the drawers I'd just filled, I threw the contents on to the bed. Ten minutes later I'd left the house, armed with a bulging black bin liner which I dumped in the dustbin. Hopping in the car and tooting cheerily to let her know I was away, I purred off down the long drive.

And an hour or so later, I was back. As I blew in with a gust of wind, the front door slammed shut behind me.

'Phew! Quite a storm brewing out there!'

Flora didn't look up. She was spread-eagled face down on the old leather sofa, her head firmly between the pages of *Jamaica Inn*.

I cleared my throat and struck a nonchalant pose. 'Whadya think?' I drawled. Still no response.

'Flora, what d'you think?' I resorted to finally, and slowly she turned. She gaped. Dropped her book.

'Pretty hot, huh?' I twirled.

'I'm not sure "hot" is the word. Preppy, or Sloaney perhaps but—God, you look like Clare. Clare on holiday!'

I beamed down at the navy-blue polo shirt tucked neatly into crisp cream trousers with a smart leather belt. Flexed the squeaky new deck shoes on my feet and swung my bulging carrier bags.

'I've got a whole wardrobe in here. Shirts, trousers, shorts, pleated skirts, all brand-new, and all my old summer clothes are in the bin.'

She blinked. 'All of them?'

'Pretty much. Except the underwear. Crew Clothing didn't quite run to that, but I'm sure somewhere in Wadebridge will oblige tomorrow.'

'Mum, could you untuck your shirt?' she said, circling me. 'And take your hair out of that band. You really do look like Clare like that.'

'Oh, well.' I shook my curly dark mane back over my shoulders. 'Might get it all cut off tomorrow.'

'No! Don't,' she said, alarmed. 'I mean . . . not until you see what David thinks. He may not like it. Any of it.'

'Nonsense, he'll love it. And anyway, it was your idea.'

'I know, it's just you don't look like you.'

'Of course it's me,' I scoffed, marching past her and heading for the stairs with my bags. 'The new improved, organised, dynamic me. We'll get the Hoover out tomorrow, Flora,' I warned as I bounced upstairs. 'Just because we're on holiday there's no reason to let standards drop.'

That night we fell gratefully into our soft, plumped-up little beds, tired after the long journey. The wind had whipped up into quite a storm, and the rain was beating a fast tattoo on the black windows. I lay there and listened for a while, loving that feeling of being snug within while it raged without.

Up above me I heard Flora get into bed, and then, predictably, get out again. I listened as she rearranged the curtain—there had to be a carrot shape of light at the top—turned round twice, touched the floor, muttered a Hail Mary; turned round again in the opposite direction, and then got back into bed. A little ritual, among others, that had to be performed every night of her life, or who knew what horrors would befall her or her loved ones.

Yes, I thought, turning on to my side, this was just what Flora needed: a break from the stresses and strains of London life. A break from keeping up, fitting in, getting on, being cool; a licence to be young and free, with world enough and time to enjoy it. In my mind's eye I had her rambling the cliffs, picking wild flowers, until my eyes closed and Morpheus led me tactfully away down the dark corridors of sleep.

It was some time later that I heard footsteps in the passage. I opened my eyes, unsure why I'd woken, and then . . . yes. There they were again. I turned my head and peered at the illuminated hands on my clock. Two thirty. Still the footsteps continued, getting closer now, coming towards my door. I sat up in bed, my heart hammering. Slowly, the door handle turned. I held my breath. The door opened and, in a long white nightdress, her eyes huge and staring, Flora wafted towards me, looking exactly like a ghost.

'Shit! Flora, you frightened the life out of me! What the hell are you doing creeping around like that?'

'There's someone downstairs!' she gasped.

'Oh, don't be ridiculous!' I spluttered, terror turning to anger.

'No, but, Mum, there's creaking and bumping and all sorts!'

'Well, of course there is! There's a ruddy storm raging outside and this house is three hundred years old. Go back to bed.'

'No, Mum, I can't,' she whimpered, climbing in. 'I'm too frightened up there. Can I sleep with you?'

'Oh, *Flora!*'

But it was a foregone conclusion and I knew it.

As ever, with Flora, I lurched between supreme patience and out-and-out frustration. I clamped an arm round her shoulders and glared at the ceiling. God, when would she grow out of this? She was nearly a teenager, for heaven's sake. She'd be dating boys soon; would they be in bed with me too? I sighed and turned over. And the worst thing was, I knew it was my fault. Mine and Adam's. Knew that she was fall-out: a timorous casualty of our terminal marriage.

'Sorry, Mummy,' she muttered.

'It's fine,' I muttered back. 'Not your fault.' I squeezed her shoulder tight. We were silent.

'There it goes again.'

'It's the wind, you wretched child.'

A pause.

'Well, what's that then?' She raised her head sharply from the pillow.

I have to say that, even to my cynical ears, it sounded very much like a chair scraping back from a table. I threw back the bedclothes. 'Right. Let's go down and see them, shall we?' I snapped on my bedside light but nothing happened. 'There's no power.'

'Why not?' Flora yelped.

'Clearly there's been a power cut, darling. These things happen in old houses in a storm. We're in the country now.'

'So how are we going to see?' she whimpered. 'How are we—'

'Come on, we'll manage.'

I got up, irritated beyond belief, and groped for the door.

It was pitch black in the passage outside. Together, we slithered along the landing wall towards the head of the stairs. Then with Flora behind me, gripping onto my T-shirt with both hands, we shuffled, like a pantomime horse, across the landing towards the banisters.

I grasped them firmly. 'Got them.'

With Flora still clinging to me, I groped my way down slowly, slowly, step by step. All the curtains were closed in the hall and, apart from a chink of light coming through a leaded pane in the front door, all was blackness. I kept my eyes firmly on that chink.

'See, Flora?' I said in a loud voice as we reached the bottom step. 'There's no one here. No one at all. Come out, come out, whoever you are!' I sang jovially, as I'd done when she was small, rattling broom handles under her bed at imaginary monsters.

'And there's a torch in the car,' I went on as we shuffled as one towards the door. 'If I get that, at least you'll have a light in your room.'

'Your room,' she corrected.

'All right, my room, just for tonight.' I patted the door, searching for the doorknob. 'But, Flora, you really must get a grip, you can't keep creeping into my— *Aaaaaggh!*'

I let out a shriek of terror as a hand closed over mine on the doorknob.

'Not so fast,' breathed a man's voice in my left ear. 'Hold it right there.'

The scream I emitted was worthy of a B-movie actress in a Hammer House of Horror. I snatched my hand away and leaped backwards into Flora, who was also squealing like a banshee. In the dark, I could just make out a man's shape, with a huge hunched back, by the door. I shrieked again, backing furiously and pushing Flora back with me.

'Get out! Get out of my bloody house or I'll call the police!'

'Your bloody house?' drawled an American accent.

A yellow flame snapped up in the gloom. In the light of a Zippo lighter, I found myself looking into a pair of bright blue eyes in a brown, weathered face.

'Where the hell are the lights in this place? Don't they run to electricity in this part of the world?'

'There's been a power cut,' I breathed, trying not to scream again. 'Who the hell are you? What are you doing in my house?'

I was still scared, but not totally terrified. He didn't have the face of an axe murderer: more of a Red Indian actually, with those slanty cheekbones; and the hunch turned out to be a backpack.

'*Your* house again. Jesus. Well, what I'm trying to do is occupy the accommodation I took for my summer vacation. Listen, are you sure the lights have gone? Haven't you got any candles or anything?'

'There's some in the drawer,' said Flora. She fumbled over to the hall table. 'I saw them while I was looking for some matches.'

It occurred to me to wonder what she'd wanted matches for, but I had other things on my mind.

'How did you get in?' I demanded.

'With a key, of course. How did you?'

'With . . . a key,' I faltered, as Flora produced some candles.

I stood, bewildered and open-mouthed, as he expertly lit four or five, holding them in a bunch in his hand. He glanced about, then, seeing nowhere to put them, strode into the sitting room and set them carefully in line on the mantelpiece. I scuttled in after him.

'But where did you get the key?' I yelped.

'From Mrs Fetherston-Hall. She mailed it to me. Together with confirmation of the dates I booked, and handy hints on the location of the butcher, the baker, the candlestick maker and other local amenities. I'm sorry, ladies, but it seems to me you're in the wrong place. I took this house for a summer vacation and that's just what I intend to have. I've also just got off a flight from Boston and driven five hours down your so-called freeways, and what I didn't expect to find when I got here was two shrieking females in white winceyette playing Lady Macbeth in stereo. Now, before you shift your asses down to the nearest motel, perhaps you'd be good enough to show me where the fuse box is so I can get this place illuminated.'

'Ooh!' I bristled when I'd finally found my tongue. '*Mrs* Fetherston-Hall just happens to be my fiancé's aunt, and she has kindly lent me this house, not just for a vacation, but for the entire summer! Clearly there's been some mix-up with your dates, but I think you'll find that if there's anyone's "ass" that needs shifting, it's yours!'

He frowned. 'She's your aunt? Mrs Fetherston-Hall?'

'My fiancé's aunt,' I hissed.

'And you've paid good money?'

'Well, no,' I faltered. 'Obviously I haven't paid money—'

'Because I have to tell you'—he whipped a letter from a pocket and waved it rather rudely in my face—'that a financial transaction has taken place here. It's here in black and white. Clear and binding.' His blue eyes challenged mine.

I snatched the letter. I began to read it: 'Dear Mr Malone . . .' Then I glanced up warily. 'That's you? Mr Malone?'

'My passport is only moments away in the car, lady,' he said testily.

'My name is Mrs O'Harran,' I snapped back, wishing I had a dressing gown over this stupid short nightie. I tugged it down and read on.

Further to your letter of the 4th, I'm writing to confirm your stay in Taplow House. The key is enclosed. The place is a little hap-hazard, as you'll discover, but charming, and I think you'll enjoy it. I've enclosed a list of reliable local shops, and an inventory. If you have any problems, please don't hesitate to telephone.

Yours sincerely,

Gertrude Fetherston-Hall

'She's made a mistake,' I said defiantly. 'She's getting old and rather dod-dery, and clearly she forgot she'd promised the house to me. I'm sorry, but I think you'll find that when we iron this out in the morning and speak to Mrs Fetherston-Hall, you'll appreciate the situation. I'm sure she'll refund you in full, Mr Malone. Meanwhile, I suggest you drive back down the road and follow it into town. There's a very pleasant hotel called the Priory Bay on the corner. We'll speak again when I've contacted her tomorrow. Good morning.'

His blue eyes, in the candlelight, hardened.

'I'm not driving anywhere, Mrs O'Harridan, or whatever the hell your name is. I told you, I've just driven five goddamn hours from London. It's two-forty-five in the morning, for Chrissake. I'm staying right here, in this house, that my family and I rented for two weeks!'

'Don't be ridiculous,' I retorted, 'of course you can't stay! *We're* here, my daughter and I. This is *our* house. We've unpacked, made up beds—'

'Mum, we can't just turn him out in the middle of the night,' mut-tered Flora at my elbow. 'He's got a letter. From Gertrude. Something's obviously gone wrong.'

'Finally, the voice of reason,' he snapped. 'Something *has* gone wrong, very wrong, the bottom of which we will get to in the morning, be sure of that, Mrs O'Have-a-go. Meantime, since you ladies are presumably occupying the first-floor accommodation, I will unroll my sleeping-bag on this couch.' He unhooked a sleeping-bag from his backpack and threw it on the leather sofa. 'I haven't put my head down in thirty-six hours and I sure as hell could use some sleep.'

'But I can't have a perfect stranger down here while my twelve-year-old daughter sleeps upstairs!' I spluttered. 'You can't just—'

'Watch me.' He unbuckled his belt and dropped his trousers.

'Oh!' I yelped and hurriedly turned Flora round. She giggled and glanced back. He winked.

'Now. Bathroom?'

'*Mr Malone*,' I seethed, 'there is a downstairs lavatory that I suggest you use. I do not want you prowling upstairs while my daughter and I are asleep. Kindly do not take one step in the direction of my quarters.'

'Mrs O'Harrods,' he said, looking me up and down, 'I swear to God your quarters are the last thing on my mind.'

'Oh!' I clenched my fists impotently. Glared at him. He grinned back.

Seething, I snatched up a couple of candles, handed one to Flora and pushed her ahead of me, towards the hall and up the stairs. 'Go on, Flora,' I hissed. 'Up, up!'

God, the *nerve* of the man. Barging in here. I strode—as defiantly as I dared in a T-shirt that just about covered my bottom—on up the stairs. And Jesus, what the hell was Gertrude up to? Had she really got her wires so comprehensively crossed? No, of course she hadn't. It was unthinkable. And she'd get rid of him, too, or David would. Golly, yes, it was practically David's house, since it was Gertrude's, which made it . . . yes, as David's prospective wife, almost mine really!

'Where are you going?' I hissed as Flora went on up to the attic.

'Back to bed.'

'But I thought you wanted to sleep with me?'

She turned on the stair to look back at me. 'Oh, that was when I thought there was a mass murderer lurking downstairs. I'm fine now.'

'But, Flora—!'

'Mum, don't fuss.' She grinned. 'Looks a bit like George Clooney, don't you think?'

I stared at her, horrified. 'Nothing *like* George Clooney!'

But she'd gone on, up to her room.

Except perhaps in that TV horror movie I'd seen him in, way before *ER*, I thought suddenly. The one where he'd played the neighbourhood nutter. That sinister smile. Horrified, I raced up after her.

'Flora, lock your door!' I panted.

'What? But, Mum—'

'Lock it!' I instructed again. Finally I heard her sigh, and then a click.

'Satisfied?' she muttered.

I nodded grimly and hurried down to my room again. Red-hot candle wax dripped over my hand, and, swearing with pain, I got into bed. I lay still for a moment, picking the wax off my hand, listening for sounds downstairs, listening for—God forbid—his tread on the stairs. But at length, in the silence, I blew out the candle. Bloody, *bloody* man.

Hours later, I woke to find the sun streaming through my window, filling the room with a golden glow. I sat up, gazing out at a sparkling lawn, and then the sea: blue, limpid and calm beyond the trees. It was a fabulous day. The storm had indeed abated and, for a glorious moment, I completely forgot about Mr Malone downstairs. And then I saw him. Emerging from the back door below me with a plate piled high with bacon, eggs, fried potatoes, baked beans and tomatoes. In his other hand he held a sloshing mug of coffee, and behind him was Flora, dressed, and carefully carrying a similarly laden plate and a mug. They made their way, the two of them, clutching knives and forks, to a table and chairs I'd never seen before set out on the lawn.

Hurriedly I lunged for my clothes. I threw them on, splashed water on my face, and then—catching sight of my reflection as I spun out of the room—hastened back to drag a comb through my hair. I ran downstairs, my feet echoing loudly on the wooden stairs. Through the kitchen I sped, and out of the back door, where, the pair of them sat, making serious inroads into their groaning platefuls.

'What the *hell* d'you think you're doing!' I panted, hands on hips.

He looked up surprised. His dark hair was tousled and unkempt, and he had an old blue fishing jersey on.

'Having breakfast.' He waved a fork towards the kitchen. 'We left some fries in the pan for you. You just need to slap another egg on the griddle.'

'I will not "slap another egg on the griddle",' I gasped. 'One of *my* eggs no doubt. I told you, I want you out of here! Not enjoying *my* sunkissed garden with *my* daughter, eating *my* bloody breakfast!'

'Ah.' He wiped his mouth with the back of his hand. 'I rang the Priory Bay, incidentally. They've got a couple of rooms vacant.'

'Excellent,' I snapped.

'They don't come cheap though,' he warned. 'It's high season now. I reckon you'll be paying upwards of a hundred and fifty pounds a night.'

I opened my mouth to speak. Finally made it. '*I'll* be paying? I'm sorry, Mr Malone, *you'll* be paying!'

He regarded me for a full moment above a forkful of egg. 'No, I don't think so, Mrs O'Haggard.'

'*O'Harran!* And we'll soon see about *that!*'

I went inside and made for the phone. The kitchen, as I stalked through it, was a profusion of greasy pots and pans, empty bean tins, egg shells, crusts and dirty mugs. The sitting room was equally chaotic: clothes were strewn all about; a half-unpacked suitcase spewed out on-to the floor; a sleeping-bag lay in a heap; and papers from a case had been knocked over onto the carpet. It looked as if we'd been burgled.

'Bloody *hell!*' I seethed as I picked my way precariously through the debris to the phone by the sofa and dialled.

Gertrude answered almost immediately, her distinctive, cut-glass tones echoing musically down the line. 'Helleau?'

'Hello, Gertrude? Oh, thank goodness you're in.'

'Annabel! My dear, how lovely. How are you?' she bellowed. 'Enjoying the weather? Glorious here, and hopefully with you, too?'

'It is, Gertrude, it's lovely, but listen. We have a slight problem.'

I briefed her elaborately, explaining at length, exclaiming, protest-ing—but not too vehemently because it was, after all, a pickle of her making—and then paused, waiting for her indignation to match mine.

'Oh. Oh, dear . . .' she faltered eventually. 'What a dilemma.'

'Well, no, not really. I'll just tell him to go, shall I?'

'Well, you see, my dear, it's all rather awkward. As a matter of fact I *do* remember meeting him now, him and his family, a couple of years ago, in Cornwall. They were staying further along the coast from Taplow House, with the Masterses. Tom Masters was an old pupil of Hugh's and a great friend. If I remember rightly, Mr Malone was a cousin of theirs, American fellow, I believe. Anyway, you're quite right, I did offer him the house this year—he contacted me recently about it . . .'

'Well, offer, yes,' I spluttered. 'But, Gertrude—'

'But, my dear, he's paid me, you see,' she said anxiously. 'Quite a lot of money. Sent a cheque, and all gone, of course, on the blasted roof. Oh, my dear, I'm most dreadfully sorry. Perhaps the Priory Bay? For a week or so, maybe? It is frighteningly expensive, though.'

'You mean . . .' I swallowed. 'For me?'

'Well, and Flora, obviously. It's just, well, now that you're down there, it does seem awfully silly to come all that way back again, doesn't it? Oh, dear, how perfectly stupid of me. I do apologise. What a forgetful old fool I am! Do forgive me!'

She was genuinely distressed now. I gazed out through the bay window at the other end of the room. In the garden I could see Flora and Mr Malone scraping their plates in the sunshine. I gulped. All my dreams for a productive summer in this glorious house by the creek: writing, fishing with Flora, teaching her to sail, all turning to dust and ashes.

'Never mind, Gertrude,' I said quietly. 'It's not your fault.'

We said goodbye and I replaced the receiver. Blinked hard, willing back the tears. By the phone, a small local guide book lay, interspersed with adverts. Slowly, I picked up the phone again. Made a few more calls. Finally, I replaced the receiver and walked back to the garden.

Mr Malone was leaning back in his chair, which he'd clearly found in an outhouse I hadn't discovered, stretching languidly and letting out a deep sigh of contentment after his heavy artillery breakfast.

'Well?' He grinned as I approached. That maddening, blowtorch grin.

'Well.' I swallowed. 'Yes. It seems you're quite right, Mr Malone. You do, indeed, have a right to this place, because a financial transaction has taken place. And I don't.'

'Great.' He grinned some more. 'So you'll be off then.'

'Yes.' I averted my eyes to the grass. 'So we'll be off then.'

I felt Flora's huge brown eyes upon me. 'You mean . . . we have to go?'

'I'm afraid so, my darling.' I raised my chin and gave a brave smile. 'It seems Gertrude forgot she'd already rented the house out to this gentleman when she offered it to us. You know how forgetful she is.'

'Oh!' Her face fell. 'So . . . where will we go? Priory Bay?'

I gave a bleak little laugh. 'What, at two hundred pounds a night? No, I'm sorry, darling, it's way out of our league. They've only got suites left, and all the bed and breakfasts are full—I've tried. High season, you see. I'm afraid it's home time for us. Back to London.'

'But, Mum—'

'Come on, my darling, chop-chop. You go and pack, and I'll do this.'

I bustled over to the table to clear the plates, to avoid her eye. Avoid saying sorry. I knew my voice would crack, and anyway, I could do that in the car. Say sorry I'd mucked things up for her, as usual. Mucked up her holiday, just as I'd mucked up her short life. I turned for the kitchen.

Mr Malone cleared his throat. 'Er, listen. This place is huge. I'm not expecting company for a while, why don't you stay on 'til you find someplace else?'

I turned. Gave a tight little smile. 'Mr Malone, that's extremely kind, but we couldn't possibly accept.'

'Why not?' said Flora.

'Because . . .' I turned to my daughter. 'Well, darling, we just can't! We don't know this man and—'

'Oh, not that old baloney again. Whadya want, a formal introduction? My full résumé?' He got to his feet and stuck out his hand—then, realising my hands were full, thrust it in his pocket. 'Matt Malone, OK?

THE WEDDING DAY

So quit with the Mr Malone routine. I head up the psychiatric department at Boston University Hospital. I'm here to get some peace and quiet and to do some work. By day I'll be working on a thesis I should have had finished months ago as it's getting published in the fall—I might, incidentally, commandeer that study I spotted earlier—and when I need a break, I might get a bit of fishing in. Unless you're the house guests from hell, I can't see our interests are going to conflict that much, since I guess you'll want to be either out on the beach or on the ocean. Am I right?'

'Yes! Yes, you are right. We will be out for most of the day, won't we, Mum?' Flora turned to me eagerly.

'Yes, but—'

'And since the house is on three floors, I suggest I take the top one—which I see has a tub but no shower in the quaint old English style—and leave you the first floor, which also has a bathroom. Would that suit?'

I stared at him speechless.

'Midday meals could be taken on the beach for you, and on the hoof for me—unless we happen to coincide in the kitchen, in which case it might be friendly to open a can of beans together like Flora and I did this morning. Am I going too fast for you?'

'N-no, but . . .' I put my fingertips to my temples and shut my eyes. 'Hang on, what about your family? Gertrude said she'd met you with your wife. Surely she'll be coming out? Surely she won't want—'

'Not for some time,' he interrupted, shortly. 'She's working.'

'Oh. Right. What as?'

He paused. Raised his eyebrows. I blushed at my nosiness.

'As a consultant radiologist, since you ask.'

'Oh, right,' I mumbled, taken aback.

'I, on the other hand, being semi-academic, get a much longer semester break, which is why I took this place on in the first place.'

'You're . . . a psychiatrist?' I ventured. 'A shrink?'

He gave a glimmer of a smile. 'I'm a clinical practitioner specialising in drug research. I treat psychotically ill patients in a high-security hospital.'

'Oh!' I stepped back in alarm. Nearly dropped the bloody plates.

'Wow.' Flora blinked in awe. 'Real psychos.'

He smiled. 'Not necessarily.'

I straightened up. 'My fiancé's a doctor too,' I said importantly. 'A general practitioner. In London. Belgravia, actually.'

'Excellent news,' he said quickly, 'I'm delighted for him. And now I must go commandeer that study. Do I take it you accept, Mrs O'Harran?'

I licked my lips. 'Annie.'

'Annie.'

'I'd . . . obviously have to pay you?'

'Why? This place belongs to your relative. You expected to have it free. I didn't. All I ask is for some peace and quiet and to be left alone.'

I bristled. 'Certainly I'll leave you alone! You may have a thesis to deliver, but I'll have you know I have a novel to finish. A London publisher is clamouring for my next chapter, and if anyone needs peace and quiet, it's me!'

'Fine, whatever,' he said brusquely. 'Do we have a deal?'

'Golly.' I swallowed hard. 'I suppose we do. But I don't know what David will say . . .' I dithered for a moment. 'Maybe I should . . .'

'Well, go ask his permission, for God's sake,' he said, exasperated.

I stiffened. 'I don't have to do that!' I snapped, raising my chin. 'Yes, Mr Mal—Matt. You have a deal.'

It was only later that evening, as I went to ring David, that I realised the enormity of what I'd done. What would he say? How favourably would he react to the news that I was sharing a house with a complete stranger? David was an easy-going man, but he did marvel at my impulsiveness sometimes. Lunacy, he'd called it on occasion. Would this be just such an occasion? I wondered. It was.

'You've done what?' I held the receiver a couple of inches from my ear. 'Annie, are you mad?'

'No, no, listen,' I insisted, 'it's fine, really. He's right at the top with his own bathroom. I promise you, we hardly see him. We've spent a whole day together and I swear you wouldn't even know he was here!'

This much was true. Matt had indeed holed up in the study as promised with a pile of books and files, emerging only occasionally to make himself cups of strong black coffee. Slightly unnerved by his presence, and not being able to get straight down to work as smartly as he had, I'd hovered, on the pretext that I was dusting or hoovering the sitting room, but actually wanting to be around in case . . . well, you know. In case he made improper remarks to Flora or something. Not that Flora was around to hear them. Having discovered the bookcase from heaven, she'd taken a pile and decamped down to the creek with her boogy-pack, her Ambre Solaire and a bottle of Evian.

I crept down mid-morning and found her lying on a towel in a bikini, engrossed in Daphne du Maurier. She looked up when she saw me.

'Everything all right, darling?' I called. 'Not bored? Or lonely?'

She regarded me witheringly. 'No, Mother. I thought you were going to work in the summerhouse?'

This we'd discovered at the bottom of the garden, a little green wooden slatted affair, with a view of the sea. And since Matt had commandeered the study, it seemed the perfect place for me and my laptop.

'I was. I mean . . . I am.'

She nodded, and went back to her book.

I crept back up the hill through the leafy glade. She was right, I should get on with some work, but hell, it was nearly lunchtime. Flora would be hungry soon. I'd better make her some sandwiches. Oops, no butter in the fridge. Better nip to the shops.

I knocked tentatively on the study door.

'Yep!' he barked. I jumped. Popped my head round.

'Just going to the shops,' I said brightly, eyes roving quickly round the room, taking in the chaotic mess he'd made of the place already.

'And your point is?'

'Well, you know,' I said quickly. 'I've left Flora on the beach. Thought she might wonder where I was.'

'She's thirteen, isn't she? Can't she handle being alone for five minutes?'

I bristled. 'She's *nearly* thirteen, and rather immature, actually. I also thought we should discuss shopping.' I sidled inside. 'If you like I could buy a load of groceries and we could halve the bill. Only it seems rather silly for us both to buy food when—'

'Whatever domestic arrangements you'd like to implement will be just fine. Only please . . .' He jerked his head eloquently towards the door.

'Well!' I shut the door soundly and stood, fuming, on the other side.

'I promise you, David,' I echoed down the phone, 'we don't see him at all. He's writing some paper, totally wrapped up in it.'

'But you don't know him, Annie. He could be anyone!'

'But he's not anyone, Gertrude's met him, and he's the head of the psychotic—or whatever—department at Boston Hospital.'

'He's a bloody shrink, you mean,' he retorted.

'Well, yes,' I said nervously. 'But on the academic side. Research and all that. You can look him up.'

'Thanks. I will. I can't quite believe you've done this, Annie. Why didn't you go to a hotel?'

'Because all the cheap ones were booked up and . . . Oh, David, the thing is, it's so heavenly here: the house and the creek and the beach, and Flora's loving it and . . . well, we'd unpacked and everything, you see. We'd got used to the idea of it being ours, I suppose,' I said lamely. Like a child, not wanting to give back a toy.

He sighed. 'Oh, well, what's done is done, I suppose. But—how does it work? I mean, what's happening this evening, for instance?'

'Oh, that's easy,' I said eagerly. 'He worked for most of the day, but this afternoon he went out fishing and caught loads of mackerel. He's cooking them now on a barbecue for our supper.'

'Is he. How cosy.'

'Oh, no, not at all. Not cosy. I mean . . . he's not like that at all, David. He's much older than me—well, about ten years, I suppose—and quite sort of . . . thick set. Not my type at all.'

'Now there's a relief,' he said wearily. 'As long as you're happy, Annie.'

'Oh, I am, I am, but I'd be so much happier to see you. When are you coming, David?' I asked eagerly.

'Not for a bit, I'm afraid. Things are difficult at work at the moment.'

'Oh? Why?'

It suddenly occurred to me that his voice was strained. And it wasn't just to do with me sharing a house with a total stranger. I frowned.

'What is it, David?'

'Um, nothing really. But . . . remember I told you about Mr O'Connell? The jeweller? The one who drank a lot?'

'God, yes. The one who was convinced he had every medical condition under the sun. Didn't he think he was having a heart attack the last time he came to see you?'

'Yes. Well, he did,' David said shortly. 'He died.'

'What!' I gasped.

'He came to see me again this morning, still reeking of the night before, and complained of a pain in his arm. I sent him home to sober up and he collapsed on the stairs outside as he was leaving.'

'Oh my God. You mean he died there?'

'Almost. Laura heard him cry out and shrieked for me to come. I ran downstairs and tried to resuscitate him, tried everything. We called an ambulance, but he died on the way to hospital.'

'That's not your fault, David.'

'Isn't it? I'm a doctor, aren't I? He comes to see me for the second time, suspecting a heart attack, and this time with a pain in his upper arm. And I send him packing.'

'Yes, but he was drunk, and—and he's been coming to you for years like that. Plastered, imagining things . . .'

'Not really years. Months. And his wife says he drank out of fear. Says he knew he was dying.'

'His wife?'

'She rang me. An hour or so ago. She was almost incandescent with rage and emotion. Telling me I was a fraud. A quack. Saying I'd effectively killed her husband. Saying . . .' he struggled.

I was appalled. How dare she! David, my sweet, kind . . . I licked my lips. 'David. David, listen to me. This is ridiculous. Outrageous! God, how on earth can it be your fault? You did what anyone else would have done, you sent him home to sober up! Relax, darling, it'll be fine.'

'That's not really the point though, is it, Annie? Yes, professionally, and in the eyes of the BMA, I'm sure it will be fine. But a man's dead. It's how I feel about it that's important.'

I swallowed, humbled. Anything I said now would be wrong.

'Anyway,' he rallied slightly, 'the point is I don't think I should just swan off on holiday at the moment. It wouldn't be right.'

'Oh. Well, no, I can see that. But maybe next weekend?'

'Maybe. I'll ring you, darling. Sorry to sound so gloomy. Doesn't help that I miss you so much too.'

'Oh, and I miss you!' I said enthusiastically. '*So* much. Think of the wedding, David, the honeymoon in Mauritius. Think how happy and relaxed you'll be then!'

'Yup.' He sounded unconvinced. 'Bye, my darling. I love you.'

'I love you too. Bye.'

I hung up. Stared dismally out of the mullioned window into the front garden, at the wind-tossed, overgrown lawn. Poor David. How awful. And how unfair. He was such a dedicated man. And he was always so careful. Always sought a second opinion if necessary, and sent patients straight round to Harley Street specialists if he wasn't sure. His uncle, Hugh, had impressed upon him the importance of doing that, when he took David on as a partner, when he'd worked alongside David for a few years before he died.

Pensive and maudlin now, I let myself out through the front door, and wandered slowly round the side of the house to the back garden. On the terrace, Matt, who made such a colossal mess inside, was making an equally spectacular one outside. Bags of charcoal had tipped out onto the York stone, and a white-wine marinade and piles of slimy fish were slopping from a dish over onto a table he'd set up beside a brick barbecue. I sat down at the table and chairs, slightly apart from the action, and bit my thumbnail anxiously.

Matt looked up as he took a fish out of the marinade. Saw my face.

'Problems?'

I hesitated. It would be nice to share it, to talk it through with someone who knew the territory, but . . . no. No, I wouldn't tell him. God, I didn't even know him, and it would be the last thing David would want.

'No. No, it's nothing.' I smiled. 'Wedding plans, actually. Not a big do, of course, because I've been married before, but it all needs doing.'

'Ah.' He went back to his fish.

I felt myself flushing. Why was I blurting all this out? I reached instinctively to pour a glass of wine from the bottle on the table, then realised I hadn't bought it.

'Oh. Sorry, I—'

'No, go ahead.' He waved the barbecue tongs. 'I noticed you'd missed it off the groceries, so I bought a few bottles on the way back from fishing.'

'Thanks.' I took a large gulp. A silence ensued.

'So,' I said brightly, keen to deflect the conversation his way. 'When will your wife be joining us exactly? I mean'—God, that sounded awful—'joining you.'

'When she can,' he said shortly.

Another silence. Was it because I'd been too nosy about his wife, I wondered? Or prattling too girlishly about my wedding? In an effort to appear serious, I adopted a creative slouch in the chair.

'And of course my book is such a worry, too,' I confided. 'My publisher is desperate for it, but I can only work if the muse is with me.'

He nodded. 'Naturally. How many books have you had published?'

'Oh. Um, none. I mean, one. Hopefully. This is the first one.'

'And how far have you got?' He expertly turned the fish on the rack.

'Er, well. Three chapters so far. In my head. One, actually on paper.'

He smiled. 'I see. Maybe if you did a little less vacuuming the muse would come back to you?'

It was said pleasantly enough, but I bristled at the audacity.

'I'm sorry?' I said, with measured quietness.

'Well, I couldn't help noticing you spent a lot of time keeping house this morning.'

I stared. 'Yes, because this house is so dreadfully dusty. And, yes, I did hoover, but only—' I broke off. Shook my head in wonderment. 'Good grief. I certainly don't have to explain my movements to you.'

'No, ma'am. You don't.' He turned the rest of the fish over.

I stared at him. Licked my lips. 'And it doesn't just happen, you know,' I said testily. 'This writing lark. There's a lot of thinking involved. Ruminating over plot lines, characterisation, that sort of thing.'

He smiled down at his fish. 'Ah.'

Ah. Now what the hell did that mean?

'Anyway.' I glanced at my watch, determined not to rise. 'Suppertime. I'll get the plates, shall I? Where's Flora?' I glanced around anxiously.

'She's making a salad in the kitchen. I asked her to.'

'Oh!' I got up hurriedly. 'She doesn't have to do that. I'll do it.'

'Sure, take over. I guess she's too young to make a salad.'

I'd risen from my chair, but now I stopped. Turned.

'Right,' I said quietly. 'I see. You're making some big assumptions about me, aren't you, Mr Malone? You're suggesting, for the second time today, that I mollycoddle my daughter.'

He shrugged. 'I'm just saying she's not a baby.'

'And you're also saying that when I'm not fussing over my offspring,

I'm cleaning the house and making excuses for not working. Is that it?'

He smiled. 'Let's just say I know the type.'

'Type?' I bridled. 'What type?'

He paused in his cooking and looked straight at me, his blue eyes bright and slightly mocking. 'Well, you know, you've got a child, growing out of your jurisdiction, but you're still hanging on to her. Half of you knows you shouldn't, 'cos she needs to spread her wings, so you're desperately looking around for something else to do besides nurturing her. You hit upon writing'—he shrugged—'but it could be anything. It could be painting, or pottery, or mosaics, but it's an occupation, not actual employment. It's to fill a gap in your life.' He paused to push the fish around on the barbecue rack.

'So, OK, you give this writing lark a go,' he went on. 'But your heart's not in it, because all you've ever done up 'til now is keep house. Either that or go shopping at the mall in your squeaky clean car'—he nodded over to my gleaming Fiat—'in your neat clothes'—he gestured at my outfit. 'So work comes as something of a shock. Am I right?' He grinned.

I gaped at him, horrified. Appalled. 'No, you are not right. You are so wrong. And—and—so *rude* . . . Flora! *Flora!*' I bellowed, fists clenched.

She appeared at the kitchen door, clutching a bowl of salad.

'What?' she called. She took in my furious face, hurriedly set aside the salad and hastened across the terrace to us. 'What is it? What's happened?'

'Flora,' I said, breathing hard, 'please tell this—this know-it-all shrink the state of our house at home. Do I keep it tidy? Do I "keep house"?'

She blanched. 'Well . . .'

'*It's a bloody tip, isn't it, Flora!*' I roared.

'Er, yes.' She blinked. 'A bit.'

'And the car?' I breathed. 'Tell him about the car.'

'Oh, yeah, the car's really dirty, usually,' she said cheerfully. 'But Mum washed it on the way down. Oh God, it was so funny, she got out in the car wash to put the aerial down and—'

'*Never mind!* And my clothes? Prior to yesterday?'

'Your clothes? Mum . . .' She looked confused. 'I thought the whole idea was to turn over a new leaf. Impress people, not—'

'My *clothes*, Flora!'

She shrugged. 'OK. Really tatty. Holes in the sleeves—bit like you actually.' She glanced at him. 'Old trainers, odd socks, a mess.'

'I've a good mind to show you my underwear, Mr Malone,' I seethed. 'A good mind to show you my old grey pants, right now!'

'Hey,' he murmured, palms raised. 'No need.'

'You think you're so clever,' I spat. 'You think you can meet someone for five minutes and do a quick thumbnail sketch of the little English memsahib—just like that!' I snapped my fingers under his nose. 'But you're way off, *way* off, because, actually, you've been dealing in appearances. You think I spend hours constantly tarting up myself or my house because I have no other interests, but I'll have you know I've worked hard all my adult life.'

'Hey, Annie, I didn't mean to—'

'You think that this . . . this occupation of mine, this "writing lark", is a little bland diversion, but it's actually the result of years of hard graft. Years of selling stories to magazines to pay the mortgage, because I wasn't just supplementing my ex-husband's income, Mr Malone, I was the bloody breadwinner! I've kept our heads above water for twelve years with this "dilettante" occupation, and all by writing about a life I didn't have. A romantic life, full of happy endings, a life that didn't exist for me.' I was horrified to find my voice breaking.

'Mum!' Flora stepped forward in alarm.

'Hey, look, I—'

'And sometimes,' I went on tremulously, 'it would have been a pleasure to have had the smart lunch-and-shopping existence you describe, Mr Malone, but it was never an option. Only now it is.' I raised my chin. 'Now, I have a lovely, respectable doctor boyfriend who wants to make my life a bit more comfortable, and d'you know what? I'm going to let him, because I've worked hard and I deserve it! So the next time you think you "know the type", and want to get analytical with someone you've known all of five minutes, *pick on someone else!*'

And with that, I burst into tears and raced back into the house.

Chapter Three

THE FOLLOWING MORNING, Matt knocked on my door. Happily I was up and dressed. I opened it an inch. He cleared his throat.

'I, um, came to apologise. I upset you last night, and I'm sorry.'

He regarded me steadily. Clear blue eyes in a tough, lined face. I nodded. Twelve hours later, I felt faintly stupid.

'It's fine,' I muttered. 'Forget it. I probably overreacted.'

He shrugged. 'Maybe, maybe not. Leastways, I had no idea I'd hit such a sore spot. In fact'—he scratched the back of his head—'I don't remember hitting a few of those spots at all. All that stuff about your boyfriend, Jesus. I don't even recall *mentioning* him.'

I took a deep breath. 'No. No, you're absolutely right. I brought him up. It's just . . . well, he seemed part of what you were accusing me of, somehow. Funding my leisurely lifestyle. Something like that.'

He shook his head. 'Hey. I've never met the guy, and like you said last night, I've only known you five minutes. It was crass of me to over-generalise, and also to knock your writing like that. I'm sorry.'

I recognise a genuine apology when I hear it. I glanced down at my feet. Nodded curtly. 'Forget it.'

There was an awkward silence. He made as if to go, then turned back. 'There's, uh, some bacon on the stove, if you like. Only you didn't get to eat last night. Have some.'

'Thanks. I'll do that.'

He withdrew and, a few moments later, I heard the study door shut downstairs behind him.

It was true, I hadn't come down for supper last night, because once I'd bolted to my bedroom and punched a few walls, it was slightly diffi-cult to save face and extract myself. So, I stayed in my room and tried to work out exactly why I was so angry.

Clearly, Mr Malone had unwittingly voiced something that perhaps I'd been aware of but had subconsciously tucked away. Now, though, there it was, out in the open, and there I was, protesting, justifying, but why? Surely my shiny new lifestyle with David was only what I deserved after all those lean years with Adam? But did I secretly feel uncomfort-able about it? And had a stranger inadvertently lit the blue touch paper, failed to stand well back, and taken a bit of heat?

Now, this morning, as I emerged from the bathroom, I bumped into Flora coming out of her new bedroom, having shifted down a floor to accommodate Matt.

'Oh, hi, Mum.' She tottered sleepily. 'We were worried about you last night. I didn't like to come up, though, 'cos you were so stressed. Are you OK, or have you still got a bastard on?'

'Don't use that expression, darling, you sound like your father. No, I'm fine. Sorry, Flora. Something . . . set me off.'

'Phew, just a bit. Scary. You didn't have any supper either. We couldn't believe you didn't come down. Aren't you starving?'

'I am, and I'm going to have some of that yummy sausage and bacon I can smell down there. What are you going to do today, sweetheart?' I linked arms with her chummily as we went downstairs, wanting to dispel all memories of the mad, unhinged mother, spilling out her life story in front of a total stranger.

'Well, isn't it today that the others are coming? I'm going to cycle round to Rock to see them.'

'D'you know, I think you're right,' I said slowly. 'It is today, isn't it? You do that, darling. I'm going to be working in the summerhouse.'

'OK.'

We went arm in arm to the kitchen, where she plucked a couple of pieces of bacon from the pan with her fingertips and sandwiched them together with two slices of bread. She took a huge bite. 'First, though,' she mumbled through her mouthful, 'I'm going back to bed with this and *Northanger Abbey*. See you.'

Armed with a cup of coffee, a bacon sandwich and my laptop, I set off purposefully across the garden, past Matt's study window and down to the little summerhouse that Flora and I had discovered yesterday.

I pushed open the creaky green door. Inside, it smelt of musty deckchairs and wooden-framed tennis rackets and old summer holidays. The past. There were three chairs with faded, chintzy cushions, and, in the window, a small, rather rickety bamboo table. I pulled up a chair and sat down delightedly, arranged my laptop and switched on. Through a gap in the trees, the sea could just be glimpsed. Perfect.

I turned on my screen and read my first chapter. My only chapter. In which Lucinda De Villiers, my elegant, highly strung heroine, had just discovered—courtesy of a hotel bill found in husband Henry's suit pocket—that while Henry was closing a multimillion-pound deal for Chase Manhattan in New York last week, he might also have treated his attractive female assistant, Tanya Fox, to more than just a celebratory plate of sushi at the Waldorf Hotel. Pacing her Holland Park mansion now, waiting for him to come home from work, Lucinda was unsure how to handle the situation.

I tapped my fingers on the bamboo table and gazed out at the view. I was unsure how I was going to handle it, either. I mean, sure, on the one hand, the man was a complete bastard. But on the other, there were her three gorgeous children asleep upstairs. OK. I raised my hands. Tapped.

Lucinda paused for a moment by the Adam fireplace in her eau-de-nil drawing room. She glanced up and regarded her reflection in the antique overmantel mirror. Her face was pale and her grey eyes huge with fear in her heart-shaped face. She glanced down at her Cartier watch again. Ten fifteen. Where was he? With her, Tanya? In a hotel bedroom in the West End, somewhere? Suddenly, she heard a key in the door.

I broke off exhausted and pushed back my chair. Phew. Golly. Seven lines had taken all morning. This creative malarkey was jolly hard work.

Perhaps I needed a coffee. Or some chocolate. I scraped back my chair and got up. I was uncomfortably aware, too, that I wasn't quite sticking to the brief as outlined by my new editor, Sebastian Cooper. After his fulsome letter of praise and acceptance some time ago, I'd rung to introduce myself properly, and he'd praised my style, my dialogue—but he'd also volunteered a hope that we might see the story from Henry's point of view. Maybe even see him in action with Tanya.

'You mean . . . you want sex?'

'Sorry?' he'd said startled.

'No no,' I'd said hurriedly. 'In the book.'

'Oh. Oh, in the book! Yeah, definitely,' he'd agreed. 'Why don't you, like, chuck it in all the way through? A bit in each chapter?'

'Er, well . . .' I'd faltered. 'I'll . . . do my best.'

'Great. T'rific. Just let it, you know, flow. Go with the flow.'

He'd sounded awfully young, I'd thought as I'd put down the phone. It was important to keep him happy though, I decided, as I took my mug and left the summerhouse. Perhaps we ought to see him in his boxer shorts? Henry, I mean. Maybe he could have a bit of a raunchy tussle with Tanya in chapter three. But I wasn't convinced I could keep it up for twenty chapters. Wasn't convinced Henry could, either, so to speak.

In the kitchen, Matt was pouring boiling water into his own mug.

'Phew. See you've taken a break too! Hard work, isn't it?'

He looked at me blankly, grunted, and went back to his study

I cradled my coffee and sauntered out of the back door, down the stone steps and into the sunshine streaming across the daisy-strewn lawn. It was a beautiful day. Not a cloud in the sky. Such a waste to be shut up in the summerhouse like that. Maybe I'd just sit out here for a bit, take a break in the clover and recharge the old batteries. Give Lucinda some thought.

I went to the far edge of the lawn where it met the long grass, lay back with my hands locked behind my head, and contemplated my heroine. The sun was in my eyes though, so I shut them. Fatal, really. The next thing I knew I was waking up to sounds of shouting and whooping coming from people messing about on a boat, below in the creek. I sat up with a start. Felt hot and sweaty. My face felt burnt, too. I touched it tentatively. God, how awful. Had I really fallen asleep?

I swung round to make sure no one had seen, and realised I'd chosen to kip, albeit at a distance, but pretty much in a beeline from Matt's study. Behind the bay window his head was bent studiously to his task, but he'd have to raise it occasionally to breathe, wouldn't he—if indeed he did breathe. He'd have been unable to miss me, spread-eagled on the grass, legs splayed, mouth open, snoring loudly.

I brushed myself down. Damn. *Damn*. And damn the fact that I couldn't just do that. Couldn't have a kip on my holiday on my own sunny back lawn if I felt like it. Irritated now beyond belief, I realised that those raised voices were awfully familiar. They were getting closer too, and louder, and through the gap in the trees, I could just see the top of Flora's head as she came up the steep slope through the woods, pushing her bike. I stood up and craned my neck. Down below at the water's edge, I could also see Michael, trousers rolled up to his knees, steadying a boat on the shore in which Rosie and Clare wobbled precariously, shrieking with laughter, as they tried to climb out.

God, already? It hadn't taken Clare long to offer to bring Flora back in the boat and take a quick shufti at our house, had it? I thought drily. I went to meet them. They'd left Michael in charge of the boat, and the pair of them came puffing up the hill towards me through the woods, Flora arriving just ahead of them.

'Mum, look who I found!'

I forced a grin. 'So I see.'

She disappeared towards the house as I went across to kiss my sister, then Rosie, who was panting hard. She stopped, clutching her knees.

'God, what a hill!'

'Steep, isn't it? Sorts the men from the boys, we find.' I shot Clare a look. 'Come to spy on me already?'

'There's no "already" about it,' snorted Clare, gasping. 'We got here yesterday morning, actually, came a day early because the weather was so glorious, and left it a whole day before coming to see you.'

'Where are the others?' I asked.

'We left Dan in charge of the children. There wasn't room in the boat with Flora's bike.' Clare was still panting. 'Blimey, is this it?' She squinted up into the sun at the house. 'Shit, it's all right, isn't it?'

'Pretty,' agreed Rosie, shading her eyes with both hands. 'And so out of the way, too. The rest of the north coast is heaving, let me tell you, but you wouldn't know it here. God, it's no good, I've got to sit down.' She flopped dramatically on her back in the long grass.

'I know, and so few people come down to this creek,' I enthused, kneeling down beside her. 'It's incredibly private.' I was keen to show off.

'Well'—Clare made a face—'except that it's not now, is it? Flora says you've got some man living here with you. Honestly, Annie, you are extraordinary, I can't quite believe it!' Her eyes were incredulous.

'Yes, well, it was a misunderstanding,' I said quickly. ''All Gertrude's fault, but not a problem in the least. He just keeps himself to himself.'

'Yes, but he's living here!' insisted Clare. 'With you and Flora! I mean, does David know?'

'Yes, he does, and shush, would you?' I glanced nervously back to the house. 'He'll hear you. He's working in the study. And he's married.'

'So where are you working then?'

'In the summerhouse.'

'That grotty old thing? That's a bit rough, isn't it?'

'No, it's fine.'

'So what's he like, then?' asked Rosie, sitting up to cup her hands round a match and light a cigarette.

I hesitated. 'Nice,' I said, finally. 'I mean . . . fine.'

'Really?' She glanced across, catching my tone.

'You'll meet him later,' I said quickly. 'Anyway, how's life down at Penmayne Terrace? Children thrilled to be here?'

'Delighted,' said Rosie. 'We've been down on the beach from the moment we got here, and we haven't been off since, have we, Clare? Splendid. We are having,' she enunciated carefully, 'the time of our lives.' There was an edge to her voice which didn't escape me. I had to look away quickly before I laughed.

'And so this is, what—how many bedrooms?' Clare was surveying the house pseudo-casually, head on one side, like a prospective buyer.

'Four. No, five, I think. Have a wander, if you like.'

'I might just do that,' she mused. 'Yes, I could do with a pee. Back in a mo.' She sauntered nonchalantly up the lawn.

'She is driving me mad,' muttered Rosie in measured tones.

'I gathered,' I muttered back.

'She won't let me smoke,' she exclaimed. 'I mean, even on the terrace! *And* she told me off for drinking too much last night.'

'Well, she doesn't drink, you see.'

'Clearly. And then this morning she woke us all up at eight o'clock— *eight o'clock!*—to send Dan off to get the papers, and me to the bakery. '"Got to get in that bread queue, or it'll all be gone." For a moment I thought I was in Poland, with a coup on or something. Anyway, ten minutes later—no cup of tea, mind—there I was, standing in this queue of women who, spookily, *all look just like Clare!* It was like something out of *The Stepford Wives*. I promise you, there they all were in their immaculate sailing shorts and sporty little polo tops—not dissimilar to yours, actually.' She eyed me with dismay.

'It's a long story,' I muttered, hurriedly untucking my shirt.

'And there am I in Dan's old shirt and ripped jeans with sleep in my eyes and a bloody shopping list in my hand!'

'Ah, yes, the bread queue.' I nodded solemnly. 'That's all part of the ritual, I'm afraid. Part of the initiation ceremony.'

'And then it was back to the kitchen to join a production line of bap-buttering while Clare filled them with one hand, washed fruit with the other, and simultaneously, it seemed, poured coffee into a Thermos, while the men sat in the sunshine with the papers and did bugger all!'

'Hm. She has rather got that fifties mentality. Very like my mother.'

'And then off we all trooped to the beach—at nine thirty, mind, sharp, to bag the best spot—where the intention was to stay all day. Just a sandy ham roll, a force-eight gale, and a hard rock to sit on, followed by a game of rounders with the children, French cricket, more rounders, more French cricket—*all bloody day*! It was only when Flora arrived and we had the idea of coming up to see you that the nightmare ended. Please tell me it's not going to go on like this?' she begged.

I giggled. 'But this is a Cornish holiday, Rosie. Surely you know the rules? *We* did it as children, and have glorious, rose-tinted memories, and now we have to ensure that *our* little darlings have them too. Bugger the fact that the world has moved on and it's not just the rich and pampered who are renting villas in Portugal, but Tracy and Wayne too. And, of course, the children really do love it, so Clare can smugly say: "Oh, they'd much rather to to Cornwall than to Italy."'

'Well, I think she's mad,' Rosie said shortly. 'What—she'd rather sit on a windy beach than stroll to the harbour arm in arm with Michael, and then back to the villa for a *siesta complet*?'

'Oh, I think the *complet* bit would be right out of the question,' I said drily. 'Clare's off games. At least as far as Michael's concerned.'

'So we noticed. He's grovelling around for some attention like a dog hoping to be tossed a bone. And, meanwhile, she's been putting lipstick on on the beach, in case a certain Todd family appear.'

'Ah, yes. The Todds.'

'Which as yet, they hadn't, but good old Clare looks up expectantly from the sandy rug that we call home every time another familiar family droops past, weighed down with windbreaks and chairs and dogs and buggies and kites and God knows what else, poor bastards. And then, finally, the Todds *did* drip past with Mr—who I assume is the object of Clare's desire—so engrossed in chat with the French au pair that he didn't even see her. She nearly spat her ham roll in the sand, she was so livid. What's that all about, then?'

'Oh. Yes.' I shifted uncomfortably. 'Well, Clare's trying to get at Michael, you see.'

'Ah. After his fumble with the fund manager at the Christmas party.'

'Who told you that!'

'You did.'

'Did I?' I was horrified. 'God, I'm so indiscreet. And the thing is, Rosie, I just don't think she's terribly happy. She has to do this frantic earth mother bit every year, because she works so hard in the City and feels guilty about it. She's a bag of nerves, actually. It's all a big cover-up. And Michael's terrified of her, of course.'

'Aren't we all,' she muttered. 'I tell you—Oops, look out, here she comes. Just tell me quickly, what's he really like, this lodger chappie?'

'Frightful,' I muttered back. 'Really bolshy and chippy and opinionated, and frankly downright rude. He makes a terrible mess, too.'

'Well, so do you, don't you?'

'That's not the point. The only good thing is that he doesn't actually appear very often.'

She smiled. 'So you're selling your soul for the sake of a luxury holiday?'

I raised my eyebrows back. 'And you're not?'

'Lovely house,' Clare conceded as she approached. 'Charming.'

'Thanks.' I smiled.

'And he's sweet.'

'Sorry?'

'Matt. In the study.' She sat down beside us.

'Oh, Clare, you didn't go in, did you?'

'Certainly I did.'

'But he's working!'

'Yes, on some paper or other. Anyway, I wanted to find out more about him. Can't have my little sister living with just anyone, can I?'

'So what did you say?' I breathed. 'You . . . knocked first?'

'Yes,' she said wearily, 'I knocked first, *and* stuck out my hand politely and said: "Hi, I'm Clare Faraday, Annie's sister." So he stood up and introduced himself and was perfectly pleasant. And you're right, he is married, but separated. His wife is living here in Cambridge, with their son.'

'Oh!' My jaw went slack. 'But . . . hang on, he said his wife was coming. He said—'

'Well, perhaps she is, perhaps she's delivering the son or something, perhaps she'll stay the night. Golly, I don't know, Annie, I'm not that nosy.' She smartly swatted a fly on her leg. 'Gotcha. Anyway, I asked him to come to our barbecue tomorrow night, and he said he couldn't. Got too much to do, apparently.'

'Blimey, Clare!' I snorted. 'You might have asked me first!'

She blinked. 'Well, I rather assume *you're* coming.'

'No! I mean, if you could ask him!'

'Why? I thought you liked him?'

'I do, I just—well I don't want to get too matey, Clare. We're lodgers, for crying out loud!'

'Lodgers?' Clare raised her eyebrows. 'Right. I'll remember that. Remind him of his place, next time I meet him.'

'Oh, for God's sake! Anyway, who's coming to this barbecue?'

'Well, the Elliotts, the Fields, the Todds—'

'Ah, the Todds.' I couldn't resist it. She ignored me and swept on.

'The Frasers, hopefully, and you and David—'

'Oh, no, David can't come down this weekend.'

'Why not?'

'He's working.' I said shortly. 'But he'll be down the weekend after, for sure, and that suits both of us, actually. I've got so much to do.'

'Ah, yes, the famous book,' she drawled. 'How's it coming along?'

'Lucinda got her rocks off yet?' asked Rosie sleepily from the grass.

'Lucinda? Who's Lucinda?' demanded Clare, irritated that Rosie knew more than she did.

Rosie turned her head in the grass. 'The manicured wife of Henry the investment banker, who's been caught in flagrante with some tart from the office. Isn't that it, Annie?'

'Investment banker? Tart from the . . .' Clare stared. 'Right,' she said softly. 'So it's about me, is it?'

I stared back, horrified. 'No, of course not!'

'Really? But he's a City boy, is he?'

'Well, yes, but—'

'Three or four children? Large house in London?'

'Yes, but—'

'Great,' she fumed. 'Really, really great, Annie. Positively sisterly of you. Loyal.' She stood up. She was trembling, she was so angry. 'And this is the one they're so enamoured with at the publishing house, is it?'

'Clare—'

'Well, good on you, Annie. Well done. Nice to know at least someone's going to benefit from this family's misfortunes!'

And with that she turned on her heel and strode back down the hill.

'Bloody hell,' muttered Rosie.

'Bloody, *bloody* hell,' I agreed.

'But you didn't, did you, Annie?' Rosie swung round to me, bewildered, when Clare was out of earshot. 'I mean—'

'No, of course I flaming well didn't!' I said hotly. 'Not deliberately, anyway. Would I do that?'

'No, but . . . subconsciously?'

'Who knows?' I ran my hands despairingly through my hair. 'But what am I going to do? I can't change it now, they love it at the publishers.'

'Easy,' said Rosie suddenly. 'You just change the characters a bit. Instead of Lucinda being a successful businesswoman in a Holland Park mansion, she's a—I don't know—a Colour Me Beautiful rep. In Leighton Buzzard. Chigwell, even.'

I blinked. 'Colour me what?'

'Beautiful. You know, they pick out the colour that suits you, tell you what to wear; that sort of thing. Waft different coloured scarves in front of your face, then boss you into lilac because of your insipid complexion. And the husband,' she went on, warming to her theme, 'doesn't have to be a City chappie like Michael, does he? He could be . . . a Burger King chappie?'

'You think that has the same cachet?' I asked.

'Well, it's not cachet you're after, is it?' Rosie insisted. 'It's pulsating passion played out in sensual suburbia with real people doing real jobs. Oh, no, this is much more gritty and realistic, Annie. Much better than sex among the smart set. Anyway, I'd better go,' she said getting to her feet. 'I've got to help with the shopping for the barbecue. Will I see you before then?' She gave me a pleading look.

'I'll try,' I promised. 'But obviously now that I've got to rewrite my entire novel, time is not exactly on my side.'

'Sorry,' she muttered and, looking severely chastened, followed Clare through the trees.

I watched her go. After a while, I heard subdued voices coming from the creek, and the sound of a motor starting. Hopefully Clare had calmed down a bit and wasn't actually killing anyone yet.

I wandered back to the summerhouse, shut the blistered green door behind me, sat down at my little bamboo table, and stared at the screen. Could Lucinda become Lorraine, I wondered? Not pacing her Persian carpets, but nervously touching up her roots in Chigwell? And could Henry really look dashing in a polyester shirt complete with Burger King logo and a jaunty little red and white paper hat?

No, I decided firmly. Clare could think what she bloody well liked. I was keeping my Holland Park ménage—who, to my mind, had never remotely resembled my rather boring sister and brother-in-law—and she could lump it. This was my story, and I was sticking to it.

I tapped away furiously—and eloquently, actually, now I'd got up a head of steam—with purple passages flowing. I'd just got to the bit where Henry is mounting the stairs looking postcoital, while Lucinda awaits him in the marital bedroom looking wide-eyed and vulnerable in her Rigby & Peller nightie, when someone rapped loudly on the door.

'What!' I barked, swinging round in annoyance in my chair.

'Sorry, Mummy.' Flora turned to go.

'Oh! No, darling. Sorry. I was miles away. What is it?' God. *Constant* interruption. How on earth had Jane Austen managed it, I wondered?

'I was just wondering if you wanted to come for a swim. The tide's right up now, Mum, and it's like our very own swimming pool.'

I took a deep breath. Squared my shoulders and forced a smile. 'Lead on, MacDuff. Nothing I'd rather do.' I glanced longingly at my screen as I turned it off. 'I'll just nip up to the house and get my things, and then I'll see you down there.'

'Got them!' She smiled smugly, holding a towel and swimsuit aloft. 'And we can change in here, can't we?'

We could, and we did, and then, taking our clothes with us, picked our way gingerly in bare feet down the granite steps and the twisting sandy path, to the water's edge. As we emerged through the trees, I was startled by the transformation.

'Oh!' I breathed. 'Isn't this beautiful?'

But Flora had already raced ahead of me, running a little way along the bank to a rock. Moments later, she'd climbed up and dived off into the water. I, meanwhile, shrieking my way in gingerly from the bank, held my arms up high as the water crept up my swimsuit.

'It's freezing!' I gasped, turning blue with cold.

'Not once you're in. Come on!' She did a splashy crawl across to me, grabbed both my hands and pulled. I shrieked again as we both went under, but she was right, and after the initial shock, we were both swimming delightedly in beautifully clear water.

'Isn't this heaven?' I shouted to Flora, bobbing beside me.

'Total!' she yelled back, and I could tell she meant it. 'You were so clever to get this place, Mum.'

Despite the freezing water, I glowed with pleasure. We ducked down and swam to the sandy bed below, trying to do handstands and pick up shells, then soaring up and breaking through the surface to the cloudless sky. When we were beginning to feel the Cornish water penetrate our very bones, we clambered out onto the bank again.

'That was brilliant,' I panted. 'And presumably we can do that every day, at high tide.'

'Exactly, and then lie on the bank to get dry!'

'This isn't the Mediterranean, Flora,' I said, trying to dry myself on the ineffectual scrap of towelling she'd brought down and watching her shake with cold. 'Where's your towel?'

She shivered. 'Only brought one.'

'Oh, Flora!' I threw it at her. 'Come on.' I picked up my clothes. 'Back to the house to get dry.'

'I'll race you, OK?' she said, teeth chattering.

I grinned. 'OK.'

She stopped and got on her marks. 'Ready, steady— Oh, cheat!'

But I was off. Knowing my daughter at nearly thirteen believed that she could beat me, I sprinted ahead. Flora, shrieking with indignation behind me and yelling that she hadn't said go and wasn't ready, was nevertheless gaining on me. We raced past the summerhouse and up the back lawn, screeching with laughter, neck and neck, up to the house, and were just hurtling round the corner, yelling at the tops of our voices and heading for the back door—when suddenly we skidded to a halt in our tracks. Flora cannoned into me, nearly knocking me over, and we held on to each other, gulping and wheezing, as we gaped, horrified. For there on the terrace in the sunshine, round a wrought-iron table and sharing a jug of Pimm's, sat Matt, Adam, and a girl of quite astonishing beauty. My jaw dropped.

'Well, hey,' drawled Adam, looking me up and down. 'Look at this. What have you come as, Annie? Lady Godiva?'

I glanced down at my white swimsuit, which, being old and thin, had become completely transparent in the wet. Horrified, I snatched the scrap of towel from Flora and dangled it ineffectually in front of me.

'Adam!'

'Daring, Annie, at your age, don't you think?' he mused. 'But, actually, I'd say you pretty much pulled it off, wouldn't you, Matt? Oh, this is Cozzy, by the way, who's totally intrigued by the cool little ménage à trois thing you and David have got going here. She's dying to find out more. Hi, Flora, darlin', how ya doin'?' He broke off to kiss his daughter who'd draped wet arms delightedly round his neck.

'Daddy!' She kissed his cheek. 'Didn't know you were coming!'

'I'm going up to change,' I muttered as I sidled past them. Matt, I noticed, tactfully averted his eyes. I darted through the back door and scurried through the house to the hall and on up the stairs, appalled.

When I got to my room, I recoiled in horror as I gazed at the apparition in the mirror. I ripped the wretched costume off and threw it angrily on the floor, grabbing a towel. Damn. *Damn.* What the hell was Adam *doing* here, for Christ's sake, without even ringing me, sitting on my back step with Matt, sipping a glass of Pimm's? Matt, for crying out loud, who wouldn't even stop for a cup of *cof*fee with me. And—and her, Cocksy or whatever the hell her name was: God, she was gorgeous. I breathed hard. Shut my eyes tight.

When I opened them again, I regarded my reflection in the mirror. My dark eyes looked wide and scared in my pale face. My heart was racing. Hardly surprising, I thought grimly. I'd never actually trod this territory before, had I? Because in all my years of anguish with Adam, all my years of broken hearts and dreams and promises, although I'd known about the other women, I'd never actually seen him with one.

Steady, Annie. Take it easy. Get dressed, and go down. Slowly.

A few moments later I was walking back out, nonchalantly drying my hair with my towel, dressed in a linen shirt and silk trousers, going for sophistication in the face of her youth. God, how young *was* she, I thought as she smiled up at me. Nineteen? Twenty? She didn't look much older than Flora, with her long blonde hair and those endless legs coming out of tiny frayed denim shorts. I breathed deeply as Matt pulled out a chair for me.

'Thanks.'

I smiled and turned to my ex-husband with what I hoped was breezy confidence. 'Adam, you should have warned me. I didn't know you were coming. I would have stocked up the fridge. Got in some alcopops or whatever it is you youngsters drink.'

He grinned good-naturedly. 'Didn't know your number. I only had your address, and your mobile was turned off, so Cozzy and I thought we'd head on over. I had no idea your place was so close. We're literally only about half an hour away, aren't we, honey?'

He turned to honey, slumped as he was in his chair in his baggy cargo pants and white T-shirt, and stretched out a tanned hand to take her tiny one. He looked gorgeous, as ever. *They* looked gorgeous.

'Thanks,' I muttered as Matt poured me a Pimm's.

'And when I looked it up on the map, I thought, well, hey, that's so close. I know, we'll pick Flora up and have her here for the night. Take her out for a curry or something. Would you like that, sweetheart?' He turned to look at her.

'Oh, Mum, can I?' Flora, curled on the grass between Adam and Cozzy's feet, glanced up.

'Of course.' I smiled. 'But don't forget there's Clare's barbecue tomorrow night. You might like to be back for that. See all your cousins.'

'Oh, I'll drop her back, don't worry,' Adam said. 'And you'll be going to that with Matt here, will you?' He jerked his head and winked. 'Matt very kindly explained your domestic arrangements. Exotic, I must say.'

'I think you'll find your husband's setting you up,' said Matt, easily. 'I certainly explained the circumstances, but I don't recall mentioning anything exotic.'

'Oh, don't worry,' I said, hopefully equally easily. 'Adam delights in setting me up. It's his speciality. And he's my ex-husband, incidentally.'

'Only according to a bit of paper,' said Adam quickly.

'A legal and binding bit of paper,' I retorted. Then I remembered Flora. No fights. 'So,' I went on brightly, 'you're close by. That's nice.'

'Not as nice as this,' he said, looking around in grudging admiration. 'I can see why you didn't want to give it up, although I'm surprised the good doctor condones this arrangement. Cozzy was pretty staggered by that, weren't you, sweetheart?'

'Well, I jus' thought it was everso funny, that's all. I thought it was reelly reelly strange, like, all three of you sharin' together!' She giggled, and I nearly went down on my knees with joy. Oh, thank you, God, thank you. A truly terrible voice. *Terrible!* A high-pitched, Liverpudlian whine that would make even Cilla wince.

I cleared my throat. 'Well, Flora.' I turned to my daughter. 'If Daddy's taking you off for the night, perhaps you'd better go and pack a bag?'

'OK. Oh, Cozzy, d'you want to see my room?'

'Oh, yeah, I'd reelly love to. Thanks, Flora!'

And up she bounced from her chair in her tiny denim shorts and followed Flora inside. They looked like a couple of schoolgirls. It hurt me though, to see how well they got on. I could see how Flora might adore having this big girl around, as younger girls did. I breathed hard.

'Annie?'

I came to, and realised Adam was talking to me.

'I said, where's the good doctor? Isn't he gracing us with his presence this afternoon?'

'Oh, no, not for a while actually. He's got a problem at work,' I said, without thinking.

'Oh? Not another misdiagnosis, I hope?' He laughed and turned to Matt. 'David had an unfortunate episode last year when he told a mate of mine he had herpes, when in fact he had impetigo. Quite a lot of steroid cream was rubbed into delicate parts for no good reason and my mate, understandably, was not exactly chuffed.' He grinned.

I felt myself turning scarlet. 'Impetigo and herpes are actually incredibly similar, and the fact is he's simply got too much work on at the moment to be swanning off on holiday. Too many patients!'

At that moment, Cozzy reappeared on the terrace with Flora, their arms linked, giggling, although Flora hastily withdrew hers when she saw me. I glanced away, wishing she hadn't. Children are incapable of subtlety and Adam and Matt had both noticed.

'So,' I said crisply, getting to my feet. 'Packed a bag, Flora?'

'Yep.' She grinned and held up a floral rucksack. 'And, yes, before you ask, I've got my toothbrush, and everything else.'

She eyed me, letting me know that yes she'd got her eczema cream and the three teddies she had to sleep with, *and* the scrap of old blanket to wind round her finger. My heart lurched for her though, as she jauntily swung the bag on her back. She could just about manage her father's for the night—nowhere else—but even then, only with a huge dollop of nerve. And this was a strange house, I thought anxiously as I walked her to Adam's car. Where would she sleep?

Behind Flora's back, I exchanged a quick glance with Adam. It said it all. No, it's OK, I'll put her next door, and no, of course I won't go to bed until she's asleep. Relax. Of course he knew. He was her daddy. I thanked him with my eyes as we walked round to the front drive.

'Bye, Mum!' She hugged me breezily, and ran across the gravel to the black convertible Jeep.

'Cool. New car, Dad?'

'Well, hired actually. Just for the holiday.'

I stood there for a moment, in the empty drive, blinking in the cloud of dust Adam had left in his wake, then turned to go back to the house.

As I walked round the side to the terrace, I was surprised to see Matt still sitting there. He hadn't, as I'd expected him to, bolted back to his study. As he glanced across, he gave the first approximation of a friendly smile I'd seen since I'd met him, and let the Pimm's jug hover over my glass. He cocked an eyebrow enquiringly.

'Drink?'

I hesitated. What I really wanted to do was to go to my room, throw myself on the bed and howl, but actually, I could do with a drink too. I sat down. 'Thanks.'

He poured out the Pimm's and we were silent for a moment. The heat had gone out of the day now, and the sun was low in the sky.

'How's the thesis coming along?' I said.

He smiled. 'It's more of a book, actually. It began as a thesis, but has grown rather.'

'Oh, a book! That makes two of us. Have you got a publisher?'

'It's an academic work. It'll be published by the university press in Boston.'

'Ah. Called?' I enquired brightly even though I couldn't care less. My hand was shaking, I noticed as I picked up my glass. Just keep up the chitchat, Annie, get the booze down your neck, then go for a lie-down.

'It's called *Molly goes Mental*.'

I glanced up.

He smiled. 'Only kidding. It's essentially a collection of papers on the extensions of clinical psychosis in the paranoic mind.'

'Oh. Heavens.' I sank humbly into my Pimm's.

He smiled. 'And yours?'

'Oh, er, *Love All Over*, at the moment. But it's um, a working title.' I nodded. 'Might change it.'

'Ah. A romantic work.'

'Well, among other things,' I said haughtily. 'There's, you know, mystery and intrigue in there as well, a bit of pathos and, um, black comedy, that kind of thing.' I cast about wildly. 'Not an entirely intellectual work, like yours, of course, but hopefully not too, well . . .'

'Trashy?'

'God. Hope not. Probably will be though.'

'I doubt it.'

I squinted up at him through the sun's rays, thinking he was being uncommonly nice to me all of a sudden. It also occurred to me that, actually, he wasn't unattractive, in a last of the Navaho Indians sort of way, if only his hair weren't so long and wild-looking and he brushed it occasionally. Oh, and changed out of that horrid old fishing jumper.

'And is it autobiographical?'

'Hm? Oh, heavens no, I make it up.' I gave a hollow laugh. 'Golly, if I wrote something autobiographical it would be about me and Adam, and that would run into volumes.' I took a big slug of my drink.

'And is that the first time you've seen him with anyone? I mean'—he jerked his head eloquently—'with that floozie?'

I grinned, grateful for his support.

'Yes, it is as a matter of fact.' I sat up a bit and flicked back my hair. 'But . . . it's fine. I've done it now, and it feels OK. Another hurdle over.'

'And for him, too. I mean, he's seen you with David, presumably?'

'Oh, yes, a few times, but that's not the same.'

'Really? But you are getting married?'

I laughed. 'Yes, but I assure you that wouldn't impinge on Adam's consciousness one iota. He couldn't care less.'

'That's not what I observed.'

I glanced up sharply. 'What d'you mean?'

'Annie, in my experience, middle-aged men only flaunt their young girlfriends in front of their ex-wives for a reason. He didn't have to bring her along today, did he? Could have picked Flora up alone?'

'Yes, I suppose, but—'

'And all his derogatory remarks about your fiancé: he wouldn't bother to denigrate him unless he was jealous or unhappy, believe me.'

I stared at him intently. Suddenly I laughed. 'Nonsense. Adam doesn't give a fish's tit about me. Oh, he would prefer to live with his wife and child and he's sad about the break-up of all that, but that's the only reason he'd want me back. He fell out of love with me years ago.'

'People don't bother to hurt each other unless they care.'

I regarded him, slumped casually in his chair, narrowing his eyes thoughtfully into the sunset, cradling his glass in his hand.

'In your experience.'

He nodded. 'Sure.'

'As a psychiatrist.'

'Well, no, not just that. My experience of life too.'

'Ah, yes, life too. Which, according to my sister Clare, has not been so dissimilar to mine. A few casualties along the way? Like a wife and child?'

He smiled. 'Ah, yes, your sister. Very different to you, if I may say so. A very . . . direct lady. Forthright. In control.'

Well, he was spot on there, but—what, and I wasn't?

'And they're over here, I gather?' I went on doggedly. Yes, quite forth-rightly and in control, actually. 'Your family?'

'They are.' He conceded. 'In Cambridge.'

'Ah, so—'

'My wife and I are separated,' he interrupted shortly. 'As I'm sure Clare told you.' He regarded me steadily over the rim of his glass. 'And Tod, my son, lives with her. And with her boyfriend, an English psychi-atrist by the name of Walter Freedman. He's a doctor at the university hospital there.' With that he threw back his drink, draining the glass.

I watched him. Right. So that hurt.

'She . . . left you?' Awful, but I wanted to know.

He looked down at the ice left in the glass. Swirled it around. 'Walter Freedman and I had an exchange professorship going on. The idea was that I'd go to Cambridge for six months and work alongside him, see how his department ticked and how he ran it, which I duly did, and then he'd come to Harvard to work alongside me, which he duly did too. Except that—and this is where he deviated from the script—when he went home, he took my wife with him.'

'And she took your son with her?'

He glanced down. I realised he couldn't speak for a second. 'Yup. Took Tod too.' I saw his eyes penetrate his glass to the grass below. He recovered. 'He's not far off the age of your Flora, as a matter of fact— who's a great kid, incidentally.'

'Flora?' I beamed. Knew he wanted to change the subject, but he'd chosen a good one. 'Yes, she's getting there. Gradually. She's had some tough times, though. You know: me and Adam . . . the split. You can't always shield them . . .'

'Oh, sure,' he nodded. 'And neither should you. Not entirely.'

'But she's coming through. And David's helped enormously. It's just . . . she's so anxious.'

'Sure she is; I've watched her. She has some compulsive obsessive tendencies, but it's understandable.'

'What?' I looked at him sharply. 'Compulsive what?'

'Obsessive. But hey, so mildly. Nothing major. And most kids have it in some small way; they grow out of it. You know, the way kids have to eat their food in strict rotation: peas, carrots, chicken. Well, Flora won't pick up something she's dropped unless she counts to ten first. And she has to tap her spoon three times on her bowl before she starts her cereal.'

I stared. 'Yes, you're quite right. Both those things. And more.' God, he'd noticed all that, already.

'It's fine, relax. Trust me, she'll grow out of it.'

'Will she?' I panicked. 'Not necessarily. I mean—God, look at me. I still can't get into a strange bed at night unless it's pushed right up into the corner of the room with walls on two sides. We're freaks, both of us, Flora and me,' I concluded miserably.

'Quirky,' he said. 'Not freaks. Believe me, I've seen a lot of those, and that, lady, you ain't.'

'And horribly impulsive, too,' I went on, knocking back the Pimm's, 'which David just can't understand. He's so organised. So steady. And I just get carried away on a strange impulse. I *do* things, like—'

'Throw all your clothes away?'

I was startled. 'Exactly! Things like that, or that stupid car wash, or—'

'Your clothes are in the closet, incidentally.'

I blinked in astonishment. 'Which closet?'

'The one in the spare room. I found them in the garbage and took them out. Figured you might regret it later.'

'Oh!' I stared. 'Oh, well, thank you. I looked, actually, but assumed the dustmen had been and . . . Thank you.' I regarded him for a moment. 'I hate all these new clothes, actually,' I confessed, tugging viciously at my top. 'So conservative. I feel like a prison warder.'

'You look like one.'

I giggled. 'Thanks.'

The atmosphere had indeed lightened perceptibly. Whether it was the drink or just the fact that our jaw muscles were loosening with practice, I don't know, but when he refilled my glass I didn't try to stop him.

'So when are you going to see your son?' I asked, suddenly brave. 'I mean, is he coming down?'

He took a moment. 'He is,' he said carefully. 'In a couple of days.'

'Oh! Great. That'll be nice. Nice company for Flora. I mean—assuming you don't mind this arrangement,' I added hastily.

'I don't mind at all.'

'Good.' I smiled. 'So, is his mother bringing him?'

'Yes. His mother is bringing him to Bodmin. To his aunt's house.'

'He has an aunt in Bodmin?'

'She's my cousin, actually. Louise is married to an Englishman, a GP. Tom was a friend of your Gertrude's late husband. That's how we met Gertrude, two years back. My family and I were visiting Tom and Louise when we lived in Cambridge.'

'Oh, yes, of course. I remember Gertrude saying now.' I waited. No more was forthcoming. 'And . . . he's staying there in Bodmin? Or here?'

He hesitated. 'That's where Madeleine—his mother—thinks he's staying. For a week. Louise has three boys, you see. But I'm gonna pick him up from there as soon as she's dropped him off.'

I was confused. 'But why? Why doesn't he just come straight here?'

'Because he's not allowed to. I'm not allowed to see him.'

'Why on earth not?'

'Because we had to go to court over Tod. Madeleine got sole custody.'

'*Sole* custody? God, how awful! But presumably you can still see him occasionally? I mean—'

'No. I have no access.'

Suddenly the garden seemed very still. Very quiet. I went cold.

'But why? I mean . . . why won't they let you see him? At all?'

'Because Madeleine has a scar at the base of her throat. Which I allegedly inflicted on her when I attacked her with a piece of glass.'

I felt ill. 'You . . . attacked her?' I said, appalled.

'I said, allegedly. Of course I didn't. It happened the night Madeleine finally told me about her and Walter. We were back home, at our house in Marblehead. It was late, around eleven, and Tod was asleep upstairs. She was sitting opposite me on our deck overlooking the sea. We'd been having a brandy together after dinner, which was quite normal. There was nothing unusual about the evening at all.' He narrowed his eyes into the distance. Went on softly.

'I can see her now, perched on that calico couch, elbows on her knees, talking to me softly—calmly even—as she sat there in the moonlight, telling me her plans. Breaking my heart. I couldn't believe what I was hearing. That she loved another man, that she was planning to live with him in England. That she was leaving me. When she told me she was planning on taking my son too, I slammed my hand on the table between us and put my fist right through the glass. A great shard flew up and hit Madeleine in the neck. Cut her badly. There was blood everywhere, she was screaming and I was trying to help her when Tod came running downstairs. Madeleine was crying hysterically, pushing me off.'

'God. And he believed her?' I whispered.

He shrugged. 'His mom was covered in blood. At the time, I think he did, because that's what it looked like, but not now. Now he knows. But what Tod believes isn't the point. The courts are behind her, you see.'

'She went straight to court?'

'Oh, sure. To get an order. And when she got up there, in the witness box, her neck still bruised and bandaged, this tiny, petite figure with a quavering voice, telling the judge how I'd attacked her . . . Oh, boy, there wasn't a dry eye in the house. She gave an Oscar-winning performance. And she had to. She had to fight dirty like that, because she knew she was the adulteress. She was the one leaving, going to England, taking her son out of school, and she also had a full-time job lined up, whereas I, on sabbatical from Harvard and writing this book, could quite easily have looked after Tod. Kept his life on track. The cards were stacked against her and she had to use every trick in the book to get that judge alongside her. And boy, did she.'

'When did all this happen?'

'Over a year ago.'

'And you haven't seen him since?'

'Haven't seen him since. And let me tell you, Annie, you think you've got it tough sending Flora off with Adam and that bit of skirt every couple of weeks, but Jeez, I look at you guys, shuttling that child between you, exchanging glances to ensure she'll sleep well at night and not be frightened in the dark, and I think: Hey. That's civilised.'

I swallowed. There was a silence.

'So, Madeleine has no idea? That Tod's coming here, to this house?'

'None at all.'

'But Tod does?'

'Oh, sure. We email regularly.'

I nodded, getting the picture. 'He wants to see you.'

He looked stunned. 'Sure he wants to see me, we miss each other like—' He stopped. 'Listen, Annie, he's my son. I haven't seen him in over a year. And I've done nothing wrong. I've done nothing, other than look after him all his life, and his mother. Love them, protect them.'

He looked very pale. Suddenly I realised what the tough mask was all about. What a vulnerable core he was protecting by distancing himself. What the habitual darkness in his face, which only occasionally lifted, was hiding. It was pain. A pain that wouldn't go away, and was so deep-rooted it wouldn't abate for a moment, either. He'd lost his wife, and then his child, in one fell swoop. He was watching me.

'Tod's coming here on Sunday, Annie. But that's not on general release. No one else knows. Aside from Tom and Louise, of course. It's a secret.' His blue eyes regarded me intently. 'And I need to know that you can keep it that way.'

The following morning I was woken by a rousing knocking on my bedroom door and Matt's voice shouting, 'David's on the phone for you downstairs.'

I unstuck my eyelids and peered around. Morning? Surely not. I'd only just gone to sleep, and—David? So early? I flung back the covers and stumbled out of bed like some rough beast, fumbling my way along the gallery, tottering unsteadily downstairs eyes half-closed.

'Hello?' I mumbled as I picked up the receiver.

'Morning, darling. Another beautiful day!'

Golly, he sounded chipper, but then he liked mornings. 'Yes, isn't it.' I yawned. 'Where are you?'

'At work, have been for ages, but I just thought I'd ring and see if you'd got any news.'

I scratched my leg. Frowned. 'News?'

'Yes, you know!'

I concentrated like mad. 'Do I?'

'Well, come on, darling, you're late, aren't you?'

I blinked. Christ. Was I? Where was I supposed to be? 'Late for what?' Heavens, I wasn't even dressed.

'Your period's late, silly! Wasn't it due yesterday?'

'Oh!' Blimey, was it? I hadn't the faintest idea. 'Oh, er, yes. Probably. You may be right.'

'I know I'm right, because yesterday was precisely fourteen days since ovulation, which we carefully pinpointed with a rather hot little baby-making session, if you recall.'

'Oh. Yes. Right.'

'So you haven't started?'

'Um, no. Not to my knowledge.'

He laughed. 'Well, darling, you are fairly clueless but I think even you'd know that. How d'you feel?'

'Fine, thanks.' I yawned.

'How about your breasts?'

'Sorry?'

'Are your breasts sore?'

'Um, I don't think so, David.'

'Well, check,' he said impatiently. 'It's always a good sign.'

A good sign. Right. I had a quick feel. 'Er, bit sore, yes.'

'Good. Particularly the nipples?'

I felt again. 'Yes, very.' I could smell bacon. I turned towards the yummy smell, obediently fiddling with my other nipple, but realising, as I did, that Matt's study door was open and he was at his desk, watching me in the mirror above it. My hand flew from my breast in horror.

'Mucus?'

'David, stop it!' I hissed, hurriedly turning my back on Matt. 'I am not giving myself a gynaecological examination at this hour of the morning on the telephone!' God, what must he think? That I was feeling myself up as I chatted to my boyfriend? I went hot with shame.

'You women never cease to amaze me,' sighed David. 'You don't even know how your own bodies operate throughout a monthly cycle. Darling, there are signs of menstruation and signs of impending pregnancy. They are similar, but different, and you should be on the lookout for both.'

'Right. Yes, I'll . . . be very alert,' I flustered. 'From now on. Only please, David, I've just woken up. What time is it?'

'Nine thirty. If you've just woken up you've had a jolly good lie-in.'

Lie-in? I called eleven o'clock a lie-in, and what was he so chirpy about? 'How are you, David?' I asked. 'No more news of Mr O'Connell?'

'Not a word,' he said happily. 'It's all blown over rather satisfactorily, actually. I realise now I was worrying unnecessarily. After all, these things do happen, in medicine.'

'Of course they do,' I said warmly. 'Except they don't usually happen to you because you're such a good doctor!'

'Well, thank you, my darling, for that vote of confidence, and on that note, I really must get back to my administerings. I've got a patient waiting in reception.'

'OK, but I'll see you next weekend?'

'Definitely at the weekend. I'll drive down on Friday.'

'Good,' I beamed.

'And fingers crossed.'

'Sorry?'

'About . . . you know!'

'Oh! Oh, yes, definitely. Fingers crossed.'

I put the receiver down and sat gazing distractedly into the floodlit garden. Narrowing my eyes at the silvery-blue water that glistened through a gap in the trees, I thought how stupid I'd been to have my guts wrenched by Adam last night. So idiotic to care, when I had the lovely David. Suddenly I wished we could hurry this wedding along. Everything would be so much simpler when we were finally Dr and Mrs Palmer. I smiled. That had a lovely ring about it, didn't it?

And, actually, it wasn't that far off, now. The wedding. Only six weeks to go, and we'd be bowling back down the aisle in that dear little church in Cadogan Street, grinning from ear to ear at all our delighted friends in their smart hats, cameras flashing, and then off to Claridge's, David had booked a private room, even though I'd favoured something a little less grand like a knees-up in the Nag's Head. I knew someone who would have enjoyed that.

On an impulse, my hand strayed back to the receiver and I dialled a familiar number. I was aware, as it rang, that the study door was firmly shut now. Too much frivolous chitchat going on, no doubt.

'Hello?' A familiar voice echoed far away.

'Mum? It's me!'

'I know that, love, I was hopin' you'd call. Clare said you were down.'

'How are you, Mum?' I asked anxiously.

'I'm fine, Annie love, an' you? Enjoyin' the sea air? And Flora?'

'Oh, Mum, it's so lovely here,' I gushed. 'You'd adore it. Right by the sea and so tranquil and pretty; I wish you could see it. In fact, why don't you? Take a few days away and come and stay with me and Flora?'

I glanced nervously at Matt's door wondering how he'd take to this invasion, but my mother chuckled predictably.

'What, who would feed the ducks and hens? Don't be daft, love. No, I'll stay put, thank you.'

Mum had sold most of the livestock when Dad had died and she rented the fields out to a neighbouring farmer, but she'd kept the poultry.

'Well, in that case I'll come and see you,' I said decisively. 'Probably next week, because we're here for ages. But, Mum, I was really ringing about the wedding.'

'Oh, yes?'

'We've booked a table at Claridge's,' I said happily. 'And the church is booked in Knightsbridge, so everything's organised!'

'Claridge's, eh?'

'Oh, and it's going to be in the evening. There'll be forty-two people there, and everyone will change into black tie—you can get a new dress!'

'Black tie. And you're right, I would need a new dress.' She sounded worried. 'Oh, I don't know, love. You young are much more used to all that razzmatazz. And it will be all young, aside from me.'

My heart lurched. 'No! Gertrude will be there, too.'

She chuckled. 'Gertrude, who was born and bred in Knightsbridge. She'll be right at home.'

My mouth dried. 'But you will come? You will, won't you, Mum?'

'Now, don't you fret, Annie, I'll think on it, all right? Leastways, you'll have a lovely party. Forty-two in black tie at Claridge's, eh? Your dad would've been right proud, love.'

'Yes,' I said. 'Yes, he would.'

I said goodbye and, chewing my thumbnail again, moved on upstairs. I reached my room and began mechanically to wash my face and get changed. I had a feeling Mum would find some reason not to come. And not because she didn't want to, but because somehow she felt she might let me down. And I thought of her in Claridge's, in her good suit that she'd had for ever. Thought of her sitting at a long table covered in white linen and silver, surrounded by braying young things, gloves tightly clasped in her lap, nervous, uncomfortable and I thought: How stupid of me. *Stupid!*

I trudged gloomily downstairs, drank a cup of tea and ate a bacon sandwich, then set off down the garden to the summerhouse. Angrily I kicked open the green door. I sat down and flicked on my computer.

Stared at the screen. Damn. And now it was all arranged. All organised. And I so badly wanted her to come! My eyes burned. I gulped down tears and scanned the screen in a desultory manner. Blinked hard and made myself reread yesterday's offering. Somehow, in my present mood, the prose didn't seem quite so sparkling.

Henry had finally slunk home smelling like Harrods' perfumery, and Lucinda, after a sleepless night, had risen to find that the nanny had taken the children to school, Henry had gone to work, and she, with a throbbing head, had one hell of a day ahead of her. A lunch date with her best friend in Harvey Nichols followed by a spot of shopping.

Talitha was late as usual. Still ensconced with her personal trainer, no doubt, thought Lucinda as she perched her pert little Versace behind on the banquette seating. Her hand trembled slightly as she picked up the menu. She was tempted to go mad and have a spritzer instead of her usual mineral water, she felt so low.

'Are you ready to order, madam?' said a badly disguised northern voice at her elbow. As she turned, she was surprised to find herself looking into the steady hazel gaze of one of her employees. It was Terence, her dog-walker-cum-window-box-gardener.

'Terence!' She was startled. 'What on earth are you doing here?'

'Mrs De Villiers! Eh oop! Ay, well I'm doin' a bit of moonlightin', like, as a waiter. But now the game's oop and I expect you'd like me to go. Leave yer employ.' He cast his eyes down morosely.

Lucinda looked up at his anxious young face. So appealing and open, and those heavenly long lashes brushing his cheek. Her gaze travelled over his muscular legs to his tight little backside, protruding provocatively, like a Masai warrior's, from the long white apron wrapped round his washboard middle. There was something about a man in an apron. Lucinda's eyes widened.

'Now why would I want you to do that, Terence?' she murmured huskily.

'Well, I thought, you know, you'd be angry, like. Mr De Villiers would be, I know. 'E'd 'ave me sacked!'

'Mr De Villiers isn't here,' she murmured. A girlish blush spread over her face as, impulsively, she reached out her hand and caught his rough brown one. 'Don't worry, Terence,' she breathed. 'Your secret is safe with me. What you do in your own time is your own affair. Your affair . . . and mine.'

With a deep sigh, I leaned back in my chair while my eyes scanned the screen again. At the end, I smiled. Filled my lungs. At last. Perfect. Here we go.

Chapter Four

THAT EVENING, to my surprise, I found myself almost looking forward to Clare's barbecue. It was one of the compulsory rituals of a Rock summer, and whenever I'd rather glibly snatched a few days at my sister's seaside house in the past, sometimes with Adam, sometimes just me and Flora, I'd always felt that, aside from Clare, who ran about beaming madly and organising everyone, there was a distinct air of forced jollity about the whole event. This evening, however, as I made my way across the golf course, following the sandy path as it wound its way down the sand dunes to the beach at the foot of Brea Hill, I decided that a bit of jollity would do nicely thank you, forced or otherwise.

Now, as I stood at the very top of the dunes with the wind in my hair, my rug under one arm, cooler bag full of mixed salad and garlic bread under the other, I gazed down at the scene below. It comforted me to see that on the stretch of pale sand, the evening was running true to form. About a dozen or so adults stood around in little clutches, chatting, laughing, and holding plastic champagne glasses. Most of them I knew: the Fields, the Stewart-Coopers, the Todds, the Elliotts, the Frasers. Masses of children frolicked around; the younger ones making sandcastles and damming moats, while the older ones sloped off to chat in little huddles, hunkering down in the dunes where I walked now. I nearly fell over one little clutch, and recognised Theo Todd's boys from his first marriage, who must be fourteen or fifteen by now, giggling with two blonde girls in a bunker.

I tactfully averted my gaze and walked on. I spotted Clare instantly and was surprised. She usually looked like a lifeguard at this event, uncompromising in navy shorts and a white T-shirt. This evening, however, she was looking extraordinary in a swirling sarong skirt and a low-cut black bikini top. The sun was going down and it was getting quite chilly, added to which she was a heavily breasted woman.

As she tasked a couple of the men off to light a bonfire—always crucial to the ambience—I saw that Theo Todd was one of them: tall and greying in a biscuit linen jacket with a bright blue shirt, but carrying a paunch before him these days, and redder of face—a drinker. His voice boomed out as Clare gave him the matches, waving her arms extravagantly as she explained which way the wind was coming from, and giving him ample opportunity to view her cleavage.

Quite apart from the main group, in a little huddle of dark baggy jumpers, like Albanian refugees, sat Rosie, Dan and Michael, heads down in a powwow as they tried to light a cigarette between them. I grinned and raised my arm, and Rosie looked up and waved back. I kicked off my shoes and made my way towards them, the sand cold between my bare toes, and dumped down my bag, breathless.

'God, you'll get shot sitting here, you lot. Don't you know the rules? House guests must pass round drinks and nibbles, and, Michael, I'm surprised at you. Barbecue duty, surely?'

'I know, I know,' he muttered, getting wearily to his feet and brushing sand off his legs.

At that moment Clare turned. 'Michael!'

'*Arrivederci*, my friends,' he murmured. Then: 'Coming, my darling!' as Clare frantically beckoned him over.

I sat down beside Dan, who was huddled with his back to the wind, arms round his knees.

'How's it going, Dan?' I grinned sideways at him as I handed him a Pils from my bag.

'Well, obviously, it's going swimmingly,' he said, taking the beer gratefully. 'Simply splendid of your sister to invite us chickens down, and the kids are having a ball, but'—he looked around despairingly—'Jesus Christ!' He lowered his voice. 'It's this wretched obsession with sand! We've been on this sodding beach all day, battered and windswept, shivering and wet, and lo! Eight o'clock at night, and here we are again. *More* bloody beach, and more bloody beach rounders, no doubt.'

'The children love it,' I soothed. 'The barbecue, the volleyball, being up late with their parents, all of that.' I looked around for Flora. Not here yet, but Adam had said he'd bring her, and he'd know where.

'Yes, but I'm not a child!' he said petulantly. He ran his hand despairingly through his mop of dark, shaggy hair. 'Anyway, thanks for smuggling in the beer, Annie. We're only allowed warm pink fizz in Stalag Faraday, you know.' He pulled gratefully on his Pils. 'I put a six-pack in Clare's cooler bag this evening, and she took it straight out again, saying crisply, "It's not really that sort of a party, Dan," and giving me a look that said who the devil was I to make catering suggestions anyway? I am, after all, only Dan, Dan, the Redundant Man, not a financial adviser or a theatrical impresario like that tosser over there.' He nodded across to where Clare was flirting wildly with Theo over the cricket stumps.

'What is she wearing?' muttered Rosie in my ear, looking at Clare. 'And is it all for him?'

I glanced over as Clare bent forward unnecessarily low to hold a cricket stump as Theo obligingly banged it in.

''Fraid so,' I sighed, as Theo boggled into her cleavage. 'And his wife, of course, couldn't care less. Turns a blind eye. Seen it all before.'

'Which one?'

'Helena. Short blonde hair, pink linen shirt.' I nodded over at an elegant but pinched-looking girl, struggling with a recalcitrant toddler.

'Quite young,' remarked Rosie.

'Second marriage. Fifteen years younger than him, and jaded already.'

'Come on, everyone!' Clare called sharply, cupping her hands round her mouth like a loudhailer. 'Let's get things under way! Michael and I have picked teams, so everyone should know which side they're on. Now, we'll bat first, so my team—behind me. Dan, come on, you're on Michael's side, so you're fielding. First base!'

'First fucking base *again*!' Dan fumed, savagely biting his beer can.

'Come on, darling,' muttered Rosie. 'Keep the peace. You'll enjoy it.'

'Oh, I'd adore it, if only I hadn't been first base five times today already.'

Nevertheless, he trudged off, hands thrust deep in pockets, tattered jeans trailing in the sand.

'Doesn't exactly look the part, does he?' said Rosie fondly. 'Among all these Boden types. You're looking more relaxed today, incidentally,' she said, eyeing my frayed old Monsoon shirt approvingly. 'You looked terrible yesterday.'

'Thanks,' I grinned. 'That was me trying to smarten up my act. D'you think I can get out of this game by dint of the fact that I arrived late? I don't think I'm on a team, and I've just come on, too. Doesn't that incapacitate me?'

'Course it does. Always used to at school, and anyway, you can be deep square leg with me.' She got up and hauled me to my feet. 'We might stand, though, just to show willing. Over here, Clare!' She grinned and did a mock catch to show she was prepared. Clare nodded approvingly and, when she turned away, Rosie lit a fag.

'Might I join you ladies? Out in midfield?' Theo was suddenly upon us, appearing from nowhere. His hair was greyer than I remembered. Longer too. He kissed my cheek, unnecessarily close to the mouth.

'I must say, Annie, you're looking quite lovely this evening,' he purred. 'And if I'm not very much mistaken this is Rosie Howard, who I distinctly remember trying to chat up at a dinner party at the Osbornes' once, to no avail.' He twinkled lecherously at her. 'And I thought I was being charming and amusing!'

Rosie smiled sweetly back. 'Are you sure you weren't being drunk and outrageous?— Ooh, I say, good shot, Clare!'

We watched in awe, as Clare sent the ball sailing way up to the sky and into the dunes. Roared on by the crowd of excited kids behind her, she set off for first base.

'Drop the bat, drop the bat!' they all yelled, as she tore past Dan, and as, unbeknown to her, one of her pendulous white breasts dropped out of her bikini top.

'I've dropped it!' she yelled, throwing down the bat.

'Hasn't she just,' murmured Theo as she pounded along the sand.

'Clare! Darling!' Michael's hands went up in horror as he tried vainly at last base to intercept her.

'Oh, no, you don't!' she cried, shoving him roughly aside. 'I'm going for a second!'

'By golly, she is too,' muttered Theo excitedly in my ear. 'Look, the other one's come out!'

Sure enough, Clare was streaking now, bare-chested like a bust on a galleon's prow, as she set off on a lap of honour, tits swinging joyously, impervious to her husband's and children's horrified faces.

'Clare!' Rosie and I shouted, frantically clutching our chests.

'Can't stop me!' she chortled, streaming past us.

'Why is Auntie Clare running around with no clothes on?' said an awestruck voice in my ear as Michael finally, with a valiant lunge, rugby-tackled his wife to the ground at last base with a mighty 'Ooomph!' I turned to see Flora wide-eyed behind me.

'This isn't one of those embarrassing grown-up parties where you all chuck your car keys in the sand, is it?' she said in disgust.

'Sadly not,' murmured Theo. 'Although I must say, I'd snap up the ones to your auntie's Volvo any day. Magnificent,' he purred.

I looked anxiously back at Clare, who, puce in the face with horror, was smartly swatting away Michael's attempts to restore her modesty and frantically pulling her top up herself.

'Thank you, Michael. I *can* manage.'

'I wonder if I can be of any assistance?' Theo mused quietly. 'Smooth ruffled feathers and all that?'

He reached into the cool box at his feet and pulled out a couple of glasses which he dexterously filled with champagne. 'Excuse me, ladies.'

Rosie giggled as Theo sauntered over with the bottle under his arm, just as Michael was being shooed away like a dirty fly.

'Looks like she's unwittingly played her trump card,' she observed. 'Snared her prey in one fell swoop and—oh God, look!' she said in awe. 'Now she's going to get pissed!'

We watched as Clare took the glass and, uncharacteristically, knocked it back in one. Theo proffered another and, pink with humiliation, but not objecting to the arm he put round her shoulders, she allowed herself to be led away to be commiserated with on the rocks.

The rounders match continued; in a less professional manner without Clare at the helm, perhaps, but with more enjoyment from the kids, who, after all, it was supposed to be in aid of. Flora ran off happily to join in with her cousins and other friends she hadn't seen since last summer, and I watched her go, pleased.

Without the gym mistress's beady eye upon us, Rosie and I sank down in the sand again, leaning back on our elbows, legs stretched out before us, happily dissecting the rest of the assembled party, analysing marriages, clothes, highlights—before I stopped suddenly. At first I'd assumed Adam had just dropped Flora and gone, but then I saw him over by the fire, chatting amiably to Dan and snapping open a can of beer. He was alone. Cozzy wasn't with him, and for that I was grateful. Adam and Dan rocked with laughter at something one of them had said, clearly delighted to see each other again.

'I'm afraid Dan's got no sense of propriety,' muttered Rosie uncomfortably. 'He doesn't know he's supposed to knee him in the balls.'

I smiled. 'I wouldn't expect Dan to take sides. They were always friends. Why should they stop now?'

It was lovely to see Adam here, actually; greeting other fathers who wandered up, men he'd known for years and whom he hadn't seen for a while, and who, I noticed, all drifted up to say hello, while the women kept their distance, out of loyalty to me, perhaps.

More than anything though, I saw the pleasure on Flora's face. It brought a lump to my throat. Yes, both my parents, her expression seemed to say, as she chatted, glowingly, to a friend she hadn't seen for ages. Mum's over there, and that's my dad. They get along fine.

The evening sailed on into a beautiful sunset. The barbecue was loaded up with steaks, chops and sausages. Children were fed first, a few younger ones tired, hugging blankets and sucking thumbs, and being shepherded onto rugs to eat and spill their orange squash. I moved around, reacquainting myself with people I hadn't seen for ages, drinking and laughing, and it felt good, with the gunmetal sea stretching out like a ripple of silk before us, the gulls swooping and calling, to be among friends and family.

Through my sozzled haze, I was dimly aware that Flora had joined Theo's boys and another couple of older girls for an illicit swig of beer in the dunes. I hoped it wasn't more than that. I swung round anxiously to see, and caught Adam's eye over the fire. In one eloquent exchange I knew that he had his eye on her. Extraordinary, that when it came to Flora, he could be so responsible. I leaned back in the cold sand with a sigh, and gazed up at the dark vault of the heavens above. I listened to the sea, beating its endless rhythm against the shore as it had since time immemorial, and wished that life could always be this simple.

The following morning, Flora and I sat side by side on the warm back step that led from the kitchen to the garden, pulling at croissants and sharing a pot of tea. Aside from the house martins and the swallows swooping low over feathery whirls of grass, all was still and quiet. In fact, it took me a moment to realise we had the place to ourselves.

'He's not here,' I observed, peering cautiously round into the study window, which protruded to the left of us in a wide bay. 'He's usually in there, tapping away by now. Must have gone for a walk. It is a lovely morning. Probably down on the beach.'

A silence ensued as we gazed into the hazy horizon.

'Mum?'

'Hm?'

She drew up her bare knees under the T-shirt she slept in. I knew by her tone it was something heavy.

'I had a chat with Dad last night.'

'Oh, yes?' I said lightly.

'Yeah. Well, in fact, he had a chat with me. He'd had a row with Cozzy. That's why she didn't come last night, and when he drove me to the beach, he was just, well, talking about what might have been if he hadn't . . . you know. Messed up.'

'At least he sees it as *his* mess,' I commented.

'Oh, he does,' she said eagerly. 'He knows he was at fault and irre-sponsible, and—and something about a terrible betrayal of trust, but— well, what he did say was that you and him got married awfully young. And that he hadn't exactly played the field.'

'What are you saying, Flora?' I said evenly.

'Well, just that I think he—you know—regrets it. Regrets what a bish he made of it, and really wishes it was different.'

'Really.' My hands were tightly clasped. 'And what about Cozzy?'

'Oh, I don't think he's ever really been serious about Cozzy. I mean, she's fun and nice and pretty, but, you know, she's very young.'

I nodded. My throat felt tight.

'Well, it's just that . . . I think if you played your cards right, I think Dad would come back for good. He really misses you, Mum. Both of us.'

I turned to look at her for the first time. Her eyes were wide and earnest. 'Flora, we had all this a year ago, remember? Remember he rang? Begged us to have him back, and you shook your head and we both agreed?'

'I know, but it was different then. You were so low. So sad.'

'Pathetic?'

'No, but it wouldn't have been right. But now you're much more, like, up. Together. You could, like, call the shots more.'

I marvelled at my adolescent daughter's knowledge of relationship games. From whence did it spring? *EastEnders*, or *Northanger Abbey*?

'Flora,' I boggled, 'one small point. I'm marrying David. Where exactly is this conversation going?'

'Nowhere. I'm just telling you, that's all, before you do get married. I mean . . . better I tell you before than after, surely?'

I struggled. 'But . . . but you like David?'

'Yes, of course I like David! But I'm not the one marrying him, am I?'

She turned angry, tear-filled eyes on me, and I gazed back, digesting this non sequitur, as a car tore briskly up the gravel drive beside us. I gulped. Turned to look.

'He's back,' I muttered. 'It's Matt. Must have been shopping.'

Flora frantically blinked back her tears. 'There's someone with him.'

'Oh,' I breathed, staring. 'I forgot. He's been to pick up his son.'

We watched as a small, fair-haired boy in glasses got out of the passenger door, pulling a huge backpack after him.

'His son!' echoed Flora in disbelief.

'Yes, I forgot to tell you,' I said hurriedly. 'His son's staying for a week. He lives over here with his mother. He's about your age, I think.'

'Oh, terrific!' she stormed. 'That's all I bloody need. Some arrogant gum-chewing Yank hanging around for my entire summer holiday—thanks, Mum!' And with a strangled sob, no doubt due to a combination of factors, she got up off the step and fled back into the house.

My heart still beating fast, I stood up to greet them. What had Adam been saying? And why was he fostering false hope in her, for something he had no intention of following through?

I swallowed hard as they came towards me, trying to forget my inner turmoil and to smile kindly at the boy, whose eyes didn't leave the grass. He was small for his age, and skinny, wearing jeans and a blue T-shirt.

'Tod, this is Annie,' said Matt. 'And if you're quick, you'll catch the back of Flora, just pounding up the stairs, there.'

'Tired and bolshie,' I said apologetically to him, holding my hand out to Tod. 'Hi, Tod, good to see you.'

'Hi,' he muttered, raising huge blue eyes for a second from the grass.

'I'm going to show Tod his room, and then take him round the place.'

'Good idea,' I agreed, my eyes glued, now that I'd greeted the boy, to Matt. I couldn't get over the change. He was wearing a cornflower-blue shirt I'd never seen before, and his hair had been washed and cut. Gone were the dark locks straggling round his brow, and his eyes, as he looked down at Tod, had lost their haunted look. The effect was staggering.

I watched them go, then wandered down to the summerhouse to turn my attention to Lucinda De Villiers.

Actually, her needs were quite pressing. Having spent an hour in here last night after the barbecue, I'd manoeuvred Lucinda into a tantalising position in her garden shed. Terence was expected at any moment, to prick out the dahlias, and she was draped seductively against the potting bench, wearing only the skimpiest of Joseph shirt dresses.

I rested my chin in my hands, and gazed out of the window. When Flora went past a few minutes later, en route to the beach, I raised my hand, but she stalked haughtily on. I sighed. Then, raising my hands for all the world like a weary concert pianist forced to embark on yet another ground-breaking symphony, tapped away.

Lucinda paced the tiny shed, wishing she'd thought to install a bigger, more sumptuous one, with a sofabed perhaps. Why were these structures so rudimentary? She'd have to lure Terence into the comfort of the house—thank God it was Consuela's day off—but her bedroom was so overlooked. That sinister artist chappie, Justin Reynolds, who lived at the back, was bound to be painting in his studio again. It would have to be the spare room at the front. She tapped her foot impatiently. If only Terence would hurry up! Her new thong was killing her. Suddenly she heard his masculine tread echoing across the York stones. The door handle turned.

'Mrs De Villiers! By 'eck, what are you doin' 'ere!'

'I was . . . looking for a reference book, for plants,' she murmured, letting her manicured nails linger over a pile of Suttons Seeds catalogues. 'Thought we might have some of that topiaried box in pots on the terrace.'

'Oh, aye. Golden balls?'

Lucinda blinked. Golly. Quite forward.

'Why not?' she purred. 'And maybe some pointy dwarf conifers as well?' She edged closer, letting her Poison waft towards him.

'Could do, but the common dwarf's only semi-erect. You might want summat more upright.'

Lucinda caught her breath. 'Yes!' she breathed. 'Yes, definitely. Don't want anything . . . semi . . . about it.'

'Aye, well, you'll be looking at summat more vigorous then. I've got one in mind that shoots up a treat. It's a big 'un.'

'Splendid,' she gasped wantonly, and wondered how on earth she was going to lure him housewards, away from these dirty, uncomfortable surroundings . . .

I glanced up thoughtfully and gazed out of the window to the seascape beyond. Beside me was a pile of poetry books, and, on top, my favourite, Emily Dickinson's. I reread a classic for the thousandth time, wishing, as ever, I could write like that, when something made me glance up. Tod was passing by my window, hands deep in his pockets, his thin shoulders hunched, making for the beach.

I read a bit more, choosing her later poems, which usually inspired me to mediocre things, but, after a while, could resist it no longer. I put the book down, turned off my computer, and crept out, shutting the door softly behind me. I picked my way carefully down the steep winding path until I came to a clearing.

I crouched down, shaded my eyes, and peered. There was Flora, standing on a rock at the water's edge, with . . . yes, Tod beside her. I sat down quietly, careful not to snap any twigs. They were plunging their hands into rock pools searching for smooth stones, then skimming them across the estuary. I watched as one jumped three—four times. There didn't appear to be much chat going on, but quite a lot of shrugging and toe-scuffing, the adolescent equivalent of communication. Good. That was a start. Mindful of being seen I stretched out my legs and leaned back in the soft emerald ground cover. I watched a while longer, then held my face up to the sky. I had shut my eyes, and was savouring the dappled sun on my face, when suddenly I heard a rustle behind me. I sat up and swung round, just as Matt, silent as a cat, crouched beside me.

'Oh! You startled me!'

'Shh . . .' He put a finger to his lips. 'Seems we had the same idea. Indulging in a spot of spying?'

I flushed. 'Well, I wasn't spying exactly, but I just thought I'd see . . . you know . . .' I gestured vaguely beachwards.

'Whether or not left to their own devices they could perform the human equivalent of canine bottom-sniffing?'

I smiled. 'Something like that.'

He peered through the trees. 'They appear to have achieved it. Gratifying to know they've acquired a few social skills along the way.'

We watched as, tiring of their stone-skimming, they squatted down together on a rock. They appeared to be intent on drawing some sort of hieroglyphics on it, with sharp stones.

'Odd age,' I reflected. 'This stage. Neither a child, nor an adult.'

'True,' he muttered back. 'Old enough to know what you want, but not old enough to make any choices.'

I glanced across at his moody profile; his eyes fixed on the beach and wondered what he meant by that? He caught me looking.

'Just the one?' he murmured.

'Sorry?'

'I can't help noticing Flora hasn't got any siblings.'

'Oh. Oh, no. Well, I had her very young, when I was only twenty-three. And it was such a struggle, we didn't have any money, so we thought we'd wait a bit. Have a couple later on, when we were more sol-vent. Of course we never *were* solvent, but when we tried again later, I lost them. Lost three, actually.' I swallowed.

'Miscarriages?'

'Yep. And the last one'—I sat up and hugged my knees hard—'well, it was at twenty-two weeks. We . . . named him. And I had to deliver him. Then bury him.' I breathed hard, remembering. Adam and I, in a heap, sobbing on the bed in the ward with the curtain closed around us.

'I couldn't face going through it all again after that. Neither could Adam.' I shook my head.

'But . . . I thought you were going to try again? Didn't you say—'

'Oh, yes, with David.' I turned to him. Smiled. 'But that's different. David says obstetrics has come on leaps and bounds since then, and there's all sorts of things we can do to ensure I hang on to them. He's very clued-up of course, being a doctor. Knows all the right people.'

'Of course.'

'Emotionally he's very different from Adam. Adam and I both went to pieces. Like a couple of kids. We couldn't even help each other.'

'Well . . . naturally.'

'Yes, but David's much more of a rock. So much more stable. Which is what I badly need. And he's much more pragmatic too. He says if it doesn't work, we don't collapse in a heap, we just try again.'

'You try again.'

I glanced at him. 'Hm?'

'Nothing.'

He pulled a beech leaf from a low branch on a sapling beside us and began shredding off the green with his thumb and fingernails, revealing a skeleton. I laughed.

'He seems like a nice guy,' he said, at length.

I frowned. 'You haven't met him, have you?'

'No, I meant Adam.'

I gave a hollow laugh. 'Oh, Adam. Yes, men always like him.' I shifted my bottom on the hard ground. I didn't want to talk about Adam. Didn't want to think about him, after what Flora had said.

'And you?' I said quickly. 'Only one, yourself?' I shaded my eyes with my hand. Don't come the personal questions with me, mister, without getting one winging straight back in return.

'Yes,' he agreed, 'just the one. Madeleine . . . well, she found Tod quite a handful. And he was a tricky baby, up at night for years.' He spread his hands. 'And, of course, as things have turned out . . .'

'Quite,' I agreed softly.

We gazed down at the beach below, where Tod and Flora had rolled up their jeans and were wading in the shallows, trying to catch crabs with their bare hands. Tod dropped a rock into the water causing a huge splash and making Flora shriek as the water sloshed up at her, whereupon an even louder shriek went up behind us.

Matt and I swung round, then looked down at the water again to check it hadn't echoed up from there, but the children had heard it too, and had turned, shading their eyes and gazing up at us.

'Annie!'

I stood up and turned round.

'Annie!'

This time, as my name rang out, I saw Clare, plunging through the trees into deep shade, looking wildly about for me, then spotting me. Ignoring the winding path, she came crashing straight from the top, through the brambles and branches, towards me. Her face was scratched and her hair all over the place. She was covered in mud, but still in the ridiculous clothes she'd been wearing the night before.

'Clare!' My hand shot to my mouth, appalled.

'Oh, Annie, thank God! Thank heavens I've found you, something terrible's happened.' She clutched my wrist, trembling, her voice cracking.

My heart stopped and I went cold. 'What!'

Her eyes were huge in her grubby face, and they gazed out at me, anguished. She swallowed hard.

'I think I've slept with Theo Todd!' she gasped.

I stared at her, horrified. 'Think? What d'you mean, *think*?'

She collapsed on my arm. 'Oh, Annie, it's awful,' she sobbed, tears streaming down her cheeks. 'I got so horribly drunk, and you know me, I've never been drunk, never!'

It was true, she hadn't. Hardly touched a drop.

'And . . . and Theo, well, he led me away, up the dunes, and I was so excited. It was so exactly what I'd fantasised about for ages, and he kept pouring me drinks—he had a bottle of vodka and some orange juice— and the thing was, we could see you all, sitting by the fire, happy and singing, and the children were fine and no one seemed to have missed us, so we crept even further away, giggling and holding hands like a couple of teenagers, right up onto the golf course. And it was so dark and thrilling and—oh, I felt such a rush, Annie! We found this bunker—'

'A bunker!'

'Yes, and we lay down in it . . . collapsed into it . . . and then he was all over me. His hands were everywhere, and—'

'Er, Clare?' I jerked my head, at Matt, but she was unstoppable.

'And I remember him taking off my bra top—I still had this ghastly bikini on—and I kept giggling and thinking it was terribly thrilling and romantic, and he had his face buried in my bosoms going "brrrmm-mmm"?'—she vibrated her lips—'like that, and and—'

'I'm out of here,' muttered Matt, turning away.

'And there we were lying in this bunker,' she gasped, 'and rolling around and kissing and, oh God, I don't remember if he took his trousers off, and I don't know what happened to my sarong, but it's all torn and . . . I just don't know!' she wailed, wringing her hands.

'Of course you'd remember if you *slept* with a man, for crying out loud,' I said aghast. 'So . . . presumably you did!'

'Presumably I did,' she sobbed, raking her hands desperately through her hair, 'but the next thing I knew, I was being shaken awake by Michael, in the back garden!'

'Michael found you in the garden?'

'Yes, at four o'clock this morning!'

'And you can't remember how you got there?'

'Well, I vaguely remember Theo and me staggering back there from the golf course—I mean, it's only down the lane—but other than that, no, not a thing.' She dropped her voice very low suddenly. 'And Michael's so furious. *So* furious.'

'Well, I'm not bloody surprised!'

She put her hands up to cover her face, then sank down on her knees to the ground. 'He's thrown me out!' she sobbed through her fingers. 'Told me to go. Sent me home, says he doesn't want me here, says he'll tell the children Mummy's been called back for an urgent meeting in London.' She took her hands from her wet face and wiped her cheeks with the inside of her wrists. 'He says it happens all the time anyway,' she said bitterly, 'so they won't question it.'

I crouched down beside her. 'Yes, well, of course he has to say that, Clare. He has to save face. But, don't worry, he doesn't mean it.'

'He does though, he does!' She turned her grubby, tear-stained face towards me. 'He means it this time. What am I going to do!'

She started pulling up clumps of grass in a tortured fashion, just as, through the bracken, Flora and Tod suddenly materialised, having climbed up the path from the beach.

'What's wrong?' asked Flora in astonishment.

'Never mind,' I muttered briskly, getting to my feet and ushering the pair of them quickly on past her. 'Now, listen, Flora. Clare's had a bit of a shock and I need to talk to her in private. Why don't you take Tod up to the house and play table tennis in the garage or—'

'Tod's brought his surfboard. I'm going to get mine and we're going to go round to Polzeath to surf. Can I have some money for a burger?'

'In my purse on the hall chair,' I muttered. 'Take a tenner, and be careful. Take your mobile, too. How are you going to get there?'

'We'll walk across the cliffs,' she yelled back at me, as they raced as one up the path towards the house, taking advantage of my abstraction to surf alone and have money.

'Come on,' I said firmly, squatting down beside my sister again and taking her arm. 'I'm going to get you into a nice hot bath.'

I hauled her to her feet. She was heavy and dumbly quiescent now. As we got to the house, I glanced nervously in at the study window. Matt, happily, had his head down, deep in the paranoia, and had the tact not to look up as I led her past and in through the kitchen door.

Once upstairs I started running a bath for her. When she'd taken off her clothes and got in the bath, I flew downstairs, and rang Rosie.

'What the hell happened last night?' I demanded.

'Ooh, Annie, it's awful,' she breathed excitedly. I could tell she was horribly gripped. 'Well, after you and Flora went, we all started packing up, putting the barbecue stuff away and everything, and then we suddenly realised Clare and Theo were missing. It was all a bit embarrassing actually. Michael was wandering round the dunes looking for them, and everyone was packing their cooler bags, exchanging knowing looks. And all the time Michael was trying to pretend to the children that it was quite normal for Mummy to go for a walk with Mr Todd.'

'Oh God,' I groaned. 'Giles and Becky and Luke!'

'Well, Giles guessed immediately, of course, and went very pale and started whacking the sand with a cricket stump and swearing softly, and then Becky started to cry because she was frightened and didn't know where Mummy was. And of course Michael knew. And we all knew that he knew, that was the worst thing, and then someone muttered something stupid about calling the police.'

'Oh, for God's sake.'

'At which point Helena gave a strange, hollow laugh, like a bark almost, and said that if she did that every time her husband disappeared she'd be on intimate terms with the police by now, and that she for one was going home. And she stalked off to her car with her children and her nanny, at which point Michael said quietly, "Right. Let's go too."'

'So we all drove back, and Dan and I put all the children to bed and Michael went out looking for her again.'

'And that's when he found her? In the garden?'

'Much, much later, at about four in the morning, having been searching all night. He said he knew she was with Theo, but he was worried in case they'd gone for a swim. And knowing she was pissed—'

'Rosie, she's *still* pissed,' I insisted. 'Honestly, she stinks, and you know Clare, she doesn't even *drink*, for heaven's sake. And she says she can't even remember if she slept with him!'

'Course she bloody did,' retorted Rosie caustically. 'Convenient amnesia. Christ, she was with him all night! Anyway, Michael's livid. I mean really fire-breathing livid. Didn't think he had it in him, to tell you the truth, in fact— Oh. Gosh, sorry Michael. I didn't . . . No, no, it's Annie.'

There was a muffled exchange. A pause, then: 'Annie? Is she with you?' I hardly recognised his voice. It was harsh and rough.

'Yes, but, Michael, listen,' I said quickly. 'I know you're furious and I don't blame you, but honestly, she was so out of it.'

'Oh, she's out of it, all right. She's out of it full stop,' he said tersely. 'I've had it with her, Annie, after this. Completely had it. For precisely seven months she's broken my balls over one inadequate fumble with a girl at a Christmas party, which, stupidly, I admitted to. She's made my life a total misery, to the point where I'm scared to open my mouth for fear of her biting my head off, or the children's heads off, and then she bloody well fucks Theo Todd at a family beach party. With all our children present, and our friends, and in a completely tarted-up, tits-out, premeditated way. Well, I'm thrilled actually, Annie. Best thing that ever happened to me. I didn't know I was looking for an excuse to get away from her, but now I've got one. Tell her to go back to London and pack up, and make sure she's out of our house in two weeks when I get back with the children. I'll speak to her through my solicitor then. I'll sue her for adultery. We'll have a nice, old-fashioned, no-holds-barred divorce.'

'Michael, you don't mean that,' I breathed. 'You're just upset.'

'I bloody do mean it, Annie.'

'Michael—'

'Tell her goodbye, Annie. And tell her I'll see her in court.'

I breathed in sharply as the line went dead. Stared at the receiver. There was a sound behind me. I turned to see Clare, hair wet, eyes wide, wrapped in a bath towel.

'Michael?' she breathed.

I nodded. Licked my lips.

'And?'

'And . . . he's a bit cross.'

'How cross?'

'Well,' I struggled, 'he wants you to go home.'

'I know,' she nodded. 'Back to London. And then?'

'He wants you out of the house. But he doesn't mean it,' I said quickly, seeing her face collapse. 'He's angry, that's all. He'll come round.'

She shook her head dumbly. 'No,' she whispered. 'He won't. I know Michael. Once he's decided something, set his mind to it . . . he's much stronger than you think. Not really a timid little man at all.' She stared beyond me. 'But you wouldn't know that, because I've knocked all the gumption out of him,' she said flatly. 'Been needling him for years. This isn't just about last night. But now I've pushed him over the edge!'

'But . . . why, Clare? Why have you been so hard on him?'

She shrugged hopelessly, tears streaming unheeded down her face now. Clare never cried. 'Because . . . because *my* life is such a misery!'

She buried her face in her hands and wept. I put both arms round her heaving shoulders and held her close.

'It's always been such a misery,' she sobbed, 'for as long as I can remember, and I've always had to pretend it was so bloody perfect! Right from way back, when I swotted for exams and was hassled by Dad, and got into a better university, and got a better job, and a richer, more successful husband than anyone else, and had more children and a brilliant full-time career and up and up the sodding ladder of life I went, climbing at quite an astonishing rate, like a bleeding mountain goat I was so flaming agile.' She paused for a moment, wiped her nose with the back of her hand, sniffing loudly. 'God, Annie, I'm so tired. So utterly exhausted, and actually, not ever even remotely happy.'

Her face was empty, naked almost in her despair.

'And Michael was, you see,' she went on sadly. 'Before I squashed it out of him. He was often happy. Larking with the children, enjoying them, and I hated that. Resented it.' She looked bleakly into space. 'All rather unattractive and undernourished, isn't it?' She gave a wry smile. 'But it's the truth. And I resented you, too.'

'Me?'

'Yes, you. In your scruffy clothes and your terrible car with your one child and your little house and your failed marriage—'

'Oh, thanks!' I blinked.

'Because even though you've been through some ghastly times,' she ploughed on regardless, getting it all out, 'you've had some really riotous, throw-back-your-head-and-roar times too. With Adam, in the old days, no money, no cares, just lots of laughter and sex and having—well, *fun*. With Flora too, and hopefully with David, and—and I've never had that! Do you know, last night, in those dunes with that ghastly, groping, geriatric pisshead, Theo, it was the first time in years that I've felt free. Happy. Just being pissed and taking my clothes off and laughing and . . . Oh, I don't know,' she trailed off miserably.

'But . . . why don't you do that with Michael?'

'Because Michael has to suffer!' she screeched, fists balled. 'Michael has to suffer because I have to suffer. Don't you see?'

I blinked. 'I . . . think so, Clare. A bit. But . . .what will you do? Will you go home?'

'I'll have to ring Donna first. She's at her mother's. Ask her to come and help Michael. He'll never cope, never. Four children—'

'He'll cope,' I interrupted softly. 'Let go, Clare.'

She stared at me. 'Yes,' she said flatly. 'You're right. He will cope. That's the awful thing. It'll be me who won't be.' Her voice was very small. 'But I can't just leave!' Her face crumpled. 'Can't I stay here?'

'Yes, of course, but . . .' I hesitated. She needed to get away. Michael needed her to get away. 'Why don't you go to Mum's?'

She gave a hollow laugh. 'What, alone? Home to Mum without my husband and kids? Hi, Mum, Michael's kicked me out?'

I shrugged. 'She's never judged. Always just been there.'

'For you, maybe.'

'And you. It's just you've always been too proud to ask.'

'Such an admission of defeat . . .'

'Dad's not there, Clare,' I reminded her softly.

She met my eyes. Nodded. 'No. Dad's not there. Just his ghost.' She shivered. 'Right. Well, maybe. Maybe tomorrow. But . . . tonight?'

'Of course. Of *course* stay,' I assured her, hugging her hard. My eyes filled as she rested her damp head on my shoulder. My big sister. So humbled through her colossal, misplaced pride.

'Come on,' I urged gently, helping her back upstairs to a bedroom. 'Sleep. You're exhausted.'

'Don't think I will,' she muttered dully, but she let me fold her legs up anyway, her face pleated with fatigue.

'Try,' I insisted, lightly crossing the room and closing the shutters, instantly plunging the room into darkness.

Leaving her murmuring bleakly to herself, I tiptoed from the room, shutting the door softly behind me. Even if she didn't sleep, I thought, she needed to be alone. I went downstairs with a heavy heart, desperately sad for her.

The sun had gone behind the clouds now, and I shivered, reaching for a cardigan on the hall table as I went on through to the kitchen. I poured myself a large glass of wine, then padded back to the sitting room. Climbing up into the bay window seat that overlooked the garden and the creek beyond, I gazed across to the little church buried in the tawny landscape.

I hugged my knees and shivered as I looked out to sea. The wind was whipping up the trees to a frenzy, swirling their tops as they danced among the gathering clouds, and beyond, the surface of the water was making white horses farther out in the mouth of the estuary. Suddenly, I went cold. The house was so quiet. So still. I leaped off the window seat and reached for the phone on the bookcase, my heart pounding. It rang for ages, twenty rings or more. I held on though, pacing the sitting room, worry stealing over me like a shadow. Then her answer machine: 'Hi, this is Flora, please leave a message—' Panicking, I ran through the hall to Matt's door and knocked.

'Matt?' No answer. 'Matt! Are you there?' God, what was he doing? Asleep at his desk, or . . . No. Just not there.

I dashed back in a panic to the sitting-room window, clutching the tops of my arms tight as I gazed out at the surf, breaking out there in the distance. Hurriedly snatching up my shoes, I ran to the kitchen and through the back door, not bothering to shut it behind me.

As I fled down the garden towards the woods, I peeled off at a tangent to the right, following the path that ran, not down to the creek, but up the hills to the cliff path beyond. My heart was pounding high up in my throat as I belted through the rough, scrubby grass, the wind streaming into my open mouth as I climbed, panting, up and up round the head-land. Then, suddenly, as I rounded a bend high up on the cliff top, I stopped. Swayed almost, in the wind. Because there, coming round the top of the cliff, in a row—in formation almost—were the three of them.

Flora and Tod were in wet suits, laughing and soaked, caked in salt and sand; Matt was between them. His hair was wet, and he was wearing old shorts and a T-shirt. He was laughing, head thrown back, his eyes as bright and blue as the sky he lifted them to. As he raised his face and roared out loud to the heavens, it seemed to me his face was alive with happiness.

'Hi, Mum!' Flora ran ahead to greet me as I stood there, holding my sides and panting with the uphill exertion.

'Hi.' I smiled, hugging her, but my smile was for Matt. A beam, actually. 'You went with them.'

He shrugged. 'Well, I figure the creek is fine, but surfing . . . You know, bashed heads, all that stuff. The current—'

'I know,' I said quickly, 'and I would have gone. I always go with her, only Clare was so upset and—'

'Mum, chill. Matt came, OK? Stop fussing,' interrupted Flora, embarrassed. 'And you should see Matt surf, he's ace. No wet suit or anything!'

'Well, where I come from wet suits are for pansies, but I gotta tell you, in these Cornish waters I can almost see the point.'

'Freeze your knackers, eh, Dad?' grinned Tod.

He winced. 'More than that.'

I fell in beside them as we walked down the cliff path towards the garden, sneaking a sideways look at Matt as we went. He looked absurdly young suddenly, his hair wet, joking with his son.

'Hose off those wet suits,' Matt instructed as they began peeling them off as soon as we reached the terrace. 'And then later on we might go see if we can get anything for supper.'

Tod turned, half out of his suit. 'What, fishing?'

'Well, I'm not going hunting. I've seen the size of the rabbits round here and you couldn't make a sausage out of them.'

'And could Mum come too?' Flora asked. 'We've never been fishing, have we, Mum?'

'Sure. If she wants?' He half turned, enquiringly.

Unaccountably, I found myself flushing. 'I'd love to. Why not? I've done enough work today, and Clare should be sleeping, so . . . lovely.'

'Good,' he said shortly. 'The wind's dropping now, so I reckon in a couple of hours we should be fine.'

In a couple of hours we were fine. Dandy, in fact, in his parlance. There we were, right out near the mouth of the estuary on the left bank, the trees with their arching green limbs like a shady umbrella over us, in a little blue boat called *Pandora* which Matt had hired from the pontoon. An anchor had been tossed over the side and the boat rocked gently in the swell. Matt and I were in the bows, Tod and Flora on the centre thwart, and each of us was equipped with a vast orange life jacket and a fishing rod, which he'd also managed to hire from somewhere.

Tod's face was intent on the water and, as I rested back in the prow, I took a moment to study him. He was a beautiful boy, his eyes huge and blue behind his glasses, his features thin and refined in his pale face. He sat passively, while Flora, I noticed, shifted about, impatiently tugging her line up every now and then to examine the hook. The worm remained untouched, but for a dark ribbon of seaweed.

'You're letting it touch the bottom,' Matt murmured from under his hat, which was pulled down over his eyes. 'Here.'

He reached across and pulled it in a length or two, then he continued with his own fishing, quietly content. At length, I found my own line slipping. I let it slide and, out of the corner of my eye, considered the line of his jaw, the set of his shoulders, the shape of his hands. Strong, capable hands, my mother would have called them. It's fair to say I wasn't exactly fishing in earnest, which was why it came as a shock when something tugged.

'Oh!' I stood up in excitement. 'I've got one!'

'Steady,' he said as the boat rocked madly from side to side.

'But I can feel him there!' I began to reel frantically, laughing at Matt over my shoulder. 'I'm not kidding, he's there, on the end of my line!'

'Brilliant, Mum!' squealed Flora.

'Not so quickly,' Matt said quietly. 'Bring him in gently.'

But I wasn't listening and, still standing, I jerked harder than ever, and caught the flash of a silver fish streaming to the surface, head first. I felt a tug, saw its underbelly gleam as it streaked sideways, and then away into the depths.

'Oh! I've lost him!' I turned to Matt, absurdly disappointed.

Matt looked up at me, laughing, pushing his hat up out of his eyes. 'You got overexcited!'

'Damn. And it was such an amazing feeling when it tugged. Now I want to catch another.'

But I didn't, of course. The children did, though; they got two apiece; Flora pink with pleasure as she hauled hers in. Matt bashed its head on the side of the boat, which made her squeal, then showed her how to take the hook out, which, to her credit, she did.

We fished a bit more, and when Tod had caught another, Matt deemed it enough for supper.

'How are you going to cook them?' asked Flora. 'On a campfire down on the beach?' she teased.

'Sure, why not?'

Flora looked taken aback.

'Dad and I often do that back home,' explained Tod. 'I mean in Connecticut.'

'Golly,' I boggled. 'Very Huckleberry Finn.'

Matt sat back in the stern and pulled the string hard out of the outboard motor. It spluttered into action. 'Hardly. I tend to use a cutting-edge nonstick pan, a firelighter and lashings of olive oil, but other than that it's authentic.'

I watched as he guided us round some rocks and back along the more populated side of the estuary. I wanted to ask him about his life now, since the split; since the days when he caught fish with his son and cooked them on the beach. He steered us expertly along the shoreline towards the creek, one hand on the tiller, his eyes, far beyond me, searching the distance.

It was a very giggly supper we prepared in the kitchen at Taplow House that evening. Clare had presented herself as we were all gathered there round the kitchen table, Matt instructing the children in cleaning and gutting the fish with plenty of squealing from Flora as she pulled out bloody entrails, while I whisked up olive oil and balsamic vinegar to make a dressing for the salad. She'd appeared in the doorway, politely refusing our invitation to join us for supper, and affording a very different picture from the one she had earlier. Clean, and wearing some old blue trousers of mine and a T-shirt, her face devoid of make-up, hair swept back in a band off her face, she looked more like her usual self; but there was a sheepishness about her, a new humility.

'No. Thank you, though. You're very kind, but I'm not particularly hungry. I'm going to go for a long walk, actually. Round the headland. I need some time to myself at the moment.'

'Did you sleep much this afternoon?'

'No, but I will tonight, I'm sure. If I walk enough I'll be exhausted.'

I nodded. Exorcise the memory of last night and everything that went with it. Get that bracing sea wind in her face; force some uphill exertion until her legs ached. I remembered doing that in the face of Adam's affairs.

'Well, we'll be down on the beach, if you need us.'

'OK.' She turned to go. 'Oh, and I've rung Mum. I'm going to the farm tomorrow.'

I crossed the kitchen quickly and gave her a swift hug. 'Well done. It's what you need. Some time at home with her.'

She smiled ruefully. 'Home. You still call it that.'

Supper on the beach was a raucous affair. Tod and Flora had been allowed a lager apiece and were now attempting to catch peanuts in their mouths and falling in a heap in the sand. Tod's glasses went flying, perilously close to the fire, and Matt yelled for calm as he expertly cooked the fish. He'd built a wall for his fire with stones to protect it from the wind, and put a barbecue rack on top to balance the pan. He turned the fish carefully, then slid them onto plates. Sprinkled with herbs and lemon, and with a salad, olive bread and new potatoes to go with it, it turned out to be a splendid feast, and I told him so later, when we were all sitting round the fire, plates balanced on our knees.

'So this is what you did in Connecticut? On the beach?'

'At weekends, sure. Tod and I made it a regular Saturday night fixture, didn't we?'

'Yeah, it was wicked. The house was right on the ocean.' Tod turned to Flora. 'You could be on the beach in seconds.'

'Cool,' she agreed. 'Have you still got the house?'

'Yeah, but we don't live there.' Tod looked out to sea.

'I still own it,' Matt explained, 'but it's rented out. I live in Boston these days. In an apartment.'

'Did your mum like the beach house?' persisted Flora with the tactlessness of youth, but Tod didn't seem fazed.

'No, it wasn't really Mom's thing. She preferred the city.'

'Madeleine finds the country dull. She calls herself a people person,' offered Matt, without rancour.

It was the first time he'd volunteered information about his wife. I wiped my plate with some bread and waited until the children had finished their meal; until they'd moved further down the beach to talk, to drink Coke, and cover their legs in sand.

'Do you miss her?' I ventured bravely.

He considered this. 'Miss is perhaps the wrong word. If she'd just walked out and left me, sure, I'd miss her. But she took Tod too, so any feelings I had for her were overwhelmed by anger and longing for him.'

'But you did have feelings for her?'

'For the girl I'd married, yes. But I have to force that image from my mind and remember the faithless woman she turned into.'

I nodded. 'I have to do that too. Force myself not to remember Adam as he was, but look at what he became.'

'Exactly. And that's not easy, because you don't just stop loving someone. But their changing into people you don't recognise helps. It hardens the heart. What you're left with is a longing for how things were long ago, not for the more recent past.'

'Does . . . your work help you do that?'

He gave a short shout of mirth. 'What, my work as a psychiatrist? You think it gives me inner vision?'

'Well, you're used to delving into other people's minds—'

'No, Annie,' he said kindly, 'it doesn't. It simply highlights the fact that I'm not doing so well. I cling to my hate because it helps, but of course I shouldn't, I know that. And not just because I'm a psychiatrist. It stands to reason. Hate leads to bitterness about everything. You feel quarrelsome, hostile, guarded, intolerant. It turns you into a deeply unattractive human being.' He smiled. 'Ring any bells?'

'Oh, absolutely. Only I never had the guts to harden myself as comprehensively as you did. I was pathetic. And I went to pieces every time Adam called for Flora, in the beginning.'

'Yeah, I guess that's one blessing in disguise. Madeleine took off so comprehensively—emigrated, in effect—that I don't have to see her.'

He stoked the fire with a stick and I thought about what he'd said. About his toughness, his shell, which I'd originally thought was the real man when I'd first met him: gruff, belligerent, angry, barking at me and locking himself away in his room; and yet there'd been moments even then when his sudden, blowtorch smile would explode across his face and I'd think: No. That's not him. There's someone else in there, hiding. I looked up. He was poking the fire, watching me.

'What?'

'I was just thinking how today was a blast. First day I've enjoyed for a long while, actually.'

He carried on stirring the embers, and somehow I knew it was very important that we both stared hard into that fire and didn't look up. We steadily contemplated the gleaming twigs simmering in the white hot ash. A log shifted suddenly in the fire, breaking the moment, and I looked across to the shore, where the children had lain down in the sand and were staring up at the stars. Their eyes were shutting and they were murmuring only occasionally to each other under the inky sky. I glanced at my watch. God. Half-ten.

'Yeah, come on, kids,' called Matt, reading my mind. 'Bedtime.'

Uncomplaining and clearly whacked, they dragged themselves to their feet and trudged towards us.

'How come?' whined Tod, but it was a token gesture.

'Because you're bushed, that's how come. Now, go on.' His father reached out and patted his leg affectionately. Tod leaned down to kiss him. Flora bent likewise to say good night.

'Will you come up?' she murmured anxiously in my ear.

'Course I will. In about ten minutes.'

I watched as she followed Tod, climbing up through the dark wood behind him, with only the light from the fire and the moon to guide them, something she'd surely never do on her own. I hugged my knees and gazed out to sea, where the moon on the horizon was sending a shimmering ribbon of light towards us.

'Your sister's in a mess, I gather,' observed Matt at length, reaching for the wine bottle and refuelling our glasses.

'Yes,' I sighed. 'Michael's chucked her out. And quite right too, in a way. She did behave badly.' Without being too disloyal I gave him a quick sketch of last night's events. 'And, actually,' I went on, leaning back on my elbows in the sand, 'she needed this kick up the backside. But the problem is, it might not just be a kick. It might be permanent.'

'Once he realises what a relief it is not to have her around, you mean.'

I glanced across, startled. 'Well, yes. But how did you—'

'Because that's another emotional target I hit with a bull's-eye after Madeleine left. Having a secretive affair had made her tense, nagging at me and Tod, and that part of her I sure as hell didn't miss. Felt something like the surge of relief Michael might be feeling now, as he throws his clothes on the floor, and watches the ball game all day on TV if he feels like it.' He lay back in the sand beside me, propped up on his elbows.

'Yes, that's what bothers me,' I said nervously. 'That he'll think: Yippee. Toss his bonnet, as my mum would say. Anyway, it's a good

411

thing she's going there. To Mum's. If anyone can talk some sense into her it'll be . . . God, what's that!'

I swung round. There was a crashing and rustling coming from the woods behind us: the sound of snapping branches and heavy breathing. Matt and I got to our feet as one. It was as if an animal was moving directly through the wood towards us, crushing everything in its path, except that an unsteady, wavering light, which I suddenly realised was a torch, told me it was human. The beam emerged at the bottom of the wood, coming towards us fast, blinding me. I put my arm up as a reflex, and as I blocked out the white glare, saw the face behind it.

'David!'

'God, David! You gave me a fright. What are you doing here?'

He switched the torch off. 'Well, I've come to see you, obviously. Came a few days early, that's all.'

'But—I thought you were on call today . . .' I felt flustered standing here on the beach with Matt, round a campfire. What must he think?

'I was, until six, then I got a locum to take over. I've just got here.'

'But why didn't you phone?'

'I tried all day, but you were out. And your mobile's off.' He turned to Matt with a smile. 'David Palmer.'

'Matt Malone,' Matt responded immediately, shaking his hand. 'And, uh, I'd offer you some supper 'cos I guess you could use some after your drive, but I'm afraid we're all cleaned out here.' He gestured hopelessly to the empty pan and plates. 'Those kids have appetites.'

'Kids?'

'Um, Matt's son is here as well,' I faltered. 'He's come to stay.'

'Ah. That explains the boy asleep in the upstairs room. I must say I was quite surprised to arrive at a darkened house and find three sleeping bodies, but not the one I expected. Seems you have a pretty full house party here, Annie.'

For the first time I detected a hint of rancour in his voice.

'Oh, well, Clare's here too, yes. She's, um, had a bit of an argument with Michael. Nothing serious, but she's off to Mum's for a bit tomorrow.'

'I see,' said David, although he clearly didn't. 'Well, obviously much has gone on here in a short space of time, but I think I'll catch up on the minutiae of it in the morning, if you don't mind. I'm ready for bed. Are you staying down here, or . . .' He gestured casually to the fire.

'No, no,' I said quickly. 'We were . . . I mean I was just on my way up.'

I was flushing to my roots, but hopefully he couldn't see in the dark.

'You go on up,' said Matt quickly. 'I'll just put the fire out and gather these plates together.' He bent down to chuck stones on the fire.

'Right,' I said gratefully.

David put his arm round my shoulders and led me away.

I glanced fleetingly back at Matt, but his head was lowered to the business of clearing up. David and I went on up the beach together and then, out of necessity, walked single file through the woods, up the sandy path in silence.

'Very cosy,' he murmured when we got to the top.

'Oh, not really,' I said uneasily. 'It's just it makes sense for us all to eat together. And since we caught some fish today,' I rushed on nervously, 'we thought we'd cook them on the beach.'

'Right. Very Ging Gang Gooly.'

He held the back door open for me and I went through, still flustered.

'I must say, I was surprised to find it all unlocked,' David remarked. 'You don't lock up, if you're down there at night?'

'Well, I'm not normally down there at night, David.'

'Ah.'

We climbed the stairs, wordlessly.

'Strange house,' he commented, when we reached the landing. 'Rather small windows. Gloomy, I'd imagine, during the day. All that wood panelling.'

'It is quite dark,' I admitted, 'but lovely when the sun streams through. You need to see it in daylight, David,' I said eagerly.

'Oh, but I have. Many times, when I was young. I'd just forgotten about the panelling.' He ran his hand along it pensively as we went down the corridor. 'Haven't been here since I was about ten.'

He was being studiously polite, and I felt unaccountably nervous as we reached my room. Wished I could break the tension.

'It's lovely to see you,' I said, putting my arms round his neck when the door was shut behind us. 'I'm so pleased you came early.'

He held me tight. 'It's lovely to see you, too,' he murmured.

'And . . . I'm sorry about being on the beach with Matt.'

'No, not at all.'

'But it must have looked . . .' I trailed off miserably.

He pulled me down to sit on the bed beside him. 'You're here now, with me. That's all that matters.'

He kissed me warmly, and I responded, perhaps over-enthusiastically, still feeling horribly guilty.

'But, David, why did you decide to set off so late?' I asked, when our lips had parted. I stood up and started peeling off my clothes to get into bed. 'It's a long journey to contemplate at that time of night, isn't it?'

'Oh, I don't know,' he said wearily. 'Stupid, really.' He put his head in his hands, clearly exhausted.

I went to the little basin in the corner to brush my teeth. When I'd finished, I looked back at him in the mirror. He was still sitting on the edge of the bed, staring down at the carpet, head in hands.

'David?' I came back, frowning. Sat down beside him. 'What's wrong?'

He looked up. Gave a thin smile. 'Nothing, really. I've just had a hell of a week, that's all.' He reached out and squeezed my hand. 'I don't particularly want to go into it, because the whole point of coming here was to forget the bloody surgery.'

'I know, but if something's bothering you—'

'Hey.' He stopped my mouth with a kiss. 'Shush. Let's go to bed.'

He took off his clothes, brushed his teeth, and slipped into bed beside me. He held me close. Slipped a hand up the back of my T-shirt.

'Mmm . . .' he murmured sleepily, nuzzling into my hair. 'If I wasn't completely knackered, I'd make love to you.'

I was appalled to feel a surge of relief flood through me. 'Plenty of time for that,' I whispered back, hugging him hard.

'Exactly. Anyway, I always wonder if it's a good idea. When it's so tiny.'

'You're not tiny, David,' I murmured sleepily.

He laughed. 'No, I mean, when the egg's so tiny. Just a speck of life.'

I froze in his arms. 'Oh, David, I forgot to tell you. It's not. I mean—I started.'

He went very still beside me. 'You're not pregnant?'

'No. No, I'm not. Such a shame,' I hastened on quickly, 'and I would have told you, only—'

'Bugger.' He sat up suddenly in the dark. 'Bugger!'

I sat up beside him, dismayed. 'I . . . I know. It's very disappointing. But, David, we've got so much time.'

'Yes, but it is disappointing, nonetheless.' He turned to face me, to look at me. 'Only you don't seem to think so.'

'David, I do!'

'Don't you want a baby, Annie?'

'Of course I want a baby! Of course!'

We stared at one another in the darkened room.

'Rather puts the kibosh on any imminent nookie, too, doesn't it?' he said bitterly.

'Yes. I suppose it does. I wasn't thinking.'

'Wasn't thinking. As usual.'

'David!' I was shocked.

Suddenly he drew his knees up, put his head on them, and cradled it in his arms. 'Sorry,' he said in muffled tones into the bedclothes. 'I didn't mean that. I just feel everything's going wrong at the moment. You telling me that was the last straw, really.'

I instantly swooped and hugged him hard. I'd never seen him so upset. Felt bewildered by it. 'Everything's not going wrong,' I soothed, 'it's all fine! We're getting married soon, and—and then we'll have a baby. Which is, after all, the right way round. You're just tired, darling.'

He raised his head. I saw him swallow. Compose himself. 'Yes, you're probably right,' he nodded. 'I am very tired. Let's go to sleep.'

We lay down and held each other close. Before I dropped off, I heard Matt climbing the stairs up to the top floor. Heard the taps running in the little bathroom up there, then his door softly close. David was asleep, and I gently disentangled myself and moved across to the other side of the bed. For a long while my eyes were wide open as I lay on my back, staring into the darkness. Eventually, I fell into an uneasy sleep.

Chapter Five

THE FOLLOWING MORNING, David seemed much chirpier. The three of us, David, Flora and I, had breakfast in the garden together, sitting at the table on the terrace and looking out over the clover and the buttercups. David had got up early and been out to buy croissants and fresh bread which we sat down to now. Flora reported that she'd seen Matt and Tod go off fishing together early, and Clare too, it seemed, had risen and left for Mum's before I was awake. Rather tactful of everyone, I thought nervously as I sank into my cappuccino.

Mmm . . . proper coffee. Well, naturally, now that David was here. And a table laid with a cloth, complete with marmalade, cups and saucers.

'You're a little wonder.' I twinkled at him over my cup. 'Normally we sit in a slovenly fashion on the back step in our jim-jams, eating greasy bacon and beans.'

He winced as he buttered his croissant. 'Not convinced my digestive system could cope with that.'

I grinned and regarded him over his propped-up *Telegraph*, leaning back in his cane chair. He looked different. But then I'd never seen him in holiday gear. Never seen him in shorts. They were pressed, and khaki, and his legs were very white. His deck shoes were pristine, as was his pale pink polo shirt, still with two fold creases down the front, and likewise his hair, parted immaculately. I giggled.

'Presumably you didn't feel out of place in the bread queue?'

He glanced up, smiled. 'Sorry?'

'I was just remarking on your sartorial splendour. Very North Cornwall.'

'Hm. I don't know about that.' He went back to his paper. Winked at me over the top of it. 'Unlike you, you mean.'

I glanced down at the faded orange T-shirt of Flora's I seemed to be wearing with inexpertly cut-off jeans. 'Working gear,' I retorted.

'Quite right,' he grinned, still reading. 'And will you be working this morning?'

'Oh, no. Since you're only here for a couple of days, I'll give it a miss.'

'Won't lose the thread?' he murmured.

Thread? What thread? 'Er, no. Don't think so.' Didn't sound terribly professional, did it? 'Anyway,' I hurried on, 'what would you like to do today, David?' I put my cup down eagerly. 'We can show you the creek, or any number of beaches—'

'Oh, yes, Polzeath!' said Flora, looking up from her book. 'You'd love it, David, the waves are huge!'

'Well, I know it sounds dreary but I've actually got to work this morning. Patients don't take kindly to holidays. I've got to enquire about hospital beds, operation lists, that sort of thing, but it won't take long. Why don't you work for an hour or two, Annie, and then I thought we could all go to Tintagel? It's only forty minutes away, and there's a terrific ruined castle there reeking of Arthurian legend. Flora would love it, and I haven't seen it since I was a boy.'

'Fine,' I said in surprise. 'But it's going to be boiling hot today, are you sure you wouldn't rather flop on a beach?'

He cast his eyes about. Narrowed them warily out to sea over the treetops. 'Not much of a beach man, to be honest,' he reflected.

He got up and ruffled my hair as he went past. 'I'll be on my mobile in the dining room. I can spread my papers out in there. That is, since Matt seems to have commandeered the study.' It was said lightly, but I glanced nervously after him as he went in.

'Mum, do we have to go to that castle thing?' hissed Flora, the moment he was out of earshot. 'Tod and Matt are going to Polzeath later, the surf's meant to be wicked today.'

'Well, yes, I think we do, darling. If that's what David's got planned.'

'Oh, Mu-um!'

'Although . . .' I hesitated. 'Maybe he'd like some time alone with me.'

'Exactly!' she said eagerly.

I looked at her expectant face. 'Hang on.'

I got up and nipped inside, through the kitchen to the dining room, hoping to catch David before he started his calls. The door was shut. I knocked and went in. David swung round quickly, mobile to ear.

'Hang on, Hugo,' he said into the mouthpiece. Smiled at me encouragingly. 'It's OK.'

'It's just . . .' I hovered in the doorway. 'Well, Flora quite wanted to go surfing with Matt and Tod today, and I wondered if you'd mind. Thought we could have some time alone together.'

'I think not, Annie. We're a family, after all. No. Flora comes with us.' He turned and went back to his phone call. 'Sorry, Hugo . . .'

I gazed at his back for a moment, feeling like a fourth-former in the headmaster's study. Dismissed. I shut the door quietly, and went back to Flora in the garden, biting my thumbnail.

'Um, he thinks not, sweetheart. After all, we are a family now.'

'But, Mum, you said!'

'I said I'd ask him, darling. But, actually, I think he's right. We are a family, and—'

'And a boiling hot car all the way to some crummy castle is just what we need to bring us together, is that it? To bond us? Terrific!'

She grabbed her book and ran off into the house.

I sighed as I watched her departing back. Heard her thump-thump-thump upstairs. Waited for the door to slam. There. Hormones, I decided wearily, picking up a tray from the grass and clearing the table, had an awful lot to answer for.

In the event, of course, she was right. We didn't set off until nearly midday, when the sun was at its hottest, since David's phone calls took longer than expected. Flora had stayed in her room all the while, with a book, and I'd got so bored with hanging about I'd taken to the summerhouse, even though I didn't feel remotely in the mood for work.

Trouble was, Lucinda De Villiers seemed like such an old tart this morning. Trying to seduce her gardener in the potting shed, I ask you. Didn't she know there was more to life than a quick bonk? Yesterday that had seemed exactly what she needed, but today . . . Oh, today, as I gazed out of the window, over the treetops to the beckoning water beyond, knowing it was shimmering out there, full of sparkle and promise in the sunshine, today she needed romance in her soul, passion. Love, even . . .

Hastily I had her enquire as to whether Terence would like a latté on the terrace. Yes, that's it, I thought, tapping away confidently. Get to know him first, Lucinda.

'Well, I dunno,' stammered Terence. 'I've never 'ad one.'

'Surely they serve them at Harvey Nichols?' said Lucinda, a trifle irritably. 'It's just a milky coffee. Come.' She called him crisply to heel and he fell in meekly as they adjourned to the terrace.

Without Consuela to help, though, Lucinda couldn't work the wretched machine, so they ended up with lemon barley water, which Terence gulped down in one go, making a rather common 'Ahh . . .' noise as he drained the glass, wiping his mouth with the back of his hand. Golly, a very rough hand, thought Lucinda nervously. Didn't he use an emollient?

'You were thirsty, Terence,' she purred. She was sitting alongside him in a steamer chair.

'Terry,' he grinned, stifling a burp. 'Only me mam calls me Terence.'

'Is that right, Terence?' Lucinda said distractedly, her eyes narrowing into the distance, her mind suddenly on other things. Justin Reynolds, for instance; the neighbouring artist, who even now was up in his studio again, looking down at her from the top-floor window. She shivered. But something stirred deep within her. Writhed, almost.

Terence was easing back in his chair a mite too casually now, Lucinda thought. She felt relieved she hadn't let his tongue loose in her throat, or his hands on her silk undies. The dear boy was beginning to get on her nerves. She turned on him a dazzling smile.

'My husband called, Terence, from New York. Asked how his water feature was coming along. Any progress?'

'Oh, aye.' Terence got stammering to his feet. ''E asked me to plant it out for 'im. Only, I don't rightly know if 'e means with bog plants, or aquatic.'

'Whatever,' she purred, eyes back on the studio window. But it was empty. Justin had gone. She felt an odd little pang of disappointment, again somewhere rather agricultural.

'Aquatic? You think?' Terence asked anxiously.

'Perfect,' she said dismissively.

Heavens. She sat up. Was that her garden gate opening? Down there, in the wall? Her heart pounding, she watched as Justin Reynolds emerged, framed in the gateway. Tall and chiselled, his arty chestnut curls blew in the breeze. He paused for effect, before making his way up the garden towards them.

'Go now, Terence,' she breathed as Justin approached.

'I'm sorry to barge in like this,' Justin murmured, looking deep into her eyes, 'but I'm having an exhibition at the Le Touche Gallery on Friday, and I wondered if you and your husband—'

'We'd love to,' she broke in happily. 'At least, I would. My husband's away. All week, in fact.'

'Is he indeed!' said Justin huskily, his dark eyes smouldering.

Lucinda felt the heat penetrate her very bones.

'I've got a stiffy for you,' he murmured.

'A . . . what!' she gasped, as he pushed a stiff, formal invitation into her hands. 'Oh! Oh, a—gosh. How lovely, yes!'

'Who's Justin? I thought she was getting her rocks off with Terence?' I swung round to find David peering over my shoulder.

'David!' I stood up quickly, knocking my chair over in my haste. 'You startled me.' I scrambled to pick it up.

'Could have sworn you told me it was Terence the gardener she was after.' He grinned. 'Now that she's sussed her husband's such a rat.'

'Yes, yes, it was,' I flustered, fumbling for the switch to turn off the screen. 'Is, I mean.'

'But now she's got her eyes on someone else?'

'Um, no. No, not really. Are you . . . you know . . . ready?'

'All present and correct.' David smiled, straightening up and clicking his heels together, which he did occasionally. It drove me slightly mad, but then he had been in the Blues and Royals. 'And ready to drive the O'Harran contingent to Tintagel Castle.' He offered me his arm and grinned. 'Shall we?'

I beamed back, took it and, with my heart pounding mightily, sailed out of the summerhouse beside him, and up the lawn to the house.

Flora's words were worse than prophetic. Horribly accurate, in fact. We finally crawled through the castle walls, having sat in a two-mile queue in order to gain entry, and emerged from the car, gasping with suffocation and dripping with sweat, at half past one. Flora crowed but got short shrift from David and me, because, by now, we'd both decided that this trip was going to be a success if it bloody killed us.

As we paid for our tickets at the little kiosk at the bottom of the hill on which the castle sat, I gazed around, marvelling at the spectacular coastline. It was all rather majestic and suddenly I felt a bit more jaunty and optimistic.

'All right, my party?' called David, who'd gone ahead to another booth to secure the guidebooks.

'Fine!' I smiled, marshalling Flora onwards.

The jaunty optimistic feeling was short-lived, however, as it soon became glaringly apparent that if this castle was to be viewed properly, it could only be done so by mounting the five hundred granite steps that led to the ruin itself.

We toiled upwards, me practically carrying Flora. And neither were we alone, I couldn't help noticing. The place was crawling with other pilgrims who, unaccountably, had also deemed this the perfect day, at thirty degrees in the shade, to climb a one in four gradient.

Half an hour later, when we'd got another hundred-odd steps under our belts and reached the second set of ramparts—where, happily, the castle shop was conveniently placed—I buckled pathetically beside Flora on the grass.

'Not sure I can go much further, David,' I gasped, as Flora emitted a death rattle beside me. 'Why don't you go on and we'll wait for you down here?' I looked up at him pleadingly.

His face was bright red against the blue sky, and he was panting with exertion and mopping his brow. The next stage was another three hundred steps away and a coronary looked imminent, but I could tell he didn't want to be beaten.

'I might just have a little look at the turrets,' he panted. 'Seems crazy not to, while we're here. But you wait here. Catch your breath.'

We did just that, arms and legs splayed out like starfish on the grass, while David trudged on.

'Two more minutes,' I groaned, 'then I'll get us some water from the shop. I promise.'

'Now,' she moaned. 'Please, Mum, I'm dying.'

My temples were beginning to throb rather ominously, and I had a nasty suspicion I might be on the brink of a thumping headache. I shut my eyes tentatively. Ah, yes, something up there was definitely beginning to bite; a paracetamol was crucial. I sat up slowly, scraping myself gingerly off the grass, knowing any sudden movement was fatal. Pausing only to bully Flora into the shade, I tottered off into the shop.

Naturally it was heaving, and naturally there was no air conditioning, but I forced my way single-mindedly through the throng. As I was paying for the water and simultaneously popping down a handful of paracetamol from my bag, I spotted Theo's wife, Helena, just to the left of me by the till.

I pocketed my change and moved across. 'Hi. Not here doing sightseeing duty alone, surely?'

'Oh, hi, Annie. No, Theo's around somewhere; he's got Rollo with him. But I wish he'd hurry up, I'm dying to go home. It's far too hot for this one.' She glanced down at her toddler.

'I know, I've got Flora complaining like mad outside.'

'Well, at least you got her to come along. I couldn't persuade the older ones. Not that they ever do much that I ask them,' she added bitterly.

'I suppose they are rather beyond the sightseeing stage,' I said.

'They're beyond anything, except nicking cigarettes from my bag and helping themselves to beer from the fridge,' she snapped. 'At least we're off to Corsica tomorrow.'

'You're off tomorrow? I thought you usually did three weeks here?'

'We do normally, but this year I put my foot down. I wanted a hot holiday as well, because, as you know, it usually rains here. Little did I know we were in for a sodding heatwave.'

Suddenly I felt a bit alarmed. God, if they were off tomorrow . . .

'There's Theo,' I said suddenly, spotting his greying head right over the other side of the shop, a changing bag over one shoulder, buggy with sleeping child in the other hand. An idea occurred to me.

'Tell you what, Helena, if you take this bottle of water out to Flora, I'll push across and tell him you're waiting for him.'

'Oh, would you, Annie? Thanks.'

She took my water bottle and, picking up her daughter, moved gratefully away towards the door. I put my head down and squirmed through the multitude, all avidly poring over clotted cream, and assorted pixie memorabilia, and finally made it to Theo, who was flicking wearily through some postcards.

'Hi, Theo.'

He looked up. 'Oh, hello, Annie.' He glanced round warily for his wife, not wanting to be caught talking to another woman. 'You've been press-ganged into this wretched trip too, have you?'

'Well, it was David's idea, but we've rather enjoyed it,' I lied loyally.

'Ah, the good doctor. Yes, well, it's all highly educational, according to Helena. She's been shoving flashcards under the kids' noses as we hustle them round in the heat. Seem to remember we let the last brood grow up rather more casually,' he said wistfully. 'Anyway, I must go and pay for these. No doubt you came over to tell me The Power And The Glory is tapping her foot outside, waiting for me?' He made to move on.

'Yes, she is, but the thing is, Theo, I wanted to talk to you about the other night.'

'The other night? Oh . . . you mean with Clare.' His already ruddy face coloured up quickly. 'Yes, that was badly done. Got it in the neck for ages afterwards, as you can imagine.'

'Yes, but the thing is, Theo, Clare can't remember whether or not anything . . . you know . . .'

He frowned. 'What?'

'Well . . . whether or not you did it,' I said desperately.

He blinked. 'Well, bugger me. That memorable, am I?'

'So you did? Oh God, Theo, Clare was so pissed she can't remember!'

'And so was I, if you must know,' he said huffily. 'Otherwise I'd never have let that lardy old she-devil—' He stopped. Cleared his throat. 'Sorry,' he mumbled. 'No, we didn't as a matter of fact. We had a bit of a fumble, and then she threw up all over my trousers.'

'Oh!'

'Not the most seductive come-on I've ever had, and funnily enough I resisted the temptation to take it any further. I frogmarched her home across the dunes and dumped her in her back garden. Didn't particularly want to bang on the door and face Michael.'

'Which is where she passed out.'

'Lucky her. I went home to Helena, who'd put the babies to bed but not the teenagers, who rolled about clutching their sides, having a great laugh at Dad being so pissed he'd been sick down his strides.'

'Ah.'

'Well, I could hardly say it was Clare's puke, could I? What would she have been doing in such close proximity to my groin? So no, I didn't get my leg over, Annie. And neither would I have tried, actually. She was slaughtered. Now, if you'll excuse me.' He stomped off.

Well, that was something, I reflected, biting my thumbnail as I pushed my way out of the shop. Clare would be hugely relieved.

The house was empty when we got back, although not locked, of course, because Matt never bothered. This infuriated David as we walked straight in.

'I mean, anyone could wander in,' he said incredulously, standing in the middle of the sitting room and holding his arms out in wonder.

'Hardly likely though, is it?' I said wearily, sinking down exhausted into an armchair in the corner of the cool, darkened room. 'I mean, it's pretty remote,' I went on, 'and this is the country, for heaven's sake.'

'Fine. No need to snap.'

I opened my eyes, surprised. 'I wasn't. I was just saying it's not exactly very accessible.'

'No, and not ideal either, is it, Annie? Not for six weeks, or however long you plan to be here.'

'What d'you mean?'

'Well, with that . . .' He waved his hand. '. . . character. Matt. I mean, it's all very well for a few days while you get yourself sorted out, but any longer is absurd. I rang the Complete Angler this morning, and they've got a couple of very reasonable rooms. I booked them for you.'

'What!' I sat up.

'Only on the phone, no deposit or anything, but honestly, Annie, what does this arrangement look like? To Matt; to everyone?'

'Oh, David, you're completely overreacting. And I can't believe you booked rooms without telling me. Why shouldn't I stay here? I like it, and Flora likes it, and the house is huge, for heaven's sake!'

'And creepy.' He shivered.

'It's not creepy! What have you got against this place, David?'

'Oh, never mind.' He sank gloomily into the armchair opposite me. 'Fine break this is turning out to be,' he muttered.

I stared at him. Don't say anything, Annie. Just . . . don't speak. At length he leaned forward and picked up a piece of paper by the phone on the low table between us.

'David, ring Hugo,' he read aloud. He glanced up quickly. 'Did you take this?'

'No,' I muttered, still cross. 'Must have been Matt. Who's Hugo, anyway? Wasn't that who you were speaking to this morning?'

'Oh, he's . . . an old friend,' he murmured. 'I'll just go and ring him back.'

Ignoring the phone in front of us and digging his mobile out of his pocket, he disappeared into the dining room, shutting the door firmly behind him.

I sighed again and slumped back in my chair, leaning my head against the old leather. I shut my eyes. Well, my headache had abated, that was a relief, but everything else felt—so wrong. So tense, somehow. Not how I'd planned this bit of the holiday at all. I stayed like that for a few minutes, then, after a while, my eyes flitted to the telephone. I should ring Clare, of course. Give her the good news. I dialled her number but her mobile was turned off, and I didn't like to ring the farm in case she picked up in the kitchen and Mum was there too. No, I'd ring later, I thought.

Instead, I phoned Rosie. I had a sudden urge to see her and Dan tonight, make a party of it. Have a jolly barbecue here in the garden with all the kids. I had an idea David'd perk up with a bit of company and a few drinks; we both would. Yes, and I could see Michael, too. Gauge whether he'd calmed down a bit, and hopefully report back positively to Clare when I rang her later.

'God, I'd love to, Annie,' Rosie said, 'but we've said we'd go to Rick Stein's with the Hamiltons. The five of us are going. Michael's treat.'

'Golly,' I boggled. 'That's big of him. It's pricey.'

'I know, but he's in such a good mood.' She lowered her voice. 'Honestly, Annie, I've never seem him so chipper, and I can't tell you what a nice day we've had today.' She giggled guiltily. 'We all had a lie-in while the children watched telly, then we read the papers in the garden, declared an early drinks at eleven thirty and went off to the pub. You know, that really pretty one at Port Gaverne. Then, on the way back, we got fish and chips from the shop and ate it from the newspaper with *no napkins*! It's been so relaxing. I now get this place, whereas a couple of days ago, I didn't get it at all.'

'Because Clare insists on doing it so flat out,' I said ruefully. 'Well, maybe tomorrow night, Rosie. Why don't you all come over at about seven? Bring some booze and I'll get some sausages and chicken legs and we'll—Oh! Darling? What's wrong?'

I broke off to stare at David who'd emerged from the dining room. He looked as white as the walls behind him.

'They're going to do it,' he said incredulously, oblivious of the fact that I was on the telephone. 'They're actually going through with it.'

'What? Going through with what?' I said, bewildered.

'They're going to sue me for professional misconduct. And not only that . . .' He struggled for composure. His eyes found mine. 'They're suing me for manslaughter, too. Manslaughter, Annie!'

I stared at him aghast, as to my horror he put his hands over his face, sank down into a chair, and wept.

'I'll ring you back,' I muttered to Rosie.

'Manslaughter!' she gasped, agog. 'But who—why—'

Brutally I cut her off, dropping the phone and flying over to David's side. I knelt beside him, cradling his head in my arms, horrified. 'David, don't! What's happened, why—'

'They're suing me, Annie.' He jerked up suddenly, his face wet. 'The wife, the family of the man I told you about. The one who died on my surgery steps.'

'Yes, but . . . David, it wasn't your fault! And . . . and so what if they sue? So what? It was just a misdiagnosis.'

'Which is medical negligence.' He got to his feet abruptly, wiping his face savagely with the back of his hand, pacing around the room. 'And it's quite possible I'll never be able to practise again, and just remotely possible I might go to prison.'

I stared at him, horror-stricken, as I knelt there on the floor.

'Don't be ridiculous,' I spluttered. 'They don't send doctors to prison for missing something. And you said yourself he had a history of—'

'I have a history,' he interrupted, stabbing his chest viciously with his forefinger. 'I am the one with the fucking history, Annie.'

I'd only ever heard him swear before once.

'I have a history of misdiagnosis,' he said with a terrible crack in his voice. 'Remember last year, that woman with a lump on her neck, and I told her it was a harmless ganglion and it turned out to be malignant?'

'Yes, but you said anyone could have made that mistake.'

'But I should have had it looked at. Should have had a biopsy done. And then back in January, the old lady in Battersea who died of pneumonia, who'd refused to come and see me, said she was fine even though when she'd been in previously I'd detected something on her chest—'

'But she wouldn't come in! You said you asked her, and she wouldn't—'

'Yes, but I should have gone to her, shouldn't I? She was eighty-two. I shouldn't just have taken her word for it. I'm the bloody doctor!'

My throat felt dry and constricted.

'Hugo only just managed to keep me out of court that time,' he said, turning his back on me and raking a despairing hand through his hair.

'Who's Hugo?' I whispered.

'My solicitor. And an old friend.' He was silent a moment, then he turned. 'I'm not up to it, Annie. Never have been.'

I stared, horrified. His face was pale but composed. There was a terrible clenched calmness about him. I got up from the floor and went to him; I shook his arm.

'That's nonsense, David. You're a wonderful doctor, everyone says so!'

He gave a tight smile. 'You say so. I say so, occasionally. But not everyone says so. In fact a lot of people say it's not so. Ask Gertrude.'

'Gertrude?' I was stunned.

He looked out to the horizon again. 'I was so desperate to be a doctor, Annie,' he said softly. 'So desperate. Like my father, a great surgeon. Well, it was clear early on I could never be that, didn't have the brain power, but . . . well, OK, like my uncle then. Gertrude's husband, Hugh. An excellent general practitioner. So I trained. And failed my exams. And trained again and failed, but eventually . . . eventually I got those precious letters before my name, changed the boring Mr for something more sonorous.' He put a hand to his brow. Stretched it across and rubbed his temples wearily. 'But you know, Annie, the awful thing was, I always knew I'd be terrified when it came to actually doing it.'

'Bu . . . but Hugh took you on. You were fine! And he must have trusted you to work with you.'

'Well, he'd brought me up from the age of eight,' he said bitterly. 'He was like a father to me. Who wouldn't do that for their nephew? Let them into the family business in Sloane Street? Also . . .' He wrestled with something. 'It meant he could watch me, you see. Keep an eye on me. But when I'd been with him a year or two, I saw the worry in his eyes.' He swallowed. Fixed his gaze on a small red boat out at sea. 'After he died, I started sending patients straight round to Harley Street for a second opinion if I wasn't sure about something. Pretending to the world that it's because I'm a cautious chap. But actually . . . covering my back. And it's worked. Mostly. I've muddled through. Because you see'—he turned back and looked at me beseechingly—'I'm not a bad doctor, Annie. I'm just—not a very good one.'

I put my arm round his neck, holding him close. 'Oh, my darling.'

He rested his head on my shoulder and, to my distress, sobbed again. I held on, very tight. After a while, he recovered. Composed himself.

'Sorry,' he muttered, turning away. He tugged a hanky from his pocket and blew his nose noisily. Moved over to the fireplace. Gazed into the grate. 'Can't think what's come over me. Blubbing like a baby.'

I crossed the room and put my arms round him from behind. Laid my head on his back and squeezed hard.

'I should go,' he said suddenly. I felt his back muscles tense. 'Hugo said he'd see me at his office tomorrow.' He turned.

'Go in the morning,' I urged. 'Sleep on it and go tomorrow.'

'No, I—'

'Please, darling, don't go now.'

In the event, I persuaded him to stay. That night, in bed, he held me very close. 'I don't know what I'd do without you, Annie,' he said into my shoulder. 'I need you, Annie. I really do.'

'And I need you too,' I murmured, but there was a desperation in his voice that unnerved me.

'I want to make love to you tonight. Please.'

'Of course. I do too,' I assured him, wishing he hadn't said please.

His lovemaking was intense, desperate even, with a ferocity about it that alarmed me. I tried to come up with some kind of reciprocity of scale, but found after a while that he was almost oblivious of me anyway. He was in a world of his own, or trying to be. Losing himself in me. Possessing me.

Eventually, he flopped round on his back, sated; exhausted; his body heaving. I lay quietly beside him and, after a while, I heard deep, rhythmic breathing as he sank into a heavy sleep.

I, meanwhile, for the second night in succession, lay awake for hours, eyes wide and raw in the darkness, listening to the waves lapping gently in the creek and the wind rustling the treetops. My mind was racing. So much I didn't know. I didn't know Hugo had had to keep him out of court. I hadn't even heard of Hugo. I didn't know he'd repeatedly failed exams—not that it mattered a jot—but why hadn't he told me? I didn't know of Gertrude's misgivings. Round and round went my mind, until, eventually, Morpheus rescued me and I fell into a fitful sleep.

The following morning, I awoke to find the bed empty beside me. David had gone. On the duvet was a note. I snatched it up.

My darling,
I'm so sorry for all the histrionics last night. I'm sure all will be well. I love you.
David

I sighed and lay back on my pillows for a moment. Then, with a mammoth effort, swung my legs round and pulled on my dressing gown.

The house was full of sleep as I crept downstairs. Certainly Flora's door was shut as I passed, and Tod wasn't around. I made myself a cup of coffee, and leaned back against the yellow Formica worktop, cradling my mug and wondering what to do with myself. My eyes unaccountably filled with tears. Still tired, I reasoned, swallowing hard. Lack of sleep. What I needed was to work. Needed the single-minded focus that writing afforded, so that my mind took refuge in someone else's fictitious life. I remembered Adam asking me once why I wrote, as I scribbled away furiously in an exercise book. I'd replied, without thinking, that it had always been a safe place to go.

I made a fresh cup of coffee and took it out into the garden. As I passed the study window, I saw that Matt, head down, had had the same idea. His window was open and, as I went by, he glanced up.

'Everything OK?'

Not 'morning', or 'hi', or even just a grunt to indicate he'd registered but was busy, but: 'Everything OK?' Quietly. Solicitously. In that soft, melodious accent.

I nodded, gave a weak smile, and passed on.

Tears were welling again, and I couldn't speak. Mustn't speak. Mustn't even think. He would, of course, have noticed that something was wrong last night. Would have noticed when he and Tod returned from the beach. Glancing into the sitting room, he'd tactfully ushered Tod and Flora out into the garden to eat the pasties they'd bought on the way home, claiming food always tasted better in the fresh air, even if it was a bit windy. And all the while David and I had sat huddled inside, talking in tense whispers, me clutching his hands, trying to shake some confidence into him and banish the demons. Nice of Matt to shield Flora for me, I thought. To feed her, and take her off later with Tod to look for cormorants on the cliffs with binoculars.

I shut the summerhouse door behind me and sat down. As I switched on my computer a sea of words filled the screen, but I stared, almost unseeing, feeling sick inside for poor David, but also so horribly, horribly confused.

'Everything OK?'

Swallowing hard, I pulled myself together. Right. Now. Lucinda. My heroine. I had to get a move on with this wretched book, or my editor would be wondering what the hell was going on. And Lucinda hadn't even got her kit off yet. She was still wandering round her empty house, Justin's invitation clutched to her heaving bosom, eyes shining, her heart full. Oh, no, I thought, rereading the last paragraph in panic, that wouldn't do at all! I quickly erased a few lines. She wasn't supposed to fall in love, for heaven's sake, not with Justin Reynolds! That way madness lay. I tapped away furiously.

Lucinda stalked into the drawing room and cast the invitation ruthlessly aside, pushing it behind a stack of similarly embossed cards on the mantelpiece. She regarded herself sternly in the mirror above it. Certainly her husband's faithlessness had to be avenged, certainly a dalliance of some sort was in order, but allowing another man into her heart could only lead to more pain. Terence, on the other hand, was an entirely different proposition. Her heart would slumber peacefully while her body did all the work. Even now she could hear his heavy tread in the kitchen as he came to collect the dogs for their afternoon walk. She flew to intercept him.

'Have a nice walk, Terence,' she purred.

'Aye, I will,' he said, surprised by her change of mood.

'And, I wondered, would you like to do something tonight? Only my husband's still away and I thought . . . we could go out.'

'Aye, we could.' He brightened. 'We could get a bite to eat, like. That'd be grand.'

'Yes, that would be . . . grand.'

Later that evening, in a shimmering, low-cut Ungaro gown, she swept into the eatery on his arm.

''Ave you ever been to an 'Arvester before?' he enquired, proudly pulling her chair out for her.

'No, never.'

'Only I wouldn't want you to be spotted, like.'

Lucinda gazed around at the simple polyester-clad folk, who appeared to be helping themselves at something called a salad bar.

'I don't think there's any danger of that,' she murmured.

The evening grew even more novel as Lucinda was encouraged to wander around, join queues and use tongs. As she returned to her seat to toy listlessly with a lettuce leaf, Terence sat down opposite her, aghast.

'Is that all you want, lass?'

Lucinda blinked at the tottering pagoda of sausage, beans, chips, eggs, beans and more beans on Terence's plate.

'By 'eck, you can 'ave as much as you like! It's all the same price.'

'Thank you, Terence. This is sufficient.'

As she sipped her mineral water, she wondered nervously what such a colossal helping of fibre would do to his performance later? Would the duvet literally hover?

As it transpired however, her fears were groundless. Once she'd led him to the suite of her choice at the Savoy and shut the door firmly behind them, although unnerved that Terence insisted on removing her Ungaro gown over her head—'Arms up, luv!'— instead of letting it drop gracefully to the floor, when he dropped his trousers all was forgiven.

He advanced towards her, staggeringly priapic, and spectacularly hirsute, too, Lucinda thought, marvelling. Playfully she reached out and grasped his—

'Mum!'

I jumped, hands flying, and knocked my coffee cup for six.

'Shit!'

Desperately mopping the keyboard with the bottom of my T-shirt, I turned to find Flora's astonished face in the doorway behind me. I shielded the screen, at the same time trying frantically to wipe up.

'What?' I yelled.

'Clare's on the phone, that's all. Why are you so jumpy?'

'I'm not!' I bellowed. 'I'm just trying to work, that's all. Can't anyone leave me in peace just for five minutes? God, *cons*tant interruption!'

'Sorry,' she said sarcastically, letting the door slam. Then 'Stressy or what?' I heard as she went up the garden path.

I flicked off the computer and flew after her.

'Sorry, darling,' I panted as I caught up with her. 'I was just a bit—you know. Into it, that's all.'

She flashed me a smile. "S all right. Thought maybe you were in the middle of a steamy sex scene or something.'

'Ha!' I attempted a hollow laugh. 'As if I'd know about that.'

'Well, I should jolly well hope you do,' she retorted as she wandered in the direction of the garage to resume her table-tennis game with Tod.

I went through to the hall and picked up the phone.

'Hello,' I said absently.

'Oh, Annie, sorry. I know Flora said you were working, but I just wondered . . . only she mentioned you'd seen Theo at Tintagel and—'

'Oh, yes! No, you're fine, Clare. In the clear.'

'You mean—'

'I did talk to him, and no, you didn't sleep with him. You did throw up over him, though.'

'I didn't!' she gasped, as I simultaneously heard a small cough behind me. I swung round. Matt's door was ajar. I cringed. Damn.

'You did,' I hissed, turning back. 'Have you spoken to Michael?'

'No, but I'm about to write to him. What d'you think?' she asked anxiously. 'Thought I could, you know, grovel more on paper. Any tips?'

'Not really, but be sure to mention that nothing went on between you and Theo. Believe me, it'll make a difference. For all Michael's posturing, this is all about whether or not you bonked Theo Todd.'

'You're getting awfully perceptive in your old age.'

'It's this writing lark.' I sighed. 'Makes me think far too clearly. And, Clare, if you don't mind I'll ring you later for a chat, I was in the middle of it when you rang.'

'Sorry, yes, you go. We'll speak later. And Mum sends her love.'

As I put the phone down I could have kicked myself. I *could* have had a quick word with Mum. It was just if I didn't get back to Lucinda, I'd start thinking about my own life again, and that would be fatal.

That evening, Flora and Tod were clamouring for a fishing trip and a campfire on the beach again. Matt and I exchanged the briefest of glances. Almost by tacit consent we'd avoided each other for most of the day, but now he was at the kitchen table reading the newspaper, and I was at the sink. Tod and Flora were eating crisps on the back step.

'Come on, Dad, let's go down and get a fire going.'

'I don't think so, guys,' he said quietly, not looking up from his paper.

'No,' I muttered. 'Not tonight.'

Definitely not tonight, I thought as I scrubbed the living daylights out of a saucepan. Not a cosy beach barbecue. I didn't want to be alone with him under the stars, gazing into the embers when the children had gone to bed. Interesting that he should feel that way too.

'Oh, Mum, come on, it was fun last time!'

'No, Flora, we'll eat here, at the house,' I said firmly.

'Well, let's at least have a barbecue out in the garden,' said Tod.

I busied myself in the sink. Didn't look at Matt.

'Sure,' he said lightly. 'We can do that. I'll go get some steaks.' He reached over my head to the shelf where his car keys hung on a hook. The sleeve of his jumper inadvertently brushed my hair. I carried on scrubbing as if my life depended on it.

In the event, though, that plan seemed to strike the right chord. We sat, just outside the back door, plates on our laps, the children's music playing loudly through the open French windows. Matt joked around with Flora and Tod as we let them cook for us, complaining we'd be dead soon if they didn't feed us. Finally, with a fanfare, the food arrived.

'I've got half a cow here,' I observed, picking up an enormous T-bone steak in two hands.

'No point lighting the thing for a few chipolatas and a potato like a bullet.'

'Ah. You've been to a few English barbecues, then?'

He grinned and perched on the back step, balancing his plate on his knees. 'My cousin's husband, Tom, likes to look mean in the garden with prongs and meths. Hell of a nice guy, but boy, does he go to some lengths to produce a burnt chicken leg.'

'Tom who's married to Louise? Where Tod is supposed to be now?'

'Exactly.'

'How much longer have you got him for then?'

'Just a couple more days. Louise is coming to get him on Thursday. He'll have a day with her boys, then back to Cambridge.'

'And Madeleine will be none the wiser?'

'Nope.' He stabbed a forkful of salad viciously.

'You'll miss him,' I said at length. 'I mean, having spent all this time with him. Having him around.'

He glanced up. 'I miss him, period.'

'Of course,' I said quickly. 'Course you do.' Stupid, Annie. 'And that's where you met Gertrude? At Tom and Louise's?'

'That's it. Two summers ago, when she was down. Tom had known her late husband pretty well. A brilliant man by all accounts.'

'Yes, he was,' I mused. 'Which may be . . . the problem,' I said sadly.

He looked at me. The children had finished their steaks and were busy burning bananas in tin foil.

'Whose problem?'

I shook my head. Swallowed. 'Nothing. I shouldn't have said that.'

Matt laid his plate aside and narrowed his eyes into the setting sun. 'Annie, I couldn't help noticing David left in one hell of a hurry this morning. You want to tell me about that?'

'Yes, he . . . had things to do. In London. He, um—'

'Because if not, don't bother. You see I can already detect a half-baked lie forming on your lips and I gotta tell you, I can spot it a mile off.'

I smiled, despite myself. 'You know me too well already.'

He didn't reply to that. In the event, I broke the silence.

'Well, OK. David misdiagnosed a patient who ended up having a heart attack and dying.'

Matt calmly wiped some bread round his plate. 'He's not the first doctor to do that, and he sure as hell won't be the last.'

'No, but there have been others. Other mistakes.'

'Lots of others?'

I put my plate on the grass. Found myself flushing. 'Enough for him to be worried. Very worried. And, Matt'—I turned to face him—'that's what bothered me more than anything about last night. His reaction. He completely went to pieces. Really broke down.'

'Cried?'

'Well . . .' I hesitated. Felt disloyal. 'Yes, actually.'

He shrugged. 'For some calm, collected people that acts as a release. We all do it, it's just you're not used to seeing it in David.'

'Yes,' I agreed quickly, relieved. 'Yes, you're right. I'm sure that's it.'

'Are you sure,' he said carefully, 'it wasn't your reaction that bothered you? How it felt to see him like that?'

I lowered my eyes, ashamed. 'Yes, that too. It unnerved me. But the awful thing is that even before it happened, I was unsettled by my feelings towards him in so many ways. I . . . can't explain, really.'

I pulled savagely at some dandelions growing by my chair, tugging them up by the roots. I felt awful. It was so treacherous sitting here discussing David, yet, in another way, it seemed Matt was the only person I could do it with.

'How did you meet David?' Matt asked.

'Oh. He saved me from sudden death.' I grinned. 'Pushed me out of the way of some falling glass. But not just that. He saved me from myself, too. I was a mess when I met David. Still grieving for Adam. Not eating properly, getting sick, going under, almost at rock bottom, basically.'

'And now you're better?'

'Well, yes,' I said uncomfortably. 'Thanks to David. And now he needs me,' I said determinedly. 'And I'm going to be there for him.'

'Just at a time when perhaps you were ready to move on?'

'No. Of course not!'

'Annie, sick people need to be saved sometimes, but savers often need to do the saving. They need to rehabilitate others.'

'Are you suggesting that that's what attracted him to me? The fact that I was a wreck? A bit of a basketcase? That's balls.'

He shrugged. 'Vulnerability can be awfully attractive.' He looked at me steadily. 'But for others it's a turnoff.'

'You mean me.' I reddened. 'It's not that I find him unattractive now that he's down,' I said angrily. 'That's awful. An awful thing to say!'

''Night, Mum.' I jumped. Flora was at my elbow, bending to kiss me. I hadn't heard her come up behind me.

''Night, darling,' I said quickly, recovering. 'You're going up early?'

She looked at my watch. 'I know, but I'm bushed. So's Tod. And anyway, we might get up early tomorrow to go water-skiing. The boat leaves the jetty at nine.'

'OK, darling.'

I kissed her and felt angry tears welling. I turned away from Matt to hide them, pretending I was watching Flora go into the house. After a moment Tod followed suit.

'I'm not saying you find him unattractive because he's down,' Matt said in a low voice. 'I'm saying you're a different person now than when you first met him.'

I fought hard with this, but it was undeniable. I had changed. I was stronger, happier, but surely that was because of him? Because of David?

I reached down and tugged at some more dandelions, knowing he was stumping me with common logic.

'Annie'—Matt cleared his throat—'I was badly hurt too, like you were with Adam. And I didn't find a saviour like you did, although I had a few kind offers. A couple of them I took up, too. One was a female registrar with great legs; another, a cute neighbour two blocks down with a shy smile and a cat that jumped on the bed at inopportune moments. But both of them purely transitory. Both on a ships-in-the-night basis. A physical healing, sure, but I never let my heart get involved. It wasn't ready. Wasn't fit for action.'

'Wasn't?' I made myself look up from the grass. 'You mean it is now?'

'Oh, sure.' His eyes collided with mine. Blue, focused, and very frank. 'Road-tested and everything.'

The blood stormed into my cheeks and the silence that ensued was alive with intensity, crackling with electric current. I held his gaze.

'Annie, I think there's something going on here that both of us are denying. Some subject we're skirting politely around, which has nothing to do with David's relationship with you, but more to do with something the two of us have thrown into the equation.'

All of a sudden the garden seemed oddly still. Unnaturally quiet. The CD had come to an end inside, but I knew that was immaterial. No amount of teenage music and bright lights and jolly banter on the terrace could blanket this moment. It was out there suddenly, in the open, like a shining sea creature coming up out of the water through the murky weed and plankton. The rising up of a truth. He was right. This was something undeniable, and of our making.

I stood up quickly and stooped to pick up the children's plates from the grass, hoping to break the intimacy of the moment. I made a stack of crockery on the table, but was aware that he was standing behind me, and that my hands were trembling.

'Annie.'

I turned and, in that instant, when he looked at me, I was in pieces. He folded me in his arms, and the world as I knew it burst like a bubble. His lips found mine, warm and responsive; his hands held me close. He smelt of the sea, grass and fresh air as I kissed him. This man, this stranger, who'd strolled into my life and rocked my world. As one long kiss unfurled after another, it seemed to me I was going into a forbidden place. As we paused for air, I simultaneously came to my senses.

433

'We're right under Flora's bedroom!' I breathed.

'So we'll go inside,' he reasoned, hands in my hair, lips softly touching mine again. 'God, you're lovely, Annie.'

And the thing was, I felt lovely in his arms. And so we went in, making it just through the French windows, where his hands cupped my face again, kissing my neck, tasting me, savouring me inside my shirt, my shoulder.

'We can't!' I gasped. 'The children—upstairs.'

'Of course we can't,' he agreed. 'But I can kiss you, can't I?'

'Oh, yes,' I panted. 'You can kiss me.'

And so he did, until a ring on the doorbell had me flying from his arms and shooting across the other side of the room.

'What was that!' I gasped.

He shrugged. 'Doorbell, I guess. Strange time to call.'

I flew to the little bay window that overlooked the porch, wiping my mouth in horror, tugging down my shirt, convinced it was David. My heart was racing. I peered around.

'It's Adam,' I breathed in relief.

'Oh, OK.' Matt was clearly relieved too. He scratched his head. 'Boy, you sure have a full quota of admirers. I never know which Romeo's gonna show up next.'

I turned to him anxiously. 'What shall I do?'

'I guess show him in, Annie.' He went into the kitchen and started to fill the kettle. 'Be hospitable, get the cookies out. If you leave him standing out there any longer he'll stroll right round the side of the house thinking we can't hear the bell 'cos we're in the garden, and come in anyway, so— Ah, Adam. Welcome!' Matt stuck out his hand and beamed widely as Adam appeared through the French windows.

Adam shook the proffered hand, nonplussed. 'Hi.' He frowned. 'Sounds suspiciously like you were expecting me.'

'No, no, not expecting, but certainly a pleasant and delightful surprise. Just making coffee: will you have some?'

'Sure, why not.' Adam ran his hand through his curls, taken aback. 'Blimey, I'd forgotten you were still here, actually. Forgot you two have this weird kind of modus vivendi.'

'Oh, not weird,' said Matt, shooting him a blowtorch grin. 'Not when we have so many unexpected visitors keeping us sane and normal. Pretty much open house here in the summer season, eh, Annie? Party's never over. Coffee for you too?'

'Please.' I suppressed my amusement. Suddenly felt brave. If he was going to brazen this out, then I could too. I folded my arms and watched as Adam strolled speculatively round the sitting room, hands in pockets. As he stopped to stare up at a print of a gull above the fire-place, it struck me that he was really quite a small man. And going a bit thin on the back of his head. Why had I never noticed that?

Adam turned and fished in his pocket. 'Here.' He handed me Flora's watch. 'She left it behind. I was passing, so I thought I'd drop it in.'

'No one "passes" this place, Adam,' I said, placing the watch in an ashtray. 'It's pretty much off the beaten track.'

'No, well, I . . .' He looked almost uncomfortable. 'I wanted to see you. Have a word.'

There was a pause.

'Oh Lord, don't mind me.' Matt threw up his hands in mock horror. 'I'll check out the sunset.'

He placed a tray of coffee in front of us, flashed Adam another smile, then took his own mug and sauntered out into the garden. I watched him go. My eyes were shining. I turned to look at my ex-husband and felt an almost airborne quality. I perched on the edge of a table.

'So. What was so urgent that it couldn't wait until morning?'

He slipped into the sofa, cradling his mug. 'Well, not urgent, as such. I just . . .' He stopped. Scratched his chin ruefully. 'You know, Annie, this isn't quite how I envisaged this little tête-à-tête. I mean, you perched up there and that guy hovering down the garden. Come and sit by me.' He patted the sofa, grinning slyly.

I smiled. 'No, thanks. Look, Adam. If you've come here to say what I think you have, that things aren't going too well with Cozzy, that you've realised the error of your philandering ways, that you're sorry you let our marriage slide, but that was then and this is now and you're no longer emotionally immature and pretty sure you've got your shit together and let's have another stab at it, then I have to tell you you've picked a bad moment.' I stood up. 'I was just washing up the supper things and, as you know, I can't abide an untidy house. So unless you'd like to dry up?'

He regarded me in astonishment. 'Well, stone me,' he said finally. 'I seem to be about as irresistible as a greasy plate.'

'Oh, don't take it personally. It's just I've heard it all before. And the thing is, Adam, I *know* that right now you really do want me to come back, and sincerely believe it'll be for ever, but you just can't help it, can you? The fact is that some people are born with honour, and some aren't.'

He blinked. 'What?'

'It's true. You either have it, or you don't—like good health or an Irish accent or blonde hair or an artistic eye. But never mind, it's not your fault.' I gave him a bright smile. 'Come on, Adam, come and dry up for me, there's a good chap. There's something terribly attractive about a man at the draining board, and you never know'—I twinkled at him—'I might change my mind and give you a quick one anyway. For old times' sake.'

He stared at me, slack-jawed. Poleaxed. Then he stood up.

'Right. Well, if that's the way you want to play it, Annie, taking the piss out of the sanctity of our marriage vows, our—'

'Ooh, there's only one person who took the piss out of those, Adam.'

'And won't even consider the happiness of our daughter, our child, the saddest casualty in all of this mess—'

'And the only person I've *ever* really considered. Look.' I strode to the door, flung it wide. 'I'm sorry you've fallen out with Cozzy, and I'm sorry this Cornish holiday isn't working out for you, but it's working out for me. So please take your sentimental heart and your bullying ways and dump it all on someone else's doorstep!'

Something flashed in Adam's eyes. I'd slipped up, and he knew it. He sauntered towards me, a smile playing on his lips.

'Ah, so it's working out for you, is it? Yes, well, clearly. You're not clutching the furniture like you usually do in my presence. Not blushing and running your hands through your dishevelled hair, trying to look at me with loathing when any fool can see the longing in your eyes.' He was standing very close to me now. He reached up and stroked my cheek. Then he let his hand fall gently to my breast.

I slapped it away angrily. 'Piss off!'

He raised his eyebrows, still smiling. 'Hm, interesting. Not even a frisson. I'm impressed. Tell me,' he drawled, cocking his head down the garden in Matt's direction, 'does the good doctor know about this?'

He winked at me. Then, whistling softly, he strolled out of the door, and round the garden to his car. I stood and watched him go for a moment, then slammed the door hard. It rattled in its frame. I stared at the wooden panels, fists balled to my sides. Suddenly I put them to my eyes, burst into tears, and ran up to my room.

I tossed and turned that night, and finally heard Matt come up at about midnight. His door closed softly above me. Thereafter, I slept fitfully, dimly conscious of my dreams billowing around, of even a few pertinent images. I woke again, suddenly, at six thirty, eyes wide open. I lay there, staring into the darkness, waiting to be filled by tears and terrible regret, or by relief—whichever it might be. I waited and waited, but all I felt was a ghastly, mind-numbing confusion.

The reason last night had happened, I figured, was all to do with proximity. Yes, that was it. It was well documented. When people of the opposite sex were cooped up together for any length of time, things that wouldn't normally happen happened. A holiday romance. Where all the senses are heightened by the sun and the sea and romantic fishing trips and beach picnics, and where no proper work or routine intrudes.

This would never have happened had I not been sharing this wretched house. If only I'd listened to David, I thought miserably. I should have gone to the Complete Angler, but I hadn't wanted to. Not just because of this gorgeous house, but . . . because of the gorgeous man in it. I froze as I admitted it to myself. Yes. Yes, he was gorgeous. *Damn.*

Oh God, what had I done? Well, I'd kissed a man, that's all, I reasoned soberly. Golly, hardly a heinous crime. But it was made worse, somehow, by the fact that it had felt so right. So good.

And then, I knew. I had to get away. Go to Mum's. I got up, woozy with lack of sleep, but heady with resolve as I rang Mum.

She was having her breakfast. Five minutes late, by her standards.

'Of course you can come, love,' she'd said in surprise. 'I'll make up the beds. This is very sudden, isn't it?'

'Not really, Mum. I just felt the need to see you.'

'Funny that. Clare felt the need to see me a couple of days ago.'

I shut my eyes tight. Swallowed. No flies on Mum.

I started to pack. An overnight bag, definitely, but actually, enough clothes for a few days. I'd sneak some in for Flora too, without her seeing. And we'd leave before Matt and Tod were awake.

When we arrived at Mum's, I felt heady with relief. An ancient stone farmhouse with two small gables sat before us, and in the yard, encircled by a low, dry-stone wall, the chickens and bantams poked and strutted around. A delicious silence enveloped us.

'Clare's here,' said Flora in surprise as she spotted her car in the drive.

'Yes, she . . . had some work to do. Needed some peace and quiet, but didn't want to traipse all the way back to London.'

'Oh, look! One of the bantams has had chicks. It's Madame Blanche.' She got out excitedly as the pure white French Silky with elaborate pantaloon legs fussed over her chicks by the edge of the pond, urging them to drink, but not to follow the duck's example and take to the water.

In the Dutch barn to the left of the yard I spotted Ted Philpot, the neighbouring farmer to whom Mum rented the land and sold the stock when Dad died. He was pitchforking hay into a trailer—no doubt inexpertly, since, according to Mum, no one forked, or furrowed, or for that matter did any manner of farm work or animal husbandry half as well as Dad had. He raised his hand when he saw me, and I waved back.

As I walked towards the house Mum appeared in the doorway.

'Madame Blanche's had chicks, Granny!' Flora called, dispensing with any formal greeting to her grandmother.

'I know, love. I thought that would please you, but she's that fussy with them.'

'That's because the fox got them last year. She remembers.' Flora abandoned the chicks for a moment to kiss her granny, and I followed suit.

'Hello, Annabel, love. Everything all right?' Her sharp grey eyes scanned my face anxiously.

'Fine.' I smiled. 'Just woke up this morning and felt like coming to see you, that's all. You look much better, Mum. You've put on a bit of weight.' It was true, her face had recovered its bloom and her eyes were brighter. Dad had died four years ago now, but it had really knocked her for six.

She chuckled. 'Eating too much, probably. So used to baking for a family, I do it out of force of habit, then eat it all myself.'

'How's Mr Philpot doing?' I teased, ducking my head as I followed her through the low doorway.

'Oh, he's not doin' too badly.'

'Oh, right,' I said, surprised not to get the usual tirade about how he only banged in post and rails and didn't use the more traditional dry-stone walling, but perhaps she was getting more tolerant in her old age.

Inside, the kitchen gleamed. The waxed terracotta floor shone up at the solid fuel black Rayburn that Mum still filled and stoked by hand, which sparkled at the blue and white delft china on the pine dresser on the opposite wall. Ralph, the border collie, was snoozing peaceably by the Rayburn, thumping his tail on the floor by way of apology for being too old to get up and greet us properly. All was exactly as it should be: home. I sank gratefully into the Windsor chair by the Rayburn with its faded gingham cushion, and Flora bent to make a fuss of Ralph.

'No Clare?'

'She's upstairs tryin' some clothes on. We went into Exeter yesterday and she went mad.'

'Any other babies, Granny?' asked Flora.

'Yes, love, there are ducklin's out back, an' if you go into the barn you might find Cinders with yet another litter of kittens.'

Flora slipped off eagerly, persuading Ralph to accompany her.

'How is Clare?' I asked as Mum poured boiling water into the old brown pot waiting on the stove.

'She's fine,' she said shortly. 'Now. She wasn't though, when she came. She was beside herself for a bit. Haven't seen her like that since she got a low mark in her geography mocks on account of flu. And I haven't had her open up to me, neither.'

'She did that?'

'Not entirely. But a bit. Well, she said she'd had an altercation with Michael, and you know Clare. That's shorthand for he's left me.'

I looked up. 'She told you that?'

'No, but I guessed as much.' She settled down opposite me in the other Windsor chair and let the pot sit on the Rayburn between us for a bit. 'All that walkin' she's been doing since she got here, been goin' for miles, she has. An' she's not herself, either: not tellin' me what to do and where to live and what to eat. Been better company, actually,' she said thoughtfully, getting up to pour the tea.

I smiled. Mum told it like it was.

'And as I say, shoppin' like her life depended on it yesterday. Like a thing possessed. But then, this morning, well, I don't know,' she pondered, taking a moment. 'She seems a bit perkier. More relaxed, somehow.' She paused to sip her tea.

'Perhaps country air and home cooking is finally working its magic?'

'Oh, yes, it'll do her the power of good, but it won't mend hearts.' She eyed me beadily. 'How's David, love? Knows you're here, does he?'

I breathed in sharply at his name. 'Um, no. Not yet. I'll ring him.'

'I should.' She reached out and passed me the phone from the side. 'Or he'll worry.'

I stared at it in my lap. 'Yes. Yes, he will.'

'Only I know you've got your mobiles an' that, but if he rings that house in Cornwall an' finds it empty . . .'

'Well, except it's not empty, there's someone else . . . someone else staying there,' I faltered.

'Oh, yes. Clare said.'

She sipped her tea quietly, watching me. I could feel my face burning. I took a deep breath and tapped out David's direct line under her steely gaze. Thank God. The answer machine. I didn't have to speak to him and feel even more duplicitous than I already did. I cleared my throat.

'Um, David, hi, it's me. Just to let you know I'm staying at Mum's for a few days, so you can reach me here. I'll speak to you later. Bye!'

'A few days?' said Mum in surprise when I'd hung up.

'Well, I'll . . . see how it goes.'

'Ah. That's just what Clare said. Talk of the devil.'

The door opened and Clare appeared in the doorway, looking as if she were going to Ascot. She was wearing a shocking-pink suit, black stilettoes and a huge black hat. 'Da-daa!' She struck a pose, then nearly tottered off her heels when she saw me. 'You're here! Blimey, you weren't supposed to see this!'

I boggled. 'What have you come as?'

'I've come as the sister of the bride,' she declared, giving a twirl. 'Like it?' She struck another pose. 'It's for your wedding.'

'Oh!' I spilled my tea in the saucer.

'Mum and I went into Exeter yesterday and we went completely berserk. You should see what Mum bought. Honestly, Annie, I've never seen her look so smart. It's stunning. And a bag too, and shoes to match—and a hat!'

I turned to Mum, feeling the colour drain from my face. 'But I thought you'd decided . . . since it was Claridge's . . .'

'Oh, that was just nerves talkin'.' She brushed some crumbs briskly from her lap. 'No, I put down that phone and said to myself: Marjorie Hooper. Of course you won't miss your daughter's weddin' on account of it being in London and havin' nothin' to wear. And Ted said the same.'

'Ted?'

'Philpot,' put in Clare, giving me a look.

'No, I wouldn't miss it for the world, love,' went on Mum smoothly, 'and I apologise if I gave the impression otherwise.'

'Honestly, Annie, Claridge's!' Clare said incredulously. 'I nearly fell over when Mum told me. It's so un-you.'

'It was David's idea,' I muttered, sinking into my tea.

'Obviously. Now, come on, Mum, show her your things,' Clare urged.

'Later, love,' Mum demurred.

'Oh, no, go on, now! Tell you what, I'll get them. Don't move!'

She teetered out of the kitchen and off up the stairs on her heels. We heard her clip-clipping across the landing above us. I stared dumbly into my tea. A moment later she was back, holding a dove-grey suit from a hanger, a hatbox and a pair of blue shoes. Mum stood up and Clare held the suit against her.

'What d'you think?' Mum asked shyly, taking the hanger.

'Oh, and the hat. The hat makes it.' Clare got it out and placed it carefully on her head. Adjusted it, then stood back to admire.

I forced a smile at Mum; my mum, standing proudly before me, with her mother-of-the-bride outfit.

'Lovely,' I gulped. 'Mum, you look gorgeous.'

She bent her head and stroked the cloth reverently. 'Never had anythin' like it in my life, not even when I married your dad.'

I couldn't speak.

'And you did cheat us out of a wedding the first time round,' Clare warned. 'Oh, and we saw a lovely dress for Flora, didn't we, Mum?'

'What's that?' Flora came in breathless, being pulled along by Ralph who'd clearly got his second wind. 'Oh, Clare, look at you! You look like Cruella de Vil!' She giggled.

'It's for your mum's wedding,' Clare said proudly, giving another twirl. 'And, actually, if Mummy says it's OK, I'll take you into Exeter and see if you like this dress I saw. It's a floaty Ghost number. You'll love it.'

'Oh, cool! Can I, Mum?'

'Yes, of course,' I breathed. My throat felt inexplicably dry.

'I was wondering what I was going to wear,' said Flora. 'Do I have to have a hat?'

'I wouldn't have thought so, love,' said Mum, 'but, Annabel, you ought to ring that girl who's makin' your outfit. See if it's finished. You've only got a few weeks to go now.'

'Yes, you should have a fitting,' agreed Clare. 'You might have lost a bit of weight; most brides do. And what are you having exactly? Ivory silk?'

'Yes. It's . . . a shift dress.' I stood up, ostensibly to pour some more tea, but actually to turn my back to them. My hands were trembling.

'With pearl buttons?' Clare was prattling on.

'Yes. Down the back.' I gazed out of the back door at the hills rising in the distance. I wanted to be out there now, on top of the furthest one.

'Flora, love,' Mum was saying, 'come and help me get your bags from the car an' I'll show you your room. It's the usual one, up in the rafters.' She went out with Flora in tow.

I felt my heartbeat come down slightly, now Mum had left the room.

'You're chipper,' I remarked to Clare as we both sat down.

'Oh.' She blushed. 'Yes. Well, I wrote to Michael. He called first thing this morning, as soon as it arrived.'

'Did you tell him about Theo?'

'I did.'

'And what did he say?'

'He said: "Ah, just a fumble. That makes us even."'

I smiled. 'Told you.'

'Yes. But he also . . . laid down a few conditions.'

'Such as?'

'Such as I give up work.'

'Clare!'

'But I'd already decided to do that anyway,' she said quickly.

'But you love that job!'

She looked at me squarely, eyes wide and frank. 'I love my husband more. And my children. And that hasn't come to me in a blinding flash; I've always known it, Annie. And I can't have both. Don't want to have both. Not if it means going at it all half-cocked, half-crazy with tiredness and not enjoying any of it, which was what I was doing. I'm going to take a break, and then . . . well, then we'll see.' She grinned. 'Anyway, we're having dinner tonight, in Exeter,' she said shyly.

'Oh, Clare, I'm so pleased,' I said, relieved. 'He wouldn't have agreed to that unless he was reconsidering, surely?'

She shrugged. 'Either that or he's going to issue me with divorce proceedings over the prawn cocktail, but he did say the kids were missing me. He also said that they were breaking all the rules: putting milk bottles on the table and throwing leftovers away without covering them in cling film and putting them in the fridge.' She grinned.

I smiled. At least she could laugh at herself. 'And, Clare'—I took a deep breath—'if it does work out, don't go back all guns blazing and—'

'I know,' she interrupted quickly. 'You don't have to tell me. Not so full on. Turn it down. Let them all chill. I *know*, Annie. What d'you think I've been doing on these windy hilltops these past two days, apart from reassessing my life? I tell you, all this fresh air is very good for the soul; I highly recommend it.' She eyed me carefully. 'Although I wasn't aware that you were in need of this place's healing properties.'

I glanced quickly down at my tea. Aware of her gaze still on me.

'What brings you down to the re-hab clinic then? What made you hurtle down to Exeter's answer to The Priory at such short notice, hm?'

Luckily Mum and Flora came back at that moment, and I didn't have to answer; I could get out of the beam of her enquiring stare and back to ordinary things, like making a salad and laying the table for lunch.

The day drifted on; Clare washed her hair and lay in the sun to dry it and top up her tan, then she painted her nails, all in preparation for her dinner that evening with Michael. I lay beside her on an ancient, creaking sun lounger in the back garden, and asked her about Ted Philpot.

She shrugged. 'Mum's said nothing. All I know is her attitude's changed towards him. She says his farming methods are different from Dad's, more modern, but that that's no bad thing, and that now he's on his own, she asks him in for lunch most Sundays.'

'He's on his own?'

'His wife died last year. Didn't you know that?'

'So . . . is there something?'

'You tell me. You know Mum, she wouldn't say, but her attitude has certainly softened towards him.'

I sighed. 'Convenient, I suppose. Both losing their partners and living at neighbouring farms . . .'

She shrugged. 'Nothing wrong with convenience. Look how many happy marriages are born of it. Mum only married Dad because their parents were best friends, and again, had neighbouring farms, and how many people meet someone at work or on holiday? I met Michael on holiday and— Why are you going all pink?'

'I'm not,' I said, hiding my face as I bent spuriously to tie the laces of my deck shoes. 'Anyway, Mum will make up her own mind. Nothing we think or say will make any difference, happily.'

'Exactly.'

Later that day, as I drifted aimlessly about, wandering from the house to the garden and back again, Mum shooed me out for a walk.

'Go on, love,' she said, kindly. 'The air will do you good.'

And I did go. I walked right to the top of Biggen Tor, where only a few intrepid sheep grazed, and then stood panting, holding my sides and gazing down at the glorious view before me. Devon was at its most biscuit-tin-like at this time of year: green and lush and gentle, with only a few grey farms sprinkled in the folds of the valleys. I breathed in, knowing I could lose myself in this special place and find peace, had always done so, but it failed to work its magic. Still Matt's face, his gentle blue eyes, his voice, the touch of his hands last night came to me. There was no escape.

Give it time, I told myself grimly, walking back down, as troubled as when I'd gone up. Give it time. You've only been away a few hours.

When I got back, Mum was just putting down the phone in the kitchen. 'Oh, you've just missed him.'

'Who?' I said stupidly, my heart pounding.

'David. That was him callin' you back, but he said not to ring just now, as he was dashin' off for a game of squash with Jamie after work. He said he'd call you later.'

That was good. A good sign. He only played squash when he was feeling up and buoyant. Hopefully he'd got things more in perspective.

That night, knowing I wouldn't sleep, I stayed up late pretending to watch a late-night film. When the final credits rolled I climbed the stairs to my old room. Everything was as it had always been: the books in the shelves, the faded rose wallpaper, the dressing table with its floral skirt, behind which I'd hidden all manner of secrets, including letters from Adam, all were exactly the same.

I undressed and slipped into the little single bed, feeling wretched with exhaustion.

'Annabel. Annabel, wake up!' It was Mum. She had hold of my shoulder and was shaking me vigorously awake.

I opened my eyes blearily, and saw her anxious face leaning over me.

'Listen, love, Gertrude's been on the phone. She's just rung.'

'Gertrude?'

I raised myself up on to my elbows.. 'Why? What's happened?'

'Annabel. I'm so sorry.' Her eyes filled with tears. She put a hand to her mouth. 'It's David. He's taken an overdose.'

I stared at her, horrified. 'An overdose!' My heart stopped. 'Is he dead?'

'No! No, he's not dead, he's been taken to hospital. He's alive, but they're pumping his stomach.'

For a moment I could only gaze at her in frozen horror. Then I snapped to, flinging back the bedclothes and swinging my legs out. 'Is Gertrude still on the phone?'

'No, she had to go, she's at the hospital. But, Annabel, love, she said David didn't want you to know.'

'What?' I paused to snatch up my jeans.

'Said he'd begged Gertrude not to tell you, but she felt that you should know.'

'Of course I bloody should!' I cried, flying across the room to grab a T-shirt and some shoes. 'Where is he?'

'He's at the Chelsea and Westminster, I've written it down. Oh, my love, why on earth would he do such a thing?'

'I don't know,' I muttered, diving into my clothes and knowing full well that I did know but . . . God, not to this extent, surely?

'But he's getting married in a few weeks,' wailed Mum, still clasping and unclasping her hands. 'Why would a young man with a weddin' coming up, with his whole life ahead of him—'

'It's not to do with me.' I swung round suddenly and gripped her shoulders. 'At least . . . I don't think it is.' I let her go. 'It's to do with work, Mum. Something at work. He . . . made a mistake, you see. Someone died. It upset him terribly.'

'Oh!' She sat down abruptly on a chair. 'Oh, I see. Poor David.'

'Yes. Poor David.' I ran my hands through my hair despairingly. 'And I should have been there for him, Mum,' I choked and burst into tears. She flew to sit by my side.

'There now, don't take on so,' she murmured, her arm firmly round my shoulders, squeezing hard. 'You weren't to know this could happen.'

'But, Mum . . . I should have gove back to London with him.' I looked up at her beseechingly, my face wet with tears. 'If things had been different, I *would* have gone, wouldn't I?'

'What things, love?' Her anxious eyes searched my face, uncomprehending. 'I don't know what you mean.'

If it had been Matt, was what I meant, I thought horrified. If it had been Matt in trouble, would I have gone? Yes, like a shot. Terrified by my own feelings, I got to my feet.

'I must go,' I muttered, heading for the door. 'Must go to him. Now.'

'Of course you must, an' he'll be fine, don't worry. It's you I'm worried about,' she said as we reached the hall.

I turned quickly. 'Why?'

'Well, first off, I don't want you drivin' all that way all upset like this. You'll have an accident. Have a cup of tea an' put somethin' in your stomach before you go. Calm down a bit.'

'Oh. Yes, you're right.' I followed her numbly into the kitchen and watched as she poured from a pot already brewed.

'Where's Clare?' I glanced nervously about.

'Still asleep. Flora's asleep, too.'

'Good.' I swallowed hard. 'Mum, don't tell them, will you?' I looked at her pleadingly as she put a cup and saucer in front of me. 'I mean, I'm sure you're right and he'll be fine, and so . . . so there's no reason for anyone to know really, is there?'

She fixed me with her grey eyes. 'No. No reason.'

She reached into the fridge for ham, and I watched numbly as she quickly sliced the bread, buttered it and cut sandwiches into triangles before packing them neatly in foil, setting the package on the table in front of me.

'I can't eat,' I muttered.

'I know, love, that's why I've packed it. Eat some on the way.'

I nodded, then got up. 'I'd better go. You'll look after Flora for me?'

'Of course.' She followed me to the door.

As I kissed her floury cheek on the doorstep, she put a hand on my arm. 'Think very carefully, my love,' she said. 'Really carefully. Nobody wants you to be a martyr.'

'What d'you mean?'

'What I say. One in the family's quite enough. An' you're very like me, Annabel. Too like me. Very biddable. Malleable.'

I held her eyes, and it seemed to me all her years with Dad rolled back before me. I wondered how much she'd suffered in silence. Clare had certainly been bludgeoned with education, but . . .

She smiled, reading my mind. 'Oh, no, love, nothin' terrible. Your dad and I rubbed along quite happily as it happens, an' I never let him think otherwise. Companionship gets a very bad press these days, yet sometimes it's worth fightin' for. But you, Annabel, you've got more choice than I had. An' I don't think you're lookin' for companionship.'

'Mum.' I licked my lips, knowing this moment might not come again. 'Mum, with Ted, is that companionship, or . . .'

She stopped in the yard. Looked ahead. 'I've known Ted all my life,' she said quietly. 'Longer even than I knew your dad. Went to school with him. But Shirley set her cap at him, an' Ted was an easy-goin' young man, easily flattered, so he married her. And I married your dad. And very happy we all were too, on our neighbourin' farms.' She walked on and opened the car door for me.

'But you always loved him?' I stared at her back, horrified. 'Ted? But, you were always criticising him, always needling him, and—'

'We must shield the heart somehow, mustn't we, love?' she said softly.

I stared at her for a long moment. 'So—so then why didn't you . . . I mean, Dad's been dead four years now, why didn't you—'

'An' Shirley's not been dead a year,' she said quietly.

'Oh,' I breathed. 'Yes, I see,' I said, our eyes still locked.

'Now come on,' she said brightly, breaking the moment, 'be off with you. An' as I say, whichever way you go, whichever way the wind takes you, all will be well. You'll be as happy as I was. It's in your nature to make the best of things, just as it is in mine. All I'm saying is, never forget you have a choice.'

Chapter Six

WHEN I GOT TO LONDON, some hours later, I wove my way through the busy streets to the Fulham Road and parked behind the hospital, in the underground car park. I ran up the ramp to the main entrance. Taking a deep breath, I pushed through the plate-glass doors and went into the cool, marble, minimalist interior.

When I asked the girl on reception, she looked at me in surprise. 'Dr Palmer?'

'Yes, he's . . . he's a patient.'

'Oh. Yes, of course.' She flushed with recognition, embarrassed. 'He's on Parthenon Ward, fifth floor.'

The lift took for ever to come, so I ran up the escalator and then down the shiny linoleum corridors flanked by vast floor-to-ceiling windows. I arrived panting at another desk. Clutched it.

'Could you tell me, I'm looking for Dr . . . Oh. No, don't bother.'

A tall figure rose from a chair at the far end of the corridor. Gertrude was coming slowly towards me, her usually erect figure slightly stooped, a lace hanky clutched in one hand. I ran to her.

'Gertrude!'

We embraced.

'Annabel, my dear,' she said softly. 'I'm so sorry.'

'Is he all right?' I gasped.

'Asleep,' she said, motioning her head to a room behind us. 'We won't disturb him. Come. Sit by me.'

She took my arm and led me wearily back to a line of grey plastic chairs outside his door, sat down and patted the one beside her.

'I blame myself,' I whispered, realising I did. This was all my fault.

'Don't be ridiculous,' she said crisply. 'This has nothing whatever to do with you.'

Her words stung, almost like an insult. I turned. She laid a hand on my arm. 'And everything,' she went on more gently, 'to do with David being David. So much of which he should have told you.'

'Oh, but he did, Gertrude, he did!' I insisted. 'He told me about the patient dying, about the possible court case. And he told me all about Hugh, too, his reservations about David becoming a doctor, David's own worries about not being good enough. I know all of that.'

She nodded. 'And you think that could be enough to tip him over the edge like this?' She regarded me keenly. I blanched.

'Well . . . no. I didn't really think so, to be honest. I'm surprised. Which is why I thought maybe it was me . . .' I trailed off.

'No, Annabel, it's not you. It goes further back than that.' She sighed. 'You know I brought him up, of course. Inherited a little eight-year-old boy who'd lost his parents. A very bewildered, frightened child.'

'Yes, I know that. They died in a boating accident, but—'

'One died in a boating accident,' she interrupted quietly. 'His mother. She dived off a boat far out in the middle of the Camel estuary one evening. Never came back.'

'The Camel—' I stared. 'But I thought . . . David said it was abroad. At least I thought it was. Or someone said . . .'

'Well, he never really says, if you think about it. He deliberately keeps it vague. And I do too. For his sake. But I should have told you where it happened when you came to see me to ask about the house. But he'd expressly asked me not to.'

'So . . . Taplow House? It happened there?'

'On a family holiday. David was on the boat with his parents one evening; they had a little dinghy that they kept in the creek. His mother was swimming from it and David and his father were fishing. Pammy obviously got into difficulties and they didn't notice. David had caught something and Angus, his father, was helping him reel it in. When they turned round, she'd gone. There was no sign of her, just empty sea. Angus dived in and swam around desperately, and finally he found her, floating among a mass of driftwood and seaweed, face down. Somehow he managed to haul her back on board and then rowed like crazy back to the shore.'

'Was she alive?'

'Just, apparently. Angus tried to resuscitate her on the shore, but failed, so he carried her up to the house, up to their bedroom, sobbing, panicking completely, demented with grief, trailed by David. He laid her on the bed, still desperately trying to resuscitate her, shutting David out of the room when he tried to come in. She was his whole life, you see. A strong, beautiful, vibrant woman, and he of course was a brilliant man. Brilliant doctor. But he couldn't save her. It was David who finally dialled nine-nine-nine, downstairs on his own, trembling, terrified.'

'Oh God . . . how awful!'

'But then when the ambulance came, ten minutes later, the sirens wailing up the lane, which Angus must have heard, there was a loud bang from upstairs. David ran up and found his father lying in a pool of blood. He'd shot himself.'

'Oh dear God!'

'David was there for a few minutes on his own with them before the ambulance men arrived.'

'Gertrude, how awful! He never told me. I never knew!'

'I know, and he should have done. Of course he should. But who's to say it's the genesis of all of this?' She waved her jewelled hand despairingly at the door behind which David lay. 'We're now surmising, or at least I am, that because he was at that house again, it triggered all this off.'

'But why *go* to the house?' I said, baffled. 'Why encourage me to take it when presumably he hadn't been back there since . . .'

'Only once, since it happened. Hugh and I took him one year, hoping for the best, but it was a disaster.' She sighed. 'I *was* astounded when David rang me and said you wanted it for the summer, but you know, my dear, I think he wanted to face up to the demons. Banish them.'

I thought back to that little boy, standing over the bodies of his parents at that scene of horror. Suddenly my mouth dried. I swung round to her. 'Gertrude, where—which bedroom was it in?'

'The main one, with the picture window, looking out over the bay.'

'Yes,' I breathed, remembering our two nights in there together. How must he have felt? I remembered his bout of passionate love-making. Was that banishing the demons? I shivered.

'I think I shall sell it now, however,' said Gertrude, straightening up in her chair. 'I'm getting too old. And after all this . . .'

We were silent for a while. Each staring bleakly out of the window at the rooftops of London beyond. The sun hung in a misty haze over them. I felt my own mood, too, suspended, floating.

'I'm going in now, Gertrude. Going to see him.'

She nodded. 'And I'm going home for a bit. I'm exhausted.'

'You must be.'

I went to the door and stared through the circle of glass at David's sleeping profile. Took a deep breath.

'Remember,' Gertrude cautioned, coming up behind me, 'he didn't want me to tell you. He doesn't know you're here.'

'I know.'

I turned and squeezed both her hands. She squeezed mine back and we traded brave smiles, both with watery eyes. Then I reached for the handle and went in.

As I shut the door softly behind me, David's eyes flickered. He was lying on his back, his head slightly elevated by the bedhead. It took him a moment to wake up and register, but then he groaned.

'Oh God.'

'I know,' I said, crossing the room and slipping quickly into a chair by his bed. 'Gertrude said you'd told her not to tell me, but she had to, David, you must see that.' I took his hand, lying limp on the blanket.

'Why?' he said harshly, turning his head away.

'Because . . .' I faltered, then tried again. 'Well, because if I don't know, I can't help you.' I squeezed his hand. 'Oh, David. Why did you do it? Was it just the court case?'

'*Just* the court case?' he said with heavy emphasis. 'My professional reputation dragged through the mud? Unable to work as a doctor again, everything I've worked for—*just* the court case?'

'I . . . I know,' I stammered. 'Awful. But it hasn't happened yet, David. They've only threatened legal action, haven't they? And you're innocent until proven guilty, and they may not even find you guilty!'

'They will,' he said flatly, turning away again. 'But it wasn't just that,' he added bitterly. 'Since you ask. It was everything.'

I felt scared. Licked my lips. Tried again.

'David, Gertrude told me about your parents. I'm so sorry.'

'But, you see, that's not what I want,' he said quietly. 'Your sympathy.'

'N-no, I . . . I'm just saying.' I swallowed, hunting for the words. 'I'm just saying I couldn't come in here and pretend I didn't know.'

'Why not? I did. For years. Why does everything have to be put out and aired on an emotional washing line?'

I inhaled sharply. Everything about his demeanour was hard and knowing. I tried a different tack.

'I'm so glad you didn't do it, David,' I said warmly. 'So glad you called an ambulance.'

'I didn't. My neighbour in Islington found me. She'd taken delivery of a registered parcel and used her key to let herself in and put it on my kitchen table. She walked past me lying on the sofa. Dropped the parcel and screamed the place down, apparently. Then called an ambulance.'

I stared at him, horrified. 'You were going to do it?'

'Oh, yes. I was.'

'And . . .' I tried to scramble my thoughts together. 'N-no note, or anything?' I stammered. 'I mean . . . what about me?'

Awful. He'd wanted to end his life, and all I could think was: What about me? It hung in the air, suspended. I couldn't take it back.

He kept the expressionless mask in place as he stared at the ceiling. Suddenly it buckled. 'That's what I said,' he gasped, 'when it happened to me. What I said when my father did it. What about me!'

Tears began to flood sideways out of his eyes, streaming down on to the pillow. He covered his face with his hands. I swooped to hold him, cradling his head in my arms as he sobbed.

'I'm so sorry, Annie,' he choked. 'So sorry!'

'Don't. Don't!'

He sobbed on and on, and we stayed like that, me holding his head tightly until, at length, he recovered. I took his hand again as he rested his head back on the pillow.

'And I'm sorry I didn't tell you,' he said, wiping his face roughly with his forearm. 'I wanted to, so many times. Wanted to get over the past once and for all, and I thought I could do it with you beside me, you see. Thought I could draw strength from you, because I loved you so much.' He was quiet for a moment. 'But when I got back here, to London, I felt this wave of terror literally sweep from my head to my toes. Because I knew that having faced it and failed, I was hollow.'

We were both silent for a while and I digested what he'd said. After a while, a nurse popped her head round the door.

'Everything all right?'

David didn't answer. Continued staring out of the window.

'Yes, we're fine, thank you,' I said swiftly.

She went away again.

I took his hand. 'Are they nice to you in here?' I asked anxiously.

'Not particularly,' he said wryly. 'Suicide cases are always treated with disdain. And a doctor who tries it, well . . .'

I took a deep breath. Let it out shakily. Oh, David.

'Anyway. I won't be here for long. I can discharge myself tomorrow.'

'Exactly.' I raised a smile. 'And then you'll be back in Sloane Street again, where you belong. When you've had a bit of time off.'

He gave a thin smile. 'No, I'm not going back to the surgery.' He turned to look at me. 'I'm going to Nicaragua, Annie.'

'Nicaragua!' I was startled. 'Why?'

'Because there's a terrible famine unfolding over there and the Red Cross are desperate for doctors. I think I could be of some help.'

I stared. He looked back at me. Composed. Implacable.

'Right.' I swallowed. Did he mean him, or all of us? I thought of the three of us out there, crowded into a little mud hut in the jungle—or was it the desert?

David was watching me. He smiled. A proper, gentle smile, for the first time since I'd been in that room. 'No, you were right the first time, Annie. It's what *I'm* going to do, not what *we're* going to do.'

'You mean . . . on your own?'

He held my gaze. 'Do you love me, Annie?'

I opened my mouth to speak. His eyes were challenging. Not hostile, but challenging. I glanced down.

'I . . . Well. Of course I—'

'Hey,' he interrupted softly. Squeezed my hand. 'That's enough. Let's not go there. We both know the truth. I love you to pieces, to distraction, always have done. But you've met someone else.'

I glanced up in terror.

'I know,' he said gently. 'I could tell. In Cornwall. And it's all right, my darling, I promise. Yes, I'm sad, but it wasn't the catalyst for all of this.' He looked beyond me. 'Another phase of my life is unfolding, and, because it's something I've always wanted to do, I can face it alone.'

I bent my head. Rested my forehead on his hand in shame.

'Oh, David, I'm so sorry,' I whispered. 'I'm so ashamed.'

'Don't be. You can't help falling in love. You met me when you were so low, Annie. I was just what you needed at the time. Necessary ballast to keep you afloat. Keep you safe. And I badly wanted to keep you. Thought marriage, babies—lots of babies, quickly—would do the trick. Bind you to me. But I see now how hopeless it was.'

He gave a wry smile. 'This may sound ridiculous, but I'm actually glad I took an overdose. Glad I was rescued too. By doing something so drastic, I've stared rock bottom in the face, and now I can only go up. I'm so glad I didn't die. Hugo says the court case will be short with possibly an out-of-court settlement. As soon as it's over, I'll be off. But I can't say I'm letting you go with joy jumping in my heart, Annie, because I love you so much, but this is the only way.'

I gazed at him, silent. Marvelling at him. Suddenly I was overcome with tears that fled hot and salty down my face. David held out his arms and I clung to him as we mourned what we'd nearly had.

After a while, though, after much nose-blowing and exchanging of shaky smiles, he patted my hand. I knew it was my signal to go.

I sat in my car in the hospital car park for a long while, my head resting on the wheel. It was tempting to wallow in emotion, in profound regret for what we'd lost, David and I, and I sat there, waiting for it to happen, waiting to feel bereft. Instead, as I lifted my head at last, something else flooded through me: something that felt profoundly like relief—albeit guilty relief—yet it was there.

I swung out into the busy main road. In my heart I knew I couldn't have gone through with it. Would have put a stop to it eventually, but probably right at the last minute. And the reason I couldn't have gone through with it—this, again, came to me with all the subtlety of the Rank gong—was because the force driving Matt and me together was already far too strong. We were already too deeply in . . . what? Was it love? I nearly drove off the road. Yes. Yes, that was it. I'd fallen in love.

Swallowing hard but feeling horribly euphoric, I beetled off down the Fulham Road towards the M4. Towards the sun. If any sense at all prevailed, everything told me that after a four-hour drive from Devon I shouldn't even be contemplating doing the same again plus another hour to Cornwall, and should be heading for my home round the corner to spend the night before setting off the next morning. I dithered for a moment at the junction to my road. OK. I'd pop home and collect the post, I decided, but that was all.

The familiar road was dry and dusty, suffering in the late July heat, and on my doorstep the geraniums and petunias wilted forlornly in the sun. As I went in, the mustiness closed around me like a shawl. It all looked so small, so dingy. Familiar, but in a long ago, regretful sort of way. It made me feel sad. I stooped on the mat to collect the sea of post, then went down the passage into the kitchen. A coffee cup David had used was in the sink, and I gulped when I saw one of his cashmere sweaters hanging over the back of a chair. No doubt he would come in and pick up his things when I was away, I thought. Yes. Much easier. A clean break, no fuss.

I had a quick glass of water then headed purposefully back outside, double locking the front door behind me and walking to the car.

My mobile rang as I drove off down the road.

It was Mum. 'How is he, love?'

'He's . . . fine, Mum. Fine. Recovering.'

'And you?'

'Yes, I'm OK, too. We've sorted everything out. There . . .' I faltered. Licked my lips and started again. 'There isn't going to be a wedding.'

She paused. 'I thought not. And how do you feel?'

'Well, the awful thing is, I feel rather relieved.'

'Not awful,' she said slowly.

'How's Flora?' I asked.

'Well, that's what I was ringin' to tell you, love. She went off with Clare, back to Rock. Clare had a lovely night out with Michael by all accounts last night, very starry-eyed she was at the breakfast table this mornin', very unlike Clare. I don't know what their bust-up was about, but it's done them the world of good. Anyway, she couldn't wait to get back this mornin', and she took Flora with her to stay with the cousins. We didn't know how long you'd be, love, and Flora seemed keen enough. An' I thought: Well, if you was heading back to Cornwall, silly to make a detour here. Flora's got your bags an' that, so you'll need to pick her up first . . .' She sounded anxious.

'No, no, quite right, Mum. You were right. I would have been going back there. I need to . . . sort some things out.'

'I thought as much,' she said. 'Well. Good luck. I hope he's worth it.'

I stared into the receiver. My mum. My wise old mum.

'He is,' I breathed.

It was a long drive but I didn't mind. In fact I felt quite energised. I was hungry too, and suddenly glad of the sandwiches Mum had packed and which I hadn't been able to face on the way up, but polished off now with alacrity. Finally, just as the evening sun was setting and the sky turning a dusty pink, I rounded a bend and there was the sea.

When I got to Clare's house in Trebetherick, all was quiet. The back door was open though, so I went in and almost tripped over. Buckets and spades littered the sandy kitchen floor, and surfboards and wet towels were draped decoratively on the table. In all the time Clare had been taking this house I'd never seen it submerged in such glorious two fingers existence, and yet Clare had beaten me back here: I could see her overnight bag. She'd had time to clear up. Progress, I thought with a wry smile as I went out into the garden. Definitely progress.

I sauntered down the lawn. It was a beautiful evening, and I knew they wouldn't be far away. As I walked across the dunes, I saw two familiar figures huddled by a rock, gazing out to sea, while the children made sandcastles nearby. Dan had his arm round Rosie's shoulders, which, for some reason, brought a lump to my throat as I approached.

'Hello, young lovers,' I said, settling down in the sand beside them, hugging my knees. 'Admiring the sunset and counting your blessings?'

Dan looked round with a smile. 'Spot on, actually. And, to our surprise, we find we have more than we thought.'

'Where've you been then?' asked Rosie, peering round Dan to look at me carefully.

'Oh, here and there,' I said lightly. She caught my eye and I had a feeling she knew. 'So come on, then,' I went on quickly, 'what are they, these blessings?'

'Dan's been offered a job,' said Rosie excitedly.

'Oh, Dan, that's marvellous.' I put an arm round his neck and gave it a squeeze. 'Congratulations! Back in the square mile? Dusting off your pinstripes and flogging insurance?'

'No, in a white coat flogging shellfish, actually.'

'*Shell*fish?'

'Well, oysters, primarily. But I'm happy to turn my hand to all manner of crustacean.'

'But . . . Hang on, where? Billingsgate market or something?'

'Wadebridge, actually,' put in Rosie helpfully. 'On the industrial estate. Not the most salubrious of locations, but jolly convenient.'

'Convenient!' I stared. 'Well, hardly. Only about a four-hundred-mile commute. Are you two on drugs or something?'

Rosie grinned. 'Oh, no, something much more intoxicating.' She leaned forward excitedly. 'Remember that supper we had the other night at Rick Stein's? When we went out with Michael's friends, you know, the estate agent and his wife?'

'Er, yes.'

'Well, the estate agent's uncle, who joined us later for a drink, runs this seafood business down here, only he wants to retire. He's looking for someone to run the business.'

'But you can't do that from London!'

'Oh, no, we'd have to move down here. Sell Fulham for a fortune, hopefully, and buy ourselves a lovely old cottage and then Dan can drive to work instead of sitting on a sweaty tube.'

'But . . .' I blustered. 'Hang on. Won't you miss London?' I knew as I said it they wouldn't, but I felt desperate. Horrified to lose her.

'Not a bit. Except for friends, but even then only a few. Most have moved out. The only person I'll really miss is you.'

A great lump came to my throat. I knew she was right, that they should do it, but the idea of London without Rosie appalled me.

'We were at our wits' end, Annie,' Rosie said softly. 'Really desperate. We were sinking in London. Ploughing into savings and going under the waterline. Dan's been out of work over a year now, and the City's in turmoil, so even if he got back in, what security would he have?'

'I'd be constantly watching my back, knowing that when heads started to roll again, mine would be first. Last in, first out, that's the rule. Well, I'm never going through that again, Annie. Never. I'm going to run my own show and I don't care how hard I'll have to work to do it.'

They looked at each other and exchanged smiles. And I smiled too. Forgot my selfishness and how much I'd miss them, because I knew they were right. They would thrive down here, I thought. I could just see Rosie lovingly transforming a neglected old house, just as she had in

London. There would be tough times ahead, but I knew, too, that love conquers all. Believed that. I dredged up a great sigh of longing.

'And you?' said Rosie, softly.

'Hm . . .?'

'Annie, Clare told us. About David.'

'Oh.' So. Mum had told Clare after all. Perhaps it was just as well.

'Annie, I'm so sorry.' Rosie laid a hand on my arm. 'Is he OK?'

'He's fine,' I said shortly. 'Feels a bit sheepish, I think.'

'And the two of you . . .?'

I heaved up another great sigh. Seemed to have a surfeit of them these days. 'He's very kindly let me go, as I believe they say in the city, Dan.'

He smiled down at the sand.

'Ah. I hoped he would,' Rosie said.

'You're not surprised?' I turned to her, astonished. 'You were very fond of David.'

'Still am. I like him enormously, but I wasn't marrying him, you were. And he was . . . not right for you, Annie. I can't say I'm desperately surprised, no. And neither will Clare be.'

I felt quietly shocked. My best friend and my sister were in agreement. Had they discussed my fiancé's unsuitability? Or mine perhaps?

'We were worried about your lack of enthusiasm,' she said gently. 'Lack of . . . I don't know, wedding mania, *joie de vivre*, excitement. God, you hardly even told me what you were going to wear, for heaven's sake, You hadn't bothered with the flowers, hadn't even booked a reception, left it all to David. I know it's your second time around, but even so.'

'And I don't know many blushing brides,' put in Dan quietly, 'who could happily spend the entire summer apart from their fiancé.'

'He was supposed to come down for weekends,' I said defensively.

'Weekends,' scoffed Rosie. 'God, if you were mad about someone, you wouldn't want to waste a moment out of their sight. you'd come dashing down to see them rather like you've just done today,' she added craftily.

I flushed.

'And I haven't even met this guy. Clare's certainly beaten me to it on that score. Says he's something of a dish.'

I caught my breath. 'You mean you both suspected?'

'Oh, we suspected all right. What, all those quiet suppers and little fishing trips and the general lack of your company?'

'Didn't realise it was that obvious,' I muttered.

'Only to the initiated. Dan didn't twig but then he's only a fishmonger. I, on the other hand, am the fishwife.'

I smiled. 'He'll stink, you realise that?'

Dan waggled his eyebrows. 'Some women find it very alluring.'

'And stop changing the subject,' put in Rosie. 'Oh, look, here's Clare, she'll pin you down.'

I turned as Clare, arm in arm with Michael, came strolling across the sand, for all the world like love's young dream. Suddenly she threw back her dark head and laughed uproariously at something he said. I hadn't seen her do that for ages. Years. God, all these happy loving couples— suddenly I didn't want to be here. I felt my heart pounding.

'Where's Flora?' I called, when she was in earshot.

'Oh, I took her back to Taplow House!' She walked towards me quickly. 'Sorry, I thought that was where you were going. Only I rang Mum, and she said you were on your way back, and you know what Flora's like, she got funny about staying the night here.'

'Oh! Did she?' I got up anxiously.

'Said she'd rather go back and wait for you there. I left her with Matt and Tod. I hope that's OK?'

'Yes, fine. But I'll get back if she's a bit jumpy.' I made to go.

'Annie.' Clare stopped me, resting her hands on my shoulders for a moment. 'I'm so sorry. Mum told me about David.'

I lowered my eyes to the sand. 'Yes. Well, he's going to be fine.'

'And . . . she told me everything else, too. About the wedding.'

I glanced up. 'She told you it's off?'

She nodded. 'Thought it would be easier coming from her.'

I swallowed. 'And I gather from Rosie it doesn't come as a huge surprise to anyone.'

She shrugged. 'We were all . . . well, very concerned. About certain aspects. The frenetic baby-making, for instance.'

'I know,' I said softly, looking down again. I sighed. 'Anyway. Good to see you two back in one piece.' I slid a grin in Michael's direction. He smiled back and hugged Clare's shoulders.

'As I said to you on the phone, Annie, best thing that ever happened to us. But now for different reasons.'

'Knocked some sense into her is what he means,' said Clare drily.

'I'll second that,' I said, giving them all a backward salute as I moved away, on up the beach, towards the car.

I was desperate to get away from them. Longing to see Matt. To have my own deeply romantic happy-ever-after experience. I hastened to my car, but as luck would have it, when I hit the road I got stuck behind the slowest tractor in the West Country. As I crawled along behind it, down the narrow, winding lanes, the floral banks rearing up mockingly on either side of me, I banged my fist on the wheel in frustration.

'Oh, come on. Come on!'

But time, for this farmer, was not of the essence, and every time I tried to overtake, a car sped towards me. Finally I gave up and sank back in my seat, willing myself to be patient.

With nothing else to do, I opened my post from London. It was bills, mostly, but there was also a thick creamy envelope, recognisable from the in-house stamp as being from my publishers. *My publishers.* I tore it open and propped it up on the steering wheel as I drove.

Dear Mrs O'Harran,

It has recently come to our attention that a temporary member of staff has been commissioning manuscripts when he had no authority to do so. Sebastian Cooper was doing work experience here in his gap year. His task was to read unsolicited manuscripts and pass on anything of interest to a more experienced member of staff. Unfortunately, it seems he took it upon himself to write personally to prospective authors, encouraging them with offers of potential advances. We are also deeply embarrassed to learn that these prospective authors—all female—were encouraged to write as salaciously as possible. We understand you are of their number, and would like to offer our sincere and profound apologies. An experienced editor has since read your synopsis, and I'm afraid we will be unable to publish your manuscript. Once again, we offer our deepest apologies.

Yours sincerely,

Emma Tarrant (Head of fiction)

I stared. Read it again. Then my jaw dropped. Bloody hell. Bloody *hell*! God, the little toerag was a ruddy schoolboy getting cheap thrills from urging frustrated housewives to pen their sexual fantasies! I nearly went up the back of the tractor I was so livid. How dare he? My blood boiled as I put my foot down and sped, with an alarming lack of thought, past the tractor. I missed an oncoming car by inches and, as it swept past me, horn beeping angrily, I flushed hotly. All that work, I seethed. Wasted! But narrowly avoiding a head-on collision had sobered me up a bit.

Perhaps it was for the best, I reasoned bitterly. I mean, had I, in all conscience, felt very comfortable with my work recently? Had it sat easily? Oh, it had flowed all right, like an oozing wound, but perhaps it *had* just been the sexually frustrated outpourings of a woman engaged to the wrong man, and not actually something I'd be proud to see in print? Let alone for anyone else to see. Flora, for instance. Or Mum.

No, I decided hastily. No, this was a blessing in disguise.

I felt sad, though, as I turned into the narrow lane that led to Taplow House. Sad that my secret dream of becoming a novelist was in tatters. But maybe I should try again? Write not romantic fiction, but something that truly fired my imagination? Something I really wanted to write?

I sighed as I pulled into the drive and crunched slowly up the gravel. I was surprised to see an ancient blue Volvo already sitting in pole position, so I swerved and parked alongside it. I frowned. Then it came to me. Of course, it was Thursday, so Tod was due to be collected by his aunt. By Louise. No wonder Flora had been keen to get here before he went, to say goodbye.

The green front door under the little wooden porch was ajar in the sunshine, lobelia nodding from the hanging baskets, blowing in the breeze. I ducked underneath the blue petals, and felt a sudden rush of relief as I pushed through the door. Nothing mattered. Not really. Not David, not the book. I was back, you see. Back where I belonged in this heavenly house. This was where I wanted to be, and it felt good.

'Flora?' I called as I went into the dim, flagstone hall, the Cornish slate cool beneath my feet. 'Matt? I'm back.'

My heart leaped ridiculously as I said that. As if I were home, and he were a part of it.

As my eyes adjusted to the gloom of the timbered sitting room, I saw someone silhouetted in the bay window. A pretty, dark-haired girl with merry brown eyes glanced up at me. Smiled. 'Hi.'

'Oh, hi.' I smiled, dumping my bag on a chair. 'You must be Louise.'

She stood up slowly, the smile fading slightly.

'Uh, no,' she said hesitantly. 'No, actually. I'm Madeleine Malone?'

I stared at her. Couldn't speak for a moment. Then I found my voice. 'Oh! You mean—' I broke off, astonished. 'Matt's wife.'

As I said it, the implication horrified me. My God. Tod.

'Ex-wife, actually, but yes.'

My mouth went dry. Matt's wife. And where the hell was Matt? Tod?

'I . . . thought you lived miles away,' I said, managing a nervous smile. 'In Cambridge.'

'I do, and I've just driven all the way down from there. Might I ask who you are?' she said a trifle impatiently.

'Oh, I'm Annie. Annie O'Harran.'

'Well, nice to meet you, Annie O'Harran, but I'm none the wiser.' She gazed at me steadily. 'Where exactly do you fit in? You see, I'm somewhat nonplussed by what's going on around here. Could you enlighten me? I'm looking for my son.'

I looked back at her. Her eyes were very unusual: amber, intent and focused. Very pretty, but in a petite, fragile sort of way; with chestnut curls and a pale, heart-shaped face. She was wearing a baggy checked flannel shirt, loose over jeans and trainers.

'I've just arrived back from London. I don't know where he is.'

'But he is here? I mean—living here?'

I took a deep breath. Walked over to the heaving bookcase and stared at the dusty spines. I ran a finger down one of them. Oh dear God. Where are you, Matt?

'Mrs O'Harran, do you have any children?' The voice, when it came, seemed to come from far away.

'Yes. Yes, I do,' I admitted into the ranks of books.

'Then perhaps you'll appreciate how I felt when I called Tod's cousins in Bodmin this morning in order to speak to Tod, and was informed by the housekeeper that no one of that name was staying. No Tod. Oh, but hang on, this woman said, last week, there had been a boy. A cousin, but only for one night. He'd left to go to Taplow House with his father the next day. Well, I tell you, Annie O'Harran, my blood ran cold.'

I turned sharply. 'Why? Is that so terrible? For a father to want to spend time with his son? To collect him for a holiday?'

'You bet your life it is.' She raised her chin in an effort to control her emotion, but I could hear it in her voice.

'At first I couldn't think where in the hell Taplow House could be, but you know, as I racked my brains, I remembered . . . remembered meeting this eccentric old English lady. She had a quaint old house on a creek by all accounts, which Matt thought sounded so cute and was real keen to rent. At first I didn't believe it, didn't believe he'd be capable of such a thing, but then I thought: Jesus, Madeleine Malone, you'd better believe it. And you'd better get yourself over to that quaint old house right away.

'So, my mind racing, I got in the car, and I drove down here. No real address mind, just a village and a house, but there aren't many houses at the end of a creek, and sure enough, after quizzing a few locals, I found it. Empty. Deserted. But that's OK because I find a room, right at the very top, that's clearly Tod's, with all his stuff in it. And you know what? I sat down on that bed and I clutched his sweatshirt to me and I burst into tears I was so damn grateful.'

I took a deep breath. Let it out shakily. I felt her eyes on me.

'And then, as I moved round this kooky old house, it got stranger and stranger. Matt's clearly living here. I figure that out because I find his stuff in a room upstairs. But there's a woman too. Not with him, in his bed, but down a floor. And another child, a girl.'

'I can explain that,' I said quickly. 'Matt rented this house, but there was a misunderstanding because I also—'

'Oh, please'—she held up her hands—'spare me. Matt's domestic arrangements became a matter of indifference to me a long time ago.'

'So then I find this note, fixed to the fridge in the kitchen, which is so damn cute, and, I guess, addressed to you.' She reached into the back pocket of her jeans and handed me a piece of paper.

I read it: *Gone fishin'. Got cabin boy, and Girl Friday too. Wish you were here. Matt.* My heart leaped ridiculously. Couldn't help it. I glanced up.

'Touching, isn't it? And clearly you are touched, although I think you should know what you're dealing with here.'

'What I'm—' I started.

'So then,' she went on, cutting me off, 'then I go into the study. I mean, I could just sit tight because by now it's dawned on me that Louise and Matt have pulled a fast one and I'm the dupe, but at least Tod's here and that's all that matters. But, you know, something makes me want to keep looking round. I just have this feeling, this hunch there may be more. And how right I am. Because in his study—which I know is his because it's so chaotic—I search through the drawers, and find these.'

She dipped into her handbag and pulled out an envelope. Handed it to me. 'Open it.'

I did. Slowly. Stared at the two pieces of paper in my hands.

'Two tickets to JFK from Heathrow for tomorrow afternoon,' she said, carefully. 'One way.'

I swallowed.

'Now. Who d'you suppose those are for?' she drawled softly, head tilted to one side. 'You and Matt?' She reached out and took them from me. 'No. I don't think you're going anywhere with him, honey.'

I licked my lips. I'd already read them. Mr M. Malone, and Mr T. Malone. I sat down slowly on the arm of the sofa.

'Matt and Tod,' I said softly.

'Exactly. Matt and Tod. So what we have here is not just a little vacation with his daddy, which anyone who didn't know Matt's full history of abuse might say was only fair since he hadn't seen his kid in over a year, but a deliberate, calculated plot to abduct my son.'

I stared at her. Her face was white, bloodless.

'Abuse?' I whispered. 'What d'you mean? Matt wouldn't . . . '

'Wouldn't do this?' She quickly unbuttoned her shirt and revealed a scar, livid and red, running from the base of her throat right down to her breast. I gasped, horrified.

'Pretty, isn't it?'

'Yes, but he told me about that,' I said quickly, averting my eyes. 'About the glass table smashing, about it flying up at you—'

'And you believed him?'

'Of course I believed him,' I faltered at last. 'Of course I did, I—'

'Even though a jury in a court of law, two police officers, a judge and a probation officer didn't?'

I met her gaze. 'Yes,' I whispered. 'I believed him.'

She buttoned up her shirt. 'More fool you. The judge called him a dangerous man. A danger to children. A danger to his own child.' She took a step closer to me, her face inches from mine now. 'He's not well, Annie. Really not well. And he's out there now, somewhere, with my boy, planning on skipping the country. And he's got your daughter—who I take it is Girl Friday—with him too.'

She'd deliberately phrased it like that to frighten me. Ridiculous. Nonetheless, anxiety accumulated in my chest, one grain at a time. Where were they? Nonsensical thoughts spun round my head like a kaleidoscope, about them heading out to sea, crazy, irrational thoughts that made my head whirl, but that was how this strange, beautiful, amber-eyed woman was making me feel. That Matt was capable of anything. I had to get away from her. I made quickly for the kitchen, for the back door. Wrenching it open, I hastened across the terrace and down the garden towards the creek, my heart thumping somewhere high up round the base of my throat.

At the end of the lawn I plunged straight into the woodland, ignoring the path and taking the shortest route straight down as the crow flies. I shielded my face from branches with my arms, but was almost oblivious of the boughs and brambles, my mind racing. Could it be true? A whole courtroom of people, a jury, and that appalling scar. I'd no idea it would be like that, so huge, so disfiguring, and yet— 'Oh!'

As I crashed through a bush, I ran slap into Matt coming up the main path, his tall frame taking the force of our collision.

'Hey, steady!' He laughed, catching my arm.

'No!' I pulled away roughly. Our eyes met in that terrible moment. His, bewildered. Mine, fearful.

'Flora!' I panted, looking frantically around. 'Where's Flora? I—'

'Here,' she said, as she rounded the same bend, carrying a bucket of water and sloshing fish, jeans rolled up, feet bare, with Tod beside her.

'Oh, darling!'

'What's up, Mum?' She too looked bewildered.

'Matt, I'm sorry, I—'

I turned back, but the damage had been done. I saw it in his face. I saw him stiffen too, as he looked beyond me over my shoulder. He'd glimpsed Madeleine, standing at the top of the garden, high up on the terrace steps, her brown curls blowing in the breeze. His eyes hardened.

'Tod,' he said softly, keeping his eyes on her. 'Tod, listen.' He reached a hand back to grasp his son's arm, but Tod had already seen her.

'Oh, shit,' he breathed, backing away.

Matt turned to him urgently. 'Tod, you can do this.'

'I can't!' he gasped, pulling away.

'Sure you can.' Matt reached out his other hand and, in one swift movement, grabbed Tod's shoulder and pulled the boy to him with not a little force. 'And you know what?' he said, his arm tight round his son, his face close but his eyes back on Madeleine. 'We should have done this a long time ago. This isn't the way, Tod. Sneaking around like this, hiding. We need to face her, OK?'

'She'll make me go back,' Tod whimpered.

'Not if you stand up to her. Come on. It's time.'

'I can't, Dad, you know I can't.'

Flora and I watched in astonishment as this normally cheerful, albeit shy boy shrivelled before our eyes. We followed at a distance as father and son walked up the path, Matt's arm round Tod's shoulder, then up the lawn towards her. As they got closer, Madeleine suddenly flew down the terrace steps, ran down the garden and scooped Tod up in her arms.

'Oh, baby. My baby!'

Tod seemed to go limp in her arms. Then she let him go and stood back, holding him at arm's length, her eyes scanning his face anxiously. 'You OK, honey? He hasn't hurt you or anything?'

Tod shook his head.

'OK then,' she breathed in relief, clasping him briefly to her again. 'Let's go. I've packed all of your stuff up from your room and put it all in the car. Let's get going and we'll ring Walter on the way back and tell him you're safe and we're on our way home.'

I watched in disbelief as Tod, without a backward glance at his father, or me or Flora, let himself be led up the garden, his shoulders encircled by his mother's arm, towards the car in the drive.

'Tod,' Matt called softly. His son didn't turn. 'Madeleine, wait, please.'

'For what?' She spun round abruptly, spitting the words out, her eyes bright and furious. She reached into her bag, pulled out the airline tickets, and tossed them angrily in the air. They fluttered to the ground. 'For you to abduct my son?' Her voice rose shrilly.

'I bought those tickets over a month ago,' Matt said carefully. 'Because Tod asked me to. Emailed me. Said he couldn't take it any longer and was desperate to come home. It wasn't supposed to be as furtive as that, but we knew of no other way. He's not a child any more, Madeleine. He'll be thirteen in the fall, old enough to decide, with or without the court's blessing, who he chooses to live with. And he chooses to live with me.'

'How dare you!' she breathed. She was trembling with emotion and her grip tightened on her son's shoulder as Tod continued to stare at the ground. 'How dare you tell such flagrant lies in front of him, put words into his mouth, when you know he adores me, would do anything for me.' She gazed down at her son's bent head. Brushed the fair hair out of his eyes. 'Tod? Honey, you want to come home now, don't you?' She gave his shoulder a little squeeze. 'Home with Mom?'

There was a silence. We waited.

'Tod?'

He nodded. 'Sure,' he whispered.

'Don't do this to him, Madeleine,' said Matt in a low, dangerous voice. 'Don't play this card. He came here of his own volition, because he wanted to. He stays with me.'

'The hell he does!'

'He's staying here.' Matt took a step towards her.

'Dad, please,' whimpered Tod. 'I'll go. Please, just let me go.'

Matt looked at his son's white face. 'OK,' he nodded. 'I understand.'

'But he wants to stay here!' cried Flora suddenly, shrilly. 'I know he does, we've talked about it loads of times and he's told me. Tell her, Tod. Tell her where you want to be!'

She gazed at him incredulously, but Tod's eyes were blank.

'Ready, honey?' murmured his mother.

'Ready,' he said flatly.

Without another look at his father, he allowed himself to be helped into the passenger seat. After she'd shut the door, she quickly ran round to the other side and got in. Without a backward look, Madeleine started the engine and drove off down the drive. Flora and I watched in astonishment. When the car had disappeared from sight, I turned.

'Matt, I don't understand. Why—'

But he'd gone. I just caught a flash of him heading for the creek.

'Mum, I don't understand.' Flora turned huge eyes on me. 'What's going on? Why has he gone with her?'

'I don't know.' I stared through the gap in the trees where Matt had disappeared. 'Wait here,' I muttered. 'I'll be back.'

I set off quickly, following Matt's tracks down the garden, through the woods and to the creek. When I emerged out into the dusk on the other side, I found no trace of him. The tide was low, and the creek one long stretch of grey wet sand, with only the gulls and cormorants, heads tucked under wings, waiting for night. Then I saw him sitting on some rocks at the farthest point of the creek, arms locked round his knees. I started quickly towards him, running clumsily through the claggy sand, then scrambling over rocks to reach him. I was almost there—when something made me stop short. I steadied myself, wobbling precariously on the slippery rocks.

'Matt?'

He must have heard me, but stayed motionless, head turned res-olutely out to sea. I felt my heart lurch in my throat. I'd doubted him, you see. Pulled away from him in the wood. I was about to turn back, misery rising within me, when he said my name.

'Annie.' Softly.

Relieved, I turned back. I picked my way over the rock pools and sat quietly beside him, following his eyes out to the horizon, sensing he was fighting with emotion and didn't want me to look at him.

Eventually, Matt broke the silence.

'So. It's over.'

I fought to comprehend. 'But why? When he wants to be with you?'

'It's not as simple as that,' he said slowly. 'You're assuming he hates his mother. For taking him away from me, for forcing him to live in England, but he doesn't. He loves her. She's his mom. The only one he's got, and, for all her faults, he won't hurt her.' He struggled to explain. 'You can't just reject your parents, Annie, because they're not perfect, because they don't match up. You darn well get on with what you've been allocated.'

'Yes, I agree, but he does have a choice. He has you!'

He shrugged. 'Just as Flora has Adam.'

'Yes, but the point is she wouldn't choose to live with him!'

He turned to look at me. 'Did you ask her?'

I faltered. 'Well . . . no. But then I'm—'

'Her mother. Exactly. And that's how it works.' He smiled ruefully. 'A child's attachment to its mother is indestructible. Something has to go seriously wrong for it to break.'

'Yes, but something *has* gone seriously wrong, and now Tod would rather live with you!'

'But he won't tell her that,' he said patiently. 'Won't hurt her to that extent. He's too . . . kind. He's all she's got, you see, and he knows that.' He sighed. 'He was the only child she could have, and she loves him with a passion. Too much, probably. We both love him too much. And children can't cope with that sort of spotlight,' he added soberly.

'Flora's said that too,' I reflected sadly. 'That sometimes I overdid it. That she longed for a brother or a sister to take the heat off her. It was one of the reasons I agreed to have more children with David. Even though I knew my body wasn't up to it and I was only shoring up more grief for myself. I desperately wanted some company for Flora.' I smiled wanly into the sunset. 'Although I realise a twelve-year age gap isn't exactly what she had in mind.'

He smiled. 'No. I'm not sure the little guy in the diaper would be up to chucking a frisbee with her, or sharing her first illicit cigarette.'

'Well, quite.' And then of course my mind flew insanely, ridiculously, to Tod. Tod, who would be up to it. I saw the pair of them tussling and laughing together in boats, on the lawn, at the table-tennis table, almost as if they *were* brother and sister— Oh, no, Annie, *no*. I gasped almost audibly at my audacity. Too much. Far too much. There weren't going to be any fairy-tale endings here, nothing so neat. Real life wasn't like that.

Suddenly I remembered something. I had to ask.

'Matt, that scar. She showed me. It's horrific.'

'I know. Appalling. And I've wondered about that too.' He paused reflectively. 'Got to thinking that it wasn't possible. A shard of glass flying at whatever velocity through the air wouldn't have inflicted such damage, or caused such a long deep cut. So I asked a pathologist friend of mine at the hospital, showed him the pictures. I even went so far as to put my fist through a couple of glass tables, and no. It couldn't have happened.'

I stared at him, horrified. 'You mean . . . you think *she* did it?'

'Made it worse.'

'Oh God.' I looked down quickly.

'Because she was desperate,' insisted Matt. 'Desperate to get Tod.'

'Yes, but—'

'And she knew I might get him.'

'Why?' I looked up. 'I mean, she's the mother after all, and, as you say, the courts tend to lean in that direction, so—'

'She is the mother, sure, but she was also a patient of mine. A psychiatric patient. That's how we met.'

'A patient!'

'Yes. Not entirely ethical, but not unusual in psychiatry circles. Although not something, frankly, that the courts would have looked kindly on from her point of view. Madeleine knew that, which is why she went to such elaborate lengths to get Tod.'

'What did she have? I mean, what was her illness?'

'Acute paranoiac depression.'

'Oh.' I swallowed. Out of my depth.

'Eminently treatable, in most cases. Including hers.'

'And you fell for her . . .what, straight away?'

My chest felt absurdly knotted with jealousy.

'Not straight away, no,' he admitted. 'I noticed she was beautiful, naturally. No, it was later on . . . when I started treating her on a regular basis. I felt such admiration for her. At how she'd coped with her illness, hidden it. Carried on working. She's a doctor herself, you know.'

'I know. You said.'

'And she was . . . so beguiling. Enchanting.' His eyes swam as he gazed into the distance.

My heart felt heavy, like a colossal lead weight inside me. I had an awful, awful feeling he still loved her. 'Beguiling.' 'Enchanting.' I curled my legs round and tucked my size seven feet firmly under me. Nothing beguiling about them.

'And, Annie, I apologise for my behaviour the other night,' he went on in a low voice. 'I was out of order. Forgive me.'

He did look at me when he said that, but distractedly. Through me. As if he'd remembered to apologise, but his mind was elsewhere. And why apologise? For what? For that glorious, endless kiss? That heavenly embrace? Surely we were ready to embark on more of the same, and then who knows what of a more permanent nature? But to *apologise* . . . I felt as if I'd been kicked in the teeth. Wondered if I'd ever get over it, actually. But I wasn't even allowed the luxury of wallowing in my misery, because suddenly a shrill whistle rang out from above.

Recognising the summons, I swung round quickly. Back down at the other end of the creek and high above us, at the bottom of the garden behind the treetops, stood Flora. She took her fingers out of the corners of her mouth, cupped it with her hands, and yelled, 'Matt! Someone called Louise is here!'

Matt stared at her, then: 'Coming!' He got quickly to his feet.

I watched numbly as he crossed the rocks in his deck shoes, leaping from rock to rock, until he reached the sand. He crossed the flatland at a trot, dodging the pools of water, and headed for the path through the woods. As I saw his back disappearing through the trees, it occurred to me that he was about to disappear from my life as abruptly as he'd entered it. That in a very short while, in a matter of hours perhaps, he'd return to America and I'd never see him again. I stood up slowly and followed at a distance. Suddenly I felt very small. Very stupid. How could I have got it so wrong? How could I have imagined anything could come of us? He lived in America. I lived in England. He was still mourning the loss of a beautiful, tragic woman who'd walked out on him when he still loved her, not to mention a son. Why would I even come close to compensating for that loss?

You fool, Annie, I thought bitterly, tears stinging my eyes as I climbed through the wood after him.

As I reached the top of the hill, a pretty blonde girl with long, perfect legs coming out of khaki shorts came running from the terrace steps down the garden towards Matt, her hair flying.

'Oh, Matt, I'm so sorry.' Her voice broke. 'This is all my fault. I just hadn't told Bernie, our help, you see, because I hadn't seen any need to involve her. But it was so stupid of me.'

'You weren't to know,' he insisted. 'And, frankly, it doesn't matter.' He held her by her shoulders at arm's length. 'This is Annie, by the way.'

'Hi.' She flashed me a smile before turning anxiously back to Matt.

'Hi,' I muttered, feeling distinctly peripheral.

'Well, as long as you're sure,' she went on uncertainly, jangling her car keys nervously in her hand. 'I just feel such a fool slipping up like that.'

'You needn't. Listen, I'll get you a drink. You look like you need one, and I sure as hell do. Come on.'

'Thanks,' she said gratefully, and she let him lead her, an arm round her shoulders, back up the garden, then up the steps to the terrace. He found her a deck chair and she sank into it. As Matt disappeared inside to get a bottle, she put her head in her hands and ran her fingers through her hair, clearly shaken. I pulled up a chair and perched opposite. She raised her head and looked at me hard.

'Bitch,' she muttered.

I started, then realised she must mean Madeleine.

'Is she?' I said hopefully.

'Oh, totally. First class. She had her claws into Matt from day one. No one could understand why he married her.'

I could tell I was going to like Louise.

'But he obviously still adores her?' I ventured, heart in mouth. 'I mean, she is very beautiful. I met her.'

She got out a packet of cigarettes. 'She is also completely barking mad. However much Matt protects her and maintains she isn't.'

'Oh!' Splendid.

She put her cigarette in her mouth and dug a lighter out of her shorts pocket. 'Actually, I shouldn't have said that,' she said, removing the unlit cigarette from her mouth. 'She's not a bitch, she's just a rather beautiful nutcase. And you know men when it comes to weak, defenceless women: can't get enough of them. But I still say she injured herself on purpose. I just *wish* Matt could have brought himself to expose her in court, but he couldn't, he's too darned nice. He couldn't bring himself to tell everyone his wife was a raving lunatic, and he wouldn't let Tod listen to that, either.' She paused. 'Jeez, I just wish—' She broke off suddenly. Stared beyond me, transfixed. For a moment I thought she was still musing on what might have been. Then, as the silence grew, I realised that whatever was gripping her was being played out right behind me.

I swung round. At the same time, a car door slammed in the drive. It was the old blue Volvo, back in position. And coming round the side of the house was Tod. He was walking, his head held high, way in front of his mother, who, as she felt her way slowly round the car, hands clutching the bonnet, looked very pale.

At that moment, Matt stepped out of the back door with a bottle of wine and some glasses. He saw Madeleine, and stopped still on the steps. Their eyes met across the garden and the gravel drive, and, in that moment, something unspoken went on. Something that meant a lot to them, and very little to the rest of us.

'You've won,' she said flatly.

'It's not a question of winning,' said Matt quietly.

She raised her head. 'It is to me.'

She looked terrible. Grey. All in. Matt held out a chair for her. 'Sit,' he commanded gently.

She shook her head, lips taut. Then reached out quickly and held on to the back of it for support. She took deep breaths to steady herself.

'What happened?' asked Matt.

She swallowed. 'We got as far as Launceston. Then Tod got out of the car at some lights. Started walking back. Not running, and he didn't say a word before he got out, just started walking in the opposite direction. I parked the car and ran after him. He wouldn't speak to me, but eventually I made him talk. He said he couldn't live with me any more.' She caught her breath, her voice shaking. 'Said he missed you too much and was only really happy when he was with you. Said he wanted to live with you.' Her face crumpled. 'I've lost him. I went through all that, the court case, the agony of it all, and now I've lost him after all.'

She hung on to the chair with one hand and covered her face with the other as she wept. Her shoulders shook. I waited for Matt to fly to comfort her. He didn't. He turned to Tod.

'Tod? Is this how you really feel? Or just an overreaction because you've had another bust-up with your mom?'

'You know it's how I feel, Dad,' Tod said in a low, almost angry voice. 'It's just . . . I've never been brave enough to say it before. Just gone along with what everyone says I should do.'

'It's nothing to do with bravery,' Matt said more gently. He glanced across at Madeleine. 'More to do with compassion.'

'And it's not you, Mom,' Tod said in a high voice, looking at her directly. 'It's my whole new life, which I don't want and never asked for. It's that creepy dark house in Cambridge; Walter, who looks at me as if I'm something that's crept out from under a stone. It's not you, Mom, you know that, don't you?' he said urgently. 'I never wanted to choose. Just wanted to go on living with my mom and dad, together, at home, as a family. When we were driving back just now, I had to get out. I felt . . . suffocated. I love you, Mom. I just can't live in that house with you.'

Madeleine's lips were bloodless. She held on to the back of the chair. Then, with an effort, she turned to Matt. Gave a strange, twisted smile.

'And, of course, it's much too late to do what Tod really wants?'

'Which is?' Matt asked, surprised.

'For you and me to be together. As a family.'

I caught my breath at the audacity. Saw Matt almost wince.

'Much too late,' said Matt firmly.

She nodded. Accepting the answer for what it was. Defeat. It had been an heroic, selfless, last-ditch attempt to save her son, and suddenly, in spite of myself, my heart went out to her. She was that desperate. That was what love did to you. Particularly the maternal kind.

'Come on, Flora,' I muttered, and we went into the house.

I headed for the kitchen where, strangely, I often found myself in times of emotional crisis, and more particularly the sink, which, naturally, was full of washing up. Turning the taps on full blast and squirting liquid over the greasy pans, I silently handed Flora a tea towel. Out of the corner of my eye, through the window over the sink, I saw Tod and his mother hug each other hard. Heard her weeping loudly, her head on Tod's shoulder, then Louise's sensible voice.

'She can't possibly drive all the way back to Cambridge now. She can come back with me. Spend the night, and then go home tomorrow.'

'That would be kind, Lou,' said Matt

After a while, when I'd scrubbed the living daylights out of those pans, I realised the garden had gone quiet. Glancing out of the window, I saw that Louise and Madeleine had gone. It was almost dark now, but down at the bottom of the garden, silhouetted against the trees, Tod's hunched figure was walking fast, heading for the gap that led to the creek. I turned to look at Flora drying up beside me, but she was already putting her cloth down. The next minute, she was walking slowly down the garden, biting her thumbnail. She turned and caught my eye through the window. I shrugged uncertainly. I don't know, darling. I really don't. She hesitated, then carried on walking, letting me know with one eloquently raised hand that she knew he needed to be alone, but that perhaps he wouldn't mind someone hovering in the shadows, should he need to talk eventually?

Quite grown up, I decided. Much more so than me. Because, frankly, I felt like picking one of these coffee cups out of the sink, hurling it at the wall, and bursting into tears, which was, of course, monumentally selfish, because I should be so happy for Matt and Tod.

Suddenly I needed the night air as much as anyone else who was fighting with their emotions around here. I pushed open the back door and walked outside, gulping back the tears as I went. There was no sign of Matt, and my heart ached for him in a way that it had never ached for anyone, I realised; neither Adam nor David.

I headed down the lawn past the summerhouse, the scene of yet another recently fostered dream that had come to nothing. The lady novelist. A deep and profound melancholy rose within me. So strange, I reflected, when only weeks ago I'd been so happy. A woman writing her book, about to become a doctor's wife, a large house in Hurlingham, more babies planned: all gone. And even though I knew it was right that it had gone, the fact that there was nothing to put in its place was hard. Real tough, as Matt would say in his dark brown accent. A ball of tears scuttled up my throat at the memory of his voice and I swallowed it down, walking quickly uphill towards the cliff path. The wind was strong now, buffeting my face, which was strangely comforting. The light was very dim too, so that when the track finally plateaued out at the top and I came across a tall figure blocking my path, I shrieked.

It was Matt, leaning back against a tree, one leg propped up. He glanced round at my cry and hurriedly stuffed some bits of paper into his pocket. The moonlight just caught them though—airline tickets, being tucked furtively away. And suddenly I was enraged.

'Going to use them?' I cried bitterly. 'Tomorrow, isn't it?'

'Sorry?' He blinked in my face.

'Well, that's when they're for, isn't it? Tomorrow afternoon, Heathrow to JFK. I'll give you a lift to the airport, if you like.'

He straightened up from the tree. 'I'm not going anywhere tomorrow.'

'But you will, won't you?' I said brokenly. I was horrified at myself, but I couldn't help it. My voice cracked. 'You'll go back to America, and Flora and I will become something that happened on a cute little English fishing holiday, a diversion while you got custody of Tod. My God, you even apologised for *kissing* me back there, as if that was completely abhorrent, a complete aberration. Well, I have no such regrets, Matt.' I was shaking now, possibly even slightly out of control. 'I enjoyed every minute of it, and was looking forward to more of the same, maybe even something of a more permanent nature, but then I haven't had the luxury of a string of affairs like you have since the end of my marriage. Add me to your list, why don't you? Pop me down as number three, straight after the radiologist with the great legs and the neighbour with the inconvenient cat: the eccentric Englishwoman who wrote cheap books. The one who threw in her chance to administer to famine victims in—in war-torn Africa, in a Red Cross uniform—'

He blinked. 'Red Cross?'

'Yes, why not!' I shrieked. 'Christ, I could be rivalling Florence sodding Nightingale! I could be handing out rice, digging wells—'

'Wells? Where?'

'In the ground!' I yelled. 'For the starving millions!'

'What, in a long white dress?'

I stared. 'What dress?'

'The one you're getting married in in five weeks' time. The one that's being specially made for you in London. You're gonna sink wells in that? After the reception at Claridge's? With your mother and sister in grey and pink respectively, both with new shoes and bags purchased from Bowman's of Exeter?' He shook his head. 'Get real dirty.'

I stared, flummoxed. 'Wha— What d'you mean?'

'I called the farm this morning. I wanted to check you were OK. You took off so suddenly yesterday, like a bat out of hell. I spoke to Clare, who'd just woken up. She said there was no sign of you, but she yelled downstairs to your mom who said you'd gone to London to see David. "Ah," said Clare, back down the phone to me. "A little romantic tryst." And then I got the whole lowdown on the wedding, right down to the colour of Flora's bridesmaid dress and the ushers' buttonholes. Oh, and, incidentally, your ma's suit is in dove-grey silk.'

'But . . . but I'm not!' I said, horrified.

'Not in silk?' He scratched his head dubiously. 'A mistake, I fear. It's very *à la mode* for brides this season.'

'No! I mean I'm not getting married! It *was* all organised like that, just as you've said, all planned without me by David, but . . . but, Matt, the engagement's off! I split up with David today in London. He's going away, to Nicaragua. We're not getting married.'

There was a silence. 'You're not . . . getting married?'

'No. I'm not.' I squinted in the dusk. Looked at him incredulously. 'You didn't *know* that?' I whispered.

'No. How could I have known, Annie, when you neglected to tell me?'

My mind spun. *Had* I? Had I neglected to tell him? 'So . . . so all the time, when you were wriggling and apologising and—'

'Trying to behave like a gentleman and do the right thing because I realised you hadn't changed your plans on account of me, and that the evening we'd shared together had clearly meant precisely nothing to you . . . yeah. Yeah, that's what I was doing.' He scratched his head. 'Felt a bit of a heel, as a matter of fact, for trying to talk you out of your big day. It occurred to me you might actually love this guy, and there I was, selfishly trying to turn things to my advantage, and all because . . .'

'Yes?' I hung on.

'Well, all because . . . I wanted you.'

'Oh!'

There was a silence. We gazed at one another.

'I love you, Annie, you must know that. And I want us to be together, you, me, Tod and Flora. But I had an awful surge of guilt there that I was prising you away from another life you'd wanted for a long time, and that even though I could see that *he* was wrong, you couldn't. You see, I've done that masterful role, Annie, the one David was doing, and it's a mistake. You don't need anyone to look after you. You need someone to look you in the eye.'

'I know,' I whispered, moving closer, holding his eye. 'I know that now, and, Matt, I love you too, so much. I just don't know how on earth we're going to . . . well . . .' I hesitated.

'What?'

'I mean, you live in America and I live here, and this isn't even our house! We're just playing at living in it and—'

'Details,' he murmured, pushing his fingers up through my hair and stopping my lips with a kiss. 'Let's worry about the details later.'

A second later I was in his arms and he was kissing the life out of me. And he was right. Nothing mattered. Nothing, except that here I was, right where I wanted to be, his lips on mine, his hands strong and warm on my back, the wind in my hair and my feet—well, was it my imagination or were my feet just slightly off the ground?

'Mum!'

We parted, panting. Swung round breathlessly. A few feet away, Tod and Flora were staring at us.

'Oh! Darling.' I hurriedly smoothed down my hair, flushing madly. 'There you are. Matt and I were just . . .'

'Your mother and I were getting some details sorted out,' said Matt as the children continued to boggle. 'And, as it happens, we have way more to discuss. Like who gets to take the garbage out and who does the dishes and—oh, boy, all manner of things. So, here.' He reached into his back pocket and drew out a wad of tenners. 'Have you guys eaten yet?'

'Er, no,' muttered Flora, dazed.

'Tod.' He turned to his son. 'Take Flora over to Padstow on the ferry, and have yourselves a pizza. Then take yourselves off around the town and spend the rest on mindless junk like CDs and T-shirts, and anything overpriced with a logo on it.'

'Cool!' Tod's eyes lit up as he took the money. 'What's the catch?'

Matt put his arm round my shoulder and led me away, walking me firmly down the cliff path and away from them, towards the house.

'The catch is,' he called back over his shoulder, 'that you're back at ten o'clock and not a moment before. Deal?'

We couldn't see their faces as we marched away from them, grinning like children, but we could hear the glee in their voices.

'Deal!'

Chapter Seven

'CALL THAT ROWING?' I murmured, leaning back in the bows of the boat and letting the sun play on my eyelids as it flickered lacily through the dappled shade of the trees. 'I've had better galley slaves.'

'Oh, I don't doubt it,' Matt said, pulling hard on the oars in his dark suit, his white rose bobbing in his lapel. 'And one of the first things we're going to address, Mrs Malone, is the question of slaves. I sure as hell ain't cleaning the bath tub every day, and knowing you as I now do, I'm pretty sure *you* aren't going to either, so my mind flies naturally to housekeepers.'

'Housekeepers?' I opened one eye.

'To keep some kind of order around the place while I'm away in Exeter curing the sick and you're penning your Emily Dickinson biography. Believe me, honey, with the detritus two kids make—not to mention one very shaggy dog we seem to have acquired—dust will gather.'

'I have to admit the whole idea of staff has always made me rather nervous,' I murmured. 'I'm too middle class to know how to deal with them. But if that's what you want, I'll happily go along with it.' I slipped a satin shoe off and put my foot in his lap. 'Frankly, my darling, today I'll go along with anything.' I wiggled my toes, watching his face.

Matt let the oars go limp in their rowlocks for a moment. He leaned forward on them, regarding me. 'Well, we sure aren't going to make it back before the guests drive round inland if you carry on like that,' he said softly, his mouth twitching. 'As a matter of fact, I'm tempted to undo all those pearl buttons which I noticed in church go right the way down the back of that dress, and let it fall in a heap in the bottom of the boat, along with that shoe.'

There was silence for a moment, while our eyes feasted and we rashly considered this option. I sat up hastily.

'If you think I'm arriving at my reception looking like a girl who's just been ravished in the bottom of a boat, you're wrong. Row on, my man.'

He grinned and picked up the oars. 'Incidentally, why can't I use the outboard motor on this thing? Get us there a whole lot quicker.'

'Ah, but it wouldn't be romantic, would it?'

He laughed. Shook his head. 'Just so long as everything's going according to plan, Mrs Malone.'

'Oh, it's going perfectly, Mr Malone,' I beamed, sitting up again.

I twisted round in the boat and gazed wistfully back at the little stone church we'd just left on the opposite shore.

'It *was* pretty though, wasn't it, Matt?' I breathed. 'Everyone said so, and everyone said how heavenly it looked inside, full of harebells and cow parsley and red campion . . . You know Rosie and I were up at dawn collecting all those flowers? They wouldn't have lasted overnight.'

'So I gather, although most brides would have let a florist do all that work, with proper hothouse flowers, but not my bride. Oh, no, she wanted the church to look like an extension of the hedgerow, without a carnation in sight.' He shook his head ruefully. 'I had no idea you had such firm views on wedding etiquette.'

I leaned forward eagerly. 'But I knew exactly how everything should be today. Right down to the provençal tablecloths in the marquee and the chocolate sponge inside the wedding cake.'

He regarded me a moment. Smiled. 'Good. I'm glad. That's how it should be.'

'We're nearly there,' I said excitedly, sitting up straight as the little blue boat drifted towards the shore. 'Oh, Matt, this is *so* special, isn't it? And look, Tod and Flora have even decorated the beach!'

He turned round to glimpse the buttercups and poppies strewn across the shore. Grinned. 'I wondered what those two were up to this morning.'

Happiness and excitement bubbling up within me, I held on to the sides as Matt, looking ludicrously handsome in his morning coat, trousers rolled up to the knees, jumped out and waded the last few feet, pulling us up the beach. He held out his hand to me as I stood up and our eyes locked for a second.

'I'm not sure whether I've mentioned this,' he said, 'but you're looking rather lovely today.'

'Thank you.' I smoothed down the vintage cream dress shyly. 'I found it in an antique shop in Helston.'

'Of course you did. No spanking new designer labels for my wife. Only the best bit of tatty old lace.'

'Less of the tatty— Oh, listen, Matt. I can hear them!'

We paused for a moment as we tied up the boat and listened to the muffled voices above us. The rest of the wedding party had gone back to Taplow House in a procession of cars inland, while we'd rowed across alone, seen off from the shore by only Flora and Tod.

We held hands as we walked along the beach and then up through the wood, following the familiar, winding sandy path to the top. There were children all over the lawn, scampering about with our newly acquired hairy dog, and as Giles, my nephew, spotted us and darted inside the marquee to report, I felt a knot of excitement grow in my stomach. A great cheer went up as everyone came out to greet us: champagne glasses were raised high as we approached, and then the throng parted and they roared us in. Blinking and laughing foolishly, I kissed Rosie and Dan, who were at the front, then Clare and Michael, who were clapping loudly behind, then more friends—some down from London who were staying in bed and breakfasts. I spotted Mum at the back, raising her glass and blinking madly, and remembered how in church she'd been unashamedly dabbing away with her hanky as Matt and I had taken our vows. I blew her a kiss. Matt's parents were here too, over from the States and staying with Louise and Tom. Everyone wanted to pump Matt's hand and kiss my cheek as we came through.

Matt's father, an extremely tall, rather distinguished-looking academic, who still lectured occasionally at Princeton, was the first to claim me, whisking me away while Matt went to see my mum.

'So, congratulations are in order on all sorts of fronts, I gather,' he said, twinkling down at me from his very great height. 'Firstly for looking like the most handsome couple I've seen in a long time, but also for becoming people of property. I understand from Gertrude over there that a little transaction is about to take place?'

I smiled over in Gertrude's direction, where, elegant in a long biscuit linen coat, with dramatic feathers looping from a tiny hat perched on the back of her head, she chatted to Flora.

'Well, she's been wanting to sell it for some time. She feels she's too old to hang on to it any longer, and since Matt's been offered the head of psychiatry at Exeter—well, we've got to have somewhere to live and frankly we can't think of anywhere nicer.'

'Oh, sure, it's a peach of a place. But all year round? Winter too?'

'Oh, but I can't wait to see this house out of season, when the waves are beating against the rocks down there and the spray comes right up to the windows. I love that feeling of being safe and warm inside while the sea whips up to a frenzy outside.'

He smiled. 'I'm with you there.'

'And I won't be remote and lonely because Rosie and Dan are just round the corner, and Louise and Tom too.'

'Whose boys, I gather, are something of a hit with your daughter?'

I laughed. 'Well, the middle one's certainly made an impression.' I turned to look as Flora chatted animatedly to a lanky blond fourteen-year-old, who was scratching his leg shyly and blushing.

'And of course they're all going to be at the same school,' said Louise, overhearing and coming up to offer her congratulations. 'My boys can't wait till next term to swagger into class with Flora.'

'Well, I can assure you the feeling's mutual. It's a dream come true for her, really. Not only to be going to a mixed school but to have Tod and the cousins there too.'

'And Tod's happy?' she asked. 'I mean, to be staying here?'

'Oh, definitely. As long as he's with his father and by the sea, he's fine.'

'And you, my dear, you're happy?' Gertrude drifted up as Louise moved away. She kissed me, and her grey eyes were kind and quizzical.

'Oh, I am, and I can't thank you enough for coming, Gertrude. It means so much to me, it really does. I thought, well, after David . . .'

'That I'd never speak to you again?' She pulled a face. 'I'm too fond of you and Flora for that, and we all know you did the right thing. David too. He wrote to me recently, incidentally, to say he's inoculated over two thousand children against measles already.'

'Golly.' I gulped.

'David needed a cause,' she said, patting my arm. 'And now he's found one. Just be glad it's not you.'

She gave me a mischievous smile and moved on, picking her way round a group of children on the lawn who were throwing a frisbee about. As Rosie's eldest leaped up to catch it, he missed, and it sailed over to the herbaceous border where Mum was chatting to Matt's mother in a patch of sunlight. Mum ducked as it looked about to take her hat off, then squealed thankfully as a man's hand shot out to grab it. She fell laughing on his arm. He threw it back to the children, caught my eye, and sauntered over.

'Adam.'

'Congratulations, my love.' He leaned in and kissed my cheek. 'You did the right thing in the end and married the right man. Bastard.'

I grinned. 'Thanks.'

'And thank you for the invitation.'

I smiled. 'Well, I have to tell you, I deliberated long and hard.'

He laughed. 'I bet you did. And Matt, presumably, couldn't care less?'

'Oh, Matt couldn't give a monkey's.'

'There's confidence for you. And yours was?'

'Sorry?'

'Your attitude?'

'Oh, that it would be nice for Flora. And it is.' We both turned to look across at her, still chatting to Tod's cousin, her cheeks glowing as she flicked her hair back from her shoulder, looking really rather stunning in her long grey dress.

'We're going to have to keep an eye on her,' said Adam as the same thought crossed his mind. 'Rather too many predatory male adolescents trailing her this afternoon for my liking.'

I smiled. 'I'm sure she'll use her father's discretion.'

He raised an eyebrow. 'And what's that supposed to mean? I'll have you know I'm a changed man since I heard about your engagement. Quite laid me low, as a matter of fact, and I haven't so much as laid a finger on—Ooh, I say. What have we here?' He stood aside to accommodate a voluptuous blonde in a very short skirt and plunging neckline.

'I know you're busy chattin' an' that, but I gotta kiss the bride, en I!'

'Of course you have. Adam, this is Lorraine, Matt's private secretary at Exeter Hospital. Lorraine, this is my ex-husband Adam.'

She turned to him, grinning coquettishly, and dug him hard in the ribs with an elbow. 'Oh, yeah, I heard all about you from Flora. Bit of a ladykiller, by all accounts!'

Adam puffed out his chest. 'Well, I wouldn't say *killer* exactly. No maiden, to my knowledge, has actually been fatally slain on account of my charms, but perhaps felled at the knees would be a better analogy?'

She chortled. 'Funny, ent ya?'

Adam was cheering up considerably now. 'Tell me, um, Lorraine. Can I get you a drink?' He gently guided her by the elbow towards the drinks table under the apple tree, a familiar light in his eyes.

I smiled at their departing backs and drifted on, nodding and thanking as, all around me, tides of greeting and congratulations flowed.

Clare and Rosie were talking energetically by the huge chocolate cake, and Rosie broke off as I approached, her face alight.

'I was just saying, my only reservation about moving down here was not knowing a soul, but now I've got my best friend round the corner!'

'I know.' I hugged her hard.

'Except, of course, I'll be the one left in London.' Clare pulled a sour face. 'I'll be no-mates Clare.'

'Oh, Clare, you've got loads of mates,' I rallied, managing to avoid catching Rosie's eye. 'And think how often you can come down now that you're not working? You can come and stay for weeks in the summer with the children.'

'That's true,' she conceded. 'And lovely for Mum to have you so close by. Now she's getting older.'

'Lovely for me too,' I said hugging her as she approached, resplendent in her grey silk suit. 'Church all right, Mum? Meet with your approval?'

'Ooh, yes, love, everything I dreamed of. And you look a picture too, doesn't she, Ted?'

'Aye. That you do.' Ted beamed.

'Your dad would have been *so* proud,' Mum went on. 'I don't know what he'd have said about this hat, though.' She put an anxious hand to her head. 'Flora made me stick this feather in the side, said it made it, but I'm not so sure myself. And I can just hear your father, Annie. "Marjorie, you look like a chicken."'

'Then I'm a lucky man,' said Matt, coming up beside her. 'Not many men can boast a spring chicken for a mother-in-law, and a glamorous one at that,' he added gallantly, making her blush delightedly. 'But now I fear I must break up the party. Michael and Tom are ready for us, honey.'

Matt took my hand and I wondered if I'd ever stop getting a thrill up and down my spine every time he called me that. I looked up at him, tall and broad beside me as we moved to the top table, where Tom, Matt's best man, and Michael, who'd given me away, were waiting. Michael raised his glass as we stopped beside him, a huge grin on his face.

'Ladies and gentlemen,' he boomed. 'I give you the bride and groom!'

Glasses were raised and a chorus of voices soared right up to the top of the marquee.

'THE BRIDE AND GROOM!'

CATHERINE ALLIOTT

When I met Catherine Alliott in a quiet French restaurant in Ivinghoe, close to her home in Hertfordshire, one of the first questions I put to her was where do the ideas for her novels come from? 'I'm often asked that question,' she replied, with a smile. 'It's strange really. Someone will tell me a funny story, or relate something about a friend of a friend, and it will just fire my imagination and I think, That could be such a good opening chapter. I find that as I get older I laugh less. I know that sounds gloomy, but it's because you feel you've heard it all before. So now if I hear a story that I think is really funny, I'll go home and write it down and I'll try to work it into the novel.'

When she started *The Wedding Day,* Catherine knew that she wanted to write about a single mother and to set the novel in Cornwall. With her husband George, and children Fred, Emily and Sophie, Catherine is a regular holidaymaker to Rock in Cornwall, taking the same house each year. 'Yes, I've stood in the bread queue with the north London mums in their pressed shorts, with their white legs on show. But I'm usually the scruffy one,' she laughs. 'Rock inspired me, though, because I thought, yes, this is all fine if you're part of a nuclear family, but I wondered how you would feel if you were a single mother there.'

I asked Catherine if Taplow House was based on an actual building? 'No. But we often cycle along the Camel Trail from Wadebridge to Padstow and there is a fantastic house overlooking the estuary, nestled in the trees. I love it, even though I have never been inside. It must be worth a fortune, like many of the properties I, and many others, drool over in the pages of *Country Life*. Middle-class porn, my brother calls it!'

Catherine has been writing for more than ten years and I asked her how she felt her novels have changed in this time. 'I think they have more depth to them now than when I first started writing—I hope so, anyway. I used to write about boy-meets-girl, go off to the nightclub, lose your pants in the ladies' loo—you know the kind of thing. But I can't write about that life now because I've moved on. I have to write about what comes naturally to me.'

After we had finished our main course and were preparing to order some coffee, our friendly French waiter walked up to our table, pulling the dessert trolley. 'That's very naughty,' Catherine said to him. 'We wouldn't normally have pudding, but now you've set all the delights in front of us, we are tempted.'

As we tucked into crème caramel and crème brulée, I was delighted to learn that Catherine has almost finished her next novel and has an idea for the one after that. 'I'm always terrified that I'll wake up one day and be unable to think of anything to write,' she told me. 'But at the moment, everything's flowing—good job too, as I've got school fees to pay!'

Jane Eastgate